W9-BOQ-791

# Antiagon Fire

# Tor Books by L. E. Modesitt, Jr.

The Imager Portfolio

Imager
Imager's Challenge
Imager's Intrigue
Scholar
Princeps
Imager's Battalion
Antiagon Fire
Rex Regis*

The Corean Chronicles

Legacies
Darknesses
Scepters
Alector's Choice
Cadmian's Choice
Soarer's Choice
The Lord-Protector's Daughter
Lady-Protector

The Saga of Recluce

The Magic of Recluce
The Towers of the Sunset
The Magic Engineer
The Order War
The Death of Chaos
Fall of Angels
The Chaos Balance
The White Order
Colors of Chaos
Magi'i of Cyador
Scion of Cyador
Wellspring of Chaos
Ordermaster
Natural Ordermage
Mage-Guard of Hamor
Arms-Commander

The Spellsong Cycle

The Soprano Sorceress
The Spellsong War
Darksong Rising
The Shadow Sorceress
Shadowsinger

The Ecolitan Matter

Empire & Ecolitan (comprising The Ecolitan Operation and The Ecologic Secession)
Ecolitan Prime (comprising The Ecologic Envoy and The Ecolitan Enigma)
The Forever Hero (comprising Dawn for a Distant Earth, The Silent Warrior, and In Endless Twilight)
Timegod's World (comprising Timediver's Dawn and The Timegod)

The Ghost Books

Of Tangible Ghosts
The Ghost of the Revelator
Ghost of the White Nights
Ghost of Columbia (comprising Of Tangible Ghosts and The Ghost of the Revelator)

The Hammer of Darkness
The Green Progression
The Parafaith War
Adiamante
Gravity Dreams
Octagonal Raven
Archform: Beauty
The Ethos Effect
Flash
The Eternity Artifact
The Elysium Commission
Viewpoints Critical
Haze
Empress of Eternity
The One-Eyed Man*

*forthcoming

# Antiagon Fire

The Seventh Book of the
Imager Portfolio

L. E. Modesitt, Jr.

A Tom Doherty Associates Book
New York

This is a work of fiction. All of the characters, organizations, and events portrayed in this novel are either products of the author's imagination or are used fictitiously.

ANTIAGON FIRE: THE SEVENTH BOOK OF THE IMAGER PORTFOLIO



Map by Jon Lansberg

A Tor Book
Published by Tom Doherty Associates, LLC
175 Fifth Avenue
New York, NY 10010

www.tor-forge.com



Library of Congress Cataloging-in-Publication Data

Modesitt, L. E., Jr., 1943–
Antiagon fire / L. E. Modesitt, Jr. — First edition.
p. cm.
"A Tom Doherty Associates book."
ISBN 978-0-7653-3457-2 (hardcover)
ISBN 978-1-4668-1417-2 (e-book)
1. Imaginary wars and battles—Fiction. 2. Life on other planets—Fiction. I. Title.
PS3563.O264A795 2013
813'.54—dc23

2012043364

Tor books may be purchased for educational, business, or promotional use. For information on bulk purchases, please contact Macmillan Corporate and Premium Sales Department at 1-800-221-7945 extension 5442 or write specialmarkets@macmillan.com.

First Edition: May 2013

Printed in the United States of America

0 9 8 7 6 5 4 3 2 1

For Susan and Gary,
who proved fast friends in time of need

## CHARACTERS

| | |
|---|---|
| Bhayar | Lord of Telaryn |
| Aelina | Wife of Bhayar |
| Kharst | Rex of Bovaria [deceased] |
| Aliaro | Autarch of Antiago |
| Quaeryt | Commander, Imager, and friend of Bhayar |
| Vaelora | Wife of Quaeryt and youngest sister of Bhayar |
| Khaern | Subcommander, Eleventh Regiment |
| Alazyn | Subcommander, Nineteenth Regiment |
| Zhelan | Major, First Company |
| Deucalon | Marshal of Telaryn |
| Myskyl | Submarshal, Northern Army of Telaryn |
| Skarpa | Submarshal, Southern Army |
| Fhaen | Subcommander, Third Regiment |
| Meinyt | Subcommander, Fifth Regiment |
| Kharllon | Commander, Fourteenth Regiment |
| Paedn | Subcommander, Fourth Regiment |
| Dulaek | Subcommander, Fourteenth Regiment |
| Fhaasn | Subcommander, Twenty-sixth Regiment |
| Calkoran | Subcommander, Fifth Battalion [Pharsi] |
| Eslym | Major, First Company, Fifth Battalion |
| Zhael | Major, Second Company, Fifth Battalion |
| Arion | Major, Third Company, Fifth Battalion |
| Voltyr | Imager Undercaptain |
| Shaelyt | Imager Undercaptain, Pharsi [deceased] |
| Threkhyl | Imager Undercaptain |
| Desyrk | Imager Undercaptain |
| Baelthm | Imager Undercaptain |
| Khalis | Imager Undercaptain, Pharsi |
| Lhandor | Imager Undercaptain, Pharsi |
| Horan | Imager Undercaptain |
| Smaethyl | Imager Undercaptain |

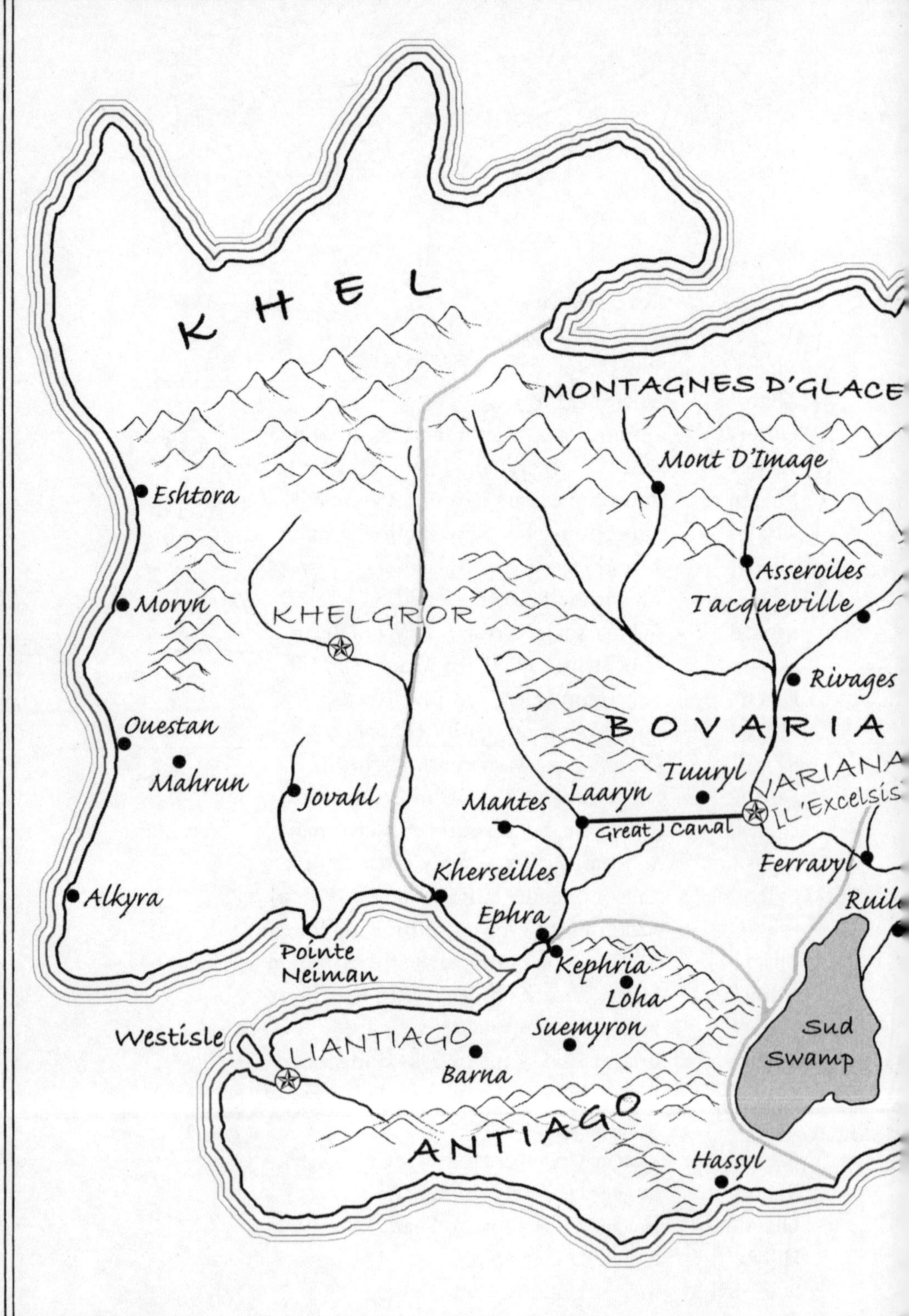
KHEL
MONTAGNES D'GLACE
Mont D'Image
Eshtora
Asseroiles
Tacqueville
Moryn
KHELGROR
Rivages
BOVARIA
Ouestan
Mahrun
Jovahl
Tuuryl
Laaryn
Mantes
VARIANA
IL'Excelsis
Great Canal
Ferravyl
Kherseilles
Alkyra
Ephra
Pointe Neiman
Kephria
Loha
Westisle
Suemyron
LIANTIAGO
Barna
Sud Swamp
ANTIAGO
Hassyl

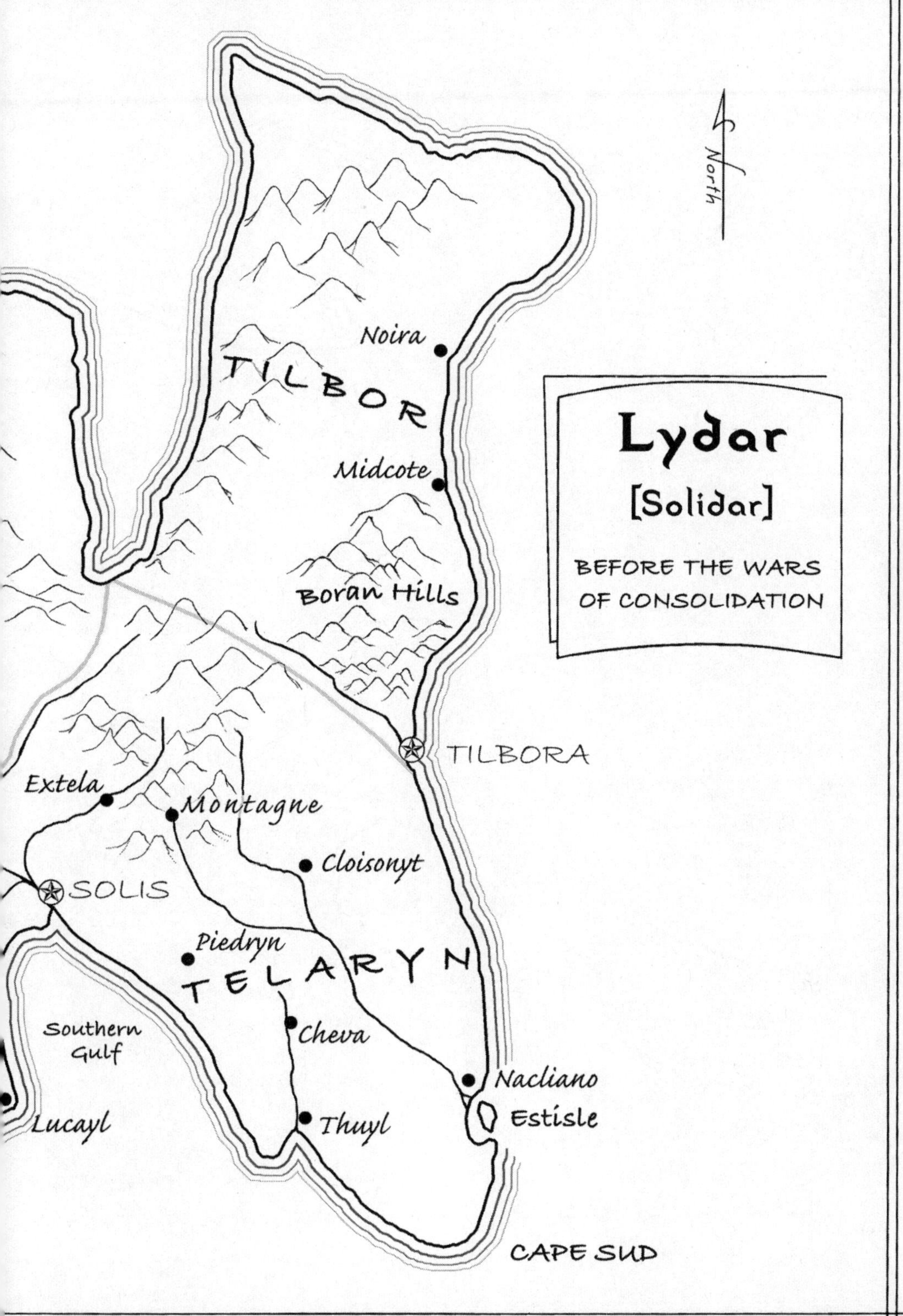
Lydar
[Solidar]
BEFORE THE WARS
OF CONSOLIDATION
North
TILBOR
Noira
Midcote
Boran Hills
TILBORA
Extela
Montagne
Cloisonyt
SOLIS
Piedryn
TELARYN
Cheva
Southern
Gulf
Nacliano
Estisle
Lucayl
Thuyl
CAPE SUD

# Antiagon Fire

# 1

Quaeryt shivered. He opened his eyes to find himself looking up into a white sky, a sky from which flakes like icy needles jabbed at his exposed face. The low moaning of a deep winter wind filled his ears. Yet, for all that the icy needles fell upon his face, each one freezing, then burning, before penetrating his skin with a thread of chill that combined into a web that bled all warmth from his body . . . there was no wind.

Standing around and above him, in a circle like pillars, looming out of the icy mist drifting down over him, were troopers in the blue-gray uniforms of Bovaria. Each Bovarian was coated in ice, and each stared down at him, as if to demand a reason why they stood there, frozen and immobile . . . why he still lived and breathed.

*Breathe?*

Quaeryt tried, but his body was so chill, with the ice creeping up from the pure white fingernails of his immobile hands and from his equally white and unmoving toenails, that his chest did not move. Nor could he utter even a sound, his words as frozen as his body.

As he froze in the whiteness, the complete and utter stillness behind which moaned the winter wind of devastation, the dead troopers reproached him with their unmoving eyes and their silence . . .

Quaeryt stretched, then rose from the table in the breakfast room in the summer chateau of the late High Holder Paitrak. Bhayar had eaten and departed before Quaeryt and Vaelora had come down from their tower chamber.

"You don't have to rush," Vaelora said quietly, in the high Bovarian she and Quaeryt always used when alone. "You should have more tea. You had another dream last night, didn't you?"

He nodded. "They're not quite as often." After a moment he added, "But I do need to get ready."

"You're not meeting with Bhayar until eighth glass."

"I worry about it."

"What can he do? You handed him a great victory, and he's now ruler of both Telaryn and Bovaria."

Quaeryt raised his eyebrows. They'd talked about that the night before.

"All right. Ruler of the eastern half of Bovaria . . . and maybe the west and north," his wife conceded. "He can't exactly punish you for success."

"No . . . but he can keep me as a subcommander and send me off to subdue the north, the northwest, the south, or the southwest."

"The High Holders of the south already pledged allegiance," she reminded him.

"Just those in the southeast."

"Has he heard anything from the lands of Khel?"

"He hadn't yesterday evening, and if the new Pharsi High Council there rejects his proposal . . ." Quaeryt shrugged.

"They'd be fools to do so." Vaelora sighed, shaking her head slightly so that the wavy curls in her light brown hair seemed to ripple. "No, dearest, you don't have to tell me how many fools there are in this world." She smiled.

As he looked into her brown eyes, he couldn't help but smile back at the woman who had raced across half of Lydar to bring him back from the near-dead. After a moment he replied, "I fear that he may send me as an envoy."

"To prove to the Khellans that you are everything that Major Calkoran was sent to tell them you are?"

"Something like that." Quaeryt walked to the window, where he reached out to pull back the curtains, then stopped for a moment to reposition his hand slightly. The two fingers on Quaeryt's left hand still didn't work, more than two weeks after Vaelora had finally roused him from a semicoma. While they didn't hurt, and he could move them with his other hand, neither finger would respond to his desire to move. At least, with his thumb and the other fingers, he could hold and lift things. *Or draw curtains.* He was still disconcerted when he saw his fingernails—snow-white, just like every strand of hair on his body.

He eased back the curtains and looked out to the west. Most of the snow and ice his imaging had created to end the battle of Variana had melted, but the land was brown and sere, and the extreme chill had destroyed or rendered unusable many of the buildings on the west side of the River Aluse, excepting, of course, the Chateau Regis, whose walls were now alabaster white and nearly indestructible, not that anyone within had survived.

"You think the Pharsi will balk?" asked Vaelora gently.

"You know they will. That's not the question." Quaeryt released the curtains and turned, catching sight of himself in a small mirror on the wall. His brown-tinted green uniform—the only one of that shade in all of the Telaryn forces, reflecting his background as a scholar—looked trim enough, although he knew it was looser than it had been, if somewhat darker than he recalled. "What happens after that is what matters."

"That's why he'll send you and no one else. Khel is two-thirds the size of old Bovaria. He doesn't want to reconquer what Kharst already bled Bovaria dry to gain."

"If he wants them to agree to his rule, he'll have to allow their High Council to act as would a provincial governor. Perhaps he might appoint the head councilor as provincial governor."

"I'm sure you can persuade him of that, dearest."

That meant, Quaeryt knew, that Vaelora was telling him he needed to. "Thank you."

"You're most welcome."

A slight cough at the archway to the breakfast room reminded Quaeryt of the serving girl. He turned. "Yes?"

"Would there be anything else, sir and Lady?" asked the serving girl in the rougher accent of low Bovarian. Even after almost two weeks, the girl would not look directly at either of them.

That was hardly surprising, Quaeryt reflected, and something that he'd likely encounter for some time to come. *But that too will pass. Everything passes in time.*

"Another pot of tea, if you would," said Vaelora, in high Bovarian.

"Nothing more for me," replied Quaeryt, also in high Bovarian.

Once the girl had provided more tea and retreated to the serving pantry, and Quaeryt had reseated himself across the table from his wife, he continued. "How would you suggest that I approach the matter? He is your brother."

"Just tell him."

Quaeryt laughed softly. "That's easier said than done."

"You haven't had problems in the past."

"That was before we wed."

"I'm certain you've done so since then, dearest."

Quaeryt shook his head. "Perhaps it's not about that at all."

"He has no other choice. Why are you so worried about it? You'll do what's necessary, and he'll accept the inevitable."

"I . . . don't want to leave you. Not after . . . everything."

"I don't want you to leave . . ." Vaelora looked down.

"But?"

"We both have to do what must be done. And if Bhayar has to settle Khel by force, it will be so much the worse."

"He still might have something else in mind."

"How likely is that, dearest?"

"With Bhayar, it's always possible."

Vaelora raised her eyebrows.

Quaeryt decided against further speculation as to what Bhayar would do, and asked, "How are you feeling now?"

"Much better . . . after the first three months, my stomach settled." She made a wry face. "Now it is merely growing. What will you do after you meet with Bhayar?"

"Return and tell you, then, if necessary, gather officers and imagers and tell them . . ."

They continued to talk until Quaeryt rose to make his way to meet with Bhayar.

At half a quint before eighth glass, Quaeryt arrived in the second-floor corridor outside the study Bhayar had appropriated until the repairs and the refurbishing of the Chateau Regis were completed.

The captain stationed there inclined his head, more than perfunctorily, "Subcommander, sir."

"Just wait until the bells strike the glass."

"Yes, sir."

Quaeryt did note that as soon as the first chime echoed down the wide hallway, the captain turned, walked to the study door, and rapped upon it.

"Subcommander Quaeryt, sir." Before Bhayar finished speaking, the captain opened the dark oak door and motioned for Quaeryt to enter.

The study of the late High Holder Paitrak was located on the north side of the chateau, designed to be cool in the summer. Overlooking a walled garden, now brown, with snow and ice in the shaded corners, the north outside wall held narrow floor-to-ceiling windows, each separated from the next by dark wooden bookshelves exactly the same width as the windows. The shelves also ran from floor to ceiling and, with the inside shutters open, the small leaded panes radiated a coolness not entirely dispelled by the fire in the hearth set into the east wall.

The wiry Bhayar rose from behind the wide table desk positioned before the bookshelves comprising the west wall. His shortish brown hair was disarrayed, as it often was, but his dark blue eyes were intent. "You're looking well this morning, almost back to your old self." His Bovarian was impeccable and far more precise, Quaeryt had discovered, than the language used by most of the chateau functionaries, unsurprisingly, since Bovarian had been the court language at Solis.

"I'm feeling well." Quaeryt smiled.

Bhayar gestured to the chairs before the desk, then reseated himself.

Quaeryt took the leftmost chair and waited for the Lord of Telaryn and Bovaria to speak.

"Matters have been going well," Bhayar said. "The shops and factorages in Variana are all open. The High Holders in the east and south, except for those in the southwest and those within two hundred milles to the north and west, have pledged allegiance. Most have remitted token tariffs."

"Token?"

"Bovarian tariffs are due in the first week of Feuillyt. Most claim, and have receipts to prove it, that they had already paid. We did recover over thirty thousand golds from the strongrooms in Chateau Regis. I insisted on a token of a hundred golds from each High Holder."

Quaeryt nodded. "What about the lands farther north and northwest?"

"Messengers have barely had a chance to reach that far." Bhayar shrugged. "There's also the far southwest. The clerks who survived claim that there are High Holders along the border with Antiago who haven't paid tariffs in years. We can't tell. Your winter freeze turned those records to mush."

Quaeryt doubted that the cold had, but most likely the thawing had rendered poorly entered ledger entries illegible. "It's sounding like Kharst didn't actually rule all of his own lands."

"He may not have. I'm not Kharst."

"Is there anything else?" *As if that weren't already more than I wanted to learn.*

"I'm pleased about the way your imagers have finished rebuilding and restructuring the interior of the Chateau Regis . . ."

"They did well. I rode there on Lundi. Or is there something else you would like done?"

"No . . . The furnishings will come as they will . . . but that's not why I wanted to meet with you." Bhayar's dark blue eyes fixed on Quaeryt, but he said nothing more.

Because he disliked Bhayar's gambit of using silence to force another to speak, Quaeryt nodded once more and smiled politely.

"There is the problem with Khel . . ."

"I can imagine. Have you heard from Major Calkoran?" The former Khellan officer had been dispatched—while Quaeryt had still been unable to hear or communicate—with the other Khellan companies to present Bhayar's suggestion that the resurgent Pharsi High Council agree to Bhayar's rule, under far more lenient terms than those imposed by the late Rex Kharst.

"I made him a subcommander and constituted all the Khellan companies as a battalion. He sent one dispatch from near Kherseilles. He was heading to Khelgror to meet with the new High Council."

"What happened to the provincial governor?"

"We can't even find any records about one. Maybe they didn't have one. Whatever happened, I doubt it was pleasant for Kharst's functionaries. Before Calkoran left, I revoked all the holdings of Bovarian High Holders in Khel. There weren't many." Bhayar frowned. "I haven't granted any of those lands to new High Holders."

"It might be wise not to," suggested Quaeryt. "Not yet, anyway."

"I'll need to create some new High Holders . . ."

"I'm sure you will. I suspect you can find enough existing high holds in the former lands of old Bovaria whose holders died or who would not fit your standards to meet that need. I even ran across a few I'd be happy to recommend."

"I've read your reports. There may not be enough."

"There will doubtless be more before the consolidation is over, but you'll only buy the same troubles you had in Tilbor—except worse—if you try creating high holdings in Khel. Besides, you need fewer High Holders, not more."

"I'm aware of your feelings about that, Quaeryt. I'm not about to do anything in Khel until the situation is clear. Calkoran won't be able to resolve the situation. I knew that before I dispatched him."

"So that's why you're going to send me?"

"I don't believe I've mentioned that to you—or anyone else. You're wrong. I'm not sending you." Bhayar smiled, the expression one of pleasure, with a hint of mischief. "I'm making you and Vaelora my envoys."

"Vaelora?" asked Quaeryt. "She is with child, you know?" He didn't keep a slight acidity from his voice.

"She rode from Solis here without stopping more than a few glasses at any one time," said Bhayar coolly, "and that didn't hurt her. She's not due until late spring or early summer. I've had Subcommander Khaern look into the fastest means of transport. You and Vaelora, as I was about to tell you, can take Kharst's personal canal boat along the Great Canal from Variana to Laaryn and then down the river. I've already arranged for the *Montagne* to meet you at Ephra and take you to Kherseilles. From there, you can take a flatboat up the Groral River to Khelgror. You'll have two regiments and what's left of your Fifth Battalion as an escort. And your imagers."

"The *Montagne* is a large vessel, but she's scarcely large enough to carry two regiments and first company," Quaeryt pointed out, "let alone mounts for the men."

"I also sent the *Solis* and made arrangements to charter ten other merchanters. You'll have to leave most of the mounts behind, but the traders in Kherseilles should have enough mounts for you there."

Quaeryt had his doubts about fitting two regiments and a company on even twelve ships, and whether all twelve would even arrive at Ephra. "How do I know we'll have enough mounts at Kherseilles?"

"I've done what I can. You'll have to do whatever's necessary when you get there." Bhayar smiled again. "There aren't any Pharsi troopers left, except the ones you commanded, and they won't attack you. I can't believe that any remaining Bovarian units in Khel, if there even are any, are large enough to give you, of all my commanders, any difficulty."

"All your commanders?"

"You've been promoted to commander." Bhayar gestured to a felt pouch on the desk. "All your insignia are there. I'd appreciate it if you'd put them on before you leave the study."

"I'll make sure I do, sir." Quaeryt had to admit that none of the Telaryn senior officers who'd covertly opposed him would be able to say a thing, not publicly, after his imaging had destroyed almost all the Bovarian defenders, as well as the late Rex Kharst, his court and family, and all the senior Bovarian officers . . . as well as more than a score of High Holders close to Kharst.

Equally important, the senior Telaryn officers, especially Marshal Deucalon and Submarshal Myskyl, would be pleased to have Quaeryt out of the way. Quaeryt had no doubts that they would be planning to reduce his influence by the time he and Vaelora returned.

"Might I know the regiment besides that of Subcommander Khaern?"

"The Nineteenth Regiment from Northern Army, now headed by Subcommander Alazyn."

"Recently promoted from major?"

"Exactly." Bhayar laughed. "Oh . . . and on the way to Ephra, you'll also be accompanied by Commander Skarpa and the Southern Army. Marshal Deucalon suggested that to keep Aliaro from getting adventurous . . . and to make certain that the southwesternmost High Holders pledge allegiance. Skarpa will also have to deal with the elveweed problem."

Quaeryt raised his eyebrows. "I didn't know Bovaria had an elveweed problem." He also didn't like the fact that Deucalon had suggested Skarpa's new assignment. *Then again, it might have been Myskyl.*

"Everyone has an elveweed problem. As I recall, there were some factors in Extela . . ."

Quaeryt nodded. He didn't like being reminded of some of the difficulties he'd encountered in his brief tenure as provincial governor of Montagne. "What is the particular problem in Ephra? Smuggling?"

"You might recall that Aliaro tried to blockade the port during Kharst's campaign in Khel . . . and that Kharst burned part of Kephria. I'm certain Aliaro hasn't forgotten that."

"But Aliaro sent troopers against us on the campaign up the Aluse," Quaeryt pointed out.

"That was then. Rulers have to be flexible." Bhayar smiled sardonically. "Then there's the problem that several High Holders have the equivalent of battalions of private guards funded by their . . . investments in elveweed and other even more undesirable substances."

"With all that, I hope you gave Skarpa another four or five regiments and made him a submarshal," said Quaeryt.

Bhayar laughed. "Once more, I see the wisdom of not keeping you too close at hand."

The silence drew out, but Quaeryt refused to speak.

Finally, Bhayar said, "I already assigned two more regiments."

"That won't be enough, for many reasons. First, Subcommander Khaern and his regiment will be with me. Second, Aliaro will look at how many regiments Skarpa has. Third, you don't need all of the Northern Army here in Variana. Fourth, you'll have to strain to keep feeding the extra regiments . . ." Quaeryt paused, then asked, "Do you want to hear more?"

"No. From what you're saying, I should give him four regiments more."

"You should. Or five. And the promotion."

"I will. I've learned that it's not wise to disregard your suggestions, even if I don't like them. But give me some reasons."

Quaeryt refrained from smiling at Bhayar's barely hidden exasperation. "First, the title will help convince Aliaro to behave, or at least to think before he tries some form of provocation. Second, it will give the local High Holders pause. Third, it will allow Skarpa the time, the men, and the position to plan for the eventual. Fourth, it will give both Deucalon and Myskyl pause. Fifth, you should also send Myskyl up the River Aluse from Variana to assure the full capitulation of the High Holders in the areas of Rivages, Asseroiles, Tacqueville, and perhaps all the way to the Montaignes D'Glace. By doing that—"

"I do understand that part," said Bhayar testily.

"It also emphasizes that you're relying on Skarpa as heavily as Myskyl—"

"And that will require Deucalon, whom you trust not at all, to be more careful in what he does."

Quaeryt nodded.

"I'll promote Skarpa, but don't you say a word. Arranging the other regimental transfers will take a bit more time. Still . . . you and Vaelora should be able to leave on Lundi." Bhayar put his hands on the wooden arms of the desk chair, as if about to rise.

"You also need to let Skarpa pick his successor as commander of Third Regiment."

"Of course. What else?" Bhayar's voice turned quietly sardonic.

"You're getting what you want," Quaeryt said quietly. "I'd like something."

"Oh? You're now a commander."

Quaeryt ignored the reference to the promotion. He'd more than earned it. "You remember that you agreed to my building the imagers into a group that will support you and your heirs, and even Clayar's heirs?"

"How could I forget?"

"They need to be gathered in a place that is both separate and isolated, yet close enough to remind everyone, quietly, that they are at your beck and call. The battle resulted in much devastation, especially along the river. The so-called isle of piers would be an excellent location for such a place. Also, by turning it into a beautiful isle scholarium for imagers, it would help reinforce both your power and your grace in rebuilding a more beautiful Variana . . . Although, in a year or so, when you officially relocate your capital here, I would recommend changing the city's name—"

"Do your presumptions never end?" Bhayar's tone was half amused, half exasperated, and followed by a sigh.

"Have I advised or done anything that was not proved to be in your interests, sir?" Quaeryt decided against reminding Bhayar that they had already discussed what he'd just said.

Bhayar shook his head, not even trying to conceal his exasperation. "I will be glad when you are off furthering my interests out of earshot."

"That is another reason why you might consider allowing the isle of piers to the imagers . . ."

"Enough!" Bhayar shook his head vigorously, but the sigh that followed was the long and dramatic one, not the short explosive one that indicated real anger. "I will hold the isle for a future reserve, for now, until you return from the so-called High Council of Khel with an agreement accepting my sovereignty."

"You won't get that unless you allow the head of their High Council to act as the provincial governor of Khel."

"I can't do that!"

"How about as princeps? That would allow your rule to be paramount, but allow the Pharsi some latitude in maintaining their way of life."

Bhayar's frown was thoughtful.

Quaeryt once more waited.

"Are you sure you didn't know you were Pharsi until last year?"

"Absolutely." Quaeryt paused. "You could use that arrangement as leverage to keep the provincial governors of Telaryn in line . . ."

"They'll have to grant more than that. At least twenty High Holdings along the coast, and two or three near Khelgror."

"I *might* persuade them to the coast holdings. I doubt that they'd agree to a high holding near Khelgror unless you made at least one of them a Pharsi holder."

"Do what you can, but I can't let it be seen that the Pharsi are dictating terms."

"In other words, you need to claim you've obtained the spoils of high holdings . . ."

"You don't have to put it that way, Quaeryt."

"I just wish matters to be clear between us. I've never spoken for you except exactly what you have stated."

"Or what you've gotten me to agree to state."

Quaeryt grinned. "You've never agreed to anything you wouldn't have granted, and you know it."

Although Bhayar grinned, if briefly, in return, Quaeryt knew he'd be in the study for at least another glass, going over details . . . and then the minutiae of those details.

As Quaeryt had suspected, his meeting with Bhayar was not short, and he did not return to the quarters he and Vaelora shared until almost three quints past ninth glass. She was waiting for him in the small sitting room adjoining their bedchamber and immediately rose from where she had been seated, setting a small leatherbound volume on the table beside her chair.

"Reading *Rholan and the Nameless* again?" he asked.

She offered a mock scowl. "Are you going to tell me how things went with Bhayar? Besides getting promoted?" An impish smile appeared as her eyes took in the gold crescent moon insignia on Quaeryt's collar.

"Did you know?"

She shook her head. "You know I've scarcely talked to him since you recovered. I did think he'd have to, but having to do something means he'll usually take his time in getting around to it. What did he say about your going to Khel?"

"About what we suspected," replied Quaeryt dryly. "Except for one thing. You're coming with me to Khelgror. We're both being named as envoys."

"I thought that might be the case."

"Oh . . . you did?"

"Think about to whom you'll be talking, dearest . . . and who often makes the decisions. Especially after what happened to most of the men."

Quaeryt nodded. He should have thought about that. Women were equal, if not more than equal, in Pharsi culture. Since much of Khel had been Pharsi—at least before the ravages of the Red Death and the bloodbath created by the late Rex Kharst's conquest of Khel—women would definitely be involved in deciding on Bhayar's offer. Sending not only a high-ranking Pharsi officer such as Quaeryt, but his wife, who was Bhayar's sister and known to be of Pharsi blood, only made sense. *If you succeed . . . only if you succeed.* "It's not likely to be as easy as Bhayar thinks."

"I doubt he thinks it's easy."

"And . . . if we don't get their agreement . . ."

"You'll end up as princeps in Tilbor again or in the far north of Bovaria when all the fighting's over," suggested Vaelora. "Or, even worse, as military governor of Khel."

"That's assuming I survive the assignments that Myskyl and Deucalon will suggest Bhayar give me."

"We'd best succeed." Vaelora's voice was firm.

She didn't have to mention that Quaeryt had barely survived either the battle of Ferravyl or the battle of Variana.

"We'll have two regiments, plus first company, after we leave Ephra." He kept a bland expression on his face.

"We're supposed to travel unescorted across Bovaria?" asked Vaelora a trace sharply.

"No . . . two regiments and first company will accompany us all the way. Commander Skarpa and Southern Army will also go as far as Ephra." He shook his head. "After that, Bhayar's arranged for ships to take us to Kherseilles. I have my doubts about whether they'll all show up, since ten are merchanters." *More than doubts, knowing what you know about merchanters. Then again, he had to have made arrangements weeks ago, even before you'd recovered, but . . .* He looked at Vaelora. "Did you tell him I'd recover?"

"Of course. I knew you would. I told you that, dearest. What about the ships?"

"His two warships will be there, but the merchanters . . ." Quaeryt shrugged. "If they all don't make it, Skarpa could use extra battalions and regiments. Then there's the problem with mounts. The ships can't carry them. Bhayar claims he's made arrangements for us to have mounts in Kherseilles, but he wouldn't tell me the details . . . and that's not good."

Vaelora shook her head. "No . . . and he probably said he had every confidence in you. But don't you think we could travel with fewer troopers, even if you don't want to tell Bhayar?"

"We could. I don't like it. Do you think I should?"

"No." She smiled. "You should have the choice of what to do if it comes to that."

"I still worry."

"You've never had enough troops, or mounts, dearest. Neither has Skarpa. This time, you might. Don't give them away because something *might* happen."

*It most likely will happen, but she's right.* In the momentary silence that filled the sitting room, Quaeryt said, "I need to find Skarpa and talk to him."

"You didn't tell me when we are leaving."

"Lundi."

"Lundi? That only gives me four days to get ready." Her eyes narrowed. "Am I supposed to ride the entire way?"

"No. We're to use Rex Kharst's personal canal boat as far as Ephra. We'll take the Great Canal from Variana to Laaryn . . ." Quaeryt quickly explained the arrangements.

"The Great Canal," mused Vaelora when he had finished. "Wasn't that where so many died in building it?"

"Kharst's father started building it. Kharst finished it. They used prisoners, captives, and some even say imagers. It took almost thirty years to finish, and at least one scholar wrote that thousands were buried under its walls."

Vaelora shivered slightly. "For a canal?"

"Because Bhayar and his father denied Bovarian traders free passage on the Aluse," Quaeryt pointed out.

"So they sacrificed thousands to avoid paying passage tariffs?"

"Some rulers find lives cheaper than golds," Quaeryt said dryly.

Vaelora shook her head, then added, "We'll still end up riding into Khelgror, I'd wager."

"But you won't be riding the whole way."

"Go find Skarpa. I need to make arrangements for more suitable clothing."

Quaeryt frowned.

"Dearest, even if all goes well, it will be winter, or close to it, before we return to Variana, and by then I will not be able to wear what I now possess."

"I understand," he said quickly. "I'll try to finish . . ."

"Take your time. And keep working on getting your shield strength back."

Quaeryt nodded. Actually, from what he could tell, his shields were stronger than ever, confirming his feeling that the more he attempted with imaging, the stronger an imager he became. *Except all the times that happened, you almost died. How long will it be before you push too hard and don't survive?* He couldn't help but think about poor Shaelyt . . . who'd tried to do too much . . . and hadn't survived.

"And even if you think your shields are back, keep them up, especially when you think it should be safe."

Quaeryt smiled sheepishly, then walked over and embraced his wife, holding her closely before kissing her cheek, and retreating to seek out Skarpa.

He'd hoped to find both Major Zhelan and Skarpa in the estate's guesthouse—temporarily being used as headquarters by Marshal Deucalon, but Zhelan was out, riding a patrol with first company, the only unit effectively left of what had been Quaeryt's Fifth Battalion, now that the Khellan companies had been dispatched with Subcommander Calkoran.

Quaeryt finally located Skarpa, sharing a small chamber with another commander at the rear of the guesthouse, a space far closer to the courtyard and stables than that of any other senior officer. The other commander was absent, but likely not for long, given the papers stacked on the second desk.

Skarpa rose. Then he saw the insignia on Quaeryt's collar and nodded. "About time, Commander."

"Quaeryt. You've been a commander longer. You still outrank me."

"Not for all that long, I'd wager." The hint of a smile lurked behind Skarpa's pleasant expression.

"You've said that before. It didn't happen. Bhayar promoted me because he had to for me to command more than one regiment." He paused. "He has told you about escorting us . . . ?"

"He hasn't. Myskyl did, this morning." Skarpa offered a wry smile. "Then, less than a quint ago, Deucalon appeared at my door here, and told me that I'd be promoted to submarshal tomorrow by Lord Bhayar and that I'll be leading a full seven regiments to Ephra—in addition to your forces. How much of that was your doing? Don't tell me it wasn't."

"It was Bhayar's decision. I did suggest that two or three regiments weren't enough for what he wanted, and that it would put less strain on the quartermasters if you took more men south. I also told him to let you pick your successor as commander of Third Regiment."

"I appreciate that."

Quaeryt raised his eyebrows.

"Fhaen. Falossn would do as well, but Fhaen has more experience. That's not all you said, knowing you."

"I did suggest that he dispatch Myskyl to the north and northwest to assure that the High Holders there, and any remaining Bovarian forces, pledge their allegiance to Bhayar."

"Like I said, in time you'll outrank me."

Quaeryt shook his head. "I'll never be a submarshal or marshal, and I shouldn't be."

"I have my doubts, but I won't argue. I've learned that I'm usually wrong where you're involved."

"That's because I don't argue when you're right," said Quaeryt with a laugh.

"And I argue when I'm wrong?" jested Skarpa.

"No. But sometimes you don't appreciate your own abilities enough." After the briefest hesitation, Quaeryt asked, "How many of your new regiments will be foot?"

"Two."

"Good. You'll need more foot in the south."

"That's why I asked for them."

"I'm glad we aren't arguing about that," quipped Quaeryt.

"There is one problem with the regiments, though," said Skarpa, "or their commanders. One of them is Fourteenth Regiment. Commander Kharllon."

"I don't know him, but I'd wager he's close to Deucalon or Myskyl. Are there any other commanders or subcommanders in the regiments he assigned to you who outrank Meinyt?"

"No. Paedn, Dulaek, Meurn, and Fhaasn are all subcommanders. One is enough, especially when Kharllon is close to Myskyl."

"Have you talked to Meinyt?"

Skarpa nodded. "He expected it. So did I, but I don't like it. Kharllon outranks you, too, but he'd likely not press that. He understands power well." Skarpa shook his head. "Calkoran won't get the Pharsi to agree to Bhayar's terms, you know?"

"I'd be surprised." Quaeryt laughed sardonically. "I'd be surprised if Vaelora and I can."

"He's sending you both?"

"Women have a stronger position in Khel . . . or they did before Kharst conquered them."

"I'd still be surprised if you can't get them to agree."

"Why do you say that?"

"Khel wasn't strong enough to stand that long against Kharst, Red Death or no Red Death. It certainly can't stand for long against a united Telaryn and Bovaria. Now is the time when the Pharsi have the greatest leverage, and you're the perfect one to point that out."

"People seldom decide such things rationally. We both know that."

"Then you need to give them a reason to decide irrationally. I'm sure you can manage that. You've done it before."

"Only with a few individuals. The rest of the time I've been far more effective at destroying things and people."

"That's true, but it doesn't mean you can't change how you operate."

Quaeryt nodded. *It does point out again that it is time to try other approaches.* "What do you know about Subcommander Alazyn and Nineteenth Regiment?"

"Alazyn . . . Alazyn . . ." Skarpa's face brightened. "He was the one who took over after Commander Kantyr got killed by that girl who claimed she was his mistress."

*That figures.* "What about Alazyn?"

"He's another one like Zhelan. Tough, fair, knows fighting men and discipline. Not much for tactics. But he's not from Nineteenth. He was the senior regimental major under Pulaskyr. Is the Nineteenth the other regiment you got? I heard about Khaern."

"It is."

"Alazyn will do fine under you. He'll have his hands full for a while with Nineteenth, not so much, though, as if they'd stayed in the Northern Army under Deucalon." Skarpa went on. "You might wish to pay a call on Submarshal Myskyl. Marshal Deucalon is touring the lands east of Variana, paying visits to the estates of quite a few High Holders."

"Mostly deceased, I presume."

"I have not heard." Skarpa offered a crooked smile.

"I will see Myskyl, then. By then, perhaps Zhelan will have returned."

"He said something about returning by the first glass of the afternoon. Please don't give Myskyl my best."

"I wouldn't dream of it, even in a nightmare. Until later." Quaeryt nodded and made his way from the small chamber toward the front of the guesthouse, where he soon located the study occupied by the submarshal.

The hard-faced undercaptain—likely a recently promoted senior squad leader—looked up, then immediately stood. "Commander, sir?"

"Would you inquire to see if the submarshal might have a moment?"

"Certainly, sir." The undercaptain moved to the door, knocked, and stepped inside, only to return almost immediately, gesturing for Quaeryt to enter the small study.

Once inside the chamber, most likely a lady's study, from the graceful carved bookcase of only three shelves to the writing table with the curved legs, Quaeryt inclined his head to the gray-haired submarshal, noting that the scars on Myskyl's left cheek, old and faded as they were, seemed more prominent for some reason . . . or perhaps Quaeryt had forgotten them, since he'd seen so little of Myskyl in the past half year. "Good morning, sir."

"Good morning, Commander." Myskyl studied Quaeryt, then smiled. "I understand that you'll be off to the west to make certain that the lands of Khel remain loyal."

"I will indeed be heading west with several regiments to persuade the High Council of Khel to accept Lord Bhayar's offer of governance. Since he did not conquer them, they doubtless believe that they owe him no innate loyalty. My task, as I am certain you know, is to make certain that they understand that accepting his kind offer and pledging their loyalty is by far the best and most prudent course of action." Quaeryt smiled. "My loyalty to Lord Bhayar goes back to when we were both students, long before Lady Vaelora and I were wed, and that bond has only reinforced my desire to dedicate myself to acting with prudence in his best interests."

Myskyl's eyes hardened, if but for a moment, before he smiled heartily.

"I'm more than certain that Lord Bhayar appreciates your unrestrained loyalty more than he will ever be able to repay, and that you will employ all your considerable talents to the end of assuring that Khel will remain loyal to him."

"I will certainly do my best to create such a loyalty, although I doubt that the Khellan acquiescence to Rex Kharst was based upon loyalty in any form. Still . . . we all do what we must, as I know you have always done, first in service to Marshal Rescalyn and now in service to Marshal Deucalon and Lord Bhayar. I have watched the care with which you have planned every strategy and can only admire your skill." Quaeryt smiled slightly more than politely.

"Alas, Commander, your skill in such is second to none, and you have mastered the art of applying force when and where it will do the most good. Of course, not all . . . difficulties . . . can be so resolved."

"I defer to your expertise and experience in that, Submarshal, and I will keep that well in mind as I deal with the Khellan High Council. Might you have any specific advice as to those points I should keep most in mind?"

"Only that agreements that cannot be enforced, in some fashion or another, will be broken as soon as it is in the interest of the parties to do so."

Quaeryt nodded. "I fear that may be a concern for those on both sides, and I will follow your observation as matters develop." He inclined his head just slightly. "I would not wish to take any more of your time, but I did want to pay my respects in case I did not have the opportunity before we depart."

"You are most thoughtful in that respect," replied Myskyl, "indeed in all respects. As you demonstrated in the last days of the hill holders' revolt."

"That thoughtfulness I learned from observing you and Marshal Rescalyn, and I do appreciate having the opportunity to learn from you both." After another nod, Quaeryt smiled politely once more, then turned and left.

From Deucalon's duty officer, Quaeryt learned that Khaern had ridden out earlier on "a routine scouting mission."

After another quint or so had passed, Quaeryt saw Zhelan ride into the side courtyard, but it was yet another quint before the hard-faced major with the slightly graying black hair left the stable and crossed to the guest house's rear entrance where Quaeryt waited.

"Sir?" Then Zhelan glanced at Quaeryt's collar. "Congratulations, sir."

"Thank you." Quaeryt paused. "Has anyone told you of our next task?"

"Our next task?" The major's eyebrows lifted, and a mild expression of puzzlement crossed his face.

"Lord Bhayar has assigned Eleventh and Nineteenth Regiments—and what remains of Fifth Battalion—to me for a mission to Khelgror."

"You're to . . . conquer the Pharsi again with two regiments?"

"No . . . Lady Vaelora and I are being sent as envoys." Quaeryt went on to explain.

Once Quaeryt had finished, Zhelan was silent for several moments.

"Go on. You can speak," said Quaeryt cheerfully.

"Lord Bhayar doesn't want much of you, does he?"

"He'd prefer not to resort to arms. So would we. So, I suspect, would the Pharsi High Council."

"But leaving on Lundi?"

"We can't afford to wait."

"I can see that. Are you . . . ?"

"I'm well. And it will be two weeks or longer before we encounter even the chance of serious opposition . . . if we do at all. The Pharsi aren't likely to attack any envoy now."

"I can see that, sir."

"Think about it. I just wanted to make sure you knew as soon as I did." Quaeryt added, "I'll need a squad to accompany me to meet with Subcommander Alazyn . . . as soon as you can provide one."

"Fifth squad is the duty squad. They can be ready to ride in less than a quint."

Not quite a quint passed before Quaeryt mounted the mare that had seen him through so much and, accompanied by fifth squad, rode out on the hazy gray day. In deference to Vaelora, rather than carrying light shields that, if anything impacted them, would trigger heavier shields, Quaeryt held full imaging shields.

They traveled more than a mille south, and another two west along a muddy rutted road to reach the smaller holding where Alazyn and Nineteenth Regiment were quartered. The hold house was old, of reddish bricks that needed repointing, and the hedges that flanked the narrow drive to the small uncovered portico had been but raggedly trimmed.

A short stocky officer with the silver crescents of a subcommander on his collar had hurried out into the cool fall wind to stand waiting on the uneven stone platform that served as a receiving portico. As Quaeryt put his second boot on the stone, a violent gust of wind whipped around him, and he had to grab his visor cap to keep it from blowing off his head.

"It's been right windy, Commander," offered the subcommander. "How might I help you?"

"Would you be Subcommander Alazyn, by chance?"

"The very same, sir."

"It's good to meet you. I'm Commander Quaeryt."

Alazyn opened his mouth, then closed it, finally saying, "Sir . . . I should have known . . . I didn't expect you to ride out here . . ."

Quaeryt grinned. "Why not? It makes more sense than sending a courier."

Alazyn gestured toward the door. "Please do come in."

Quaeryt followed the shorter officer in through the wide single and weathered ironbound oak door, closing it behind himself.

"Commander Pulaskyr has been kind enough to share the study here with me." Alazyn stopped at the door off the small entry hall, again motioning for Quaeryt to enter. "He's out with Second Regiment at the moment . . . Second Tilboran, I should say."

The study was little more than an oblong room with a hearth at one end and a writing desk at the other, with two tall bookcases behind the table desk and against the tan plaster wall. The two windows in the outside wall were chest high, with small leaded panes cloudy with age. Two armless chairs stood before the desk. Quaeryt walked to the nearer one and seated himself, then waited for Alazyn to sit down in the other.

Alazyn did so, then said, "You and Commander Pulaskyr were together in Tilbor, I understand."

"We were in Tilbor at the same time, but we never actually served anywhere together. He was in charge of all operations north of the Boran Hills, and I was with Marshal Rescalyn in the south. We never even met until after the hill holders' revolt was put down." *And even then we barely had a chance to speak to each other.* "I understand he was very effective in dealing with the northern hill holders."

"He said that you were largely responsible for the way things turned out in the south."

"He is *far* too generous. The entire campaign in the south was planned and masterfully carried out by Governor Rescalyn, and finished by Submarshal Myskyl."

"The governor died in the last battle, Commander Pulaskyr told me. Did you see any of that?"

Quaeryt smiled wryly. "No. I was unhorsed by a heavy cavalryman moments before Rescalyn fell." That wasn't quite true, but it was what Quaeryt had said all along, and what everyone, including Myskyl, believed. "Have you yet been instructed as to where Nineteenth Regiment will be assigned?"

"Just a dispatch yesterday saying that we were assigned to special duty under your command, sir . . . and that specific orders would come from you."

"Eleventh and Nineteenth Regiments, and the one company remaining from Fifth Battalion that was not Khellan, have been assigned to support Lady Vaelora and me in our duties as envoys to the High Council of Khel . . ." Quaeryt went on to explain.

When Quaeryt finished, Alazyn tilted his head, almost quizzically. "I'm not certain I understand why Lord Bhayar . . . has taken this approach. Isn't taking a woman, even Lord Bhayar's sister . . . ?"

At that moment, Quaeryt realized he'd assumed that Alazyn knew more than he did. "There are several reasons. First, both Lord Bhayar and Lady Vaelora are part Pharsi. Second, I'm the highest ranking officer of full Pharsi blood in the Telaryn forces. Third, I was the one in command of all the Pharsi officers who are already in Khel offering Lord Bhayar's terms." He paused. "And there is the small matter that Lady Vaelora is my wife."

Alazyn's eyes widened, if but for a moment.

"I take it that no one bothered to mention those facts to you," said Quaeryt dryly.

"Ah . . . no, sir."

"That's not surprising. At times, senior officers assume subordinates know everything they do." Quaeryt laughed humorously. "As I just did." After a moment he went on. "Please ask any and all questions you may have . . . even if you worry that they may indicate you don't know something. In situations like this, the only stupid questions are the ones you don't ask."

"Yes, sir." Alazyn looked away from Quaeryt. "Is it true that you're an imager?"

"Yes, but I'm one of about ten, and the other imagers will be accompanying us as well . . ."

More than a glass passed before Quaeryt had answered all of Alazyn's questions and departed the hold house for the ride back to the outskirts of Variana.

Quaeryt barely had time to wash up and change out of his muddy undress uniform into his only set of dress greens, except, as was the case with all his uniforms, the jacket shirt and trousers were green tinted with brown, to show his scholar background. Then he joined Vaelora in their sitting room—prior to walking down to the formal dining room of the estate house for dinner with Bhayar, the first dinner they had shared with him in weeks.

"You look beautiful." Quaeryt appraised his wife, who wore a long black dress with a silver and black jacket.

"I can barely fit into this."

"That doesn't show."

"It will before long," said Vaelora. "I worried you'd forgotten we were having dinner . . ."

"No. I had to meet with Skarpa and Major Zhelan. I also dropped in and paid my respects to Submarshal Myskyl, then rode out and met with Subcommander Alazyn."

"How was the good submarshal?"

"We were very polite. He intimated that Khel would be loyal to Bhayar and that if it weren't, it would be my fault. I said that Khel had never been loyal to Kharst and the Pharsi Khellans especially didn't see Bhayar as Kharst's successor, but that I would certainly endeavor to establish such loyalty. He intimated that I was a devious schemer, if one enthusiastically loyal to Bhayar. I blandly noted that his and Rescalyn's actions in Tilbor were masterful, and that I had learned much from them. We parted with amicable words."

"But far from amicably."

"Politely. He's never liked nor trusted me, and I certainly don't trust him. More important, I don't think your brother should. Ever."

"While you were ill, dearest, as I may have mentioned, we did discuss that. He will watch both Deucalon and Myskyl closely. He does believe that they have their uses."

"Don't we all?"

"Of course. Yours are just more valuable and longer lasting. And . . . we should be joining dear brother, dearest . . ." murmured Vaelora.

Quaeryt grinned. "A polite reminder to begin escorting you down the stairs and into dinner. Do you know who else will be there?"

"Marshal Deucalon, I believe, and perhaps several others."

"Officers . . . local High Holders?"

"Brother dear did not convey that information to me."

When they reached the main level and had walked a good fifty yards toward the front of the large hold house, they came to an undercaptain standing by the open door to the chamber adjoining the dining room. "Lady, Commander . . ."

"Thank you." Quaeryt allowed Vaelora to guide him while giving the impression that he was the one leading, into the sitting room . . . or reception chamber.

There, Bhayar and Deucalon stood talking, half facing the window overlooking one of the already frost-killed gardens. Near the hearth at the end of the room away from the open double doors leading to the formal dining chamber stood two other men. One was white-haired, with a lined but tanned face, who wore the vestments of a chorister of the Nameless. The other, gray-haired, wore a formal black jacket and a pale gray shirt, with a high collar.

Bhayar turned. "Vaelora, Quaeryt . . ." He smiled at her. "You are lovely this evening."

"You commanded that I look my best," replied Vaelora with an expression just short of mischievous.

"You both know Marshal Deucalon, of course. The distinguished-looking chorister there is Amalyt D'Anomen. He has been the chorister of the Anomen Regis . . . before it was damaged by the storms created in the battle. The equally distinguished personage in black is Chamion D'Council, the head councilor of the city of Variana." Bhayar turned to the two local officials. "Commander Quaeryt is the most battle-wounded and tested of my commanders, and also the husband of my charming youngest sister, Vaelora."

Both the chorister and the councilor inclined their heads.

"The commander is also an imager and a scholar," added Bhayar. "We've known each other since we were students, but that's never prevented him from disagreeing with me."

"Battle-wounded . . . ?" ventured Amalyt. "I would not have thought . . ." He shook his head and added, almost apologetically, "Scholars here are much . . . different, it appears."

"You might explain, Quaeryt," suggested Bhayar. "Briefly."

"I never set out to be an officer," began Quaeryt. "I was pressed into service in the revolt in Tilbor. After the revolt, I served briefly as princeps of Tilbor, then as temporary governor of Montagne province after the earthquake and eruption there, long enough to restore order, before being called to serve as a subcommander in the campaign that led to Variana."

"Commander Quaeryt proved most effective in leading from the front and forging somewhat inexperienced troops and officers into a most effective and devastating force," said Deucalon smoothly. "He came close to dying at least twice."

"I do believe dinner is waiting," said Bhayar, nodding toward the open double doors, standing back, and then following the others.

A shorter table had been set, with screens shortening the room and blocking off the long table. Bhayar stood behind the chair at the end closest to the double doors from the sitting room, while Deucalon took the chair at the end of the table opposite Bhayar. To Bhayar's right was Chamion, and to his left was Vaelora. Amalyt was seated below Vaelora, and Quaeryt below Chamion.

Once the others were seated, Bhayar settled himself at the head of the table and waited for the ranker in formal greens to fill the crystal goblets with a pale amber vintage. Then he raised his goblet. "My appreciation to our guests for their courtesy in joining us."

"And our appreciation to you, Lord Bhayar," replied Chamion in a raspy deep voice, "for seeking us out."

After everyone had drunk, or sipped, the toast, and as the uniformed servers began slipping soup bowls before the diners, Bhayar spoke again. "I sought you out in hopes you could provide observations and other thoughts that will make the next months . . . less disruptive for everyone."

"If I might say so, Lord Bhayar," replied Amalyt immediately, with a slightly testy edge to his voice, "the very fact of your inviting us suggests that you wish the choristers of the Nameless to be supportive of your rule. While I certainly would rather have peace than anarchy or continuing conflict, I would suggest that the Nameless cannot be invoked as supporting or opposing any ruler . . ."

Bhayar glanced to Quaeryt.

"Honored Chorister," began Quaeryt, "Rex Kharst attacked Telaryn with no warning or provocation after he learned that the former and ancient capital of Telaryn had been partly destroyed by fire and earthquake. When Lord Bhayar responded, Rex Kharst immediately threatened all his people and High Holders with death and worse if they so much as sold a single keg of flour to the armed forces of Telaryn. He had his own men burn the fields of poor tenants. He dispatched assassins against his own High Holders. Lord

Bhayar and all his commanders have taken great pains to avoid creating unnecessary suffering for the people of Bovaria, and he has treated them far more fairly than did Rex Kharst."

"I cannot dispute you, Commander, nor would I even if your words were not true, although I must admit that at least some of what you say, and perhaps more, is unhappily so. My concern and belief is that such views not be discussed in the anomen."

"I can understand your feelings, Chorister Amalyt," responded Quaeryt in as gentle but firm a voice as he could manage, "but so far as I am aware, and you may certainly correct me if I misspeak, the Nameless stands above physically taking sides in the conflicts of men. Yet . . . over time, those who have served the Nameless have often expressed their views about the practices of rulers and High Holders and whether those practices were in accord with the precepts set forth as worthy of the Nameless. If I recall correctly"—Quaeryt paused just slightly, then continued—"in olden times, the noted chorister Tharyn Arysyn barred even Rholan the Unnamer from the north anomen in Montagne, not far from Rholan's own home, saying that only those who had studied the Nameless could speak and that Rholan's teachings were not in accord with the ways of Tela. Perhaps I am misinterpreting that history, but it would appear that the chorister was using the imprimatur of the Nameless in support of the way things were, and that includes the ways of ruling. Likewise, is it not true that when barely a man, Rholan supported the Chorister Sumaal, when Sumaal allowed High Holder Quintus of Montagne to proclaim the unfitness of Lord Suffryk of Tela to rule? As I have read, Rholan declared that Sumaal was only doing what any good chorister should do in allowing Quintus to apply the precepts of the Nameless to rulers as well as to the common man, the tradesman, the factor, or the High Holder." Quaeryt looked to Amalyt, waiting.

"You appear unusually well read in matters concerning the Nameless," replied the chorister, "yet times and people demand . . . certain adjustments . . . to . . . older practices."

"Rholan had some words for that, I believe," said Quaeryt. "Justice is what men should do, while law is what codes and powers require them to do, and that is invariably less than what they should do or what the Nameless requires of them. Your words suggest that choristers must refrain from applying the precepts of the Nameless to rulers. Would it be inaccurate, or against the precepts to which you have devoted your life, to declare that, while war is indeed deplorable, and that many suffered in the conflict, Lord Bhayar has behaved more honorably than the previous ruler of Bovaria, and that you trust he will continue to do so . . . and that you will measure his behavior and acts, as you do those of all men, against the precepts of the Nameless?"

A wry smile appeared on Amalyt's lips. "You are a dangerous man, Commander, especially for one so comparatively young. If I speak against your words, I appear unreasonable to you . . . and to a lesser amount, to myself. Yet if I raise my voice in support of Lord Bhayar, most of my congregants will discredit me."

"Then do not speak in support of Lord Bhayar," replied Quaeryt. "Tell your congregants that, so far, matters have been far better than anyone could have hoped in a war of such scope and that Lord Bhayar has behaved honorably, unlike the late Rex Kharst, and that the test of Lord Bhayar's character and acts will come in the months and years ahead."

Amalyt turned to Bhayar. "He is most persuasive, is he not?"

"I have found him persuasive not because of his words, but because of his judgment." Bhayar offered a slightly crooked smile. "I will not say that I have always found his words agreeable. But his counsel is seldom wrong, even when he was but a modest scholar. Quaeryt has studied more history, and forgotten more than I ever learned, for all that his tutor and mine attempted to require us to learn."

"I suspect you know more than you allow," suggested Chamion.

"That is a trait of all rulers," said Amalyt, "and one cannot blame them."

"It's true of all men of ability," added Deucalon.

After a moment of silence, the councilor spoke again. "There was much destruction in the western part of Variana . . . of a rather strange and mysterious nature."

"There was," agreed Bhayar. "That often occurs in war."

Chamion frowned.

"Perhaps," suggested Vaelora, "the councilor meant to inquire about what you plan to do there."

"We have already rebuilt the exterior and interior of the Chateau Regis, thanks to Commander Quaeryt and his officers, and we have begun to refurbish it. We will restore the lands as time and golds permit. I will see . . . perhaps . . . about repairs to some anomens."

Quaeryt understood the implications of the word "perhaps."

"But . . . what of all the others . . . ?"

"I cannot afford to rebuild all that Rex Kharst destroyed in Telaryn. Surely you do not expect me to rebuild all that has been destroyed here as a result of Kharst's unwise decisions."

"One could hope . . . for . . . some assistance."

"On that, we will have to see once Bovaria is settled once more."

"You have said little, either here or in public, Lord Bhayar, about High Holders . . . whether they or their heirs might still hold their lands, or whether you plan great changes." Chamion looked to the head of the table.

"There will doubtless be some changes in holdings, councilor," replied Bhayar. "There were some High Holders whose behavior was so egregious as to merit loss of position and lands, and there may be others who perished in the fighting without direct heirs. In general, I do not plan to replace reasonable and effective High Holders unless they give me cause. Some may lose a portion of their lands, as I see fit, depending on circumstances, but I believe these matters will sort themselves out over the next few months."

"And choristers?" asked Amalyt.

"Unless a chorister incites against me or causes others to do so, I have no plans to replace choristers. I reserve the right to do so, but would only do so for cause."

Amalyt offered a nod that was as much grudging as accepting.

"Might I inquire as how you plan to rule both Bovaria and Telaryn?" Chamion glanced from Deucalon to Bhayar.

"As one land, with the same laws for both . . . in time, of course. Anything else would not be fair." Bhayar laughed musically. "Anything else wouldn't work well for long, either."

After another three courses, a dessert of pear tarts, and a sparkling wine . . . and more questions and much carefully worded conversation, Bhayar eased back his chair, then rose. "Chorister Amalyt, Councilor Chamion . . . it was a pleasure to get to know you. I trust that we will all be able to work together to assure that the future is more promising than the past."

"That would be our hope as well," replied Chamion.

Amalyt merely nodded and said, "Lord Bhayar."

After the two Bovarians had departed, Bhayar nodded for Deucalon, Quaeryt, and Vaelora to join him in the reception room, although once there, he did not seat himself.

"Marshal, what are your thoughts?"

"They're like all functionaries. They'll accept matters as they are going to be, and they won't openly oppose you. For now, they won't even do so behind closed doors. They will strive to position themselves favorably." Deucalon cleared his throat. "You've never said about High Holders . . ."

"That's because we don't have a complete accounting yet. It appears as though close to fifty High Holders were killed in the battle of Variana and the aftermath. Most died when the Chateau Regis froze solid." Bhayar smiled.

"That worked out rather well, because the majority of those were those closest and most loyal to Kharst."

"From what I observed during the campaign," said Quaeryt, "those most loyal to Kharst would most likely be High Holders of the kind least disposed to an honest and direct ruler."

"Deucalon," said Bhayar, nodding to the marshal, "and I made similar observations from what we saw. That is another reason for dispatching Submarshal Myskyl to the north and west and Submarshal Skarpa to the south. Until they return, we will not know how many high holdings there are in which we will have to replace the holder. There will certainly be those who will need to be replaced with more reliable and loyal High Holders. Such replacement will have to wait until all is largely settled, but it will happen."

"I can see that," said Deucalon, "and I am glad to hear it."

"I'm sure you can, and I'll be taking your counsel in that." Bhayar smiled at Deucalon. "I'll be walking back to my quarters with Vaelora and Quaeryt."

"Yes, sir." Deucalon smiled politely, bowing slightly before turning and departing.

"That went about as well as it could have," observed Bhayar.

"You've been having dinners like that for weeks?" said Quaeryt.

"Not every evening, but more than I'd like. How are your imagers doing?"

"They all recovered far more quickly than I did. Would you like me to see if they can make some repairs to Amalyt's anomen?"

"If it does not strain them for the journey west."

"Are you sending them all with me because I'll need them, or because you want to see how matters are here without us around?"

Bhayar shrugged. "There are reasons. Those are some of them. Imagers are another form of power. I'd like to believe that they're the kind of power the Pharsi can respect."

"Once the imagers are settled, they should wear gray."

"Settled?" The Lord of Telaryn raised his eyebrows.

"On the isle of piers," Quaeryt reminded Bhayar.

"Gray?" Bhayar frowned.

"The black of mourning mixed with the white of ice. Call it a reminder of what the excesses of imaging can do. The imagers will need that reminder. So will a few others."

Bhayar looked at his sister. "He doesn't give up, does he?"

"You wouldn't be here, dear brother, if he were a man who did."

Bhayar winced at the polite chill in Vaelora's voice. "I can see I'm outnumbered." He laughed softly. "The isle of piers and gray uniforms it is, but only after you and I—and Vaelora—are all agreed that matters are settled. Is that all?"

"For now," said Quaeryt cheerfully.

"I fear I may hear that from you two for some time."

"It was your idea that we wed," said Vaelora sweetly.

"It was a good idea," replied Bhayar, "but even the most beautiful rose has thorns, and the most useful knife can slice the user." He walked toward the door. "Tell me what you expect from the Pharsi while we walk back to our quarters."

"They will expect to be treated with respect, and most likely, as you pointed out, many of those on the High Council will be women. They will be leery of a strange Pharsi officer from Telaryn, but Vaelora will help . . ."

By the time they reached the landing leading up to their tower chamber, where they parted with Bhayar, Quaeryt felt he had offered more qualifications and generalizations and fewer concrete observations and expectations than he would have preferred. He said little more until he and Vaelora were alone in their sitting room.

"I was surprised that he actually accepted my suggestions about Myskyl and Skarpa. I'm even more surprised that he mentioned what he'd done at dinner."

"Oh? How do you think he could admit you were right without actually saying so?"

"There is that. But I've never thought of myself as a great speaker."

"You? After giving all those wonderful homilies?"

"Homilies are different from conversations at dinners involving matters of state where every word and expression is weighed and analyzed."

"You remind me of Rholan," said Vaelora.

"Me?"

"Wait a moment." She walked to the table that held the small brown leatherbound volume and began to leaf through it. "Here. Just listen to this."

Quaeryt listened.

> "To hear Rholan converse, one would never have guessed at his power when he spoke to believers or to deliver a homily. Some years back, when Rholan was visiting the small hamlet of Korisynt on the lands of High Holder Klaertyn, the people gathered to hear Rholan, and they petitioned him to beg for flour from the High Holder, for drought and burning heat had scorched their fields. They had already been refused by Klaertyn, who claimed that he had no flour or grain to

spare. Klaertyn heard that the people had gathered, and he rode down to the hamlet with a score of armsmen to disperse them. When they saw the High Holder, they once more begged for flour so that they could have bread, and again he said he had none.

"Then Rholan stepped forward and said to Klaertyn in that strangely powerful voice, 'Tell your people that you have no grain for them, or no flour. Tell them, when this very day you have sold barrels of fine flour to the factors of Cloisonyt. Tell them that your armsmen did not see this.' Klaertyn could not say such without branding himself a liar. So he made the best of it, and told the people of the hamlet that his steward would deliver barrels of flour on the morrow. And he did. But he never forgot, and, subsequently, when an outbreak of the Red Death struck Korisynt, leaving no family unscathed, and some with no survivors at all, High Holder Klaertyn removed the survivors, razed all the structures, and planted saplings, primarily oaks and goldenwoods, so that by the time of his grandsons, no one would know that such a town had ever existed, and already, as I write this, few remember, and some choristers believe that Rholan made up the entire incident."

When Vaelora finished, she looked at her husband. "You see?"

"I'm not Rholan."

"No . . . you could be more . . . if you let Bhayar claim much of the credit for what you do."

Quaeryt decided to let her have the last word on that . . . because, much as it sometimes galled him, he knew she was right. So he put his arms around her and embraced her gently, holding her silently for a long, long time.

Sunlight poured in through the small leaded panes of the tower window on Vendrei morning barely after dawn. The diffused illumination turned the top of the ancient oak bedstead a dark gold, a gold Quaeryt had restored from the white to which his semiconscious imaging had turned everything around him after the battle. He still wasn't certain that their chambers looked as they once had, although he had needed to re-image the finish of the stone walls and the floor more than once to meet Vaelora's standards.

Quaeryt turned slightly, reaching for her, only to find that she already had moved to a sitting position in the wide bed and was propping another pillow behind her back.

Quaeryt smiled broadly at her.

"Not this morning, dearest. My back is aching, and I'm sore all over. No one mentioned that those sorts of things happened when you're with child."

"I wouldn't know," he admitted.

"Both Bhayar and Deucalon were eager to mention you are an imager, but neither mentioned that you had acted as a chorister? Bhayar even made sure that never came up."

"You know exactly what that means, devious woman."

"Me? Devious? How could you say that? I was the one who approached you in the beginning, was I not?"

"I stand corrected. Perhaps you'd prefer 'deceptively direct,' dear one?"

Vaelora laughed, that low husky sound that Quaeryt had always liked. "For all that you protest, dearest, you do have a way with words . . . and not just in delivering homilies."

"I wish you were receptive to my other ways . . ." Quaeryt grinned, mock-lasciviously.

Vaelora arched both eyebrows. "What are your plans for the day?"

"I have to plan for the day?" When Vaelora only replied with a despairing look, Quaeryt finally answered her question. "I will rise, wash up, dress, eat breakfast, and proceed from there."

"What about the nineteen glasses you've left out?"

"And when I finish, I'll try to get seven solid glasses of sleep."

"Dearest . . ."

Because that long-drawn out word was not an endearment, Quaeryt capitulated. "I need to meet with the imager undercaptains individually, especially Khalis and Lhandor. Skarpa and I also need to talk over the arrangements for travel for nine-odd regiments. If the day goes the way they usually do, I'll discover more that I will have to deal with. Oh . . . and I may send imagers to repair an anomen." He smiled as cheerfully as he could. "What about you?"

"Trying to get the estate seamstress to sew some riding clothes that will fit me in the months ahead."

"In three days?"

"I can be persuasive, you've always said."

"That you are, and you've persuaded me that it's time to get up." Quaeryt did not quite bound from the bed.

"Of course, dearest."

Quaeryt didn't bother hiding the wince, especially since Vaelora left the bed in a movement carrying hints of a flounce . . . and disapproval.

Washing up and dressing were accomplished with polite phrases.

Early as they were in getting to the small breakfast room that served only the three of them, Bhayar was getting up from the table when Quaeryt and Vaelora appeared.

"You're up earlier today."

"Quaeryt is feeling much more energetic these mornings," said Vaelora brightly.

This time, Quaeryt managed not to wince.

Bhayar laughed. "I've heard those words from someone else. At least, you're still talking to each other. Or should be." With a smile he glanced at Quaeryt. "We'll talk before I have dinner. I'm entertaining several High Holders from the northeast of Variana—at their request."

"After you sent an indirect invitation?" Quaeryt doubted any Bovarian High Holder would request a meeting with Bhayar without some indication of receptivity and personal safety.

"Something like that."

"You'd like to see me at fifth glass?"

"Around then."

Once Bhayar had left them alone in the breakfast chamber, Vaelora said quietly, "You are fortunate, dearest, that I am slightly more forgiving than Aelina . . . but only slightly."

"I've always said I was fortunate in you," Quaeryt murmured in reply, breaking off what else he might have said as the serving girl appeared with two mugs.

"Tea, sir and Lady?"

"Please," said Vaelora.

Quaeryt nodded, then added, after the server had set the mugs before them and departed to bring breakfast, "Very fortunate, but it is difficult at times not to appreciate you excessively."

"I do appreciate your affection. I cannot always accept it in the spirit in which it is offered."

*Those words hold all too many meanings.* "I understand." *How could you not, even if you don't like it?*

Vaelora offered a smile. "You are a very stubborn man."

"You wouldn't wish me otherwise."

"Nor I either, dearest."

He chuckled ruefully.

After breakfast, Quaeryt made his way from the hold house and was waiting in the foyer at the estate guest house and staff headquarters when Zhelan returned following muster.

"Commander?"

"It will be a busy day. I'll start with the imagers . . ."

"They're in the second tack room off the main stables. That was the best I could do."

"That will be fine. After that, I'll need an escort squad to the boat piers serving the Great Canal. Have you seen Kharst's canal boat?"

"No, sir."

"Good. That might be the first thing in weeks where you haven't anticipated me. Have you been able to locate a scholars' house, or a scholarium?"

"Yes, sir," replied Zhelan. "There's one some four to five milles up the river, on this side. There's also one, I'm told, that's even larger in Laaryn."

"I'll need a squad to accompany me to the one upriver tomorrow. I need to see the scholars before we leave on Lundi. Are there any supplies we're short of that you need me to persuade someone to release or find?"

"No, sir."

"Good." *Not that it's as good as all that.* Quaeryt suspected that Zhelan was having little difficulty because any senior Telaryn officer would be pleased to see Quaeryt leaving Variana. "Plan on two glasses before I'll need to leave for the piers. Oh . . . and some of the imagers will need a squad to escort them to the Anomen Regis . . . the one across from the Chateau Regis."

Zhelan offered a look of inquiry.

"Lord Bhayar would like to offer some repairs to the chorister there. Let's go and see the undercaptains." Quaeryt turned and walked toward the door. When he stepped outside, back into the cool late-autumn air, he saw several commanders walking toward them.

"Greetings," offered Pulaskyr, one of the few Quaeryt knew by more than name.

"Greetings."

Pulaskyr stopped a yard from Quaeryt. "How are you finding Subcommander Alazyn?"

"He seems well grounded and not difficult to work with." As Quaeryt spoke, he couldn't help but notice how the other three commanders eased away from them and slipped into the building serving as headquarters. "I believe that's your doing, and I do appreciate it."

"Thank you. I did tell Skarpa that I thought he'd do well under your command."

"He'd mentioned that."

"You're heading west?"

"To try to persuade the Khellans that they'd do better under Bhayar. It's better than another campaign," Quaeryt said.

"If it doesn't turn into one," replied Pulaskyr with a laugh. With a smile the older commander turned and continued into the building.

Quaeryt and Zhelan turned and walked toward the main stable, then through the open sliding doors and to the second tack room.

When Quaeryt stepped into the small room, with its racked saddles and bridles and other gear, the eight imager undercaptains all stiffened to attention.

"As you were." Quaeryt stood just inside the door and waited a moment. "Among other things, I wanted to tell all of you how impressed I am with the work you did in restoring and repairing the Chateau Regis. I was there the other day and had a good look around. You did yourselves proud, all of you." He smiled broadly, then went on to explain the mission assigned by Bhayar . . . and the day's chore of accomplishing what repairs they could on the Anomen Regis. When he finished, he asked, "Do you have any questions?"

"Just two regiments and first company heading into Khel, sir?" asked Desyrk.

"And all of you. That should be sufficient." *I hope.* "Besides, bringing a larger force would suggest we intend to fight. We may have to, but that's not Lord Bhayar's intention. I'd like to think that the High Council will prove reasonable. I'm not much interested in slaughtering people who should be allies, but the last thing we need is another independent country in Lydar, and the last thing the Khellans need is to make Bhayar angry. Our job is to get those messages across."

The questions after that involved details, the answers to some of which Quaeryt referred to Zhelan. When there were no more questions, Quaeryt announced, "I'll be meeting briefly with each of you, beginning with Undercaptain Voltyr. The rest of you can wait outside."

In moments Quaeryt and Voltyr stood alone in the small tack room, Quaeryt half marveling at how much had changed in the year and a half since the summer day when Voltyr and Quaeryt had been sitting on the porch of the scholarium in Solis and Voltyr had asked Quaeryt, then a mere scholar assistant to Bhayar, what he hoped to gain from traveling to Tilbor.

"You did an outstanding job in supervising the others in refinishing the inside of the Chateau Regis. I hope you can do something with the anomen today, as well."

Voltyr shifted his weight from one boot to the other, smiling almost sheepishly, although Quaeryt thought he saw a certain spark in Voltyr's gray eyes.

Finally, the undercaptain replied, "I kept them on task. I'm no crafter. Baelthm was the one who made sure all the imaging was perfect, and he did most of the final smooth-imaging, if you will. They also had to repair some of the outside ornamentation as well."

"I appreciate the honesty. Is there anything he did that was particularly outstanding?"

"The frieze over the main entrance was totally destroyed. Baelthm and Lhandor created the entire scene from nothing."

"That scene of the chateau rising above the gardens? They did that?"

"Yes, sir." Voltyr smiled slightly. "You might not have noticed, but . . . do you recall the riders on the left side, opposite the images meant to be Bhayar and the senior officers?"

"I recall the hunters. A small grouping . . ."

"Their leader bears a remarkable similarity to a certain recently promoted commander. Baelthm told me he would prefer you not know."

"Thank you for letting me know. How were the other imagers?"

"Threkhyl was most helpful in rearranging the exterior steps and walls, as was Horan. Smaethyl helped all around. So did Desyrk. Khalis was almost as good as Baelthm with the details, and he works hard, harder than the others. He reminds me of Shaelyt."

"I miss Shaelyt," replied Quaeryt. "He was a good imager, and he would have been a superior officer." *Is that why there are so many like Myskyl and Deucalon as senior officers? Because the ones who won't order their men to do anything unless they've done it or are doing it have a greater chance of getting killed before they can get promoted out of danger?*

The next undercaptain Quaeryt saw was Threkhyl.

"I understand you were most helpful in restructuring the front area of the Chateau Regis."

"The whole front of the chateau was a mess. That wasn't from our imaging, either. Chateau that big, and a narrow drive barely wide enough for a single carriage . . ." Threkhyl shook his head and continued on.

After listening to Threkhyl, Quaeryt talked to Desyrk, always reserved and polite, and then waited for Baelthm, the oldest of the imager undercaptains, and by far the weakest imager.

"Good morning, Commander." Baelthm inclined his head.

"Good morning. Undercaptain Voltyr has told me, without your artistic talent, refinishing the interior of the Chateau Regis would have taken longer and been of far lesser quality."

"Some of it, sir, was just using imaging to strengthen what was there and to bond it back to the stone, especially on the inner outside walls . . . not all that bad. Smaethyl and Horan, even Threkhyl, helped with the heavy imaging. You taught me how to do more than I thought I could. Still needed help."

"You and Lhandor had to recreate the main entry frieze?"

Baelthm snorted. "No one could tell us even what had been there. Now that, sir, I'll have to say, took some doing. Whatever you did to the outer walls . . . well, it made them harder than any stone I've ever seen, and whatever was there before collapsed. I think it was a plaster cast or carved plaster or something just as soft. Took both me and young Lhandor, sir. I'm a crafter, maybe an imager crafter, but a crafter. No artist. Lhandor, he made the design and drew the figures, and then we worked on it together. Solid young fellow, he is . . ."

Quaeryt mostly listened, as he did with Horan and Smaethyl.

After them came Lhandor, one of the two remaining Pharsi undercaptains.

"Lhandor, Baelthm was most complimentary of your design of the ornamentation . . ."

"Thank you, sir. I've always liked to draw." The young Pharsi officer looked down for a moment.

"Where did you learn that?"

"At home. My mother . . . she has skill along those lines. Her uncle was a cartographer back in Khel."

Quaeryt had suspected something along those lines, but Lhandor and Khalis had arrived in the middle of the campaign, and Quaeryt hadn't had the time to draw them out as much as he would have liked. "Where in Khel did your family come from?"

"Pointe Neiman. She came with my aunt as a child when my uncle had to . . . leave Khel many years ago. She never said why. I was raised near Estisle."

"Not Nacliano?"

"Oh, no, sir. They can't abide Pharsi there. A hamlet south on the south end of Estisle. It's mostly rocks there."

"What did your uncle do?"

"He drew maps for Ghasphar. He was the High Holder who owns all the diamond ships out of Estisle. I helped him, my uncle, some for the last year before . . . before I was sent to serve."

Quaeryt couldn't help but ask, "Does High Holder Ghasphar have ties to Khel?"

"I heard that his grandfather was from Ouestan, but when I asked Uncle Haelyn about it, he told me not to say a word, especially not in Estisle."

"But you liked drawing things other than maps?" asked Quaeryt with a slight smile.

"Yes, sir."

"I'd like you to give some thought to something larger. If we are successful in bringing peace to Khel, Lord Bhayar is likely to be amenable to our creating something like a scholarium for imagers here in Variana. We would have to build it, of course, but . . . Is coming up with a rough design for that something you'd be interested in?"

"Yes, sir!" Lhandor paused. "But . . . where would it be? I mean . . . designs aren't much good if they're not suited to the place they'll be built."

"I don't know for certain, but the isle of piers is one possibility."

"Could I ride over there and look?"

"Of course. But you'll have to do it today . . . after you work on the anomen."

"I can do that, sir."

Quaeryt couldn't help but smile as the young Pharsi undercaptain departed with a spring in his step.

Khalis was the last of the undercaptains to enter the tack room, and the youngest. While he reminded Quaeryt of Shaelyt, with the exception of the light amber-honey Pharsi complexion and dark hair, there were few physical similarities. The resemblance lay more in the quiet thoughtfulness.

"Where will we be going in Khel, sir?"

"Generally up the Groral River from Kherseilles to Khelgror."

"That's a long way, farther than from Ferravyl to Variana, sir."

"True enough, but I'm hopeful we won't have to fight our way up the river."

"No, sir." Khalis moistened his lips. "Didn't Subcommander Calkoran . . . isn't that what he was supposed to be doing?"

"Lord Bhayar is concerned that the subcommander isn't likely to be believed without a certain . . . reinforcement."

"Even if they believe him, sir, they will likely want to talk and talk and talk."

"You've seen that?"

"Not in Khel, sir. Only in my family, but my grandpere said his father left Khel because he could never get anyone in the family there to agree with him."

"So he came to Lucayl where there was no one older to disagree?" Quaeryt smiled.

"Something like that, sir." Khalis paused, then added, "Except my great-grandmere."

*More likely it was the great-grandmere who wanted to leave.* "That happens in some families."

When Quaeryt finished, he met briefly with Zhelan again.

It was well past the first glass of the afternoon before Quaeryt and fourth squad reached the river piers just north of where the Great Canal diverged from the River Aluse, heading westward across the mostly level lands south of Tuuryl to where, hundreds of milles farther west, it ended at the River Laar.

He made a careful inspection of Kharst's canal boat, then spent time seeing to the arrangements for supply boats, and the mules to tow all those required. After that, for close to a glass, he studied the master map of the canal, checking the distances and planning stops, then rode back to the hold house. Once there, after stabling the mare, he met again with Skarpa to talk over the logistics and the timetable for travel to Ephra.

He was waiting in the corridor outside Bhayar's study by two quints before fifth glass. He waited another quint before Bhayar summoned Quaeryt into the study.

"What have you been doing today?" asked the Lord of Telaryn.

Quaeryt told him, briefly.

"That sounds better than my day." Bhayar paused. "You've alluded to this before, but Myskyl cares little for you. Is there more to this than what happened with Rescalyn?"

"Does there have to be more than that?"

Bhayar laughed. "What happened today wasn't why I wanted to see you, but you might get a chuckle out of it." He motioned to the chairs in front of the table desk, then seated himself and waited for Quaeryt to sit down. "Myskyl accompanied Deucalon to the marshal's morning briefing here. Deucalon held up a letter and read from it. It was from a factor in Villerive. His name was Farrcoyn or Saarcoyn . . . something like that. This factor was professing his loyalty to me, but he also wrote to express his appreciation for one of my senior officers, a subcommander named Quaeryt, or some such. He wrote that you took possession of his dwelling and grounds after the battle of Villerive in a most professional manner, and that when you and your battalion departed, you left almost no trace of their occupation. He appreciated that."

Quaeryt frowned. "I recall that, but . . . what was the problem?"

"Deucalon was most displeased. He insisted that there was a vast difference between professionalism and unwarranted leniency. Myskyl said nothing." Bhayar smiled. "If you had been here, what would you have said?"

"Something along the line that I would agree wholeheartedly with the marshal, that had the factor been uncooperative, my efforts not to destroy his livelihood would definitely have been unwarranted. But I would have pointed out that a number of High Holders who stripped their holdings of everything, including provisions we could have used, are being allowed to retain those lands and holdings. I don't believe that you, or those of us serving you, should employ one standard for factors and another for High Holders, especially when the factor in question was nearly as wealthy as some lesser High Holders. Doing so would undercut your support among the factors without gaining you any more support at all among the High Holders."

Bhayar nodded. "I thought your reply might be something like that. I merely thanked the marshal for his concerns and said I would bring the matter up with you."

"I suspect Myskyl brought the matter to Deucalon's attention. I would not wish to speculate on why that might be."

"Vaelora would . . . and has."

"She is often more perceptive than I . . . and more careful in her words."

"And if Myskyl did suggest Deucalon's words?"

"You would know far better than I," Quaeryt pointed out.

"What I do know is that I'll be relieved when my submarshals are away from Variana and you are on your way to Khel." Bhayar sat back slightly and tilted his head to the left. "That leaves another matter. Do you honestly believe that you and your imagers can rein in the High Holders in the years to come?"

"Don't you?"

"You weren't exactly as effective as you could have been in Montagne."

"I was as effective as necessary in order to restore order. And . . . I was acting alone. The outcry would have died away."

"Especially if something . . . an accident or sickness . . . had happened to another High Holder?"

Quaeryt nodded.

"You are capable of that. I know."

"I'd prefer not to act that way, but it's far better to remove one man than fight uprisings and rebellions."

"How long will it take?"

"As necessary, we can begin to do what needs to be done once I return from Khel."

"Not until then?" A faint, almost humorous smile flitted across Bhayar's lips.

"You need to give the High Holders time to misbehave. That way, any accidents or illnesses will be seen as a result of their actions and not mere greed for their lands on your part."

"But not too much time."

"No." Quaeryt shook his head. "But you will need to allow us the resources to build the scholarium. The imagers cannot be seen as merely your tool. We need to prove useful to many, so that the people, especially in Khel and Bovaria, will support them."

"And not in Telaryn?"

"That will come, but it is not as necessary."

"I suppose not." Bhayar stretched, then stood. "I'd best ready myself for a long dinner."

"Better you than me."

"Your turn will come, right after you return."

*If I return successfully.* "We'll face that then."

"Along with more than you ever dreamed possible, Quaeryt."

"You're so encouraging."

"What else can I be when you're married to Vaelora?"

"Remind me to talk to Aelina when she arrives."

"Don't worry. You won't have to. Vaelora will tell you everything." Bhayar gestured toward the study door. "Go."

Quaeryt grinned, then bowed, turned, and made his way out.

At two quints before ninth glass on Samedi morning, Quaeryt had just stamped and then brushed his muddy boots off on the stone floor of the south-facing covered porch of the scholarium some five milles north of the Chateau Regis.

*Nearly two glasses to cover four milles on what wouldn't have been called a path in Telaryn.* Were all the side roads in Bovaria that bad, or was that because the scholars were in as much disfavor in Bovaria as in Telaryn? *You may find out shortly.*

He glanced back below the porch at the terraced gardens, their low walls composed of local stones stacked and barely fitted together. The ground between the walls was bare, and the stalks and stubble had been turned under the soil, crudely, for Quaeryt could see parts of stalks protruding.

He turned. Two rankers, hands on the hilts of their sabres, stood behind him as he crossed the porch to the door, still carrying full heavy imaging shields. Before Quaeryt reached the door, it opened.

"Who might you be?" offered the lean, almost emaciated, man with straggly blond hair, who wore scholars' browns of a somewhat different cut than those worn by the scholars of Telaryn.

"Quaeryt Rytersyn, scholar and commander in the Southern Army of Telaryn. I'm here to see the maitre."

The scholar glanced at the two armed rankers and the mounted squad drawn up at the foot of the stone steps, then back at Quaeryt. "I don't suppose we can exactly stop you."

"I have no ill intentions."

"I suppose not, not if you are asking. If you would follow me, sir . . ."

Quaeryt ignored the grudging tone of the "sir" and followed the scholar into the two-story oblong brick structure. The rankers followed, the second closing the door.

The scholar walked through a square entry hall floored with boot-scarred slate and down a narrow corridor to a dark gold oak door, half ajar. "Maitre, there's a Telaryn commander here to see you. Says he's a scholar."

"Then have him come in, Brialt."

"Thank you." Quaeryt image-projected absolute authority and stepped past the scholar, ignoring the audible gulp, and closed the door behind himself. "I'm Quaeryt Rytersyn, maitre, a scholar from Solis." *Among other things.*

The white-haired and bent scholar did not rise from the narrow desk, but peered up at Quaeryt, his eyes wide as he took in the brownish green uniform and the commander's insignia. Finally, he spoke in Bovarian. "You command a powerful presence, a strength of purpose I have never sensed before."

"I am who I am."

"You wear a uniform, yet you say you are a scholar."

"I was raised a scholar in Solis, then was a scholar assistant to Lord Bhayar before serving in the Tilboran rebellion and becoming an officer."

"You know we are not scholars like those in Solis."

Quaeryt was only slightly surprised at the standard phrasing, and he replied in kind. "I did not expect that you would be exactly the same. Nor does the moon have sons she acknowledges openly, yet learning exists under moonlight or sunlight, for all that the hunter may be Artiema's guardian."

"I suppose I must welcome you, Quaeryt Rytersyn. I am Charpentier D'Scholarium, and Scholar Maitre of Variana. Might I ask what brings you here?"

"Part of my duties to Lord Bhayar is to talk to the scholars of Bovaria. You represent the scholars here."

"Only here." Charpentier offered a raspy laugh. "Only in this poor scholarium. Once this was the smallest of the three in and around Variana. Now . . . it is all that remains."

Quaeryt eased himself into the rickety-looking single armless wooden chair across the desk from the maitre. "How did that come to be?"

"It is a long story . . . and a sad one."

Quaeryt nodded.

"In the time of Rex Haarl, the father of Rex Kharst, the scholars were respected. Every scholarium received golds from the nearby anomens. Not many, but enough to supplement what we earned from the schools and to maintain the scholarium. Then . . . when Rex Kharst succeeded his sire and took the Chateau Regis, things changed." The maitre sighed. "Had we but known, but yesterday is always so much clearer than tomorrow. You would think we go through life like a man riding backward in a coach, seeing everything after we pass it, if not later, facing where we have been, rather than where we are headed."

"And what happened?" prompted Quaeryt.

"Rex Kharst . . . he ordered that the anomens not give golds to the scholaria. He said that worship belonged in the anomens, and scholars in the scholaria, and choristers should not use their golds to influence what scholars taught, and scholars should not teach what choristers wanted students to believe. The choristers were not unhappy, for they had never cared much for the old custom."

"And the choristers and the anomens prospered?"

"You should see behind the walls of the modest dwelling of Chorister Amalyt . . . or Chorister Bruisn." Charpentier gave a sniffling snort, then wiped his nose with his sleeve. "When Rex Kharst raised the tariffs on the local crafters and merchants, and the factors, fewer would send their boys to the school . . . and there were not even silvers to spare. We expanded the gardens and sold our beer, and it was a fine beer, but the brewers of Variana complained, and the armsmen of the rex came and smashed the brewery. That was three years ago."

Quaeryt nodded slowly. "Kharst was not good for scholars or for Bovaria."

"Who could say such?" The old scholar looked at Quaeryt, then said in a lower voice, "We prayed to the Nameless to grant us a scholar with the power to advise our ruler. Or even for another rex." He laughed, his aged voice cracking. "From what I see of you, we received what we prayed for. Exactly what we prayed for."

"Have you no students?"

"We have no students, and but a handful of scholars remaining, for that is all our modest lands will support. I hear that the scholarium in Laaryn has fared better. The others here in Variana are no more. About those elsewhere"—Charpentier shrugged—"I have not heard."

Quaeryt stood. "Thank you for seeing me. I am sorry to hear of your troubles."

"What will you do, Commander Scholar?"

"For now . . . I will report to Lord Bhayar. What he will do, I do not know, save I doubt that he will visit more tribulation upon the scholars or any scholarium that accepts his rule."

"What else would we do but accept what we cannot change?"

Quaeryt nodded once more, then took his leave of the old and tired building. Once outside, in the muddy space below the front steps, he mounted the mare, then gestured for the squad to ride out. At the foot of the low rise where the lane from the scholarium joined the road that was barely more than a path, he glanced back, his eyes taking in the sagging roofline of the old building and the wooden shutters that doubtless covered windows whose glass the scholars had been unable to replace.

*What has happened to the scholars all across Lydar? Or is it that the rulers changed?* Quaeryt wasn't certain that he knew. What was becoming increasingly clear was that he would receive little or no support or assistance from the scholars . . . and that he was likely better off without what they might offer. *Except that the scholars in Tilbor had refused to accept being impoverished . . . and that had created a different and more difficult situation.*

Both situations saddened him.

*But that is why what you plan must come to be . . . must . . .*

Solayi morning, Quaeryt and Vaelora slept late, if seventh glass could be considered late by any standards except that of the military—or by Bhayar, who seemed to rise glasses before anyone else. They had breakfast, and then Quaeryt headed out to meet with Zhelan to go over details of their departure on Lundi morning. Next came the session with the imager undercaptains, conducted in what had likely been a walled garden of the late High Holder Paitrak. First, Quaeryt received a report from Voltyr on the anomen repairs, indicating that such had been limited to strengthening the walls and repairing cracks in the masonry.

Then Quaeryt surveyed the eight remaining undercaptains before going on. "Because of various things, I have not had a chance to formally evaluate how each of you has progressed in terms of your imaging ability since before the battle of Variana." *And you should have, and now you're squeezing this testing in because you didn't get to it earlier.*

Zhelan and several rankers stood to Quaeryt's left, holding various weapons, as well as a large wooden bucket filled with smooth stones.

"Undercaptain Threkhyl . . . step forward."

The ginger-bearded Threkhyl did so, trying to conceal a smile.

"Your ability to create and move material is prodigious," Quaeryt began. "In the past, however, you have had difficulty in maintaining and holding personal shields . . ."

Threkhyl suddenly had no trouble maintaining an unsmiling expression.

"This could be a problem, since it renders you vulnerable to attack. So . . . I'd like you to raise whatever shield is appropriate." Quaeryt stepped forward and took the staff from the nearest ranker, then motioned for Threkhyl to move out onto the open ground. "You're to hold your shield as long as possible. If they fail or collapse, step back immediately. I'm only interested in your shields. You've already proven your courage in battle. Do you understand?"

"Yes, sir."

Quaeryt squared his stance, holding the staff easily, with his own imaging shields almost against his skin in order to allow himself the ability to use the staff as freely as possible. Then he struck Threkhyl's shields, a blow not particularly hard, because he knew the undercaptain's shields could withstand almost anything—so long as Threkhyl could hold those shields.

The staff rebounded, and Quaeryt tried a thrust toward Threkhyl's legs, then one directly at his chest, moving the staff in a blur, again because he knew the undercaptain had difficulty in maintaining a comprehensive shield and compensated by creating a smaller moving shield. As Quaeryt suspected, after almost a full quint, abruptly Threkhyl stepped back, his face bright red. He was panting heavily, and sweat streamed down his face.

"That's better, Threkhyl. When you practice, I'd like you to try a larger moving shield a bit farther from your body."

"Yes, sir." The burly undercaptain's raspy voice was just short of surly.

*And that hasn't changed much, either,* thought Quaeryt. "Undercaptain Voltyr . . . forward."

Voltyr stepped out and into the clear area Threkhyl had left, his gray eyes on Quaeryt.

Quaeryt motioned for the ranker with the bucket to join him. "I'm going to start throwing stones. I want you to image them out of existence as fast as you can." He began tossing stones, quickly, and Voltyr managed to image each one away, either elsewhere or into nothing.

Abruptly Quaeryt stopped. "Now . . . I want you to hold the strongest personal shields you can. While Major Zhelan pounds on them, I want you to continue imaging the stones away."

Voltyr nodded.

Zhelan stepped forward and took the staff. Quaeryt began tossing stones. He stopped after a quint. Voltyr was breathing hard, and sweating heavily, and his face was flushed, but his shields had held.

"Excellent." Quaeryt turned to Desyrk. "We'll start with the stones." He paused and looked at the bucket, then shook his head. "Major . . . could you have one of your men gather another bucket or two of stones that are roughly fist-sized?"

"Yes, sir." Zhelan smiled.

While one of the rankers hurried off, Quaeryt began throwing the stones for Desyrk. The undercaptain with the wavy blond hair destroyed a score before he missed one, then imaged away another, and missed the next.

"Take a few moments rest, Desyrk. Then I want you to try again, while holding the best shields that you can."

"Yes, sir."

By the time Quaeryt finished evaluating all the undercaptains, well after the first glass of the afternoon, he was sweating heavily despite the cool, almost chill, fall afternoon. More than a few muscles were aching and would doubtless remind him for the next few days that while his imaging skills had more than recovered, his physical endurance had not—and that lack of endurance and physical condition would, in turn, limit the amount of imaging he could accomplish.

*You need more exercise . . . much more.*

All of the undercaptains had improved, although some, particularly Voltyr, Khalis, and Lhandor, had improved far more than had the others.

After Quaeryt had dismissed the undercaptains, Zhelan turned. "You're tired. Did you have to test each of them personally?"

"Who else would you suggest?" asked Quaeryt dryly. "Besides, I needed the exercise more than they did." He paused. "What did your rankers think?"

"Any rankers with sense have already decided that they don't want to be imagers." Zhelan added wryly, "I wouldn't wish your position for all the gold in Lord Bhayar's coffers."

*Some of us don't have that choice.* But Quaeryt laughed ruefully and said, "You're kind, Major, but I wouldn't want your position, either."

"Then it's good we each have what we do, sir."

They both smiled.

Because of the duration of the individual sessions with the undercaptains, and the need to wash up afterward, it wasn't that much before second glass when Quaeryt finally made his way to Skarpa's small study to wait for his subcommanders. Once inside the study, he sat down behind Skarpa's small table desk and took a deep breath.

It seemed as though only moments had passed before Khaern—the short and wiry subcommander with red hair shot liberally with gray—walked into the study with quick, not quite jerky, movements, his faded gray eyes taking in everything before settling on Quaeryt.

"Good afternoon, sir."

"Good afternoon. How are matters with the Eleventh Regiment?"

"We're set to head out, sir. Even managed to round up some more spare mounts, and a couple of extra tow mules for the supply flatboats. Grain's tight, but I've inquired and got the names of some grain factors in Eluthyn and Laaryn."

"You've been busy."

At that moment Alazyn entered. The junior subcommander was no taller than Khaern, but broader in the shoulders, and moved with an easy grace for all his muscularity, closing the door firmly, but so quietly that there was almost no sound. Under jet-black hair, his brown eyes took in everything without seeming to do so. "Good afternoon, Commander, Subcommander."

"Have a seat." Quaeryt gestured to the empty chair. "We were talking about arrangements for tomorrow and for moving along the Great Canal. I'd meant to ask you earlier, Alazyn, and I apologize for not doing so, but do you have a company of engineers?"

"Yes, sir." Alazyn paused. "That is, I've got a company that's on the roster as engineers, and the captain, the undercaptain, and a couple of squad leaders know their trade. The rankers, well, there are a couple of journeyman carpenters, and a wheelwright that's barely more than an apprentice . . ."

When Alazyn had finished, Quaeryt nodded. "You've got more engineers than all Southern Army had. That's good, because Subcommander Khaern only has about a squad."

"Why are you worried about engineers, sir?"

"Because I have no idea what shape the Great Canal might be in once we get farther west . . . or what the water level is in the River Laar . . ."

All in all, Quaeryt spent close to a glass with the subcommanders, going over everything from the travel route, the supply situation, payroll details, even provisions for a farrier and spare horseshoes.

Then, at fourth glass, the three of them walked to the salon in the dwelling —or what had been the salon until much of the furnishings had been removed and replaced with a long table that had likely been used for dining—for a meeting of all the regimental commanders in Southern Army and those under Quaeryt's command.

Skarpa was waiting outside the door and beckoned to Quaeryt.

"Just go on in," Quaeryt told Alazyn and Khaern. As he stopped beside Skarpa, Alazyn and Khaern nodded and stepped through the doorway into the makeshift conference room.

"Not all the other subcommanders are here yet," added Skarpa. "Just Fhaen and Fhaasn, and Meinyt."

*The one most junior and the two loyal to Skarpa.* While that didn't surprise Quaeryt, it suggested certain . . . possibilities.

"Kharllon isn't here yet, either," added Skarpa in a low voice.

"He'll be the last, but barely."

"My thought as well."

Two subcommanders approached, hurrying down the hallway from the front hall. The first was graying, the second balding and blond. Both nodded to Quaeryt and Skarpa. "Good afternoon, Commander, Submarshal."

"Good afternoon, Dulaek, Paedn," replied Skarpa. "We'll be starting in a few moments."

No sooner had the pair entered the salon than the last two officers, who had to be Commander Kharllon and Subcommander Meurn, appeared from the rear of the building, walking at a steady, but not swift pace. Both nodded politely and said, "Good afternoon, Submarshal."

Quaeryt followed them into the salon, noting as he entered that the head of the table had been left for Skarpa, and the chair to Skarpa's right for Quaeryt. Kharllon had taken the place to Skarpa's left, across from Quaeryt. Quaeryt did not sit, but remained standing as the other officers rose when Skarpa entered.

"As you were."

Quaeryt seated himself, taking a quick look at Kharllon, a clean-shaven, square-chinned man with short light brown hair shot lightly with silver, who looked to be perhaps ten years older than Quaeryt. Kharllon smiled warmly at Quaeryt, even with his pale blue eyes, and nodded. Quaeryt returned the nod and smile.

"Part of the purpose of this meeting is simply for all of you to see the other regimental commanders," began Skarpa. "Some of you already know each other, but most of you don't know Commander Quaeryt except by name, or Subcommander Khaern, Subcommander Alazyn, and Subcommander Fhaen, who is succeeding me as commander of Third Regiment. Several of you have not met Subcommander Meinyt." As he spoke each officer's name, Skarpa gestured toward the man. After his opening words, Skarpa outlined both the orders for Southern Army and those for Quaeryt and his forces, then gave the order of march for the morning, although Quaeryt knew that the submarshal had to have provided that to each officer individually already. "The regimental order will change daily, as I've discussed. Are there any questions or observations?" Skarpa looked toward Kharllon.

"Have you been given any indication how long this operation . . . is expected to take, sir?"

"Until we've accomplished what's necessary. Several months, if not longer. Commander Quaeryt will be operating independently once he and his forces leave Ephra, of course."

"I'm curious, sir," asked Meurn, "as to why seven regiments are necessary to deal with High Holders who have only a few hundred armsmen."

"Together they might mass more than a regiment. We'll also be stationed almost on the border with Antiago. Relations between Rex Kharst and the Autarch were never good. Those between Lord Bhayar and the Autarch have not been any better. Aliaro sent regiments against Southern Army on the march up the Aluse. Aliaro has attacked Ephra at least once already . . ."

"Will this operation be similar to what was required in Tilbor?" Meurn asked.

"Only in that we're likely to be dealing with rebel holders. The land is very different."

"Have you been there? Or has Commander Quaeryt?"

"Actually, I have been in both places," replied Quaeryt. "Tilbor is far cooler, and the trees are mainly evergreens, with greater ease in riding through them, with limited undergrowth. In southern Bovaria and northern Antiago the forests are thicker, the air damper, and the undergrowth almost impassable." Quaeryt was exaggerating a bit, since he'd actually only spent a few weeks over several years in Antiago while his ship had been in port in both Kephria and Liantiago, but he didn't like the intent behind Meurn's questions.

After that, there were few questions, mainly those asking for honest clarifications, and a quint past fifth glass found Quaeryt walking back toward the estate house under a sky that was threatening rain—a cold rain, from the way the wind out of the northwest felt.

*At least you don't have to worry about conducting services and giving homilies.* Yet, even as he thought that, Quaeryt realized that, in a way, he missed those aspects of acting as a chorister—or at least he missed the thought behind creating the homilies.

He found Vaelora in the sitting room of their quarters, looking at two large kit bags and a pile of garments. With a grin, he started to open his mouth.

"Don't say a word, dearest. Not a word."

Quaeryt didn't. He retreated to the bedchamber with *Rholan and the Nameless*, the only volume in sight. He began to leaf through the pages. In light of Vaelora's terse command, he found one passage amusing, not that he would have dared to show or read it to her.

> Men think women vain when they fret over their appearance and their clothing, and Rholan was little different. Any woman could have told him that what a man calls vanity in a woman is not undue worry over her appearance, but an attention to detail to assure that her personal presentation will enhance her power and control. Yet the men who belittle a woman's concern over her dress would think nothing

amiss about fretting over who owes them as little as a copper or whether the cooper or the tanner or the wool factor treats them with proper respect. What is the difference? A woman's appearance is so often the measure of what small power she may have, and that power may be diminished if she fails to match or exceed in appearance and demeanor another woman. Many have noted that a man's power is measured by the respect he is accorded by others, and in the world in which women dwell, respect is seldom granted to women except in their appearance. As the son by blood, if not by inheritance or recognition, of a High Holder, Rholan was less than cognizant of this difference in how power is established, and that may explain in part why so many who followed him so faithfully were men . . .

There was something about the passage, though, that nagged at him, and he was still pondering what it might be and why it bothered him when Vaelora indicated they should leave their quarters just before sixth glass. With only one of Vaelora's kit bags packed, Quaeryt refrained from any comment as he and Vaelora descended to the second level and the small family dining room, where Bhayar, alone, was already waiting.

"I did insist on game hens this evening," Bhayar said. "It will be a time before you'll have a chance for such delicacies."

"You're most thoughtful," replied Vaelora.

"I try, for if I did not, Aelina would discover it sooner or later."

As they seated themselves at the table, Quaeryt heard the pattering of raindrops against the dining room window and glanced briefly toward the ancient leaded panes.

"With luck," Bhayar said, "the rain will have passed before you depart in the morning." He took the carafe of white wine, filled Vaelora's goblet, then his own, and handed the carafe to Quaeryt. After Quaeryt filled his goblet, Bhayar raised his. "To a safe and successful journey."

Once they had finished drinking to the toast, one of the uniformed servers presented each of them with a bowl of a soup.

Vaelora tasted it first and nodded. "A pumpkin soup. It's particularly good for an evening like this. We haven't had that in years."

"Pumpkins don't grow well near Solis."

Vaelora nodded in return, then looked squarely at her brother. "I have my ideas, but what do you expect of me on this journey?"

"To be yourself, and to offer your best judgment to Quaeryt. I do not expect you to efface yourself when you deal with the Pharsi High Council.

That is why I have named you both as my envoys in the documents you will carry."

Vaelora glanced at her husband.

"I haven't seen the documents."

"Did you think he was placating you, sister dear?" asked Bhayar.

"That thought had crossed my mind, foolish woman that I am."

Quaeryt winced.

Bhayar laughed softly. "Your husband would not placate you in something that important."

"Oh . . . does that mean I should not worry if he attempts to placate me?" Vaelora's smile was mischievous.

For her expression, if not her words, Quaeryt was grateful.

"I think, sister dear, I am most grateful for the man to whom you are wed." Before Vaelora could reply, Bhayar gestured toward the server who entered with three platters. "And also grateful for the arrival of the game hens."

"They'll be far more tender than any fowl we'll have for some time," added Quaeryt quickly, "and better prepared."

"Not if I supervise the cooking," said Vaelora.

Quaeryt and Bhayar exchanged knowing glances, then busied themselves with the fare on their platters, which included lightly boiled fresh green beans with almonds, sage-herb rice, and an apricot glaze on the game hens.

After a time and several pleasantries, Bhayar cleared his throat. "The return from Khelgror may be far more dangerous than the journey there, especially if you are successful."

"Because many would prefer that Telaryn be excessively occupied with Khel for years to come? Do you think Aliaro would actually send troops into Khel?" asked Quaeryt.

"Troops?" Bhayar shrugged. "I'd wager against it, but I wouldn't put it past him. I wouldn't put anything past him, even secretly supplying elveweed to Skarpa's troopers."

Quaeryt sensed the undercurrent in Bhayar's words, not that such was surprising, given the way Aliaro had treated Bhayar and Vaelora's sister Chaerila, and how he had dismissed her very existence after her death in a childbirth that had been fatal to her and the infant.

"I do want you both to take care." Bhayar looked from Quaeryt to Vaelora. "And since neither of you takes enough care of yourself . . . Vaelora, try to keep him from doing too much. And you, Quaeryt, keep reminding her that she is with child, and that, even if she can do something, she needs to think about whether she should now that she has to worry about more than herself."

Bhayar laughed. "I've said my piece. I have my doubts that either of you will fully heed my words . . . but try."

The wry irony of his words brought smiles to the faces of both Quaeryt and Vaelora.

"Oh . . . there's one other matter," said Bhayar. "I said I'd have the funds for you for the expedition. Skarpa will have the pay chests for all the men, including your regiments, and the golds for food and supplies until you reach Ephra. You can't be commandeering food and lodging in Khel—unless and after they refuse terms, and even that wouldn't be good. So, along with the documents naming you envoys, I'll have three hundred golds for you in the morning. Make it last as long as you can."

"I definitely will," promised Quaeryt.

The dessert was an apple tart with a flaky crust just a shade overcooked, Quaeryt thought, both from tasting it and seeing the brief frown from Vaelora after her first bite. Still, he thought it tasty and far better than what they would be eating in the weeks ahead.

Later, after they had sipped brandy with Bhayar and then parted, neither Quaeryt nor Vaelora said anything as they climbed the steps to their tower quarters and then made their way into the small sitting room. Vaelora settled into one of the ancient armchairs. Quaeryt did not, walking to the window and then back toward his wife.

"You're pacing," Vaelora said quietly.

"Your brother's never expressed that much concern before."

"That worries me," Vaelora replied.

"He's worried. I don't think he wants to send us, but the last thing he wants is to fight in Khel. If the High Council refuses his terms, he'll either have to fight or resign himself to an independent Khel . . . and that will lead to battles that he or Clayar will have to fight later."

"Can't we use that point with the Pharsi leaders?"

"What point?"

"If they agree to his terms, there won't be any more wars and deaths, and right now, Bhayar is inclined to be more generous."

"We can certainly try." Quaeryt could see Vaelora's eyes narrowing. "I know. Merely trying isn't enough. We have to make it work, some way or another. I just hope whatever way it is doesn't turn out to be too bloody."

"We'll have to see that it doesn't, dearest, won't we?"

Quaeryt nodded, wondering, not for anywhere close to the first time, just how he and Vaelora could do that.

Well before seventh glass on Lundi morning, Quaeryt, Vaelora, and first company left the hold house where Quaeryt had spent more than a month, and began the short ride of a half mille south of the hold—and two milles or so north of the Chateau Regis—to the piers serving both the River Aluse and the Great Canal.

The sky held high thin gray clouds, and the road was muddy, but not excessively so. Quaeryt could only hope that all the mounts and marchers of the regiments would not turn the canal towpath into slop, although it appeared well packed and graveled. The two kit bags containing Vaelora's garments were bulging, and Quaeryt avoided even looking close to where they were strapped behind Vaelora's saddle.

"What can you tell me about the canal boat?" asked Vaelora as they turned on to what passed for a main road.

"Well . . . the squad leader who's been caring for it said that it was fancy and clean. It's not leaking, and all the fittings look to be sound."

"Dearest . . ."

"It's some twenty yards long, and barely five wide, and there is a small galley, a salon, and a small sleeping cabin. The crew quarters are cramped."

"You're not saying much, dearest. How is it furnished? How large is the bed? Is there a wash chamber?"

"The furnishings are adequate, and the bed is wide enough for two. There is a small space barely a yard square in the corner of the bedchamber for bathing."

Had Vaelora's glance at Quaeryt been a quarrel, he would have perished on the spot. Instead, he grinned. "My dear . . . it matters little, since the accommodations are what we have and are far better than most we have endured in past travels." He paused just slightly before adding, "But they look to be quite comfortable. I did make sure that there were enough quilts and blankets."

"I'm sure *you* will need them." Vaelora sniffed.

Two quints later, Quaeryt and Vaelora rode past the squad serving as the vanguard and reined up at the lower pier where the canal boat was tied up.

"It's gorgeous." Vaelora looked at Quaeryt accusingly.

The canal boat was indeed striking, with a well-oiled and glistening oak hull and superstructure. The main cabin structure occupied fifteen yards, perhaps slightly more, with the flat roof of the cabin rising less than two yards above what would have been the main deck, if the forward deck had extended from stem to stern. The short front crew deck extended less than three yards from the rounded bow to where the main cabin began, and the steering deck aft of the cabin was closer to a yard and a half in length.

Quaeryt dismounted, handing the mare's reins to one of the rankers, and then stepped back to Vaelora's mount, holding out a hand for her to dismount. "Lord Bhayar's orders," he said solemnly, before grinning.

Vaelora shook her head in a short gesture, but she did take Quaeryt's hand as she dismounted.

Quaeryt escorted her to their transportation and quarters for the next weeks. On the starboard side of the canal boat, some seven yards aft of the stem, was a set of narrow doors, swung open to reveal a set of steps down into the main cabin. At the bottom of the steps, to the right, or forward, was another narrow pocket door, leading into the cabin that was the bedchamber.

Vaelora moved carefully down the narrow steps and into the sleeping cabin, taking in the paneled walls and the built-in bed, with the headboard against the bulkhead set between the two narrow and angled windows. Beneath the windows were built-in cabinets.

"For travel, this is well appointed," Vaelora said. "There's little space for clothing, though."

"There are large drawers under the bed," replied Quaeryt. *They likely won't hold everything you brought, though.* "Let's move into the salon, so the rankers can carry our gear into the sleeping cabin." He stepped back out of the smaller cabin, almost tripping as the boot heel of his bad left leg caught the edge of the bottom step. He caught himself smoothly and pivoted into the salon.

The salon was paneled in goldenwood, and had wide windows that could be blocked by folding shutters, but those windows only began at what would have been the deck level. A small writing desk stood in the starboard aft corner, with a lamp on a brass mount above it. A space slightly starboard of the middle of the salon was occupied by a narrow oblong goldenwood table with chairs for eight, clearly more for officials or officers to meet than for regular dining. In the forward port corner was a comfortable armchair, with a pair of lamps above it. A second armchair was set next to and aft of the first.

"Everything's aboard, sir," announced the squad leader from the salon entry.

"If you'd tell Major Zhelan to give the word to the boatman to get under way."

"Yes, sir."

As the squad leader vaulted up the steps, Vaelora turned to Quaeryt. "What will you do now?"

"Sit with you and watch the canal go by for half a glass—until we join up with Skarpa and the regiments."

The next four days were uneventful, with cool but not immoderate weather, and no rain and no problems with the canal or the towpath. Quaeryt had just dressed and finished eating an overcooked cheese omelet and bread with bitter peach preserves on Vendrei morning, perhaps two quints before the army and the canal boat were due to head out, when someone rapped on the side door of the boat.

"That doesn't sound good." Across from him at the narrow table in the salon, Vaelora lowered her mug of tea, tea that was lukewarm at best, Quaeryt knew.

He just shook his head, stood and walked across the salon and up the narrow steps, then pushed open the doors and stepped out onto the stone coping on the top of the canal wall. The vertical gap between the boat deck and the coping seemed larger than the night before.

Zhelan stood waiting. "I'm sorry to bother you, sir. The submarshal's scouts have reported a breach in the canal some five milles ahead. The canal's dry there, and the boats from the west are all backed up at the next locks. Those are at Eluthyn . . ."

Quaeryt nodded, then glanced at the hazy early morning sky. He saw no sign of rain. He looked to the west and the water level in the canal in front of the boat. While it was lower, the canal was not empty. Still, if they couldn't fix the breach, he supposed that they didn't have to take the canal boat to get to Khelgror. He'd rather not do that, because Vaelora would have to ride a great deal more, especially on the way back.

"The local canalman managed to close one of the emergency gates near the east end of the breach," Zhelan went on, "and the lock at Eluthyn keeps the water from there from draining, but there are more than twenty boats lined up to the west, bringing harvest grain to Variana. Submarshal Skarpa says that all the boats on the canal will be stopped before long."

Quaeryt took a deep breath. "That's all we need . . . people short of bread just at the beginning of winter." *And Bhayar won't be happy if he finds out you didn't solve the problem.* "Are the imagers ready?"

"Yes, sir."

"I'd like to bring Alazyn's engineer as well. He might be able to help in telling us how best we can repair the breach. How did it happen?"

"Heavy rains four days ago, the canalman said, but the berm side of the canal didn't give way until yesterday."

"I can be with you in a quint or so."

"You don't need to hurry that much, sir. It'll take longer than that before everyone's ready to mount up."

Quaeryt had another thought, one he should have had first. "I'll need to meet with the submarshal before we head out."

"I thought you might, sir. He said he'd be here in a few moments."

Quaeryt didn't have to wait long for the submarshal. Skarpa arrived within moments of the time that Zhelan had left to inform the undercaptains and engineers.

"You know I'd hoped we could reach Eluthyn by last night," began Skarpa.

"I know, but it was better to stop than settling nine regiments on the town in darkness."

Skarpa cleared his throat. "With all the delay . . . it might be best to march ahead today to Eluthyn. It's only seven miles. That way we'd have more time to arrange for supplies and quarters. It would also give the mounts and men at least a day's rest . . ."

Quaeryt grinned. "You scarcely need my approval for that. Except you're suggesting that Eleventh and Nineteenth Regiments accompany Southern Army as well."

"It would rest them more as well."

"By all means. First company and Vaelora and I will have to stay with the boats, though, and I'll need the imager undercaptains and the engineers to deal with the breach in the canal."

"I'm not comfortable with just one company. I'd thought to have two companies from my forces remain here as well."

Almost half a glass passed before Quaeryt, the imagers, first company, and Captain Neusyn from the Nineteenth Regiment engineers rode west, leaving the regiments, the canal boats—and Vaelora—temporarily behind.

It was well past eighth glass when Quaeryt and Neusyn reined up and dismounted on the towpath on the north side of the empty canal, a good five hundred yards east of the leaking emergency water gates, and several hundred yards from the nearest canal post building.

Quaeryt looked at the south side of the canal, the so-called berm side, where the stone walls were backed by the spoil dug from the canal itself. The stone blocks had collapsed into a rough heap. He turned to Captain Neusyn. "Didn't something besides rain have to cause this?"

"Almost looks like someone blasted the underburden away, so that the water leached out and eroded the support under the lowest course of stones until they collapsed." Neusyn frowned. "But that . . . I need to look at it more closely."

Quaeryt looked skeptically at the muddy bottom of the canal.

"Better to cross through the mud," said Neusyn. "I wouldn't want to walk across that emergency gate." He gestured vaguely with the iron-tipped staff he carried. "It's barely holding, and if it goes, the water will widen the breach and drain more of the canal."

Quaeryt could see that, but he didn't like it. He and the engineer had to walk almost a hundred yards farther west until they reached a set of stone steps that allowed a short jump down to the mud of the canal bottom. Quaeryt's boots sank into the mud not quite to midcalf, and dark globs of mud sprayed up onto his trousers. He wasn't terribly happy as he made his way through the mud after the engineer, trying not to spray more of the smelly mud on himself.

Once Neusyn reached the far side of the canal, he stopped short of the hole in the bottom of the canal that extended to the south and all the way through where the stone walls and the stone and earth berm beyond had been. There, only a long pile of cut stones lay toppled and half buried in muck and mud. After studying the toppled stones for several moments, the engineer captain walked around the stones, prodding them and the area around them with the iron-tipped staff. He shook his head as the staff revealed a length of bone, then another.

"The stories were true, it would seem," said Quaeryt. "That looks like a human bone."

"There are others over there at the other side of the gap . . . just short of where the wall is sagging," said Neusyn.

Quaeryt looked in the direction the staff pointed. He couldn't be certain, but he thought there were enough bones there to account for several bodies.

"The clay preserved them for a time," added the engineer. "But bad engineering tells in the end."

"What was so bad about it?" asked Quaeryt.

"Do you see these white chalky flakes and grains?"

The white fragments that Neusyn pointed out obviously meant something, but what that might be Quaeryt had no idea. So he just nodded.

"They're gypsum."

That didn't explain any more to Quaeryt. "I'm afraid I don't understand."

"It dissolves when there's a lot of water around it. When they built the canal, after they laid the stone walls and mortared the stones in place, they sealed the bottom of the canal itself with clay. That's usually enough to keep seepage to a minimum, but if anything happens . . ."

"The rain couldn't have done that in a few days, then?"

"No. It's been sinking for years. You can see the way the canal walls have sunk. Might have been the runoff from the berm funneled down there, or maybe even rodent holes . . ."

Quaeryt looked at the stone courses. From what he could see, the stones had sagged in various ways for more than fifty yards on each side of the gap in the wall and berm.

". . . wouldn't be that obvious with water in the canal, but now . . ."

"So . . . what will it take to put it right?" asked Quaeryt.

"The footings under the stone courses need to be replaced, with solid stone, if we can find any. The part of the canal bottom that's been eroded needs to be replaced with solid fill, with at least half a yard of good clay on the top, and then the stones reset and mortared. A good half yard of clay on the outside of the south wall, and the same on the bottom of the canal where it's been washed away. Stone rip-rap or backing on the outside before the berm is replaced . . ."

"All right. Let's go back. You explain that carefully to the imagers, and we'll get to work."

"Can they . . . ?"

"That's what they're here for. This can't be any harder than what they've done before, and they'll be doing it without having an enemy attack them while they're working."

As the two waded through the mud to the north side of the canal and then climbed up to the towpath, Quaeryt couldn't help but think about the bodies buried under the walls. *But you've killed far more men than this canal did . . . and for what?* He didn't have an answer to his own question . . . only a hope that the deaths might lead to a more peaceful and united Lydar. *Does that hope justify what you've done?*

Quaeryt pushed those questions into the back of his mind and gathered the undercaptains, listening as the engineer had explained what was necessary.

Then Quaeryt turned to the imagers. "Horan . . . image those stones in the breach, the pile of muddy ones in that hole in the bottom of the canal, onto the berm. That's the flat raised part beyond the wall. Put the stones, say, fifty yards west of the westernmost part of the breach."

"Yes, sir."

Once those stones had been moved, Quaeryt turned to Desyrk. "If you would begin to image away the muck in the breach, in small amounts so that no load tires you too much."

Desyrk nodded, then began to concentrate. Bit by bit, the muck began to vanish. After less than a quint, the first riders of the Southern Army began to ride past, along the towpath and the ground to the north of the canal.

After a quint Quaeryt said, "You stop for now. Smaethyl, you take over with the muck."

As he could, Quaeryt alternated between imagers, but it was past the first glass of the afternoon before they finished cleaning out the breach. By then Skarpa's forces and Quaeryt's two regiments had all passed and were, Quaeryt hoped, settling into Eluthyn.

When he was satisfied with the cleanup and removal, Quaeryt summoned the engineer.

Neusyn looked at the gaping gash where, two glasses before, there had been a breach, uneven courses of stone, toppled stones and muck. "That would have taken at least several days with all my men."

"Imagers do offer some advantages." Quaeryt glanced over at the undercaptains, all of them sweating somewhat despite the cool breeze out of the northwest, then at the gash. After several moments, he turned to the engineer. "You need a stone footing, don't you?"

"Yes, sir."

"It should run from one end to the other, but how high should the stone be?"

"About a digit below the bottom of the lowest course of the stonework on each side."

Quaeryt studied the gash, and the hundred or so yards between the undamaged canal walls, thinking. Then, he reached out into the lands to the south of the canal, lands he hoped had been warmed by the weak autumn sun during the morning. Carefully, he visualized a smooth stone footing, filling the lower trench, and stretching from one wall to the other.

A flash of light and a wave of chill swept over the group, and a slight feeling of dizziness struck Quaeryt . . . and passed. He looked across the empty canal at the smooth expanse of gray stone, then at the sparkling ice and frost stretching southward across the stubbled fields beyond the canal for close to half a mille. After taking a deep breath, he said to Neusyn, "That will have to warm up, I think, before the others begin to image the walls back in place."

The captain swallowed. "As you say, Commander."

Quaeryt looked to the undercaptains. "We all need a break, and some rations, before we go back to work on the walls."

In the later part of the afternoon, after a break of nearly a glass, Quaeryt directed the undercaptains in their imaging to replace the stonework, then the clay, and finally the berm. They did not finish until well after fourth glass. While they made ready to return to the regiments, Quaeryt and Neusyn walked the several hundred yards to the small canal house. The weathered canalman was standing outside, waiting.

"The repairs are finished," Quaeryt said.

"Sir . . . never seen anything like that," said the weathered canalman, looking westward at the stonework, then back at the commander.

"It's not something imagers usually do," replied Quaeryt, "but Lord Bhayar needs the Great Canal in working order. I don't think you should open the locks and emergency water gates for another glass or so." Quaeryt was being cautious, but he couldn't help but worry that some of the material might be chill and should warm before coming in contact with water.

"Whatever you say, sir."

Quaeryt nodded, then headed over to where the mare and the undercaptains were mounting up.

On the ride back to the canal boats and first company, Quaeryt took some time imaging the dried mud off his trousers, but being careful not to image away any of the fabric. When he finished, he realized that he was tired, but only physically so, and that he was having no trouble with his shields. That was good, especially after imaging a massive section of stone into place.

"Well?" said Vaelora when Quaeryt returned. She wrinkled her nose. "What . . . ?"

"Canal mud. It's not exactly perfume. I imaged away the worst of it."

"How bad was it?"

"One of Kharst's engineers cut corners . . ." He went on to explain what had happened and what he and the other imagers had been forced to do, then finished, "It will likely be tomorrow afternoon before the springs refill this section of the canal, and we'll have to wait until at least some of the cargo boats—"

"Why do we have to wait?"

"Because they're all jammed up at the locks in Eluthyn. We couldn't get through until they've moved." Before Vaelora could say more, he went on. "Since we're going to be here for another day, we might as well visit Eluthyn tomorrow. The locals should be getting used to a Telaryn force of some size by now. There might even be an inn with decent fare." He paused. "I do think that the accommodations here are likely to be better than in the town."

"In that, dearest, I would agree, but it would be nice to see more than water and canal walls and fields and small towns."

"We can manage that."

Vaelora smiled.

Quaeryt woke up with a start, lying on his back. He could not move, except to breathe, and his breath was a thin white cloud above him that crystallized into fine needles of ice that stabbed at the flesh of his face as they solidified and fell. The chill seeped over him like ice water, but without any sense of wetness as it bit into his exposed flesh.

Standing in the ice mist facing him were white figures, assemblages of bones, angular skeletons. The sightless eyeholes of the skulls looked at him, accusingly. As he lay there, Quaeryt became aware that standing on each side of where he lay were men in the blue-gray uniforms of Bovaria. Each Bovarian trooper was coated in ice, and each stared down at him, as if to demand a reason why he stood there, frozen and immobile.

"No . . ." Quaeryt could barely choke out the words. "No . . ."

Then . . . the skeletons and the ice-covered troopers faded away, and Quaeryt lay in the icy sheets of the wide bed in the canal boat's sleeping chamber, with Vaelora's arms and warmth around him.

"Dearest . . . dearest . . ."

"I'm here," mumbled Quaeryt.

"The windows . . . They're coated with ice." Vaelora wrapped her arms even more tightly around Quaeryt. "Another terrible dream, dearest?"

"I was frozen in ice . . . again. This time . . . there were skeletons, bones of ice, and they were all looking at me."

"Bones, skeletons?"

"Yesterday, when we repaired the canal, we discovered bones, bones of the workers who died building it and who were buried under the walls and the bottom of the canal."

"You didn't say anything about that last night."

"No," he admitted. "I didn't want to think about it."

"You didn't have anything to do with them."

"No . . . but I couldn't help thinking about how they died for a purpose. Have the thousands I've killed, more than those Kharst and his sire killed in building the canal, died for any real purpose?"

"You can't think that way, dearest. You can't."

"I keep telling myself that. I keep saying I've had to do what I've done, but sometimes I'm not very good at persuading my dreams to consider things that way." Quaeryt shivered.

"Thousands would have died if you hadn't done what you did. In the end, it might have gone the other way, and thousands more in Telaryn might have died. Bhayar is far more merciful than Kharst ever was. Neither he nor Father nor Grandsire killed thousands to build canals. They didn't employ assassins to kill uncooperative High Holders."

Quaeryt sat up slowly, looking around the sleeping cabin. The frost that had coated the inside of the shutters and the paneled walls was beginning to melt, but the air was still far cooler than it should have been, even in late fall. "Are you all right?"

"Me? I'm fine." She paused. "Are you?"

"I will be . . . thanks to you." He turned and put his arms around her.

Somewhat later, after Quaeryt had stopped shivering and both were dressed, they sat across from each other at the narrow table in the salon, sipping tea and finishing the remnants of egg toast drizzled with an apple-berry syrup.

"I wonder how Skarpa is doing in finding supplies in Eluthyn," mused Quaeryt.

"He won't be having that much difficulty. It would be rather hard for factors to deny someone with nine regiments." She paused. "Didn't you get a message while I was dressing?"

"I did. It just said that he had established quarters in the north of Eluthyn and that the town was calm. The factors wouldn't cause problems, but purchasing their supplies could be hard on the town if there aren't High Holders with supplies. I should have mentioned that. Then . . ."

"Then what?"

"Purchasing supplies from either holders or factors will drive the costs of goods up here, no matter how it's done."

"There are costs to war that no ruler can pay." Vaelora smiled. "I have no doubts Submarshal Skarpa will have done what he can, dearest. If he hasn't, you can always go to the High Holders. You have a way with them."

Quaeryt made a sour face. "Just another form of coercion."

"All power is a form of coercion," she pointed out.

"It is," he agreed, "but the problem is that you can't get much done without power, and the less power you use, in whatever form, the longer it takes to get things done. The more you use, the more likely people are going to get hurt or killed."

"Sometimes, using more quickly hurts fewer people than not acting." She looked at him. "A man who doesn't act can claim he didn't do anything to hurt people, but what happens if more people die because he doesn't want blood on his hands?"

"I understand that argument all too well, dear. It's why I have nightmares."

"No . . . you have nightmares because you understand the costs of power. Those who don't sleep soundly. You've often wondered why Bhayar is up so early every day. It's because he worries himself awake."

Quaeryt hadn't even considered that, he had to admit.

"Now . . . dearest . . . shall we prepare to ride to Eluthyn?"

By way of an answer, Quaeryt stood and extended his hand to Vaelora.

Two quints later, as they rode westward on the towpath, escorted by first squad from first company, Quaeryt looked at the canal water level, which seemed to be almost as high as it had been before the breach—until they reached the closed water gate. While water was filling the space between the easternmost lock and the water gate, it was less than a yard deep, needing another yard before it reached a level equal with that behind the emergency water gate to the east.

Before long, they began to ride past more and more cots set in the fields, both to the north and the south of the canal, and then the towpath was bordered by warehouses and factorages, stretching for the several hundred yards leading to the first lock just east of where the canal crossed the Phraan River. The water level remained about a yard deep, and most of the canal boats tied to the bollards on the canal wall tilted slightly one way or the other, indicating that the water had not yet risen enough to lift them off the bottom of the canal.

They rode up the ramps beside the two locks, both empty of boats, and then to where the canal crossed the Phraan River. The river was narrower than even the canal, and Kharst's engineers had resolved the problem of crossing the river simply. They'd just created a stone culvert under the canal, so that where the canal crossed the river, it was effectively a stone tube above the culvert.

To the west of the river, the canal widened to almost twenty yards across for close to half a mille, and canal boats were tied end to end and two deep for most of that distance. A hundred yards ahead, a large stone plaza extended north from the canal towpath, and beyond it a wide paved boulevard, the first paved street or road Quaeryt had seen since leaving Variana. He gestured to the squad leader and Vaelora, then turned the mare north and led the others across the plaza. Because it was Samedi, a market day, there were carts and stalls and vendors set up all around the plaza. Quaeryt also noted more than a few men in the garb of boatmen, but that was to be expected, given that Eluthyn was a stop on the canal and that more than the normal number of canal boats were tied up because of the breach in the canal.

More than a few people glanced at the uniformed riders, particularly those closer to the center of the plaza as they edged back from the armed troopers, but most soon looked away once it was clear that the riders were passing through the plaza.

"They don't seem terribly worried," said Vaelora quietly.

"Most likely because of the way Skarpa handled things." Quaeryt's words were supported by the fact that he saw no Telaryn patrols riding the boulevard. If the people in Eluthyn had accepted Bhayar's rule, patrols were not called for unless there were disturbances.

Beyond the plaza the boulevard gradually narrowed, although there remained enough space for several wagons abreast. The shops and crafting establishments that stood back of the wide stone sidewalks were modest, but well kept. Quaeryt noticed two coppersmiths in the space of a long block, as well as a silversmith.

"You! The Telaryn officer!"

Quaeryt turned and reined up the mare, gesturing for the squad to halt. Then he rode over to a gray stone building on the east side of the boulevard, roofed with gray slate, old enough that the slate tiles were green with moss in places. There on the limestone steps stood a heavyset man in a stylish gray coat and matching trousers.

"You had a question?" asked Quaeryt, looking at the older man, who was likely half a head taller than Quaeryt himself.

"What are you doing here? You and all the other Telaryn troops? The war's over, isn't it? We agreed to accept your lord's rule."

"You haven't heard?" asked Quaeryt mildly. "Although Lord Bhayar defeated Rex Kharst at Variana over a month ago, not all parts of Bovaria have been as agreeable as you have. As for why we're here, we're in the vanguard of the Southern Army headed for Ephra. Some regiments will be posted there to watch Autarch Aliaro's forces. Some others will be heading to the lands that were once Khel, since they have not yet agreed to Lord Bhayar's terms. The troopers here will not remain long, most likely only another day . . . unless there are severe storms." Quaeryt smiled politely. "Might I ask your name, sir?"

"My name is mine, not yours."

Quaeryt refrained from sighing. While image-projecting both absolute authority and well-meaning friendliness, he spoke again. "I certainly mean you no harm, sir, but as an officer of Lord Bhayar, I cannot accept the way in which you replied. So I will offer my name and ask once more for yours. I am Commander Quaeryt Rytersyn, in command of the Eleventh and Nineteenth Regiments. You are?"

The large man paled slightly, then swallowed. "Grekial D'Factorius, Commander."

"Thank you. I wish you well, Factor Grekial. Good day." With a nod Quaeryt turned the mare and rode back to where he rejoined Vaelora.

"You were powerfully mannered, dearest," she murmured.

"I wish I had not been required to do so."

"He will remember both your power and your forbearance."

Quaeryt certainly hoped so.

After several blocks the shops gave way to two-story dwellings, and then to those of one story, and before long they were nearing what looked to be the northern end of Eluthyn proper. Ahead was a squad of Telaryn troopers, heading southward, with an undercaptain in the lead.

"Commander! Sir!" The undercaptain rode forward and reined up as Quaeryt signaled his own troopers to a halt.

"Yes, Undercaptain?"

"We just left the submarshal, sir, with a dispatch for you." The officer handed a folded and sealed paper to Quaeryt.

Quaeryt broke the seal and read the message.

*Commander—*

*We have availed ourselves of the generosity of High Holder Cleotyr.*

*He has hopes that he might make your acquaintance and that of Lady Vaelora . . . if such is possible.*

Underneath the brief lines was Skarpa's signature.

Quaeryt handed the missive to Vaelora, who read it and handed it back.

"Lead on, Undercaptain," said Quaeryt.

"Yes, sir!" The undercaptain turned his mount, and called out orders to his squad, his voice enthusiastically cheerful. "To the rear, ride!"

"He is most cheerful," observed Vaelora, easing her mount closer to Quaeryt's mare, so much that their boots nearly brushed.

"Of course. We saved him a ride of more than ten milles, and he can report success."

"I'm not dressed for calling on High Holders."

"We don't need to ride seven milles back and then another seven milles to return here," he pointed out reasonably.

"I'm only wearing good riding clothes," murmured Vaelora.

"What else would you be wearing for riding?" he replied, adding in a voice below a whisper, "That kind of riding, anyway."

"Dearest . . ."

Quaeryt did not wince at the icily exasperated tone, but he did manage to grin.

"You are impossible."

"That is quite likely, as you well know."

Ahead of them, a trooper galloped away, heading northward along the road that had become merely packed clay beyond the edges of Eluthyn.

*No doubt to tell Skarpa that we're on our way.* Quaeryt glanced toward Vaelora.

She looked straight ahead, clearly refusing to look in his direction, although he thought he detected the faintest hint of a smile at the corners of her lips.

After riding another mille or so, the undercaptain and his squad rode through a set of gates guarded by a squad of foot troopers. Quaeryt and Vaelora and their troopers followed.

The graveled drive that led from the dull red-brick entry gates with their black iron grillwork toward the hold house curved through gently rising grounds that were largely meadows, although Quaeryt wasn't totally sure about that because much of the grass had been flattened, either by winds or late and heavy rain. Several hundred yards back from the drive on each side rose tall trees, mainly oaks, set in what was clearly parkland, for there was little undergrowth.

Nearly half a mille up the drive was the hold house, a moderately sprawling two-story structure constructed largely of the same dull red brick as the gates, with limestone cornices, arches, and window ledges.

Skarpa was standing in the midday shade under the small covered portico.

"I had hoped you might appear," he offered, looking to Vaelora and adding, "and especially you, Lady Vaelora."

"How could we not?" replied Vaelora brightly.

Quaeryt merely nodded as he dismounted and handed the mare's reins to the nearest ranker, before moving to offer a hand to Vaelora in dismounting. As usual, she needed no assistance, but took his hand, if putting no weight at all on it while alighting on the lowest step of the brick and stone steps up to the main entry.

"High Holder Cleotyr and his wife are most hopeful that you will accept their hospitality for midday refreshments," Skarpa added.

"We would be delighted," announced Vaelora, "although we are dressed for riding." She did not glance sideways at Quaeryt, although he felt that she did.

"I am quite certain that they understand you are traveling, Lady. I assure you that you look beautiful."

"You are most kind."

"No. I'm honest. Your husband knows that."

Quaeryt grinned. "I told her that she was beautiful in riding clothes. She didn't believe me."

"She should. You're too honest for your own good, Quaeryt." With that, Skarpa turned and led them up the low steps to the entry doors, opened by a footman in maroon livery.

Waiting in the square receiving hall beyond the entry foyer were a man and a woman. The man was likely five or six years older than Quaeryt, and his wife close to the High Holder's age. Both immediately inclined their heads as Skarpa, Quaeryt, and Vaelora halted.

"High Holder Cleotyr, Lady Cleonie, might I present Commander Quaeryt and his wife Lady Vaelora? She is the sister of Lord Bhayar, as you may recall."

The faintest look of puzzlement crossed the face of the ample High Holder as he looked at Vaelora, but his eyes widened as he beheld Quaeryt, especially after he had removed his visor cap and tendered it to the footman.

By comparison, his petite wife smiled warmly and stepped forward immediately, inclining her head. "Lady Vaelora, you and your husband grace us with your presence."

"We are pleased to be here, and you are most kind to receive us with so little notice," replied Vaelora.

"It is not kindness, but what you are due," added Cleotyr. "Come . . . we should retire to the salon while refreshments are made ready." He stepped aside and gestured toward the larger of the three corridors leading from the receiving hall, the one that led straight back.

Lady Cleonie and Vaelora led the way, followed by the three men, to an oblong chamber with large square windows set waist high in paneled light oak walls and comprised of leaded panes that looked to be even older than those in the hold house of the late High Holder Paitrak. Cleonie settled herself on a loveseat upholstered in a green velvet, a velvet that had seen its youth before Quaeryt was born, he suspected. Vaelora sat beside her.

Cleotyr did not sit, but moved to a carved oak sideboard and turned. "I can offer you a lovely white wine, an exuberant red, or some of the best amber lager in Bovaria."

"The white, if you please," said Vaelora.

"I must say that I'd prefer the best amber lager in Bovaria. Good lager is even harder to find than outstanding vintages," noted Quaeryt.

"Ah . . . a man after my own heart."

"The lager, if you would," added Skarpa.

Cleotyr nodded to the footman who stood at the end of the sideboard, then gestured to the wooden chairs, with seats and backs upholstered in the green velvet, set in a semicircle, with a low table midway between the loveseat and the chairs.

Quaeryt took the chair across from Cleonie, Skarpa the one facing Vaelora, and the High Holder the one between them.

"Quite a surprise to have such distinguished personages appearing without notice here in Eluthyn," offered the burly Cleotyr, shifting his weight in the chair and glancing toward Skarpa. "We have not seen such in many years."

In turn, Skarpa looked to Quaeryt.

"Many things may occur without notice for some time to come," said Quaeryt. "Lord Bhayar has no wish to unsettle the High Holders, factors, and people any more than necessary, but he also will make changes, and some of those changes may come with brief notice."

"What kind of changes might those be?" Cleotyr's voice was pleasant, but held an undertone.

"There are always changes when those in power change," replied Quaeryt. "Some will happen just because Lord Bhayar is in power. I suspect that merchants along the River Aluse will find it easier and less costly to use the river ports in the cities of old Telaryn, for example, and traders and merchants will find more places to sell goods now that Telaryn and Bovaria are no longer enemies."

"And do you anticipate changes in the laws of the land?"

"There will doubtless be some. Lord Bhayar would not wish to have to administer one set of laws in one place, and another somewhere else. How those changes to a more consistent set of laws will be made . . . that I could not tell you, since I doubt Lord Bhayar has yet had the chance to consider the matter beyond the fact that some changes along those lines will be necessary."

"Such speculation right now would be useless," added Skarpa firmly.

Cleotyr turned as the footman appeared with a tray on which were set three beakers of lager and two goblets of white wine. "Ah . . . you must tell me what you think of the lager."

Vaelora received her wine first, then Cleonie, with the lagers going to Skarpa, Quaeryt, and Cleotyr in turn. Quaeryt was careful to take the crystal beaker in his right hand, since he still had no real control of the two fingers on his left.

Once everyone had a beverage, Vaelora lifted her goblet. "Our thanks and appreciation for your gracious hospitality."

"It is more than our pleasure," replied Cleonie, also lifting her glass.

When they had all sipped, Vaelora said, "As you said, this is a lovely white wine."

"And the lager is indeed one of the best I've tasted," added Quaeryt.

"I agree with Commander Quaeryt," said Skarpa, "and we've tasted lager all the way across Lydar."

"You're most kind," replied Cleotyr.

"Truthful," said Skarpa.

After a slight moment of silence, Cleonie again spoke, looking to Quaeryt. "I could not but notice that your uniform differs slightly from those of other officers, Commander. I know little of such, and I beg your indulgence for my ignorance."

Quaeryt smiled, managing to conceal his amusement at the manner in which she had offered the question to obtain an answer most likely desired by her husband. "It is not a matter of ignorance. You are most observant to note that the shade and color of my uniform differ somewhat from those of other officers. The color reflects my background as a scholar."

"And as an imager," added Skarpa.

High Holder Cleotyr moistened his lips. "There was mention of an imager commander . . ."

"Yes, there was," replied Skarpa. "Commander Quaeryt has been most effective. Now he is on his way to Khelgror. Lord Bhayar named him and Lady Vaelora as his envoys. Southern Army is accompanying his forces as far as Ephra."

"Again," interjected Cleonie sweetly, "I fear I lack the knowledge to understand these military matters as I should. But . . . if Commander Quaeryt is so accomplished . . . and he is married to the sister of Lord Bhayar . . ." She let the words trail off with a puzzled expression.

Quaeryt wanted to laugh. He did not. "I did not plan to be an officer. I was a scholar advisor to Lord Bhayar, and I was sent to Tilbor to advise the princeps there. During that time, the hill holders revolted, and I ended up in service, just in order to survive. I proved somewhat effective, and after the revolt was put down, I was appointed princeps. After the eruption and earthquake leveled part of Extela, Lord Bhayar's ancestral home, he sent me and Vaelora there. For a short period I was provincial governor until Rex Kharst attacked Ferravyl, and I was once more pressed into service in charge of a battalion. I fear I lack the experience to command more than a few regiments, and Lord Bhayar is wise enough not to tariff me beyond my abilities."

Cleotyr frowned. "So you have worked your way up to commanding large forces in only a few years?"

"Commander Quaeryt is unduly modest," replied Skarpa. "He is the most effective commander in Lydar today. He was responsible for the destruction of Rex Kharst's forces at Ferravyl and at the battle of Variana. He has survived wounds and experiences that would have killed lesser men. They have taken their toll in other ways, you might notice."

Quaeryt appreciated the tactful allusion to his brilliant white hair.

"Still . . ." pressed Cleonie.

Cleotyr's glance at her was like a crossbow bolt.

Cleonie smiled. "There must be a story behind how you two came to be wed."

"There is," said Vaelora. "I wrote him letters until my brother commanded me to wed him."

The High Holder's wife blinked.

"And Lord Bhayar told me that he would have my head if I ever disrespected her," added Quaeryt with a low laugh.

"That is indeed quite a story," said Cleotyr, "and someday we hope to hear all of it . . . if you wish, of course."

"As a High Holder"—Quaeryt turned in his chair to the burly man—"you must have spent some considerable time in Variana."

"More than I would have liked, I must admit, but one's attendance was often required, if only to show . . . a modicum of support for the rex."

"All Lydar has heard rumors of the, shall I say, stringency of the late rex toward those who disagreed or were less than eager to cooperate with his wishes." Quaeryt almost said "whims," but decided against it. "I also talked with a number of High Holders on the way to Variana. I got the impression that being a High Holder, especially when in Variana, could require . . . great skill and delicacy . . ."

"Great skill and delicacy!" Cleotyr laughed heartily, if with a slight undertone of bitterness. "You do have a way with words. Yes, skill and delicacy . . . but better than that was silence except when addressed and a look of thoughtful consideration, no matter how outrageous the conversation . . . or the proposed diversions. But then . . . as a High Holder of modest means in the country, it was . . . useful . . . to be overlooked."

"How did you find Variana, when you were there?" Vaelora asked Cleonie. "Were some of the more noted High Holders as polished and scheming as has been said?"

"Those in favor were most polished," replied the petite woman. "The most despicable were the most mannered. High Holder Ryel . . . they said he was Kharst's spymaster, for all that he was the minister of waterways. I never saw his wife, though she was supposedly an outland beauty of wealth, but any of that wealth went toward his schemes." Cleonie glanced at her husband. "I don't care. He's dead, you said, and he wasn't as bad as the other ones, the one Kharst banished to his lands, or the one who walled up his wife . . ."

*Ryel?* Hadn't Eluisa D'Taelmyn, Rescalyn's mistress, said something about a High Holder of that name? Quaeryt couldn't remember what, though. *And so did someone else . . .*

"He is dead, as are all those High Holders who were most polished," said Cleotyr heavily. "Rex Kharst summoned them to him when he heard Lord Bhayar was marching on Variana."

"Why?" asked Skarpa.

"To see his triumph over Lord Bhayar with the trap he had laid. He could not conceive that a ruler so much younger could have developed a greater trap." Cleotyr looked at Quaeryt. "You were the one who executed it, were you not?"

Quaeryt offered a puzzled expression.

The High Holder chuckled. "I'm not much of a man for fighting. I know lands and how to run them, but I know men, and I've watched rulers. From what the submarshal has said, and from the way he defers to you, and from the woman to whom you're wed, and from the mission you're on with only a modest army, I'd judge you had much to do with Lord Bhayar's success."

"None of it would have been possible without Submarshal Skarpa," Quaeryt demurred, "or without the leadership of Lord Bhayar."

Cleotyr nodded slowly. "I can see that Lord Bhayar will have a long and peaceful rule, and I would appreciate your conveying my support of that rule." He offered a laugh that was somewhat forced. "And now . . . might we talk of the weather, the best in wines and lagers . . . until the refreshments are ready?"

"Do you have your own vineyards?" asked Vaelora gently.

"Alas, no. The wine comes from the lands of my distant cousin . . . but the lager . . . all the grains and hops are grown here, and the lager is indeed brewed here . . . in the fashion developed by my grandsire . . . although I will say that I have made some modest improvements over the years, and even my son, who is visiting relatives in the north with his bride, has been most helpful in that regard . . ."

Quaeryt could not help but note the wary expression in Cleonie's eyes whenever she looked in his direction, but he sensed that little more of import would be mentioned for the duration of their visit.

# 11

Quaeryt and Vaelora did not return to the canal boat until well after sixth glass and only ate lightly, given that High Holder Cleotyr's "refreshments" had been endless and lavish. Solayi morning, they set out early because they had to cover more than six milles to pass through the two locks at Eluthyn and cross the Phraan River in order to meet Skarpa's Southern Army and the Eleventh and Nineteenth Regiments by eighth glass.

They had covered close to three milles before they encountered the first of the grain boats heading eastward, followed by several others, which slowed their progress. The lockmasters did give them priority, that being assured by Zhelan riding ahead with a squad of first company, so that they cleared the second lock slightly before eighth glass.

At a quint past eighth glass Skarpa arrived at the moving canal boat and swung himself onboard. As he entered the salon, Vaelora began to rise from where she had been reading while Quaeryt sat at the narrow salon table, poring over a map of the lands of Khel.

"Please don't leave because of me, Lady," Skarpa said immediately. "As an envoy you need to hear anything I say. If you do not, then Quaeryt will not have your best judgment for counsel." He held up a hand. "Do not tell me that you are but a woman or some such nonsense."

Vaelora laughed. "I will not." She moved to seat herself at the table beside her husband.

"How did matters go after we departed?" asked Quaeryt.

"Quietly." Skarpa barked a harsh laugh. "You two terrified them, you know?"

"Cleonie was wary," said Quaeryt.

"Her husband was far more than that. When he said good evening to me last night, he offered some words to the effect that he had seen more capability in his salon yesterday than in the entire Chateau Regis in the past ten years."

"That has to have been an exaggeration. A number of the Bovarian officers were quite good tacticians and strategists," returned Quaeryt dryly. "I know, unhappily. So do you."

"That's not the same thing," interjected Vaelora. "A bad ruler can have good officers."

"Especially lower-level senior officers," pointed out Skarpa, with a quick look at Quaeryt.

"At times." Quaeryt's words were equally bland.

"You two." A certain disgust colored Vaelora's short response. "What else did he say?"

"He suggested, very indirectly, that when an effective commander married to a ruler's sister was not a marshal, that alone was enough to treat the ruler with respect. He did say that sending you as an envoy, Lady Vaelora, showed a ruler well in control of his land."

*For now.* Quaeryt did not voice that thought

"That is a useful impression," she said.

"What else?" asked Quaeryt.

Skarpa smiled. "We did get quite a lot of supplies, especially grain for the horses. Sometimes, respect pays in more than words."

"Not often enough," replied Quaeryt, "but it's good when it happens." He fingered his chin. "I fear that the farther we travel from Variana, the less people, even High Holders, will know, and the less respect we will receive, and the more power we will have to display."

"Even along the Great Canal?" asked Vaelora.

"Even here as we go west," replied Skarpa. "As Cleotyr pointed out, the High Holders with the most power were gathered in the Chateau Regis. They would be the most knowledgeable. Few Bovarian officers survived the battle, and news travels slowly. More slowly here than in Telaryn, except along the Aluse."

"The roads . . . ?" inquired Vaelora.

"Your brother, your father, and your grandsire spent golds on good roads," replied Skarpa. "Except for a few roads along the River Aluse, more and more we are discovering that Rex Kharst and his forbears did not."

Vaelora looked to Quaeryt. "You wrote about roads and canals."

"They date back to the Naedarans, and they are all along the River Aluse. Kharst and the Bovarians only used them, and the Naedarans never ruled even as far west as Variana."

"But how could he rule so vast a land . . . ?"

"Through the High Holders, I would judge, although that is just a guess. He had nothing like your brother's provincial governors. That is why he needed a corps of trained assassins—and a spymaster—to assure that the High Holders followed his dictates . . . at least mostly."

At that moment Quaeryt realized where else he had heard the name Ryel—from Lady Fauxyn after he had crippled her husband—and that mention had been anything but favorable.

After that, the three of them looked over the canal map and discussed possible stops on the way to Laaryn and then the possibilities for heading downriver.

After Skarpa departed, Quaeryt looked to Vaelora.

"You're worried about something else, aren't you, dearest?"

"Why do you say that?"

She just looked at him, her brown eyes conveying amusement.

He shook his head. "Several things. First, I read over the documents appointing us as envoys again this morning—very carefully." He nodded to the document on the table.

"And?"

"I'd like you to read this section. The same wording is in your document, by the way." Quaeryt pointed, then waited as Vaelora read through the words.

> . . . he is empowered to treat for and make agreements with those required or empowered to make and comply with terms of allegiance to Lord Bhayar of Telaryn, save that no terms hereunto entered into may be construed as limiting the existing powers and authorities of Lord Bhayar . . .

She looked up, puzzled. "He's just saying that we can make agreements for him, but those agreements can't limit his existing powers in Bovaria and Telaryn."

Quaeryt nodded. "But . . . what's interesting is that those powers are not limited to dealing with Khel. They would also allow us to gain agreement with High Holders who do not think they are part of Bovaria, or . . ."

Vaelora's eyes widened. "You don't think?"

"I don't know what to think, except he is very careful about what power he grants. And he did say that some of the southern High Holders and some in the north may not have paid tariffs in years. You see why I was concerned?"

"I can see that, but it may never come to such. What else?"

"I need to ride with first company and the regiments, at least for most of the day."

"We'll ride with them. I'm an envoy, too."

"Only when you feel good. If you don't . . ."

"I promise."

Quaeryt had his doubts about that, but refrained from voicing them.

"There's more, isn't there?" pressed Vaelora.

"Nothing I can put a finger on . . . I still feel uneasy. Have you had any farsights?"

"Besides the one where I saw you surrounded by ice? I'm not so certain I want to see any more like that . . . except . . ."

"That farsight saved my life, dear."

"I know. That's why I said 'except.' "

Quaeryt frowned. "You didn't answer my question. Have you—"

"Yes . . . but I'm not going to talk about it. You know why. Anything you say about it might color what I recall—and that would be dangerous because I might not recall it accurately when the time comes to understand what it means. That was something Grandmere was very firm about."

"She was firm about many things, I have no doubt."

Quaeryt rose. "Are you ready to ride?"

"Are you?"

They both laughed.

# 12

For the next three days, almost all that Quaeryt and Vaelora did was ride with one of the companies, either first company or one of those in Eleventh or Nineteenth Regiment, and occasionally with Skarpa and his forces; share rations with the officers; and retire to the canal boat to sleep, then wake and begin the same pattern once more. The one other duty to which they attended was to write their respective missives to Bhayar, ostensibly reporting on what they had observed so far in their travels . . . and then dispatch them with a trooper courier and his escorts.

By midafternoon on Meredi, a chill wind blew, and light flakes of snow drifted intermittently out of light gray clouds, flakes that melted when they touched the towpath or the mare's mane or the sleeves of Quaeryt's uniform jacket.

"First snow of the year," observed Zhelan, riding to Quaeryt's right.

"Here," added Vaelora from his left. "It's likely snowed in Tilbor. More than once."

To Quaeryt, the snow was a reminder that the beginning of winter was just a bit more than three weeks away, and that they would be heading north from Kherseilles . . . and that Khelgror was as far north as was Tilbora. That meant riding into snow.

*If only you had recovered sooner.* But there was no way to undo what had been done, and waiting until spring would make matters worse, far worse.

He glanced ahead to see more than a score of people standing on a rise to the north of the towpath, watching as the vanguard rode westward. Many, if not all, appeared to be crofters and peasants from their worn trousers and shirts, the colors of which ranged from faded tans to washed-out grays and blues. Behind them were others bending and stooping among the stalks that remained green. Most of them, Quaeryt realized, were women, and those that were not were old men or children. The children were either shoeless or wore rags wrapped around feet.

"Who are they?" murmured Vaelora.

"Field workers, likely gleaning the fields after the harvest, trying to grub up the leftover grain or beans or whatever," replied Quaeryt.

"Autumn beans," added Zhelan quietly. "They're sweeter, but they're often frost-killed."

"I've heard of gleaning," said Vaelora, "but . . . it's different when you see it."

"When you see so many gleaning, especially soon after harvest, that's often a sign of famine . . . or a greedy High Holder," said Zhelan.

"It wouldn't hurt to learn whose lands they glean," said Quaeryt.

"It might be better if I asked, sir, or had a squad leader ask."

"Try with a squad leader," suggested Quaeryt.

Zhelan turned in the saddle.

Quaeryt did not catch all the words but overheard the gist of the orders. ". . . don't press . . . just ask whose fine fields we're passing . . ."

"Yes, sir."

The three watched as the squad leader rode forward, behind the scouts, and then slowed. Several of the gleaners immediately moved away, but a tall woman with streaks of gray in her hair remained. Her posture was upright, and while Quaeryt could not hear what she said, he could tell that whatever she said was uttered emphatically. After a time the woman gave an abrupt nod and stepped back, her eyes fixing on the approaching riders, although Quaeryt could not determine at which of them she was looking.

The squad leader turned his mount and rode back to rejoin first company. When he reached the head of the column, Zhelan motioned for him to ride alongside, then asked, "What did she say?"

"She said that the lands belonged to High Holder Raynd. She also said that he was a disgrace to both the High Holders and to the Nameless because no just Almighty would let such an abomination live, let alone prosper."

"She said that?" asked Zhelan.

"Sure as I'm here riding, sir. Those are the words she said."

"We need to keep that name in mind." Quaeryt looked to Vaelora.

"I won't forget."

Quaeryt doubted that she would, not with such words from the gleaner and not when it was Vaelora's first sight of such countryside poverty. It was also another reminder to him of how she had been sheltered from certain cruel realities of the world, while being exposed to other cruelties and considerations that the gleaners could not imagine.

"We can't do anything . . . either . . ." murmured Vaelora to Quaeryt.

"Not now." *And perhaps never . . . or enough to help these poor folk, either.*

The dark-haired woman did not move from where she stood, watching as Quaeryt and Vaelora rode by and remaining motionless as the intermittent snow swirled around her and as the rest of the Southern Army rode and marched onward along the towpath toward Laaryn.

Slightly before eighth glass on a cool and hazy Samedi, Quaeryt once more looked to the Great Canal, empty of boats. He turned to Vaelora, riding beside Alazyn at the head of Nineteenth Regiment. "How long has it been since we've seen a canal boat?"

"We haven't seen any today," noted Alazyn.

"Midafternoon yesterday, I think," said Vaelora.

Quaeryt nodded. "Then there's some sort of problem, most likely with the locks, since the water level seems to be all right. I'm going to ride ahead and talk to Skarpa."

Vaelora glanced sideways at him.

"We'll ride up to talk to the submarshal."

Alazyn managed not to smile. "Yes, sir."

A quint later Quaeryt and Vaelora reined their mounts in beside Skarpa.

"What's on your mind?" asked the submarshal.

"That there aren't any boats on the canal." Quaeryt went on to explain. "So I think we should sent someone ahead to see what the problem might be."

"Meinyt. Just this morning he was telling me he wasn't used to riding in Bovaria without being attacked." Skarpa chuckled. "Besides, that will irritate Kharllon."

"Is he getting to you?" asked Quaeryt.

"Only in the quiet way that he's looking to find any mistake I might make."

"Him and Meurn," said Quaeryt.

"Would you have expected anything less of Deucalon?"

Quaeryt laughed.

In less than half a quint, Meinyt and one of the companies from his Fifth Regiment were moving westward at a good clip along the towpath. Almost two glasses passed before the subcommander and his company returned. Skarpa called a halt and let the troopers rest while the three senior officers and Vaelora met at the edge of the towpath.

"There aren't any boats because there's trouble in Laaryn," Meinyt began. "That's what the town councilor told me. An old white-bearded fellow. He came out to meet me with some factors. They said a full company of Bovarian foot has occupied the lock houses." Meinyt shook his head. "Sounds like an alehouse tale, but I thought I'd report and see what you thought."

"They must want something," said Vaelora.

"Supposedly, they want Bhayar to allow them to rule western Bovaria as independent. The councilor says that they've drained all the locks and put barrels of gunpowder against the lock gates to destroy them."

"Did you see that?" asked Skarpa.

"The locks are empty of water—one is, anyway. The councilor didn't want me closer. He said the troopers would kill some hostages. They kept looking back at the lock houses. I didn't see anyone moving—except for one trooper at the door of the closest lock house."

"What's to keep us from just moving in and taking them out?" asked Skarpa.

"They say they've captured the firstborn sons of fifty factors and merchants, and if their terms aren't met, they'll cut all their throats." Meinyt shook his head. "I don't like people who hold others for ransom. Don't like folks who tell stories like that, either. Just as soon take 'em all out. Besides, I can't believe they'd let their own troopers take so many hostages."

"The locals can't expect Bhayar to give in," Skarpa pointed out.

"That doesn't matter," said Vaelora. "What matters is that we can't appear weak."

Quaeryt frowned. *But why block the canal? It would take weeks for Bhayar to find out.* He looked to Meinyt, then Skarpa. "Would any company you've ever commanded do something like this? Would anyone who's ever commanded come up with a story like that?"

"It's not likely," said Skarpa.

Meinyt shook his head.

"Given the way Kharst punished men . . ." suggested Vaelora.

"So what do we do?" mused Skarpa.

"Did you see any troopers . . . or any men with arms? Besides the one?" asked Quaeryt.

It was Meinyt's turn to frown. "No. The councilor begged me not to approach the lock houses too closely."

"What are we supposed to do, then?"

"Send their request to Bhayar and wait for a response."

"I'd like to try something different," said Quaeryt.

Vaelora offered a concerned glance.

"I'd like you to march one of the regiments toward the locks. Stop a good half mille short and hold them there. Tell the councilor that you will wait there for Lord Bhayar's reply."

"And?"

"I'd like to see what is actually happening."

"I take it," said Skarpa dryly, "that they won't happen to see you?"

"I'd be very surprised if they did."

"We'll just take the whole army until we're about two milles from the edge of Laaryn," Skarpa announced. "Fifth Regiment will be the one making the appearance."

Meinyt nodded, as if he had expected nothing else.

"And your imager undercaptains will be in the van with Subcommander Meinyt and me," Skarpa added.

A quint later Fifth Regiment rode westward at the front of the long column. Quaeryt and Vaelora rode behind Skarpa and Meinyt, with the eight imager undercaptains following them.

Vaelora eased her mount closer to his. "What are you thinking, dearest?"

"I think you know. Troopers wouldn't take a canal, or hold the firstborn sons of factors for ransom. Who benefits from closing the canal, especially in wartime?"

"And they didn't expect an army?"

He nodded.

"Then why not . . . ? Oh . . . we'd have no idea . . ."

"Exactly, and it will be better if . . ."

Vaelora nodded, but said no more as they continued riding.

Noon had come and gone, and it was close to the first glass of the afternoon before they could see the buildings ahead spreading away from the Great Canal.

"The first lock house is a bit more than two milles from here," Meinyt declared.

"Column! Halt!" ordered Skarpa.

In moments, or so it seemed to Quaeryt, he and the imagers were moving out with Skarpa and Fifth Regiment, leaving Vaelora with Zhelan and first company.

When the vanguard of Fifth Regiment reached the millestone with the number two on it, roughly a mille from the lower lock, Skarpa called a halt and looked to Quaeryt and Meinyt.

"Submarshal, I'd suggest that you ride forward with a squad and two imager undercaptains who can provide shields. I'd recommend that you announce to the town councilor that you're stationing one regiment here for the moment, with the others slightly farther away, and that you'd like to talk to the leader of the mutineers."

Meinyt raised his eyebrows as if to ask why Skarpa would be doing the talking.

"I'll be there," said Quaeryt. "The submarshal just won't see me. I'd rather not walk that distance." He turned to Skarpa. "I doubt that you'll have to say much more, but if you do, just tell whoever it is that you'll have to send a dispatch to Bhayar."

"They'll claim they won't wait for that. They'll threaten to kill people."

"Then say that any deaths will be on their heads. Stall them however you can." Quaeryt turned in the saddle. "Voltyr! Desyrk! Forward."

Before long, flanked by the undercaptains, Skarpa rode forward. Quaeryt rode just behind Desyrk, and following him was a squad of troopers. Quaeryt held a concealment shield only in front of himself and the mare, so that the troopers saw him perfectly, although Skarpa and the undercaptains could not.

To Quaeryt's right was a lane that paralleled the canal. The riders continued on the towpath for another hundred yards before the lane curved away to the west-northwest, and Quaeryt rode past the first of several structures that looked to be traders' or factors' warehouses. As seemed to be common along the Great Canal, they were constructed of the same dull red brick that Quaeryt had observed day after day in the small towns through which they had ridden. Unlike in many towns, though, the buildings appeared to be roofed in fired clay tiles.

As Quaeryt had suspected would happen, when they neared the section of the towpath some fifty yards short of the lock gates of the lower lock, the white-bearded town councilor, accompanied by two muscular young men, hurried forward.

Skarpa reined up, as did the group. Quaeryt dismounted and walked the mare forward and to the right side of Desyrk, so that the undercaptain could see him. There he handed the reins to Desyrk, before stepping to the side and extending his concealment shield to surround himself. He stood, waiting to hear what the white-bearded man had to say.

"Sir . . . I told the other officer . . ."

"I'm Submarshal Skarpa of the Southern Army. There are nine regiments behind me. Who are you?"

"Town councilor Moraes . . . Please, sir, do not approach closer. They will kill too many."

"Who are they?"

"The soldiers who hold the locks . . . and our sons."

"What do you expect us to do, Councilor?" demanded Skarpa coolly. "I understand from Subcommander Meinyt that these mutineers have some ridiculous idea about governing their own land."

"Yes, sir . . . yes, sir."

"Then it's our duty to remove them," Skarpa declared. "Lord Bhayar isn't about to stand for something like that."

"Please, sir . . . please wait . . . please."

"I'll give them a glass to come out and talk to me. No more."

"But . . . sir . . ."

"Tell them what I said."

The councilor's shoulders sagged. "Yes . . . yes . . . I will tell them." He turned and began to trudge back, with the two muscular men, each with a truncheon, walking on each side of him, perhaps a pace back.

As Quaeryt followed them, he noticed a single canal boat, well appointed, tied to the wall just below the lower lock. When he was almost abreast of the boat, he saw that the shutters were closed and locked, and the hatches or doors were chained shut. Yet he could see marks in the towpath that indicated cargo had been rolled or carried to the boat, and that it rode lower in water, with the canal water slightly above its waterline. The doors of the warehouse across from it were chained shut as well.

*Probably a factor trying to save his cargo from the rapacious Telaryn barbarians.* Quaeryt shook his head and returned his attention to the men he followed.

The three were silent until they reached the long stone ramp that angled up beside the lower lock.

"You should have tried harder, Moraes . . ." said the taller younger man.

"With a Telaryn submarshal?" The older man's voice was plaintive. "You heard what they did at Variana."

"What do we care about that?"

The other man with the truncheon turned and looked back.

Quaeryt froze.

"What is it?"

"Coulda sworn I heard someone else."

"There's no one else around, not close enough you could hear steps. Just keep walking," said the tall man.

The north side of the lower lock was almost ten yards wide. Quaeryt glanced up. From what he could see, a lock house stood at each end, one just short of the eastern lock gate and one just below the western lock gate. The ramp rose until it was level with the top of the lock at the west end, and then flattened out for some fifty yards. Besides of the one trooper standing outside the easternmost lock house, Quaeryt saw no one else near the locks or the canal.

That single trooper standing by the lock-house door paced back and forth. *Pacing . . . not marching.* Quaeryt frowned.

The lower lock looked to be largely empty of water, although he could not see the bottom of the lock from where he was. *At least one lock empty, the one that leads to Eluthyn. What about the one that serves that part of the canal that meets the River Laar?* The town councilor had said that both lock gates were charged with gunpowder. Quaeryt wanted to shake his head. Just placing bags of gunpowder against oak-timbered locks and lighting them off might only create superficial damage and might not even strain the lock-gate timbers. He glanced toward the closed gate to the upper lock, but there was no way to tell whether it was full or empty.

Abruptly the three men turned to the right, walking toward a narrow stone-paved lane between two brick buildings.

At the far end of the lane, Quaeryt could see that the street was blocked with barrels set on their butts, with ropes wound around each barrel and then stretched to the next. Behind the barrels stood men with truncheons and clubs, facing north and away from Quaeryt. Beyond them were more than a few men and women.

As Quaeryt stepped into the partly shaded lane, he strained to see if he could hear some of what was being said. Most of the words were lost, but he did catch a few louder phrases.

". . . no, you can't go there. Lord Bhayar's got an army coming through . . ."

". . . you want to get trampled?"

". . . don't care if it is market Samedi . . ."

The three men he followed turned left into an open archway, and Quaeryt had to hurry to catch up to them as they stepped through two battered doors that were swung back. In the open space before rows of bales and barrels stood nine men.

Immediately a tall and stout gray-bearded man turned. He wore a rich brocade jacket and black woolen trousers, with a silver stripe down the outside seam of each leg. "What happened?"

"They've got a submarshal there, like Moraes told you. He says he's got nine regiments. He said we had a glass to get one of the mutineers out there to talk."

"We can't get everyone out that fast, not all the men who are manning the barriers."

"They'll talk . . ."

"How were we to know that bastard Bhayar would send an army this way so soon? None of those in Variana—"

"They probably traveled faster than any messengers . . ."

". . . don't know if the Telaryns let anyone ride out . . ."

". . . have to do something . . ."

Quaeryt surveyed the interior of the warehouse for several moments, before imaging a thin layer of stone across the far door, then across the two windows. A whitish mist filled the warehouse, caused by the chill of the imaging. While holding full protective shields, he dropped the concealment shields.

The factors turned. As their faces took in the uniform, several swallowed.

One younger and burlier factor pulled out a blade and charged Quaeryt. When he hit Quaeryt's unseen shields, the force of his impact threw him off balance, but the blade did not leave his hand until he slammed down on the stone floor. His head twisted, and the side of his face hit the stone as well.

Another factor raised a heavy pistol, awkwardly starting to cock it.

Quaeryt imaged the weapon out of existence, then image-projected his voice with absolute authority. "None of you are going anywhere. Not for a time."

"Who are you?" demanded the tall and stout gray-bearded man.

"Commander Quaeryt Rytersyn, in the service of Lord Bhayar. I can tell you also that he will not appreciate the attempted closure, even temporarily, of the Great Canal." Quaeryt once more studied the inside of the warehouse for several moments, then imaged more stone across two other possible exits, a boarded-up window, and what looked to be a trapdoor, behind the barrels. Then he stepped back and imaged a stone barrier to fill the archway.

Once outside, he raised his concealment shields and walked around the warehouse, sealing two other doors and three windows. Then he hurried up the second ramp to the upper lock, filled with water. He looked to the west. Beyond the upper lock were scores of boats moored to the canal walls, but very few crewmen in sight.

Quaeryt couldn't help frowning, but he turned and walked down the upper ramp, past the empty lower lock, down the second ramp, quickly, past the locked canal boat, the only one in sight below the lock, and out to where Skarpa waited, dropping the concealment as he neared Skarpa, the undercaptains, and the squad.

Even before he mounted the mare, he began to explain. "The local factors are behind this. I've sealed some of them in a warehouse, but they certainly aren't the only ones. They have men blocking off access to the canal . . ." When he finished describing the situation, he added, "I'd suggest we take over the canal and the warehouses first and then sort through who else might be part of this."

Skarpa's smile was almost predatory. "I would agree, Commander. If you would dispatch one of your undercaptains to inform the other regiments to join us."

"Undercaptain Voltyr, do so at once. Begin with Commander Kharllon and then Subcommander Meinyt."

"Yes, sir."

Once Voltyr rode back toward the remainder of Southern Army, Quaeryt turned to Skarpa. "We'll need to have companies assigned to protect the locks. From what I could tell, there are no charges, but I didn't have a chance to look closely."

"If we keep everyone away until your imagers can deal with the locks, it won't matter," Skarpa pointed out.

"We'll also need to capture the men blocking off the canal . . ."

Skarpa and Quaeryt had finished their plans a good quint before all the regiments had arrived. Once they did, Quaeryt and Skarpa rode near the head of Fifth Regiment as the Southern Army rode into Laaryn. Over her unvoiced objections—not that Quaeryt had not noticed her frown—Vaelora remained farther back with Zhelan and first company.

One of Skarpa's regiments split off to the north, moving out in order to flank the factors' men at the barrel barricades. In less than half a glass, the regiments had encircled both locks and had captured most of the men who had been behind the roped-off barrels.

Before dealing with the factors walled up in the warehouse, now surrounded by two companies from Meinyt's first battalion, and with Voltyr and Horan standing by there just in case, Quaeryt first approached and checked the upper lock, still closed at both ends and holding water, if at a slightly lower level than the canal leading to the River Laar, which he hadn't noticed earlier. He could find no sign of explosives anywhere. He inspected the smaller lock house, but it was empty. After that he approached the main lock house of the upper lock. He continued to hold full shields and hoped that there weren't any explosives inside.

Even from fifteen yards away, Quaeryt could see that the door was chained shut, with an old and rusty but large and heavy lock. He paused, then imaged away the lock hasp, and waited. Nothing happened. He moved forward, finally, unfastening the remainder of the chain and easing open the door.

Inside was a figure gagged and bound to a chair. Behind the chair were long and heavy levers, most likely for controlling the water flows into or out of the lock. Quaeryt moved to the chair, then took out his belt knife and cut the ropes binding the man's hands, then untied the gag.

The lockman, gray-haired, with a short gray and brown beard, coughed several times before he finally spoke. "Never thought I'd be thanking a Telaryn officer for saving me." He frowned. "You are Telaryn? That's no uniform I ever saw."

"I'm a Telaryn commander," Quaeryt admitted. "We have an army taking back the canal."

"Hope you get whoever did this." The lockman rubbed his wrists where the ropes had been fastened, then stood and stretched, gingerly. "Wasn't supposed to be like this."

Quaeryt thought the man was unsteady. "You need to sit down. I'll have someone get you some water or ale or something. Who tied you up? What did you mean by it not being as it was supposed to be?"

"They close the canal every so often for repairs. Never saw any repairs most times. This time, I said to Pharn—he's the head lockman—said that we didn't need repairs, and with the war, folk in Variana needed grain and food. He looked at me funny, then walked off. Next thing I knew, there were three big fellows in brown. Grabbed me and tied me up. Never saw 'em before in my life." The lockman snorted as he sat down. "That's something in a place like Laaryn."

"Did they say anything that said who or why they did it?"

"Not a word. Just told me I'd be all right if I didn't fight."

"You've been here for a while."

"Close to a day, I figure. Ruined my clothes."

Quaeryt had noted the odor, but ignored it. "Did they mention gunpowder or anything like that?"

"No. Heard some hammering and smelled coal or charcoal, like someone was forging. Don't know why, though."

"Take it easy . . ."

When he finished with the lockman, Quaeryt made his way down to the lower lock, still empty except for a few digits of water covering the bottom of the lock. As closely as he looked, he could find no sign of gunpowder or other explosives. Then he carefully approached and checked the lock houses. The smaller one was empty, as was the larger one. As he left the larger one, he couldn't help but frown. *Only one lockman tied up?* That suggested that some of the canal workers, likely the head lockman, had been cooperating with or been co-opted by the factors. *But you might never find out which.*

He shook his head. The older he got, the more he discovered that there were all too many questions to which the answers remained unknown or obscured in some fashion. He paused and looked closely at the eastern end of the lower lock gate, noticing for the first time a band of iron linking the iron plate of the housing into which the lock gate recessed to the plate at the end of the lock gate. Someone had forge-welded the lock gate closed. Trying to cold-chisel it open would likely damage the gates so much they might not hold water.

Quaeryt smiled. Imaging would take care of that.

# 14

After dispatching a ranker with a water bottle to the upper lock house, Quaeryt went to find Skarpa. The submarshal was standing in the shaded lane beside the archway Quaeryt had imaged closed with stone. Predictably, by then, Vaelora was also there, if guarded by Voltyr, Lhandor, and Khalis, as was Meinyt.

"So far as I can tell, there aren't any explosives around the locks or in the lock houses," Quaeryt announced. "They did tie up one lockman and left him. He could have died, for all they seemed to care. He has no idea who was behind it, except that the head lockman, named Pharn, said they were closing the canal for repairs. When the lockman protested and said that they didn't need repairs, before long three men he didn't know grabbed him and bound him to a chair, then chained the lock-house door."

"It was planned, then, here in town," said Vaelora.

"By the factors. That's the way it looks."

"Your factors haven't tried to break out," said Skarpa, adding with a straight face, "I could see that they might have trouble, though. The troopers rounded up close to fifty bravos with clubs or truncheons and a score or so of factors, mostly younger men."

"We'll have to talk to all of them," said Quaeryt. "Well . . . maybe not all the bravos, but all the factors. I think we need to find a good inn and use a chamber there. I'd suggest we start with the younger ones first . . . and leave the factors inside the warehouse for now."

"They won't be happy." Skarpa grinned.

"That's the idea. I don't think they understand what they did. Or rather the seriousness of what they did." Quaeryt paused. "Either that, or they thought that in the disruption following the conquest of eastern Bovaria, no one would notice."

"Why did they do it?" asked Meinyt.

"If grain shipments to Variana are stopped, the price of grain will go up. The factors will receive more when they resume shipping," Quaeryt said.

"Why didn't they just refuse to ship?"

"They could do that, but grain likely comes down the River Laar from other growers, factors, and High Holders. Unless they take control of the canal, the shipments go on, and the prices stay lower than they desire." Quaeryt shrugged. "Then when we showed up they spread the story that mutineers did it . . . and, well, if the mutineers ran off when we approached or got tired and gave up, who's to know?"

"Why didn't they just stick to the story about repairs?" asked Meinyt.

"I'm guessing that they're saving that for all the future times when Bhayar doesn't have an army near. Even if people suspect, who is going to accuse any group of factors who can raise enough muscle to seize the canal? The High Holders won't care. The price for their grain goes up as well. Besides, there's grain and flour here in Laaryn, and the local price will likely go down for a time, and most people don't care that much if it costs more somewhere else."

"Real bastards," offered Meinyt in a low voice.

Vaelora nodded.

"We need to find an inn and quarters for the regiments," Skarpa announced.

Close to another glass passed before Skarpa, Vaelora, Meinyt, and Quaeryt stood just inside the entry hall of the Canal Inn, located on the east side of the square set just to the east of the point of land that overlooked where the canal joined the River Laar. The inn was not that ancient as Bovarian inns went, Quaeryt judged, likely only thirty years old and probably built not that long after the Great Canal had been completed. The three-story squarish structure with the dull red brick walls that seemed so prevalent along the canal boasted a large public room, two plaques rooms, one larger and more elegantly appointed than the other, a good-sized entry hall, and an imposing facade with stone columns flanking the entry, and two covered side porches.

Khaern remained in charge of the canal area, and Zhelan and first company had taken over the exterior of the warehouse imprisoning the local factors, with Voltyr in charge of the imager undercaptains, who remained there in order to assure that the factors remained behind the walls.

"How do you think we should handle this?" asked Skarpa, looking to Quaeryt.

"You shouldn't be the one questioning all the factors. That makes them feel too important. They should be almost beneath your notice—at least until their punishment is announced."

"What about justicers?" asked Vaelora.

"Blocking the Great Canal isn't a matter for a local justicer, assuming Kharst even had them. Besides . . ." Quaeryt smiled.

"You've acted as a justicer for Bhayar," she finished.

"And you're a full commander," added Skarpa.

"We'll just take over one of the plaques rooms and bring them in one at a time," said Quaeryt. "By the time I finish with the younger ones, the ones in the warehouse might be getting a message."

In less than a quint, Quaeryt was seated behind a table in the more luxurious of the plaques rooms, waiting.

The first of those captured to appear before Quaeryt, escorted by two solid rankers, did not look much older than Khalis, the youngest of the imager undercaptains, a beardless youth with well-trimmed brown hair and matching gray trousers and jacket . . . not to mention a bruise along his left jaw and a slight scabbed cut on his forehead. His hands were bound behind him.

"Who are you, and what were you doing with the bravos who were blocking people from getting near the canal?" asked Quaeryt.

"Might I ask who you are and what your authority over me is?"

The question was worded politely enough, but the condescending arrogance behind the words grated on Quaeryt. He smiled politely, projecting absolute authority and total contempt before he uttered a single word. "I'm Commander Quaeryt Rytersyn, scholar, former justicer, and officer in the Telaryn Southern Army. My authority comes from Lord Bhayar and the nine regiments that have occupied Laaryn after some group unlawfully blocked the Great Canal. Now . . . answer the questions."

The youth staggered back a step, then swallowed. "You can't . . ."

"This is wartime. You were part of a group that was caught blocking a canal to cargo and supplies. That's treason. If necessary, I can order your execution. I will if I have to. I'd rather not, because you're not worth the time or effort." Rather than say more, Quaeryt waited.

"I'm Coryal D'Coryt. I was trying to get to my father's warehouse when your men snatched everyone in sight. I have no idea what you're talking about."

Quaeryt sighed, loudly, then looked to the two rankers. "Put him in the empty cellar. We'll take care of him later, along with the others. Have the major send in a few of the bravos."

"You will be sorry," said the youth.

Quaeryt shook his head sadly.

The next man was a broad-shouldered bravo in brown, with a wide leather belt and well-trimmed hair and beard.

*He's too well groomed for a typical bravo.* "Your name?" asked Quaeryt.

"Huddn."

"Why were you blocking off the canal?"

"Why not? The swells paid half silver a day for me to hold a truncheon and keep folks off."

"Did they tell you why they wanted the canal blocked?"

"Yesterday, it was for repairs. This morning they said it was because Lord Bhayar's army was coming."

"Who do you work for?"

"Whoever pays me."

"Who paid you yesterday?"

Huddn shrugged. "Don't know his name. Young fellow dressed like a factor. Blond, short beard. Probably not old enough to grow more. Didn't give his name. Paid all of Voryn's crew."

Quaeryt asked more questions, but it was clear that Huddn knew little more than he'd revealed at the beginning. The same was true of the next five bravos. The sixth gave his name as Voryn.

"So you have a crew," said Quaeryt. "What do they do for you?"

"Work. Most times, we load or offload the canal boats. Other times, we'll keep order for factors, like when they have a fest for their help."

"Or when they want people kept away from the Great Canal?"

Voryn nodded, his wide-spaced eyes wary.

"How often does that happen?"

"Not often. Maybe three-four times in the past few years. Called in more muscle this morning, though."

"Who pays for you and your crew when that happens?"

"Factors' council."

"Who's on the council?"

"Don't know them all. Old factor Coryt . . . Aelsam, Yudrow . . . Barkudan. Those are the ones I know."

"What other factors use the canal for shipping, enough to need a crew . . ."

Quaeryt continued with his questions.

Three glasses later, Quaeryt decided he'd heard enough. He'd also finished quick interrogations with those the rankers had rounded up—more than ten young factors or factors' assistants, and more than a score of hired bravos or loaders.

Once the last of the assistants was out of the chamber, he sent word to Zhelan to have the imagers open the sealed warehouse and to bring all those inside to the inn for questioning. Then he requested that Skarpa and Vaelora join him. He was pacing around the plaques table when they arrived and closed the door behind themselves.

Skarpa said nothing, just looked at Quaeryt inquiringly.

"I'm sure we don't know everything. From what I've heard, this isn't the first time the factors have closed the canal. They've done the same thing before, once for almost two weeks."

"Just to keep their prices higher?" asked Skarpa.

Vaelora only nodded, sadly.

"The one thing that's strange is that someone called in more bravos—and paid them—this morning. None of the bravos knew who had paid. They didn't recognize the man who had the silvers." Quaeryt frowned. "That doesn't make much sense. Why would they do that with Southern Army marching toward Laaryn?"

"Maybe someone else did," suggested Vaelora.

Quaeryt shook his head. "Of course."

Skarpa glanced from Quaeryt to Vaelora and back again. "Of course?"

"Someone who's not happy with the canal closings paid for more bravos . . . either to make things seem worse than they were or to make certain we did something to stop the closings." Quaeryt shrugged. "We may have trouble finding out who that was. I think it's time to talk to the factors we walled up. I've already sent for them."

"Do you want either of us there?" asked Skarpa.

"Not now. I might need Vaelora before long, though."

"Me? A mere woman?"

Quaeryt managed to avoid wincing. "An envoy and sister of the mighty Lord Bhayar, far more prestigious than a mere commander, of whom there are many."

Vaelora did smile. "I'll take my leisure in the other plaques room."

"That's a very good idea . . . but not until we get word that the factors have arrived." He turned to Skarpa. "What do you think about the whole matter?"

"From what I've seen, the factors here are wealthy. They were surprised that we offered no deference to them."

"I don't think many of them have ever seen troopers," added Vaelora. "The children peer out of windows at them."

Quaeryt found himself frowning. *How had Kharst kept order, especially given the nature of his High Holders?*

"There are also no High Holders close to Laaryn," added Skarpa. "The scouts report that the closest high holding is fifteen miles north."

The silence that followed was broken by a knock. Then Zhelan eased the door open. "Sirs, Lady Vaelora . . . the captives from the warehouse are outside on the porch."

Skarpa rose, as did Vaelora.

"Send in the white-bearded town councilor first," instructed Quaeryt as he rose, "after the submarshal and Lady Vaelora leave."

"Yes, sir."

Vaelora gave Quaeryt a parting smile. Skarpa shook his head as he left.

A short time later Moraes—the white-bearded town councilor—stepped gingerly into the plaques room. He peered at Quaeryt, then shuffled forward. "Sir . . . you're the officer who walled us up. I tell you, sir, it wasn't my idea to close the canal."

"This time or all the other times?" asked Quaeryt dryly.

Moraes was silent.

So was Quaeryt.

Finally, the older man cleared his throat. "What would you have me do, sir? No one dares go against the factors' council."

"Why not?"

"Things . . . happen to those who do. Unfortunate things . . . dwellings burn . . . dray horses sicken . . . accidents happen to children . . . shipments of goods vanish . . ." Moraes did not meet Quaeryt's eyes.

"Who serves on the factors' council?"

"The wealthy factors."

"Who?"

"Aelsam, Fuadan, Coryt, Barkudan, and Yudrow."

"Just five men?"

"There have always been five."

"Moraes . . . do you have civil patrollers here in Laaryn?"

The councilor looked totally confused. Finally, he asked, "How did you know my name?"

"I'm good at listening. About the patrollers? Do you have them? I didn't see any."

"Yes, sir. We do."

"Why weren't they blocking off the canal?"

"The piers and warehouses in the town alongside the canal belong to the factors' council or to various factors. The patrollers only keep order on the streets."

"The factors' bravos were on the streets blocking access to the canal. Where were the patrollers?"

"I'm certain they were there somewhere." Moraes wet his lips nervously.

Quaeryt couldn't help but wonder if some of the bravos were actually patrollers, especially given how suspiciously well groomed a number of them had been. He decided to keep those thoughts to himself. It wouldn't have been the first time patrollers supplemented their pay by using their skills in other capacities. Or that those with wealth or power subverted the patrollers to their own ends. "How is the town council chosen?"

"The guilds choose two members, and the factors three. It's always been that way. As long as I can remember."

"You were chosen by the factors, I take it?"

"Yes, sir."

"And the factors tell the town council when to close the canal?"

"No, sir. The canal in Laaryn is under the authority of the factors' council."

More inquiry revealed little new, but that might well have been because he didn't know enough to ask the right questions, and he finally dismissed Moraes back to custody. The next factor—thin, brown-haired, and intense in his expression—gave his name as Phaelan.

"What was your role in closing the Great Canal?" asked Quaeryt.

"My role, sir? I had none. The factors' council decides when to close the Great Canal."

"And you agreed with that decision?"

"I didn't question the factors' council, sir."

"Why not?"

"Because they're the council." Phaelan's expression conveyed a very definite message that questioning the council just wasn't done.

"Which factor is the head of the council?"

"There's no head. I suppose Barkudan has the most influence."

"Were they all caught with you in the warehouse?"

Phaelan shook his head "Barkudan and Coryt were there. I didn't see Yudrow or Fuadan. Aelsam wasn't there. He's recovering from a flux, I heard."

"Who pays the patrollers?"

"The town council."

"Where do they get the funds?"

"Most of the silvers come from the canal passage tariffs."

Quaeryt questioned Phaelan for another quint, then sent him back to the other captives.

The next two captives he saw were the two bravos who'd escorted Moraes. They had little to add, except that they'd been paid to protect the councilor.

Quaeryt had some thoughts about what was meant by "protection," but both men insisted that their only task had been to accompany Moraes and to escort him back to report to Barkudan . . . and Barkudan was among those Quaeryt had not yet questioned.

After that, a younger factor with bruises on his face appeared. While Quaeryt couldn't be certain, he thought the man was the one who had attacked him with a blade.

"Your name?"

"Yudryt, Commander."

*At least he recalls what I am.*

"Can you tell me why the factors thought to deceive us about the reason why the Great Canal was closed?"

"They were worried. They thought that you might delay in arriving if you thought there were armed men holding innocents."

"Why were they worried?"

"I could not say."

*That's a lie.* "Why might they have been worried?"

"There was word that when people resisted, Lord Bhayar froze them to death."

*That's not much better.* "If they believed that, why did they not immediately just say that the canal had been closed and would reopen shortly?"

"I don't know. No one said. They were worried, but no one could say why."

"Are you the son of one of the factors on the council?"

For a moment Yudryt was silent.

Again, Quaeryt waited.

"Yes. Yudrow is my father."

"And he didn't tell you why the council had the councilor tell the submarshal the lie about rebel Bovarian troopers?"

"He didn't tell me anything except to meet him in the council warehouse."

Quaeryt strongly doubted that.

Young Yudryt had very little else to reveal, and Quaeryt dismissed him.

The next factor was Coryt, the man who had pulled the pistol on Quaeryt.

"Why did you tell the submarshal that stupid story about rebelling troopers?"

"I didn't. Barkudan told Moraes to stall—"

"Why?"

"We didn't expect a Telaryn army marching along the Great Canal and demanding that it be opened immediately. If Lord Bhayar wanted to change the way the canal is operated, he should have let us know." Coryt's tone was polite, with an undercurrent of puzzlement, and a faint hint of the accusatory.

"He did. He sent us. Instead of saying that you'd open the canal immediately, you came up with a stupid story and tried to stall us. When I announced who I was, you tried to shoot me." Quaeryt smiled coolly.

"We didn't believe you, I'm sorry to say, but brigands have tried ruses for years."

"I take it that you close the canal whenever prices get too low in Variana?"

"No. Just when we believe that closing it will stabilize prices and keep grain and flour from flooding the market."

"And Rex Kharst was aware of this?"

"Of course. We'd have been fools to do something he didn't approve of."

*Kharst approved of this?* Quaeryt managed to keep his expression impassive. "Why did you order the lockman bound and chained in the lock house? He would have died."

"The lockman was bound and chained? That's not anything I know about."

"You didn't know? And you're on the factors' council?"

"The lockmaster handles things like that. I've told you what I know."

Quaeryt had his doubts, but he didn't know enough to ask the questions that would trip up someone as smooth and sharp as Coryt.

The last factor was the tall and stout graybeard, whom Quaeryt recalled from the warehouse by the brocade jacket and black trousers with a silver stripe. "You are?"

"Barkudan D'Factorius of Laaryn. Might I ask why you have treated us so shabbily?"

Quaeryt ignored the question and the condescension behind it, as well as an arrogance that suggested Barkudan was used to being able to order Kharst's officers around. "Why did you close the Great Canal?"

"For the usual reasons."

"The usual reasons?" asked Quaeryt ironically.

"To keep the price of grain and flour up. That way, Commander, Rex Kharst received more golds in tariffs when the goods were delivered and sold in Variana."

*Kharst agreed to that scheme?* "The problem with that is that everyone else is inconvenienced, and those who are the poorest pay the most." That had been one of the problems in Extela. *And here it is again in a different guise.*

"That is indeed a problem if one is poor, but we should not have to lose golds because there are those who are poor."

Quaeryt decided to be dense. "Lose golds? How can you lose golds when you already have the grain? If the price is lower than what you purchased it at, all you have to do is wait."

"We might wait months, Commander, and we still have to pay our warehousemen, our loaders, our drivers . . . We might have to let them go, and that means more people are poor and without food. No . . . it is much better to keep the prices as stable as we can . . . not that such would be a concern for a fighting man."

"All of that makes sense from your point of view, but there are several things that don't. For example, why was a lockman bound and gagged and left chained inside a lock house?"

"I doubt that was the case," Barkudan replied smoothly. "If someone was there when the canal was closed, they should not have been. The man doubtless was drinking and fell asleep there. No one noticed him when everything was locked up. It would have been an unfortunate accident, except for the fact that your men came along. He should be most grateful."

"Men who are drinking don't tie themselves to chairs and gag themselves."

Barkudan shrugged. "I wouldn't know about that."

*Yes, you would, you slimy bastard.* "To whom does the lockmaster report?"

"To the factors' council. We pay them for doing their duties."

"And you knew nothing about the lockman?"

"I knew nothing until you told me."

Quaeryt could see that none of the factors were about to admit or acknowledge anything about the unfortunate lockman . . . or anything else, regardless of any pressure he could apply. He smiled, coldly. "You have repeatedly told the people of Laaryn and those trying to ship cargo from other places that the canal was closed for reasons that were untrue. You attempted to increase the golds in your coffers by lying. That is fraud, whether or not Rex Kharst approved or not. Doing so in war amounts to treason. The penalty for treason is death."

Barkudan swallowed. "You . . . you do not have the authority . . . not when we were carrying out Rex Kharst's wishes."

"Assuming that happened to be the case, that argument only had validity until you were aware that Lord Bhayar wished otherwise, yet all of you did nothing to accede to his requirements. Instead, you compounded your failures by lying to Lord Bhayar's representatives. As for authority, I have the authority of a senior officer commissioned by Lord Bhayar."

"That should not apply to a civil matter."

Quaeryt smiled once more. "I could dispute that. I won't. Instead, I will ask Lady Vaelora Chayardyr, an envoy of Lord Bhayar, and also his sister, to pass judgment on the matter."

"And when might this be?" asked Barkudan warily.

Quaeryt paused as the bells outside the inn began to ring—six chimes. *Is it that late already?* When the sound of the bells died away, he continued. "Shortly. Southern Army is escorting her to deal with the lands of Khel."

Sweat began to bead on the factor's forehead.

"Until then, you will remain in custody, and we will also seek out the other members of the factors' council so that all of you may share in that judgment."

Quaeryt could see Barkudan pale, if only slightly. He nodded to the troopers. "Take him out."

For several moments Quaeryt just sat behind the plaques table. After glasses of questioning people, he still had far too few answers. *You might have gotten more by using imaging . . .* He shook his head. The factors were far too cold and too experienced to be affected by his imaging feelings at them, and using some form of force against people who weren't using arms against him would only lead to more trouble than he wanted to deal with. He'd just have to find another way of discovering what he wanted to know.

He stood and walked to the door, opening it slowly and looking at the ranker outside. "If you wouldn't mind asking the submarshal and Lady Vaelora if they would join me."

"Yes, sir."

Quaeryt just stood by the plaques table, waiting, until the other two joined him, then gestured to the chairs.

"What did you find out?" asked Skarpa after he and Vaelora had seated themselves.

"Not enough." Quaeryt took a deep breath. "If I can believe what all of these factors are saying, their council has been closing the canal as they think necessary in order to keep supplies of grain and flour from flooding into Variana. I wouldn't be surprised if the factors in Eluthyn might not have been doing the same thing, but we didn't catch them at it. The factors I questioned all claim that Kharst approved of this because the cargoes are tariffed when they're sold in Variana and he received more tariff golds that way . . ." Quaeryt went on to summarize what he'd learned, then waited for their response.

"It makes sense, in a way," said Vaelora. "It doesn't raise prices here. So people don't get upset . . ."

"But what about goods headed here?" asked Quaeryt. "I'd think . . ." He shook his head. "You're right. Most other things people need are made locally. Still . . . there's something that's not right about it."

"More than something," added Skarpa.

"What do you think we should do?" asked Vaelora.

"Summon the factors' council and order them not to close the canal except for repairs, and then for as short a time as practicable."

"If we're not here," said Skarpa, "they'll just claim the need for repairs and do the same thing."

"We may have to leave a company or a battalion," said Quaeryt, "but I can't see having the canal closed while we're still dealing with possible holdouts, rebels, Khel, and the border with Antiago. Can you?" He looked to Skarpa.

The submarshal shook his head.

"There's one other thing. These factors are hiding something. I don't know what. I think the imagers and first company should search every warehouse along the canal around the locks." *For starters.* He paused. There was something . . . something that wasn't quite right, that he was overlooking.

"That will take time," Skarpa pointed out. "Where should they start?"

*The one boat! The only boat.*

"What is it?" asked Vaelora.

"Have them start with the one canal boat below the locks and the warehouse across from it, then move west."

Skarpa nodded.

*It's probably nothing except a concerned factor. Still . . .*

"Oh . . . we need to find out if any smiths have been doing work on the canal locks lately."

"Smiths?"

"Someone forge-welded one of the lock gates shut."

"What about the factors' council?" asked Skarpa.

"We need to round all of them up and have them meet us here at ninth glass tomorrow. We only caught two of them in the warehouse. Maybe by the time we meet with them tomorrow we'll know more." He shrugged. "If not, we'll still likely have to be here another day." He paused. "We might as well get something to eat. Have the officers and men eaten?"

"I took care of that while you were dealing with the factors," said Skarpa. "It was the easier task. By far."

Quaeryt didn't argue. As he stood, he realized he needed to send one of the undercaptains to image away the steel plate on the lower lock, so that it could be used and the canal reopened. *Among other things.*

On Samedi night Quaeryt and Vaelora stayed in the largest and best appointed chamber in the Canal Inn. They woke early on Solayi, and Quaeryt washed, shaved, and dressed quickly, then headed downstairs to get a report from whatever officer had the duty. That turned out to be Captain Belaryk from Nineteenth Regiment, who could only report that Major Zhelan and a squad, with Undercaptain Voltyr and Desyrk, had departed the inn almost a glass earlier to complete tasks that had been halted by darkness and rain the evening before.

Quaeryt couldn't help feeling guilty, especially since he hadn't even noticed the rain.

"If you would have someone let me know when he returns, Captain, I'd appreciate it."

"Yes, sir."

After leaving the captain, Quaeryt arranged and paid for breakfast to be carried up to Vaelora, then followed the server back to their chamber, where, just before seventh glass, he barely finished eating before a ranker knocked on the door and announced that Major Zhelan had returned.

"Tell him I'll be right there." Quaeryt turned to Vaelora. "I might be back in less than a quint . . . or I might not be back until close to ninth glass."

"Try not to be late. Those factors might not appreciate facing me without you there."

"Skarpa wouldn't mind."

"Go!"

Quaeryt grinned, then left and hurried down the steps.

Zhelan was waiting in the hallway between the staircase and the doors to the plaques rooms. "You were right, sir. About the canal boat."

"What did they find?"

"Twenty kegs of dried elveweed, some ten half kegs of a tannish powder. They were sealed with wax, but I thought we should open one. When I slit the wax and pried it open, the factor's guard started babbling that he didn't know."

Quaeryt shook his head. "I'd wager that it's curamyn. That's a powder that they have pleasure girls snort . . . or so I'm told. Another Otelyrnan drug. Not that I've actually seen it, but I'm told it's quite expensive."

Zhelan nodded. "There was also a chamber with a heavy lock. It had eight narrow bunks in it, and very small portholes."

Quaeryt could guess who would have been quartered there.

"To what factor does it belong?"

"The warehouse guard said both the boat and the warehouse belonged to Factor Aelsam."

"The one who wasn't with the others because he had the flux," mused Quaeryt. "Did you find him?"

"No, sir. He and his son left in their wagon yesterday afternoon. He's a widower, and his daughter lives elsewhere, according to the steward. He was so upset that we put guards around the house, and quite a dwelling it is, too, sir . . . one that you might inspect, sir."

Two "sirs" in the same sentence indicated more than a suggestion.

"Is it far? We're supposed to meet with the factors' council at ninth glass. With those factors we've been able to find, that is."

"Less than a quint's ride to the north, sir. I have a squad standing by." After a slight pause, Zhelan added, "There were two other strange things. The first one was that last night a boy came up and told me that he'd been given a silver to tell me that the submarshal should look in the canal boat below the locks."

"He didn't know who had told him, I assume?"

"Just a man with a raspy voice and a cloak with a hood that covered his face."

"So someone wanted us to inspect the boat. What else?"

"Undercaptain Voltyr did remove the iron plate that kept the lock unable to open. You asked us to seek out smiths who might have worked on the canal. We couldn't find all of them last night, but the two we did talk to hadn't worked on the canal. The third one wasn't at his smithy. This morning, the patrollers found him in the alley behind The Brass Tankard. His head had been bashed and his throat cut." The major offered a crooked smile. "The canal lockmaster can't be found, either."

"That doesn't surprise me, unfortunately." *He was likely either part of the plot or dead, if not both. But which plot?* It was more than clear to Quaeryt that there had been more than one set of plotters. "We'd better go now."

"I did take the liberty of having your mare saddled, in the event you wished to inspect the dwelling."

Quaeryt couldn't help but smile at that. "Thank you, Zhelan. That will save some time." He couldn't help but wonder if that was a harbinger of things to come.

Both the squad and Quaeryt's mare were waiting in the courtyard just beyond the north porch to the inn, as was Zhelan's mount. Quaeryt mounted quickly, although he fumbled slightly when he took the reins in his left hand because the two lower fingers still didn't respond. *Will they ever heal fully?* He had the sense that they wouldn't, but he could hope.

Early as it was on Solayi morning, the main street heading north from the Canal Inn was largely deserted, and all the shops remained shuttered. The eastern sky held a silvery haze that had begun to fade into thin off-white shreds of clouds. In the quiet of the early morning, the clopping of the horses' hooves echoed off the fronts of the shops, but faded as the riders moved northward, where the small houses were set farther back from the street. After they had ridden not quite a mille, they passed two stone pillars, signifying the edge of the town proper. On the right were cots with small plots, and on the left, an open expanse of overgrazed pasture.

"The factor's place is up on the left, sir, behind that wall," Zhelan said quietly.

Quaeryt looked farther north. After what Zhelan had told him about the contents of the canal boat, Quaeryt had expected a large dwelling. He had not expected one that was the size of a High Holder's hold house, if one of the smaller hold houses. The wall was of the dull red brick, close to three yards high, without any openings, except for the heavy black iron gates, through which Quaeryt, Zhelan, and the squad rode, after the troopers on duty had swung the gates open.

The three-story dwelling was also of brick, but the window ledges, cornices, and the tops of the low walls at the edge of the porches that surrounded the three-story dwelling were of gray stone. The roof tiles were of a light gray slate, and the wide windows had shutters painted a dark green. The dwelling itself ran nearly a hundred yards from end to end. The roof of the receiving portico on the south side of the three-story dwelling extended over the area where carriages would halt to discharge their passengers. In addition to the stable, there were two other blocklike buildings set farther behind the mansion, behind a large walled garden.

"Rather impressive for a factor," observed Quaeryt dryly.

"I thought so myself, sir."

Quaeryt dismounted under the portico, as did Zhelan, and the two walked up the gray stone steps to where two troopers stood stationed beside the door from the portico into the mansion. The brasswork on the door gleamed, and light shone through the narrow stained-glass windows flanking the wide single door.

Quaeryt lifted the brass knocker and let it fall.

The door opened, and a narrow-faced man in dark green livery peered out. "What do—" He stopped when he saw the uniforms, then swallowed, and said, "Yes?"

"We're going to need to look through the house, since it appears that Factor Aelsam is not here," said Quaeryt pleasantly.

"Sir . . . that is . . . most unusual."

"The times and circumstances are most unusual. You are?"

"Dallaen, sir. The steward."

"Excellent," said Quaeryt cheerfully. "You can show us through the dwelling."

The steward opened the door, reluctantly, and stepped back to allow the two officers to enter, his head slightly down. His eyes took in Quaeryt's ungloved hands and flickered, widening as he got a better look. Then he swallowed.

The side entry hall was a square five yards on a side with an off-white plaster ceiling a good yard above Quaeryt's head. The walls were finished in a pale green silklike paper that stretched from dark floor moldings to the crown moldings framing the green tinted off-white ceiling. Immediately beyond the entry along the wide corridor that ran the length of the house were a pair of studies, a lady's study on the right and across from it a much larger library and study. Both were furnished with various pieces of polished goldenwork in a spare style that was far more to Quaeryt's taste than the ornate furnishings in the hold house of the late Paitrak.

*A lady's study? For a widower? Or is it for a mistress?* Quaeryt said nothing, but let Dallaen show them the rest of the main floor, which held a large dining chamber with a long goldenwood table and matching chairs, the adjoining salon, and a pair of parlors, or perhaps a parlor and a morning room off the smaller front entry to the mansion. Then came a breakfast room, and opposite it a music room with a clavecin and several settees and chairs upholstered in a pale green silk. Beyond the music room was another study, small and dark paneled, with but a small writing desk and a table . . . and a green hanging in the middle of the side wall.

Quaeryt walked over to the hanging and drew it aside to reveal a heavy brassbound door with a brass-plated keyhole for a built-in lock. He looked to Dallaen. "Please open the door."

"I can't, sir. Only the master and the young master have keys."

"Are you certain?"

"Oh, yes, sir. They never let anyone have the keys to either this door or the outside door to the lower level."

"Have you ever been down there, Dallaen?" asked Quaeryt.

"Only in the lower study, sir, the chamber at the bottom of the steps."

"What else is down there?"

"I wouldn't know, sir. There's another locked door that leads to the rest of the lower level. That was what the master said."

Quaeryt had his doubts about the accuracy of Dallaen's words, but let that pass. "Then, I guess we'll have to let ourselves in."

"The door is iron-backed, sir. I would hope that you would not create great destruction."

Quaeryt smiled. "So do I." He looked at the door and concentrated on imaging away a thin section from the top to the bottom on the side facing the lock. Then he tried the lever handle. It depressed and the door opened.

Dallaen's mouth opened and shut silently.

"Shall we see what lies below, Major? Please follow me."

"Yes, sir."

Holding full shields, Quaeryt stepped down on the first step—and found himself hurled backward into the iron doorjamb. *Frig! You should have thought about traps.* He straightened, ignoring the soreness in his shoulder, and looked at the still-vibrating and massive morning star that had swung down out of a concealed recess in the staircase ceiling.

He stepped back into the rear hallway and looked at Dallaen.

All the color had drained from the functionary's face.

"I think you should precede us down the stairs," Quaeryt said quietly.

"Sir . . . I beg you . . . please . . . I knew nothing."

"Down the steps."

Dallaen glanced from Quaeryt to the morning star and back to Quaeryt, then shuffled to the steps and began to descend, turning his body to pass the suspended weapon. Quaeryt followed, with Zhelan behind him.

The windowless and stone-walled chamber at the bottom of the steps contained a single writing desk with one side against the wall, two wooden chairs, one set behind the desk, and a bronze lamp in a wall sconce above the side of the desk, all barely illuminated by the light from the room at the top of the stairs. Quaeryt imaged the lamp into light, surveying the room as he turned up the wick for more illumination. As Dallaen had said, there was another door, ironbound and secured by both a heavy padlock running through iron hoops and another in-door lock.

"You have no idea what lies behind this door?" Quaeryt's voice was soft.

"I've heard voices, at times, sir. Women's voices," Dallaen admitted in a resigned tone.

"And you've sent down food?"

"Yes, sir. But only to one of the factor's guards. Usually, it's Wharfyl."

"Where is Wharfyl now?"

"He left with the master."

*I'll wager he did.* Quaeryt saw no point in questioning the steward more at the moment since he already had a good idea what he faced. Instead, he stepped to the door and imaged away the padlock hasp and the iron-edged part of the door where the lock bolt had to be. Then he opened the door. A sour odor assaulted him when he stepped through the door, only to see a second door less than a yard beyond the first. The second door had no locks, only a heavy latch, but when he pushed open that door, the odor became far stronger. There was no light in the second room, except that seeping through from behind him, but that was enough for him to make out the four women—scarcely more than girls, he thought, chained to iron rings set in the stone walls. All were naked, and all were cringing back against the stone, their faces averted.

". . . Namer-frigged bastard . . ." muttered Zhelan from behind Quaeryt.

". . . please . . . no more . . ."

". . . do anything . . ."

The pleading murmurs from the girls were desultory, the tone of faded desperation.

Quaeryt spied the single wall lamp and image-lit it. As the faint light filled the chamber, he saw that there were five unused rings set in the wall. He also saw that each girl wore a harness with a lock in the back that connected the chain from the wall ring to the harness.

One of the girls squinted at Quaeryt. "Sir . . . please!"

"We'll have you free in a moment."

". . . just another trick . . ." That murmur was so low Quaeryt couldn't tell which of the four had uttered it.

"Zhelan . . . escort the steward upstairs and have him provide blankets for the girls. We'll worry about garments after I get them out of here. If he shows the slightest inclination to be less than cooperative, run him through."

"Sir . . . I didn't know . . ." protested the steward.

"Sowshit!" snapped Quaeryt. "I don't want to hear another word. Get those blankets."

"Yes, sir."

Quaeryt's head was aching faintly by the time he'd imaged away the harness locks and guided the trembling girls up the steps into the study, where Zhelan immediately wrapped a blanket around each girl.

Leaving the four stunned and trembling girls in the main floor study, Quaeryt drew Zhelan out into the corridor.

Zhelan was silent until Quaeryt closed the door to the study. "The fellow is more than . . ." The major seemed unable to come up with a word adequate to describe the missing factor. "He just left them to starve . . . to die."

"He might not have. He might have thought that we'd move on and he could return."

"He had to know that might not happen."

Quaeryt nodded. "That's possible. I need to leave all this in your hands. Get them fed, washed up and clothed . . . and keep them safe."

"Yes, sir. What about the house staff?"

Quaeryt shook his head. "For now, keep them all here. Except Dallaen. Tie him up. He, of any of them, should have known. I need to think about this."

"Sir?"

"We're not justicers." *Not anymore.* "But I don't trust the locals to handle it, either."

The major nodded sadly.

Quaeryt left Zhelan at the mansion, as well as all but two troopers of the squad that had accompanied him, to deal with the factor's mansion staff and former captives. As he rode south along the road that led back to the Canal Inn, he thought about what he'd just discovered. There weren't any laws that he knew of that prohibited girls from becoming pleasure women, and even in Tilbor parents could sell their daughters—or sons—into indenture for up to five years.

What Aelsam had done went far beyond that, but . . . in any justicing hearing, he would doubtless claim, and the locals would likely support that assertion, that he had only been disciplining girls who had refused to live up to the terms of their indenture. Quaeryt hadn't seen any bruises or welts or cuts on the girls when he'd freed them, not that he'd looked closely, and he suspected that less obvious means had been used on the girls. Three of them had looked dazed, and he couldn't help but wonder how much curamyn had been in their food. But, again, feeding them curamyn wasn't against any law he knew. *Despicable . . . but not against the law.*

Even if he persuaded Bhayar to decree changes in the law, how long would it be before such changes were accepted by the factors and High Holders?

And even if he were successful in setting up the imagers as a force, it would be years . . . if not longer . . . before they could make significant changes. *It will be hard enough to get compliance with what laws there are now.*

He was still thinking about what he might be able to do when he walked into the larger plaques room of the Canal Inn, where Vaelora and Skarpa waited.

"I was wondering, dearest, if you were going to return in time."

"There was another . . . difficulty." Quaeryt paused, then went on. "Zhelan sensed that there was something . . . unusual . . . about Factor Aelsam's dwelling. He suggested an inspection might be in order. It was." Quaeryt went on to describe what he had found.

"He had those girls chained up?" asked Vaelora.

"He did. Zhelan is arranging for them to be brought here to the inn. I don't know what we'll do, but I don't think they want to go to the pleasure houses or wherever Aelsam had in mind for them."

"Variana, I would imagine," said Vaelora tartly.

"What I don't understand is why the canal boat was left," said Skarpa.

Quaeryt laughed. "The good factor Aelsam had two warehouses, one on each side of the locks. The one to the west of the locks likely held grain that he bought cheaply from growers whose shipments were held up when the lock was closed for repairs. The one on the east was for goods destined for Variana in times both good and bad—for either Rex Kharst's pleasures or for the pleasure houses catering to a more wealthy clientele. But when Aelsam discovered an army was coming, everything was reversed, and he ran out of time, and he certainly couldn't have escaped us heading east, especially since he would have had the only boat for more than twenty milles. I'd guess that one of his enemies hired the smith, for a goodly amount of golds, to forge-weld the canal lock just so that Aelsam couldn't move his more luxurious goods back west. I also suspect that enemy was one of the factors on the council, most likely one of the two whom we didn't pick up, because they knew who Zhelan was and that he could get word to the submarshal. The two we have in custody know that, but they haven't had a chance to talk to anyone else."

"And anyone else who could tell us is dead," concluded Vaelora.

Quaeryt nodded. "But I'm certain that Aelsam is accompanied by a considerable amount of gold, and likely headed west."

"Not downriver?" asked Skarpa, who immediately shook his head. "No, he'd have guessed that we'd have to take a large force south."

"We can't chase him west, but there may be some things we can do to make sure he can't return to Laaryn," said Quaeryt. "We'll have to talk about those later."

Vaelora gave Quaeryt a look that told him he would be explaining a great deal later.

The bells had not finished chiming ninth glass when Major Aernyt, an officer Quaeryt did not personally know, ushered the four remaining members of the factors' council into the plaques room, led by the narrow-faced Coryt. The stout gray-bearded Barkudan was last, and that meant the two in the middle were Yudrow and Fuadan.

"You can just stand before the table," said Quaeryt.

"It is most . . . untoward . . . to be summoned to a hearing on a Solayi morning," the stout Barkudan said in a quietly aggrieved tone.

"It was most untoward for you to have a city councilor lie to a submarshal," replied Quaeryt. "It was most untoward for you to attack me."

"All of that was a grievous misunderstanding," said the sallow brown-haired factor smoothly. "Had we but known . . ."

"You are?" asked Skarpa.

"Yudrow D'Factorius, Submarshal." Yudrow inclined his head politely. "We received no word about the approach of your forces. Nor did we receive any instructions that our past practices were no longer to be sanctioned by Lord Bhayar. Had we but known—"

"We attempted to let you know," said Skarpa dryly. "I would have thought that the approach of an army would have been sufficient to convey that matters had changed. Instead, you all immediately lied. Two of you tried to kill a Telaryn senior officer who had not even lifted arms against you. One of your number fled."

"Now that we know, sir," added the black-haired and green-eyed Fuadan, "we will certainly comply with all laws and rules you and Lord Bhayar specify."

*The implication there is that they shouldn't have to comply until they are told.* Quaeryt wanted to snort. *Since when is shooting at authority allowed once the war is over?*

Skarpa smiled. "Please explain why you lied to me and fired upon Commander Quaeryt." His eyes fixed on Barkudan.

"Sir . . ."

Quaeryt image-projected the feeling that more dissembling might well lead to executions.

A sheen of perspiration began to appear on the stout factor's forehead. Finally, he continued. "Sir . . . there . . . is no explanation save that we did not know what to expect. The fact that we could not even come up with a good explanation is proof enough of our confusion."

"Would you have lied or fired upon Rex Kharst's officers?" pressed Skarpa.

"I could not say, sir. In my entire life, I have never seen such."

"You've never seen a Bovarian officer?"

"Not in Laaryn, sir. I have in Ephra and in Variana, but never here."

"What about the rest of you?" interjected Quaeryt.

"No, sir."

"Never, sir."

"How have you paid your tariffs to Rex Kharst?" asked Quaeryt, ignoring the puzzled look from Skarpa.

"As always," replied Barkudan. "The factors' council receives them from all crafters, merchants, and growers in Laaryn and the surrounding area. We send them with guards by canal boat to Variana by the end of Feuillyt every year."

"Do the tariffs from the High Holders go on the same boat?"

"Of course. It would be a waste to send two boats."

"Is this the same method used in most of Bovaria?"

"I believe so."

"Who checks the tariffs for the rex?"

"If the regional tariffs don't match the yearly requirement, the head of the factors' council can be executed. That happened once eleven years ago. If the discrepancy is great, all can be executed. High Holders can lose all or part of their holding if they fail to meet their tariffs. They also can be executed."

*That explains a great deal . . . and it's going to make Bhayar's life—and yours—a lot harder.* "You sent your tariffs this year?"

"Of course, sir. We dared not do otherwise."

"And you'll keep sending them to Lord Bhayar?"

"We wouldn't think otherwise."

"Do any of you have any questions or anything else to say?" asked Quaeryt.

The four exchanged glances, then all shook their heads.

Quaeryt glanced to Skarpa and then to Vaelora. "I'd suggest we excuse the factors and review what we know. When we come to a decision, we'll summon them back."

Vaelora nodded. After a moment, so did Skarpa.

"Major . . . if you'd escort the factors out," said Quaeryt.

Once the plaques-room door closed, Skarpa looked to Quaeryt. "Why did you stop questioning them?"

"Because what they said changes everything. Much as I dislike the way they run Laaryn, they largely behaved as they had been told by Kharst. Aelsam is another story, and he knows it. That's why he fled. It's also why one of them made sure that the canal locks couldn't be opened quickly and why Zhelan was informed about Aelsam and his boat." Quaeryt coughed to clear his throat. "We can't afford to kill off or punish the people who are collecting tariffs just because we don't like the way Kharst governed. Bhayar will have to decide how to change matters once he understands exactly what's going on, but it's not our job to make those changes." He looked to Vaelora. "What do you think?"

She shook her head. "Kharst only cared about the tariffs. So long as the locals and the High Holders paid, they could do what they wanted. It's no wonder the factors closed the canal to keep prices up. Still . . . we need to discuss some sort of token tariff for the factors, the same thing that Bhayar imposed on the High Holders, only not as much. Golds are all they seem to understand."

Quaeryt nodded.

"It also explains about the roads," mused Quaeryt. "The rex has never worried about them. Most of the trade has been by water. The lack of good roads is another reason why Kharst wanted to control the River Aluse all the way to the southern Gulf."

"His father built the Great Canal," Vaelora pointed out, "and he finished it."

"Only because he had to," Quaeryt countered, "because of Chayar's tariffs on Bovarian traders using the River Aluse. He likely used prisoners and impressed the poor, and it was cheaper and faster than using the roads."

"But . . . how could he convince people to pay the tariffs?" asked Skarpa.

"Remember the crossbowmen? The ones who tried to kill us?"

"Oh . . . they were used to assassinate any recalcitrant High Holder, weren't they?"

"Exactly. And with the factors largely running the towns . . ."

"Most High Holders couldn't afford to raise large numbers of armsmen or build an impregnable chateau," concluded Skarpa. "That meant that Kharst could turn his army against the few who did have those kinds of resources. And Telaryn and Khel."

Quaeryt nodded. "It's not the way I'd run a land, but it appears to have worked for Kharst and his predecessors . . . although I suspect that Khel was plundered pretty thoroughly after Kharst conquered it. He probably intended the same for Telaryn."

"So what do we do about the factors' council?" asked Vaelora tartly. "Let them off with token tariffs and a feathered lash?"

"No. I'd suggest that we also make them pay in other ways, where it pains them the most," replied Quaeryt. "They will have to supply us fully for the journey downriver, with additional flatboats as well, as well as support the force we leave here to keep order. I would suggest you leave Subcommander Meinyt and Fifth Regiment, with him as the acting regional governor . . . unless you want to leave Commander Kharllon."

"I doubt Myskyl and Deucalon would approve of that," said Skarpa wryly. "Or of leaving Meinyt. That would leave me with one less regiment."

"We may be able to remedy that," said Quaeryt, thinking about the likelihood that he would never have the ships to transport two regiments, no matter what Bhayar had promised.

"How?"

"I'd rather not say. It is possible."

"Possible or not, what about Bhayar?"

"Do it subject to Lord Bhayar's approval. Send a courier, notifying him of your action and the reason why. Vaelora and I will send separate missives supporting that. Then say that if he feels a short occupation by Fifth Regiment is sufficient, he can order Subcommander Meinyt to move downriver and rejoin you at Ephra. Or, if he agrees with our recommendations, he can confirm Subcommander Meinyt as the temporary regional governor." Quaeryt paused, then added, "I think we should leave Meinyt two imager undercaptains. And I intend to detach two for your use with Southern Army as well." Quaeryt could see Vaelora nod, if only slightly.

Skarpa frowned. "Will Meinyt really need imagers?"

"He may not, but I want the Bovarians to learn about them, and to see their abilities. There will be times when they will be useful in resolving problems with less use of weapons."

"I can see that, but the regiment business . . ." Skarpa smiled. "I won't wager against you, not ever."

*Let's just hope my feelings are right about this.*

"I'll send for Meinyt, and you can brief him here later." Skarpa paused. "You know Kharllon will say something."

"Just tell him what I know you would anyway."

Skarpa raised his eyebrows.

"That he's the only seasoned full commander that you have, and that Meinyt's already dealt with patrolling duties."

"You know me too well. What about you?" asked Skarpa. "Will you have enough imagers for your mission in Khel?"

"That will still leave me four, and that should be more than sufficient in dealing with the High Council. Oh . . . and we can declare Aelsam an outlaw, subject to immediate execution, with all his golds, goods, and property forfeit."

Even after that, it took the three another quint to agree on the exact terms and to wait for the factors to return.

When the four factors stood again before the table, Quaeryt let the silence draw out for more than just a few moments before declaring, "The decision will be announced by Lady Vaelora Chayardyr, Lord Bhayar's sister and envoy."

Vaelora studied the four, one at a time. Finally, she spoke.

"I will not pretend that I am pleased with either your actions or your behavior, but much of that behavior resulted from the demands and lack of care on the part of the previous ruler of Bovaria. For that reason, what is required of you is this. First, each full factor who is a member of the factors' council will remit, without delay, a token tariff of ten golds to Lord Bhayar. Every other factor will remit five golds, and the council will submit a listing of each factor and his payment. If, by chance, any factor is not listed, then each member of the factors' council will be required, during the next annual payment of tariffs, to remit an additional ten golds for each missing factor." Vaelora paused, letting the weight of those words sink in. "Second, you are not to close the Great Canal for any reason other than repairs. Such repairs will be made expeditiously. Third, for your acts in failing to receive Southern Army and for your attempted deception, you will provide the following reparations. You will supply, without recompense, all provisions and equipment required by Southern Army. You will provide whatever number of flatboats for use by Southern Army is required by Submarshal Skarpa. Such boats will be left at Ephra or elsewhere for your recovery only when Southern Army has no further need of them. We will also be leaving a regiment to assure compliance with that and to assure that order is maintained in Laaryn. You will supply that regiment, without recompense, until Lord Bhayar determines otherwise.

"For his considerable crimes, Factor Aelsam's life is forfeit. His golds, property, and goods will revert to Lord Bhayar, and his dwelling and grounds will become the headquarters for the Telaryn regiment that will remain in Laaryn to keep order. If you fail to keep these terms, or leave Laaryn to avoid fulfilling them, your lives and all that you or your families possess are forfeit." Vaelora paused, then added, "So be it, in the name of Bhayar, Lord of Telaryn and Bovaria."

"So be it," added Quaeryt, his voice quietly firm, image-projecting the sense of absolute authority and certainty.

The four factors shuddered slightly. So did the major, standing by the plaques-room door.

"That will be all," announced Quaeryt.

The three at the table watched silently as the factors and Major Aernyt filed out of the chamber.

The remainder of Solayi promised to be uneventful, if busy, for Quaeryt. Once the three finished with the hearing, Quaeryt and Skarpa met to work out what supplies would be necessary while Vaelora wrote out a record of the hearing and the findings to include with the dispatch Quaeryt would be sending to Bhayar, including the reasons for the "token" tariffs, and a suggestion that it be applied to other factors besides those in Laaryn. Next, while she talked with the girls rescued from Aelsam's cellar prison, Quaeryt summoned the imager undercaptains to the Canal Inn, where they met in the smaller plaques room.

He stood before the circular table, waiting until all eight undercaptains had entered and stood silently. Only then did he speak.

"I'm sure all of you know what has happened here in Laaryn, but to make sure that there's no misunderstanding, I'm going to go over a few things. The most important of these is something that you all have experienced, but we haven't talked much about it directly. That is the fact that Bovaria has been governed very differently from Telaryn. Rex Kharst and his predecessors demanded comparatively less of factors and High Holders than does Lord Bhayar, but in those matters that were important to the rex, absolute obedience was demanded, and failure to comply meant loss of everything, and most often death . . ." From there, Quaeryt explained how that had led to the situation in Laaryn. ". . . because this city is critical to trade and control of the southwest of old Bovaria, we have decided that, at least for a time, one of Submarshal Skarpa's regiments will remain here, and I will be detaching two imager undercaptains to support Subcommander Meinyt and Fifth Regiment. Once we reach Ephra, I will be assigning two others to support Submarshal Skarpa and Southern Army." Quaeryt paused and looked over the imagers. "Those of you who are detached have a great responsibility—to me, to Lord Bhayar, and to yourselves. You must conduct yourselves with the full awareness that not only your future but that of all imagers in Lydar rests on your conduct and your success. That does not mean concealing your abilities, but using them wisely in support of your commander. Wisely, but not excessively.

"The two undercaptains who will be assigned to Subcommander Meinyt are Undercaptain Desyrk and Undercaptain Smaethyl. Desyrk will be in charge and all imaging acts must be with his knowledge and approval, except in combat situations where that is not possible. I will make the decision on which imagers will support Southern Army once we reach Ephra." Quaeryt paused, then asked, "Any questions?"

"Why'd you pick Desyrk, begging your pardon, sir?" asked Threkhyl.

*Always trying to stir the pot and make trouble.* Quaeryt smiled. "Because his talents suit Subcommander Meinyt's needs, Undercaptain. I always try to fit the task to the capabilities, and Undercaptain Desyrk has shown that he can maintain his composure under all sorts of stress, especially the stress required in the kind of situations likely to occur here in Laaryn. I'd be happy to discuss your strengths and capabilities privately, if you so desire. Any other questions?"

"What about Ephra?" asked Voltyr.

"Nothing new. You may recall that, several years back, Autarch Aliaro had his imagers and his cannoneers blockade Ephra. That lasted several months, until Rex Kharst used the River Laar to send troopers downstream. He landed them in Kephria and fired the port quarter there."

"They didn't go to war?" asked Horan.

"Kharst was still engaged in fighting in Khel. Aliaro was angry because some of the Bovarian forces along the border with Antiago had harassed Antiagon traders and confiscated their goods. He figured that Kharst didn't want to fight two different wars. Kharst didn't, but he did deliver a warning."

"Why didn't Aliaro attack?"

"He did use imagers against the Bovarian troopers and imagers and killed the attackers in Kephria. That was bad enough from Kharst's point of view that he let it go. Aliaro didn't do more because the Antiagons' strengths are more defensive. They've developed their imagers and Antiagon Fire, and a huge wall encircles Kephria, except for the side on the River Laar. Now that Kharst is dead, there's no telling what Aliaro might do." Seeing that there were no more questions, Quaeryt said, "That's all for now. Desyrk . . . if you'd remain."

Once the others had left, Quaeryt pulled two chairs out from the table, gestured for the undercaptain to sit, then seated himself.

After seating himself, Desyrk looked at Quaeryt. "Sir . . . if I might ask . . ."

"Why I selected you and Smaethyl?" Quaeryt smiled. "Because you're levelheaded and competent, and Smaethyl's a strong imager who will listen to you. I could be wrong, but I think any imaging required in Laaryn is within your capabilities, even without Smaethyl, but your safety as an imager is greatly enhanced by having another imager undercaptain with you. So is the impression of imager presence. You can project a shield somewhat, I know. There may be times when you should accompany the subcommander closely . . ."

"To keep people from attacking him, you mean?"

"It's better to prevent an attack with locals than to allow it and have to kill people in order to maintain authority," Quaeryt explained quietly.

Desyrk nodded. "I can see that, sir. You've shown that."

*And I've also killed more people than I should have, far more, because of what I didn't know.* "I also want you to brief Smaethyl. I'm having you do it, because that reinforces your position and authority." Quaeryt looked at Desyrk. "One other thing. If you and Smaethyl come across young imagers, and they and their parents are willing, take them on as apprentices."

"Sir?"

"As Voltyr may have told you, I'm interested in what will happen to all imagers in Lydar, both now and in the future. If we are successful in dealing with Khel and possibly Antiago, Lord Bhayar has agreed to let us have the isle of piers for a scholarium of imagers and scholars. We need to gather as many imagers as possible, but not through force."

"If anyone can assure that, you can. I'll keep my eyes open." Desyrk paused.

From there Quaeryt went on to reinforce specifics of what he expected of Desyrk.

A quint later, when Desyrk had left, Quaeryt went to see if Meinyt had arrived, only to find him in the public room. Quaeryt decided to join the older officer there, gesturing to the server. "A pale lager, if you would."

Her eyes took in the collar insignia. "Yes, sir."

Then Quaeryt slid into the chair across the square oak table from Meinyt. "Thank you for coming here. Things have been a little . . . hurried."

The grizzled subcommander barked a laugh. "They always are around you. Skarpa said I'd be holding down this area with Fifth Regiment and that you had a present of sorts for me."

"I wouldn't call it that. I'm detaching two imagers to report directly to you."

"Which two?" Meinyt's voice was wary.

"Desyrk and Smaethyl. Desyrk's the senior . . . very levelheaded."

"Heard good things about him."

Quaeryt waited as the server neared and set down a beaker of the pale lager. He set three coppers on the table. The server nodded and scooped them up. Quaeryt took a slow swallow to ease a throat dry from talking.

"Why imagers here?"

"They can be useful in situations where force would be awkward. They're very good at opening locked buildings without making messes, and providing certain kinds of protection."

"The way things that should have wounded you never seemed to reach you?"

"Something like that. Desyrk probably couldn't stop an attack of massed crossbows or muskets, but should be able to handle single weapons."

"That might be handy."

"Especially in dealing with recalcitrant factors or High Holders."

"You know I'm not good at politely telling people to do what they should."

"You're polite enough, and having a regiment behind you should mean that they'll have to be polite. If they're not . . . well . . . things could happen to them. After all, you do have to establish and maintain Bhayar's authority. Quietly and gently, if possible."

"He said something like that," Meinyt said with a wry smile. "Why did you pick me?"

"It was Skarpa's decision in the end."

"You suggested me, didn't you? Why?"

"Because you're honest, loyal, trustworthy, and good at whatever you do. And you have a good feel for things."

"I'm supposed to live up to all that?" Meinyt's tone was wry.

"You have so far. Now you have to while surrounded by corrupt factors and sleazy High Holders."

"I knew you'd be trouble the day you pulled a crossbow bolt out of your chest and rode back to base without collapsing."

"I should have listened more carefully to you. I wouldn't have been hit in the first place."

"You had to get hit. That way, I can tell every junior officer and ranker that even commanders get wounded and survive and that they've got no cause to bitch." Meinyt grinned.

"Just for that, I'll hope that there are some local beauties who are attracted to a subcommander."

"I've seen what you've done for your lady. Don't wish that on an old subcommander."

Quaeryt couldn't help but laugh, and Meinyt joined him.

When Quaeryt finished with Meinyt—and his lager—he set out to check the canal. The rest of his day was consumed with minor activities of all sorts.

By the time he and Vaelora had eaten a late supper with Skarpa in the smaller plaques room and then retired to their chamber upstairs, Quaeryt was trying to stifle yawns.

Vaelora checked the bolt on the door and turned to Quaeryt. "What did you decide about that horrible steward?"

"The one who insisted he knew nothing?"

"He had to know!"

"I'm certain he did. That doesn't mean he could do anything about it. Zhelan and I decided that he and the housekeeper, who also had to know, will be exiled from Laaryn, and that they'll be allowed to take nothing. If they return, they'll face floggings and branding. The others will lose their positions when Meinyt takes over the mansion as the regimental headquarters."

"You're being too easy on him."

"How do we prove he knew? I could flog and execute all the factors in the town on those grounds. The only thing we can do that's practical is have Meinyt here to change things."

"I know, dearest." She sighed. "You're right. I don't have to like it, though."

"What did you find out from the girls?" Quaeryt sat on the straight-backed chair, letting Vaelora prop herself up in a sitting position on the bed, with her legs stretched out.

"They'd been kept there for over a month, more like two, and they were only fed when they did what Aelsam wanted." Vaelora's voice was cold.

"What he wanted were acts expected of women in pleasure houses?"

"What else? The longer they were there, the more often they had to perform."

"Then he had to be giving his guards their favors." *And that meant Dallaen and others definitely had to know, not that you didn't suspect that all along.*

"Or others. The girls have no idea who, only that it seemed endless. They've been drugged. With curamyn, I'd suspect, to get them to associate sex with pleasure . . . or forgetfulness. I wish you'd caught Aelsam."

"It might be for the best that he fled."

"How can you possibly say that?" Anger colored her words.

"Because his life is forfeit because he fled. In either Bovaria or Telaryn, drugging indentured girls to induce them to do their chores is not against any law. Nor is requiring them to serve in a pleasure house. The most he might have been charged with is cruelty and battery—and that *might* require loss of a hand and a large penalty payment."

"That's all?" Vaelora's voice held a mixture of aghast amazement and iron anger. "That's it? For what he's done to so many? I can't believe it."

Quaeryt smiled sadly. In some ways, Vaelora was still far too innocent. "Even High Holders' wives can be punished by their husbands without legal recourse under the High Holders' low justice. Do you think indentured servants would be treated better?"

"But they were held captive."

"He would have claimed he was disciplining them for failing to carry out their duties as pleasure girls."

"You could have done something."

"I could. If he'd remained in Laaryn, I could have set it up so that he attacked me, and killed him in self-defense. Even were I a justicer, I couldn't have sentenced him to execution. Not without risking being disciplined by Bhayar for exceeding my authority. Why do you think there are some things I've done about which no one knows anything?"

Vaelora sighed. "I don't like to think about that, either. It's terrible that so much of what Aelsam did isn't considered wrong."

"Most people would think it wrong, but the law doesn't," Quaeryt pointed out. "Especially the way Kharst viewed ruling. All this is just another example of all the changes Bhayar will have to make, and why uniting Telaryn and Bovaria will be anything but easy."

"Do you think putting Khel under Bhayar's rule will be as bad?"

"No. Pharsi laws are closer to those in Telaryn. I just hope we can get their High Council to see it that way." He paused. "Do you have any ideas about what to do with the girls?"

"I've talked to them about what else they can do. I've also talked to the innkeeper's wife. I'll try to find places for them. One of them, the little blonde, I worry about her, especially."

"Every time we try to make something better, there's more to worry about." Quaeryt shook his head.

"You need to worry about getting some sleep," Vaelora suggested.

"Sleep?" asked Quaeryt dryly, looking intently at her.

"Sleep," she said firmly . . . but her face softened after the single word.

Quaeryt blushed.

# 17

Much as Quaeryt worried about spending the time, early on Lundi morning he and Vaelora—supported by first company and second company from Nineteenth Regiment—set out from the Canal Inn to pay a visit to one High Holder Delauck, the closest High Holder, whose hold was some twelve milles north and, unsurprisingly to Quaeryt from what he had learned over the past few days, more than a mille east of the river.

"Why?" Skarpa had asked.

"Why not?" Quaeryt had replied. "We won't be ready to leave until tomorrow, and I need some questions answered. They're questions I didn't know enough to ask until yesterday."

"You think High Holders here are different, don't you?"

"They're not different, except more arrogant—in general—but I think their position is much different. If I'm right, that will affect how Bhayar has to deal with them." *And how the imagers will, as well.*

After riding for more than two glasses through a cold mist that occasionally turned to a drizzle, Quaeryt couldn't help but have second thoughts about his impulsive decision to see Delauck, especially if the High Holder didn't happen to be available. *Still . . . you could learn something from his steward and the staff.*

"Is that it?" asked Vaelora, pointing eastward toward a pair of stone pillars set at the side of the muddy road several hundred yards ahead.

Quaeryt could make out a graveled lane that led from the pillars at an angle up a rocky hillside to a walled structure on the north end of the hill. The hold house resembled Quaeryt's concept of the hold of an ancient Yaran warlord—a stone structure perched on top of a rocky rugged hill, reached only by a winding narrow road, crossing at least two wooden bridges. Yet the lands to the west, through which they had just ridden, were wide and sweeping, and clearly fertile. "I'd guess so, but we'll see shortly."

Less than half a quint later, they reined up at the foot of the high rocky hill. "Chateau Delauck" read the letters chiseled into the stone pillars flanking the narrow lane.

"You can't put more than two men abreast on that road," said Zhelan. "I'd wager that there's no other way up, either."

"That's not a wager I'd take," replied Quaeryt, turning to Vaelora. "What do you think?"

"There's no point in wasting a day. At the least, you can make him an example."

"My thoughts as well." Quaeryt gestured to Zhelan. "We need to send some scouts up the road. It's likely designed with weak points. As soon as they reach one of those places, I'll have the imagers strengthen it. Imagers forward!"

Once the imagers had ridden forward, Quaeryt began to explain. "We're here to visit High Holder Delauck, and I think we'll offer him a few tokens of goodwill." Quaeryt wiped his forehead and adjusted his very damp visor cap. "We'll need to improve the lane to his hold, and turn some of the rickety spans I can see into good stone bridges."

They'd no more than started up the hillside than one of the scouts returned.

"Sir . . . there's a gap in the road, a yard wide and a third of a yard deep."

*To slow wagons or carts or fast-riding armsmen.* Quaeryt nodded and called back, "Desyrk."

Once Desyrk had imaged stone pavement in place, the climb continued, for another fifty yards, to a wooden span across a gap dug out of the hillside.

This time, Quaeryt summoned Threkhyl. "If you would see what you could do."

"Yes, sir." Threkhyl looked both irritated and puzzled as he eased his mount around Vaelora's gelding and then Quaeryt's mare.

Behind him, Khalis suppressed a smile, as did Lhandor.

The imagers dealt with two short wooden spans, strengthening the roadbed and creating solid stone bridges, and the column rode forward, for a hundred yards or so before Zhelan rode back once more. "Sir, around the next turn there are timber supports below the road."

"The kind that can be removed quickly, I would venture."

"Yes, sir."

Quaeryt gestured. "Horan . . . this repair is up to you."

After Horan's repairs and reinforcements, and another quint, the upward ride continued.

As much as Quaeryt understood the reasons for the fashion in which the road had been constructed, he was getting more than a bit irritated, since they still had several hundred yards to go before they reached the drawbridge over the gorge that separated the walled hold and the leveled-off peak from the rest of the rocky hill. Still, he decided against pressing too quickly, and he had the imagers firm up anything that looked suspect.

More than a glass and a half after they had started up the winding lane to the hold, Quaeryt and first company rode to a halt just short of the wooden drawbridge across a gorge, close to twenty yards deep. An iron portcullis dropped into the stone slots of the gate towers on the far side, and the iron-bound gates swung shut. The bridge retracted slightly, then dropped, swinging down so that it extended straight down into the gorge below the gate towers, leaving the walled hold isolated.

"Not exactly friendly, is he?" asked Zhelan.

Quaeryt snorted. "I wouldn't be either with a company of armed men at my gates." He walked to the end of the road, standing on the paving stones where the end of the bridge had been, took a deep breath, and then spoke, image-projecting his voice toward the walls of the hold. "High Holder Delauck, Lady Vaelora of Telaryn and Commander Quaeryt are here to pay a friendly visit. We would appreciate your receiving them."

A man appeared at the top of the tower. "High Holder Delauck receives no one he does not know and has not invited."

"He can receive the commander and the lady in friendship and offer his allegiance to Lord Bhayar, or he can suffer the consequences."

"He will receive no one. Do as you please."

Quaeryt concentrated, trying to draw what heat he could from the clouds overhead, and from the trees and growth on the hillsides around the hold. Then, he imaged.

The gate towers vanished, as did the walls extending from them, and a walled stone bridge spanned the gorge. A thin sheen of white ice, unfortunately, also covered the bridge and the flat expanse of stone that remained where the towers and walls had been.

Quaeryt's head throbbed, but only slightly, and he reached down and pulled out his water bottle, then took several swallows of the lager within. Vaelora handed him a biscuit, which he slowly chewed.

"Now, sir?" asked Zhelan.

"We wait." *For the ice to melt and for Delauck to reconsider.*

Shortly, an armsman walked forward through the remnants of what had been a walled formal garden in front of the hold house. He carried a blue-edged white parley flag on a staff.

Quaeryt beckoned for the armsman to cross the stone bridge.

Warily, the man put one foot on the gray stone, then another, then walked swiftly across the span, coming to a halt a yard before Quaeryt and setting the butt of the parley flagpole on the stone approach to the new bridge.

Quaeryt waited.

"High Holder Delauck would like to know your intentions, sir." The armsman's eyes went from Quaeryt to Vaelora, then back to Quaeryt.

"We're here to meet with him and to obtain his allegiance to Lord Bhayar," said Quaeryt.

"And his understanding that Lord Bhayar, while far less petty than Rex Kharst," added Vaelora, "expects not only allegiance but compliance with the laws he will be setting forth."

The armsman blinked at Vaelora's words.

"You can also convey to your master," said Quaeryt, "that Lady Vaelora is Lord Bhayar's sister, his envoy to Khel, and his personal representative. We expect him to lay down any and all arms and step forward to meet the lady outside the hold house. Any further delays in his hospitality will result in further removals of his hold." Quaeryt smiled.

"Yes, sir." The armsman inclined his head. "I will convey your terms to High Holder Delauck." He turned and strode back across the stone bridge.

"He didn't look happy," observed Zhelan.

"No, but these High Holders need to respect Lord Bhayar, without qualifications and without hesitation," replied Vaelora.

"And since they only respect force applied directly to them and their property, we must show we can apply such force." Quaeryt's voice was dry.

Almost half a quint passed before a group of men walked through the remnants of the walled garden and toward the stone bridge. An angular black-haired figure, wearing black trousers and a crimson shirt, with an open black jacket, was trailed by ten armsmen, their blades unsheathed and held at the ready. The man leading the others stopped at the far side of the bridge. "Since I cannot stop you, I suppose I must invite you in, whoever you are."

Quaeryt sighed. "Zhelan, Voltyr, follow me. If you would remain here, Lady, I would appreciate it. Undercaptain Ghaelyn, when I beckon, if you would have a squad escort Lady Vaelora across to join me."

"Yes, sir."

Vaelora offered a smile, slightly sad and knowing.

Quaeryt rode across the fifteen yards of the span, halting several yards short of the man in black. "Quaeryt Rytersyn, commander in the forces of Lord Bhayar, and protector of Lady Valelora."

"Delauck D'Alte. High Holder of Lauckan." The holder looked squarely at Quaeryt.

"The Lady Vaelora wishes to accept your allegiance to her brother Lord Bhayar of Telaryn."

"For someone who is entreating my allegiance—"

"I don't think you understand, Delauck. She is not entreating. She is allowing you to offer that allegiance. You invite her in and pledge complete allegiance to Lord Bhayar."

Delauck glanced at the stone span and then back to Quaeryt. "Your imager is rather accomplished."

"Imagers. Lord Bhayar has a number of imagers." Quaeryt smiled. "You will find the road to your hold much improved and strengthened. Call it a token of goodwill."

"The goodwill of making my hold easier to take."

"Oh . . . no. Any who attempt to take your hold will find that they lose everything, beginning with their lives. Excepting Lord Bhayar, of course."

"Northern Bovaria is a rugged land, Commander."

"Not nearly so rugged as the lands of Montagne, where Lord Bhayar was raised. You might consider that Rex Kharst sent close to sixty regiments against the forces of Telaryn. Something like fifty-eight perished to the last man. Lord Bhayar lost at most four regiments."

"You leveled my towers and killed two score or more of my men . . . and I'm supposed to be grateful and plead allegiance?"

"Yes." Quaeryt looked beyond Delauck, concentrating as he imaged away ten lifted blades. "Behold your armsmen."

Delauck turned, then looked back at Quaeryt. He started to speak.

"Say nothing you will regret." Quaeryt image-projected both authority and sadness with the words.

The holder paled, but only momentarily.

Quaeryt could see the rage held in check, but he raised his hand, and waited as a squad escorted Vaelora forward.

"My lady," offered Quaeryt, "might I present Delauck D'Alte, High Holder of Lauckan?"

"You might indeed." Vaelora smiled politely, looking down at the black-haired Delauck. "I look forward to seeing your hold house."

Delauck hesitated only for an instant. "I am pleased that you would like to see it. If I might show you . . ."

"A moment," Quaeryt said. "Major . . . Undercaptain Voltyr . . . should any force or unfriendliness be directed at you, begin to remove buildings around the hold until those directing such force desist. Is that clear?"

"Yes, sir."

Quaeryt turned to Delauck. "Is that clear to you, Holder Delauck?"

"Yes. I do not have to like it, but I understand."

Quaeryt shook his head. "You only think you understand, but that will suffice for now. Please show us your hold."

"You have no fear of entering my domain?" Delauck's voice held a trace of ironic mocking.

"My only fear, dear holder," replied Quaeryt, "is that I will be forced to destroy you and bring down the entire hold."

For an instant Delauck said nothing. "Why don't you do it and get it over with?"

"Because the Lady Vaelora would prefer that we do not wreak unnecessary damage on holds, and also because I'd have to seek out another High Holder and do the same with him, and since you're the closest to Laaryn, I'd prefer not to waste time in escorting Lady Vaelora to Khel. But she can tell you about that in due time."

"Of course . . ." Delauck turned.

Quaeryt, Vaelora, and the escort squad followed the holder and his men over the bare stone that remained where the towers and entry courtyard had been and then along a path through the remaining section of the walled garden. Once they reached the entry to the stone keep, for it was a keep, rather than a hold house, Quaeryt immediately dismounted and offered a hand to Vaelora, making certain that his shields enfolded Vaelora.

Delauck stood on the stone stoop and gestured toward the open iron-bound door. "I suppose I must bid you welcome, not that I have much choice."

"We appreciate your welcome," replied Vaelora, her voice containing only grace and not the slightest hint of irony or condescension.

Although he should have followed both Vaelora and Delauck, Quaeryt eased into the narrow entry hall behind Vaelora and before Delauck, in order to make certain she remained shielded. As if she understood, and she doubtless did, reflected Quaeryt, once inside Vaelora stepped to the side to face Delauck, as if waiting for him to conduct her to the parlor or great hall.

"If you would show the way," she said.

"My pleasure," Delauck replied, not quite curtly.

Beyond the narrow entry hall was a larger square hall, and from there Delauck turned to the left, striding down the bare stone corridor to the first archway on the right, where he halted and gestured for them to enter. Quaeryt followed Vaelora into a chamber with a hearth at the far end, but with large windows overlooking another walled garden, one in which there remained some fall flowers. Standing beside the hearth was a gray-haired woman.

"Lady Vaelora, Commander, my mother, Aenitra D'Alte. I trust you will pardon me, but my wife is recovering from a difficult time . . ."

"I am sorry to hear that." Vaelora's voice was warm, with the slight huskiness that Quaeryt loved to hear.

"She almost died," said Aenitra, easing forward and stopping so as to place a settee between her and Vaelora. "I fear my son did not have a chance to inform me of what you are, Lady."

"She is Lady Vaelora Chayardyr of Telaryn," offered Quaeryt, "sister to Lord Bhayar and his envoy to the High Council of Khel. While on her way, and stopping at Laaryn, she heard of Lauckan and decided to travel here to receive High Holder Delauck's allegiance to Lord Bhayar. Given the rather treacherous approach to the holding and the unsafe nature of the drawbridge, she ordered that you receive a much safer and more secure way to your holding."

"I am certain it is, from what I have seen of the stone bridge you created," said Delauck, his voice flat, "but it was never intended to be either."

"We know. That would suggest that you were not a favorite of Rex Kharst."

"We've never been fond of any rulers."

"I suggest that you will find Lord Bhayar far more fair in his judgment of High Holders," said Quaeryt. "Some holders, of course, do not appreciate fairness, but they also do not appreciate life."

The gray-haired woman's eyes focused on Quaeryt. "Might I ask you, sir, why you, only of those here, paint your nails?"

"You might. I don't paint them. They are like that."

"Your face is young, but your hair is white. Is all your hair white?"

By way of an answer, Quaeryt eased back his left sleeve.

"What is all that—" began the holder.

"Delauck . . ." said the older woman, "swear whatever allegiance they require and mean it. If you want your hold and your family to remain."

The holder turned. "You've never presumed . . ."

"Swear it. You don't want to anger a hand of Erion."

"A hand—"

"Who else brought down your mighty towers and walls and created a bridge across the gorge in instants? Don't be an idiot." She turned back to Quaeryt. "Are you a hand of Erion or the lost one?"

"I have no idea. I've been called both."

"Who are you, truly?" asked Delauck.

"As I said, Quaeryt Rytersyn, commander for Lord Bhayar, and husband of Lady Vaelora."

"Yet she is the envoy?" Delauck's face screwed up in puzzlement.

"She is indeed." To Quaeryt, the scene in the parlor was getting more surreal by the moment.

"If you will pardon me," said Aenitra, "it might be best if I explained to my son." She turned. "Lord Bhayar holds Pharsi blood in his lineage. You can see it in the Lady Vaelora. The commander bears the traits of a lost one of the Pharsi, with the white hair of Erion and the dark eyes. He also limps slightly. The Pharsi High Councils have always been headed by women. Lord Bhayar clearly knows this, and has sent his sister to treat with them. The commander is more than a commander, and he and his men are here to make a point—that Bhayar will tolerate none of this feuding foolishness that has gone on . . . and more, I suspect." She turned back to Quaeryt. "Is this not so?"

"You are most perceptive, Lady Aenitra," replied Quaeryt. "Lord Bhayar intends that the laws will apply to all, and to that end, for the time being, a regiment will be stationed in Laaryn."

Delauck frowned slightly. "You did not bring a regiment here."

"No. We judged two companies to be sufficient. Were they not? But Lady Vaelora is being escorted by my command of two regiments and the Southern Army of seven regiments. The one to remain in Laaryn will be Fifth Regiment."

"What do you require of me?"

"Your statement that you will be loyal to Lord Bhayar and that you will not engage in any hostilities against him, his forces, or any other High Holders or groups, such as factors."

"That . . . I can pledge . . . and I do so."

Vaelora smiled. "I accept your allegiance on behalf of Lord Bhayar."

"You don't require some oath on paper?" Delauck's voice was almost light.

Quaeryt looked to Vaelora.

She smiled at Delauck. "Only the words written in the heart count. Paper burns in an instant. You agreed to be loyal to Lord Bhayar. So long as you are, he will support you. If you are not, you have seen what can happen."

Aenitra nodded.

"Will you stay for refreshments?" asked Delauck.

"Much as Lady Vaelora would enjoy such," replied Quaeryt, "her time here is limited, and she needs must return to Laaryn to deal with other matters before dark." *Besides which, imaging isn't proof against poison and other less obvious treacheries.*

"We have caused you much concern," added Vaelora, "but I do trust that the unpleasantnesses of the day will be the last, and that at some time, when matters are settled, we will see you in Variana." She smiled warmly.

Behind Delauck, his mother nodded ever so slightly, before saying, "We will see you out and wish you a fruitful journey."

"Thank you," replied Vaelora. "We wish you and your mother well, and your lady a quick return to health."

"I appreciate your thoughts," replied Delauck.

Quaeryt *thought* the High Holder was resigned to the change in his position, but he remained close to Vaelora all the way out of the keep and until they were mounted and across the bridge and on their way down the improved lane.

"You were worried about poisoning and the like, weren't you?" Vaelora asked as the hold disappeared behind them.

"I don't think he would have," replied Quaeryt, "but I couldn't be certain. That was a risk you didn't have to take."

"What about you?"

"I worried more about you."

"Bhayar said—"

"I know, but . . ."

"Dearest."

"Yes, dear one," Quaeryt said quietly.

Vaelora laughed. After a moment so did Quaeryt—even as he hoped that word of the visit to Lauckan would spread, and that they would only have to make a few more such visits to High Holders in the weeks ahead as they headed downriver from Laaryn. *If there are even any holdings close to the river.*

All in all, it wasn't until Meredi morning that Southern Army and Quaeryt's regiments pulled out of Laaryn, heading down the River Laar toward Ephra. While the factors of Laaryn had provided more flatboats, they were only used for supplies, and the troopers were forced to ride—or march, in the case of Skarpa's two regiments of foot—along a very rough road on the east side of the river.

There had been one sad reminder that no matter how hard Quaeryt and Vaelora tried, sometimes there was no remedy for some ills. The small blond girl, about whom Vaelora had worried, had slipped out of the inn on Mardi night and thrown herself in the river. One of the squads riding patrols had seen her running toward the water, but hadn't been able to reach her before the current pulled her into deep water, where she vanished in the darkness. The other girls hadn't heard her leave.

The better side was that Vaelora had found families willing to help the other three, and had persuaded Meinyt to have an officer follow up to make certain they had kept their word. Even thinking about what he had found left Quaeryt discouraged, especially since he doubted that the situation was all that rare in Bovaria, perhaps even in Telaryn.

By Samedi noon, the Telaryn forces had weathered a chilling rainstorm that had halted their progress on Vendrei for several glasses, gusty fall winds, and two broken axles on supply wagons. They had covered close to a hundred milles, passing through hamlet after hamlet. Quaeryt and Vaelora also discovered that Kharst's comparatively narrow and flat-bottomed canal boat rolled considerably even in the gentler waters of the River Laar and that the rudder was too small for quick response. In the end, Quaeryt ordered the canal boat lashed to a flatboat, and he and Vaelora rode with the troopers—although Quaeryt had to admit he did enjoy sleeping comfortably at night.

As they left another riverside village, called Croilles, Quaeryt looked to Vaelora. "Have you noticed that we haven't seen anything even faintly resembling a high holding?"

"You've mentioned that every day, dearest."

"I just wanted to keep reminding you of that."

"You're doing well. Why don't you tell me what that means. You're dying to do so, I think."

"I well might"—Quaeryt grinned sheepishly—"especially since the weather has been nothing to talk about." He ignored the fact that the morning was sunny and pleasant, with just enough breeze to be cooling without chilling.

"Well . . . go on."

"Since you insist."

Vaelora rolled her eyes in an exaggerated fashion.

Quaeryt grinned, then said, "When we traveled up the River Aluse—Southern Army, that is—we didn't find many high holdings there, either, and there were far more ruined holdings than I would have expected, a number of them burned out or abandoned. In fact, I saw more ruined high holdings there than I have in all of Telaryn. When I think back on it, there was something else I didn't see—and that was that people weren't particularly afraid of the High Holders. The majority of the High Holders were afraid or worried about Kharst, and the larger and richer the hold, the more worried they were. Then there was something else"—Quaeryt looked to Vaelora—"something we saw again in Laaryn."

"Powerful factors?"

"*Rich* and powerful factors. Some of the factors' dwellings in Bovaria are the size of hold houses in Telaryn . . . and all of them are in towns or very close to them . . . and then there are the roads . . ."

"You keep saying that Kharst and his forbears didn't build roads, except for the one from Nordeau to Variana."

"Exactly. Almost all the trade and commerce in Bovaria has gone by the rivers, not by roads, and what good roads there are flank the rivers. Kharst's power was limited by those facts. Telaryn is different, and so is Tilbor. Except for the Aluse, we don't have that many long navigable rivers, and the ones we do have are separated by mountains and the like. So rulers built roads. They had to in order to be able to control their people and even the High Holders. Kharst used his assassins to rule the High Holders by fear, and granted the factors more power in order to collect tariffs through them. Bovaria doesn't even have a government in the sense that Telaryn does. I'd assumed that Kharst had some sort of regional governor in Khel, but Bhayar couldn't find any record of that, and all the messages in the Chateau Regis . . ."

"You destroyed them, didn't you?"

"Those that survived were unreadable," Quaeryt admitted.

"You think that the powerful High Holders in Bovaria were either favorites of the rex and close to rivers, or located in places where the rex would have great trouble attacking or assassinating them?"

"It makes a strange sort of sense." Quaeryt shrugged. "I'm sure there are High Holders that don't fall into that pattern, but too many of those I've encountered or observed do."

"That also explains the Great Canal," Vaelora said. "When Father started tariffing the Bovarian merchants using the River Aluse, that meant Kharst's father couldn't tariff his merchants as much. He didn't build roads, though. He didn't even think that way. He built a canal from Variana to Laaryn to get goods to and from the port at Ephra."

After a pause, Vaelora asked, "Then why aren't there more high holdings in the hills to the north of Lauckan? Those places would be even harder for any rex to have reached. Or is it because the ground is not only rocky and rugged, but poor?"

"That would be my guess. From the maps, it looks like all the lands north of Laaryn and Tuuryl are rather hilly and inhospitable. And the richer high holdings are those located at the hilly or rocky edges of flatter and more fertile lands—usually away from the rivers."

"That explains Lauckan. It doesn't explain why someone else didn't do what you did, though."

"I think it does."

"It does?" Vaelora's tone conveyed considerable doubt.

"Kharst and his predecessors ruled through the factors and through fear and assassination. He used crossbowmen and armsmen to carry out his wishes. Those are forms of violence against which a ruler can take precautions. We—the other imagers and I—have been effective only because Bhayar has gathered us and because I'm loyal to him. That's because he's a good ruler . . ."

"Kharst couldn't trust any imager powerful enough to do what you can, could he?"

"I'd be very surprised." Quaeryt sighed. "That's why I have to build the imagers into an institution that has to be loyal to Bhayar and his successors, and one that is strong enough to assure that his successors are good rulers, in a way that will never tempt future imagers into trying to rule."

"That sounds more difficult than unifying Lydar."

"I doubt Lydar will remain unified if we don't succeed." Quaeryt couldn't keep a certain bleakness out of his voice.

"If anyone can, you can . . ."

"No . . . it will take you, me . . . and Bhayar . . . and all the imagers." *And even that might not be enough.*

# 19

The following Jeudi evening found Quaeryt, Vaelora, and Skarpa seated in a small private room in the Grande Laar Inn, located in the town of Daaraen, situated on the point of land between the Phraan River and River Laar just before they met—some seventy milles north of the port of Ephra. The Grande Laar Inn was located off the main market square on the west side of the city, not that far from the river piers and warehouses—a number of which Skarpa had commandeered temporarily for Southern Army and Quaeryt's regiments, as well as three other inns and their stables.

In the interests of both security and privacy, the three had decided to have their meal brought to them while they discussed what had occurred during the day, although none of them spoke much until they had largely finished eating.

"Lots of little towns along the river," observed Skarpa, "ever since Croilles, anyway."

"The maps don't show more than hamlets farther from the river," said Vaelora. "Is that because the maps are bad or because no one really knows . . . or doesn't go there?"

"With roads like they have . . . ?" Quaeryt shook his head. "Most of the crofters don't need good roads, and many of the High Holders don't want them."

"We've only seen a handful of high holdings," mused Vaelora.

". . . and we only saw one that was devastated," Quaeryt observed after taking a last bite of a fowl pie that was a touch spicier than he might have liked.

"It had been that way for generations," Vaelora pointed out. "That wasn't Kharst's doing."

"That might have been his grandsire's doing. I don't think the way Bovaria's been ruled has changed much over the years. There certainly wasn't another one near . . . and we have seen many fine dwellings here in Daaraen, certainly belonging to factors."

"Not a sign of any Bovarian armsmen. Not at all." Skarpa shook his head. "You'd see more in the mountains of Montagne . . . or in the north of Tilbor. Still say it doesn't make sense."

"It makes sense," said Vaelora firmly. "Fear and treachery . . ."

Quaeryt nodded. "The Khellan majors all pointed out that Kharst had little success in conquering Khel until he used traders and others to spread the Red Death. In most of the high holdings we visited on the way to Variana, the holders were terrified—gravely concerned, anyway—that they not anger him. And when they could, even the Bovarian commanders used tactics like that."

Skarpa frowned . . . then slowly nodded. "When you put it that way, they used musketeers from ambush in mass firing and tried to get us fearful and confused . . . or Antiagon Fire . . ."

"They weren't ready for us to attack through those," Quaeryt pointed out. "They expected to weaken us through fear."

"They might have, except your imaging turned fear against them," Skarpa pointed out.

"They didn't expect that, just the way the factors in Laaryn didn't expect what you did," added Vaelora.

For several moments none of them spoke.

"I was thinking we should stay here tomorrow and head out on Samedi," suggested Skarpa, his words carrying a hint of deference.

"We might even want to stay a day longer if the drizzle turns into a downpour," replied Quaeryt. "If it's sunny and clear, then I'd definitely think Samedi."

Skarpa nodded. "Leave early though. We'll have to cross the Phraan, and neither bridge looks that sturdy."

"We need to meet with the local factors in a town, really a small city, this big, but we haven't heard from them."

"You will," prophesied Skarpa. "You will."

"Even after that . . . we need to make a statement of some sort." Quaeryt looked to Skarpa. "A bridge might be just the thing. Call it a gift to Daaraen. It might lead to better roads, and it certainly will leave a lasting reminder."

"Won't that tax your imagers?"

"The Phraan's pretty narrow where the lower bridge is. Threkhyl could handle that himself. I could have Lhandor draw out a plan for one that's not plain . . ."

"They don't need fancy," Skarpa retorted.

Major Aernyt eased the door open slightly. "There is a Factor Jarell who would like to speak to Lady Vaelora on behalf of the factors' council of Daaraen."

"Have him enter in a few moments, after someone clears the platters," said Quaeryt.

"Yes, sir."

Two rankers appeared immediately and took the platters, while Quaeryt stood and moved his chair, then motioned for Vaelora and Skarpa to change seats, so that she was seated between them and facing the door.

Several moments later the door opened, and a man in a dark brown jacket and trousers entered, with a white shirt and highly polished boots. Jarell appeared to be only a few years older than Quaeryt, clean-shaven, with straight brown hair slicked back from a high forehead. His smile was winning as he bowed before the table, his eyes directly upon Vaelora.

"We had heard that there was a grave misunderstanding by the factors' council of Laaryn, Lady Vaelora, and we wished to make certain that no action of ours might be associated with any error on our part . . ."

"You have not presumed, but you are here to inquire," replied Vaelora. "Unlike the factors of Laaryn, who lied, and then attempted to cover their falsehoods with greater deception. What do you wish to know?"

"What do you expect and require of us?"

"You have paid your tariffs, I trust?" asked Vaelora.

"They were paid, alas, to Rex Kharst, before . . . the recent . . . unpleasantness."

"Lord Bhayar may require a token tariff . . . as a gesture of loyalty."

"We have heard that such was required in Laaryn, but was that not for the failures of the factors in Laaryn?" Jarell's tone was apologetic, as if he were asking for clarification of something he did not understand.

"Much more than that was required of the factors of Laaryn," replied Quaeryt. "Much more. As for tokens of allegiance, Lord Bhayar has already required a token tariff of High Holders. He granted Lady Vaelora the authority to impose such where necessary, while he considers the matter for all factors in Bovaria."

"The tariff system here is most fair . . . or so many have said."

"It may well be," agreed Quaeryt. "I would suggest, however, that you provide a reasoned argument for the system to him, because those of us from Telaryn are not so familiar with the methods of tariffing used in Bovaria." *That will also explain the system to him, which will be useful, since not much in the way of records survived the ice in Chateau Regis.* "Even so, do you not think some token of allegiance would be merited?"

"We have pledged that allegiance in full and good faith."

Vaelora smiled. "That pledge is most welcome . . . but as factors you well know that pledges alone do not pay for goods. You do not sell your goods for pledges, and a land cannot be governed on pledges alone. In ruling and in trade, without coin or golds, pledges are empty."

"That is most true, Lady . . . most true. Yet one would hope not to pay for the same goods twice, nor the same governing."

"That is also true," said Quaeryt, "but there are times when one pays for a good and it is not delivered, and to obtain the good one must pay again. The same is true in ruling. Rex Kharst delivered bad governing, and Lord Bhayar has had to pay twice. He is not settling the cost upon you, but he may well ask for a token amount against what he has paid. Since the factors of Daaraen have not flouted his authority or lied to his officials, no tariffs are due now. Whether a token tariff for the past year will be required will be Lord Bhayar's decision."

"Thank you for clarifying that." Jarell bowed.

"We will require some additional supplies," noted Skarpa. "We will talk of that later. Where might we find you tomorrow?"

"One of the factors' council members will be at the council chamber on the main market square from eighth glass to fourth glass." Jarell bowed again. "If there is nothing further with which I can assist you . . ."

"Thank you for your courtesy," replied Vaelora. "You may go."

Once the chamber door closed behind the factor, Quaeryt shook his head.

"It didn't take them long," said Skarpa dryly.

"The factors in Laaryn must have sent a fast boat down the Laar—without stopping," mused Quaeryt. "This is going to create some considerable problems for your brother."

"Factors can be worse than High Holders, it appears," said Skarpa.

"That wasn't what I meant," explained Quaeryt. "The factors of Laaryn immediately sent word to the factors here, and most likely to those all along the river. That suggests that they can and do work together, more so than the High Holders. That also explains why the factors in Laaryn were so surprised. I would suspect that all of the factors' councils, at least along the River Laar, cooperate in managing the flow and pricing of goods."

"They're all in on it, the greedy bastards," murmured Skarpa.

"That's not always bad. It could result in more flour and grain in bad times as well." *Although the price would be higher.* "But it does mean that Bhayar will have to be consistent in his dealings with all factors, and not play off one area or group against another—unless he wants some very dissatisfied factors . . . and that's not a good idea."

"Inconsistency isn't a good idea in anything," said Vaelora.

"Except occasionally in battle," pointed out Skarpa.

"Your point is taken, Submarshal, and that reminds me." Quaeryt rose from the table. "I need to take care of another matter."

"Where are you going?" asked Vaelora.

"To talk to the imagers, and have Lhandor design a better bridge. It will give him and them more practice for what they'll need to do when they return to Variana."

"Do I want to know what else you have in mind?" asked Skarpa gruffly.

"Probably not." Quaeryt grinned. "But if they build solid bridges across the Aluse and roads in places that need them for trade, that will show that imagers can benefit everyone. That can't hurt." *Assuming we all can survive to return . . .*

By midafternoon on Vendrei the skies over Daaraen had cleared, and on Samedi morning, after checking with Skarpa to determine that Southern Army was indeed riding out, Quaeryt dispatched rankers to inform the factors' council that their presence was expected on the city side of the lower bridge over the Phraan River at eighth glass. Then he summoned the imager undercaptains to meet him in the plaques chamber in the Grande Laar Inn.

While he ate quickly with Vaelora, in their chambers, she looked at him and smiled. "You like doing this, don't you?"

"I'd rather impress Bovarian factors by creating things." *Besides, there's already been enough destruction.* "It's also more impressive, because what you've created remains."

"Dearest, you're an optimist. People fear destruction, not building."

"So . . . I should just destroy parts of the city?" His tone was ironic.

"No. I'm just telling you what people are like."

"Then it should help if I have the imagers destroy the old bridge first."

"That would be better."

"And I don't want to portray Bhayar like Kharst."

Vaelora shook her head.

"I'd best be going to meet with the undercaptains." Quaeryt swallowed the last of his tea.

"I'll take care of getting all our gear out and ready, dearest."

Quaeryt had his doubts about that, but merely said, "Thank you," and then headed down the stairs to the plaques room. All the imagers were present when he walked into the chamber and closed the door behind himself. With Desyrk and Smaethyl remaining in Laaryn with Meinyt and Fifth Regiment, that left just six imagers.

Not for the first time, Quaeryt wondered if what he planned with the imagers was the best strategy. *Yet . . . if you keep them all together, then you don't create the impression you need . . . and Skarpa will need imagers in Ephra.* He offered a smile he wasn't sure he felt, then said, "Good morning. The skies are clear, and we're heading out. As I told you yesterday, we need to provide a certain demonstration for the locals." *And for a few of the regimental commanders . . . like Kharllon and Meurn.*

He looked to Threkhyl. "Threkhyl . . . you've studied the plan Lhandor gave you thoroughly?"

"Yes, sir. That shouldn't be a problem."

"And you can image the basic structure?"

"Yes, sir. Could do more, sir."

"I'm certain you could, but I don't want any of you unable to image after we leave. With less than eighty milles to Ephra, there's always the possibility of running into something unexpected, especially since there aren't any other Telaryn forces in this part of Bovaria . . . and there are High Holders reputed to have forces the size of several companies, if not larger."

"You don't think . . . ?" began Horan.

"I'd doubt it, but we've been attacked by smaller forces than those might be, and I'd rather not lose troopers when some effective imaging could prevent it."

Most of the undercaptains nodded.

"There will be one change. I'd thought just to have you replace the old bridge. The Lady Vaelora pointed out a problem with that. Since she has seen the effects of what rulers do for far longer than I have, I do listen to her. Most people tend to forget that the power to create is also the power to destroy, and they fear destruction more than creation. So . . . Horan, before Threkhyl and the others image the new bridge, I'd like you to destroy the old one."

Horan smiled. "I can do that, sir."

"Good. Otherwise, we'll proceed as planned. Any other questions?" Quaeryt looked across their faces. "Then load out and mount up. I'll see you in the side courtyard shortly."

Once he left the room he hurried back up the stairs to the chamber where he'd left Vaelora, only to find it vacant. He laughed softly and headed back down to the courtyard and the stables beyond, where, indeed, Vaelora was mounted with her single kit behind her saddle, holding the reins to Quaeryt's mare.

Quaeryt just grinned at her and shook his head. "Sometimes . . ."

"Dearest . . ."

When Quaeryt saw her expression, and that of Zhelan beyond her, he could only laugh and mount. In less than half a quint, first company was riding away from the inn to meet up with the other two regiments at the northern market square. While there were some people on the streets, most moved away from the riders, although quietly.

Although he had a greater force to gather, Skarpa reached the square within moments of the time that Quaeryt did, more than a quint before eighth glass.

"Would have liked to have moved out earlier," said Skarpa.

"I know, but we need the factors to see this. At seventh glass, many wouldn't have come. The council would, but not some of the others, and the more that are here, the better." Quaeryt glanced to the southeast side of the market square, where more than a score of factors stood, many with frowns and quizzical expressions on their faces. "I'll think I'll ride over there for a moment. If you would position the column, with the imagers in front, the way we planned."

"I'll take care of that. Be a pleasure to see their faces." Skarpa snorted.

"Zhelan! The submarshal will be positioning first company." As he called out to the major, Quaeryt could see Vaelora beside Zhelan. She gave Quaeryt an amused smile.

"Yes, sir."

Quaeryt turned the mare and rode across the square to where the factors had gathered. He'd barely reined up when Jarell stepped forward.

"Might I ask, Commander, the point of requiring the factors' council to be here this morning?" Jarell's voice was polite, but there was a tension in it. "I doubt that the factors need to see your arrayed forces to understand the power of Lord Bhayar."

"There is power, and there is power, Factor Jarell. But in answer to your question, we did not request your presence merely to see our troopers depart Daaraen. We had another purpose, which will become clear in a few moments. If you and the others would move a few yards farther north, to where you have an unobstructed view of the bridge, everything will become most clear very shortly." Quaeryt smiled politely, but he did image-project a sense of reasonable authority. "The matter will not take long, and I appreciate your diplomacy in dealing with a difficult situation." He had no doubt Jarell had been chosen to treat with them just because the factor was calm and diplomatic, but it didn't hurt to recognize it.

Quaeryt eased the mare along the edge of the paved portion of the square, then waited for the gaggle of factors to follow, listening as he did.

". . . don't see the reason . . ."

". . . power's its own reason, Vauxal . . . its own reason . . ."

". . . be thankful you're not watching executions . . ."

". . . just glad they're leaving before they require all the provisions we have . . ."

Once Telaryn forces were in position, the imagers at the head of a column that stretched for a good half mille, if not farther, back through the streets, Quaeryt guided the mare to a position between the imagers and the factors, then reined up. The undercaptains waited no more than thirty yards from the approach to the old bridge and less than ten from the gathered factors.

"Factors of Daaraen!" Quaeryt projected authority, then waited for the murmurs and conversations to die away before continuing. "We requested your presence here this morning for a specific reason. In coming to Daaraen, we could not help but notice that the bridges across the Phraan were in less than perfect repair. Therefore, as a gift to Daaraen, and as a reminder of the beneficence and power of Lord Bhayar, we have decided to remove this bridge and replace it with another . . . one that is . . . sturdier. Much sturdier."

Quaeryt turned and gestured to Horan. "If you would remove the present bridge."

"Yes, sir." Horan gazed at the narrow timber span, barely wide enough for a single wagon, with narrow railings and planks separated enough that anyone on the bridge who looked down could easily see the gray waters of the river.

A single flash of light flared across the river, and thin sheets of white fog rose from the water, immediately dispersing to reveal . . . nothing. Where the old timber bridge had stood, supported on two stone pilings, nothing remained, not even the pilings.

Quaeryt said nothing, just waiting, again listening.

". . . what happened . . ."

". . . Namer-flamed imagers . . ."

". . . do that?"

Quaeryt again spoke, image-projecting his voice. "Now that the old bridge has been destroyed totally, it is time for a new and stronger bridge to replace it." He gestured to Threkhyl.

Another series of light flashes flickered across the river, followed by a white fog that filled the air above the water, water now covered with a thin layer of ice. The fog immediately began to disperse under the bright morning sun, revealing the solid structure that arched over the river with enough clearance for the largest of river and flatboats—but not enough for tall-masted sailing craft, since Quaeryt doubted that few would attempt sailing up the narrow and shallow Phraan. As Quaeryt had suggested and Lhandor had drafted, the bridge supports were of black granite. The side walls and the pillars at each end were of image-hardened white alabaster. The roadbed was wide enough for two large wagons side by side, with room to spare.

Quaeryt studied the faces of the factors as they beheld the bridge that seemed to rise out of the white fog. Most showed no initial expression, as if they could not quite comprehend what had occurred before their eyes. One—Jarell—frowned, nodded, then turned to the older factor to his left, murmuring something. The thin sheet of black ice on the river, which extended several hundred yards upstream and downstream of the new bridge, began to crack into fragments that shimmered in the sun, and more wisps of fog rose from the ice and the water.

Quaeryt waited, watching to see what ice, if any, remained on the bridge roadway, but the thin rime quickly dispersed, far more swiftly than the ice on the river below. He looked back to face the gathered factors. "To prove the strength of this bridge, we will leave Daaraen by crossing it on our way to Ephra." Turning from the factors, Quaeryt eased the mare over to ride beside Vaelora, flanked by Zhelan on the far side.

Then he gestured and ordered, "First company! Forward!"

The roadway's black stone did not even vibrate as the riders of first company, and then of Eleventh and Nineteenth Regiments, rode across, four abreast, filling the span from end to end.

When they reached the middle of the bridge, Vaelora leaned toward Quaeryt. "Very well done, dearest. They will remember the day."

"And the power of Lord Bhayar." He grinned.

# 21

By ninth glass on Lundi morning, the Telaryn force had passed through a score of hamlets and villages, the last being Ghaern, a largish village where they had spent the night on Solayi. They had reached a point some fifteen milles north of Ephra, and while the troopers watered mounts and took a break, Quaeryt, Vaelora, and Skarpa stood under an oak tree that was shedding leaves with each gust of a damp wind that felt only a trace less than raw.

"So far as I can tell, there's no way to cross the river except by ferry," said Skarpa. "The maps don't show any bridges. None of the locals know of any, and the only ferry is supposed to be at Geusyn. That's maybe five milles north of Ephra." He gestured to the far side of the river. "Over there all I can see is marsh and swamp and trees . . . and sometimes our supply flatboats."

"We should think about building a bridge somewhere," suggested Quaeryt. "If you need to deal with the Antiagons, you don't want to rely on ferries."

"Needs to be closer to Ephra," said Skarpa. "We'd have to slog through swamp on the west side."

"We'll have to see if there's any place with solid ground on both sides and where the river's not too wide," added Quaeryt. *If there even is such a place.* He was already worrying about saying that he and the imagers could build a bridge to Ephra. *What if the river gets even wider and the ground stays swampy?*

"I'd not want to wager on that," replied Skarpa.

"Nor I, either. It might not be practical, but I can hope." Quaeryt refrained from shaking his head. "Have either Meurn or Kharllon said anything about the bridge Threkhyl imaged?"

"Not a word. Not where I've heard anything."

That wasn't surprising.

In another quint Southern Army was again riding along the rutted road south, with first company in the van, followed by Eleventh Regiment. Skarpa and Quaeryt rode side by side, with Vaelora and Zhelan behind them. Quaeryt couldn't help but glance continually at the river, and at the far side, but the western shore seemed an unchanging welter of low trees, reeds, and high grasses, stretching west as far as he could see. *Does it go on all the way to Ephra?*

After another glass or so, his intermittent study was interrupted by the sound of scouts galloping back toward the vanguard.

"Sirs! Raiders ahead! Attacking a wagon."

"How many?" demanded Skarpa.

"A squad. Couldn't be more than that."

Quaeryt turned in the saddle. "Major . . . take first company. Lhandor and Threkhyl, you go with them!"

"Yes, sir!"

"First company! Forward!" ordered Zhelan.

Quaeryt forced himself just to watch as first company headed out at a measured pace.

"Very good," murmured Vaelora as she eased her mount forward until she was riding almost at Quaeryt's shoulder.

"I agree, Lady," added Skarpa, with a laugh.

"Thank you both," replied Quaeryt dryly.

"Can't say I'm surprised that there are raiders here," Skarpa finally said, easing his mount almost to the left shoulder of the road to allow Vaelora to ride up between him and Quaeryt. "No large towns, no sign of High Holders."

"But what are they raiding?" asked Quaeryt. "The most valuable goods are on the river . . . or in Ephra or Kephria."

Skarpa frowned. "If they're raiding, they aren't doing it for nothing."

The column continued southward, and a mille later, as the road curved back eastward around a low hill, two scouts rode toward them, reining up and then riding beside Quaeryt along the shoulder on the east side of the road.

"The raiders were gone when first company got there. They attacked a wagon."

"Who were the riders?" asked Skarpa. "Could you tell?"

"No, sir," replied the scout. "They wore dark green, all of them, like uniforms."

"Someone's private army," ventured Quaeryt. *But that raises even more questions.*

Ahead, Quaeryt saw a wagon, and first company, formed up on the road to the south of the wagon, with a squad of rankers and Zhelan surrounding the wagon.

The first thing that Quaeryt noticed as they rode closer was the blackened area around the rear of the wagon, as if someone had started a fire that had failed to ignite the broken tailboard. The wagon itself was small, half the size of a dray with large high wheels supporting a body barely three yards long and perhaps half as wide. The wagon bed was a yard deep and a canvas sheet had been tied across barrels and kegs set on their butt ends, but the containers had been smashed open and their contents strewn across the road and the west shoulder.

Quaeryt had no trouble smelling the overpowering odor of what had been in the wagon. "Elveweed," he said to Vaelora.

"All those barrels?"

"It looks that way."

The single draft horse lay on its side, unmoving in its traces. Seeing the dark stain on the dirt, Quaeryt reined up beside Zhelan and looked closely. One side of its skull was crushed in.

"What sort of weapon . . . ?" He shook his head.

"Something like a morning star," answered Zhelan.

"But . . . does anyone use those anymore?"

"Someone did here."

"They had to be carrying it on purpose—just for that." Quaeryt couldn't think of any other reason for carrying such a heavy weapon, one unnecessary in warfare when almost no one wore armor any longer. Then he noticed the body of the man in gray, sprawled on the road in front of the dead horse. His skull was also crushed.

A woman knelt by him, her body shaking.

Vaelora dismounted, handing the reins of her mount to one of the scouts, and strode over to the woman. Quaeryt followed, still mounted.

"We weren't doing nothing," sobbed the woman, looking up to Vaelora. "Traes, he was just trying to put food on the table."

"With elveweed?" murmured Quaeryt.

"Why did you need the elveweed to do that?" asked Vaelora.

"Only thing folks'll pay for hereabouts. Traders sneak north from Antiago. Elveweed don't grow there."

Quaeryt frowned. "You couldn't sell it in Ephra?"

"How'd we get there? Can't afford the ferry. 'Sides, factors . . . holders don't let no one doesn't hold a medallion sell nothing there. Who's got silvers for that?"

"What about selling it yourself farther south?" asked Quaeryt.

"You crazy? Antiagons fry anyone selling elveweed . . . except some of their own. That's why we sell to their traders."

"Who attacked you?"

"Friggin' holder. Had to be Chaelaet. Dark green." The woman's eyes took in Quaeryt's uniform and then that of Zhelan. "Who are you?"

"Commander Quaeryt of Telaryn. We're headed to Ephra."

The woman turned to Vaelora. "You help me, Lady . . . please . . . You are a lady?"

"I am."

"Don't let them . . ."

"They won't touch you. They're not like the Bovarians or the holders here." Vaelora paused. "They know they'd answer to my brother . . . and to my husband."

". . . husband?"

"The commander is my husband. You can ride with us so long as you wish."

Interestingly enough, the woman did not ask who Vaelora's brother was. *Or perhaps she thought that Vaelora's husband was also her brother.* Quaeryt had heard that such marriages occasionally occurred among the oligarchs in Jariola, but why would a Bovarian woman think that might happen in Lydar . . . unless she knew so little of geography that all places outside of Bovaria were the same?

By the time the troopers had cleared the road and brought up a spare mule to hitch to the wagon, which was unharmed, Vaelora had calmed down the woman and had her riding beside her while a trooper drove the wagon, along with the supply wagons. Vaelora said little, and whenever Quaeryt glanced in her direction, she shook her head, indicating that the woman was not ready to say more than she had.

Quaeryt motioned to Skarpa, and the two rode farther ahead, putting more distance between their mounts and those of the women.

"Have the scouts found out more about those riders?" asked Quaeryt.

"I was about to ask you."

"Zhelan said they were long gone by the time first company reached the wagon, but the woman said the riders had to belong to a holder named Chaelaet because they wore dark green."

"That's a start. Don't care much for elveweed, but I care even less for holders sending armsmen out to smash heads."

"From what Bhayar intimated, some of the High Holders here may be trading in elveweed themselves. It could be that they don't want anyone else doing it."

"That would make sense." Skarpa snorted.

"That means you're going to have trouble with them as well as with Aliaro."

"And if I come down on the High Holders, they might just decide to make this part of Bovaria part of Antiago, you think?"

"They might threaten that. If they do, you'll have two strong imagers. Don't argue. Just have Threkhyl topple their holds in on them."

"You're sounding like Meinyt again."

"There are times when young commanders can learn from grizzled old subcommanders," retorted Quaeryt. "But then, the more I see of Bovarian High Holders, the less I'm impressed."

"You've never been impressed by most High Holders."

"I'm even less impressed by those here in the south."

"I can't imagine why."

Both men shook their heads as they continued to ride southward.

By fourth glass on Lundi evening, Southern Army reached Geusyn, the largest town they'd seen since leaving Daaraen. While there were actually nine inns in the town of various sizes, all with stables, in the end Skarpa, Quaeryt, and the senior officers had to work hard to get all the troopers and mounts in what passed for quarters, with Kharllon gently pressing for his regiment to use the northernmost inn.

Skarpa had arranged for the senior officers to be quartered in the River Inn, and Quaeryt couldn't help but wonder how many inns there might be of that name all across Lydar. The one in which he and Vaelora were staying was an oblong two-story structure, solidly built, clean, and with little else in terms of architecture or design to distinguish itself—except that it had three plaques rooms, suggesting to Quaeryt that more than a few traders engaged in plaques.

While Vaelora dealt with the widowed woman, and tried to help her . . . and learn what she could, Quaeryt sought out the inn's stablemaster. Ostler, really, he reflected as he sized up Haern, a wiry man a good ten years older than himself.

"What'd you be wanting, sir, besides the grain and fodder for your mounts?"

"Information."

"Don't know as I'd be the best for that."

"I'm sure you would be for what I'd like to know. You've seen people come and go for years here, I'd imagine."

"More 'n ten years, sir."

"Do most traders stay here in Geusyn as long as they can . . . or do they go to Ephra as soon as possible?"

Haern laughed. "No one'd go to Ephra sooner than they had to . . . or stay long there, not given a choice. Place is filled with red flies, green skeeters, and flux. A night at an inn not so good as here costs twice as much, and the food's worse. Only reason traders go there is to get their goods on an outbound trader or buy and off-load from a spice ship from the south. Otelyrn and the like, you know. Wouldn't say that there might not also be curamyn and a few other things, either. Course the traders'd go to Kephria if they could, but with the walls and the guns and the imagers . . ."

"Do the Antiagons fire at everything coming down the river?"

"Aye . . . well . . . sometimes, mostly at vessels not showing an Antiagon trade flag . . . that's why fewer and fewer trade ships call at Ephra, and why most leave on the early morning or early night tides. Been that way ever since Rex Kharst sneaked imagers near the piers at Kephria and they fired warehouses there. Say that none of the imagers and boats escaped, not that their deaths stopped half the port quarter from burnin'. Could see the flames all the way up here that night . . ."

"What about the ferries? How do they avoid the Antiagon guns?"

"The current and the tides. They use the current to cross the river heading downstream, then wait for the tide coming up the Gulf so that they can cross the river to the towpath below Geusyn, and mules tow them back up to the piers here."

After another quint's worth of questions, Quaeryt thanked the ostler and headed back into the inn. There, he met with Zhelan, Alazyn, and Khaern. He still waited a quint longer for Skarpa to finish meeting with his senior quartermasters before he could draw the submarshal away and relay what he'd learned so far.

When Quaeryt finished, Skarpa looked at him. "The more I learn about Bovaria, the more I wonder how Kharst governed it at all."

"He didn't. He tariffed it and used the tariffs to build an army to plunder elsewhere and to terrify High Holders into paying the tariffs to support him and the army." Quaeryt knew he was oversimplifying, but he wasn't sure that he was that far off.

"Do we even want to go to Ephra?" asked Skarpa.

"I don't think you should," replied Quaeryt. "You'd just have your army trapped there, and all the real problems you face are on this side of the river. I don't have much of a choice."

"Are your ships there?"

"I don't know. There was no one at the ferry piers when we got here, and no one else seems to know. I can only check tomorrow."

Skarpa nodded. "I've arranged a senior officers' mess—that includes Lady Vaelora—in the large plaques room at sixth glass. We need to go over what you and I and the other commanders have found out, and what everyone thinks."

"We'll be there."

After leaving Skarpa, Quaeryt turned and headed up the narrow stairs,

stairs that creaked with every step, to find Vaelora. She unbolted the door when she heard his voice.

He smiled, seeing her in a camisole.

"Dearest . . . not now. I've been washing up." She stepped aside and re-bolted the door behind him.

In order to take his mind off what he'd just seen, he looked around the corner room, large enough for an inn, but without curtains, only inside shutters, and a wide bed that sagged slightly in the middle. "What do you think of the quarters?"

"They're more spacious and less gracious than the canal boat. What are you going to do with it now?"

"Leave it at the piers with the supply flatboats. They're all guarded. I suppose I should see if it can be towed upriver, although I don't see how, given the lack of towpaths and the state of the roads." He shook his head.

"That's a pity. It's a beautiful boat, and I'd hate to see it rot away."

Quaeryt agreed, but he didn't have a ready solution. "What happened to the woman?" he finally asked as Vaelora walked back to the table that held a washbasin and pitcher. He removed his visor cap and set it on the plain square table at the side of the bed.

"She left. I couldn't persuade her to stay. She said she had an aunt. I doubt she does, but I don't think she trusts anyone, especially troopers and officers from Telaryn, and she would have felt like a captive if I'd insisted."

"We rescued her. You know—she knew—what those troopers—raiders—would have done."

"She did, and she was grateful. She was also afraid our kindness wouldn't last."

"Mine, you mean?"

"Most likely," Vaelora admitted. "I gave her some coppers and silvers. She didn't refuse."

"What's her name?"

"Willina," replied Vaelora. "She's younger than I am."

That surprised Quaeryt, given that Vaelora was not quite twenty-two, and Willina looked ten years older than his wife. *Just how hard has the woman's life been?* Quaeryt was all too afraid he knew. "How long has she been married?"

"I don't think they were married. She lost a child to the flux in Agostas. Her man grew elveweed in the swamps on the other side of the river and rowed it across on dark nights."

Quaeryt almost asked why, before recalling that there were no towns—except Ephra—on the west side of the River Laar anywhere near. "Dangerous business to grow it in the swamps, row across the river, try to avoid the High Holders' patrols, and sell it to Antiagon traders." He nodded as he recalled the wagon—light, high-wheeled, able to cover rough ground, and built more for speed than for capacity—a smuggler's wagon. "Why were they on the road, then?"

"She said something about having to make up time to meet the traders. They'd had to travel around Ghaern because another High Holder had set up road blocks to see if anyone was carrying contraband."

Quaeryt wanted to shake his head. In Laaryn, the factors controlled trade, but near Ephra, it sounded like the High Holders—or some of them—did so. *But Bhayar told that they might be a problem for Skarpa.* "I'm beginning to wonder if Kharst really even governed down here."

"His wanting to take Ferravyl makes more sense now," offered Vaelora.

"In a way, it does," mused Quaeryt, "but he'd still have had to take the whole river and occupy Solis. That would have cost him dearly, even if Solis is a better port. Here, all he'd have to have done is take Kephria and some territory to the south to get a decent port, not an entire chunk of another land. He already controlled the river—except for this part."

"You don't know how strong the Antiagon defenses are . . . or how much the local High Holders were paying him in tariffs. You've told me how much in golds elveweed brings. What if all the High Holders along the Lohan Hills, from here to the Sud Swamp, have interests in elveweed . . . and their own armies?"

"There can't be that many."

"There could be enough."

"It doesn't make sense," Quaeryt asserted. "Kharst raised a huge army against us. Less than ten years ago, he did the same and took over Khel. Surely, he could have lopped off a chunk of Antiago, the part with Kephria in it, and fortified it."

"Kharst didn't have many imagers, and Aliaro does. At least, he's supposed to. The Autarch also has Antiagon Fire. You've told me what damage that could have done if it hadn't have been for you and the imagers. When Kharst attacked Ferravyl, he had no idea that you and the imagers even existed. Have you forgotten that?"

Quaeryt had. He laughed. "I've been thinking about what Kharst and his commanders knew after the war started, not before. I hadn't thought of it that way."

"And if the High Holders here were paying higher tariffs . . ." added Vaelora.

"And other High Holders and marshals wanted lands in Telaryn . . ." Quaeryt nodded. "I suppose it makes sense in a strange way."

"Dearest . . . things are never as direct as one might think."

Quaeryt smiled. Vaelora might not know all he did about life beyond a capital city or a palace, but she'd seen and heard far more than he had about what went on around a ruler. "I forgot to tell you. We're going to eat with Skarpa and the regiment commanders and subcommanders in one of the plaques rooms."

"I thought we might. He hasn't had much of a chance to sit and talk to any of you."

"And you," Quaeryt added.

"If I know you, you've been making inquiries. What did you find out?"

"Nothing that pleases me," he admitted.

"Why don't you tell me while you wash up?"

Recognizing the gentle double command, he grinned. "As you wish, my lady."

"I do, indeed . . ." She smiled. "Later . . . dearest."

He began to explain what he had learned.

Before that long, he finished washing up, and they walked down the creaky narrow stairs to the large plaques room, where Skarpa was waiting outside.

"The others are already inside, even Commander Kharllon."

"Of course," replied Quaeryt lightly. *He wouldn't want to slight Vaelora.*

"If you would lead the way, Quaeryt, and if you would accompany me, Lady?"

Quaeryt understood. He was junior, but Skarpa could afford neither to place himself above Bhayar's sister, nor himself below her.

All the regimental commanders stood as Quaeryt entered, followed by Skarpa and Vaelora.

The large circular table was set for eleven, with the three vacant places facing the door. Vaelora sat on Skarpa's left, with Quaeryt on his right. Kharllon was located beside Vaelora, and Paedn beside Quaeryt.

Once everyone was seated, and the two trooper servers had filled all the goblets, Skarpa raised his and offered the toast. "To our safe arrival in Geusyn and to the effective accomplishment of the tasks ahead."

"To arrival and accomplishment," replied Quaeryt, leading the response, then taking but the smallest sip of the wine, a pungent red.

Kharllon turned toward Vaelora, asking, "How have you found the journey so far, Lady?"

"Far easier than riding across Telaryn," replied Vaelora.

Quaeryt refrained from smiling and turned to Paedn, the older subcommander to his right, as the two troopers began to serve, beginning with Vaelora and Skarpa. "What strikes you about southern Bovaria?"

"It's poor."

"What else?"

"It shouldn't be. Good rivers, good land." The balding subcommander absently brushed back a wispy lock of blond hair, his fingers not quite twiddling with the stem of a goblet still nearly as full as when it had been poured for the first toast.

"Why do you think that is? That it's so poor?"

"No one cares. Not the High Holders. Not the rex."

"Things should get better under Bhayar, then."

"It takes time. People don't change. Their children sometimes do."

While Quaeryt could overhear some of the conversation between Vaelora and Kharllon, who was being politely most solicitous of Lord Bhayar's sister, he quickly gave up trying to make sense of those phrases, since it was a strain to converse with the clearly laconic Paedn.

"What did you think about a holder's men attacking that cart?"

"What cart?"

Quaeryt went on to explain.

Paedn nodded when Quaeryt finished, then said, "Elveweed's more profitable than anything else. The High Holder will only hear your men attacked them. That will make getting allegiance harder."

"We were supposed to let them get away with it?"

Paedn laughed, just a short soft bark. "No. It just works that way."

"It's always that way," interjected Skarpa from Quaeryt's left. "Sometimes, the more you try to help people, the more they blame you."

Paedn nodded.

"The whole matter is disturbing," Skarpa added. "Either the High Holders don't have control of their armsmen, or they don't care about the people around Geusyn. Either way . . ."

"It's not good," said Paedn.

The fowl casserole provided by the River Inn was adequate and filling. The rest of the dinner conversation was pleasant and polite, and Quaeryt learned little more than he'd already learned from previous meetings of the regimental commanders. He was more than ready to go upstairs with Vaelora when the meal was over, but neither spoke until they were alone in their chamber and he had imaged the lamp on the narrow writing table into light.

"What did Kharllon have to say?" asked Quaeryt.

"He was most charming," replied Vaelora. "He's intelligent and knowledgeable. I did ask him what he thought of Rholan. He said that Rholan was likely a scoundrel who lacked golds and talent with anything other than words. So he turned to selling faith as a way to make his living."

"Did you ask him what he thought of scholars, then?"

"I did." Vaelora grinned. "He said the best were useful, the worst only misguided. I didn't press him on that. I think he actually believes what he said."

"Anything else? Of import?"

"He doesn't much care for Skarpa, but respects his skills. He didn't say it that way. It was more like, 'Lord Bhayar needs the best commanders he can find in times like these.' "

"And the implication is that it's unfortunate, but necessary."

"Something like that . . . all unsaid."

"Did he mention Deucalon or Myskyl?"

"No. He did say your forces would have had a more difficult time fighting your way up the Aluse if the Bovarians had had better marshals. For that, he was most grateful. He also conceded the same was true of the Bovarian leaders the Northern Army faced as well."

"An interesting way of putting it," mused Quaeryt.

"He did mention how strange it was that the Bovarians didn't use cannon against you until you were close to Variana."

"It only seems strange. Cannon are heavy. They're hard to transport, and you've seen how bad the Bovarian roads are. Kharst doesn't have much of a fleet, either, so the Bovarians haven't that many cannoneers with experience. Kharst was saving those to defend Variana." Quaeryt yawned.

"You're tired."

"Not that tired."

"You . . ." Vaelora shook her head.

"A man who has a beautiful and loving wife likes to appreciate her."

"You've made that quite clear . . . dearest." But she did smile . . . warmly.

On Mardi morning Quaeryt rode south from Geusyn with Skarpa and the first battalion from Third Regiment. The two imager undercaptains who rode behind them and in front of the first squad of rankers were Voltyr and Threkhyl. Quaeryt had left the others in the town to practice imaging skills, but he wanted the two he planned to leave with Skarpa to see as much of the area as possible before he and the other imager undercaptains departed.

After seeing the dark circles under Vaelora's eyes that morning, he'd also insisted that she remain at the inn and rest. The fact that she hadn't protested showed how tired she was . . . and that worried Quaeryt. *And you shouldn't have kept her up so late.* He winced at that thought and concentrated on studying the road and the terrain.

The road south from the town hugged the eastern shore of the river, close enough that Quaeryt could see the narrow towpath used to pull the flatboat ferries back to Geusyn. For the first mille or so, he saw no ferries, but several hundred yards later, they did pass a smaller craft drawn up on a mud flat adjoining the towpath. Two men were working on what Quaeryt thought was the tiller post. Neither looked up.

After riding another mille Quaeryt could see gray stone walls ahead, stretching for a good mille from the water's edge to a rocky hill and partway up the hill. Across the river to the west, almost a mille away, there was a raised area, surrounded by reeds and swamp, on which perched an odd assortment of buildings and roofs. Below them was a harbor, but Quaeryt could only see two merchanters, both sloop-rigged, suggesting coastal traders . . . and no sign of either the *Montagne* or the *Solis.* Just ahead was a set of piers, most likely where ferries unloaded on the return trip from Ephra. A packed clay ramp led from the end of each empty pier up to the road.

"Battalion! Halt!" ordered Skarpa.

Quaeryt could see why. South of where they had halted the road turned into a narrow rutted track that looked not to have been traveled in years, although the lower growth flanking the track showed that at one time the road had been used more.

"Well . . . what do you think?" asked Skarpa, turning in the saddle toward Quaeryt.

"The walls ahead look to be some ten yards high, if not more, and solid. The Antiagons have fortifications back into the hills as far as I can see."

"None of this makes sense." Skarpa shook his head. "There's never been a border wall you couldn't march far enough to get around, except on an island. I can't believe that wall extends all the way to the Sud Swamp. That's some five hundred miles."

"The ground isn't that level, and it's heavily wooded, at least near here. Do you want to cut a road more than a mille through it?"

"Isn't that what imagers are for?" Skarpa grinned.

"Of course," replied Quaeryt, "but Bovaria's never had that many imagers."

"Still . . ." Skarpa gestured to the west. "Ephra's an island of solid land in the middle of a swamp. Why did the Bovarians build Ephra on the west side?"

"Where else could they have built it with access to the ocean that they wouldn't have to worry about Antiago?" asked Quaeryt.

"But they have to get back upstream, some as far north as Laaryn."

"Most of them don't get back that way. They load the goods on ships at Ephra and sell the flatboats for lumber. Then they take the ferry to the east side, where they buy some horses. There are more than a few stables in Geusyn. They ride back north with small high value goods . . . probably in groups for safety." Quaeryt gestured back upstream. "The piers down there are pretty solid, and the road toward Geusyn has been well traveled."

"Do you really want to image a bridge across the river to Ephra?" asked Skarpa.

"I'm not sure that we could. You'd need a lot of piers, and trying to image them into water would be hard. If the river bottom is all mud, they'd just sink and keep on sinking. Ephra might be on solid ground and so is Kephria, but the channel between is pretty deep, and more than a mille wide. Besides, even if we could image that massive a bridge, we'd have to take Kephria to get that close to Ephra."

"And I take it you don't want to start another war right now."

"I wouldn't want to think about that, not until matters with Khel are settled." *One way or the other.*

"You'd think about it . . . if it's necessary. So would Bhayar," said Skarpa.

"Any strong ruler considers everything," temporized Quaeryt.

"Don't see any sign of large ships over there, either."

"No. They might be holding offshore, though. I'll have to take a ferry later today and see if they already arrived and moved offshore. If I were captain of the *Montagne,* I wouldn't want to be anchored for long that close to Kephria. Then, they might not have arrived yet."

"I'd wager on that."

"So would I, but I still need to find out." Quaeryt gestured toward the walls ahead of them to the south. "Do you want to ride farther and get a better look at Aliaro's defenses?"

"We might as well, but we need to be careful. I can't believe that they don't have cannon. Catapults with Antiagon Fire, too. No sign of either, though." Skarpa raised his arm, then ordered, "Forward!"

Over the next quint, Quaeryt kept an eye out, looking for gouges in the ground, broken trees or limbs, or other signs of cannon having been fired, but even when Skarpa called a halt, what had been a road had become an overgrown wilderness, and Quaeryt had to strain to see such signs—and they were years old.

"No one's even tried to come through here," snorted Skarpa after they'd reined up a good three hundred yards short of the walls, where the underbrush effectively made the road impassable. "Not in years. Hard to believe."

"Kharst didn't want to deal with the walls. He attacked Aliaro the way the Bovarians prefer. He came down the river, probably in darkness, and used imagers to set fire to the port. That way, all he lost was the force that set the fire." *And got rid of the imagers as well, no doubt.*

"Be a struggle to bring cannon down here, too," said Skarpa.

"If you have to deal with Aliaro, it might just be easier to have Threkhyl punch a big gap in the walls here."

"It might at that. Don't know as it will come to that, though. Those walls would show that Aliaro just wants to be left alone."

"So long as he can control the Gulf and the ports here," replied Quaeryt. "I can see why Kharst wanted Ferravyl, though. And Khel."

"His factors and traders couldn't cart goods from Bovaria across the hills and the western coastal mountains to ship from places like Eshtora and Ouestan."

"He could have cared less about that. He just wanted the tariff golds from the merchants shipping from those ports, and if he gained control of the Aluse all the way to Solis, then that would have made things easier for most of the merchants, traders, and High Holders in Bovaria."

"You know . . . when you talk like that, I'm glad I'm just a soldier."

"I'm glad you are, too, especially when I think about Deucalon and Myskyl. I hope Myskyl has a long hard winter in the north of Bovaria."

"He'll find a way not to get that far before the snows hit."

"You're probably right about that. Let's hope it's a ways from Variana, though."

Skarpa looked back at the Antiagon walls. "Don't even see anyone up there. There's probably some poor ranker posted there who's filled his britches seeing a battalion down here on the road. First one in years, I'd wager." He shook his head. "Might as well head back."

Quaeryt nodded, even as his eyes scanned the massive walls that stretched eastward to the rocky hill a good mille away, then turned his mount and accompanied Skarpa as the battalion reversed its order and began the ride back to Geusyn. He kept looking out at the river, and finally caught sight of a ferry angling its way toward Ephra, but that was the only craft he saw.

For a time, neither officer spoke.

"Have to say that, at times, I had my doubts about Chayar and then young Bhayar," mused Skarpa.

Quaeryt didn't mention that he'd had a few as well. "And now?"

"The more I see of other places in Lydar . . . well, let's just say I'm glad to be serving under him."

Quaeryt understood that, although he'd known it for years. He just hoped the Khellans would . . . and that he could convince them of that. *If you can ever get there.*

The road back to Geusyn was without riders until they were within a half mille of the dwellings on the south side of the town.

Vaelora was standing on the front porch of the River Inn when Quaeryt returned just after ninth glass. Even before he stepped up onto the porch he could see that the circles under her eyes were not so dark as they had been.

"You're looking better. The rest helped."

"What did you find out?"

"That things are worse than we thought . . ." He went on to explain, ending by, "That's why I need to take the next ferry to Ephra."

"I'll come with you."

"Ephra isn't a healthy place. Everyone I've talked to says so. It's dirty and filled with sicknesses, and I intend to stay only long enough to find out what I need to know."

"You're going. Why shouldn't I?"

"Because you'll be safer here."

"I'll be safe with you."

"I can't protect you from sickness and flux. You know that."

"You're making me sound unreasonable! I'm not. I can ride as well as you can, and there's no reason—"

"Vaelora . . . did you look in the mirror this morning? You have to be careful for two people, not just yourself . . . and your brother told me to remind you of that."

Vaelora made a face. "You'd better not say that too often."

"I hope I don't have to. I don't mind saying that I don't want to go, and I don't want to stay any longer than I have to."

"You'd better not."

"I won't." Quaeryt held back a sigh of relief.

In the end, when he boarded the ferry at two quints past noon, Quaeryt took just one squad from first company, as well as Khalis and Horan. The ferryman only grunted when Quaeryt paid the copper a head fee, perhaps because Quaeryt's squad comprised the only passengers. The ferry was a modified flatboat, if deeper of draft and roughly seven yards wide and fifteen long, guided by a large sweep rudder. Quaeryt saw two lockers aft of the square prow, long enough to contain either oars or poles, but neither compartment looked to have been opened recently.

Once they were well away from the pier at Geusyn, Quaeryt noted that the ferry immediately headed toward the far shore. When the craft's heading was established he eased over to the man at the tiller. "How many passengers can you take at once?"

"Maybe three score."

"How many ferries are there this size?"

"We run two at a time when we need to. The factor has four."

To transport just first company and one regiment meant eight trips with all four ferries, assuming the factor who owned them could be persuaded to use all—and that could take days.

The tillerman glanced at Quaeryt's gold crescent moon collar insignia. "You a Telaryn marshal or something?"

"Commander."

"You thinking of transporting some of your men to Ephra to board a ship?"

"That's possible. I won't know until I check with the portmaster in Ephra." Quaeryt laughed. "Is there one?"

"Old Haasyn was, last time I heard. Mostly just posts what ships are tied up or moored to the south, out of range of the Antiagon long guns."

"Can they reach the harbor?"

"Not quite. Any ship that gets within a half mille, though, and it's another story."

Quaeryt nodded. "At what glass will you be returning to Geusyn tonight?"

"Around midnight when the tide's flooding. You be heading back then?"

"That's what I plan, but it depends on what I find out in Ephra."

The tillerman nodded. "Like that with a lot of folks."

As the ferry neared the northern end of the harbor, more like a semicircular indentation in the swamp, Quaeryt could see a number of ships farther to the southwest, two of which looked large enough to be warships, possibly the *Montagne* and the *Solis.*

Even before the ferry reached the mossy timber piers, the mixed odors of dead fish, swamp, greasy burned cooking oil, and others even less definable oozed over him, creating the impression that the ostler's description of Ephra might be generous. *More than generous,* he decided, as a cloud of green mosquitoes appeared from nowhere.

"These piers aren't where the merchanters tied up, are they?" Quaeryt asked the tillerman.

"Nope. Those are on the south side, far as possible from Kephria. Deeper water there, too."

Two men hurried toward the bow, where they pulled long poles from the lockers and used them to guide the ferry toward the nearer pier. The poles told Quaeryt just how shallow the water was. One of the men laid down his pole and leapt across a yard or so of water to the pier, holding a coil of line attached to a cleat on the ferry. Once on the pier, he ran the line around a bollard, then braced his feet, letting the bollard take the weight of the ferry and bring it to a halt, before removing one turn of line from the bollard and slowly bringing the ferry to rest in the slip.

"Here you are, Commander," announced the tillerman.

"Thank you. Which way to the deepwater piers?"

"See the lane one in—not the one by the seawall—but the one by the public house there? Follow that as far as it goes, and you'll end up on the south harbor square."

With all twenty rankers, the squad leader, Quaeryt, and the two undercaptains on the pier, Quaeryt felt as though the timbers moved with every step any of them took, and he was more than happy to set foot on the lane heading south. The weathered public house, with its sagging salt-grayed shutters and crooked windows overlooking the ferry slips and piers, made the meanest taproom in Solis look like a High Holder's salon by comparison.

"This is a port?" murmured Horan from behind Quaeryt.

"What passes for one in old Bovaria," replied Khalis.

"How did they ever . . ."

Whatever Horan might have said was lost as they walked past a pleasure house with open windows . . . behind each of which stood a woman barely clad, or wearing a shift of fabric so fine that she might have been wearing nothing at all. Quaeryt smiled wryly. Even had he not met Vaelora, he wouldn't have been tempted. As a young seaman, he'd seen and heard too much.

After Quaeryt walked another block, slightly uphill, the lane flattened out, and several blocks ahead, down beyond the gently sloping lane, he could see grayish water, and a pair of masts above the low roofs of the harbor area. The shops were slightly less weathered and somewhat less rundown in the blocks closer to the harbor, but the lines of warehouses bordering the harbor made it clear that Ephra was a port of necessity, and little more.

Quaeryt walked up to the timbered building at the shore end of the second pier, a structure no more than four yards on a side, with a single door, open and tied back to the wall, with a frayed rope around a cleat that looked ready to pull out from the graying wood. He stepped inside and saw a burly man sitting on a high-backed stool looking out through an unglassed window at the harbor and the Gulf waters to the south.

The man turned his head, but did not speak.

"I'm looking for Haasyn, the portmaster."

"You've found him." The gray-bearded burly man studied Quaeryt. "You must be the commander the captain of that Telaryn ship's been looking for."

"Most likely. How long has he been here?"

"Three days . . . maybe four. Sends in a pinnace every afternoon, around third glass. They wait for a glass, maybe two, till the last ferry from Geusyn comes in."

*Almost another glass before the captain sends in the pinnace . . . and that's if he's prompt.* "Where do they tie up the pinnace?"

"End of third pier." Haasyn pointed.

"Thank you." Quaeryt stepped out of the building, then looked at the squad. "The *Montagne* is anchored out to the south. They've been sending a pinnace in late afternoon. While we're waiting, we might as well walk around and see what we can see."

Unfortunately, there was little to see, except more of what they had already seen, and Quaeryt and his group ended up well before third glass standing near the end of third pier.

"Never seen so much of nothing," said Horan.

"You haven't seen that many small towns, then," replied Khalis. "This is a small town that's a port."

"It wouldn't even exist except that Kharst didn't want to let his traders pay tariffs to Aliaro or Bhayar," added Quaeryt.

"Why didn't the traders just pay them anyway, sir?" asked Khalis.

"I wondered that myself . . . until what happened in Laaryn. It's pretty clear that any factor or High Holder who went against the rex just ended up dead. Since he gave them pretty free rein in other matters"—*including various depravities*—"they tended not to go against his will. I'm sure many smuggled things and went around his 'requests,' but since any word of defying him had rather harsh consequences, that kept the defiance down. I'm only guessing at that, but it fits what I've seen."

Quaeryt stopped talking as he saw a pinnace under sail angling past the southwest breakwater, running largely before the wind. Absently, he wondered if another reason for the afternoon run from the *Montagne* was because the winds tended to be more favorable. "It looks like that might be the pinnace from the *Montagne*."

Little more than a quint later, the pinnace eased up to the pier, and two Telaryn seamen immediately secured the small craft to the pier, while an ensign who looked to be a few years younger than Quaeryt stepped out.

"Ensign Paolyn, sir. You're Commander Quaeryt, sir?"

"I am."

"Captain Nykaal's been hoping you'd show up before long, sir."

"We got here as quickly as we could. Most of the forces are still in Geusyn."

The ensign nodded. "The captain said that was likely."

Quaeryt looked at the pinnace, some seven yards long, with a single mast, although he also saw three sets of long oars as well. "Can you take the entire squad?"

"Yes, sir. In this weather. If the swells were higher, I'd want two trips, but the water's calm, and looks to remain that way."

Quaeryt could see that Horan and several of the rankers were looking dubiously at the small craft.

For all that, in short order, everyone boarded, and Paolyn had the pinnace headed back southward in less than half a quint. The trip out to the *Montagne* took longer, Quaeryt suspected, because Paolyn headed eastward to pick up the river current, and they had to tack back and forth before they neared the warship, one of the bigger vessels Quaeryt had seen, for all his past merchant experience. *Close to sixty yards stem to stern, if a bit less at the keel.*

Paolyn eased the pinnace up to a boarding platform that had been lowered. "If you would, Commander."

"Thank you." Quaeryt stepped onto the platform, then asked, "Permission to come aboard?" as he headed up the ladder to the quarterdeck.

"Welcome to the *Montagne*," said the short officer in the uniform of a ship's captain, although he also wore the gold crescents, signifying that, technically, they were of equal rank.

"Thank you, Captain. Quaeryt Rytersyn, commander and envoy to Khel."

"Nykaal Kaalsyn, commanding. I doubted you could be anyone else."

Quaeryt wondered why, but didn't ask, and the two waited as the other two undercaptains came aboard, followed by the rankers. Two of the rankers looked slightly green, and Quaeryt wondered how they might do on the much longer and likely much rougher voyage to Kherseilles.

"Ensign Paolyn will see to your officers and men, Commander. If you would join me in my stateroom?"

"I'd be pleased to."

Quaeryt followed the captain aft across the main deck and up the ladder to the top deck of the sterncastle. The quarters comprised a cabin roughly four yards by three with a wide bunk against the aft bulkhead and a circular table, firmly affixed to the deck, farther forward.

A steward stood waiting.

"Lager or wine, Commander," asked Nykaal.

"Lager, please."

"Make that two, Vessyn."

The steward nodded and moved to a built-in cabinet.

Nykaal gestured to the table.

They both seated themselves, and the steward set a crystal beaker holding an amber lager in front of each of them and then left the stateroom.

"I understand that we'll also be carrying Lady Vaelora, and that she's accorded the status of an envoy as well."

*That bastard Bhayar! He decided that even before you recovered and never said a word.* "Not quite. She is an envoy in duties and capabilities. Bhayar decided that was necessary because of the composition of the new High Council of Khel."

Nykaal frowned.

"They're all Pharsi. Pharsi women often govern, and since they lost so many men, the Council is likely predominantly women."

"Oh! And with Lord Bhayar's ancestry, the selection of the two of you . . . I see."

Quaeryt wasn't certain Nykaal saw completely, but he wasn't about to alienate the captain by explaining because that would likely be taken as condescending. "Lord Bhayar would prefer to obtain agreement without fighting another war."

"I can understand that." Nykaal smiled. "Since you are both envoys and married, you will have my quarters for the voyage. No . . . don't protest. I still have my sea cabin near the helm and for a week or so, that's more than adequate. Besides, I'd certainly not be the captain who did not give up his quarters to the sister of Lord Bhayar and to the commander who destroyed the Bovarian armies twice."

*Does everyone know that?* More than likely, Quaeryt reflected, if Nykaal had learned that in port in Solis. "I can't say that my wife won't appreciate that."

"There is one difficulty. Lord Bhayar . . . ah . . . his dispatch mentioned two regiments."

"That might be a problem, I take it?"

"If you were thinking of transporting them all at once. The *Montagne* and the *Solis* can each carry about four hundred of your troopers for the week or so it will take to reach Kherseilles. The merchanters . . . there are only four of them, and, well, they'll average two hundred, maybe a bit more."

"So I can take one regiment and my command company in one voyage and then wait three weeks and perhaps longer, given that it's almost winter, if I want the second regiment?"

"That's about it," agreed Nykaal. "Lord Bhayar requested ten merchanters if possible, and a minimum of four. We were lucky to impress four, and none of them are happy about it, even for the golds Lord Bhayar promised."

"With winter coming on, we'll have to chance it with one regiment and the command company. It's going to take several days just to get the men to Ephra, I fear, even one regiment."

Nykaal nodded. "We can't help much there, but we've got two pinnaces, and we can get them from the south pier to the ship fairly quickly."

"Did the dispatch you received say anything about arrangements for mounts in Kherseilles?" Quaeryt asked.

"No. It just said that those arrangements would be taken care of by others."

*Which others?* Quaeryt didn't ask, since it was clear Nykaal didn't know.

In less than a quint, Quaeryt and the captain had worked out a tentative schedule for boarding and for the voyage to Kherseilles.

At that moment, Nykaal cleared his throat. "If I might ask . . . how do you plan to return to Geusyn?"

"I'd thought to take the ferry . . ."

"Nonsense. We've got a good south wind, and Paolyn can take the pinnace on the tide just before it turns, and then come back. Be a good exercise for him as well."

"If you're certain . . ."

"No one should have to spend any more time in Ephra than absolutely necessary."

"You've seen it?"

"I landed when we got here on Vendrei. Once was enough. That was true for the crew as well." Nykaal laughed. "You can eat with me, and your officers with the mess, your rankers with the crew, and then we'll send you off."

"I appreciate that." Quaeryt truly did. *The less time we spend in Ephra, the better.* Nykaal seemed a good sort, and the ship's fare was bound to be better than anything in Ephra.

Quaeryt took another swallow of the lager.

# 25

Quaeryt returned to Geusyn so late on Mardi evening that he had to rise early on Meredi morning to meet with Skarpa. Even so, Skarpa was waiting when Quaeryt joined him in the inn's public room.

"You must have come in late last night," observed the submarshal as Quaeryt slid into the chair across from him.

"More like early this morning." Quaeryt gestured to the server. "Tea, please."

"What did you find out?"

"The ships are here. They're anchored southwest of Ephra. Captain Nykaal has four merchanters in addition to the *Montagne* and *Solis*. That means they can only transport first company and one regiment—unless they make two trips, and that will take another month . . ." Quaeryt went on to explain.

When he had finished, Skarpa fingered his chin. "You wouldn't have to take the ships at all. You could ride along the coast to Kherseilles."

"At this time of year?" Quaeryt shook his head. "In good weather that would take three weeks, if not longer. Now . . . who knows?" He paused to take a swallow of the mug of tea the server had set on the small square table. "Besides, if the Khellans aren't in a fighting mood, I won't need a second regiment. If they are, I can't conquer the entire land with two. Besides, I'll be fortunate if Bhayar's 'arrangements' result in enough mounts for one regiment, let alone two."

"You'll take Khaern and Eleventh Regiment, then?"

"Unless you have an objection. I also thought I'd leave Voltyr and Threkhyl with you. They might prove helpful."

"They might indeed." Skarpa paused. "You know that nothing at all might happen here?"

"Aliaro may do nothing, but if he does, you'll need imagers. I also have the feeling you may need to act against some of the local High Holders. Imagers can prove useful in making a point without losing troopers."

"Do you think they'll try anything with this many troopers here? I have my doubts."

"I'd suggest you visit each of them and see what you think."

"You do that better than I do."

"I won't be here . . . and what do your orders say?"

Skarpa snorted. "You know as well as I do. Don't remind me. Doesn't mean I have to like being polite while leaning on those condescending snots."

"Don't worry about leaning hard. They won't think you mean it unless you do, not after dealing with Kharst."

"What a frigged-up land." Skarpa shook his head.

Quaeryt wasn't about to disagree. "We'll just have to set it right." *If we can.*

"What are your plans?" asked Skarpa.

"We'll start transferring troopers to Ephra as soon as we can today. It's likely to take several days, if not longer, even using the pinnaces from both the *Montagne* and the *Solis*."

"You honestly think you can get mounts in Kherseilles?"

"One way or another. I just hope it's not the hard way."

"Good fortune on that."

When he and Skarpa had finished, Quaeryt arranged for some breakfast to be sent up to Vaelora, gulped down some egg toast and ham rashers, then waited for Alazyn and Khaern to join him in the smallest of the plaques rooms.

Both entered together, and Quaeryt gestured to the chairs on the other side of the circular table. Once they were seated, he began. "Subcommanders . . . you may have heard that the *Montagne* and the *Solis* are anchored south of Ephra. I met with the lead captain yesterday."

The red-haired Khaern nodded.

"Yes, sir," replied Alazyn.

"We've run into some difficulties. There are only six ships, rather than the twelve that we had planned for . . ." Quaeryt quickly explained, then went on. "That means I can only take one regiment in addition to first company. The other regiment will remain with Southern Army."

"You're leaving Nineteenth Regiment with Commander Skarpa, sir?" asked Alazyn.

"I'd thought so. Unless either of you has a reason why it would be better otherwise?"

"No, sir," replied the stocky Alazyn. "That makes more sense. You've worked more with Eleventh Regiment. But this will only be for as long as you're in Khel?"

"That's my intent. Lord Bhayar can always change assignments, but I doubt that he'd see any reason for that."

"When will we be embarking?" asked Khaern.

"As soon as we can . . . after I talk with the imager undercaptains."

Once Quaeryt had dismissed the subcommanders, he then sent for Voltyr and the imager undercaptains, but met with Voltyr first.

Quaeryt gestured for the undercaptain to take a seat across the circular table. "You know why I requested that we meet, don't you?"

"I suspect so, sir. You intend to detach me to serve with the submarshal, do you not?"

"You and Undercaptain Threkhyl. The submarshal may need two strong imagers, and you're the only one able to keep Threkhyl in line."

"You think so, sir?"

"Your shields are stronger than his, and he knows that."

"He also knows you'd destroy him if he misbehaves." Voltyr's voice was dry.

"I'll talk to him next, and then everyone together." Quaeryt paused. "There is one other thing, and it's what I told Desyrk. If you happen to run across any young imagers, make them apprentices or trainees, and make sure they're paid. Before everything is all over, not that it's ever all over, we'll need as many imagers as we can gather."

"Yes, sir." After a moment Voltyr asked, "How long do you think you'll be in Khel?"

"I'd like to say a few weeks, but it could be all winter, the way things are going."

"Is there anything I need to look out for?"

"Nothing that we haven't talked over already. I would like to emphasize that you're to be very polite to any High Holder, and you're not to trust any of them."

"You don't think much of them, do you, sir?"

"Any of them who survived need to be watched closely. I've gotten the feeling that the most trustworthy ones seldom survived Rex Kharst."

They talked for another quint before Voltyr left.

The plaques-room door had barely closed before it opened once more and Threkhyl stepped inside.

"Take a seat, Undercaptain."

"Yes, sir." Threkhyl nodded and seated himself.

"I'm certain you know what I'm about to say. You and Undercaptain Voltyr are being assigned to the submarshal while Eleventh Regiment and first company are dealing with the Khellan High Council. The reason why I chose you and Voltyr is because you two are the best imagers, and the submarshal will need both your skills. Voltyr is in charge, because he knows how to deal with the submarshal and others."

Surprisingly, to Quaeryt, Threkhyl only said, "Makes sense, sir."

"I'd also like to remind you that you are valuable to me, and to the submarshal. For that reason, when you are called to image something, please think how you can get the greatest effect with the least strain. This will be important because you and Voltyr will only have each other."

"Yes, sir."

Once Quaeryt had finished with Threkhyl, he summoned the other five undercaptains into the plaques room. This time he stood and left them standing as he surveyed them.

After several moments of silence, he said, "Some of you know what I'm about to say, but not all of you, and there are matters that will affect you all that we need to go over. First is the matter of who is going to Khel . . . and why. Because Lord Bhayar could not obtain enough ships, only a single regiment will be accompanying us . . ." He went on to explain his decision and the arrangements he had made. "Do any of you have questions?"

"How far will we have to travel once we reach Kherseilles, sir?"

"We may have to travel all the way to Khelgror, where their High Council meets."

"Have you had any word from Subcommander Calkoran?"

"Not since we left Variana . . ."

"What about mounts, sir?"

After almost a quint, Quaeryt dismissed the undercaptains. Then he made his way to the stairs. He needed to see how Vaelora was coming along, as well as to pack his own gear.

All in all, the transfer of the troopers and their equipment, including riding gear, took more than three days. Quaeryt had arranged for first company to begin the transfer, sending Vaelora with the second set of ferry trips so that there would be troopers already waiting for her, while he moved back and forth, along with Zhelan, to try to keep the transportation moving smoothly. While the factor owning the ferries hadn't been especially enthusiastic about using all four at once, Quaeryt managed to persuade him, if with a touch of authoritative image-projection.

The breeze off the shore was light as the *Montagne* weighed anchor and spread sail at eighth glass on Samedi night, just two glasses before the first day of winter. Quaeryt and Vaelora wore their riding jackets and stood on the upper deck of the sterncastle of the *Montagne,* looking northward at Ephra, and then to the northeast at the somewhat brighter lights of Kephria.

"It's getting chill," she said.

"We've been fortunate with the weather so far, only a few rainstorms and a touch of snow flurries in the north."

"That likely won't last."

"I'd be surprised if it did. With the clear skies ahead to the southwest, we'll likely have at least a day without storms on the voyage. After that, who knows? How are you feeling?"

"Like all my clothes are shrinking."

"They're not."

"I know that, but it's the way I feel. Pretty soon, I'll have to start wearing the other garments, and I'll look like I'm wearing a canvas sail."

"You'll never look like that."

"I feel that way."

Because Quaeryt had no answer for that, he did not respond immediately.

Vaelora grasped Quaeryt's arm as the *Montagne* pitched forward slightly. "It will get rougher than this, won't it?"

"More than likely, dear."

"I hope I don't get sick from it. I was sick enough for the first two months."

Quaeryt turned as he heard steps on the deck, watching as Nykaal joined them.

"Beautiful evening, isn't it?" asked the captain.

"It is," replied Quaeryt. "Your men got everything stowed quickly."

"That had something to do with the way the gear was organized. You know something of ships, don't you, Commander?"

"A bit. I was a seaman and then quartermaster apprentice on a merchanter for several years before I became a scholar."

"And yet you're a commander now, not to mention an imager."

Quaeryt wondered how Nykaal had learned that. *Possibly from Bhayar's dispatch . . . or from his officers or crew listening and asking company officers or men.* It really wasn't a secret, although that was something Quaeryt still wasn't totally used to, not yet. "I was pushed into leading troops in the Tilboran uprising, under Submarshal Skarpa. One thing led to another."

"How did you become captain of the *Montagne?*" Vaelora looked to the ship's captain.

Nykaal laughed, quietly. "You're most protective, Lady."

"Only because my husband has been most protective of me and of my brother and his interests."

"I would doubt that is solely the reason for your protectiveness, but I admire and commend you for it."

"It's far from simple, Captain," said Quaeryt. "After we ended the uprising, I was acting princeps of Tilbor before Bhayar confirmed me in the post. I was ordered to become temporary governor of Montagne after the eruption there, and was then ordered to form imagers into a fighting force against the Bovarians. I was successful—"

"Exceedingly successful, according to Lord Bhayar. But no one ever suspected . . . your talents?"

"Lord Bhayar and I have known each other since we were students of the same tutor. He suspected I was more than a scholar, but Lady Vaelora was the one who discovered the usefulness of my abilities. Lord Bhayar punished us both for that by insisting that we wed."

"Such punishment!" Nykaal laughed, but the laugh faded. "How effective are your imaging abilities at sea?"

"I have no idea. Why do you ask?"

"I hope they will not be necessary, but the Antiagons do have fast vessels with their Fire, and a good captain always seeks all possible defenses."

"It's likely we can mitigate such an attack. If you need imaging, let me know, and we will see what we can do."

"I do appreciate that, Commander, Lady, and I will bid you good evening." Nykaal inclined his head, then turned and walked back toward the wheel and the steersman.

"He's worried," said Vaelora.

"Wouldn't you be? He's carrying Bhayar's sister, and he has two warships, the only ones your brother possesses, and four merchanters, and Aliaro has a fleet of warships. In his boots, I'd be worried, too."

Vaelora shivered, possibly not from the cold.

"Are you ready for bed?"

"I am. I get tired more easily."

"I haven't noticed that."

"You have. You were insisting I needed more rest just days ago."

"I haven't noticed that in the past few days."

She smiled. "You haven't been here much . . . and I did get some rest. The bed in the stateroom is more comfortable than those in the inns."

"It should be." Quaeryt took her arm.

As they headed for the ladder leading down to the hatch that afforded access to the captain's stateroom, Quaeryt gazed briefly off to the starboard, and the dark line of the shore that marked the southern edge of the Gulf of Khellor.

*Can you fit everything together? So that it will last?*

Vaelora squeezed his hand before she released it to start down the ladder.

On Solayi morning Captain Nykaal had insisted on having Quaeryt and Vaelora served breakfast in his stateroom, and Vaelora had insisted that Nykaal join them. In turn, Quaeryt had added his invitation, not only out of courtesy and thankfulness, but also because he sensed a certain tenseness about the compact captain. The steward served tea to everyone, and set platters with egg toast, biscuits, and ham slices before the three, then slipped out of the stateroom.

Quaeryt sipped the tea, then said, "The weather's holding so far."

"The test of that will be when we round Cape Morain and set a northwest course." Nykaal took another swallow of tea from his porcelain mug before continuing. "We may have another more pressing problem."

"Antiagon warships?" asked Quaeryt.

"There are sails to the southeast, and they're closing. Five vessels. The *Montagne* and the *Solis* could put on more sail and likely outrun them, but the merchanters can't . . ."

Quaeryt nodded politely, but privately doubted that the two warships could outrun Antiagon warships designed for speed.

"If they're Antiagon, and with five ships they're not likely to be anything else, they'll insist that the merchanters pay passage tariffs. That's just an excuse to board and pillage."

"Aliaro's still insisting that the Gulf waters belong to Antiago?" asked Quaeryt.

"When it suits his purpose," replied Nykaal dryly. "Or that of his captains. They're more like pirates at times."

"How long before we're in range of their cannon?"

Nykaal shrugged. "If the winds hold, midafternoon. They must have set sail within a glass of when we lifted anchor. The tides would have been against them for the first few glasses." He took another swallow of tea. "Can you and your imagers do something about them?"

"How close can you get without endangering the ship?"

"There's always danger, but their cannon are limited to about six hundred yards, and they're not very accurate above four hundred."

"I heard that some of the cannon from Kephria could almost reach ships anchored at Ephra."

"They've got one or two huge long-barreled things at Kephria that might reach half a mille on a good day with the wind behind them. They've occasionally hit or come close to careless captains. But on board a ship . . ." Nykaal smiled ironically. "Anything with that range would be too heavy or too small to fire a ball heavy enough to break a ship's timbers."

"They don't have Antiagon Fire shells?"

"They say some of their ships do. There's a merchant fleet out of Estisle or Nacliano that has cannon like that. Wouldn't carry those for the world. Too easy to set the entire ship ablaze."

Quaeryt nodded once again. He saw no sense in mentioning what the Diamond ships could do, especially after seeing how careful the captains had to be.

After Nykaal had finished breakfast and excused himself, Vaelora looked to Quaeryt. "You didn't agree with some of what he said, did you?"

"I don't think a vessel this big with this broad a beam could outrun an Antiagon warship. They're designed almost as pirates and raiders."

"So Nykaal either doesn't know or is misrepresenting what his ship can do?"

"One or the other."

"Then we must be even more careful." She paused before going on. "Dearest . . . whatever you do . . . do what is necessary with the smallest effort possible on your part. Use the other imagers as much as you can."

"Yes, dear."

"Quaeryt Rytersyn, husband dearest . . . do not condescend to me, and do not patronize me!" Vaelora's eyes flashed.

Quaeryt winced. "I'm sorry."

"You should be. I rode across most of Lydar for you."

"I am truly sorry," he replied. "I was thinking about how it never ends."

"Dearest . . ."

He laughed ruefully. "You're right. I was condescending, and I shouldn't have been."

"No . . . you shouldn't." She smiled. "But since you admit it, I'll forgive you. This time."

Quaeryt managed not to wince again.

Somewhat later, he met with Zhelan and then went through the troopers' quarters, undertaking an informal inspection.

When he returned to the upper deck of the sterncastle, he could see that the sky remained clear, especially to the northwest, and that the wind had shifted slightly, coming from more to the south. The Antiagon ships were closer, but still several milles astern.

Nykaal crossed the deck. "The wind shift will favor them a bit more than the merchanters. We'll need to drop back slightly before long. What they'll do is send two or three of their ships to engage us and the *Solis,* while the other ships pick off the merchanters."

"So we need to stop the ones readying to attack the *Montagne* as quickly as possible?"

"Anything you can do would be most useful," said Nykaal dryly.

"If you can get us as close as possible, but just out of cannon range, we may be able to take care of several of them. We'll have to see, but I have several things in mind."

Over the next several glasses, as the *Montagne* reefed sail enough to slowly drop to the rear of the Telaryn formation, Quaeryt kept track of their pursuers. In between that, he checked with Vaelora, who alternated resting and reading *Rholan and the Nameless.* He refrained from asking her what she thought, fearing such a question might be thought patronizing.

Before he knew it, or so it seemed, the ship's bells were striking third glass, and Quaeryt and the four imager undercaptains stood on the port side of the upper deck of the sterncastle. He could hear the commands and the movement of sailors and gunners on the lower decks, as well as see the men stationed by the lighter guns on the main deck.

The lead Antiagon vessel was perhaps eight hundred yards away, two hundred south and six hundred off the port quarter of the *Montagne.* The ensign flying from a jackstaff was large and clear—a jagged lightning bolt of green and yellow crossed with a stylized halberd, all against a bright maroon background.

The second Antiagon ship was less than a hundred yards astern of the first, with a third behind, and two others moving northward, as if trying to close on the *Solis* and the four merchanters ahead of and to the north of the *Montagne.*

Nykaal crossed the deck to Quaeryt. "They're getting close enough to range us with their bow gun."

"We'll see what we can do." Recalling Vaelora's advice, Quaeryt again studied the Antiagon ship, clearly narrower in the beam than the *Montagne,* with a lower fo'c'sle and gun ports not that much above the waterline. He thought about imaging out a chunk of the lead vessel's keel, then recalled Vaelora's advice.

"Imagers! Stand by."

Quaeryt concentrated on removing a section of the hull perhaps a yard square, just below the waterline immediately aft of the stem, then followed up by imaging out a chunk of the mainmast. A flash of light and pain seared across his eyes, then vanished. He watched as the mast swayed, then slowly toppled back, smashing through the sails and the yards of the mizzenmast. As it did, the upper section of the mizzenmast snapped as well.

The second Antiagon vessel turned in toward the *Montagne,* just enough to clear the faltering first vessel.

After another quint, the second ship was close to cannon range. Quaeryt turned. "Horan . . . image out a chunk of the mainmast on the nearest vessel. That's the second mast," he explained.

"Lhandor . . . can you put a large hole in the hull below the waterline just aft of the bow?"

"Yes, sir."

The young undercaptain swayed, then grabbed the railing, but straightened. "I think I did it, sir."

"Good."

Quaeryt looked to Khalis. "We'll wait a moment or so." His eyes went back to the first Antiagon ship, whose crew was trying to cut away the tangled mass sails and rigging, as well as the shattered and fallen masts. The bow was definitely lower in the water, and dropping, if not as much as Quaeryt would have liked.

After a moment, he imaged again, this time concentrating on creating a smaller hole, perhaps a half yard across, midships and below the waterline. He scarcely felt the effort. *Smaller holes are better.* Then he shifted his attention to the second ship, smiling when he saw similar damage there, as the second ship seemed almost to stop dead in the water.

Even so, the third ship began to close on the *Montagne,* continuing past the first two stricken vessels under full sail. Quaeryt considered the distance, almost a half mille, then concentrated, wincing, and watching as another mainmast toppled backward, snaring the mizzenmast. He didn't want to try holing the third ship at that distance. Still . . .

"Khalis . . . a hole in the third vessel there, below the waterline and as large as you can make without overstraining yourself."

"Yes, sir."

Quaeryt turned his attention to the two vessels that had been angling northward toward the *Solis,* but as he did, Nykaal issued an order to the steersman, and the *Montagne* eased onto a more starboard heading, as if to close the range to the two remaining Antiagon vessels. He wondered if the two remaining Antiagon ships would continue to pursue or whether they would break off the engagement and see to the three sinking ships.

After perhaps half a quint, both remaining pursuers reefed sails and turned, heading back toward the stricken vessels. Quaeryt watched for a time, but it was clear the two surviving ships were trying to aid the others.

"Imagers, take a break. Get some lager or ale and biscuits, but stand by . . . just in case."

As the *Montagne* swung back to the northwest to move up on the slower merchanters, Quaeryt crossed the deck to where Nykaal stood to the side of the steersman. "I think we've removed that threat . . . for now, anyway."

"How did you break their masts?"

Quaeryt smiled. "We just imaged out sections of the mast. We also put some holes in their hulls. I don't think the first ship will make it back to port. I don't know about the others."

"How big a hole?"

"One a yard square in the lead vessel, and a second one midships half that size."

"You can image away things?"

"Sometimes."

Nykaal shook his head. "With two masts gone . . . and that kind of holing . . . they won't be going anywhere."

*Except to the bottom of the Gulf.*

"They might try a night run, though."

"Not tonight," said Quaeryt. "They're not that much faster than the merchanters, and by the time they deal with the damaged ships . . ."

"They might be waiting for us to return."

"What are your orders?"

"We're to see what the situation is in Kherseilles. I'm to consult with you, then decide."

"That makes sense."

Vaelora appeared, holding his water bottle. "You need this."

"You shouldn't . . ." He decided against saying more.

"I didn't come up here until the steward told me the Antiagons had turned away."

"You told him that would happen, didn't you? And that he should tell you when it did?"

"Of course . . . dearest."

Quaeryt didn't know whether to laugh, groan, or shake his head.

Instead, he took a long swallow of lager from the water bottle.

By the fifth glass of Solayi afternoon, the sails of the Antiagon ships had vanished below the horizon to the southeast. From what Quaeryt had seen, two of the three ships that the imagers had attacked had sunk, but it appeared as though the Antiagons had managed to save the third. While he was relieved that the imaging had not resulted in many, if any deaths, he also worried that by not having destroyed all five vessels, the *Montagne* and *Solis* might face greater problems from the Antiagon fleet in the future. *No one talks about the price of mercy in warfare.* But then, technically, Bhayar and Aliaro weren't at war, at least not so far as Quaeryt knew, even if Antiagon troops had fought against Southern Army in Bovaria.

At sixth glass the steward appeared with dinner, and with Captain Nykaal.

Once dinner had been presented—mutton cutlets with a brown sauce, fried potato slices, and pickled cabbage, along with freshly baked bread—the steward departed.

Nykaal flourished a bottle of red wine. "From my private stock, with thanks for your success in dealing with the Antiagons." He filled each of the goblets halfway, then seated himself, then raised his goblet. "My thanks and appreciation, Commander."

"That wouldn't have been possible without your ship handling," demurred Quaeryt, lifting his goblet in return.

Vaelora nodded as she raised her goblet, although Quaeryt knew her nod likely meant that she appreciated the captain's skill because it had resulted in less strain on the imagers, on Quaeryt in particular.

"This is excellent wine," said Quaeryt after taking his first swallow. "Where did you come by it?"

"My cousin has a vineyard in the hills north of Cheva, and he occasionally gifts me with bottles . . . now and again."

"It's very good," added Vaelora.

"From you, Lady, that is high praise."

"Indeed it is," said Quaeryt. "She has excellent taste."

"The wine is doubtless better than the fare, but the cooks are decent and sometimes better than that."

After several bites, Quaeryt had to agree with Nykaal's assessment. *Decent and filling, but not much better.*

"I must admit that I don't fully understand why Lord Bhayar would . . . allow . . ." Nykaal did not finish his words.

"Why he would risk so many imagers in one command when there are so few of them?" suggested Quaeryt.

"Or why he would hazard his sister in marriage to an imager?" added Vaelora softly. "Or dispatch her as an envoy to a land that might become an enemy?"

"You must admit that those are questions many would ask." Nykaal sipped from the crystal brandy snifter engraved with the letter "M."

Quaeryt finished a mouthful of potatoes, then laughed softly. "No. They're questions many might wish to ask, but few would dare."

"I would judge that you have thought through such questions," said the captain blandly.

"More than a few times." Quaeryt glanced to Vaelora, who gave the barest of nods.

Nykaal smiled. "I think you have provided one answer already."

"That is possible," replied Quaeryt. "I will offer another. While imagers can have a great impact on a battle, Bhayar observed years ago that no imager, no matter how talented, who was sent out into combat without other imagers for support survived for any length of time." *Since no one ever sent more than one, none ever survived.* "He also observed that no single imager who has been involved in the daily affairs in the court of a ruler has managed to long survive."

"And?" pressed Nykaal gently.

"When I came close to dying several times in the Tilboran uprising, he decided it might be best to find other imagers to work with me. His willingness to try such a strategy has thus far been effective. Part of that also suggests another strength of Lord Bhayar. He is willing to try new strategies and take reasonable risks, but not exceedingly unreasonable ones."

"He has also followed the example of his sire as well," mused Nykaal, "in that he requires as much of himself and his family as of others."

"If not more," said Quaeryt.

"I doubt that he requires as much of himself as you do of yourself, Commander, not if a fraction of what I've heard about you has any truth to it at all."

"There are always exceptions, Captain," murmured Vaelora.

"You are both exceptions, but is that not why he trusts you with great responsibility?"

*That, and because Bhayar has few alternatives.* "I observed years ago that those who are unwilling to undertake tasks which involve danger should not be trusted with great responsibility. Nor should those who go out of their way to seek and surmount danger." Quaeryt smiled.

"One might suggest that you have sought danger, Commander."

Quaeryt shook his head. "I have not shied from danger, when necessary, but I have tried to accomplish what was necessary with the least risk possible. Avoiding risk for the sake of avoiding it may well create more risk in the long run, while accomplishing little."

"You could have destroyed those ships, I think."

"Even if we could have, to what end? The effort required might well have endangered one or more of the imagers. Would you have lost the *Montagne* to destroy all five of theirs?"

"Hardly. I would not willingly lose one of the two great warships Lord Bhayar has for five ships, not when Aliaro has a score or more."

"Exactly," replied Quaeryt.

"Yet you are accompanied by a full regiment, four imagers, and Lord Bhayar's sister on this mission to Khel at a time when Bovaria has not yet been fully subdued."

Quaeryt nodded. "It would have been better to have left earlier, but that was not possible. It is preferable to make offers before the positions of others rulers have been allowed to set."

"I may be less than optimistic, Commander, Lady, but the Pharsi have always struck a hard bargain. They know that Bhayar cannot send his armies into Khel with winter upon us."

"That's true. That is why he sent us."

Nykaal laughed softly, if somewhat uneasily. "You are suggesting . . . ?"

"I'm suggesting nothing. Bhayar would prefer a willing agreement to a forced conquest. If the Khellan High Council will not agree to terms, then, within a few years, there will be a forced conquest. That is why we are going to Khel."

"Your wine is indeed quite lovely," said Vaelora sweetly. "I cannot tell you how much I appreciate your kindness in sharing it with us. That kindness is particularly noteworthy when such a splendid vintage comes dear, and from a family vineyard."

Nykaal froze for just a moment, then blinked . . . and laughed heartily.

"You're most gentle, Lady Vaelora. For that I am thankful. It is a good vintage, and I'm more than happy to share it. The memories I will have of sharing meals with you will be far more dear than the wine." He lifted his goblet. "If you would tell me how Extela fared after the eruption . . ."

"Of course." Vaelora smiled warmly. "You must know that I spent much of my youth there, as did Bhayar and our sisters . . ."

More than a glass later, after cheerful conversation, Nykaal slipped away, and the steward reappeared briefly to remove platters and the remnants of the meal.

When they were alone, Quaeryt turned to Vaelora. "Do you think I was too indirect? Or the opposite?"

"I think you conveyed what he needed to understand without actually saying it."

"What? That at times five imagers represent more power than regiments, especially when there aren't enough ships to carry those regiments?"

"You made that point."

"You emphasized it with your sweet comments." Quaeryt grinned.

"People want to know what is happening. They also like to hear what they wish. That has not changed since the time of Rholan, and long before." She paused. "You are like Rholan, in some ways . . . if the book is correct."

"Oh? I'm like Rholan?"

"Let me see if I can find that section of the book." Vaelora hurried over to the built-in drawers on the right side of the captain's bunk, opening the narrow top one and extracting the small leatherbound volume.

Quaeryt waited while Vaelora paged through the book.

"Here . . . listen to this."

"Do I want to?"

"Dearest . . . listen . . ."

Quaeryt decided further comments and protests were futile. He nodded for her to begin.

Still standing, Vaelora cleared her throat, then put out a hand against the bulkhead to steady herself as the *Montagne* pitched, then rolled slightly. She began to read.

> "Rholan's insights often conflicted with not only the views of the powerful, but at times with folk sayings and what some have called common sense. One saying that incensed him was the Montagne fatalism that 'rivers run where they will,' or the observation that rivers run free. In a homily in the small mountain town of Yanaes, accord-

ing to reports from those who were there, he went so far as to call both sayings complete rubbish. He pointed out that water or rivers always seek the easiest path downhill, and that was why the waters often dropped great distances over falls. He went on to say that rivers were a poor example of guidance or freedom that, if anything, the Nameless provided their twisting courses as an example of how following the easiest path not only often did not take one where one wished, but usually took longer and put one through needless falls and trials. Needless to say, he was never asked back to Yanaes."

"You see?" Vaelora closed the book, but remained holding it.

"Well . . . it is true that no one wants to ask me back." He grinned.

"Dearest . . ."

"That's why we need to create a scholarium for imagers. That way, we'll always have some place where we can return when the invitations run out . . . which they will rather quickly once Bhayar establishes his reign and there's a lasting peace."

"Lasting peace?"

"Well . . . for a few hundred years, anyway."

Vaelora frowned.

"It's simple enough. Once he unifies Lydar, there won't be anyone to fight here, and no one's likely to create a fleet big enough to ferry an army large enough to attack . . ."

"You are an optimist."

"Why not? It's less depressing, and it might even come true."

"Have you told him that he's supposed to unify Lydar?"

"Of course not. That way, when it's done, he can tell himself that he never intended to conquer the entire continent. No one will believe him, but they never believe rulers in those matters anyway, and once it's done, no one will dare to complain."

"Enough of your grand dreams, dearest."

"Plans, not dreams."

"Don't plan too elaborately. Things never work out as planned."

"That's why I just keep the goal in mind. I can always change the plans."

She shook her head.

Quaeryt wasn't certain whether her expression was one of resignation, concern, or veiled amusement. *She's entitled to all three.*

While the weather cooled over the next few days, and the wind shifted until it blew largely out of the northeast, the Telaryn convoy saw few other ships, and no warships or raiders. Late on Vendrei morning, Vaelora and Quaeryt stood on the upper sterncastle deck, close by the starboard railing, where they could see in the distance to the north the rolling hills southeast of Kherseilles. The Gulf waters were rougher than they had been, and Vaelora kept one hand on the railing as they talked.

"There aren't many towns or ports along the coast here, are there?" asked Vaelora.

"There are more than a few fishing villages, but that's about it. The southern hills here are rugged. They don't get much rain, and there aren't many streams. From what I've heard, the lands to the north and west of Ephra don't grow much of anything."

"Didn't Kharst do something . . . you told me about the Pharsi . . ."

"Oh . . . according to Major Arion, years ago he drove the Pharsi traders out of Laaryn and marched them to the barrens north of Mantes. Most of them just kept going and crossed the Groral and settled in Khel. That was part of what started the first war against the Pharsi . . ."

"You told me. That was the one they won, and then Kharst sent all sorts of blankets and goods used by people who'd died of the Red Death." Vaelora shook her head. "Compared to what he did to others, he had an easy death."

*Easy? Freezing to death?*

"Dearest, you suffer more over what you did than Kharst ever felt from what you did to him. And that was the most he likely ever suffered."

From the corner of his eye, Quaeryt caught sight of Nykaal crossing the deck toward them. "Here comes the captain."

Vaelora turned and the two of them waited.

"It's been a pleasant voyage the last few days," offered Nykaal, with an easy smile. "Well . . . except for that squall the other afternoon, but it didn't last long. Didn't even break any sheets or rip any sails."

"How much longer to port?" asked Quaeryt.

"If the wind holds, a glass before sunset."

"I've not been in Kherseilles in more than ten years," began Quaeryt. "The port had ample piers then, but . . ."

"There are still ample piers. Not much else, I'd wager." Nykaal offered a crooked smile. "I doubt that we'll need to anchor offshore."

"Oh?"

"Kharst seized or burned all the local trading vessels. And the Bovarians . . . or Aliaro . . ."

"Likely more berths than even we'll need, then?"

"That's the word." With a nod, the captain headed back toward the helm.

After Nykaal returned to his position near the helmsman, Vaelora stepped closer to Quaeryt and said in a low voice, "I don't like it when you talk as if I'm not here. A few words of explanation wouldn't have cost you much."

"I'm sorry. I thought you knew. I didn't mean . . ." Once again, Quaeryt was reminded that while Vaelora was a very bright woman, her upbringing had left large gaps in her knowledge. *The problem is that you don't know where they are, and if you overexplain everything you come off as patronizing and make her look stupid.* "Because Kherseilles was a Khellan port, it's on the west side of the Groral River. It used to be as big a port as Eshtora and Ouestan, and all the trade in eastern Khel came down the river to Kherseilles. They even built some ships here from the timber that they floated down on the spring runoff. But when Kharst conquered Khel . . ." Quaeryt shrugged.

"All the traders were Pharsi, and they were killed and their ships burned or taken?"

Quaeryt nodded.

"And there weren't many people left to trade?"

"Between those who were killed and those who fled, I'd doubt it. That's another reason why I've been worrying about whether we can gather enough mounts for both first company and Eleventh Regiment." He shrugged. "I couldn't very well refuse to come on the grounds that your brother couldn't have made sufficient arrangements for mounts."

"He wouldn't have taken that well." She paused. "There isn't a Bovarian town on the east side of the river? One where . . . ?"

"There was. It was never a port. Suppose it's still there, but there's not much growing in the coastal hills between Kherseilles and Ephra."

"You just said that. I don't need repetition. Once is enough."

"Would you like some biscuits?"

"I can find them myself." Vaelora left Quaeryt standing there.

He knew better than to follow her immediately. He should have realized that she needed to eat. *She gets cross when she's hungry, far more than she used to.* He smiled wryly. Another aspect of her being with child that he hadn't known about until it happened.

Over the next three glasses, Quaeryt spent a great deal of time being pleasant and thoughtful, and making sure Vaelora had frequent biscuits, so that by fourth glass, she was again speaking warmly to him when they returned to the upper deck to watch as the *Montagne* neared the harbor under minimal sail.

The two long stone piers nearest the river were empty, except for a small fishing shack that was tied almost at the seawall at the base of the pier. Where the warehouses had stood along the stone boulevard behind the seawall and facing the harbor, all that remained were the blackened stone foundations, stretching for almost half a mille. The two smaller piers, the ones that had been timber, had burned down to blackened and weathered pilings. The third stone pier, farther west, was the only one that showed any activity, with a coastal schooner near the end on the east side, and a single-masted craft perhaps twice the size of the *Montagne*'s pinnace.

For all that he thought he was prepared to see what had happened to the harbor, Quaeryt could only look. *There's no way we'll have enough mounts . . . not with the destruction here.*

"Kharst did all that?" asked Vaelora.

"I don't know. It could have been Aliaro. Once the Khellans were defeated, he could have landed a few ships and fired the entire place. Or it could have been Kharst's men, or factors or officers acting for him. They both wouldn't want an open port here, and in a few years, the Pharsi survivors could have been back trading. They will be, anyway. It'll just take longer."

"They all hate the Khellans that much?"

"I doubt it. Just business. The Pharsi are better traders. So, when the Pharsi couldn't do anything, whoever it was fired the entire port. If they left the warehouses and all the piers, in months some trading would have resumed."

"Lines out!"

As seamen scurried about, sails reefed in, and as Nykaal issued the orders to ease the big vessel up to the stone pier, Quaeryt looked beyond the harbor. From what he could tell, most of the shops and dwellings farther from the water and the river looked to be largely intact, although he did see one or two that had been burned out. There were people on the streets . . . but only a fraction of the numbers he recalled from when he'd ported at Kherseilles so many years before.

*We're supposed to find mounts here?* He couldn't help but keep thinking about that.

By the time all six ships were secured along the stone piers at Kherseilles, the sun had dropped behind the hills to the west of the port. Although Quaeryt had sent out Zhelan with a squad to look into whether any factors or stables had mounts available . . . or if anyone knew about Bhayar's purported arrangements, the two stables nearest the harbor knew nothing about such an arrangement—as Quaeryt had feared.

By the time Zhelan had returned, Quaeryt had decided against searching out suppliers of horses—or whoever might have the mounts that Bhayar had purportedly arranged for—until Samedi morning. He only told Vaelora that Zhelan had been unable to locate the mounts and that further efforts would have to wait.

Samedi morning dawned cool and foggy enough that when Quaeryt peered out one of the stateroom portholes he could barely make out the ships at the next pier. "It's a good thing we made port last night. We'd still be out in the Gulf waiting for the fog to burn off."

"You didn't want to talk about the horses last night," ventured Vaelora as she pulled on riding trousers.

*Neither did you.* "There wasn't much to talk about. Zhelan couldn't find anyone who knew anything. We both worried about that from the time we left Variana. But Bhayar brushed off my questions . . . and you know how he can be."

"Yes, dear. I do know. I grew up with him."

"I don't think we'll have much fortune in finding mounts for Eleventh Regiment."

"What will you do?"

"What comes most unnaturally to me. Wait to see what happens while Zhelan looks into finding mounts. We might as well have breakfast." He walked to the hatch to the passageway, where he tugged at the bellpull.

"You didn't ask if I was ready."

"I'm sorry. You looked ready."

"You might have asked."

"I'm sorry. I'm worried."

Vaelora opened her mouth, then shut it. "I'm sorry, too. I didn't mean to be so sharp with you. I don't know what's come over me."

"Being with child, being hungry, being on a warship in a strange land trying to do things for your brother and your husband where more and more often matters are not proceeding as planned . . . those might have a little something to do with it. Just a little."

Vaelora offered a faint smile. "They might."

Moments later Nykaal arrived with the steward and breakfast. "Good thing we ported yesterday. The fog looks to be thickening. Sure sign of winter."

"You sound almost cheerful about it," said Quaeryt.

"No sense in complaining. The Nameless won't do anything about it, and the Namer doesn't care."

"Spoken like a true captain," replied Quaeryt, stepping back and letting the steward set platters and mugs around the circular table.

"Will it snow here, this far south?" asked Vaelora, waiting for the steward to set her platter down before seating herself.

"Probably not," replied Quaeryt. "We're about as far south as Solis, and we're on the water. Fog and cold drizzle are more likely."

"It's chill as it is." Vaelora cupped her hands around the mug.

Quaeryt hid a smile. The night before she'd been complaining about how hot she'd felt.

The way she looked at him suggested he hadn't hidden the smile that well.

"What are your plans, Commander?" asked Nykaal.

"We'll need to see how many mounts we can round up, and what we can learn about whether the High Council is presently gathered in Khelgror. I'm hopeful that we might get a report from Subcommander Calkoran."

Nykaal nodded. "I had one of the ensigns check with the portmaster this morning. There weren't any messages or dispatches."

After breakfast Quaeryt met quickly and in turn with Zhelan, Khaern, and then the imagers. He dispatched Zhelan to continue looking into the possibility of finding mounts, listened to Khaern's report on the regiment's readiness, and told the imagers to stand by. Then he stationed himself on the upper deck, where he could see at least the nearer part of the pier while the fog continued to burn off . . . and to wait. Vaelora joined him for a time, then repaired to the stateroom. Quaeryt couldn't blame her. The air was raw, and he wasn't good company.

Almost another glass passed before he heard the sound of hoofs on the stone of the pier. Then he saw a squad of riders in Telaryn uniforms. Through the drifting fog, he couldn't make out the officer at the head of the squad, although he had the feeling it might have been Arion. Even before the riders drew up on the pier opposite the gangway for the *Montagne*, Quaeryt was hurrying down the ladders to the quarterdeck.

As the officer walked up the gangway, Quaeryt recognized him. "Major Arion!"

"Subcommander . . ." Arion looked puzzled. "I did not see you . . . after the battle."

The Pharsi's accented Bovarian caught Quaeryt by surprise for just a moment, but he quickly replied in Bovarian, "It left me somewhat . . . whiter."

"More like the lost son of Erion." The major's eyes went to Quaeryt's collar insignia. "Excuse me, Commander."

Quaeryt decided not to protest anything associated with being a lost one. Not at the moment. "It happened after you left for Khel. If you'll come aboard, we can talk in the captain's stateroom. He's lent it to Lady Vaelora and me."

"Your lady is with you?"

"Lord Bhayar appointed us both as envoys to the High Council."

The dark-haired and black-eyed Arion smiled. "He was wise in that." The smile faded.

Quaeryt led the way to the upper sterncastle and the captain's cabin, then knocked before opening the hatch, a door really, but Quaeryt couldn't help but think of it as a hatch.

Vaelora rose from where she had been writing at the circular table.

"Dearest, might I present Major Arion?"

Arion bowed deeply. "I am most honored, Lady."

"It's good to meet you, Major." Vaelora smiled warmly. "My husband has spoken well and often of you and your abilities."

"He may have been generous, Lady."

"Kind, perhaps," she replied, "but he is honest in his assessments of others."

Quaeryt gestured to the table. "Please sit down."

Once the three were seated, Arion glanced from Quaeryt to Vaelora, then smiled. "Since you are both envoys, I should report . . . and then deliver a message."

"Please."

"We suffered no attacks on the ride west, but we did not ride far toward Khelgror. We had barely left Kherseilles when a messenger from the High Council reached Subcommander Calkoran. The Council requested that we ride to Saendeol to meet with them."

"Where is that?" asked Quaeryt.

"A week's ride north and west of here, in the warm hills. It was the old winter meeting place of the High Council, back in the times of my great-great-grandmere. Even then, they did not like to meet in the winter ice and snow of Khelgror."

"How long were you there?"

"More than two weeks before the subcommander dispatched us to await you."

"It sounds as though he wanted to make certain we were met as soon as we arrived," said Quaeryt. "Are . . . there difficulties? How has the Council received Lord Bhayar's suggestions?"

"They have not shared their views on what Lord Bhayar proposed. They were less than kind to Calkoran for presenting them."

"What did they expect? Is he all right?"

"Thank you for asking. He will be pleased that you inquired about him. He is in good health, but some have accused him of being a traitor, especially the . . . Selenorans."

"Selenorans?" asked Vaelora.

"The believers in the moon goddess—Artiema. They believe Lord Bhayar is the agent of Erion, and that Artiema, and Khel, must never be hostage to the Great Hunter and lesser moon."

Quaeryt shook his head. "Then they do not understand the world as it is."

"Is not that why Lord Bhayar has sent you both?" Arion's words were wry.

"It might have something to do with it," Quaeryt admitted. "Matters have not gone as well as we might have wished. We were attacked by Antiagon ships on the way, and we've had a little difficulty in locating mounts." Quaeryt kept his voice bland.

"That is not surprising. As soon as the High Council read Lord Bhayar's message, they issued an edict forbidding the sale of any horses to anyone from Telaryn, Bovaria, or Antiago."

"I understand why they might do that," Quaeryt said. "I can also say that it might not have been the wisest of decisions."

"They doubt that Lord Bhayar will soon send an army to Khel, not when he has not fully conquered Bovaria."

"They're right. He won't. But he does not forget, and if he does have to send an army . . ."

"Calkoran suggested that. They did not believe him."

"What do you suggest, Arion?"

"The High Council has agreed to meet you in Saendeol. I think you should do so. They have sent with me enough mounts for one company." He paused. "And for the undercaptains."

"We only brought four of them. The other four are in Bovaria with Submarshal Skarpa's forces."

Arion raised his eyebrows.

"Yes, I did bring Lhandor and Khalis, as well as Horan and Baelthm."

The major nodded.

"When do you suggest we depart?" asked Quaeryt.

"When you are ready."

"This afternoon at first glass?"

Arion smiled. "You do not wish to tarry."

"Lydar cannot afford delays. Or other mistakes. Neither can Khel."

"Then I will have the mounts here at noon. Did you bring saddles and riding gear?"

"We did." Quaeryt stood. "Thank you for all that you've done. We look forward to talking with you on the ride to Saendeol and hearing what else you've learned."

Arion rose quickly. "I do as well, sir. Until later, sir."

Once the major left the *Montagne*, Quaeryt summoned Khaern and requested that Nykaal join them as well.

The ship's captain arrived first, but only a fraction of a quint before the subcommander.

When Khaern entered the stateroom, he inclined his head first to Vaelora, then Quaeryt, and then Nykaal. "You requested my presence, sirs and Lady?"

"Please have a seat." Quaeryt gestured to the vacant chair at the circular table. "You may have heard that we've had some difficulty obtaining mounts."

"There's been some word about that, sir."

"You may also recall that Major Arion served under me before he was dispatched with Subcommander Calkoran to suggest an agreement with the High Council of Khel. He rode into Kherseilles a short time ago with his company. He informed me that the High Council has effectively prohibited the sale of any horses to anyone not serving the High Council. The Council is willing to provide us enough horses to mount up first company—and Lady Vaelora and the undercaptains—so that we may travel to Saendeol to meet with the Council."

"If I might say so, sir, that doesn't appear to be the most conciliatory of acts on the part of the Council."

"That was my first thought," replied Quaeryt. "Yet, from their point of view, landing two warships and troops in Kherseilles might not be considered terribly conciliatory, either." He turned to Nykaal. "What are your thoughts on the matter, Captain?"

"You're not going to make that strong an impression with one mounted company. On the other hand, I doubt that they can force us out of Kherseilles."

"I wouldn't want it to come to that, for a number of reasons. What are the arrangements for the merchanters?"

"Their contract is over once your troopers disembark, and they'll leave on that night's tide, I am more than certain."

"And your orders?"

"Both the *Solis* and the *Montagne* are to support you for so long as you require."

"Will that be a problem in terms of supplies?"

"No, sir."

"Then it appears that our immediate course is set."

Nykaal frowned, if briefly. Vaelora nodded.

"I have no mounts for Eleventh Regiment, and no way for Eleventh Regiment to return immediately to Ephra or Geusyn. We are charged with meeting with the High Council. They are amenable to meeting. So first company, when appropriate but as soon as practicable, will ride to Saendeol to meet with the Council. I'm planning on departing at first glass this afternoon."

"With but one company?" asked Nykaal. "You can't even be certain that the Khellan battalion won't attack you if their Council decides you're a danger."

"They've seen what the commander can do, sir," replied Khaern, "and they're not stupid enough to bring his wrath down on them."

Nykaal frowned. "But if they believe that . . ."

"Why doesn't the Council?" asked Quaeryt. "Because no one believes much of anything until they get burned or watch someone else get burned, frozen, or otherwise destroyed. Some don't even understand when they do see. Those are the ones who have to experience it firsthand . . . and too many of them don't learn from the experience because they don't survive it."

Nykaal still wore a puzzled frown.

"Captain, there are forty thousand dead Bovarian troopers and officers," said Khaern. "That doesn't include a rex and most of his court. There's scarcely a building left standing in a space three milles wide and a mille deep. You probably think I'm telling tall tales. I'm not. My men had to help bury all those bodies. So did the Khellan troops."

"If you're wondering why we didn't do something like that to the Antiagon ships," added Quaeryt, "there wasn't any need to, and it's better to save extreme measures for extreme situations." He smiled. "Now . . . we need to discuss how you feel we should handle the *Montagne* and the *Solis*."

"I'd prefer to have one at sea off the harbor at any time. The Antiagons have been known to sneak in vessels and fire them before they could raise sail."

"That shouldn't be a problem. You and Khaern can work out details for what troopers you need aboard. First company, Lady Vaelora and I, and the imager undercaptains will be riding out at first glass. We will send dispatches, although I doubt that you'll learn much until we reach Saendeol. Unless you have any questions, several of us need to ready ourselves for another ride." Quaeryt glanced sideways to Vaelora, and the two of them rose.

By a quint past first glass, Quaeryt, Vaelora, and first company were riding away from the pier and the *Montagne*. Arion had insisted that Quaeryt ride a large black gelding and Vaelora a matching black mare.

*So long as it's not a white stallion,* Quaeryt had thought when he'd saddled the gelding.

Arion had not brought all of fourth company to Kherseilles, just two squads, both of which rode rearguard, while Zhelan dispatched first company's second squad as the vanguard, with scouts from both first company and from Arion's squads. Quaeryt and Arion rode on each side of Vaelora, with Khalis and Zhelan following, and the other undercaptains after them.

As they rode away from the burned-out warehouses that still lined the harbor, Quaeryt began to count the houses and shops that appeared ruined or vacant. After three blocks he stopped. Roughly one in every three or four structures appeared deserted and looked to require significant repairs to make it livable once more.

"Did all the destruction happen during the war?" asked Quaeryt.

Arion laughed harshly. "Almost none of it did. There weren't any battles fought here in the south. Kharst just marched an army from Laaryn to Khelgror, and then shipped forces to Ouestan and Eshtora. Those forces closed the ports and waited. Factors from all over Lydar descended on Kherseilles with their own guards and armsmen and took whatever they wanted. Sooner or later, that happened to all the port cities. It happened sooner in Ouestan and Eshtora. After the Red Death, we did not have enough men to send to every port, so we fought the Bovarians near Khelgror. We fought until we had but a few companies left. We almost won, but there were too few of us. Once we were defeated, they removed any Pharsi factors who had survived and replaced them with people of their own. Except in the coastal hills in the west, they didn't create high holdings. Anyone who complained was executed. For any Bovarian trooper or functionary who was killed, they killed five people at random. So . . . troopers and factors began to disappear. For every Bovarian who vanished, they killed three people."

"How many troopers or factors vanished, and then reappeared?"

"That happened once or twice. After that, they still killed three people—and they also killed the people who vanished if they showed up again."

"How many of the people are left?" asked Vaelora.

"The Red Death took one in three. The war took one in four of those remaining. The factors and the troopers that supported them took one in four from those survivors—and then those who remained killed all the troopers when we learned that Bovaria had fallen to Lord Bhayar. That cost us many people, mostly women."

Quaeryt attempted to make the calculations in his head. "Based on those numbers, today you have about four out of every ten who lived in Khel ten years ago."

Arion shrugged. "It is what it is."

"Do you know why the High Council is opposed to Lord Bhayar's terms?"

"They have not spoken to me, or to any of us who served under you—except for Subcommander Calkoran."

"Then tell me why you think the Council opposes Lord Bhayar's rule."

"Wouldn't you?"

"I might have ten or fifteen years ago. Today . . . no."

"They do not see it that way. They trust no one. Many would rather die than be ruled by an outsider. The Selenorans believe Lord Bhayar would be as bad as Kharst, if not worse."

"Would that be so even if the Council were given some authority for what happens in Khel?"

"There is a saying about a ruler's promise lasting less time than a black coney in winter."

"Is a black coney the sign of bad luck?" asked Quaeryt.

The slightest hint of a frown crossed the major's face. "Not that I know . . . well . . . there is the saying that he who hunts only black coneys will soon starve."

"For more reasons than one, I'm sure," said Quaeryt dryly. "How is Captain Stensted doing? And your men?"

"All are healthy, and all are pleased to be back in Khel."

"But . . . there are some matters that are unclear?" suggested Quaeryt. "Such as whether your allegiance is to Lord Bhayar and how long you'll be paid, especially since there are few coins indeed in Khel? And since you agreed to fight against Rex Kharst and he's dead?"

"Those things have been mentioned."

"I thought they might have been," replied Quaeryt.

Arion said nothing, but kept riding, avoiding looking at either envoy.

"Lord Bhayar did promote Subcommander Calkoran. To me, that suggests he believes all of you are still serving him and will be paid as such. Unless, of course, that allegiance is repudiated. I imagine the High Council sees it that way as well, and that could place the subcommander in a difficult position. A most difficult one."

"He has said as much to me."

"But not to Major Zhael, I would guess."

"I do not know, but Zhael has said nothing."

"So you're to find out what you can?"

Arion grinned, somewhat sheepishly.

"I think Bhayar would like to keep paying you all for as long as you would serve him."

"That would mean Khel would become part of Telaryn."

"That is his hope . . . and mine. I do not think the future of Khel will be very bright without Bhayar's support."

"Would you turn against Khel, Commander?"

"I'm not interested in turning against anyone. Lady Vaelora and I are here to try to find a way that Khel can agree to become part of Telaryn so that all Lydar is united and there will be no more wars among its people."

"Do you think the Autarch Aliaro will accept that?" Arion's skepticism was more than clear.

"One way or another, he will."

"You mean dead or alive?"

"It might come to that. I would not wish the same for Khel."

"How can Bhayar promise a fair rule when he does not yet even control all of Bovaria?"

"I'd like you to think about that for a while, Major. And I hope the Council will as well." Quaeryt smiled warmly. "In the meantime, can you tell me a little about the Selenorans? I've never heard anything about them."

"There have been those who believe in the power of the moon goddess since as far back as there has been a Khel. Much longer, I would think. Most of them are hunters and herders and stay far from the cities and larger towns. The most dangerous are the Eleni, the wise women to whom the others listen and who tame the great eagles to hunt for them. There are tales . . . they are only tales . . . but you do not wish . . ."

"Tell me of the tales," said Quaeryt. "If they oppose a union of Khel and Telaryn, I should know more of them and why they are so opposed."

"In the time of the first great council, the first of the High Councils, the people of Moryn sent a councilor to them who was said to be a hand of Erion." Arion paused. "You did say . . ."

"Go on."

"This councilor wished to extend the laws of the High Council to the wild ones, the ones like the Eleni, who lived away from the towns, and cities, and even the hamlets. He refused to listen to the Eleni who approached him and who claimed that they lived under the laws of Artiema and that they had no need of the laws of the High Council. Three times, the wise women of the Eleni approached him, and three times he turned them away. When he dismounted below the Mound of Truth and began to walk up the steps of truth, one of the great eagles appeared in the sky and swooped down upon him and killed him with a single blow.

"The eldest of the Eleni appeared at the foot of the steps and declared that the same fate would befall any man—even a hand of Erion—who dared to act without even the grace to talk to the Eleni. Then she vanished where she stood, leaving the councilor's body on the stones." Arion shrugged. "Many say that his death proved he was no hand of Erion. Others say that his death proved that Erion was indeed the lesser moon."

"Are there other tales such as that?"

"Many," said Arion. "Khel is an old land, perhaps older than Telaryn."

"There's little doubt of that," agreed Quaeryt. "Go on."

"Most are of lesser happenings, but all show the power of Artiema and the Eleni. In the time of my great-grandmere, a Ferran factor seized the daughter of a Eleni herder and tried to take her back to his factorage in Eshtora. She pleaded to Artiema, and the factor was struck by a dark thunderbolt, and she escaped."

"Another eagle?" asked Quaeryt.

"I would think so, but my grandmere—she was the one who told the story—insisted it was a black thunderbolt . . ."

"How does one tell who is of the Eleni . . . truly?" asked Vaelora.

"By their deeds. Sometimes by their garb. They are always black-haired, and the huntresses wear red leather shoulder rests for the eagles and red leather gloves."

"Have you ever seen one?"

"Twice, from a distance as a boy. I had no desire to get closer."

"Are there any other stories?" asked Quaeryt.

"My friend Reybaal told me that he saw an Eleni huntress turn aside a mounted company. He did not see what she did . . ."

Just outside Kherseilles, the column turned onto a narrow road—but an ancient gray stone paved way that looked all too familiar to Quaeryt. He looked to Arion. "This is an old, old road. Was Saendeol once the capital or a leading city of southern Khel?"

The major looked quizzically at Quaeryt. "Where have you heard this? I said nothing of that."

Quaeryt smiled. "The road told me."

Arion smiled in return. "What did it tell you, Commander?"

"The stones are all the same size. They are the same size and shape as the stones used by the Naedarans in the south of Bovaria, yet I have seen no other stone like this used in the walls and buildings of Kherseilles. The road is the same width, and has been here for a long time, but there is little trace of wear. The walls of Nordeau were built in a way that suggested the builders feared imagers, but the early Bovarians had no imagers. Also, roads are built by people with power, and they connect places of power. The stone piers at Kherseilles are old and of stone. You told me that Saendeol was where the Council once met. Therefore . . ."

"Therefore . . . what?"

"The old ones of Khel had imagers. They likely fought with the Naedarans, and Saendeol was a place of power." Quaeryt shrugged. "Or it could be that the old ones of Khel came from Chelaes and Naedara. Perhaps they did not agree with the old ones of Naedara. But there is some sort of tie."

"Because of the stones?"

"Are there buildings in Saendeol built of gray stone like this?" Quaeryt gestured toward the road.

"There are a number."

"Aren't they all older buildings?"

"They have been there for years."

"Tell me, Major, where there is a quarry from which these stones could have come?"

"I do not know of any, but I am from the north."

"I take it that this road goes all the way to Saendeol."

"Yes, sir."

"Does it go anywhere else?"

"No, sir." Arion looked directly at Vaelora. "You have said little, Lady Vaelora."

"For all that you two have said, you've both talked past me, not to me."

Quaeryt winced, but said gently, "You could have spoken. You don't need to defer to me . . . as you've pointed out on a number of occasions."

Vaelora laughed softly and turned to Arion. "He is right about that." After a pause she went on. "I said little because I mostly agree with my husband. He knows that I will let him know if I don't. I worry more than he does, I think, that the High Council will not look to the future because the past few years have been so painful. Rex Kharst was a terrible ruler. He was cruel to Khel and the Pharsi, but he was cruel to all of his own people as well, save for a few favorites. My brother has been firm as a ruler, but he has been as fair as he could be. My husband has not agreed with everything Lord Bhayar has done. No honest man will ever agree fully with another, even another man who is honest and fair. But Quaeryt believes Bhayar is the best ruler for Lydar, and he believed that before he and I ever met. I can also tell you that the people of Khel have no greater champion than Quaeryt. My husband would not wish me to say this, and my brother certainly would not, but the Council would be foolish to waste Quaeryt's support and skill." She paused once more. "What else could I say?"

Arion shook his head. "I have felt all that you say, and I have said it to those who will listen, but I have not been allowed to speak to the High Council."

"The more fools, they," said Vaelora tartly. "You've seen what Bhayar and Quaeryt have done, and what they have not done. It is one thing to be cautious. It's another to be deaf and blind."

Quaeryt managed to keep a pleasant expression on his face as he continued riding.

By Samedi night Quaeryt, Vaelora, Arion, and first company were far enough from the waters of the Gulf that the evening breeze was more than chill. When they broke camp on Solayi morning, a fine white frost coated the browned grasses bordering the stone road, as well as the grasses of the open meadows between the stands of bare-leafed trees. In its construction, the road reminded Quaeryt of the ancient Naedaran stone roads, but there was one principal difference. The Naedaran roads Quaeryt had seen had largely followed or paralleled streams, canals, or rivers. The one on which Arion guided them did not, but appeared to have been laid out more directly through the hills to the northwest of Kherseilles. While it followed a stream now and again, that appeared only because the stream happened to be where the ancient road builder had wanted the road, and not the other way around.

On Lundi evening, they stayed the night in an abandoned and not quite ruined stead—a place Arion said that he and his men had used on the ride from Saendeol. On Mardi evening, just before fifth glass, they arrived in the town of Rheon, set in a gentle valley flanked by vineyards, where, once again, a number of the houses appeared abandoned, although Quaeryt got the impression that the empty houses were more on the order of one in ten, rather than one in three or four, as they had been in Kherseilles.

Arion led the column along the stone-paved road that had become the main street of the town until he reached an open square, where he turned eastward and rode toward an oblong two-story building that had to be an inn.

As Quaeryt and Vaelora followed the major past the signboard in front of the building, Quaeryt found he could read the letters on the signboard, but had no idea what the words meant, although, in a way, he felt he should, since they were Pharsi. *That just shows how lost you are.*

"One of the two towns between Kherseilles and Saendeol with a proper inn," Arion announced as he dismounted in the courtyard.

"What's the name of the inn?" Quaeryt asked, gesturing back toward the signboard.

"It means 'the warm hearth' or 'the welcome inn.' "

"I have some golds," Quaeryt said, "but my funds are far from unlimited."

"He'll accept whatever you offer."

"A copper for each man for lodging, two for the officers, and three for each meal?"

"He'd find that more than fair, especially since the men will be in the barns and stables."

"Is there anyone here who doesn't speak Pharsi?" asked Vaelora.

"No one who would likely admit it at the moment," replied Arion. "Some also speak Bovarian. Almost no one speaks Tellan." He turned and began to talk to the stable boy, who had hurried across the paved courtyard from the open stable doors.

Quaeryt swung down from the black gelding, then held his hand out for Vaelora. Surprisingly, she took it, if but for a moment, as she dismounted.

"You should meet the innkeeper," said Arion. "If you would follow me, sir, Lady . . ." The Pharsi major guided them toward the side door of the stone-walled inn.

Sandstone, not gray stone, Quaeryt noted as he eased Vaelora after Arion. He did extend his shields to cover her, just to be careful. The side door opened on a narrow corridor leading to the main hallway off the public room.

Arion offered a greeting in Pharsi as he neared the main entry hall, and in moments a dark-haired, honey-skinned man appeared from somewhere in the back of the inn. After an exchange of words, the innkeeper bowed slightly to the major.

Arion spoke a few more words, and the innkeeper turned from Arion to Quaeryt and Vaelora. He froze where he stood. His eyes widened, and then he bowed, and offered a welcome, one of the few Pharsi phrases Quaeryt knew.

Quaeryt offered a short reply in Pharsi, then had to add in Bovarian, "Thank you, but I was orphaned young and did not learn Pharsi beyond what I knew as a small boy."

"I . . . understand," the man replied in Bovarian, but his eyes fixed on Vaelora, and he bowed even more deeply, offering a more voluble greeting.

Vaelora responded with a longer phrase, and then a second, before finally saying, in Bovarian, "Those are what my grandmere taught me."

Arion stepped forward and began to talk to the innkeeper once more.

The man finally nodded, smiled, and said in accented Bovarian, "Most welcome you both are."

"Thank you," said Quaeryt, this time in Pharsi, one of the few phrases he'd learned from his Pharsi undercaptains on their long rides.

"My daughter . . . honored lady . . . she will show you . . . the way."

A young girl appeared, perhaps ten, and stepped carefully toward Vaelora. She stopped a yard short and bowed, then gestured for Vaelora to follow her.

Quaeryt followed the two several yards past the main hall and then up a set of stone steps. Halfway up, one step was a bit higher than the others, and the longer boot heel on Quaeryt's bad leg caught the edge of the riser, and he stumbled and almost fell before catching himself—and almost jamming the two immobile fingers on his left hand. At the top of the staircase, the girl turned to the right and walked to the end chamber. There, she opened the door and stepped inside, gesturing for Vaelora and Quaeryt to follow.

The chamber was modest, floored in slate tiles, with clean white plastered walls, and a double bed, with a table, an armoire, and an alcove set off by a decorative screen that held a wash table and basin and other items. The large window had no curtains, but a set of dark-stained inside shutters, swung open to admit the light.

Once they were alone, Quaeryt asked, "Do you know what the innkeeper said to you?"

"I didn't catch all of it, but he called me 'Seliora,' and I know that's the daughter of the moon. There's something about the two of us together that surprised him."

"I think I'll ask Arion while you wash up, if you don't mind."

"I don't mind, dearest. Take your time."

*Meaning, don't hurry back.* Quaeryt slipped away, closing the heavy door, and headed down to the courtyard, where he found Arion and Zhelan directing the men and mounts. He stood back in the shadows of the inn wall, watching and not wanting to interfere. Once it was clear that they had finished, he stepped forward. "Arion?"

The Pharsi major turned. "Yes, sir."

Zhelan also turned, clearly interested.

"I don't speak much Pharsi . . . almost none, as you know. It seemed to me that the innkeeper was referring to Vaelora as the daughter of the moon . . . and that he was surprised that we were together. Or did I misunderstand?"

Arion laughed softly. "You didn't misunderstand, but he said more than that. He said that few had ever seen a hand of Erion—that's the old way of saying a son of Erion—and fewer still had seen him with the daughter of the moon."

"He didn't look exactly happy about it, not at first."

"When the two are seen together, according to the old tales, it foretells great change. Great change," Arion added sardonically, "usually means war, famine, or disaster . . . if not worse."

"And you told him?"

"That you two had come in hopes of making that change as peaceful as possible."

"I hope the High Council sees it that way."

"So do I. So does Subcommander Calkoran."

"Let's hope we can convince the Council. What can we do about getting the men fed?"

"Your three cooks will help in the kitchen, and they'll feed the men two squads at a time, beginning in half a glass. There's a table in an alcove at the end of the public room that will seat ten . . ."

"That would suit the officers and Vaelora and me," suggested Quaeryt. "That's nine. We could eat together, once the last squad is fed."

Arion looked to Zhelan.

"I can take care of this," replied Zhelan. "It'd be best if you talked to the innkeeper."

When Arion had reentered the inn, Quaeryt asked, "What do you think?"

"Seems straightforward to me. Ostler and stableboy know their business. Place is one of the cleanest inns I've seen. No one looking away. Everyone's cheerful. One of the serving girls was flirting with Undercaptain Khalis. He was trying not to blush. Lhandor rescued him."

"Whether he wanted to be rescued or not, I imagine."

"He needed to be rescued. She had her blouse down so far . . ." Zhelan shook his head.

"He's a handsome young man, and sometimes too courteous."

"Except in battle . . . or protecting you."

Quaeryt didn't contradict the major. He recalled Khalis hovering over him when he'd been flattened by a cannon powder explosion.

Once the men and mounts were settled, Quaeryt walked back into the inn. As he headed toward the stairs, he saw one of the serving girls looking at him. He smiled back and started to turn when he saw a man in dark gray leathers lean toward the serving girl and murmur something. The girl replied, and the man stepped away. There was something about the exchange that troubled Quaeryt, but he couldn't have said what.

He kept walking and returned to the room, where he washed up. Then, at half past sixth glass, he led Vaelora into the public room, down one side past the tables where the last two squads were finishing their meal. He did catch a few murmured remarks.

". . . wouldn't be letting my sister ride with us . . ."

". . . would if *he* were guarding her . . ."

". . . heard the innkeeper near-on filled his britches when he saw her . . . called her a moon goddess or something . . ."

What Quaeryt did hear confirmed his faith in the ability of troopers to find out far more than their commanders ever intended.

The officers at the table all rose as Quaeryt and Vaelora approached. They had left vacant the two places in the middle of the table on the side closest to the wall. Quaeryt eased Vaelora into the seat beside Arion, while he sat between her and Zhelan.

"What are we having for dinner, Arion?" asked Quaeryt.

"Lamb. What else? For a Pharsi, the best meal is always lamb. The lamb tonight will be stew with mushrooms and potatoes and spices. With fresh-baked rosemary bread and red wine."

The wine carafes were already on the table, and Quaeryt filled Vaelora's goblet and his, then passed the carafe to Arion, who handed it back to Zhelan. The first casserole dish was set before Vaelora, but Quaeryt served her and himself, and then the two majors. That was deliberate, especially since he could see the innkeeper watching.

*The daughter of the moon should be served first, especially in Khel.*

Once all the officers were served, Quaeryt lifted his goblet. "I'd like to offer a toast, and thanks, to Major Arion, for his guidance and his knowledge . . . and for finding a good inn."

For a time thereafter, there was little conversation, but after a bit, Quaeryt turned to Arion. "What is the road like from here to Saendeol?"

"Much like it has been. If the weather holds, we should reach Saendeol by Samedi evening."

"How large a place is it?"

"Perhaps twice the size of Rheon. It does have more inns. There was little destruction."

"Why was that?"

"There is little of great value grown there, and no mining, and the Bovarians like to trade by canals and rivers."

Others asked a few questions after that, and Arion was more than happy to tell the officers about Khel.

Quaeryt and Vaelora mostly listened.

As they rose after eating, Quaeryt leaned toward Vaelora. "I need to talk to Khalis and Lhandor."

"I would have suggested it, if you hadn't."

Quaeryt gestured to Lhandor, the nearest of the two. "I'll need a moment with you and Khalis after I escort Lady Vaelora to her chamber. If you'd wait here."

"Yes, sir."

Quaeryt escorted Vaelora through the public room and then up the stairs, again shielding her until she was inside their chamber. "You will bolt the door."

"Yes, dearest. I'll even unbolt it when you return."

"I'd hope so."

"There are times, dearest, when you hope too much."

Quaeryt let the wince show.

She lifted her hand to stroke the side of his face. "Do what you must and hurry back."

Quaeryt returned her smile. "I will." But he waited outside in the hall until he heard the bolt slide into place.

The two Pharsi undercaptains were waiting at a table in the corner of the public room. Quaeryt gestured for them not to rise and eased a chair into place across the table from them. "As you both know, I speak little Pharsi. I have little idea what's being said. What have you heard?"

"I don't catch everything," replied Khalis. "They speak a bit different here, but you scared the innkeeper when you came into the inn and took off your cap and he saw you and the lady together. The serving girls were whispering about it."

"One asked me if you were a lost one," added Lhandor, "or maybe an ancient."

"An ancient?"

"One of the old Pharsi from the east."

*A Naedaran Pharsi?* "Were there Pharsi in Naedara?"

Lhandor shrugged. "I don't know. There are tales that the oldest Pharsi fled into the west."

"I never heard that," said Khalis.

"My grandmere talked about them. My father told me not to believe her, that all good Pharsi came from the west."

Quaeryt nodded. In that light, the road and some of the legends made sense. "Did they say anything else?"

"One of them asked me why all your hair and your nails were white, if you painted them to look like the son of Erion. I told her that your hair and nails turned white, that it was part of the price you paid for calling down the ice on the armies of Bovaria. It was, wasn't it?"

"It was," Quaeryt said quietly. *But only a part.*

"She got real quiet then. The other one whispered something about telling her father. I got the idea he might be the innkeeper."

"Was there anything else?"

The two shook their heads.

"I'd appreciate it if you'd keep listening. Any little thing could be important."

"Because of the High Council?" asked Khalis.

Quaeryt nodded. "I don't want Lord Bhayar to bring an army into Khel. The Pharsi don't want that. We'd all be better off if we can work something out."

"Yes, sir."

Quaeryt could sense the doubt in their voices. "It won't be easy, but it's something we have to find a way to do." *Because that's best . . . or because you don't want to destroy thousands more?* "Thank you both. I'll see you in the morning."

With a parting nod, he turned and headed back to the room . . . and Vaelora.

When he had bolted the door, he walked to the armoire and sat on the stool, where he began to pull off his boots.

"Dearest . . . I've been thinking . . ."

"Yes?" he replied warily.

"There isn't anyone, except perhaps the Autarch, who can threaten Khel. By defeating Kharst, Bhayar has removed the threat of Kharst. Weak as it is, Khel poses no threat to Telaryn or Bhayar. Not now. Why are you going to press the Council to accept Bhayar's agreement?"

"Besides the fact that he dispatched us to do so?"

"If it's not a good idea, it's not a good idea."

"You're right about that, but uniting Khel and Telaryn is a good idea, even if the Council doesn't like it."

"Go on. Tell me why. You'll have to tell the Council why."

Quaeryt turned on the stool to face Vaelora, who sat on the end of the double bed.

"First, Khel can't protect itself from the factors who flee Bhayar and move to Khel, especially those in the north and west of Bovaria. If Khel doesn't accept Bhayar's terms, he certainly won't have any interest in pursuing those factors. Why should he protect Khel from them? Second, what's to stop traders from Jariola or Ferrum or other places from trying to establish themselves in Khel? If they do, and it's against the interests of Telaryn, then Bhayar will have to do something in the future. The Khellans certainly won't like that. Third, if Khel accepts his terms, the Pharsi will have Bhayar's protection, under law, against factors and others who try to exploit them, and they will have the ability to trade freely throughout all of Lydar except for Antiago. That will make them far more prosperous.

"Equally important, Khel can get better terms now because, sooner or later, he will take over Khel. If he has to fight to do it, Khel will suffer far more than it already has. If the High Council agrees to terms he can accept, then there's no war, and everyone benefits."

"That makes sense . . . and they won't agree," said Vaelora sadly, glancing toward the window and shivering.

Quaeryt rose and walked over to close and fasten the inside shutters. Then he turned back to face her in the dim light. "I'm afraid you're right. Do you have any better suggestions?"

"Not tonight, dearest."

Later, much later, outside the window, even with the inside shutters closed, Quaeryt could hear the wind and the beat of heavy rain on the roof and the walls of the inn, but his mind drifted back, time and again, to the same words.

*What can you do to persuade them?* The question kept circling in his thoughts, and yet he had no answer—none at all.

At some point, he finally drifted into sleep with the beating of the rain on the walls and the roof.

Quaeryt woke abruptly in the darkness and turned toward Vaelora. She wasn't there. He ran his fingers over the covers, but the bed was empty, except for him, and the sheets were like liquid ice. He bolted upright and looked toward the alcove behind the screen, but there was no one there, either. The door was still bolted, and the shutters were closed, tightly fastened, just as he had left them.

*Where could she have gone?*

The chamber was so cold that his teeth began to chatter as he kept looking around, but he knew better than to try to image warmth. *No telling what damage that could do.*

Where was Vaelora? He threw back the blankets and stood. The stone tiles under his bare feet felt like ice, but he walked to the armoire. Surely she couldn't be hiding there. He opened it, and all he saw were clothes. From there he went to the screen, but the washing area was vacant.

He turned back and looked at the bed again. He could see the rumpled blankets where he had been lying, but the covers were smoother where Vaelora had been. Had she gotten up earlier? But how could that have been?

He walked back to the bed, then turned as a glimmer of light seeped into the room from the closed shutters, followed by streams of silver light flowing through the shutters of the window . . . and then the shutters melted away to reveal the figure of a man with hair like flowing silver, standing at the end of a road of reddish silver that stretched into the night sky. In one hand he held a dagger with a blade of brilliant light. Across his back was a mighty bow, and in his other hand was something shimmering so brightly that Quaeryt could not determine what it might be . . . a key, a small book, a coiled chain of gold . . . ?

The silver-haired figure smiled at Quaeryt, almost sadly, before he spoke. "You cannot hold a daughter of the moon, for not even a son of mine can do that."

"I haven't tried to hold her," Quaeryt protested.

"You have not. So far . . . but women and lands cannot be held against their will, not and prosper. Nor can you force peace with a blade or even the power I have given you. You can only stop others from fighting by destroying them or by the threat of destruction. The absence of fighting is not peace. It is only the absence of fighting that may resume at any time."

"But why won't they see?" Quaeryt finally asked.

"Do not argue over what is not and may never be," said the silver-haired man.

"What do you mean by that?"

"You have heard those words before. You know their meaning more than most."

The light faded, and Quaeryt shivered a last time, then realized that Vaelora was sitting up beside him.

"What was that light?" she asked sleepily.

*Light?* "There was light? I thought I was dreaming it." After a moment he said, "You're here. You're really here?"

"I am indeed. You were talking to someone, but there's no one here."

"I had the strangest dream . . ." Quaeryt shook his head. "You were gone, and Erion was standing in a flow of silver light before the window. He told me . . . that I could never hold you . . . because you're a daughter of the moon."

"Of course you can. You do every night."

"No . . . he was right. You choose to stay, but if you chose to go, I couldn't hold you."

Vaelora took his hand, the left one, with the two fingers that could feel but not move, and held it. "Isn't that true of you as well? I could never hold you against your will, even with Bhayar behind me."

"But I want you to hold me."

"That's not the same thing," she said softly, "and you know it."

"He also said that lands and women were the same, that with all the power I had been given, I could not force peace. That I could only use destruction to stop fighting for a short time. He was right about that . . . too."

"If it was a dream, you were telling yourself that."

"Was it a dream?" he asked. "You saw the light coming through the shutters."

She leaned forward and kissed his cheek, then put her other arm around him. "Does it matter? Truth is truth."

Tired as he was, Quaeryt felt as though more than a glass passed before he drifted back into sleep and uneasy dreams.

When he woke the second time on Meredi morning, close to sixth glass, Quaeryt thought, he walked to the window and unfastened the shutters. A wave of coldness radiated from the thin panes, completely covered with frost. He scratched away enough of the frost to peer out and to see that white covered the hills he could barely make out over the roof of the stable, and that gusting flakes continued to fall, swirled here and there by the wind. Through the swirling flakes, he found it hard to tell just how much snow had fallen or was falling.

"What is it?" asked Vaelora.

"Snow, and it's still snowing." Quaeryt refastened the shutters and turned back to face her. "We'd best get washed and dressed and see how bad it is."

"Should we be traveling through a snowstorm?"

"Probably not, but it's hard to tell from here if it's a light passing storm that's almost over, or the beginning of something bigger. I'd like to see and to talk to Arion and Zhelan. The sooner we get to Saendeol, the better, but we don't want to be frozen to death on the road."

Vaelora sat up, the covers drawn around her. "Have you thought about your dream?"

"Not much," he protested. "I just woke up. Have you?"

"Only that it means you shouldn't force the High Council to agree to Bhayar's terms, even if it means Khel will not be a part of Telaryn so soon."

"So soon?"

"It will happen. Of that, I am convinced."

"Just as you were convinced we would be together?"

"I knew that it would be so." She smiled.

"Have you had any farsight visions on this? On Khel becoming part of Telaryn."

"No, but I feel it will be so. Without force."

Quaeryt fingered his stubbled chin. "What is force? What's the difference between persuasion and force?"

"You know very well, dearest. So does every woman."

"There sometimes is a narrow line . . ." He grinned.

"Only men think it's narrow." Vaelora sniffed.

Quaeryt knew she was teasing . . . slightly. He sighed, loudly. "We need to get dressed."

Once he had washed and shaved . . . and dressed, pulling on his winter riding jacket and lined gloves last, he ended up pacing around the chamber.

"Stop pacing!" snapped Vaelora. "Or wait for me downstairs."

Quaeryt forced himself to sit down and not to say a word. Nor to sigh or groan.

Finally, in less than half a quint that felt like a glass to Quaeryt, Vaelora was ready, and they walked from their chamber down the corridor and the steps into the main entry hall. Recalling his near mishap of the night before and feeling a certain stiffness in his bad leg, Quaeryt was especially careful on the steps.

Both Arion and Zhelan were standing, talking, by the front doors to the inn. In the side corridor leading to the stable courtyard, Quaeryt noticed a man in gray leathers, talking to an older gray-haired man. Neither looked at him.

At that moment Zhelan turned. "Commander . . . we've been talking. The cooks are feeding the men, but I don't like the look of things."

"Let's walk outside," suggested Quaeryt.

"Yes, sir."

Quaeryt grinned. "I know you two have already looked, but I've only seen it from the window."

"It doesn't look any better outside," replied Zhelan.

Arion nodded.

"At least give me the illusion of being in charge." Quaeryt nodded to Vaelora, then held the door for her as they stepped into the gusting winds and swirling snow.

Once outside, he looked up and down the street. The snow hadn't piled up that much, only a digit or two, if that, but there were small drifts deeper than that against the inn and the walls of the other buildings Quaeryt could see. On the other hand, he didn't see any riders or wagons anywhere on the street.

"If you walk downhill, to your left, sir," said Zhelan from behind Quaeryt and Vaelora, "you can get a better view of the hills."

Quaeryt stayed close to Vaelora, holding shields around them both as they walked down the edge of the paved road a good fifty yards so that he could look across a meadow that showed some brown grass protruding from an uneven cover of snow. Through the swirling snow that was lighter than it seemed, he could just barely make out the outline of the hills to the west. Even through the falling snow, he could see that the higher hills were definitely snow-covered, although it was difficult to tell just how deep the snow was.

"What do you think?" Quaeryt turned to Arion.

"It doesn't look like that heavy a storm, now, but the sky to the north is darker. That's where it's coming from. It might not get worse, but you can't tell. Were I you, I wouldn't hazard men and mounts."

Quaeryt chuckled. "And if you were just you, traveling with your squads?"

"I'd stay here and wait for the weather to change."

Quaeryt looked to Zhelan. "Major?"

"I'm with Major Arion."

Lastly, Quaeryt looked to Vaelora, who nodded. "Then that's what we'll do. Let's head back to the inn and let the undercaptains and the men know."

They turned, and the majors stepped aside to let Quaeryt and Vaelora lead the way. After they had walked fifteen yards Vaelora pointed past the inn. "There's a woolens shop up there."

"How can you see that?" murmured Quaeryt.

"I can always see the important places."

He wasn't about to respond to that.

"If we're not traveling today, I can see what they have."

"I'm sure that you can, dear."

"Dearest . . . that sounds patronizing . . . disrespectful, my brother might say."

Thankfully, Quaeryt could hear the teasing note in her voice. "I'm being most respectful. I agreed that you could visit the shop."

Quaeryt and Vaelora turned toward the front door of the inn, some ten yards away. Just then a strong gust of wind swirled a wall of snow at them, strong enough that Quaeryt's shields diverted the snow, leaving them untouched as they walked toward the inn.

At that moment Quaeryt saw the two bearded men in leathers, the younger of whom had pointed at them. *More likely at seeing the snow avoid us.*

"Why are those two men looking at us?"

"My shields diverted that gust of snow. They saw it."

"I didn't notice that." Vaelora paused, then said, "They're both wearing leathers. Didn't Arion say something about that?"

Quaeryt frowned, trying to recall. "Oh . . . he said that the Eleni hunters, the women, wore red gloves and red leather shoulder rests."

"They're definitely men," said Vaelora.

"And not wearing red leather," Quaeryt pointed out.

Quaeryt watched as the two men reentered the inn, but by the time he and Vaelora had reached the door and stepped inside, neither of the men in leathers were anywhere to be seen.

"Since we're already up, and the men have been fed, we might as well eat some breakfast," suggested Quaeryt.

"I could use some tea. Then . . . what do you have in mind?"

Quaeryt said nothing.

"Besides that."

"We could walk around Rheon and get an idea of the town . . . and of Khel."

"You'll need a very long walk."

"If we're going to see the town and all the woolen shops, then I'll need a solid breakfast." Quaeryt turned toward the public room, followed by Arion and Zhelan.

"You will, dearest," murmured Vaelora.

Quaeryt shook his head.

# 34

Although the clouds began to break by midafternoon on Meredi, there was no point in starting out so late in the day. There had also been little gained by Quaeryt's and Vaelora's walking through Rheon, since there had been nothing significant to distinguish it from small towns elsewhere in Lydar—except for the woolen shop, which, Quaeryt had to admit, did have bolts of tightly woven cloth with patterns he'd not seen elsewhere.

By Jeudi morning, the air had warmed, and the snow had begun to melt. By the eighth glass the road was mostly clear, although the hillsides still held snow, and Arion proclaimed that the weather would only warm. Quaeryt wouldn't have wanted to ride on the roads of Bovaria—most of them, anyway—but the gray stone road was indeed clear in all but the most shaded of spots. As Arion had predicted, the innkeeper had been surprised, astonished, it appeared, at the five golds he had received from Quaeryt, and he bowed profusely—if with great relief, Quaeryt suspected.

Less than a glass after leaving Rheon, they came to a shady area dusted with snow. Arion's scouts called a halt and requested that Quaeryt and Arion come forward to look at the tracks in the snow.

"A single rider," said the scout. "He was moving faster than a walk through here earlier today because there's been no wind. Yesterday . . . would have been covered with blowing snow, most likely."

"It couldn't have been a dispatch rider looking for you, sir, could it?" asked Arion.

Quaeryt shook his head. "Couriers always travel with at least two escorts. Khaern would have sent at least that many."

"Wonder who it could have been in such a hurry in this weather," mused Arion. "Don't see many single riders on the roads these days, especially not at the beginning of winter."

"We could set the scouts another hundred yards farther ahead," suggested Zhelan.

"That can't hurt," agreed Quaeryt. *Hoofprints in the snow headed northwest, toward Saendeol and whatever lay along the way. Just a coincidence?* He had no way of knowing.

They kept riding, and Quaeryt kept pondering, but by midday the road was clear everywhere, although the wind from the west was still chill, if no longer as bitter as it had been earlier. The scouts reported no one, and there were no other signs of riders.

That night, they found quarters of a sort in a small town set in a wide valley that was so flat it might once have been a lake. Vendrei morning was warmer, with skies almost clear, except for a faint haze. The wind had shifted from the north to the southeast and had become more temperate, giving a more autumnal feel to the air, even though the fields through which they rode were either brown or stubbled.

Slightly after midday, as the fields gave way to sparse grassland with scattered bushes and trees, Vaelora turned to Arion and asked, "How much farther to Saendeol? How many days?"

"Tonight we will stop in Sovahl," replied Arion. "It is at the foot of the Deol Hills. From there it is a ride of five or six glasses to Saendeol."

"For what is Sovahl known?" asked Quaeryt, not that he was supremely interested in one town over another, but because any knowledge would be valuable.

"Gemstones. The hills to the north of Sovahl hold many kinds of precious stones, and the gem merchants of Sovahl are known for their ability to cut and to shape those stones."

"Why didn't Kharst occupy Sovahl, then?"

"He did. Rather, the factors who had purchased stones from Sovahl hurried to Sovahl. They found nothing, except empty buildings. Gems, even the largest, are small, and one has to know what they look like before they are cut. The tools to cut are small. Everyone fled into the hills. Not all have yet returned. Some may never return, except to sell stones."

"They just left? And no one chased them?"

"You will see," promised Arion with a laugh. "You will see."

By midafternoon, as they neared the hills to the north and west, the almost barren grasslands gave way to low, rugged, and rocky rises with little greenery except occasional scrub junipers and squat pines, with stretches of sand between the rises, various scattered bushes, and sparse stands of wild grasses, now bent and brown.

"Not exactly the most hospitable place," observed Quaeryt, leaning forward in the saddle to stretch his back. "I think I can see why the Bovarians didn't have much success in chasing down the gem dealers. Are the hills around Saendeol this desolate?"

"They are dry, but not so dry as here," replied Arion.

"And there's a town ahead?" asked Vaelora. "Where? It doesn't look like there could be anything here."

"Another glass or so, I would judge."

Vaelora raised her eyebrows.

Smothering a smile, Quaeryt asked, "Were these lands greener a long time ago?"

"I do not know. Why do you ask?"

"I just wondered. This is a very good road. It was built a long time ago, yet you tell me it only runs from Saendeol to Kherseilles, and there's nothing here except a few towns, and herders and gem miners and merchants."

"Saendeol was once very important. It was also the capital of Jovana, when what is Khel was three lands."

That was something Quaeryt had not heard. "How long ago was that?"

"Before the time of the lost ones, generations before. I cannot say. Remember I come from the north and west."

Quaeryt still thought that the lands of the south had once been more lush, but it was clear that what Arion knew about this part of Khel was limited.

Another glass passed before Arion spoke again, smiling. "The edge of the town is just ahead."

The road began a gentle descent into lower ground running between two sandstone buttes, each about twenty yards back from the road and rising no more than thirty yards above the road. Each one was shaped like a squarish ridge that extended some two hundred yards or so, Quaeryt thought. He frowned. There wasn't a building in sight . . . except he saw thin trails of smoke rising into the midafternoon sky in places—from the buttes themselves. Then, between the buttes he saw sandstone-paved lanes leading off from the gray stone of the road.

"The town . . . it's carved into the stone itself?"

"It is. Many of the chambers were cut out even before there was a road, or so they have told me."

As the column of troopers and officers neared the "town," Quaeryt could see openings cut into the reddish sandstone, on two and sometimes three levels. Some of the "dwellings" or "shops" carved out of the sandstone were vacant and had been so for some time, with shutters either missing or hanging askew, or with vacant oblongs on the ground level where doors had been. Still, most seemed to be occupied in some fashion or another. The brown-stained shutters flanking those windows or openings that had shutters were anchored into the sandstone itself.

After they had ridden several hundred yards past the first inhabited stone chambers, Arion gestured for them to follow the scouts to the right down a wide sandstone paved lane. Ahead of them and to their left, sculpted out of the stone, was a pointed arch rising some ten yards, and in the center of the base of the arch were double doors, brassbound and half open. Shuttered windows set some two to three yards apart extended for some twenty yards on each side of the arch, with three levels of windows. At the south end of the "building" toward which they rode was a set of wide stable doors.

"Welcome to the Stone Inn," said Arion as he reined up outside those doors from which two young men hurried out. "I did tell them that we'd likely be back."

"How far back does that stable go?" asked Quaeryt.

"To the other side of the butte. That way they get fresh air. The last part, well, those are really just tunnels big enough for the horses, with iron grates on the eastern end."

"You've actually looked?"

"I rode back there with a torch. It's dark after the stable proper ends before you get to the far end, and you can feel the air moving."

Quaeryt could see Vaelora shiver, but she said nothing.

"I think we'd like a chamber with a window," suggested Quaeryt.

"Oh . . . all of them do. They run along the front on all three levels. They use the chambers on the inside for storage and other things. We'd best dismount and see the innkeeper. They get offended if we don't greet them first."

"By all means," said Quaeryt, easing himself out of the saddle. By the time he turned to Vaelora, she was already standing beside him.

They followed Arion to the brassbound doors in the middle of the sculpted stone arch. Three men emerged, two younger, who stood behind the older man, presumably the innkeeper.

Arion nodded politely and spoke several phrases.

The innkeeper smiled, and nodded in return, replying with several much longer phrases.

He was a wiry man, his skin darker than that of most Pharsi and weathered, who looked old enough to be a grandfather. His eyes scarcely moved to Vaelora, which surprised Quaeryt. Instead, he inclined his head deeply to Quaeryt and spoke once more.

Quaeryt didn't understand a word.

"He says that he is pleased that a son of the north has come to grace his inn, and he will offer all that he can for your favor," said Arion.

"If you would tell him, in the proper phrases, that we appreciate his hospitality and add whatever else is customary and proper." Quaeryt wasn't so certain he wanted to promise favor without knowing what that entailed.

Arion spoke for several moments, and the innkeeper smiled and inclined his head, then gestured to the young men and spoke again.

"They will show us our places while the men stable the mounts and unload. We will eat in about a glass."

In moments Quaeryt and Vaelora were inside the sandstone inn, where the corridors were narrower and shorter than he had expected, only a little more than a handspan above his head, and Quaeryt was not that tall a man. The chamber that Quaeryt and Vaelora shared was smaller than he expected, no more than three yards by four, with two windows a yard and a half apart, each slightly more than half a yard wide. There were no inner shutters and no hangings. The furnishings consisted of a thick pallet on a stone platform that was part of and rose from the sandstone floor. There were two stools, a washstand, a chamber pot, and a set of pegs protruding from the wall. Covering the bed pallet were heavy woolen blankets woven in designs of black and white. There was a coarse linen or cotton undersheet, and two thin brownish towels, one on each side of the washstand.

"This is not Rex Kharst's canal boat," observed Vaelora.

"No. It's not even the inn in Geusyn."

They looked at each other and laughed.

After washing up as best they could, Vaelora stretched out on the bed, such as it was, on top of the blankets.

"It's not that uncomfortable. It doesn't sag, anyway, not like the inn in Laaryn."

"You never said anything about that," replied Quaeryt.

"I didn't think I had to. Besides, it wasn't as cramped as the boat."

"How old do you think this is?"

"Older than I think I want to know."

Sitting on the edge of the stone bed, Quaeryt smiled at that.

A quint later they made their way down to the public room, a chamber large enough to hold all of first company and Arion's two squads, with several of the long trestle tables still empty. The stone ceiling was supported by columns of stone that had been left in place when the space had been cut, in irregular places. The columns were darkened with the smoke of ages.

"More lamb?" asked Quaeryt as they seated themselves at a table with the other officers, one set off partly in a stone alcove with a narrow stone window above one end, through which cool air flowed, for which Quaeryt was grateful, given the smoky air.

"No. Goat, most likely," replied Arion. "The land is hard even for sheep, and the goat will be sliced thinly or chopped and cooked for a long time. But it is good."

"What is there to drink?"

Arion gave a rueful expression. "Here you have a choice of a bitter beer—I would not call it ale or lager—or fermented goat's milk." He paused. "The beer is safer, I think."

Quaeryt glanced at the column behind Arion, carved with figures in a circular scrolling pattern that rose almost to the ceiling. He saw men and horses, hunters with bows, a merchant bestowing what looked like a gem to a man in elaborate garb. What he didn't see were any women.

"I've been looking at the carvings in the stone. They look to be old, and there aren't any women shown."

"You're among the southern hill people here. They're not truly Pharsi, and the stories say that they were here from the beginning. Unless you know them well, and they trust you totally, you never see a woman, and seldom a girl."

As if to emphasize that, the servers were all men, and they set the same stoneware bowl, filled with a stew, as well as a stoneware mug, in front of each officer and Vaelora. There were two large pitchers on the table, one sandstone red, and the other white.

"The red is beer," explained Arion.

The stew was tender, tangy, and not especially spicy, with a touch of mint and a spice he'd never tasted. The beer was so bitter that Quaeryt had to force himself to drink even a swallow of it. Then he imaged away the local brew and replaced it with the lager with which he filled his water bottle, adequate but not particularly good. But then, he didn't know enough about brewing to image superb lager. Even so, he did the same for Vaelora and was rewarded with a thankful smile . . . after a briefly puzzled expression crossed her lips.

When he looked down the table, he thought that Khalis had done the same thing, and suggested it to Lhandor. While he couldn't read their lips, the looks on their faces when they glanced at the pitchers and the comparative ease with which they lifted their mugs suggested they were having little difficulty drinking what was in them.

"How was your stew?" he finally asked Vaelora.

"Not bad . . . especially with the . . . change in beverage," she murmured back.

"I thought it might help."

"It did. I just hope it's not necessary for the remainder of the time in Khel."

"That makes two of us."

"I hope we can get a good night's sleep this evening."

Quaeryt did not miss the slight emphasis on the word "sleep," but he smiled anyway.

As the undercaptains formed up on Vendrei morning outside the Stone Inn stable doors, Quaeryt rode over to where Khalis and Lhandor waited, almost stirrup to stirrup.

"How did you find the local beer?" he asked, smiling.

Khalis looked to Lhandor.

Lhandor laughed softly. "It was awful, sir."

"But I noticed you two were lifting your mugs rather often."

"So were you, sir," replied Lhandor. "How did you find it?"

"As you did," Quaeryt said pleasantly. "You seemed to find a way to deal with it. Water, wine, ale, lager . . . what did you manage?"

Khalis grinned ruefully. "Berry juice and water. I tried to image lager, but it was worse than the beer."

"And you?" Quaeryt looked to the other Pharsi undercaptain.

"Piss-poor lager, sir, but better than the beer," replied Lhandor.

"What's in your water bottles?"

"Piss-poor lager," replied Lhandor.

"Good," said Quaeryt. "Keep your eyes open today."

"More so than usual, sir?" asked Khalis.

"Call it a feeling." Quaeryt nodded, then eased his mount forward to rejoin Vaelora near the head of the column. He was pleased that the two youngest imagers were widening their skills, and not just at his urging.

As Quaeryt and Vaelora rode away from the Stone Inn, Quaeryt could see the innkeeper and the two younger men standing just outside the stone arch over the entry, watching impassively as the column of troopers passed. Very few of the doors in the sandstone cliffs that held the rest of the town had any signboards, but many of those that did bore letters or symbols that Quaeryt did not understand, leaving him with the feeling that they had not so much as ridden through Khel but through a part of Lydar's distant past.

Just north of Sovahl, the road turned almost due west up a gently sloping dry valley that was little less than a half mille across at its base. Quaeryt saw no sign of any dwellings, nor of livestock or even of goats. Yet the stone road ran straight as a quarrel up the middle of the valley that held only sparse grass and bushes, and little enough of either.

"Tell us more about Saendeol," prompted Quaeryt. "How big is it? What are the buildings like? The land around it?"

Arion shrugged, then gestured at the stony and near-barren hillsides on each side of the valley. "The land is much like this for the next fifteen milles or so. They call it the stone desert. After that, there are pines and other trees on the heights, and there are tall grasses, good forage in places. There is a small river that runs through the long valley that holds Saendeol. There are many apricot orchards, and the brandy they make from it is well known. The traders of Jariola send ships every year to Pointe Neiman to buy kegs of it."

"What about the buildings?" asked Quaeryt. "Are they hollowed into the stone?"

"No. The oldest are built of the gray stone like the road. The newest are of sandstone, but they look the oldest."

"Are there council buildings that are also old?"

"There is only one council building. It stands on top of a round hill, and it is round as well. I do not know what lies inside."

For the next several glasses, they rode along the old stone road, as level and as well crafted as any of the Naedaran roads and showing less wear, with scarcely a crack or a fissure, through the dry hills until they came to a rise with a scattering of trees, which included bare-limbed broadleaf trees as well as the previous scattered pines and junipers. When they reached the crest of the road, Quaeryt could make out below a moderately wide valley, sprinkled with the orchards of which Arion had spoken, as well as hundreds of houses and buildings set well back from a narrow river. From the highest point on the road, Quaeryt estimated that it dropped almost two hundred yards over several milles as it angled down the comparatively gentle slopes to the base of the valley.

"There is Saendeol," said Arion.

"The houses aren't that close to the river." That was Quaeryt's first thought.

"That would not be wise. At times, the spring floods are wide and violent. The buildings are all on higher ground."

That was another confirmation of the age of Saendeol for Quaeryt.

As they rode down to the town, Quaeryt noted that, unlike most towns, the streets were straight and either parallel or perpendicular to the river, creating regular oblong blocks. The buildings all appeared roofed in gray stone or tile. It took him a half quint to locate a building that met Arion's description of the council chamber, because it was on the west side of the river, directly at the end of an avenue leading westward from the single bridge over the river. There were no other structures on the round hill, and the hill was encircled by a stone avenue as well.

Near the bottom of the incline, still a mille or so from the nearest buildings of Saendeol, a handful of riders in the green uniforms of Telaryn rode toward Quaeryt and first company. As they drew nearer, he recognized Subcommander Calkoran.

"Welcome to Saendeol," called the Pharsi officer as he reined in his mount beside Quaeryt and Vaelora. "And especially to you, Lady." His eyebrows lifted slightly.

"Lord Bhayar named her as envoy as well," said Quaeryt.

"He promoted you as well, sir, I see. Well deserved, for both of you . . . and necessary."

"Thank you."

"We're here to escort you."

"Where would you suggest we stay?" asked Quaeryt.

"There is a compound to the north of Saendeol. It once held armsmen, but it has not been much occupied in recent years. We have made it usable. The main house is in good repair. We have saved that for you and Lady Vaelora," said Calkoran. "It is to the north." He gestured, then urged his mount forward gently.

Quaeryt refrained from smiling at the smoothness with which Calkoran had moved from being surprised at Vaelora's presence to his immediately accepting her presence. "We need to talk once we're where we can discuss matters."

"Yes, sir. We do. There may be . . . some difficulties."

Calkoran's mention of difficulties suggested that matters were not about to run even close to smoothly, but Quaeryt didn't want to pursue those yet. "How was your journey here?"

"Arion told you, did he not, that we did not travel to Khelgror?"

"He did. He said that the High Council was meeting here. Do you know why they decided to do that?"

"They have not said, but we have asked, as we can, for although we are Pharsi, we wear the colors of Telaryn, and we are not trusted." There was a slight edge to the subcommander's voice before he barked a laugh. "They will not trust you, either. As Pharsi we distrust all we do not know. That is one of our curses, and few indeed are left who knew any of us."

Quaeryt had the feeling that Calkoran had almost said more, but had refrained.

The first houses they neared were built of a pinkish gray sandstone, but had bluish gray slate tile roofs. They were not particularly large, perhaps ten yards by five, but neatly kept. As they entered the town, Quaeryt could see no unoccupied buildings or houses, for the first time since they had arrived in Khel. He also noted that every street was stone-paved, although some of the side streets had sandstone paving blocks with wagon grooves worn into them. The streets and the walks flanking them were not empty, but neither were there more than a few handfuls of people visible, and only two carts and a single rider. None of them gave the Telaryn force more than a passing glance.

Quaeryt found that both surprising and puzzling.

After riding less than ten blocks into the town, Calkoran gestured to a gray stone street heading north. "That is the way to the compound."

Before long, they had left the neat stone houses behind and rode through an area with orchards on each side of the road. After about a mille, they neared an enclosure of gray stone walls two yards high.

"That is the compound."

"It looks old," said Quaeryt.

"It has been here so long as anyone can remember," replied Calkoran.

Quaeryt nodded. The fact that it was on the north side of Saendeol suggested it had been built to deal with threats from the north when Jovana had been a separate land and Saendeol its capital.

The stone paving continued through the gray stone posts that bore no gates. The only sign of a road to the north was a clay track, showing little sign of use, that diverged from the paved road some fifty yards before the posts and continued northward. Beyond the gates was a paved courtyard fifty yards on a side with two long buildings south of the paved area, and two north. A single dwelling was set on the west end of the pavement. The dwelling was stone-walled, as were all the buildings, with the same slate tile roof, but was square, with eaves that extended almost two yards, allowing the roof to cover the narrow porch that ran all the way around the building. The windows were comparatively wide, and glassed, with equally wide gray shutters, now open.

"The dwelling is for you and the lady. The second long building on the right is for your officers and men. The stables are at the end."

Quaeryt turned in the saddle. "Major Zhelan . . . you have command. Settle the mounts, men, and officers as necessary."

"Yes, sir."

Calkoran, Quaeryt, and Vaelora rode straight across the paved entry square and reined up just short of the three stone posts with bronze hitching rings.

"Just inside there is a sitting room on the right, a study on the left, then a parlor on the right and the dining chamber across from it," said Calkoran. "Both have doors to the porch. Then the kitchen and serving areas are on the left, and two sleeping chambers on the right, one large and one small." The subcommander nodded. "By your leave, sir, I will return shortly."

"Thank you."

After Calkoran rode off, Quaeryt dismounted and tied his mount. Vaelora did the same, and they walked up the three stone steps to the stone-tiled porch and inside the small entry hall, which had doors on each side, and a narrow corridor leading straight back.

Two women appeared, bowing gracefully, and speaking in Pharsi.

Despite the fact that Quaeryt spoke no Pharsi beyond a handful of phrases and that Vaelora's knowledge was most limited, in a short time they had unloaded their gear and put it in the larger bedchamber, a room some four yards by six, with a small attached bathing chamber.

"The bed looks far better than the one last night," observed Quaeryt.

"The headboard is beautiful," murmured Vaelora.

Quaeryt had to agree. The oiled wood was the color of honey, but had the feel of great age, and he had to wonder if it had once been almost white. Above a center section of plain wood was a carved scene of men and women working in an orchard picking fruit and placing it in baskets, with carts at each side. Beside the carts were neatly stacked arms—bows, arrows in quivers, and lances laid upon the grass in rows.

"A bit of symbolism, there," he observed. "A good harvest, with arms at the ready."

"The Pharsi culture?"

"From what I've seen and heard . . . most likely."

Through the open window, from which flowed a cool but not chill breeze, Quaeryt heard hoofs on the stone. "That's likely Calkoran."

A few moments later they stood in the study of the modest dwelling, where Calkoran rejoined them. Quaeryt did not sit, nor suggest that they do so.

"Before we talk about the Council . . . you have a cook and a maid here for you. It is best that the lady not eat with the men, but we have set up a mess for the troopers and officers."

"I'm a bit confused," said Quaeryt. "You didn't know that the Lady Vaelora was coming, but now you're saying that she shouldn't eat with the men."

"Not if she is to be treated as your equal as an envoy. That would indicate she is not *Eherelani*."

"*Eherelani?*"

"Of the wise women . . . the ones to be revered. They eat alone or with family or equals. They are few." Calkoran paused. "I would have suggested the same for you, sir, had you been the sole envoy."

"What can you tell us about the *Eherelani?*"

"They often have the sight . . . the visions . . . one of the High Councilors is *Eherelani*." Calkoran shrugged. "The *Eherelani* speak only to whom they wish."

Quaeryt could see he wasn't about to learn more about the wise women, not from Calkoran. "What about supplies?"

"The High Council has been kind enough to provide provisions."

"We will need to thank them." Quaeryt paused, then asked, "When should we meet with the High Council, and what should we know?"

"The High Council will meet with you tomorrow, I would think. I will make certain, but Councilor Khaliost said they would talk to you on the morning after you arrived. The others . . . I am here on sufferance." Calkoran shook his head. "They believe that Khel will never fall again, that without the Red Death it would not have happened."

"The Red Death may have caused its fall," said Quaeryt, "but how many would be left if Bhayar sent his armies into Khel?"

"The question they will not ask, sir, is whether you will lead those armies."

"I would rather it not come to that. If the armies come, there will be great destruction that I cannot prevent, and there will follow a horde of factors and traders. If the High Council agrees to terms Lord Bhayar will accept, there will be no armies, and that will leave Khel free to deal with any hordes of factors."

"Do you know that?"

"That is what he has told me. In fifteen years he has never lied to me."

"Would that other rulers could have that said." Calkoran laughed ruefully. "They will not believe you, you know?"

"That is what we fear. How many armsmen do they have here?"

"None, except for us. The people in the town have arms. All Pharsi in Khel do, but there are few men left to wield them, and not that many young women. Still, the older men and women could fight. They would not do well against armsmen, and I think they would prefer not to fight."

"Do you think they're stalling, waiting for some sort of reinforcements?"

"I would think not, but as I told you, they trust me not, and they have told me little." Calkoran snorted. "We fought and fought, first here, and then later . . . to bring down the Bovarians . . . and they will say little."

For the first time, Quaeryt could sense anger and exasperation on the subcommander's part, and he certainly couldn't blame the man. "They owe you more than they know."

Surprisingly, Calkoran shook his head. "If a Pharsi of Khel acknowledges a debt, he will do much to repay it, but no Pharsi likes to be told he owes a debt when it was not his own choice to incur it. Nor will a Pharsi trust a man who has not done as he promised, no matter why."

"What did you do?" asked Quaeryt, involuntarily, wishing he hadn't as he did, and quickly adding, "Even when you all fought to keep Kharst from conquering Khel?"

"I did my best, as I saw it, and I failed. There is no debt in failure."

"But you returned to help destroy him."

"They only grudge my presence, I tell you, Commander."

"Can I find a way to make it not so?"

Calkoran's smile was wintry. "I hope so, but I have my doubts."

"We'll think it over and talk in the morning. Seventh glass?"

"I will be here. If you need me sooner, we are in the barracks to the south." Calkoran inclined his head.

After Calkoran left, Quaeryt turned to Vaelora. "Did you notice that no one in town was interested or surprised to see us?"

"Calkoran's men have been riding through town for weeks. That might be why."

"That's possible, but it still bothers me."

"What else bothers you?"

"Calkoran being here on sufferance because he failed to stop the Bovarians."

"Pharsi can be very stiff-necked, dearest."

*I do know that.* "The other thing is that everything is too quiet. We're expected. Everything is in order."

"You think that they plan a surprise?"

"I don't think they plan an attack, but I suppose it's possible."

"Why don't you go talk to Zhelan and the undercaptains while I wash up?"

"You have a double purpose in mind."

"Of course."

"But bolt the door while I'm gone."

"I will."

Quaeryt smiled wryly as he left the bedchamber on his way to the barracks or whatever the building in which first company was quartered might have been called.

By the time Quaeryt had finished discussing matters with Zhelan, then asked the Pharsi imagers to listen to everything they could, and returned to the building that had likely been the compound commandant's quarters, Vaelora had washed and changed. He did the same, and they repaired to the parlor, graced by matching wall hangings on the interior facing walls, one showing an empty courtyard garden in spring and another depicting the same garden in fall. They had barely seated themselves in armchairs before the serving maid appeared and spoke.

"I think we're being called to dinner," said Vaelora.

They rose and followed the maid across the narrow center corridor into the dining room.

Colored hangings were centered on the end walls, finished in an off-white plaster, as was the bedchamber. The table and chairs had been crafted from the same honey-colored wood as the bedstead in the main bedchamber. Into the back of each chair was carved a tree, a different variety, Quaeryt thought, from a quick glance. Two places were set, across from each other at the end of table farthest from the curtained archway to the kitchen.

The serving maid gestured to the seats, ambiguously, and Quaeryt guided Vaelora to the one facing toward the windows, although he could not have said why, seating her before he seated himself.

The serving maid half filled the two heavy goblets with a clear liquid from a pitcher, beginning with Vaelora. Then, setting the pitcher on the table, she slipped through the curtained archway to the kitchen, returning in moments with two bowls, placing one first before Vaelora, and then the other before Quaeryt. When she finished, she inclined her head to Vaelora. After the slightest hesitation, Vaelora nodded in return, and the server retreated behind the curtain, although Quaeryt had no doubt that she was still observing them.

"You're positioning me as the superior," Vaelora said quietly. "Why?"

"I can't explain, not in a logical way. It's just a feeling."

"Like why it's better that I don't eat with the officers and men?" asked Vaelora. "I've been doing that all the time. No one said anything in Sovahl, and I was the only woman there. No one in my family ever mentioned anything about that. I've never heard of either *Eherelani* or Erlani. Not before now, I mean."

"Neither have I."

"You still haven't said why you're deferring so obviously to me."

"As I said . . . a feeling . . . and because your great-grandmere was likely an imager with the farsight who had enough power to sleep alone."

"That's not the same." Vaelora sipped the clear liquid in her goblet. "This is good."

"Better than the beer in Sovahl?"

"Much better. I can't say what it is, but it's strong." She set the goblet down.

Quaeryt sipped from his goblet. "I'd guess that it's a white ice wine of some sort."

"Are these *Eherelani* the same as the Eleni that Arion mentioned?"

"I don't know. I'll talk to him in the morning before we meet with Calkoran." He looked down at orangish liquid in the bowl. "Do you want to try the soup? I think it's soup."

"The spoons are thin . . . too thin for soup. These look like the bowls . . . you're supposed to use the bowls like cups and sip it right from them."

"Something you remember?"

Vaelora nodded, then lifted the bowl.

Quaeryt followed her example. The soup tasted like a combination of apricot and squash, a mixture that was almost too sweet for him.

Vaelora, on the other hand, was smiling when she finished her bowl. "That was good. It tastes familiar, but I can't remember . . ." She shook her head.

"Something from when you were a child?"

"Probably."

Although Quaeryt had not finished the soup, and did not intend to, as soon as she was through, the server returned and removed the bowls, then appeared with two platters, again serving Vaelora first. On the platter were parchment-thin slices of dark meat, interspersed with equally thin slices of what appeared to be cheese of some sort, both covered with a light orange-colored glaze.

After his experience with the soup, Quaeryt looked at his platter closely. Vaelora had no such trepidation, taking the angular knife and equally angular two-tined fork in hand, cutting off a section, and eating it. "You should try this, dearest. The meat is some kind of fowl, I think, a little strong, but the mixture with the cheese and the apricot glaze is quite good."

Quaeryt took a much smaller morsel than she had. While he would not have been quite so enthusiastic as his wife, he did have to admit that the combination was in fact rather tasty, and better than the goat stew of the night before. "What kind of fowl, would you think?"

"Something not too tame. The meat's rather dark."

Quaeryt took another sip of the clear ice wine, if that indeed were what it happened to be, and found that it cleared the taste of the main dish. He took another bite, and it tasted better than the first . . . or he was getting used to it. "What do you think of the house?"

"It's much better than most of the quarters we've had. The furnishings show good crafting and taste, but . . ."

"But what?"

"It's a little . . . cold . . . as if . . . well . . . as if no one really lived here."

"That could be because it's been used as guest quarters. Still, that raises another question. This dwelling has been kept up. Why? For whom? Especially if Kharst was ruling all of Khel."

"It would have to have been as quarters for guests of the High Council, then," replied Vaelora.

"That would mean that Kharst never really controlled more than the larger towns and cities, then, and there has been a shadow Pharsi government here for years, most likely for the entire time Kharst claimed Khel."

"Wouldn't that make sense?" asked Vaelora.

"It would, but it's going to make our job harder. Much harder. Unless we can get the High Council to agree to a unified system of government, Bhayar will have even more problems than Kharst did."

"Because he can't seem to be weak, but doesn't operate through fear and terror?"

Quaeryt nodded.

When Vaelora had finished eating, the server appeared and removed both platters, reappearing immediately with smaller plates. On each was a small pastry, with a flaky crust, garnished with mint leaves that had been marinated in some liquid. The dessert turned out to be honeyed pastry folded around a nut-apricot filling, and drizzled with a sweet mint syrup.

"The cook has gone to great lengths on this dinner," Quaeryt said, "as has the server."

"They don't want to offend us."

"Or you," he added.

"How much do you think they worry about what Bhayar might do?"

"They do worry, I'd guess, but they'll try to avoid committing to anything without creating more reasons for Bhayar to attack. At the very least, they'll want time to rebuild Khel."

"Once Bhayar's made a decision, he's not likely to change his mind."

"No." Quaeryt shook his head slowly. "That's something we both know."

After they finished eating, Quaeryt stood, moved to the other side of the table, and eased back Vaelora's chair as she rose. "I'd like to look at each room before we retire."

"What are you looking for?"

"If I knew," he replied, "I wouldn't have to look."

She laughed gently as they moved from the dining room back to the front sitting room, sparsely furnished with an upholstered settee, two armchairs, two side tables, and a narrow sideboard before the window. The honey-colored wood had been used for all the furniture, and for the interior window shutters. As in Sovahl, there were no curtains or hangings flanking the windows. On the single interior wall without a window or a door was another hanging, this one displaying a vineyard in harvest, with golden grapes, some in baskets, some still on the vines, but without a single person.

The front study also featured the same honey-wood furniture, but the single interior wall was comprised of floor-to-ceiling bookshelves, although there were only a few dozen volumes. Quaeryt removed several and opened them. One was written in Bovarian, the others presumably in Pharsi.

Later, as he lay in the darkness beside a sleeping Vaelora, his thoughts circled back, time and time again, to the same question.

*What are you missing?*

Quaeryt woke early on Samedi morning with at least a partial answer to the question that had plagued him the night before.

"That's it," he murmured as he sat up in the bed.

"What's it?" murmured Vaelora.

"Except for this headboard"—he gestured—"have you seen a single picture, sculpture, or carving of people since we came to Saendeol?"

Vaelora frowned, then turned to study the headboard. "You can't see any faces here."

Quaeryt turned and looked at the carving on the top of the headboard. He hadn't noticed that before, but the figures were depicted in such a way that no facial features were shown. "You're right."

"What do you think that means? That showing people's faces gives others power over them? Or that the Pharsi here in Khel feel that it's disrespectful?"

"It could be either, or something else altogether. That's another question for Arion," Quaeryt said, turning and sitting on the side of the bed. "How soon do you think breakfast will be ready?" Even as he finished speaking the words, he laughed.

"Why are you laughing?"

"That was a stupid question. Breakfast will be ready as soon as the Lady Envoy indicates that she wishes it."

"*That*, dearest, is most disrespectful." Vaelora tried to pout.

"You don't pout well," he said with a grin, standing.

"That's because . . ." She shook her head, then eased the covers aside. "If the Commander Envoy requires breakfast, I suppose the Lady Envoy should wash and dress."

Quaeryt had to admit she was far better at the arching tone of mockery than pouting.

Breakfast was indeed ready in moments from when Vaelora emerged from the bedchamber. The meal consisted of fluffy eggs cooked in a cheese mixture, a small almost crispy loaf of cinnamon-like spiced squash bread, and, of course, apricots that that had been dried, and then stewed. The beverage was a strong and unsweetened hot tea.

After eating, and more than a quint before seventh glass, wearing his best remaining uniform and jacket, Quaeryt strolled in the still-chill early winter air toward the buildings that quartered the Pharsi battalion.

Before long, he saw an officer, who stopped in his tracks, turned, and then stiffened.

"Sir? Might I help you," asked the captain in accented Bovarian.

"I was looking for Major Arion . . ."

"I think he's still in the mess, sir. I'll see, sir."

"Thank you, Stensted."

The Pharsi captain looked surprised at the use of his name, but nodded and hurried off.

In moments, Arion was walking swiftly toward Quaeryt, who waited.

"Sir, you were looking for me?"

"I was, Major. I've been thinking, and I had a question. You'd mentioned the Eleni, and last night Subcommander Calkoran mentioned the *Eherelani*. Are they the same or different, and what might be the differences?"

Arion smiled. "*They* believe that they're different. The *Eherelani* are the elder wise women who are councilors or who have been councilors. Many are said to have the sight. They are few, but they all come from towns or cities or from near such. The Eleni are what . . . you might call them the *Eherelani* of the barrens or the wild places. Some of the *Eherelani* talk with the Eleni, but most do not. Some of the Eleni are said to be very powerful." He shrugged. "So are some of the *Eherelani*. I do not know what else to say because that is what I know, and I come from the cities of the north, not from the wilds . . . or from the south."

"Would any of your men and officers know?"

"I know of none who come from the south. Those who live here . . . most keep to themselves and fewer joined the forces fighting Kharst's armsmen. Those who did and survived returned to the wilds. Most of those who served under you, sir, come from the north and the port cities on the coast."

"There's something else I noticed. There are few pictures, sculptures, or carvings of people here, and none show their faces."

Arion smiled crookedly. "That is the way of the south. It has always been like that. I cannot say why."

"Why not?"

"Because the southerners will not talk of it, except to say that images of people give power to those who control the images."

*Images or imagers? They have always worried about the power of imagers?* Quaeryt nodded. That made a kind of sense.

"Subcommander Calkoran left earlier to see when the High Council will see you and Lady Vaelora. I would expect him back in a quint or so."

"I'll be meeting with my officers, and then I'll be in the main house."

"Yes, sir. I'll let him know."

"Thank you." Quaeryt nodded and turned toward the buildings to the north, conscious of the unevenness of his steps as his boots struck the stone paving of the courtyard in behind the entry and in front of the main dwelling.

One of the rankers must have alerted Zhelan, because the major met Quaeryt even before he had reached the first door to the rear building.

"Good morning, Commander."

"Good morning. Have you noticed anything, Major?"

"No, sir . . . except that we're likely the only ones here, us and the Pharsi battalion, that is. Stables haven't been used in a while. There's cut grass for fodder, but it's a wild grass. I'd be guessing the subcommander's men have been cutting it."

"Is it all right for the horses?"

"It looks to be the same as what they've grazed along the way, except it's healthier, longer stalks . . ."

"Is there any grain?"

"Some. Not so much as I'd like, but there's also some heavier grass, set in different lofts. Most likely winter feed."

"How are the quarters?"

"They're dry and solid. They're also clean. Enough space and more to spare."

"Have you seen any sculptures, pictures, or carvings that show people's faces?"

"Sir?"

"It sounds like a strange question. Trust me; it's not."

Zhelan frowned. "Now that you mention it, sir, there's no decoration at all in the barracks here. Just bunks and straw pallets, benches and tables. That's it." He paused. "The buildings here are bigger than they look. You could put a battalion in just this one, and the men wouldn't be cramped."

*Barracks to hold a regiment dating back who knows how long?* "How are things going?"

"Fine, sir."

"The undercaptains?"

"Undercaptain Baelthm's kept them in line, not that they've tried to stray. Khalis and Lhandor have been looking at everything, though."

"I asked them to . . . and to listen as much as they could."

"Begging your pardon, sir . . ."

"I'm trying to figure how to get the Pharsi High Council to agree to Lord Bhayar's terms . . . or to come up with terms he can accept. We really don't want to fight another war here." *Especially after what you're seeing.* "But if we can't get an agreement, sooner or later, Bhayar will insist on having Khel."

"Rather not be in your boots, sir."

At the moment Quaeryt wasn't exactly pleased to be in them, either.

After spending another half quint talking to Zhelan, and then arranging for his and Vaelora's mounts to be readied, Quaeryt returned to the main dwelling, where he stood, and occasionally paced, until Calkoran finally rode through the gates less than two quints before eighth glass. The subcommander caught sight of Quaeryt and rode straight to the dwelling, where he reined up, immediately dismounted, tied his horse to one of the hitching rings, and stepped up onto the narrow porch.

"What did you find out?"

"Councilor Khaliost told me that the High Council would meet with you and Lady Vaelora, at your convenience, between eighth glass and ninth glass."

"When should we show up, then? What does it mean if we're earlier or later?"

"I could not say, sir. This is the south."

*Don't any of them know anything about the south of their own land?* Quaeryt wanted to snort, but only said, "We'll leave at eighth glass, then, and split the difference."

"Yes, sir."

The moment Calkoran rode off, Vaelora appeared, wearing a striking riding outfit of black trimmed with gray. She smiled. "I take it that we should be departing?"

"Our mounts should be here shortly."

"Do you have your credentials, such as they are?"

Quaeryt held up the leather folder he had carried across Lydar. "In here." While they waited, he told her what else he had learned.

When he finished, she looked at him. "Do you think that the southerners have taken over Khel? Calkoran never did get very far north."

"Or they want us to think they have."

"How can we tell?"

"We'll just have to do the best we can and see. We can also suggest that possibility, if indirectly, and see how they react." Quaeryt turned as two rankers led their mounts toward them. Toward the north end of the paved area, Quaeryt could see first company forming up.

The ride back to Saendeol and then to the gray stone bridge took about a quint. As they rode through the town, Quaeryt could see no pictures of people and no statues at all. In fact, he realized, none of the few signboards depicted any animals, either.

The bridge itself consisted of two stone spans, joined in the center at wide pier. The river itself was comparatively narrow, no more than fifteen yards wide, if several yards deep, its waters a deep gray-blue.

"What river is this?" Quaeryt asked Calkoran, who rode behind two outriders and just ahead of Quaeryt and Vaelora.

"The Vohan," replied the subcommander. "It flows into the Neimara north of Pointe Neiman."

As they crossed the bridge, Quaeryt studied it closely, but saw no decorations, nothing besides solid stone construction—and no marks on the stone. *Just like the buildings in Nordeau.* From the bridge they rode another half mille or so until the avenue joined the stone road that circled the hill on which the council building stood. From there they took the stone lane that gradually angled up the hill so that by the time they reached the top they were at the back of the structure, a circular building no more than thirty yards across.

From what Quaeryt had seen, there were four sets of double doors, positioned on the east, north, west, and south. Two men wearing tan trousers and jackets with brown boots and belts stood by the western doors. One of them spoke to Calkoran in Pharsi.

"You may enter by any doors but these," the subcommander relayed.

"Then we'll use the north doors," said Quaeryt, dismounting, and then offering a hand to Vaelora as she dismounted.

"The north doors would be good," said Calkoran. "Not all should come."

"No." Quaeryt turned to Zhelan and the imager undercaptains behind him. "If anything should happen . . . unfortunate . . . you are to destroy this building and everyone who does not wear a Telaryn uniform."

"Yes, sir!"

One of the Pharsi guards swallowed, suggesting he understood something of what had transpired.

Quaeryt made certain he held shields around Vaelora as they followed the circular stone walk around the side of the building to the brassbound honey-wood double doors on the north, where two more Khellan guards stood. As the three approached, each guard opened a door.

Quaeryt let Vaelora lead the way into the building if but by a half step, with Calkoran bringing up the rear.

Inside was like a stone and wooden tent, with huge long beams running from the gray stone walls to a solid circular stone pillar in the middle of the building. Narrow stone-framed windows, each a half yard wide and a yard apart, were spaced equally between the northern and southern doors on the east side of the structure. On the west side, the window ran but for half the distance. A low stone platform a half yard high extended from the northwest midpoint of the wall due south to the southwest midpoint. Centered in the middle of the platform roughly two yards back was a wooden fronted counter or desk about five yards long. Seated behind that desk were four women and a man, all in tan, with red scarves similar in shape and drape to those used by choristers of the Nameless. The man sat at the south end, but he was the one to speak.

"You may approach the High Council."

"Councilor Khaliost," murmured Calkoran from behind Quaeryt.

Quaeryt eased out the leather folder, then slipped the parchment documents from it, and nodded to Vaelora, letting her precede him just slightly, as before, toward the wide stone step in the middle of the platform, but gesturing for Calkoran to accompany them. When they reached the space before the desk, Quaeryt eased both documents onto the flat honey-wood surface, then stepped back, waiting as the documents were passed from councilor to councilor and then back to the white-haired and weathered-looking woman in the center.

The central councilor took a last look at the documents and then looked to Vaelora. "Why should we even consider treating with you?"

"Because," Vaelora replied politely, "it is in your interest to do so."

"Our interest is in being free. Agreeing to any terms with Lord Bhayar will lessen that freedom."

"You need more trade, and you need more people," said Vaelora. "Lord Bhayar will have little interest in allowing either."

"How will he stop it?"

"He will not. He will merely tariff your traders heavily for any trade with Bovaria and Telaryn, and he is not likely to restrain his traders in their dealings with your people."

The head councilor turned to Quaeryt. "You have not spoken, Commander. What have you to add?"

"I would observe that Lord Bhayar wishes to see all of Lydar under one rule so that the fighting and the wars of the past will be no more. I would also observe that because he has not completed his efforts in Bovaria, Khel is currently in a position to gain many concessions and rights that may not be possible if it insists on refusing Lord Bhayar's offers."

"May not be possible?"

"Lord Bhayar is not always patient. Those descended from the Yaran warlords are known to keep their word, for good and for worse. He would prefer not to fight in Khel, but fight he will when the time comes. You thought you suffered greatly from Rex Kharst, but Rex Kharst lost over fifty regiments to the very last man in fighting Lord Bhayar. Bhayar lost perhaps five. He does not wish to invade Khel. You do not wish him to. Those are conditions favorable to seeking an agreement."

"You are said to be the most deadly fighter and commander possessed by Lord Bhayar. You are also said to be a hand of Erion. Yet any man with white hair and a bad leg can claim to be a hand of Erion. Being white-haired and young, and even an imager, does not make that so."

"I have never claimed to be anything of Erion," Quaeryt replied. "Since we are talking of claims, neither does claiming you are a High Council with dominion over all Khel make it so."

"You doubt that? Then why are you here?"

Quaeryt smiled politely. "Because you have claimed that, and one has to start somewhere."

"If you doubt this, ask the Pharsi officer with you who I am."

Quaeryt looked to Calkoran, who was plainly shaken to be noticed.

"She is Councilor Cheliendra. She was . . . she is the head councilor of Eshtora," said Calkoran quietly. "The one on the end, the oldest man . . . as I said, he is Khaliost, and he was the head councilor from Ouestan. The woman beside him is, I think, from Ackyra."

*If they don't represent Khel, it's an impressive bluff.* "How do you know them all?" asked Quaeryt in a low voice.

"They gave me my final orders before the battle of Khelgror," murmured Calkoran dryly.

Quaeryt had suspected, but not known, that Calkoran had held much higher rank in Khel, but his reply suggested he'd been the equivalent of a marshal or submarshal. *And he never said that? Except what good would it have done, except to sound plaintive? And then for them to almost disregard him?* No wonder Calkoran had been angry! "Thank you for clarifying that, Marshal," he replied, inclining his head and keeping his voice low.

Then he turned back to face Head Councilor Cheliendra. "I am somewhat puzzled by another matter. Marshal Calkoran fought against the Bovarians at Khelgror, and he fought against them more successfully at Variana. Yet you seem dismissive of him."

"He and his troops vanished for years. Because they were not here, many suffered. Only because he returned under the protection of Lord Bhayar is he even alive. We would not wish to be seen as excessively . . . arbitrary."

"Why then," asked Vaelora, almost sweetly, "are you taking a position that will arbitrarily place you and Khel in greater danger and privation? Lord Bhayar is willing to go to great lengths to accommodate your needs."

"Is he?"

"Would he send his sister and one of his best commanders were he not?" countered Vaelora. "You cannot threaten him at present or in the future."

"Then why does he insist on governing Khel . . . if we present no threat?"

"You do present a threat," said Quaeryt, almost wearily. "You present the threat of weakness. Very great weakness. More Bovarian factors, as well as opportunists of every type, will soon descend on Khel, and you will be hard-pressed to deal with them. They will have more resources than remain to you, and they will attempt to steal or swindle everything that they can because they will see no force strong enough to stop them. In the end, you will either end up killing them or having your people killed by them. And, in the end, Lord Bhayar will end up invading Khel to keep that disorder from spreading to his lands. It would appear that you have lost too many young men and young women and that perhaps as few as four in ten people remain from those who lived in Khel before the time of the Red Death. With so few young people, times will become harder and not easier."

"And Lord Bhayar would make it so much easier by flooding our lands with outlanders?" The scorn in Cheliendra's voice was withering.

"No . . . your land will have many coming here. You cannot stop this. Neither can Lord Bhayar. He can use his power to enforce those laws that your High Council and he agree upon. He can open his lands to your traders without passage tariffs, so that they and you may profit."

"You do not show us the most attractive picture of the future, Commander."

"We are not here to deceive you. We are here to try to create the best possible course for both lands in a time of trouble."

Cheliendra's eyes fixed on Vaelora again. "Did your brother pick you merely because you are his sister and a woman?"

"My brother uses all tools necessary," replied Vaelora. "He never has been known to pick weak tools."

Cheliendra offered a hard smile, then turned to Quaeryt. "Commander . . . you rode into Saendeol with a company of men. What would it take to stop you from leaving?"

Quaeryt smiled back. "No man is the best judge of his own capabilities. I suggest you ask Marshal Calkoran . . . or any of the Pharsi officers who have served under me."

"Your reply is either of confidence or arrogance." The head councilor focused on the marshal, her voice cool, just short of mocking. "Calkoran, what would it take to stop the commander from leaving?"

Calkoran replied levelly. "I do not believe there is any power in Khel that could stop the commander."

"Even from you . . . that is a remarkable statement." Cheliendra paused. "Are you willing to consider a wager, Commander?"

"That would depend on the wager."

"Very well. We will not even make it a wager. If . . . if you and your lady . . . will walk to the top of the Hall of the Heavens by yourselves and present yourself to the Eleni who holds it, then we will consider talking further with you. If you do not wish to do so, you are welcome to leave Saendeol and Khel as you wish."

"Where is the Hall of the Heavens?" asked Quaeryt, thinking that it might well be more than a thousand milles to the north in Montaignes D'Glace.

Cheliendra laughed roughly, not quite cackling. "There is no trickery. This hall is not located on Artiema or Erion or in the far north. It is less than a half day's ride to the west. Nor will there be any legions of armsmen or raiders or the like. Just you two, the Hall of Heavens, and the keeper of the Eleni and her handful of guardians. You may take what men your require to the base of the Hall, but no farther."

"Might I ask the purpose of this condition?"

"You asked proof of who and what we are. We ask proof of who and what you are, for it is clear that what you two are will determine to what degree we can trust Lord Bhayar. Or if we can trust him at all."

*After traveling all this distance, with the fate of two lands at stake . . . they want a personal trial of some sort—just to keep talking?* Quaeryt wanted to shake his head. The brief thought of just image-killing the entire High Council crossed his mind, but he dismissed it. The Pharsi would just form another High Council and refuse any overtures at all, and there would definitely be war and death and chaos.

Quaeryt smiled politely and nodded. "As you wish."

"A guide will meet you at the compound at seventh glass tomorrow morning. You may go."

Vaelora cleared her throat. "No. We choose to go. Just as we choose, out of care and courtesy, to undertake your request. While we are gone, think very carefully upon what you will say when we return. Think very carefully."

Quaeryt could sense *something* that accompanied her words, and every single face on the Council froze for an instant, even that of Cheliendra.

Then Vaelora inclined her head, barely, and turned. Quaeryt and Calkoran followed her out from the council building. Quaeryt was more than glad that she had offered the final words. He wasn't certain he could have been so politely menacing.

As they walked back from the north doors to their mounts, Quaeryt looked to the marshal. "What can you tell me about the Hall of the Heavens?"

Calkoran shook his head. "I know little of it. It is said to be the place where Erion faced the thunderbolts of the Heavens to claim the daughter of the moon as his bride. That is the old legend. I have never been there. I do not know any who have. I have heard that few return, and all who do return come back changed."

*Namer-frigged Pharsi . . . stiff-necked idiots, when we're trying to save their land and their way of life!*

"All will be changed when we return," said Vaelora quietly and firmly. "All."

With that, Quaeryt could certainly agree.

Neither Quaeryt nor Vaelora said anything as they rode down from the council building under a sky that held a haze more like autumn than winter, although the wind was definitely on the chill side. Once they were on the avenue toward the bridge, Quaeryt directed Zhelan to take a detour through all the main streets of Saendeol, beginning with the square on the east side of the river and weaving back and forth.

"Is this so that the locals can see us?" murmured Vaelora.

"One reason. I also want to see their reaction." *And whether there are any statues of paintings of people anywhere around.*

After crossing the bridge, first company rode through the main square, immediately adjacent to the east side of the bridge, with half the square to the north of the avenue and the other half to the south. There, the few handfuls of local inhabitants frequenting the carts and vendors, of which there were less than a score, were largely gray-haired and older and looked at the Telaryn riders almost incuriously, although a few children were far more interested, but only when the adults around weren't looking at them.

Once they had ridden through both sides of the square, Zhelan led the company north on the street closest to the Vohan River, only so far as the shops extended, then south on the street east of the first. The tour of the shop areas of Saendeol took little more than a glass before they were headed north out of the small city. Quaeryt still saw no depictions of humans in any form, and while he overheard occasional comments, all were in Pharsi. He hoped that Lhandor and Khalis were listening and could remember most of what they overheard.

As they rode through the stone pillars to the compound, Quaeryt turned in the saddle. "You're looking pale. You need something to eat and drink. Go inside. I'm going to talk to Zhelan and the undercaptains. Then I'll be back and join you."

"Take whatever time you need."

"It shouldn't be that long."

Quaeryt and Vaelora eased away from the company and reined up before the main dwelling, where she dismounted and handed her mount's reins to him. Quaeryt watched until she was inside, then led her mare back toward the stables.

Once he'd dismounted and unsaddled the black gelding, he summoned the two Pharsi undercaptains, and the three of them walked ten yards from the stable doors before he stopped.

"Did either of you hear or see anything out of the usual?"

"One man said something about all of us being gone in a month," offered Lhandor.

"Another argued with him," added Khalis. "I didn't hear it all, but it was about the fact that Bhayar was part Pharsi and he had a Pharsi commander, and that meant trouble."

"Anything else?"

"A lot of muttering about our riding around." Khalis laughed.

". . . one fellow said you could tell there weren't many real Pharsi in the company, because they didn't ride that well." Lhandor looked sheepish. "So I told him there were more than he thought."

"Did he say anything to that?" asked Quaeryt.

"Something about outland Pharsi not counting."

"That figures. Did you reply to that?"

"I couldn't, sir. We'd already ridden too far past him."

"That was probably for the best," Quaeryt said wryly. "Did either of you see any statues or paintings of people?"

Both undercaptains shook their heads.

By the time Quaeryt finished with the two, Zhelan was waiting by the stable door, trying to conceal a certain irritation, Quaeryt suspected.

"I'm sorry, Major. Lhandor and Khalis are the only officers I have who speak fluent Pharsi, and I wanted to hear if they'd overheard anything before they had a chance to forget."

Zhelan's face relaxed. "Worried they'd done something wrong."

"No. Now . . . things are going to get strange tomorrow." Quaeryt went on to explain what the High Council had requested.

"They want you two to do that just to keep talking?"

"I'd prefer that to fighting another war."

"Still . . . doesn't seem right, sir. Especially for Lady Vaelora."

"She issued her own challenge to their High Council. So we're both in this together. The head councilor said we could take as many troopers as we wished, but I think we'd make a better impression with only two squads, and the undercaptains. Like it or not, this is going to be about impressions as much as numbers. Which squads would you recommend?"

"Right now, sir, second and fourth squads."

"Then second and fourth squads it is."

After going over the remainder of arrangements for Solayi with Zhelan, Quaeryt walked back to the main dwelling, where Vaelora was waiting in the parlor for him.

"There's a drink for you on the table."

Quaeryt looked at the crystal beaker, filled with a pale orange liquid. "What is it?"

"It's not bad. Try it."

While he wasn't sure about anything that shade of orange, Quaeryt settled into the armchair across from Vaelora and gingerly picked up the beaker, taking a small sip. As Vaelora had said, it wasn't bad, although the closest description Quaeryt could come up with was that the beverage was a cross between brandy and apricot beer. After another sip, Quaeryt looked to Vaelora. "You're still a little tired, aren't you?"

She nodded, setting the pale orange drink on a small table beside her.

"I thought you might be after what you did. I've been meaning to ask you . . ."

"Ask me what?"

"What you did before the Council."

"At the end? I don't know. Not exactly. Except it was almost like farsight . . . where I could see the dead and dying everywhere, all because those stupid old women couldn't see what was going to happen . . ."

"But they saw it, too."

"You didn't, did you?"

"No . . . but I felt it," he admitted.

"Good. I'm glad you didn't see what I saw." She shivered. "It was horrible."

"I've seen worse," he said quietly. "I've caused worse, I suspect. Or things equally bad."

"I know you have. That's why you didn't need to see it."

Quaeryt closed his mouth. He hadn't thought of it in that way.

"You have enough to worry about," Vaelora said. "We have to find a way to get the High Council to agree to some sort of terms."

"They don't seem terribly inclined to want to talk, at least not until we face whatever sort of trial they have in mind."

"The Eleni . . . is she some sort of imager?"

"She may be . . . or she may be able to project visions, the way you did. Or something else entirely."

"They can't be that powerful . . . or Kharst couldn't have conquered Khel."

"I'm beginning to think he didn't—just the larger towns and cities and the ports. That's why we need to work out something with them. Bhayar doesn't need to be in that situation."

"Neither do we," replied Vaelora.

"Except we already are."

"You'll figure out a way."

"We will," he affirmed. *Even if you don't have the faintest idea how you're going to do it, let alone whether the High Council is willing to be reasonable.* The Pharsi weren't always known for that. Certainly, many wouldn't have thought what Quaeryt had in mind for all the imagers of Lydar was at all reasonable.

He smiled and tried another sip from the beaker.

For all their speculations on Samedi evening and after they woke on Solayi morning, Quaeryt and Vaelora still had no real idea what might face them in or on the so-called Hall of the Heavens. They dressed, Quaeryt in uniform and Vaelora in riding clothes, ate, and then repaired to the front study until Quaeryt rose to ready their mounts.

"I could—" began Vaelora.

"Not without compromising your status. Besides, you're getting to the point that you need to be a bit more careful. We'll be riding most of the day, remember."

Vaelora made a face, and Quaeryt shook his head in return.

He returned in little more than a quint with both mounts, while Zhelan was forming up second and fourth squads. Shortly, they mounted and rode toward the formation. They had only moved into place, at the head of the column when a rider, presumably their guide, rode through the stone pillars of the compound and then reined up at the front of the column.

The slim and wiry white-haired woman in dark leathers looked at Vaelora, then at Quaeryt. She smiled, then said something.

From where he sat on his mount behind Vaelora Calkoran said quietly, "She says that it's likely to be quite a day."

"Tell her we hope it will be beneficial for both Telaryn and Khel," returned Quaeryt.

The guide's response, according to Calkoran, was, "One way or another, the skies will decide."

The guide gestured and turned her mount.

"Forward!" ordered Quaeryt.

"Forward! On the guide!" echoed Zhelan, and all the Telaryn riders began to move, with the scouts falling in directly behind the guide, followed by Quaeryt and Vaelora, Calkoran and Zhelan, the undercaptains, and then the two squads.

For the first quint, they simply retraced the path back to the hill that held the council building, but rather than taking the lane up to the building, the Pharsi guide led them along the avenue around the hill to a narrow stone road little wider than a lane that headed due west toward the higher hills. That lanelike road was paved, not with the gray stone, but with a pinkish stone that looked every bit as durable as the ancient gray stone. Quaeryt saw no wear marks or gouges, and from its appearance the stone itself could have been cut and laid within the last year, though the worn and gentled appearance of the shoulders of the road gave the lie to that.

The lane continued due west, running through apricot orchards, where the branches of the trees had been trimmed back to just short of the graveled shoulder, itself only about half a yard wide. That explained to Quaeryt, at least partly, why he hadn't noticed a straight road running due west from Saendeol, since it would have looked like a space between trees.

He couldn't help but smile at that. *Hidden in plain sight*. That raised the question of what else might be so hidden.

He turned slightly in the saddle and looked back to Calkoran. "It appears we'll be on this road for a time, and there are a few things that could use more explanation."

"You wish to know why we left Khel?" asked the former marshal.

"It might help us to understand."

"I had three regiments left after Khelgror. We fell back to the road from south Ouestan. The Bovarians brought five regiments from the coast and at least ten from Khelgror. They surrounded us. We fought. We killed almost half the Bovarians, more than eight regiments worth. It was not enough. When all was over, there were less than three battalions of Khellan troopers remaining. Those are what we took to the northern mountains."

"If that was what happened, why don't they understand?"

"Because," said Calkoran slowly, "the High Council had ordered me to disband my men and to have them go to the hills in the dead of winter and fight in small groups. We had few supplies, no golds. I was withdrawing from Khelgror and trying to get the men south and closer to the coast, where they would have a better chance to survive. I did not know that the Bovarians had used Antiagon Fire to level most of Ouestan and left that city to march toward Khel. But they moved more quickly than I had thought, and we had no choice but to fight." Calkoran sighed. "In the eyes of the Council I had disobeyed. In the eyes of the Bovarians, we were to be hunted down and destroyed for the toll we had taken." He shrugged. "We decided to cross the northern lands in winter. It took much longer than that, and many died. We did not think we would survive to see Khel again, but we decided that we should die in battle against the Bovarians."

*Now what do you do or say, for the sake of the Nameless?* "Knowing this . . . you accepted a mission back to Khel?"

Calkoran straightened in the saddle. "You risked everything and saved Khel from the Bovarians. You did it many times. You did it when you could not image, when any musket ball or shaft would have struck you dead. How could I refuse? After I had failed once, already?"

Quaeryt shook his head. So did Vaelora, if almost imperceptibly.

After they had ridden at least two milles through the bare-leafed apricot orchards, at the western edge of the valley, the road swung to the north, circling around a hill into another dryish valley filled with scattered pines and junipers that angled northwest. The road rose slightly over the next mille or so, then leveled out. With little warning, just as their guide passed a grove of junipers, she raised her arm and reined up. On the right was an open area, with a low stone wall encircling a fountain that spilled down a stone trough into a circular pool.

"She says that this is the last water," relayed Calkoran.

"Then we should water men and mounts," said Quaeryt. "Major, if you would."

"Water by squads! Second squad."

Vaelora immediately dismounted, as did Quaeryt, happy to stretch his legs. Calkoran followed.

Vaelora turned to face the former marshal. "You haven't been here before?"

"Lady, I did not even know that there was a southern council building. Until yesterday, I did not know that the Hall of the Heavens was near here."

"You had heard of it?" asked Quaeryt.

"Most in Khel have heard of it. It is where the *Eherelani* and Eleni are tested, and I knew it was somewhere in the south. There are tales that there was once another Hall in the north, but that it has been lost."

"How are they tested?" asked Vaelora.

Calkoran shook his head. "That is a secret they keep to themselves. I know only that often those who would be *Eherelani* are never heard from again."

"Hard-kept secrets," said Quaeryt.

"If you return, I would not be surprised if you would be the first outlanders to walk the Hall of the Heavens and survive."

"Probably because they haven't let any others try," said Quaeryt.

"They don't have much choice with you," added Vaelora. "They need proof that you are what everyone claims before they dare even consider any serious talks about the future of Khel."

"Proof of what we're claimed to be," corrected Quaeryt.

Vaelora offered a faint smile in return.

Calkoran looked away, nervously moistening his lips.

Once all the mounts had been watered, the guide resumed leading Quaeryt and Vaelora and their squads up the valley. With each mille that passed, the valley walls grew higher, and the valley itself narrower until it was more canyon than valley. Roughly a glass and a half later, the road turned north again, up an even narrower way with the paved road only wide enough for a single mount or possibly a small cart drawn by a single draft animal. Quaeryt rode in front of Vaelora, his shields extended slightly to cover them both.

Less than two-fifths of a mille later, the road ended in a circular space at the base of a cliff that rose to the northwest. Quaeryt judged that the cliff was not that tall, perhaps twenty or thirty yards, but an expanse of the hard, pink, granite-like stone some hundred yards wide had been smoothed and polished into a mirror-like finish. In the center of that expanse was a set of stone steps, also of the hard pink stone, that had been chiseled out of—or imaged into—the sheer cliff.

When he looked up the steps, Quaeryt could see nothing but sky.

The guide called out something.

"If you choose," said Calkoran, "you are to walk to the top and meet what awaits you."

*Who knows what lies at the top of those steps?* He turned to Vaelora. "Are you ready?"

She nodded.

They dismounted, then walked toward the guide in dark leathers, who had also dismounted and now stood near the base of the steps, which followed an angled cut up through the stone of the cliff.

Quaeryt looked at the guide, then inclined his head. She nodded.

Vaelora looked at the guide. The guide's eyes widened, and she stepped back, as if involuntarily.

"Let us begin, dearest," said Vaelora quietly.

Quaeryt did not ask what she had done, although whatever it had been had clearly terrified the guide.

The steps were neither narrow nor wide, but they could walk up side by side, although there were no handrails and the treads were cut less than calf-depth into the angled passageway up toward what was presumably the Hall of the Heavens.

Halfway up, Quaeryt squeezed Vaelora's arm. "Stop for a moment. You're breathing too hard."

"So are you."

"Why do you think I told you to stop?" He offered a grin, one that faded. "I can sense . . . something . . . but I can't tell what." He felt almost stupid saying that he could feel something, yet it was that way with imaging. So why was this different?

"There's someone up there, and they have . . . power."

Quaeryt glanced back, and wished he hadn't. While they weren't terribly high, perhaps fifteen yards, it was clear enough that if they made any serious misstep, they'd tumble all the way down—and even with shields around them, they'd break more than a few bones, and that was if they were fortunate.

Could he anchor the shields to the stone?

Surprisingly . . . he couldn't. Was that because the stone was so polished that there was no way to anchor anything? *Someone planned this to be able to deal with shields . . . at least to some degree.* That worried him, more than a little.

"Quaeryt?"

"Just a moment. I need to think."

Could he anchor shields to the entire top edge of where the stone cut holding the steps emerged, spreading them far enough to provide enough support that something couldn't push them down the steps? There was nothing else to do but try.

He concentrated.

After several moments he had the feeling that the expanse of anchoring or attempted anchoring would provide protection against moderate force—such as small boulders, arrows, and crossbow bolts . . . and perhaps a musket, but not against much more. Still, that was better than nothing.

"Are you ready?" he asked.

"I was about to ask you. What was that all about?"

"Later. I'll tell you later."

As they neared the top of the steps, Quaeryt could still see nothing but the sides of the angled passage that held the stone staircase . . . and the sky, as if they were indeed walking upward into a hall that held the heavens alone. Then, as his eyes reached the point where he could look above the sides of the stone staircase, he took a deep breath. The steps ended almost in the middle of a polished flat stone surface whose edge appeared to be an oval, cut off at the end behind them by the flat cliff through which they had climbed.

At that moment a gust of wind howled from nowhere, pressing them backward.

Quaeryt linked them to the shields, because, as he'd discovered more than a year earlier, shields by themselves provided no protection against wind. Even so, the wind ripped at their jackets and trousers.

He slowly surveyed the polished surface of what had likely once been a rocky hilltop, but saw no one and nothing. *The Eleni must have concealment shields . . . or something like them.* Just to see what might happen, Quaeryt wrapped a concealment around himself and Vaelora.

As suddenly as it had come up, the wind died down to nothing.

After several moments Quaeryt let the concealment vanish.

A huge wheel, some three yards high and two wide, appeared from nowhere, only yards away, rolling toward Quaeryt and Vaelora.

Quaeryt concentrated, then imaged it away.

Instantly a chill wind swirled ice flakes around them. As the wind died, it dispersed the light fog that had momentarily enfolded Quaeryt and Vaelora.

Before Quaeryt could consciously react, a crossbow bolt shattered on his shields, the fragments dropping and skidding across the polished stone surface.

Then the entire surface before them was filled with bleeding bodies and moaning women.

Except Quaeryt could tell that he was only seeing an image. *How do you remove an image?*

*Something* radiated from Vaelora . . . and the image vanished.

A second image appeared, this one of hundreds of hard-faced, black-eyed women in dark leathers, each with a crossbow aimed at Quaeryt and Vaelora.

That image vanished as well, and as it did, something crashed into Quaeryt's shields from the side, with enough force that it shook his body, if for a moment. He glanced around, then winced as he saw the giant bird—a sun eagle—lying crumpled on the polished stone less than five yards away to his right.

He took a step toward it, and then another, hoping it was only stunned.

"Quaeryt!"

He glanced back, and then up, only to see two more of the sun eagles circling—not above him, but above Vaelora. The last thing he wanted to do was to kill another of the magnificent birds.

Abruptly he image-projected the sense of a mighty black eagle above the two eagles about to begin their dive toward Vaelora, with absolute cruelty of a pitiless predator, and the sense that Vaelora belonged to that predator. Then he added the compulsion that the pair should return to the Eleni who directed them, although he had yet to see her anywhere.

He watched intently . . . ready to image more, if necessary, but the two slowly circled down and away from Vaelora, slowly and gracefully coming to rest on the red leather shoulder pads of the Eleni woman who appeared, seemingly from nowhere, on the polished stone some thirty yards in front of Quaeryt.

Vaelora moved up beside Quaeryt. "I've never felt anything like that. I felt like the smallest of the small."

"I didn't want to kill the other eagles. They were just going to do as they were trained. Stay close to me. We're going over to see what this was all about." First, he moved forward to the crumpled form of the eagle, hoping against hope that it was only stunned, but as he knelt he could see that it was dead. Slowly, he straightened, then continued toward the Eleni in her dark leathers and red leather gloves and belt. The black-haired huntress was older than she had looked from a distance. She watched impassively as Quaeryt and Vaelora neared, still saying nothing when they halted a yard away.

Both sun eagles looked at him, their golden eyes cold.

He met those eyes and gazed back, image radiating the power of the heavens and wings broader than the skies. In moments, both birds looked away.

"They said you claimed to be a son of Erion." The Eleni's Bovarian was heavily accented.

"I claim nothing," replied Quaeryt. "I am who I am."

"You are Pharsi from the far east of Lydar." The huntress's eyes took in Vaelora. "So are you." She studied Quaeryt. "You have the hair of a lost one, and the limp." Her eyes took in his hands. "And the fingers of a son of Erion. Do you deny that?"

"I have never claimed to be other than I am. I was orphaned as a small child and raised by the scholars of Solis."

"And the woman?"

"She is the sister of Lord Bhayar of Telaryn, and she is of the blood of the Pharsi."

"Why did you kill Athyor?"

"The first eagle? Because I did not see him in time. He struck my shields before I could do anything." Mentioning shields was a slight risk, but the Eleni had to know about shields, and that he had such.

"You are protected even from what you cannot see?"

Quaeryt nodded.

The Eleni continued to study Quaeryt, her dark eyes fixed on him as if to use her gaze as a knife.

Quaeryt waited.

"You are doubly blessed, Son of Erion . . . and triply cursed. You are blessed with powers that none will dare best and blessed by the love of a woman. You are cursed because you can only use those powers for others, unless you would destroy yourself. You are cursed because to do what you must, others will be known for what you have made possible, and you are cursed to know that all this is so."

The dark-eyed Eleni looked long at Vaelora before speaking again. "You will be the greatest of your blood in this time or any other. None will recognize that, for you have wed the lost one and share his curse and heritage. Nor will any remember your names, even though your trials will be great and your deeds will change Lydar for all time."

Quaeryt could feel the sadness that radiated from her, and that surprised him. She pitied them? Still, he had a question. *But then, you always have had questions.* "I have noticed that there are no pictures or sculptures of people. Is this because the ancient ones attempted to image beyond what should be imaged? Or is there another reason?"

A faint smile crossed the lips of the Eleni before she spoke. "It came to pass in the old times that the ability to create things from where there is nothing was not accompanied by the wisdom to understand what to create and how to create, and when not to create . . . and that doomed the folk of the old south. That is why all who image must face the Hall of the Heavens, or die, for only should those such as the Eleni or the *Eherelani* be trusted with such powers. As a hand of Erion and a farseer who have faced the Hall of the Heavens, you and the lady are like the Eleni and the *Eherelani*. You must also be respected."

"But not trusted?" asked Quaeryt, raising his eyebrows.

"You can be trusted to use your powers, but no Eleni or *Eherelani* would care to trust the outcome of the use of powers by a son of Erion. You are more than a hand of Erion, more than a lost one of legend. All may hope, but to trust is beyond reason."

"Sometimes," Quaeryt said gently, "the greatest of reason is to trust."

"If one has the wisdom to know whom to trust." She paused, but briefly. "Go as you will, for the Hall of the Heavens has judged you and found you worthy. And more." The last two words were added, in a lower voice, as if unwilled and reluctant.

"We thank you and wish you well, in keeping your heritage and ours," replied Vaelora.

After that, Quaeryt merely nodded.

When they turned and walked toward the stone staircase down from the Hall of the Heavens, Quaeryt could sense the eyes of the Eleni still upon them.

For all that the Eleni had said that he and Vaelora should be respected, Quaeryt maintained shields linked to the edge of the stone staircase until they were both standing firmly at the bottom of the steps.

The woman who had been their guide bowed, as if reluctantly, and murmured several sentences.

"You are like unto the *Eherelani*," said Calkoran. "As with them, your every act will be weighed and measured, and none will wish you close, respected as you may be."

*Not that such is any different from most of the last year—except now Vaelora's facing the same thing.* But, really, was that any different for her, either?

Quaeryt could feel all the eyes on him and Vaelora, and the questions, none of which he wanted to answer. So, to break the stillness and forestall questions, he said, "We've done what the High Council asked. We're heading back. Mount up. We've got a ways to cover."

While he wanted to ask Vaelora a question, he wasn't about to until later and he could ask without everyone looking at them and hanging on every word. Later didn't come until they were on the wider road, with a barely warm midafternoon sun at their backs. "What did you do up there . . . to break that illusion?"

Vaelora smiled, a trace shyly. "I just thought . . . a different version of those words."

While Quaeryt thought he knew, he had to ask, "Which words?"

"I will not see what is not and may never be."

"How . . . ?"

She shrugged. "It seemed right. Just as I can tell between what I'd like to see and a true farsight."

He nodded. *How many people can make that distinction?* Then he smiled.

Quaeryt decided against asking for a meeting. Instead, he dispatched Calkoran and the guide with the message that since he and Vaelora had accommodated the High Council's request, they would meet with the High Council at eighth glass on Lundi morning. Surprisingly, he and Vaelora slept reasonably well on Solayi evening.

Lundi morning dawned cold but clear, with a wind out of the northeast. Usually, Quaeryt knew, that when the wind blew out of the center of Lydar, there was less likelihood of heavy rain or snow. *Usually . . . but not always.*

Immediately after a hurried breakfast, he went to find Zhelan, who was already inspecting the stables.

"Commander, you look to be in a hurry, sir. Begging your pardon, sir, but have you heard something from the Khellans?"

"Not yet. I don't know exactly how the High Council will react, but it could be that we may want to leave Saendeol immediately after Lady Vaelora and I meet with them. Just in case, I'd like to have the men ready for a departure. It might be as early as ninth glass, and it might not happen at all today."

Zhelan raised his eyebrows, wanting to ask a question, but not wanting to presume.

Quaeryt almost smiled, but replied, "The Pharsi are stubborn. Whatever happens, they're unlikely to accept Lord Bhayar's terms immediately. I could be wrong, but we're in no position to start an attack on Khel, especially at the beginning of winter, even if we are in the south."

"You're thinking of returning to Kherseilles, sir?"

"More likely to Geusyn or elsewhere in Bovaria while the Pharsi decide. If they do accept Lord Bhayar's terms, we won't stay much longer, nor will they wish us to, I suspect."

"Yes, sir."

"What are your thoughts, Major?" Quaeryt paused and added, "Your honest thoughts," emphasizing his desire for that honesty with a touch of image projection.

"I'd be agreeing with you, sir. There's little more we can do here."

"Except kill people . . . and that won't help our mission."

"No, sir."

"We'll need just a squad as an escort to the High Council, and Undercaptain Khalis and Undercaptain Horan. I'd think we should form up at two quints before the glass."

"Very good, sir."

Quaeryt returned to the main dwelling and sat in the front study and fretted until Vaelora joined him.

"You think they'll say 'no'?" she asked.

"I don't think they'll commit to anything. If they reject Bhayar's terms, that immediately angers him. If they accept them, that will anger most Pharsi."

"So what do we do?"

"Make certain, as best we can, that they commit to eventually accepting them without saying so."

"That won't please Bhayar."

"I'm sure it won't, but I can hope he'll be a realist."

"He'll blame you, you know?"

"I'm quite aware of that," he said dryly. "I can hope that, in the end, it will work out." *So long as getting to the end doesn't take too long . . . or put me in the far north of Bovaria destroying High Holders who can't or won't accept Bhayar.*

He was glad when it was time to leave for the meeting with the High Council, if only so that they could learn where they stood . . . and, hopefully, what they could do about it.

The ride from the compound was uneventful, and there were neither significantly more or significantly fewer people along the streets or in the main square of Saendeol, although Quaeryt did notice that many wore relatively heavy coats or sweaters, and even the poorest seemed to be wearing several layers of clothing.

"Is it that cold out?" he asked Vaelora.

"It's colder than it has been, but not by that much."

Quaeryt looked to the north, but the sky remained clear, if slightly hazy.

Abruptly Vaelora laughed softly.

"What?"

"We're in the south. They're not that used to cold. It was the same way when Father moved us from Extela to Solis. I kept wondering why people in Solis were wearing coats on pleasant days."

Quaeryt hadn't even considered that, possibly because he'd grown up in Solis, but had then had to get used to the bitter cold of Tilbor.

As before, when they reached the council building, Quaeryt and Vaelora walked around to the north doors, followed by Calkoran. Neither of the guards at the doors, even as they opened them, would look directly at Quaeryt or Vaelora.

*Good or bad?* Quaeryt almost shrugged. One way or another, it didn't matter.

He remained a half step behind Vaelora when they climbed the single step and stopped before the long desk and the five councilors.

Vaelora inclined her head so slightly that the motion was barely perceptible. "As you requested, we walked the Hall of the Heavens and met with the Eleni. We have returned to request your consideration of the favorable terms offered by Lord Bhayar."

"For envoys who are requesting favorable action, you are not being especially accommodating," replied Cheliendra.

"You requested that we prove we could walk the Hall of the Heavens," said Vaelora. "We did. Our request, in turn, is that you consider the terms."

When there was no immediate response, Quaeryt spoke. "We came here to work out terms that would be beneficial to both Khel and Telaryn. Thus far, we have not demanded anything more than a meeting time. You on the other hand . . ." Quaeryt let the silence draw out. "Let us just say that for the leaders of a land facing terrible problems and the threat of worse, you appear to be behaving in a manner that does not consider realistically either the situation in which you find yourself or the benefits to be gained by working out terms with Lord Bhayar."

"You claim that we will benefit because we stand alone," said Cheliendra. "Yet Antiago is not yet a part of Telaryn. You say that you do not come to threaten. Yet is not your very presence a threat?"

Quaeryt did not reply immediately, thinking for several moments. "Is it a threat to come to a neighbor and to say there is a fire burning through the grasslands that will consume you? Is it a threat to warn of an oncoming storm? Once there were many separate lands in Lydar. Once even what is now Khel was three lands, I have heard it said, and this very city was the capital of Jovana. Those three lands did not survive, but became one. So it is becoming with Lydar. It will be one land before long. You in Khel did not regain your full freedom from Bovaria because you were strong. You regained it because Lord Bhayar destroyed Rex Kharst, and that was because he was strong, not you."

"You say that you will not use your powers, Son of Erion," asked the woman to the immediate right of Cheliendra, whose name Quaeryt did not recall, "to force Khel to agree to terms with Lord Bhayar. Then why are you here?"

"Khel cannot be forced to agree to those terms, not unless the land is laid waste and even more Pharsi are slaughtered, not unless all are frozen under the lash of a winter you have not ever seen, and should hope you will never see. Your choices are simple. You can agree to work out terms with Lord Bhayar. Or you can refuse for all time, and in time, you will see that winter and those deaths." Quaeryt knew that there was a third choice, but he wanted the High Council to suggest it.

"You have said that we stand alone, but there are others not yet a part of Telaryn," replied Cheliendra.

"The time when you will stand alone, and without allies or friends, is not that far in the future," replied Vaelora, even before Quaeryt could have said a word. "Long before Rex Kharst attacked Telaryn and brought all this to bear, the Autarch of Antiago inflicted great pain upon Lord Bhayar. Even as we traveled here, we were attacked by Antiagon ships. After such provocations, how long will Antiago stand, do you think?"

"I imagine that depends on how much Antiagon Fire the Autarch has and how strong the walls of north Antiago are," interjected the councilor to the right of Cheliendra.

She might have said more, Quaeryt thought, but for the sharp glance from the head councilor.

Cheliendra cleared her throat. "There is an old saying. 'Do not argue over what is not and what may never be.' That profits no one." She looked directly at Vaelora. "Lady Vaelora, *Eherelani* and farseer that you are, we cannot decide for our people on what might be. If and when we stand alone, there will be time to consider the terms Lord Bhayar offered. Even then, it will take time for those terms to be sent to the councils across Khel. You should understand that Khel is not ruled by the will of the High Council, but that the High Council reflects the will of the people as expressed by the local councils."

"That we do understand, Councilor," returned Vaelora. "When you send those terms to the local councils, and as I stand here, you will have to do so or face even greater devastation of your land, we would suggest that it would be the better part of wisdom to suggest that some accommodation with Lord Bhayar would be greatly more to the benefit of Khel than failure to reach such accommodation."

"And what accommodation is Lord Bhayar offering, if you might tell us."

"Refraining from invading Khel and reducing it to an even greater state of ruin than the one in which it already finds itself," replied Quaeryt. In the momentary silence that followed, he image-projected a sense of destruction and devastation, of death and despair, of famine and futility.

Even Cheliendra paled.

After another silence, she spoke. "There have been others who could impose images and feelings . . . but the most appalling aspect of those you have shown us is that they come from within you and from what you have experienced. How can you live within yourself, Son of Erion?"

*With great difficulty, at times.* Quaeryt looked at her, image-projecting absolute conviction. "Why do you think I am here? Why do you think I am almost pleading with you to accept Lord Bhayar's terms? Do you think I wish more devastation?"

"Then leave us be," offered the woman who had not yet spoken.

Quaeryt smiled bitterly. "Then I would condemn the children of today's children to the continuation of war and devastation, and the same to their children. You wish a momentary peace, but given what men are, the only lasting peace within the boundaries of Lydar that can come is when all Lydar is one land under one set of laws. Lord Bhayar would make those laws fair for all, as he has done in Tilbor and as he is doing in Bovaria."

"And you would see to that?" The words were almost mocking.

"He has no choice." Vaelora's voice was like the chill of the deepest winter, immobilizing all on the High Council as if they had been turned into pillars of ice. "And Lord Bhayar has no choice but to heed him."

Quaeryt took a step backward . . . and waited. So did Vaelora.

Several low sentences passed back and forth between the three women at the center of the Council. Then Cheliendra straightened and looked at Quaeryt and Vaelora.

"The will of the High Council is to consider Lord Bhayar's terms once Khel stands alone. In the meantime, when you leave Saendeol and the lands of Khel, you are to take with you all those men who served Lord Bhayar. The one who stands behind you is never to return to Khel, even if in the future, we reach an accord with Lord Bhayar, for that will be a part of that accord. If such an accord is agreed to, all others may return as they wish. You may remain here in Saendeol for as long as a week, or as you wish."

"We will depart shortly," replied Quaeryt. "There is little reason to impose on your hospitality now that you have heard us out. We wish for all of us that we can reach a peaceful agreement."

"Until then," added Vaelora.

Then they turned and walked from the building.

Once more, on their way out, the two guards avoided looking at either of them.

Neither Quaeryt nor Vaelora said more than pleasantries until they returned to their quarters at the compound outside Saendeol and began to gather their gear for the ride back to Kherseilles.

"Poor Calkoran," said Vaelora sadly.

"You don't think they'll ever relent?" Quaeryt couldn't help but recall when Calkoran had ridden nearly headlong into a Bovarian musket ambush to warn Quaeryt because there had been no time and no other way to convey the warning. Nor could he ignore the totally dedicated support that Calkoran and the Pharsi troopers had provided. While he understood the High Council, he truly wondered how many of them had ever seen real combat.

"No. Do you? Didn't you notice that the High Council never addressed him directly? Except one time. For them, he does not exist as a Pharsi."

"And he never will?"

"Bhayar will not jeopardize an accord over Calkoran, though he will find some other recompense."

Quaeryt noted the definite, if slight, emphasis on the word "will."

Her voice was soft as she went on. "There's always someone to blame."

"Like us . . . for failing to get the High Council to agree to Bhayar's terms?"

"Once Antiago falls, they will accept terms," said Vaelora.

"And Antiago will fall?"

"Why do you think Skarpa is in Geusyn? Do you think that Bhayar sent two full regiments with you just to treat with poor battered Khel?"

"That thought had crossed my mind, but I can't see Skarpa attacking Antiago without provocation."

"We were attacked by Antiagon ships coming here. Others may attack on our return. Aliaro has been unable not to act imprudently for any length of time."

"Is this another farsight? Like the one you won't tell me more about?"

"That one is . . . I just don't think I should tell you."

Quaeryt nodded. He understood her reasons, even if he didn't happen to be certain he agreed, but his views wouldn't change hers.

"This isn't a farsight." Vaelora laughed. "It's the result of years of quiet eavesdropping. And when Aliaro has been destroyed, the High Council will haggle. They will protest, but they will agree."

"Because they see they have no choice?" Quaeryt's tone was sardonic, yet resigned.

"No, dearest. They will accept because they have seen devastation in your eyes, and heard destruction in your voice . . . and felt the honest desperation of your not wishing to unleash it upon them."

*And they heard icy certainty from a Pharsi farseer, which may have meant much more.* But he did not say those words.

The ride back to Kherseilles took six long days, a day less than the trip to Saendeol had required, partly because Quaeryt and Vaelora had not wanted to remain in Khel any longer than necessary, and partly because Quaeryt had begun to worry even more about what was happening along the Bovarian border with Antiago.

Just after sunset on Solayi evening, first company reined up short of the harbor piers at Kherseilles. As Quaeryt had suspected, the four merchanters were long gone, and the *Montagne* and the *Solis* were tied up at opposite sides of the longest stone pier. He was about to ride out to the *Montagne* when a single rider approached.

In the growing twilight it took Quaeryt a moment after the man reined up to recognize Subcommander Khaern.

"Commander, sir. We weren't certain when you'd be back. We took the liberty of turning two of the warehouses—the ones that were not in terrible condition—into quarters. The inns here . . ." Khaern shook his head. "That will leave space on the *Montagne* for first company."

Quaeryt smiled. "I certainly don't have a problem with that, but I'll need to talk with Captain Nykaal and you. Matters aren't what we'd like, and Lady Vaelora and I need to hear what's happened here so that we can decide what to do next. In a half glass on the *Montagne?*"

"Yes, sir."

"Oh . . . and you and Subcommander Calkoran will need to work out quarters for his battalion after I spend a few moments with him."

Khaern nodded.

"Good." Quaeryt turned in the saddle. "Subcommander Calkoran . . . I'd like you to join us for the meeting on the *Montagne*. I'd also like a word with you before that . . . once we've unloaded."

"Yes, sir." Calkoran's voice remained slightly subdued, as it had been on the entire journey back from Saendeol.

Quaeryt, Vaelora, and first company then rode along the stone pier until they reached the *Montagne*. After dismounting and seeing that his and Vaelora's gear, and Vaelora, were safely aboard, Quaeryt returned to the pier to meet with Calkoran.

As he stood there and the Pharsi subcommander walked toward him in the light breeze off the water, surprisingly raw to Quaeryt, although in a sense it felt warmer than the inland winds, Quaeryt couldn't help but feel compassion for Calkoran, who had been punished far more for trying to do the right thing by his men than so many officers who'd actually done the wrong things and never been discovered. *One of the ironies of war and battle.*

"Sir?"

"How fast can your battalion make the journey from Kherseilles to Geusyn?"

"A good ten days, maybe more if the weather is bad."

"Are you willing to do that? We're going to need every man possible."

"Antiago?"

"Either Antiago or the southern High Holders, if not both."

"Sir . . . we've not spoken . . . about the future."

"No . . . we haven't. Are you willing to remain in service?"

"Yes, sir."

Quaeryt understood what lay behind those words. *What other real choice does he have?* "In time, Lord Bhayar will be properly grateful. At the moment it's a good thing we're as far from Variana as we are."

"Yes, sir. I understand."

"Lord Bhayar would prefer others see what he would call reason. I believe that will happen. It just won't happen for a while, and it's better to let time and distance separate us while events make that point rather than have to explain it in person."

The faintest smile crossed Calkoran's face before fading away.

"I'll leave the arrangements to you, but I can likely spare a hundred golds from what Lord Bhayar provided to help with supplies and other necessities. I'd like you to leave as soon as possible after we depart. We'll talk about the timing after we meet with Nykaal and Khaern." Quaeryt paused. "One other thing. What about the mounts that the Council provided?"

Calkoran snorted. "We paid for them. The Council merely allowed us to purchase them."

"Then take them with you, regardless of the Council's decree. They might make the trip easier."

"If you had not suggested that, I would have," Calkoran paused. "Sir . . . there is one other matter. I would be remiss . . ."

"Go ahead."

"There have been other sons of Erion. There was Calixen, who was drowned in a flood, and Polysses, who fell from the sky and the road of Erion. They are among those we remember. Do you know why?" Calkoran's voice was soft, almost sad.

"No."

"Because they failed. They failed because they turned from their destiny and sought glory and power for themselves. We remember those who failed. No one remembers those who were true to their destiny and did not seek glory."

Quaeryt tried not to shiver at the honest certainty in the voice of the Khellan officer. Finally, he said, "Thank you."

"You should know."

Quaeryt nodded. "Until later, then." He watched as Calkoran rode back to the foot of the long stone pier.

It was close to seventh glass when Quaeryt, Vaelora, Nykaal, Khaern, and Calkoran gathered around the circular table in the captain's stateroom on the *Montagne*. Quaeryt stood, letting the others sit. He began by summarizing the events of their journey, then concluded, "We believe that, in time, the Khellan High Council will agree to some form of agreement. If they do, there is nothing to be gained by remaining in Kherseilles. If they do not, there is also no reason to remain here, since we do not have the resources to conduct or even begin a campaign, especially given the bitter winters in the north and west of Khel." He turned to the ship's captain. "Have you received any messages from anyone?"

"No, sir."

"Have you seen any Antiagon ships?"

"I've had the pinnaces patrolling. Wouldn't have wanted anyone to come in and catch us unaware. Two or three sails . . . might have been Antiagon. They didn't come close enough to the harbor to be sure."

"How many men can you and the *Solis* transport back to Ephra—or Geusyn?"

"On a single voyage?" asked Nykaal. "Might be able to handle seven hundred. Eight hundred would be pushing it."

"How soon could you leave?"

"Tomorrow morning."

"We'll have to push it . . . twice." Quaeryt ignored the captain's frown. "We can't afford to make three trips to get first company and the regiment back to Geusyn, and Subcommander Calkoran barely has enough spare mounts for a company."

"It won't be comfortable, sir," said Nykaal.

"I understand, Captain. Believe me, I do. But I have reason to believe that Submarshal Skarpa may need as many additional regiments as possible as soon as practicable, and we will accomplish nothing by remaining here."

"As you wish, Commander."

Quaeryt could tell that Nykaal was less than pleased. "You have some concerns that you have not voiced, Captain? Is there something I should know?" Quaeryt image-projected both sincerity and concern.

"Nothing that I could put a finger on, sir." Nykaal paused. "Winds might not favor us."

"At this time of year? They're usually out of the southwest on the west of Lydar," said Quaeryt.

For just a moment, Nykaal looked surprised.

"Unless they've changed in the years since I was a quartermaster," added Quaeryt.

Again . . . there was the slightest hesitation before the captain said, "You're right. Most of the time they are, but in Ianus . . . you can't always count on it."

"We'll have to chance that, and you will have imagers for protection on the first voyage."

"That'd be true enough." Nykaal smiled. "That's a comfort. Is there anything else?"

"At what glass should we begin loading tomorrow?"

"You want an early departure. Say fourth glass."

Quaeryt looked to Khaern. "I'll need you to stay here and hold Kherseilles until the *Montagne* and *Solis* return. I've leave it to you as to which two battalions you want to embark."

"Second and fourth, sir. They'll be ready to load out at fourth glass. If you wouldn't mind . . ."

"Go. You have a lot to handle." Quaeryt smiled warmly at the subcommander.

Close to two glasses passed before Quaeryt finally finished dealing with Nykaal, giving last moment instructions to Calkoran, and going over loading plans with Nykaal and Bourlyt, the captain of the *Solis*. His eyes were twitching, and he was sore all over when he finally sat on the edge of the wide bunk of the captain's cabin and pulled off his boots.

"Is everything settled?" asked Vaelora, gently in, as usual, high Bovarian.

"As much as it can be tonight." He yawned. "It's been a long day, and tomorrow will be early." *Too early.* "Do you have any idea why Nykaal is worried?"

"I don't think he wants to head back."

"Why not?"

"It could be that it has nothing to do with him, but you."

"Someone doesn't want me back in Bovaria too soon?"

"That's only a guess."

"It can't be Skarpa."

"No . . . but it could be almost any other senior officer. Deucalon, Myskyl, or one of their commanders. Or . . . it could be that Nykaal has other reasons."

"Or he's worried about what the Antiagons might do when he returns to Ephra?" Quaeryt shook his head. "I'd doubt that."

"We'll just have to watch and see."

*As with everything else.*

Quaeryt truly had to force himself out of the wide bunk in the darkness of early Mardi morning. He did try to move quietly in dressing, but suspected he woke Vaelora anyway, although she rolled over and was sleeping once more—he thought—when he left the stateroom. While he watched the onloading of the two battalions, for the most part, he let Khaern direct the operation, and by sixth glass, Nykaal and Bourlyt had ordered the gangways pulled.

As the lines were singled up, Vaelora joined Quaeryt on the upper sterncastle deck.

"You couldn't sleep?"

"With all that noise?" She raised her eyebrows.

It hadn't seemed that loud to Quaeryt, but he supposed he was more accustomed to it . . . or not so light a sleeper as Vaelora.

"Look!" said Vaelora. "Over there."

Quaeryt turned to follow her gesture. At the foot of the piers, Telaryn-uniformed riders were forming up. It had to be Calkoran's battalion presenting a departure honor guard. "I didn't order that."

"Of course not," replied Vaelora. "Calkoran wants to show his appreciation and respect for your standing behind him and his men. How else could he do it?"

Quaeryt had to agree with that. He also hoped that, somehow, he could reward the Pharsi troopers whose bravery, skill, and support had enabled the imagers to function and improve. Without them, even more of the imagers might well have perished in the campaign to take Bovaria. *Not that it's still totally taken.*

From behind them, Nykaal issued another set of orders, and the lines were reeled in, and the two seamen vaulted aboard as the *Montagne* slowly pulled away from the pier under partial sail. As the captain ordered more sail spread, the ship moved more quickly out of the harbor. Quaeryt looked back, but Calkoran's troopers maintained their position at the foot of the pier so long as Quaeryt could see them.

Quaeryt remained on deck, watching as the *Montagne* moved out into the

Gulf and steadied on a southeast heading. He saw no other sails, but that didn't mean that the Antiagons might not send more vessels against the pair of Telaryn ships.

After a time Vaelora said quietly, "I'm getting chilled. Would you mind . . . ?"

"Of course not. I'll see you later."

She reached out and squeezed his hand, then moved to the ladder.

Perhaps a quint later Quaeryt sensed Nykaal leaving his position by the helm and crossing the deck to join Quaeryt.

"Very clean departure," said Quaeryt.

"Your men loaded well. That made it easy."

"Khaern will be here when you return. There shouldn't be any problem then, either."

"You never said much about your time at sea," offered Nykaal almost jovially, even while clearly ignoring the implications of Quaeryt's words.

"It's not something I'm terribly proud of," replied Quaeryt. "I ran away from the scholars and spent more than three years on a merchanter. It took that long for me to realize what a mistake it was." He laughed. "That's not true. I realized it was a mistake in a few months. It took me the rest of the time to admit that I'd have to go back to Solis and grovel to get back to being a scholar."

"You ever been at sea since—except for coming from Ephra?"

"I took two merchanters to Tilbor. One as far as Nacliano, the other to Tilbora . . . well, not to Tilbora. We got caught in a storm and broke up on a reef north of the Barrens . . . except it wasn't a reef, but an ancient harbor wall. A place called . . ." He struggled to remember it . . . and finally did. "The Namer's Causeway."

"You fetched up along the Shallows Coast?"

Quaeryt nodded.

"Not many do that and live to tell of it."

"I did. Later, when he came to Tilbor, Lord Bhayar cleaned out the last of the ship reavers and brigands."

"I imagine a few people were pleased with that."

Quaeryt shrugged. "The ship reavers had driven out most honest folk."

"But . . . it took Lord Bhayar . . . later . . . ?"

Quaeryt understood exactly what Nykaal wanted to ask. "I was still learning about imaging. It's very dangerous, and most imagers die young. I knew that. So I was cautious as a youth, but that meant I hadn't learned much. I learned a great deal in the year that followed."

*Because I didn't have much choice.*

"That says why many of your imager undercaptains are young, I would judge."

"Either young or older and cautious. I've kept the younger ones with me until they gain more experience."

"There are others?"

"Oh, yes," replied Quaeryt with a smile, although he decided against providing more specific details.

"I wasn't aware that there were so many imagers in Telaryn."

"There aren't that many, compared to all the people, but there are a number. The ones who are careful to hide their talents are the ones who have survived. That's why you don't see or hear of very many. Lord Bhayar decided that if he offered a reward for the safe handing over of young imagers who might otherwise have perished, they might prove useful in the war against Bovaria, and they have."

"But . . . after the war . . . would they not be . . . a danger?"

"Most imagers present as much danger as perhaps a half squad of troopers. Some present no more danger than a man with a club. A very few present greater danger." Quaeryt smiled. "But then, so does a great warship, or a great commander in battle. A good ruler is one who knows how to turn such dangers into tools to support his rule. Lord Bhayar is good at that. It's one of his talents that his enemies have often overlooked."

"I can see that." Nykaal nodded. "Good leaders often have that talent. Once had a young seaman who'd been a cat burglar. Best topsail man I ever knew."

"What happened to him?"

"Served his term and left. He's likely either wealthy or dead. That's the problem with unusual talents. They're not always used in ways that those with power appreciate."

"And even when they are, others with power may not appreciate those talents."

"I imagine that is a possibility."

"That's always a possibility." Quaeryt laughed, then added, "Those in power often have dreams above their abilities, which is why they would punish others with greater abilities, if they but could. It's even more dangerous to dream above one's abilities than to rightfully pursue one's abilities."

"Too true . . . but many might question the idea of what is rightful. Does having power make it right? We all know that being right in itself does not create power."

"You've thought long on this, I'd wager," replied Quaeryt. "I don't know that there's an answer that would suit the Nameless. I'm certain that the one that would suit the Namer is that might makes right. I would say that the more power one has, the greater the duty to use it wisely. Unhappily, the greater the power, the fewer the number of people who can place a check on that power or insist that it be used wisely. Still . . . I do know that Lord Bhayar has pondered this dilemma and that he has considered ways in which he can exercise his powers wisely. One of the problems he faces, as you must have considered, is that using power wisely is not always perceived as being in the interests of others who wish to see their power and influence grow, whether it should or not."

"Is that always not in the eye of the beholder?" Nykaal's reply was sardonic.

"Always," replied Quaeryt. "That was Rex Kharst's problem. He wished his power to be greater than it was when he scarcely was able to rule his own land. Did you know that he did not even have regional governors? Or that he entrusted tariff collections to factors and High Holders with no accounting procedures?" Quaeryt shook his head. "Lord Bhayar's rule will be a blessing to most, although I do worry about the clamor for the creation of more high holdings in Bovaria."

"Is not that why many have supported Lord Bhayar?"

"That, too, is possible," replied Quaeryt, "but one thing I have learned as a commander and a governor is that putting ambition before order is always ill-considered because nothing that is not ordered endures."

"Spoken like a scholar!"

*No . . . spoken like a realist in a world of overambitious men.* "Who else would say such?"

"You have interesting thoughts, Commander, but I should check our heading once more." Nykaal smiled and turned.

Quaeryt watched the captain walk back toward the helmsman, wondering with what opponent of Bhayar Nykaal was allied or supporting.

Although the lookouts on the *Montagne* sighted sails on a number of occasions over the next three days, those vessels either kept on course away from the two warships or immediately changed headings to avoid closing. As Quaeryt half expected, the seas in the Gulf were rougher than on the outward voyage, and at times salt spray froze on the railings and deck at night, but there had been no storms . . . so far. The rough seas had resulted in many troopers hanging over the rails at times, but the numbers had decreased by Meredi afternoon.

Nykaal had been friendly, but had refrained from any more probing questions, even though he had eaten breakfast and dinner with Quaeryt and Vaelora every day.

On Meredi evening, Quaeryt, Vaelora, and Nykaal sat around the circular table after a dinner of white gravy over biscuits and mutton, filling but little more than that. The lager that Quaeryt sipped was far better than the fare.

"Do you really think that the Khellans will agree to terms with Lord Bhayar, now that they believe themselves to be free?" asked Nykaal.

"I think they will find that being free in the circumstances in which they find themselves will leave them with little real freedom." Quaeryt sipped the lager, waiting to see where Nykaal's questions might lead.

"Will that not encourage the Bovarians who are dissatisfied with Bhayar to cross into Khel? It would seem that might make taking Khel even more difficult."

"I don't think many will try that during winter, and those that do will likely not survive. By spring, matters may well be different."

"How might that be?"

"Lord Bhayar will likely have a far firmer hand on Bovaria, and many who are dissatisfied now will be less so . . . or less of a problem by then."

"Will he not have to increase tariffs to pay for the war?"

"Not more than he already has, I would wager. He recovered much of Kharst's treasury, and since Kharst's armies were destroyed, there is no need to pay them. Bhayar's forces can be paid from what Kharst had set aside." *For the next half year, at least.*

"By your own words, then Khel has little to fear from Bovaria or Lord Bhayar in the months, or even in the years ahead."

Quaeryt glanced at Vaelora, who smiled politely, then sipped a glass of red wine. She'd scarcely drunk half a goblet all evening.

"Oh . . . Khel has much to fear," replied Quaeryt. "Lord Bhayar will do nothing to stop traders and factors from overwhelming Khel. If the Khellans resort to force or try to stop trading, then Bhayar will be forced to use force, and the Khellans will lose any possibility of favorable terms. The High Council knows this, but they must convince the people. If they do not, Lord Bhayar is in no worse a position, and does not have to fight a winter war."

"I respect your scholarly reason, Commander, but I have my doubts that the Khellan Council will think it through so reasonably."

"They don't have to, Captain," Vaelora said sweetly. "Quaeryt spelled it out quite clearly for them. They were less than pleased, but they understood."

"Understanding does not always lead to the desired results, I fear," said Nykaal.

"I could not agree with you more," said Quaeryt warmly. "That is why we have armies and warships. And why rulers trust those who pledge allegiance the most who can back their understanding with power of one sort or another. There are many with power, and more than a few with understanding, but few indeed with both." He took another sip of the lager. "This is very good. Might I ask where you got it?"

"A friend sent it to me from Tilbor actually. There's a High Holder there who brews a truly fine lager. I was fortunate to receive a keg, and able to keep it cool."

"It is excellent, even after all that travel."

"I'm glad you like it."

For the next quint or so, before Nykaal retired and left Quaeryt and Vaelora to their own devices, the conversation remained firmly on lager, wines, and other matters of cuisine and cultured dining. Even as he made various comments and observations, Quaeryt kept thinking about the lager . . . and how and where it had come to Nykaal.

Quaeryt sat at the circular table, thinking, while Vaelora prepared herself for bed, noting absently that the *Montagne*'s pitching had subsided slightly.

Suddenly Vaelora appeared at his shoulder. "Oh . . . I didn't mean to give you a start. I thought you might wish to read this, dearest. Our conversation brought this to mind." Vaelora handed *Rholan and the Nameless* to Quaeryt, a thin strip of leather marking the page.

"Thank you." Quaeryt eased from the chair and moved closer to the sole oil lamp still lit, opened the volume, and began to read.

> The problem of righteousness is that while most people wish to be perceived as righteous and comporting themselves as good people, many do not wish to make the effort or to pay the prices required. This is one reason why many come to the anomen, for there, by their presence and without words or much effort, they can proclaim their goodness. This is also why, Rholan believed, those whose faith rests on the need to be perceived as good fear and attack anything that might reveal the shallowness of their belief.
>
> He was quite candid, if in private, in revealing that he was unsure of what the Nameless might wish of him, while insisting that to act for what he believed to be good, even if others did not approve, was all that the Nameless could expect, given that the Nameless had seen fit to leave the definition of good to men and women. Moreover, because in their hearts they know they are not as good as they should be, they despise those who display themselves publicly as paragons of virtue, and rejoice when those paragons fall from grace or are shown to have hidden their true nature behind a silver mask of false virtue.

He closed the book and nodded. "Yes . . . I have had some thoughts along those lines." *Long before tonight, but tonight was just another example.*

Later, when they lay in the bunk, side by side, Vaelora murmured in Quaeryt's ear, "It's a good thing you're returning to Bovaria."

"I fear that it is." *I just hope that matters, whatever they may be, have not progressed so far that more great bloodshed cannot be avoided.* But he had strong doubts about that.

Vendrei morning had dawned overcast, and by ninth glass, the clouds that had appeared out of the west had thickened, darkened, and threatened rain. Quaeryt stood on the starboard side of the sterncastle's upper deck, studying the sea to the south, where he'd glimpsed the sails of several ships, heading westward, he thought. Even after a quint of watching, the distant sails had not moved appreciably closer, but were definitely on a westerly course.

Finally, he walked toward the helm, where Nykaal had positioned himself, because Quaeryt had seen the captain receiving reports from the lookouts. When it appeared Nykaal was not unduly occupied or concentrating, Quaeryt asked, "Can you tell me about the ships to the south . . . besides their being on a westerly course?"

"Three carrack-type merchanters. They look to be Ferran outbound from Kephria. They're riding high, and they haven't ballasted heavily enough for what little they're likely carrying. If they're carrying much of anything at all."

That the vessels were Ferran, partly empty, and outbound made sense. Antiagon traders usually carried their own goods, light and high value items such as silk and fine cottons, in their own bottoms.

"That means they were inbound heavily laden." Quaeryt frowned. "I wonder if they were carrying worked iron of some sort." There wasn't much metal-working in Antiago, and the southern half of the land, that part bordering the ocean, was rugged and hilly, with comparatively fewer people, while the east backed up to the seemingly endless Sud Swamp. Quaeryt would have been astonished if the population of Antiago amounted to a tenth part of that of even old Telaryn.

"Cannon . . . muskets . . . blades, you think?"

"It wouldn't have to be that. Just tools. The Ferrans had enough time to realize that Aliaro wouldn't be getting any more iron goods smuggled from Bovaria or from outlanders who picked up iron tools in Solis and shipped them to Estisle or Kephria. Bhayar tariffs the iron leaving Telaryn heavily, but he can't prevent foreign bottoms from sailing to Antiago."

"Not unless he wants to build a fleet," replied Nykaal.

"In time, he or Clayar may have to."

For a moment Nykaal seemed to consider Quaeryt's words, as if weighing them. "You think so?"

"Once he consolidates all Lydar, he won't need as many troopers, and the greatest threats will be to traders and shippers."

"Don't know as I'll be manning a deck when that happens."

"That's why I said Bhayar or his son. It depends on how ambitious he is and how long he rules."

Nykaal nodded. "That's true of any ruler."

"Seems to me that we're making fair progress."

"A steady following wind helps." Nykaal looked back to the west. "If the winds pick up too much more, we'll have to reef sail."

"The clouds aren't that dark. You might be fortunate and just get rain and good winds."

"Still have to keep a close eye on them." Nykaal looked back and then toward the helm.

Quaeryt took the hint and moved back toward the railing once more.

Later that afternoon, Quaeryt sat at the circular table in the captain's stateroom. Vaelora sat across from him. The clouds of the morning had thickened and darkened, and cold raindrops pelted against the glass of the portholes, and the *Montagne* continued to pitch and dip with the long regular following swells as she headed southeast.

Vaelora covered her mouth, trying not to burp. "How much longer will we be on this course?"

"Until we pass Cape Morain. Then we'll have another day or so heading northeast, maybe longer, if we head into prevailing winds out of the north."

"When we get to Geusyn, what will you write Bhayar?"

"Just what happened, and the fact that the High Council is considering his terms over the winter, and that it made little sense to remain there . . . but to return to Geusyn where we can support Submarshal Skarpa in the interim. Do you disagree with that?"

"No. That's the best we can do. What will you tell Skarpa?"

"Beyond what happened? I'll just have to see. I may not have to tell him anything. If all the border High Holders refuse to offer allegiance to Bhayar or, worse, attempt to claim allegiance to Antiago, and if Aliaro won't disown or surrender them . . ."

"Then there will be war with Antiago?"

"Do you think your brother is likely to allow High Holders to secede from Bovaria and Telaryn?"

"Not once he discovers such, but it would take more than two weeks for him to discover that and issue orders."

"He has two envoys committed to speak for him in terms of pledging allegiance to Lord Bhayar and Telaryn."

"Those credentials were meant for dealing with Khel."

"Remember what we discussed while we were still on the Great Canal . . . ?"

"You think he was thinking about rebelling High Holders?"

Quaeryt shrugged. "I have the feeling he was concerned, but he didn't want to spell that out. Why else would he have waited until the last moment to provide our credentials and hand them to us personally less than a glass before we departed?"

"He's protecting himself. If what we do goes well, he can claim he anticipated it. If not, he can say we exceeded his authority."

"I don't think it's that. He expects us to deal with any such problems, but he doesn't want anyone else to know he's delegating that much authority until afterward. Then he can claim he authorized it all along."

"Why? Because you're a scholar and an imager, and I'm a woman and his sister?"

"Something like that," Quaeryt said. "Look who surrounds him."

"That's been his choice."

"Given Telaryn and Bovaria . . . has he had that much choice?"

"Probably not," replied Vaelora grudgingly.

Quaeryt nodded.

"What aren't you saying?" Vaelora's glance at Quaeryt was not quite accusing.

"Why do you think I've tried not to be too obvious in what I've done? Well . . . ever since Extela."

"Destroying armies isn't obvious?"

"Have I done a thing to claim personal credit? Haven't I always made sure that all the imagers were considered part of what happened? Weren't they the ones most visible in improving and repairing things?"

After several moments Vaelora finally spoke. "I'm not certain you've been as unobvious as you'd like, but you certainly have avoided taking credit. That's true."

"I'd prefer to build the imagers into a stronger force so that they're considered as a power in the same way High Holders or factors are . . . so that no one will think that eliminating a strong imager or a leader will destroy their power."

"That also protects us."

"That would be my hope."

Vaelora smiled, if but in passing. Then, after several moments, she spoke. "What you said about not being obvious . . . it reminded me of something else."

"What might that be?"

"*Rholan and the Nameless.*"

"I've thought a lot about it. You know that. What are you thinking?"

"I keep wondering who wrote the book."

"It had to be someone who knew him closely."

"But who knew him that closely?" replied Vaelora. "It couldn't be family . . . or children. He didn't have any."

"So far as we know," said Quaeryt dryly.

"Do you really think he had a mistress or bastard children?"

"Probably not," conceded Quaeryt.

"The writer says he never married."

"Then it had to have been one of his followers."

"That's a problem, too. If what the writer says about him is true, he could be pretty prickly. Besides, none of the other stories about him mention any devoted followers. He had admirers, but people who were close to him?" Vaelora shook her head.

"Then who did write it?"

"I don't know . . . yet . . . but there has to be a clue somewhere in the book."

"Just like everything has clues?" he asked with a laugh, grasping the edge of the circular table as the *Montagne* abruptly pitched and rolled simultaneously.

"Not everything," she replied. "Not everything."

*Especially not everything where women are concerned.* But he only said, "That's true."

# 45

Both the rain and strong following winds continued for almost another day before both subsided. Finally, on Solayi morning, the *Montagne* and the *Solis* crept up the last few milles of the Gulf of Khellor toward Ephra under hazy skies that blocked most heat from the sun and left frost on any shaded section of the ship's decks. Quaeryt stood on the sterncastle deck in the raw cold that might have been truly bitter, even in his heavy winter riding jacket, had the wind amounted to any more than the faintest breeze. Vaelora had joined Quaeryt briefly, then retreated to the stateroom when it had become clear that the *Montagne*'s progress was slow, that there was little to see, and that Quaeryt was not the best of company.

Nykaal did not move from his post near the helm, but his head and eyes never stopped searching, even after the lookouts reported sighting no ships moored either at Ephra or Kephria.

The fact that there were no ships in the harbor at Kephria or moored offshore, combined with the sighting of vessels leaving Antiagon waters lightly loaded, or perhaps without any outbound cargoes, had Quaeryt fretting. What had happened in Geusyn? Had the local High Holders turned their forces against Skarpa? Was the Autarch backing them? Or had they retreated into Antiago? Or had something even worse occurred?

Finally, as the *Montagne* neared Ephra, Nykaal crossed the deck to where Quaeryt stood.

"Commander, how do you want to handle debarkation . . . and where?"

"What would you recommend as the fastest way to get the men to Geusyn and you on your way back to Kherseilles?"

"Those aren't quite the same objectives, Commander. It would be far faster for the *Montagne* if we moored at Ephra."

"But getting the men to Geusyn would take longer?"

Nykaal nodded.

"Then we should use the best method to get the men to Geusyn quickly."

"I thought that might be your decision, given your concerns about the High Holders and Autarch Aliaro. We can sail farther north, if we stay to the west, and we can use the pinnaces . . ."

Quaeryt listened as Nykaal explained what he proposed, essentially using the pinnaces to ferry the troopers to a point south of Geusyn and then letting the river carry the empty pinnaces back out to the *Montagne*.

By the second glass of the afternoon, the first pinnace, carrying Zhelan and most of the first squad of first company, was under sail toward the lower ferry piers of Geusyn. From what Quaeryt could tell, there were no troopers in the area, and there was no cannon fire from the northern walls of Kephria. Still . . . he worried.

The second pinnace—from the *Solis*—arrived and took second squad. More than a glass later, the first pinnace returned to the *Montagne,* this time for Quaeryt and Vaelora, the undercaptains, and half of third squad.

The River Laar was choppy, and the spray from the waves was so cold that it stung when it hit the exposed flesh. By the time Quaeryt helped Vaelora out of the pinnace at the lower ferry piers, he had the feeling that his face was reddened and almost frostbitten.

Zhelan greeted them immediately.

"As you requested, sir, I sent word to Submarshal Skarpa. He holds the River Inn as his headquarters. Your mounts are waiting up on the road. His dispatch said that he looked forward to meeting with you at your earliest convenience."

"Thank you, Major." Quaeryt smiled warmly. "As always."

"My pleasure, sir, Lady Vaelora."

When they walked off the piers and up the packed clay lane to the road, Quaeryt was pleased to see his mount, the mare that had literally carried him across Lydar from Tilbora all the way to Geusyn. She looked rested and healthy, he had to admit, as did Vaelora's gelding.

From the road Quaeryt looked south, but the tall walls of Kephria looked no different from when he had last seen them, except that most of the trees had finally lost their leaves, leaving the few pines as the sources of green in the brush immediately north of the walls.

Three quints later they reined up outside the River Inn. Once Quaeryt had Vaelora settled—in the same chamber they'd occupied previously, doubtless due to orders from Skarpa—he hurried down to find the submarshal—in the larger plaques room, with maps spread across the circular plaques table.

Skarpa gestured to one of the seats. "I got word that you'd returned. What happened?"

"About what we expected. They'll consider Bhayar's terms over the winter."

"Over the winter? The winter's almost half gone."

"Not really. You know that the snow in the north lasts well into Maris." Quaeryt let a sigh escape. "They know Bhayar doesn't want to invade Khel at the moment. They also know that in the future, if they don't agree to terms, he will. The High Council can't convince the people to agree unless a threat is more imminent. They feel that way, in any case."

"And you don't want to turn Khel into a wasteland."

"Not really. But I'll do what's necessary if I have to." *Because Bhayar won't feel safe without a unified Lydar, and if he doesn't feel safe, imagers won't ever be safe, either.*

"The Pharsi can be stiff-necked and then some."

"That worries me." Quaeryt shook his head. "What's happening here?"

"The Khellans are right about Bhayar not being able to invade Khel." Skarpa snorted. "Things aren't good here, and they're getting worse."

"I had the feeling that you might be having trouble. That's another reason why we returned. Because the merchanters left as soon as we off-loaded in Kherseilles, I had to leave Khaern and half of Eleventh Regiment in Kherseilles. After the *Montagne* and the *Solis* finish off-loading the half of the regiment they could bring, they're to head back and pick up Khaern. The Khellans banished Calkoran . . ." Quaeryt went on to brief Skarpa on the rest of the situation, but not what happened at the Hall of the Heavens. When he finished, he waited for the submarshal's reaction.

"So . . . for taking care of his men, Calkoran faces death or exile?" Skarpa shook his head. "They think Bhayar or Aliaro are going to leave them alone?"

"No . . . but they'll want to haggle for a better deal."

"That could get them a sharper blade at their throats."

"But later," Quaeryt pointed out. "Most people think that delays will result in matters getting better. Even the Pharsi."

"That's like trying to harvest fodder once the snow starts falling."

"It sounds like the High Holders here are proving a problem."

Skarpa snorted. "Does it snow in winter? Does too much lager turn a man into an idiot? Oh . . . they've all been very polite. Somehow, it's never convenient for them to receive me, and when I've appeared with a battalion, the hold is open, and no one's there, and the steward knows nothing, and the High Holder has all the keys, sir. What's worse is that the roads from Geusyn are terrible. In places, they barely exist, and every hold seems perched on a rocky summit surrounded by forests that almost might be Otelyrnan jungles. It seems like that, anyway."

"They have to have roads somewhere."

"We came across one that was slightly better. It was headed south into the Lohan Hills."

"It might go all the way into Antiago." Quaeryt fingered his chin, with his left hand, again conscious of the two immobile fingers. "Perhaps we should insist on pledges of allegiance to Bhayar and payment of token tariffs. That's what Bhayar required of the High Holders in other areas."

"I've mentioned that, but they've ignored it. They claim I don't have the authority."

Abruptly Quaeryt smiled. "I think Vaelora and I might have the answers." He eased out the leather case he'd carried all across Lydar, then extracted the credentials document. He stood and walked around the table to lay the document before Skarpa. "Read this part."

Skarpa studied the words, then frowned and said, "You're empowered to make anyone comply with terms of allegiance to Lord Bhayar of Telaryn. The only restriction is that whatever you do can't limit the existing powers and authorities of Lord Bhayar . . ." He shook his head. "The High Holders will claim . . ."

"It doesn't matter. Vaelora is Bhayar's sister, and she has the same credentials, word for word . . . and you now have seven imagers."

At that, Skarpa laughed. "So how would you recommend we proceed?"

"Send a message to the nearest High Holder, saying that a special envoy from Lord Bhayar will be visiting the hold, say at midday on Mardi, to receive the High Holder's allegiance, and that his absence, given his reluctance to meet with Lord Bhayar's dutifully appointed submarshal, will be regarded as proof of failure of allegiance."

"And what will failure of allegiance result in?" asked Skarpa.

"I'm thinking the destruction of the entire hold house and outbuildings. Bovarian High Holders don't seem all that inclined to respond to anything less than death or destruction."

"You don't think we should spell that out in the message?"

"No. Lord Bhayar shouldn't have to do that. Courtesy, respect, and allegiance shouldn't be withheld until destruction is threatened."

"But that's what you're doing . . ."

Quaeryt shook his head. "The destruction is for failure to show respect. If it goes that far, we bring down the first hold . . . and send a message to the second, just like the one to the first."

"They'll all agree after that."

"I'm not so certain about that. The accounts aren't clear, but some few functionaries indicated to Bhayar's clerks that they weren't certain that some of the southern High Holders had paid tariffs in years."

"With Bhayar's crossbowmen after them?"

"They each have small armies, no roads, forests like jungles, and Kharst really didn't have much of a governing structure away from the rivers."

"You think that they've been providing a buffer between Kharst and Aliaro?"

"It wouldn't surprise me." *But then, the way things are going, nothing would.*

"What do you think Aliaro will do? That's the question, isn't it?" Skarpa paused. "You're thinking of invading Antiago, aren't you?"

"Only if necessary, and only if it appears likely we can conquer it."

"I wasn't dispatched here for that, you know?"

"I know. You were ordered to deal with any threats raised by Aliaro and the southern High Holders. But . . . what if the only way to deal with both of those is to eliminate Aliaro?"

"Do you think it will come to that?"

"I'd be surprised if it didn't. I'd also be surprised if Bhayar would be terribly astonished. After all, you're no longer under Deucalon's command, are you?"

"No. I'm to report to Lord Bhayar directly. How did you know that?"

"I didn't. But it has to be that way if you're to be effective. Neither Deucalon nor Myskyl wants you to be too successful, and Bhayar knows that."

"You're wasted as a commander, Quaeryt."

Quaeryt shook his head. "Bhayar can't afford to recognize a scholar and an imager in a position much higher than a commander." After a moment he added, "And I can't afford to be recognized, either, especially at my age."

"You can't keep what you are a secret."

"Unfortunately not. But so long as I'm perceived to be under the control of and subordinate to officers like you, it will only make the High Holders and other senior officers uneasy, rather than having them unite in opposition to Bhayar and to me." Quaeryt managed a smile. "Shall we draft a letter?"

"I suggest that we draft letters to all five of them, setting a date for meeting the second High Holder as well, and telling the others that you and Vaelora will inform me of the dates of their meetings."

"That makes more sense," agreed Quaeryt. "Otherwise, matters will drag out."

"They will anyway."

Quaeryt nodded.

# 46

Lundi morning, Quaeryt first met with Subcommander Alazyn in the smallest of the inn's plaques rooms.

"What have you been doing?" asked Quaeryt as soon as Alazyn settled into the chair on the other side of the battered circular table.

"Having the companies ride patrols. It's been quiet. Don't think the locals have seen this many troopers ever."

"What about the High Holders? Have you seen any of their men?"

"About a week after you left, we saw a squad of riders in gold and green. They saw us and took to a path through the woods. Haven't seen anyone in a uniform since. Neither have any of the submarshal's regiments, either, even when they tried to visit some of the high holdings."

"That's what the submarshal said. It's likely things will change in the next week. I'll be doing some scouting today with first company. Now . . . give me a report on all your battalions."

"Yes, sir. First battalion . . ." Alazyn offered concise and thoughtful reports on the readiness and strength of each battalion.

When he finished, Quaeryt went to find Zhelan and to inspect first company. Then, at two quints past seventh glass, Quaeryt and the imager undercaptains, as well as first company, rode out of Geusyn with Skarpa's scouts. Less than half a mille outside the town, the rutted road they followed to the east-southeast narrowed to a clay track barely wide enough for a single wagon or two horses abreast.

Quaeryt frowned. According to the map Skarpa had provided the nearest high holding was that of one High Holder Chaelaet, and it was some three milles east of the east river road.

"Undercaptain Horan, forward."

"Yes, sir."

"I'd like you to clear the area on each side of the road, so that there's ten yards beyond each shoulder. Do it in whatever way requires the least effort on your part. Begin by clearing with a stretch some twenty yards forward of us on each side."

"Yes, sir."

Horan concentrated.

After a moment a wave of cold air swept across the front of the column, and a thin misty fog filled the air to the east. As the light breeze carried it away, Quaeryt could see that Horan's imaging had removed anything that had been growing taller than a few digits and dumped the refuse into a packed mass against the remaining trees, effectively creating a barrier nearly two yards high that extended almost thirty yards ahead.

"How do you feel?" asked Quaeryt.

"I could do a few more of those, sir."

"I'll have you alternate. That way you can do more over the day. Undercaptain Threkhyl, forward!"

Threkhyl rode forward, and as the column moved down the road, somewhat smoothed out by Horan's imaging, Quaeryt explained what he wanted done once more. Threkhyl cleared the next fifty yards, and first company moved on. Even so, it took more than a glass to clear the first half mille, and Quaeryt ordered a short break after that.

The second half mille took a good glass and a half. To clear the shoulders and smooth road for the entire three milles and the hundred-odd yards up the side road to the rough stone pillars marking the hill lane leading up to Chaelaet's hold took until well after second glass of the afternoon. That wouldn't have been possible had Quaeryt not cleared several hundred-yard stretches himself.

As the weary undercaptains rested and drank from their water bottles, Quaeryt studied the area to the east. The gray-walled hold was more like a chateau fort, sitting on the top of a narrow ridge composed mainly of light gray rock that rose some fifty yards above the surrounding forest. The walls themselves didn't seem that high, perhaps three yards, but they had been constructed at the top of a steep rocky slope a good fifty yards long that had been cleared of vegetation and soil. The hold and the outbuildings weren't that extensive, making it possible that the other imagers might be able to flatten all the structures without assistance from Quaeryt.

Although Quaeryt couldn't be certain, the lack of trees on the far side of the lower slopes of the ridge suggested that large expanses of fields and meadows lay to the east on the north side of the road. That made sense, because anyone from the west—and the River Laar—would have to pass the fortified hilltop to reach the more productive lands. The narrowness of the road and the closeness of the trees—before the imagers had changed that—would also have made any attackers on the hold vulnerable to continual assault. While a regimental-sized force could have survived such an attack, the casualties would have been significant in dealing with just one High Holder.

Quaeryt nodded. That was important, given that Skarpa had identified five High Holders within a day's ride to the east, all located just north of the border with Antiago.

Zhelan eased his mount up beside Quaeryt's mare. "The scouts have found some tracks on the road. They're not that recent, and they're all headed away from Geusyn."

"Yesterday?"

"Late yesterday, most likely."

Quaeryt nodded, his eyes still on the rocky hill and its hold.

"There's a good half mille of narrow lane up to the lower gate, sir, and the lane to the upper gate is walled."

"I thought it might be. That's why I wanted the road cleared."

"Will you have to have imagers do that for the next holding?"

Quaeryt shrugged. "I don't know. The next nearest high holding is more than ten milles from here. I suspect we'll have to do some clearing in dealing with other High Holders, but how much and when will depend on what happens tomorrow."

Zhelan studied the hill hold for a time before speaking. "That hold looks like it has never been taken."

"It probably hasn't. Rex Kharst was a sovereign in name only in parts of Bovaria. That makes matters harder for Lord Bhayar."

"Begging your pardon, sir, but it makes things harder for you, the submarshal, the undercaptains, and the troopers."

"I stand corrected, Zhelan," replied Quaeryt with a soft laugh. "But if word gets out that any group of High Holders can defy Lord Bhayar . . ."

"I understand, sir."

"For your information," Quaeryt said softly, "I'm not planning on risking troopers unless we're attacked on the road. Nor will there be an attack or a siege on fortified positions if a holder refuses allegiance to Lord Bhayar." He took a deep breath. "That may be hard on some Bovarians who are innocent, but I see no point in risking men unnecessarily."

"That was why you cleared the roadway today?"

"Yes." *And also to start building up more strength in the imagers.*

"You don't think that this Chaelaet will pledge allegiance, do you?"

"No. He'll either evade pledging, or withdraw from his hold, or close his gates and defy us to do our worst." *Not understanding what that might be.*

"There are some who will not learn."

"No," replied Quaeryt sadly, "there are some who have never had to learn until it is too late."

# 47

Early on Mardi, with sky barely graying, Quaeryt pulled on his uniform and then his boots. From the bed, covers pulled up around her shoulders, in the dim light of a single oil lamp, Vaelora watched.

"You don't like doing this, do you?" she finally asked.

"No, but the High Holders here aren't any better than Kharst was. They might be worse, and letting any of them defy Bhayar will lead to more and more trouble. Our forces are spread out, and we need to end this defiance quickly while losing as few troopers as possible."

"People will say Bhayar's worse than Kharst."

"So long as it's only High Holders who say that, your brother can live with it."

"Dearest . . . what if the High Holders here were what kept the Autarch from taking over this part of Bovaria?"

"I've thought about that, but Bhayar still can't afford to have them making trouble. Or do you think I'm wrong?"

Vaelora shook her head. "But to establish his rule . . . especially with imagers . . ."

"I know. We'll be the ones feared, especially by the High Holders. That's why we'll need a safe enclave, and a lot more imagers, when it's all over." Quaeryt offered a rueful smile. "But we're also what he needs to rule, independent of the High Holders."

"You've never liked the High Holders."

"I've liked more than a few," Quaeryt replied. "I don't like the present systems of High Holders, either in Telaryn or in Bovaria. The Khellan High Council is better, but I'd worry that something like that would eventually deteriorate into something run by factors or their equivalent."

"Why? The councilors aren't factors."

"Because the factors are the future, and they'll control more and more of trade and golds. It's already happening in Telaryn and Bovaria, in different ways. High Holders who are into trade and shipping are coming to dominate Telaryn while the wealthy factors in Bovaria control many of the towns and cities. The council system will fall to wealth. The imagers won't."

"That's only if you're successful," Vaelora pointed out.

"Then *we'd* best be successful."

"And I'd best get dressed," replied Vaelora.

"Alas . . ."

"Enough of that, you lecherous imager." But she did smile as she eased herself from the covers. "We also need to eat."

By seventh glass, the force escorting Vaelora and Quaeryt to meet with High Holder Chaelaet was assembling on the main road just to the south and east of Geusyn. Skarpa and Quaeryt had decided that a single regiment and first company were more than enough. Quaeryt hadn't wanted to bring Vaelora, but there was always the off chance that Chaelaet was more intelligent than his previous behavior suggested and that he was willing to meet with Quaeryt and Vaelora and pledge allegiance to Bhayar.

By two quints past the glass, the scouts were headed out. Quaeryt, Skarpa, and Vaelora rode behind the vanguard, a company from Sixteenth Regiment, with the imager undercaptains and first company immediately behind them.

Two quints later they arrived at the point where the imagers had widened the road and the open space. Skarpa looked at the road ahead, then at the cleared area beside it, and finally at Quaeryt. "You've had the imagers busy."

"They didn't have much to do in Khel, except drills. The track they called a road was too narrow."

"What about you?"

"Some, but not enough. I was busy yesterday as well."

"You widened it all the way to Chaelaet's holding? Why?"

"To his gateposts. As for why . . . this part of Bovaria needs better roads, both for the safety of the troopers and for the future."

"After seeing this, Chaelaet certainly won't be there now."

"He might not," replied Quaeryt, "but he's more likely to be there if he happened to be there yesterday. I suspect he left earlier."

Skarpa offered a noncommittal nod.

A glass later they reached the end of the widened road, and Skarpa called a halt.

"It looks mostly empty," observed Vaelora. "It's winter, but only a few chimneys show any sign of smoke."

"He'll have left his retainers. He may have even left defenders." Skarpa looked to Quaeryt. "Do you still want to go ahead with your plan?"

Quaeryt nodded. "We can shield a company from attack for a short while . . . long enough to withdraw. Then we'll clear the road"—*as well as anyone close to it*—"and the regiment can advance to a point below the gates. From there, the imagers can destroy the hold, wall by wall, building by building."

"I'm wagering the woods are empty." Skarpa's smile was wintry.

"I wouldn't take that wager, but here in Bovaria, who can tell? If they don't attack, we'll approach the gates. What happens after that depends on what they do."

"Or don't," replied Skarpa.

Quaeryt turned and looked at his wife.

"Be careful," murmured Vaelora.

"I will," he promised, then ordered, "First company! Forward."

Quaeryt wasn't that surprised that he and first company were not attacked on the ride up the curving road to the bridge that crossed the depression between the road and the chateau gates, a space some fifteen yards wide and roughly that deep. He was surprised that the bridge was not a drawbridge and that the chateau gates were open.

Two guards stood at the far side. They appeared to be waiting, as if they'd expected Quaeryt and his men. Between them stood a white-haired man in green and gold livery. His face was pale.

*Green and gold . . . ?* Abruptly Quaeryt nodded. Then he studied the bridge. From what he could tell, it looked solid.

"Welcome to Laetor, Submarshal. You may enter as you wish," called the older man.

"First squad," suggested Zhelan quietly.

Quaeryt nodded.

"First squad! Forward!"

Quaeryt watched as the troopers eased their mounts past him and the scouts and then across the timbered and lightly railed bridge barely wide enough for two mounts abreast or a small wagon. The bridge creaked slightly, he thought, but he could see no movement of the timbers as the troopers crossed the span.

Still maintaining shields, Quaeryt followed them, with Zhelan beside him and the remainder of first company behind him.

The white-haired man had retreated to the far side of the stone paved space inside the walls and gates, gates that did not appear to have been closed in some time. Once first company was re-formed inside the courtyard, Quaeryt rode forward, reining up short of where the speaker stood before the ironbound doors to what appeared to be the main keep.

"High Holder Chaelaet requested that I tender his regrets that he was unable to meet with you, Submarshal."

Quaeryt decided against correcting him. "Who are you?"

"Loetnyn, the assistant steward." The white-haired man offered a resigned expression.

"Where might High Holder Chaelaet be at present?"

"I could not say, sir, save that he is not anywhere in the hold or in the nearby properties."

That didn't surprise Quaeryt. "Do all the High Holder's armsmen wear green and gold?"

"Sir?"

Quaeryt waited.

"Yes, sir. They always have."

That settled another question, and it definitely made Quaeryt even less sympathetic to the absent High Holder. "How many people are in the hold at the moment?"

"I couldn't say exactly, sir. There are fifty some servants, usually, but a number are with the High Holder and his family. I could not say exactly. Perhaps a score."

"And their families?"

"Most live in the village."

"That's at the end of the walled walk and steps to the east?"

Loetnyn frowned, his eyes taking in the mounted and armed men who filled the courtyard. "Yes, sir."

"You are to pass the word that everyone—every last man, woman, and child—is to be beyond the walls of the hold in less than a glass. Anyone who remains will die. While they are leaving, you will show us the items of value suitable to be saved and given to Lord Bhayar."

Loetnyn's mouth dropped open. He swallowed without speaking. Finally, he managed a weak, "But . . . sir . . ."

"What did High Holder Chaelaet expect, steward? He has not pledged allegiance to Lord Bhayar. He will not meet with his envoys."

"He said . . . sir . . . to tell you that he expected the courtesy due any High Holder." Loetnyn swallowed.

"He has offered no courtesy and no acknowledgment of allegiance to Lord Bhayar. He can scarcely expect it in return."

"But . . ." Loetnyn appeared totally aghast, as if he could not believe what was about to happen.

"Enough," said Quaeryt quietly.

It took almost two glasses to inspect the hold and all the rooms that might have held items of value. There were few of those, fewer than Quaeryt had expected, and he had not expected many given the location of the hold. Most of Chaelaet's wealth had to lie in the lands and their harvests and possibly in timber.

There were no golds or silvers in the empty strong room. There was a magnificent harp in the holder's personal quarters and a lute almost as precious, but no clavecin anywhere, not that Quaeryt would have been able to remove it. There were several tapestries, quite an array of worked silver, mainly for dining, and, surprisingly, an antique Cloisonyt vase glazed in shimmering green . . . possibly the single most valuable object in the hold, yet it had been almost buried in a cabinet holding worn silver pitchers.

All told, it took a small wagon to hold the various treasures.

The steward kept looking at Quaeryt as if he could not believe that a minion of Lord Bhayar would so casually loot a high holding.

*You're going to be even more shocked shortly. Unfortunately.* Quaeryt turned to the assistant steward. "I do hope that everyone has left the hold."

"You aren't going to fire it, are you?"

"No." Quaeryt paused. "We're going to level it into a heap of bricks and stone."

". . . No . . ." The protest was barely murmured.

"Your master does not seem to have grasped the fact that Lord Bhayar does not brook defiance or even casual disregard."

"But . . . what of the people . . . the village?"

"We have no intention of touching either. Why do you think we gave you warning . . . and insisted on people leaving the hold?" Despite the warnings, Quaeryt had his doubts that everyone had left . . . but he'd done what he could.

Keeping Loetnyn with him, Quaeryt returned to the courtyard and gathered the imagers. "We're headed to the northern end of the hold. We'll bring down the walls and the buildings starting there."

Quaeryt watched as, numbly, Loetnyn walked beside the mare along the stone lane beside the main keep and past an overgrown space that looked to have once held gardens, with two large heaps of manure on the north end, and then between a long and moderately kept barracks across from a long stable. Quaeryt reined up in the space between the north end of the stable and barracks, where he studied the low walls and the small orchard beyond the paved area. Then he turned the saddle.

"Undercaptain Baelthm, forward."

When the oldest undercaptain rode forward, Quaeryt gestured toward the small outbuilding beneath the walls. "See what you can do to bring that down."

Baelthm looked quizzically at Quaeryt.

"Do what you can."

"Yes, sir."

Although Quaeryt was ready to help, Baelthm managed to bring the walls in and down by imaging away the keystone over the door and, Quaeryt suspected, by removing a small section of a support beam. Even so, the older imager was white and shaking when he finished.

"Good thinking. Drink something, and then eat some biscuits," said Quaeryt. "Undercaptain Khalis, forward."

"Yes, sir."

"Flatten as much of the wall as you can without totally exhausting yourself. I'd prefer that it collapse outward so that all the rubble falls over the cliffs."

Khalis nodded, then turned and concentrated.

After several moments the entire north wall, from corner tower to corner tower, a length of nearly seventy-five yards, shivered and then slowly tumbled outward, leaving only a set of massive foundation stones protruding less than half a yard above the remaining ground.

"Undercaptain Lhandor, forward." Quaeryt waited, and then ordered, "The west wall from the corner back even with the north end of the stables."

More stones crumbled and then tumbled.

Section by section, Quaeryt and the imagers retreated, leveling walls and buildings, until the entire hold had been leveled except for the main keep, a four-level stone structure, and the walls and gates to the south of it. He'd also had Baelthm remove the narrow wooden bridge that led over another deep declivity to the path winding down the east side of the rocky hill to the village. The air was far colder than it had been two glasses before, and flakes of ice dropped out of the clear sky intermittently.

"Back across the bridge and hold!" Quaeryt ordered, then waited as first company crossed.

Once the entire force had withdrawn through the gates and across the bridge to the lane down to the main road, Quaeryt and the undercaptains followed them. Quaeryt doubted that any of the undercaptains were ready for powerful imaging—but they would be again by Meredi or Jeudi, when it would be necessary once more.

That meant he'd have to bring down the main keep and the remaining walls by himself. He'd studied the keep, and seen that the south wall seemed to lean. He squared himself in the saddle, then concentrated on the main keep, on drawing whatever warmth he could from the depths beneath the largely leveled hold and visualizing a seamless circular pillar in the middle of a smooth surface where there had been rubble rising skyward, composed of all the stones from the keep and the walls.

Light flared everywhere for a moment, then vanished.

Quaeryt rocked in the saddle, his head throbbing. He could still see, and what he saw was a white column some five yards across rising a good fifty yards above the flattened paved surface where there had been a hold. Surrounding the column was a white mist that slowly began to dissipate. Then the white surface split, and shards of ice cascaded down, leaving a featureless gray circular column with a flat top dominating the hill.

The wooden bridge had vanished, but so silently that, for a moment, not even Quaeryt had noticed.

Behind Quaeryt, no one said a word.

He glanced down. Loetnyn had turned pale. He stood there shuddering.

Quaeryt looked at the assistant steward. "Your master's high holding and the lands it once held are now the possessions of Lord Bhayar. Should he be unwise enough to attempt any action against Lord Bhayar, his life will also be forfeit . . . and so will that of any man who joins him or fights for him."

"You . . . you are like the ancients returned."

"No. Unlike them, we will never rule. We only serve. And we serve those we believe to be the most just. Did we attempt to harm a single person in the hold?"

Loetnyn looked down.

"Go," said Quaeryt quietly, image-projecting authority and a sense of fairness and justice.

The assistant steward remained standing at the edge of the narrow road that ended at the bridgeless gorge. Then he turned and headed into the trees, stumbling as much as walking.

Quaeryt looked to Zhelan. "Order the company to return to the regiment."

"First company! Forward!"

Zhelan did not speak again until they had ridden more than a hundred yards down the lane, letting first company lead the way. "Do you think what you did will endear the peasants to Lord Bhayar?"

"Not at first," Quaeryt admitted.

"If this High Holder gathers his men, they will not desert him."

"Then they will die." Quaeryt sighed. "Perhaps by the second or third time, some holder's followers will understand."

"Begging your pardon, sir, but some will never understand why. They will only comply through fear."

"If that fear turns to respect, and I believe it will in time, all will be well." He paused, then asked quietly, "Do you have any suggestions for dealing with the next High Holder?"

The major did not reply for a time, then finally said, "I would that I did, sir. They are all . . . if one is charitable or kindly just, they see that as weakness. Yet they see any strength that they cannot overcome as vileness."

"I've gotten that impression. I don't want to lose troopers to make holders feel better."

"No, sir. You shouldn't." Those words were said firmly.

Compared to the High Holders of Bovaria, the Khellan High Council seemed to show the height of reasonableness, Quaeryt reflected. He rode silently, still trying to think of another strategy that would not risk troopers and imagers, given what they faced. He hadn't thought of one by the time first company rejoined the regiment.

"I take it that the noble High Holder Chaelaet was not present?" asked Skarpa when Quaeryt rejoined him.

"He left an assistant steward to tell me . . ." Quaeryt explained what had happened.

When Quaeryt finished, Skarpa nodded, a gesture that was both resigned and accepting. "It won't be this easy the next time."

"It might not be that hard with High Holder Duravyt on Vendrei. He may not have word by then."

"He will. We're probably being watched right now."

"You're likely right. But he won't have much time to set a trap in the hold, and he won't want to destroy his own hold or keep. After that . . . the possibilities are even worse," replied Quaeryt dryly. *And that will mean that we'll have to be even nastier.* Still . . . what else could they do? Requests from Bhayar hadn't resulted in pledges of allegiance. Politeness hadn't worked. Nor had a show of force.

"If the others are as stubborn as Chaelaet, all of their holds may have to be reduced or destroyed." Skarpa looked to Quaeryt, raising his eyebrows questioningly.

"I don't see any alternatives—not that won't take tens of regiments and longer than it took to get full allegiance in Tilbor. Do you?"

Skarpa shook his head. "They've been allowed to be too independent for too long. Rex Kharst was too indulgent."

And that was the pity of it all. The southern High Holders—and perhaps others far from Variana—wouldn't respect anything that was a reasonable overture, and anything that they would respect was far from reasonable.

*But hasn't it always been that way with those who have held too much power or wealth for too long?* He eased his mount back beside Vaelora.

"You didn't have any choice . . ." she murmured in a low voice.

He did not look back in the direction of the gray column dominating the flattened hilltop as they rode back toward Geusyn.

On Meredi morning Quaeryt readied himself to take first company, as well as Alazyn's Nineteenth Regiment, back out to Laetor. Once on the road below the leveled hold, he and the undercaptains would begin clearing, smoothing, and improving the narrow track that led to the next nearest hold, because he wanted to clear the road as much as possible before Jeudi, especially since there was no way to meet with High Holder Duravyt on Jeudi without covering much of the distance from Geusyn the day before.

Vaelora had started to dress when Quaeryt shook his head. "You'll be coming with Skarpa and his two regiments later today. We talked about that last night, remember? You said you were tired."

"That was last night."

Quaeryt still thought she looked tired, but saying that would only stiffen her resolve. So he waited as she continued.

"You talked about leaving early. I don't remember you saying anything about my being escorted by Skarpa."

"I thought that was clear."

"Clear? How?"

"Because we're a working party, merely improving the roads for you. You're Lord Bhayar's sister and the most important envoy. Having you with me sooner than necessary for a member of the ruling family would undermine your status in the eyes of the High Holders . . . and of the Autarch."

"Merely improving the roads?" replied Vaelora with a light sardonic tone. "And what, exactly, does the Autarch have to do with it?"

"You'll need every evidence of stature when we have to treat with him."

"If we have to treat with him, and that's unlikely, dearest."

"You think so?"

"I do . . . one way or the other."

"I would strongly prefer that you rest this morning and come with Skarpa," Quaeryt said gently.

"Since you are expressing a preference . . . and not commanding, dearest . . ." Vaelora paused meaningfully before concluding, "I will rest this morning."

"Thank you." Quaeryt tried not to sigh in relief.

"You're sweet when you're concerned," she added, "especially when you stop trying to order me around." She smiled, an expression both pleased, yet appreciative. "Not that you do all that often. But still . . ."

*Bhayar said that she could be difficult.* He'd also mentioned something about Quaeryt being difficult and the two of them deserving each other.

"I'm glad you're taking a full regiment."

He looked at her quizzically.

"If the undercaptains have to clear that much road, they'll be tired by the end of the day. So will you. You might think about sending a company ahead of the clearing . . . if you haven't already."

"Farsight . . . or prudence?" he asked.

"Prudence. You know that the only farsight flash I've had since we left Variana doesn't make much sense."

"Do you want to tell me?"

"You know how I feel about that." She shook her head. "Besides, I don't think it reflects something about to happen soon."

"Like when you saw yourself entering the Telaryn Palace years before it happened?"

"You like the thought that we were destined to be together." Vaelora smiled. "You know, the idea of destiny is a bit of a conflict for a man who doesn't believe in the Nameless. How can there be destiny without some force creating it?"

"Maybe there is a force, just not the Nameless or the Namer."

"Then . . . it's still a Nameless force."

Quaeryt couldn't argue that. "I need to be moving."

She raised an eyebrow.

He flushed, then shook his head. "I'll see you this afternoon. Skarpa is planning to ride out just before noon."

"I'll be ready."

Quaeryt stepped forward and put his arms around Vaelora, conscious as he only had been recently of the physical reminder that they would be parents. He embraced her gently, kissed her, and stepped back, taking a long look at her before turning and leaving the chamber.

Less than a glass later, wearing his winter jacket, if full open, he was riding near the front of the column headed eastward once more, with Alazyn on one side of him and Zhelan on the other. With the comparative smoothness of the imager-improved road, the ride to the gateposts that marked Laetor was far easier than it would have been otherwise, and it was only slightly after eighth glass when they reined up. Quaeryt glanced toward the gray stone column. It did look ominous against the high gray clouds that he hoped did not foreshadow a cold winter rain.

"Commander . . . ?" asked Alazyn, his voice low but firm.

"Yes?"

"Begging your pardon, sir. I know you've explained that we need to clear and widen these roads, but . . ."

"Why now when, if we have to destroy more holds, there won't be any holdings left?"

Alazyn nodded.

"Because there aren't enough imagers to be everywhere. Once we leave, regular troopers can use the roads as necessary with less fear of ambush. Also, it will allow the locals to travel and trade more. The more they do that, the sooner Bovaria and Telaryn will be truly united." *You hope.* "That will, I trust, limit the years and years of skirmishes and rebellion that occurred in both Khel and Tilbora."

"Do you think . . . ?"

"That it will be that easy?" Quaeryt snorted. "Hardly. But anything we can do now that makes things easier for those who are helpful in uniting Lydar and harder on those who aren't will cost us fewer lives in the future. Especially if we can do it without many casualties."

"I can see that," said Alazyn.

"Before we begin with the imagers, I'd like a company sent out to hold a position a half mille or so ahead of us. The imagers will be concentrating on the road, and I don't want them surprised. The troopers aren't to stand and fight anyone who attacks. If that happens, they're to withdraw and let the imager undercaptains move forward to deal with the attackers . . . or at least widen the fighting area so that the attackers can't dart back in and out of the trees and entice our troopers into that sort of skirmish."

As the black-haired subcommander rode back to instruct the regiment, Quaeryt studied the road ahead. There were more southern pines in the woods flanking the narrow road than there had been nearer the river, but the vast majority of the trees looked to be hardwoods that had lost their leaves, and that might make surprise attacks easier to spot. *You hope.*

As Quaeryt had expected, the imagers were largely rested, and by half past the first glass of the afternoon, they had cleared and smoothed the road a good three milles past the village that had served High Holder Chaelaet. Thin plumes of smoke rose perhaps two or three milles farther west, possibly from a village where they could spend the night, before resuming their efforts on Jeudi. That would require less effort on Jeudi, allowing the imagers more rest before possibly having to deal with High Holder Duravyt on Vendrei.

Then, just as Quaeryt was congratulating himself, a pair of riders galloped toward the imager undercaptains and first company.

"Hold on the imaging!" Quaeryt ordered Lhandor and Horan, who had been about to clear the next section of woods flanking the road and then to smooth and strengthen the roadbed.

"Sir! Raiders in the woods. Captain Brehalt is falling back as ordered."

Quaeryt, wincing inside, turned. "Undercaptains Voltyr and Threkhyl! Forward!" He turned to Alazyn, who had ridden up to join him when he'd seen the riders. "Which battalion?"

"Second. They're standing by."

"Undercaptains, you're to accompany second battalion, Major Vhessyn commanding."

"Yes, sir!"

"Second battalion! Forward!"

Even before Brehalt's company was within three hundred yards, second battalion met and swept around them on the narrow road.

Quaeryt and Alazyn waited for the captain to report.

When he reined up, Quaeryt nodded to the subcommander.

"What happened?" asked Alazyn.

"Arrows from the woods. We never saw more than a handful of them, but they must have loosed five score arrows," replied Brehalt. "Most missed. We've got three wounded. Don't look to be serious. Even without your orders, going into the woods would have cost us more men, and likely wouldn't have got many of them."

"Good thinking," said Alazyn.

Quaeryt nodded, but he wondered how many more attacks there might be as he looked down the narrow and winding road to the east.

*Waiting won't get any imaging done.* He cleared his throat. "Undercaptains Lhandor, Horan, stand by to resume imaging."

Less than half a glass later, with another quint of a mille clear and smoothed, and the regiment moved forward, second battalion returned.

Voltyr and the major reined up before Quaeryt and Alazyn.

"Sir," reported Voltyr, "by the time we reached where the ambush took place, the attackers were gone." He nodded to Vhessyn.

"We followed some tracks, but there were only a score," added the major. "They rode southeast along a path narrower than this road."

*Southeast?* The attackers might have come from Duravyt's hold . . . or from one farther south and east. Quaeryt couldn't immediately remember whose high holding that might be.

Although only three men had been wounded in the initial attack, none seriously, Quaeryt decided to change tactics. He turned in the saddle toward Alazyn. "You've had experience in dealing with these kinds of attacks, I suspect. What would you recommend?"

"I'd place the scouts a few hundred yards out, in plain view, set your imagers in the middle of the road just at the edge of the widened sections, with a company flanking them on each side."

That was similar to what Quaeryt had done on the way to Laetor, but he merely nodded. "Thank you. That's the way we'll do it from now on. If you'd assign your troopers . . ."

"Yes, sir."

"Undercaptains . . . stand by while the regiment re-forms."

In little more than a quint, the road imaging had resumed.

Even by the two quints past the fourth glass of the afternoon, when a trooper messenger reached Quaeryt with word that Skarpa and his regiments—and Vaelora—would reach them in less than a glass, Quaeryt and Alazyn had seen no sign of more attackers, and the village that he had glimpsed earlier in the day was in sight, less than half a mille away.

Jeudi followed the same pattern as Mardi had, with two more quick attacks on the regiments, although the imagers saw some of the attackers through the trees and brought them down with iron darts. Following that greater success in dealing with the attackers, after which the troopers found eight dead men wearing gray and black uniforms, there were no other attempts on the three regiments, and by Jeudi night Skarpa had all the regiments and the imagers bivouacked in the village less than a mille from Duravyt's high holding, a holding seemingly without activity.

Quaeryt and Vaelora shared a very small hut with Skarpa. All three were more than ready to depart on Vendrei morning—as expressed by Vaelora's parting comment as she looked back at the village from the saddle of her gelding. "There's much written about the pleasures of the simple life, but most of it was written by those who have not experienced it."

Skarpa rode toward Quaeryt and Vaelora, reining up beside them.

"The scouts report that they've still seen no one near Duravyt's hold, but there are tracks and deep ruts in the road beyond the gateposts and heading east. I've sent a company to follow them and report back what they find."

Clearing the last half mille to the hold gates was far easier than previous stretches, since there was only low brush flanking the road proper, as if Duravyt had kept the trees away from the road near the hold. Even so, when the column halted short of the two stone gateposts, the holding surprised Quaeryt, because it was far more like that of other High Holders, a small limestone palace of some age set on the top of a low rise with gardens around it, and only a low stone wall circling the bottom of the rise. The lane leading up to it was paved, and lined with trimmed evergreens of some sort. The gateposts held worked iron gates, gates that were open.

"There's no smoke at all from the chimneys," said Vaelora. "No one's there."

"Duravyt got word about what happened to Chaelaet. That's clear," said Skarpa.

"But why wouldn't he even meet with us?" asked Vaelora.

"He didn't trust Kharst," replied Quaeryt. "For that, I don't blame him, but he's avoided meeting with anyone representing Bhayar, and he's refused to reply to any written dispatches."

"He also avoided me when I rode out here," added Skarpa.

"There must be some other reason," suggested Vaelora.

Quaeryt had ideas about that, but no proof, only suspicions. "We'll find out, sooner or later."

"Either way, we won't like it," said Skarpa. "How do you want to handle this? The same way as with Chaelaet?"

"We might as well."

So Quaeryt and first company, with imagers at the ready, and carrying full shields, rode through the stone gates and up the gently sloping land toward the hold house. The only sounds were those of the riders and their mounts, the loudest of which was hooves on the stone paving. When they reined up short of the main entry, Quaeryt saw that while the windows were closed, they were not shuttered. He turned to Zhelan. "If you'd send a trooper to knock on the door."

Zhelan relayed the command, and a trooper dismounted and walked toward the door.

Just out of caution, Quaeryt extended shields to cover the man. The trooper knocked. There was no response. After several moments Quaeryt called out, "Try the door."

The trooper did, with no result.

"Stand back!" Quaeryt ordered.

When the trooper did, Quaeryt imaged away the door, then asked, "Is there anyone there?"

"Sir . . . it looks like the entire place is empty. I don't see anything at all."

"Stand by." Quaeryt turned. "Undercaptain Khalis, Voltyr . . . you're to make a quick inspection. Hold shields at all times." He looked to Zhelan. "Five troopers to accompany them, if you would."

"Yes, sir."

Less than a quint later, Voltyr, Khalis, and the others returned.

Voltyr walked back to where Quaeryt had remained mounted, watching for a possible ambush or attack.

"Sir . . . everything of value has been removed. They left older furniture and common items in the servants' quarters, but little else."

Quaeryt nodded. "Thank you. Mount up. We'll ride back down the lane a ways before we level the dwelling. Then we'll inspect the outbuildings before we reduce them."

All in all, it took less than a glass to level all the structures, all essentially empty.

As Quaeryt rode back to the gates, following the imagers and first company, he realized that to remove everything from such a hold on short notice required significant resources. *A great number of men, mounts, horses, and wagons. Did the other local High Holders assist Duravyt . . . or does he possess that capability himself?*

When he returned to Skarpa and Vaelora, he gave a quick explanation.

"We might as well push on," replied Skarpa. "If we don't give Wheltar notice, we *might* find him in his hold."

"The way matters are going, I have my doubts," said Quaeryt.

"I said *might*, Quaeryt." Skarpa looked at the level top of the rise.

Quaeryt had refrained from creating another column.

"Almost a shame to destroy the hold," added Skarpa.

"We can't play favorites, and there's no point in leaving them some place where they can return without a high cost." Even as he realized the necessity, Quaeryt hated the fact that he'd destroyed such a well-kept structure. *Yet . . . what else can you do once you've started?*

"If this keeps up," Skarpa added, "the only thing we'll have for this whole campaign is some very angry High Holders and some very good roads for the locals."

"And for Bhayar's troops and tariff collectors, since it appears likely he'll end up owning all these lands . . . at least for a time."

"Maybe he should give some of them to Myskyl," quipped Skarpa.

"In time"—*after we deal with Aliaro*—"that might not be a bad idea." Quaeryt glanced toward Vaelora, who had said nothing. She was still looking at the empty low hilltop. While he wondered what she was thinking, he did not ask. Belatedly, he realized that she had never actually seen the imagers create such destruction. She'd only seen the results after the fact.

The regiments had just covered a few hundred yards from the hold gates when Quaeryt and Skarpa saw the company sent to scout the road returning. Skarpa called a halt, and they waited for the company officer to rein up and report.

"What did you discover, Captain?" asked Skarpa.

"The wagons and the riders from here only rode a half mille east. Then they took another road south, sir. It looks to head for the gap in the hills there. The part of the east road leading to the south road is a good road. The road south is even better and much wider . . ."

*Leading right through the Lohan Hills into Antiago.*

"They must have had more than a score of wagons, and there are tracks headed both ways. Some of the wheel ruts on the shoulder are shallower. I'd guess that they must have made several trips carrying things. The border is only about two milles south of the east road. At least, there are posts there with an 'A' cut into them. The road looks even better on the other side. We didn't ride past the pillars, sir."

"Good. Anything else?" asked Skarpa.

"No, sir. We didn't see anyone. No guards or sentries."

That observation chilled Quaeryt more than anything else.

"Thank you, Captain. You and your men may return to your battalion."

"Yes, sir. Thank you, sir."

"Thank you."

After the captain had eased his mount away, Vaelora urged her mount forward, closer to Quaeryt and Skarpa. "So they retreated into Antiago. What do you think that means?" Her quick glance at Quaeryt suggested she had a point beyond the obvious with the question.

"That they know they're welcome there," said Skarpa. "Or that Aliaro can't do anything to them. Either way . . ." He paused. "But why? Kharst wasn't pressing them that much."

"Maybe he was, and maybe he couldn't do much with everything else facing him," replied Quaeryt.

"Maybe he wasn't that good a ruler," suggested Vaelora.

"I think we've already established that," replied Quaeryt. "In a way, it all makes sense. There's really no other place to trade or to obtain goods."

"What about Ephra?" Skarpa frowned.

"You haven't seen the place. It's almost fifteen milles from there to the river, and two milles across and downstream. They'd have to pay to get goods carried to and from the port . . . and Geusyn doesn't offer that much for trading. If Aliaro offers the High Holders some sort of accommodation, they can trade with the towns just south of the hills. They provide a buffer against Kharst . . . and Aliaro can always deny that he knew anything about it."

"So they're really Aliaro's High Holders as much as Bovaria's?" prompted Vaelora.

"More, from what I've seen," rejoined Skarpa gruffly. "Well . . . we might as well push on and see what we find at Wheltar's holding."

Quaeryt suspected they all knew what they'd find . . . or what they wouldn't. But they needed to prove that before he, Skarpa, and Vaelora could decide on their next steps.

Over the next week, the imagers widened roads and visited three more empty high holdings. At each holding, there were tracks and traces heading south. Quaeryt and the imagers leveled them all. When they finally returned to Geusyn, with the regiments, it was more than a week later, and Skarpa, Vaelora, and Quaeryt met once more in the small plaques room in the River Inn after dinner on Vendrei evening.

"We're almost a week into Fevier, and we're in no better position than we were a month ago. You and the imagers have destroyed five high holdings, but gained little in golds and no allegiance." Skarpa took a deep breath and then a swallow of the beaker of lager before him. "Except we can't do anything more because they've all crossed the border into Antiago. Every last one of them."

"Perhaps it's time we went into Antiago," suggested Quaeryt.

"I'd ask if you're serious, except I'm afraid you'll tell me you are."

"I am. We could send dispatches to Aliaro, but he'd just reply politely and say that he doesn't have any control over Bovarian High Holders and if they choose to visit lovely Antiago, he certainly can't stop them."

"Deucalon will claim the Autarch hasn't done anything against us," Skarpa pointed out.

"Oh . . . he hasn't. Outside of sending troopers and Antiagon Fire against us in support of Kharst. Or attacking Telaryn ships in the open Gulf. Or harboring five High Holders who failed to pay tariffs to either Kharst or Bhayar," replied Quaeryt, "and who not only failed to pledge allegiance to Bhayar, but fled rather than do so."

"He'll claim that we didn't ask Aliaro for their return."

"He probably will," admitted Quaeryt. "But Aliaro will delay answering and then admit to nothing while readying his defenses, his imagers, and his Antiagon Fire. He might even make noise about the fact that Bhayar can't even control his own High Holders. Bhayar wants control over both Antiago and Khel, and he can't get Khel unless he takes Antiago. The longer he waits, the more men and time it will cost. And Aliaro has already raised arms and ships against us when we did nothing against him."

"You're intent on invading Antiago, aren't you?"

"How many troopers did we lose and how many did Deucalon lose by following Myskyl's advice?"

"Thousands," admitted Skarpa.

"If we're successful, is Bhayar going to give Antiago back to Aliaro?" asked Quaeryt.

"After the way Aliaro treated our sister?" added Vaelora sardonically.

"And if we're not successful?"

"Doing nothing but sitting and waiting will be considered failure. Is there an alternative with Deucalon and Myskyl waiting for us to fail?"

"If we succeed, Khel will have to agree to terms," said Skarpa slowly. "We either succeed mightily . . . or fail grandly."

"Do we really have another choice?" *Given who we are?*

"How do you plan to attack Antiago?"

"Quickly . . . and without warning. There are only five major cities, and that's if we count Kephria, which might not even be a large town. We take them, except for Westisle, which we can't because it's on an island . . . and take Aliaro . . . and try to make people understand that we're not out to destroy them personally."

"That's . . ." Skarpa shook his head.

"Harder than it sounds," Quaeryt admitted. "And I could be wrong." *And you often are.* "But I can't believe Aliaro's liked all that well."

"Few rulers are. Don't you think the Khellans would agree to terms anyway?" asked Skarpa.

"In a generation or so when the land is overrun with opportunists and shady merchants . . . except it won't go on that long, because the merchants and traders will all be petitioning Bhayar to do something because the Pharsi will be either driving them out by better trading or removing them by quiet force."

"What about Khaern and the rest of Eleventh Regiment? How soon do you expect them to return?"

"It could be within the week. It could be two weeks. It depends on the winds and the sea state."

"When do you want to start this assault? Tomorrow?" asked Skarpa dryly.

"I was thinking about Solayi morning. No one attacks on Solayi. Since Aliaro won't be expecting anything so soon . . ."

"You think we can take Kephra more easily."

"That's the hope." Quaeryt frankly harbored the thought that they might not encounter serious resistance until they neared Liantiago. *You're assuming that you can even get that far with seven regiments against an entire land.*

"You realize that we're likely doomed if we don't succeed," Skarpa pointed out.

"We're likely doomed if we do nothing," replied Quaeryt. "That doom will just happen more slowly."

"Would you take your two regiments alone into Antiago?"

"I'll take all that I can, if I have to," replied Quaeryt. "I am missing half a regiment and Calkoran's battalion at the moment."

"Why?"

"Because right now is the only chance we'll have to do it right."

"You can't invade another country without killing thousands."

"Exactly," replied Quaeryt. "If we don't invade Antiago now, someone will have to invade Khel and Antiago in the next ten years, and each invasion will cost more than our doing it now."

"You don't think the three lands could live in peace?"

"They never have. Even when they were supposedly at peace, there were raids and skirmishes. Every time one land has been markedly stronger than another, there was an invasion and a consolidation. It's going to take place. The only question is when and how many lives it costs. You and Meinyt told me that one of the biggest dangers for a commander was waiting too long."

*You're twisting that a bit, but . . .*

"Meinyt's always believed that."

"Do you disagree?"

"I don't disagree with his point, but we haven't been given orders to invade Antiago."

"No . . . but we have been given orders to obtain the allegiance of the High Holders, and we can't even get a hold of them without invading Antiago. So we fail if we do nothing, and if we're to succeed we end up invading Antiago one way or the other."

"And . . ." Skarpa paused before adding, "You can't get Khel to agree to terms without Bhayar having control over Antiago. So we're both frigging screwed unless we start another war . . . and win it."

"That's the way I see it. What about you?"

Skarpa shook his head. "I'd like to find Deucalon in a dark alley and put a blade up under his ribs, but then we'd have to deal with Myskyl, and that wouldn't be any better."

"Worse, more likely."

Skarpa abruptly turned to Vaelora. "Lady . . . you've been quiet. You're Bhayar's sister and an envoy. What do you think?"

Vaelora offered a sad smile, but did not speak.

Both men waited.

Finally, she spoke. "I think that if you do your best the war will be short and bloody. If you try to be kind and merciful in battle, it will be long and bloody, and more will die."

"You sound like your father," said Skarpa.

"How could I not? I've heard what he saw. I've seen what Quaeryt has done, and how worrying about what people think always makes things worse."

Skarpa looked to Quaeryt. "The plaques are red. How do you want to proceed?"

"I'd like to scout the wall early tomorrow and meet with you when I get back. I don't think we should tell any of the regimental commanders much beyond the fact that we expect heavy fighting on Lundi. It's not as though we've got any way to scout Kephria, and even if we sent a spy . . ."

"It wouldn't do much good."

Quaeryt shook his head. *Not when you plan to bring down the wall.*

"Then I'll see you in the morning. I need to think about a few things." Skarpa paused. "I imagine you do, too." He looked to Vaelora.

She took the hint and rose from her chair. "We all do, Commander. I appreciate your thoughtful questions, and my brother will appreciate all the concerns about what is in his best interests."

"Rulers don't usually appreciate much besides success," said Skarpa as he and Quaeryt stood.

"That's why you and Quaeryt will do what you must, and why I will support and aid you both as I can."

Skarpa nodded. "Thank you, Lady."

Neither Quaeryt nor Vaelora spoke more until they had returned to their chamber.

Once Quaeryt had closed the door and slid the bolt, Vaelora looked at him. "What are you thinking this very moment, dearest?"

"About the entire future of Lydar being decided in the smallest plaques room in an old inn in a run-down town on the Laar River." He shook his head. "What about you?"

"I'm angry with the High Council of Khel. They're being stupid and shortsighted, and they should know better. I don't expect more from Aliaro."

"Especially after the way he treated Chaerila?"

"She was so sweet, and when she died giving birth to his child . . . and he remarried in less than a season and only sent a curt dispatch." She shook her head. "Khel is too weak to hold out."

"Was I too hard on Skarpa?"

"It's something you two had to talk out."

"He trusts you. That's clear."

"That's because he's a good judge of character." Vaelora smiled, briefly.

"How do you think this campaign will go?"

"No matter what you do, it will be bloody. All wars are. The shorter the fighting is, the fewer people who will die."

"And the more decisive and brutal the imagers and I will have to be."

She nodded again. "But over the years fewer will die, and others will be happier. If you survive. You must survive, or all will be for naught."

"Another farsight?"

"No . . . just an understanding of what must be."

Quaeryt walked to the window, as if to look out, before realizing that the inner shutters were still closed.

"It's dark. There's nothing to see," Vaelora said gently, walking toward the narrow table that served as a desk. "For all your words . . . you're worried."

"More than worried. I *know* that taking over Antiago will be for the best for everyone in the long run. People don't think that way."

"Dearest . . . remember what I said about Bhayar not being successful without you? This is one of those times. If he makes the decision to invade, everyone will know. It will take longer and cost more lives. If you do it . . ."

"Then he can claim brilliance if it works and blame us if it doesn't."

"You don't need to keep going over it and over it tonight."

"What would you suggest I do?"

"First . . . remember to lay out your uniforms so that I can have them all washed and fullered tomorrow."

"All of them?"

"You know what I mean." Vaelora then offered an impish smile that he knew was forced as she stepped away from the table toward him. "Read this, if you would, dearest?" She extended the copy of *Rholan and the Nameless*. "It might take your mind off what lies ahead."

Quaeryt wasn't certain that anything would, but he took the book. "It's too dark to read."

"You could light the lamp on the table."

He did by imaging it into flame, then sat on the straight-backed chair and began to read at the place where Vaelora's finger pointed.

> Among the many conflicting stories about Rholan's death was that of the man in gray who sought him on the days before he disappeared, and since the assassins of Estisle always wore gray, many speculated

> that young Hengyst had dispatched one. It is not beyond the pale to entertain that notion, but Rholan had enemies other than Hengyst, and most were far closer . . . including High Holder Doulyn of Douvyt, who had wed his half brother's widow, and who had forbid her to ever meet with Rholan. While there is no record of the two meeting, there were rumors for years, although those died away quickly when Doulyn died of "bad food" less than a month after Rholan's disappearance, especially when her only son by Doulyn became High Holder of Douvyt.

When he finished, Quaeryt looked up quizzically. "Why this passage?"

"Don't you think it's rather odd?"

"What?"

Vaelora offered an exasperated sigh. "Rholan's death, her being forbidden to meet with him, and then Doulyn's death."

"You don't think Doulyn's death was an accident at all, do you?"

"Of course not. That's not the point. The writer never mentions Thierysa's name here, but she's mentioned elsewhere. Doesn't some of what's written here seem strange?"

"Right now, everything seems strange." He closed the book and handed it back to her. "I suppose all times are strange to those trying to change them. Rholan was successful in changing some things . . . and no one really knows who he was. Except for those long dead or the few that read this book."

"I wonder if she loved him."

"She didn't marry him."

"She couldn't. Not without destroying her family. I'm fortunate."

"I'm not so certain," Quaeryt said slowly. "She couldn't marry, even if she had wanted to, and we don't know whether she did. You had to marry me so that I can make your brother ruler of all Lydar. Both of you had no choice."

"But I discovered I could love you. She didn't love Doulyn. Just the way the book is written makes that clear."

"Then we're both fortunate." Quaeryt stood.

"We are." Vaelora wrapped her arms around him, holding him close.

Quaeryt tried just to concentrate on her.

Two quints past seventh glass on Samedi morning, Quaeryt, Zhelan, the imager undercaptains—excepting Desyrk and Smaelthyl, who still remained with Meinyt in Laaryn—and a company from Nineteenth Regiment, led by Captain Maasn, reined up on the rutted and now disused section of road that had once led to Kephria, some two hundred yards north of the massive stone wall that ran from the rugged hills more than a mille east of the river, right to the edge of the water. Where the land wall and the shore wall met was a low square tower. The river's waters lapped against the section of that sheer gray stone wall that ran a good half mille downstream from the tower before turning westward, where it extended some fifty yards out into the water, ending with a larger square stone tower that rose another five yards above the wall. For all its considerable length the top of the stone wall was uniformly ten yards above the road or the water. There were no gates or breaks in the stone, none that Quaeryt could see, at least.

As before, Quaeryt saw no sentries. He glanced from the wall to the chest-high brush between the road and the water at the odd assortment of buildings and roofs to the south on the far side of the river. Ephra still looked like a poor location for a port, and not a single ship was visible in its harbor. Even the piers used by the ferries returning to Geusyn were empty, although, Quaeryt supposed, that was to be expected in late morning.

Quaeryt turned to Zhelan. "Your thoughts, Major?"

"If you want quick passage, it'd be best if the imagers could topple the wall into the river. Be the Namer's time getting over all the fallen stone otherwise. Unless you have the imagers smooth the way through the middle of the city."

"There aren't any dwellings or buildings on the higher parts of those hills to the east," mused Quaeryt. "Usually folks with golds like the hills. Then again, this close to the border, I'd guess that they live farther south." On the other hand, he'd also never heard of a wall stopping trade, and that suggested the heavy forest to the east concealed a myriad of narrow roads or trails that wound back through the hills. Given the modest level of prosperity in Geusyn, that trade had to run both ways, suggesting that the wall had never been built to stop trade, but to make the cost of acquiring Kephria higher than any Bovarian rex wanted to incur.

"The scouts never see anyone on the walls. Can't believe that Kephria's that busy a port."

"It's likely not. The autarchs built it to keep the city from falling into Bovarian hands."

"When was it built, sir?"

"No one seems to know exactly, but one of the autarchs built it sometime early in the rule of Rex Haarl, Kharst's father. That may have been why Haarl built the Great Canal. Or maybe Aliaro's sire put up the wall to block access to Kephria after the Great Canal was built."

"So they traded for centuries through Kephria . . . and then the Autarch built the wall? Why didn't Kharst or his father just stop it or take it down?"

"That's a good question. We likely won't ever know why, but I'd guess by the time they learned about the wall, it was largely built, and they felt it wasn't worth fighting a war over, especially in a place so hard to get an army to and so far from Variana."

"Could it be that Kharst's sire didn't want his troopers that far from Variana?" asked Voltyr, who had eased his mount forward on Quaeryt's left.

"That's very possible." Quaeryt looked past Zhelan to Maasn, reined up on Zhelan's left. "Captain . . . if you'd send a squad east along the wall—as far as where it meets that rocky outcropping. We need to know if there are any breaks or gates in the wall—or anything unusual."

"Yes, sir." Maasn nodded and turned his mount.

While the captain moved off to give instructions to the patrol squad, Quaeryt turned to Voltyr. "What do you think about how to remove or breach the wall?"

"It might take less effort to rearrange the stone, rather than remove it," suggested Voltyr.

*Rearrange?* Then Quaeryt nodded. "That would also make our progress southward even faster."

"You ought to have Threkhyl begin the imaging," Voltyr went on. "He's the strongest, besides you, at that. You want the Antiagons to be shocked and stunned."

Quaeryt nodded, then watched as a squad moved away from Maasn's company, heading eastward along a path that might have once been a lane, or a game trail. Then he turned his mare so that he faced the undercaptains and motioned for the others to ride forward and join him.

"I'd like all of you to study that wall. We may have to remove a large section of it and use the stone to pave a causeway through the city beyond."

"May?" asked Threkhyl.

"If it appears that the Bovarian High Holders won't pledge allegiance and intend to remain in Antiago, the only way to secure the border will likely require our taking Kephria. The submarshal is considering that possibility. He wanted to know if we could open the wall. That's why we're here."

"We can do it, sir," replied Threkhyl. "We've done more than that."

"I know you can, but I'd like you to do it with the least effort possible. When we first encountered earthworks, you asked if you could just move the earth, and it turned out that was less effort. I thought that you might be able to do the same with the stone."

"You mean just pile it aside somewhere?"

"Actually," said Quaeryt with a smile, "you all have noticed how poor the roads happen to be here. I was thinking that we might just turn the wall into a stone-paved way right through Kephria . . ."

A wide grin crossed the face of Khalis, the youngest undercaptain.

Threkhyl frowned, then nodded. "Yes, sir. It'd be easier that way."

"If we remove part of the wall, sir," asked Voltyr, "how wide an opening do you want?"

"We'll start with a hundred yards, and then see what's on the other side."

"What about the Antiagons?" asked Horan.

"We won't be leading the assault, but we'll try to avoid hurting people who aren't troopers."

Quaeryt answered questions for a time after that, then filled the other imagers in on what he knew about Antiago and the Autarch, including the way Aliaro had dealt with Bhayar's sister Chaerila. After almost a glass, when Maasn's squad rode back and reined up, Quaeryt urged the mare forward to talk to the squad leader.

"What did you find out?" asked Quaeryt.

"There's nothing different there, sir. Just trees and the wall. We didn't see any gaps, no tunnels, and no gates. There aren't any embrasures in the wall, either."

"Did you see any sentries?"

"No, sir. There are small towers every fifth of a mille. Sentries might be inside, I'd guess. No way to measure exactly, but there are six from here to the end of the wall. That doesn't count the one there at the corner."

"How thick is the undergrowth?"

"It runs right up to the stone. Trees have been cut back now and again, looks like, for maybe twenty yards back from the wall."

*So they won't overtop the wall itself.*

Quaeryt asked questions for almost another quint, but learned little more. Finally, he ordered the group back to Geusyn. He reined up in the courtyard of the River Inn at two quints past the first glass of the afternoon, but had to wait until almost second glass before Skarpa returned and they met in the large plaques room.

"What did you find out?" asked Skarpa.

"It's a big wall." Quaeryt smiled sardonically. "It's a waste of good stone. Kharst and Aliaro could have paved a road for milles with all that stone and split the tariffs from Kephria. They both would have come out ahead, and Kharst and his sire wouldn't have had to pour golds into that swamp they call Ephra."

Skarpa frowned. "You're thinking of paving . . . ? Oh . . . Do you think that will work?"

"Voltyr suggested it, in a way. It can't hurt to try."

"I've set a meeting with the regimental commanders for third glass. They should know," said Skarpa. "They can keep it to themselves. Especially if you point out to them that if word leaks out, hundreds more troopers and officers might die."

"I worry about that . . . but you're right." Quaeryt paused. "Have you received any dispatches from Bhayar or Deucalon?"

"One. Just before you returned from Khel. From Deucalon, requesting that I keep him informed of our progress. I sent back a brief missive that said we were progressing as expected and that you had not returned from Khel."

"You're under Bhayar's direct command . . ."

"There's no point in upsetting a marshal when you don't have to," said Skarpa mildly.

"You're right." *And Deucalon can get upset about such things easily.*

"There's one other matter," said Skarpa. "We've never discussed battlefield succession . . ."

Quaeryt looked at Skarpa. "You're in command. Why are you bringing that up now? Are you worried about something we haven't talked about?"

"Anytime you fight, you can run into trouble. Everyone knows that, if something happens to me—it could, you know—then you're in command."

"And if something happens to us both, Kharllon is next in line."

"And after him?"

"If it comes to that . . . it's not our problem," Quaeryt rejoined dryly.

"That may be. But, just because we've never talked about it, the seniority is, in order, Paedn, Dulaek, Meurn, Fhaen, and Fhaasn." Skarpa nodded firmly. "We'll just tell them we're going to attack Kephria and why. Then we'll explain the plan . . ."

Quaeryt listened, occasionally making suggestions.

After he and Skarpa finished going over the agenda for the meeting with the regimental commanders at third glass, Quaeryt retreated to his and Vaelora's room, where she was seated at the desk, writing.

"You're back?" she asked, looking up.

"For a few quints, until we meet with the regimental commanders. Who are you writing?"

"Aelina. It's been a while. Don't worry. I'm not saying anything except where we are, and that can't be any secret." She paused. "You look worried."

"Skarpa insisted on going over the seniority . . . as if something might happen to him tomorrow or in the weeks ahead. He's never done that before."

"He's never commanded this big an army before, has he?"

"No . . . but it's not like him. I can't help but worry if it's another way of saying he doesn't like the idea of invading Antiago."

"Do you?"

"No . . . but it's the least of the evils." Quaeryt fingered his chin, then shook his head. "Everyone will think that it was foolish and unnecessary, and that all those who will have died didn't have to. But the fights and the wars will go on and on until Lydar is unified."

"If it stays unified," Vaelora pointed out.

"It has to. That's one thing the imagers can do for your brother and his son."

"Only if you survive, dearest. No one else can hold them together . . . and face down Bhayar."

"I think you've made that point before."

"I'll keep making it, too."

"What are you telling Aelina?"

"That I'm healthy, and that Geusyn and southern Bovaria have little to recommend them."

"We agree on that." Quaeryt sat on the end of the bed and glanced toward the unshuttered windows, one of which was open, with a cold breeze flowing from it. "Aren't you cold?"

"No. I get too warm if the window's not open. Aelina told me that might happen. She said I was fortunate not to have to carry a child through the summer. She had to, and she was miserable."

"Especially in Solis."

"It wouldn't be any better here."

Quaeryt could believe that. In thinking about the letter his wife was writing, he also realized that neither he nor Vaelora had received any letters or dispatches . . . and Skarpa only one of a noncommittal nature. He couldn't help but worry about what might be happening in Variana. *But there's nothing you can do about it.*

All too soon, he gave Vaelora a brief kiss and headed back down to the large plaques chamber, where he waited outside with Skarpa, while all the regimental commanders entered and took their places around the large circular table.

Then he entered, followed by Skarpa, who remained standing while all the others seated themselves.

"Tomorrow, we're going to take Kephria," Skarpa began.

Quaeryt surveyed the faces of the officers seated around the table. Kharllon revealed nothing, nor did Meurn. Paedn nodded, as did Fhaen. Dulaek frowned, and Fhaasn's brow wrinkled in puzzlement. Alazyn glanced at Quaeryt more than once. He just nodded in return.

"It's simple," Skarpa went on. "We were sent to secure the border with Antiago and to obtain the allegiance of the Bovarian High Holders in the south. All of them have fled into Antiago. When Commander Quaeryt took part of his force to Kherseilles, his ships were attacked by Antiagon warships. While he and his imagers sank three of the five attackers, that was an act of war against Telaryn. So is harboring traitorous High Holders. Previously, the Autarch has attacked Ephra as well. His cannon take aim at any ship nearing Kephria that is not Antiagon. The only way to carry out our orders and secure the border is to take Kephria."

"We don't have cannon or siege engines, sir," said Subcommander Meurn. "Or will we be marching east and swinging behind the wall?"

"Trying to ride or march through those woods would be hard on your men, Subcommander," replied Skarpa. "We'll be leaving the wall to Commander Quaeryt and his men. Once they've opened it, because there may be a fair amount of debris, we'll need a foot regiment to move in first. That will be Fifteenth Regiment . . ."

Meurn did frown at that, if momentarily, as Skarpa continued putting forth the plan of attack.

Quaeryt just listened and watched the other officers, knowing he'd need to go over details with Alazyn and Zhelan after the meeting, and then with Major Baarl, the senior major from Eleventh Regiment, since the two battalions he was temporarily commanding would be the ones guarding Geusyn—and Vaelora.

# 52

By seventh glass on Solayi morning, Quaeryt, first company and the imagers, and the three regiments Skarpa had selected from Southern Army were formed up some two hundred yards north of the gray stone wall that separated Kephria from Bovaria. The air was chill, the sky a hazy gray. To the right, and nearest to the River Laar, were Quaeryt and the imagers, with first company drawn up close behind them. In the center of the rutted road was Fifteenth Regiment, with the mounted Sixth Regiment behind them, and Twenty-sixth Regiment farther back.

Skarpa was mounted beside Quaeryt with a squad from Third Regiment to his left and slightly behind him. The remaining three regiments from Southern Army and Nineteenth Regiment were standing by, but on the outskirts of Geusyn.

"There's still no one on the walls," said Skarpa. "And no clamoring or alarms from the south."

"They may not be worried. They can't see cannon or siege engines." *They may not even know that we've used imagers to remove walls. And even if they've heard stories, most people wouldn't believe them.*

"Proceed, Commander," ordered Skarpa, nodding as he issued the order.

"Undercaptain Khalis! Clear the underbrush!" ordered Quaeryt.

"Yes, sir!" The young undercaptain concentrated. A swathe of underbrush more than a hundred yards wide and fifty deep vanished. Instantly, a thin white mist appeared above the ground where the bushes had been.

"Undercaptain Threkhyl! Forward!"

"Sir!"

"Remove the first section of wall."

"Yes, sir."

Barely had the acknowledgment left the undercaptain's mouth when a white flash obscured the gray stone barrier for an instant. When Quaeryt could see, an opening a hundred yards wide, from the ground up, had appeared in the stone. Beyond the middle of the opening was a stretch of gray stone pavement that looked to extend hundreds of yards south, almost to the edge of the harbor.

Quaeryt glanced to Threkhyl, who swayed slightly in his saddle. "Drink some watered lager! Now!"

His eyes went back to the opening in the wall. Beyond where the stone wall had stood was a welter of huts and hovels, through which wound twisted paths. The newly created and paved road had cut through a number of those dwellings, and dust swirled up through the chill morning air, made even colder by the imaging. Several women were screaming . . . and people were scrambling out of the ramshackle dwellings and hurrying southward toward the more solid structures around the harbor.

Quaeryt hadn't known what to expect, but he hadn't anticipated what he saw.

*But you should have known! Aliaro wouldn't have built the wall right beside good houses.* On the other hand, there was no sign of a nearby barracks or post, unless the wall sentries or guards were based in a modest gray stone building set against the shore wall just before the corner where it turned out into the waters of the River Laar.

A horn blared, and the troopers of Fifteenth Regiment moved forward at a trot, blades and bucklers at the ready. Not a single Antiagon armsman moved forward to meet the advancing Telaryn troopers, but the scattered screams grew more numerous as the troopers moved down the stone-paved road through the scattered dwellings and the remaining parts of some huts toward the center of the port town.

"Forward," ordered Skarpa.

"First company! Forward!" repeated Zhelan.

"Imagers! On me!" added Quaeryt.

Skarpa was careful to set the pace so that Fifteenth Regiment continued in advance of him and first company, although that caution seemed scarcely necessary as the inhabitants of the run-down taudis fled willy-nilly.

In less than a quint the Telaryn forces reached the north end of the harbor, which effectively began with the stone wall that extended out into the river. A handful of men in maroon uniforms fled from the gray stone building at the corner of the wall. One ran for the river and jumped into the water. The others began to run toward the center of the town.

"Not exactly brave defenders," noted Skarpa.

"Unless there's a garrison on the south side of Kephria, there may not be any at all," replied Quaeryt, surveying the north end of the harbor.

Against the south side of the river wall was a stone pier, at which were moored several small craft. One of them was filled with water and resting on the river mud. The shoreline angled eastward downstream of the river wall, forming the northern side of the small harbor, but there was no river wall or seawall on the northern end, just a muddy flat stretching southeast, and flanked by a boulevard paved with uneven and cracked stones on which Quaeryt certainly would not have wished to drive a wagon.

"Company halt!" Quaeryt ordered, since Fifteenth Regiment had also halted.

Several of the buildings bordering the northeast side of harbor were little more than roofless charred structures whose walls had weathered into featureless gray.

*Not even rebuilt from the fires set by Kharst's imagers?*

Farther south were dwellings and shops that had seen better days, and then the remaining intact warehouses, as well as a row of shops, a chandlery, and possibly an inn or two.

A courier galloped toward Skarpa, reining up. "Sir, Subcommander Meurn requests permission to continue."

"Have him take the city. No one is to be harmed unless they attack or offer resistance."

"Take the city. Harm no one unless they attack or resist. Yes, sir." The squad leader nodded, then turned his mount.

Quaeryt watched for a moment as the foot troopers moved forward, followed by Dulaek's mounted, and then by Fhaasn's foot.

"Did you expect this?" asked Skarpa.

"I didn't think there would be that many defenders. I told you that. I didn't expect that there wouldn't be any . . . or so few as to amount to none." Quaeryt paused, then added, "The Antiagons have scarcely been using Kephria as a port. That's what it looks like, anyway."

"Waste of a good harbor." The submarshal shook his head. "Doesn't make sense."

"In a way, it does." Quaeryt readjusted his visor cap. Even in the chill of a southern winter, he tended to sweat where the edges of the cap met his head. "The autarchs wanted to keep Bovarian traders and trade out of Kephria. I'm guessing about that, but it's the only thing that makes sense."

"But why?"

"Most ships that likely once ported here were more interested in trading with southern Bovaria. I'd guess the Bovarians built the Great Canal to take advantage of that. Aliaro's father was probably afraid that the Bovarians would take over Kephria, and he didn't want more Bovarians here. So he built the wall to keep them out. The Bovarians couldn't afford a war, or didn't want to send an army that far from Variana. So they built Ephra, and most ships stopped porting here because they couldn't pick up Bovarian cargoes."

"He put up that huge wall to stop traders? How could he have known that Bovaria wouldn't try to tear it down?"

"He didn't. I'd wager that a regiment was probably posted here for at least several years. Long enough to discourage the Bovarians from bringing an army down here."

Skarpa shook his head.

A glass later, another messenger, this one from Dulaek, reported that the port, such as it was, had been secured and that mounted squads from his fourth battalion were patrolling the streets. Shortly, thereafter, Meurn reported that the fort beside the main pier had surrendered.

"We might as well ride down there and see what the fort is like," suggested Skarpa.

Only a handful of men were out, and all of them were graybeards or older, standing on porches or looking from open windows, watching as if they could not believe they were seeing the green uniforms of Telaryn riding through Kephria.

From a closer perspective, under the high thin overcast, Kephria looked even more tired than it had from a distance, everything seeming even grayer and worn. The southernmost pier, the main pier, looked to be the best, constructed of sold gray stone and extending close to five hundred yards out into the river . . . or the Gulf, since there wasn't a clear demarcation of where one began and the other ended. Not a single craft was moored there, but Quaeryt could see several vessels under sail heading southwest, either out along the Gulf to the open sea or to Liantiago. Neither of the two nearest vessels, from their rigging, looked to be warships.

He reined up and studied the pier. The gray stone was worn, chipped, and stained, clearly weathered and old. The bollards were not only weathered, but the wood appeared wormy and rotten in places. The mooring spaces closer to the shore looked not to have been used in some time, and when Quaeryt looked more closely at the water, he could see why. The water there was less than a yard deep, suggesting that the inner part of the harbor had been silting up for years, if not decades.

Then he turned his attention to the fort, a square stone structure constructed on a raised knoll just south of the main pier. The walls formed three sides of a rectangle, with a small building with a slate roof comprising the rear east wall. The wall facing the river and the Gulf was only some twenty yards long. He couldn't see how many cannon ports there might be, but he doubted there were more than half a score.

"I'm going to ride out on the pier for a moment," he told Skarpa.

"Make it quick. You still could be a target."

Quaeryt did strengthen his shields before he eased the mare down the center of the pier. He only rode out far enough to see the gun ports. At first he thought there were ten, but then he realized that seven of those appeared to be boarded up on the inside, although he wouldn't have been able to tell that if he'd been much farther away. Shaking his head, he turned the mare and rode back to rejoin Skarpa.

"What did you see?"

"From a distance, there are ten ports. Seven are blocked."

"A sham. Like everything else here."

"It might not have been once."

"They just fired at Bovarian ships to keep the Bovarians thinking that they had a large garrison here," said Skarpa.

"Where are their real troopers?" asked Zhelan.

"They have to have some. We ran into a regiment's worth of them on the way up the Aluse," replied Skarpa. "Khaern said they had a regiment northeast of Hassyl."

"That would make sense. That's near the border with Telaryn," said Quaeryt. "Aliaro might be relying on those Bovarian High Holders we chased into Antiago as protection here."

"But why wouldn't they have some troopers here?" asked Zhelan. "They built the wall."

"Troopers cost golds. Antiago isn't that rich a land." Quaeryt was surmising from what he'd seen years earlier and from what he'd read. "The Lohan Hills are inhospitable and the southern coast is almost a high rocky desert. The area around Hassyl is fertile, and so are at least some of the lands from east of Suemyran to Liantiago. Most of the wealth comes from the sea, with their traders."

"They'll have troopers and Antiagon Fire when we near Suemyran," predicted Skarpa.

"Not too much nearer, I'd wager," replied Quaeryt. "Aliaro seems to have neglected this part of the north."

"Kephria, anyway," said Skarpa. "Once we've got everything settled here, we'll need to talk to the people before we go any farther."

Quaeryt couldn't disagree with that.

By late Lundi afternoon, Kephria was firmly in Telaryn hands, and the Telaryn ensign flew from the tower at river end of the breached stone wall. Major Baarl and the half of Eleventh Regiment with Southern Army had taken over the patrolling duties, and Vaelora was installed in the best room in the one decent inn in Kephria, looking over Quaeryt's shoulder as he attempted to draft a dispatch to Bhayar.

"I still worry about leaving you here," he said, pausing for a moment.

"You need as many troopers as possible for what you're doing. I'll be just as safe here as in Geusyn," insisted Vaelora. "And Major Baarl and you don't have to garrison two towns. Besides, it won't be that long before the *Montagne* returns with Subcommander Khaern and the other two battalions of Eleventh Regiment."

Quaeryt did not dispute her logic, but he had misgivings about anything that hadn't yet happened. Anything could delay the return of half of Eleventh Regiment . . . not to mention Calkoran's understrength battalion. Still . . . he and the imagers had to accompany Skarpa, especially since the invasion of Antiago had been his idea, and sending Vaelora back to Variana would weaken their forces. In addition, the authority they were using—or misusing—was based on both Quaeryt and Vaelora having power as joint envoys.

Vaelora looked out the inn window, then turned to Quaeryt. "Why is it so run-down?"

"Idiocy," he replied, realizing he hadn't explained to her what he'd already suggested to Skarpa. "Most ships with trade for southern Bovaria likely once ported here. I'd guess the Bovarians built the Great Canal to take advantage of that. Aliaro's father was probably afraid that the Bovarians would take over Kephria, and he built the wall to keep the Bovarians out. The Bovarians didn't want or couldn't afford a war and built Ephra, and most ships stopped porting here because they couldn't pick up Bovarian cargoes."

"It all doesn't make much sense. The autarchs built a wall that ruined the port and then largely neglected the town, and Kharst tried to burn it down, and then Aliaro shelled Ephra?"

Quaeryt offered an ironic smile. "If all goes well, we'll end up restoring

Kephria, taking trade from Geusyn, and turning Ephra into a ruin. It should make everyone better off in time."

"People don't like to wait for better times."

"They don't like to pay for them, either." He returned his attention to the document before him. "I need to finish this and have you read it . . . and make any changes you think necessary before I show it to Skarpa."

"You think he'll want to sign it?"

"We'll all be blamed if things go ill. If they go well, he might as well get the credit."

"He will get the credit, you know, dearest?"

Quaeryt nodded, then resumed writing. After a time, he laid the pen carefully on the folded paper serving as a pen rest and handed the sheet to Vaelora. "If you would?"

As she took it and began to read, Quaeryt rose and stood behind her, rereading what he had set to paper, concentrating on the paragraph following the flowery salutation and greeting.

> . . . In your wisdom, you directed Submarshal Skarpa, as well as Lady Vaelora, and Commander Quaeryt, acting as your envoys to those not within the domains of Bovaria and Telaryn, to secure the border with Antiago and to obtain the allegiance of the High Holders of southern Bovaria. Rather than pledge allegiance, those holders defied Submarshal Skarpa and even refused to meet with Lady Vaelora, then fled into Antiago. To comply with your orders, Southern Army is pursuing these traitors as necessary. In attempting to assure the safety and loyalty of the south, we have undertaken a campaign that has, of necessity, required a greater extension of your power than originally anticipated. As a result, Kephria is now a part of your domains. It may be that other areas of Antiago will also need to be subdued and annexed so that the southern border of your lands will be forever secure, and we will continue to keep you informed of events as they transpire . . .

"Transpire?" asked Vaelora. "That sounds more like 'expire.' Why not just say 'happen' or 'occur'?"

" 'Occur' is better," Quaeryt agreed.

"You also might explain that we gave the traitors every opportunity to meet and pledge allegiance over a period of more than a month."

"That's better."

All in all, after another quint of discussion, Quaeryt took the document and sat back down to redraft it. Before he picked up the pen, he looked up at his wife. "How are you feeling?"

"Well enough, except I feel like I'm wearing small tents instead of clothing, and it won't be that long before I'm wearing large tents."

"You can scarcely tell, and you still look lovely."

"I *still* look lovely? Does that mean you expect I won't before long?"

Quaeryt hid a wince and was about to issue a heated denial—until he saw the smile in her eyes. "I should have said that you will always be lovely."

"To you. Others may think differently."

Quaeryt decided there was little point in pursuing that further. "Can you remember anything else about Aliaro? Anything at all you heard in Solis or that Bhayar or your father might have said?"

"I think I've told you everything I recall . . ." Vaelora frowned. "Oh . . . there is one thing. Daesn—he died last winter—he was Father's envoy to Liantiago. He arranged Chaerila's betrothal. He mentioned something about Aliaro's imagers having to live in metal-lined chambers—"

"Cells, I imagine," snorted Quaeryt.

"No. He definitely said chambers. He said it was because they were unhappy."

*Unhappy?* Abruptly Quaeryt understood . . . or thought he might.

"What is it?"

"Imaging is much harder in dealing with metal. If his imagers were unhappy, and they lived in metal-lined chambers . . ."

"They couldn't image to harm the Autarch." She frowned. "Wouldn't it make more sense to keep them away from the palace?"

"Why do you think all the imagers report to me?" he asked.

"Oh . . . of course." She shook her head ruefully. "That's because Bhayar trusts you to keep them in line."

"And why few rulers have had many imagers." *And why all too many died in strange circumstances . . . something you'll always need to keep in mind.* He waited. "Can you think of anything else?"

"Not right now."

"Then I'd better rewrite this and get it to Skarpa."

"You should." She smiled. "You changed the subject rather deftly."

He laughed. "Hardly. If I'd been deft, you wouldn't have noticed."

Her smile grew broader, then faded. "You're still leaving tomorrow?"

"Seventh glass."

"How long will it take to reach Suemyran? If you encounter no opposition?"

Quaeryt shrugged. "I can't say. The road south looks better than those along the Aluse—except for the old Naedaran stone roads—but it might be as long as ten days. I'd be surprised if we had much opposition until we reach Barna. Aliaro's never had a huge army, and he's moved his forces by ship."

"His ships will find out that you've taken Kephria and bring him word faster than a courier could."

"That's true, but he'll have to gather forces and move them. He won't have many, if any, stationed away from the coastal cities. And he won't know if we've just taken Kephria or if we intend more. I suspect he'll have trouble believing what we have in mind."

"I do hope so, dearest."

*So do I.* With a faint smile, Quaeryt reached for another sheet of paper and picked up the pen.

Vaelora walked to the window and looked out into the early evening.

Southern Army and Quaeryt's forces departed from Kephria on Mardi morning almost two quints before seventh glass, heading south on the road to Suemyran, a road that proved over the next three days to be adequate and whose condition appeared to improve with each mille that Southern Army traveled.

Just after midday on Jeudi, a day so clear and warm that Quaeryt had removed his riding jacket, they approached a small town whose name—as chiseled on the millestone—was Clianto. To the north of the town were low hills covered with orchards, mostly of olives. Several hundred yards ahead, on the right, a young man leading a donkey pulling a cart stopped dead, as if frozen where he stood as he looked from the outriders to the troopers that followed. Then, after several moments, he immediately turned the cart down a lane and began to run, yanking on the donkey's leads, trying to get the animal to move faster.

"There's another poor boy who can't believe what he's seeing," Quaeryt said to Skarpa, riding beside him. Every day since they'd left Kephria, Quaeryt had seen similar reactions by the Antiagons, and he couldn't blame them. First was the shock, and then the fear.

"You can't blame them. So far as I know, no one's ever invaded Antiago." Skarpa looked to Quaeryt. "You're the scholar. Is that so?"

"The Naedarans held some of the Lohan Hills, but nothing this far south."

"They got around, from what you've said."

"It's hard to say, but at the height of their power, their land was likely half the size of old Tela."

"They had imagers, too. So why didn't they expand more?"

"For the same reason no one's used imagers effectively since then." Quaeryt laughed softly. "Rulers don't trust imagers, and they don't use them effectively."

"You're trying to change that."

"Trying is a good way of describing it." Quaeryt didn't want to go into more detail, not when part of the reason for invading Antiago was tied to his ambitions for assuring that life for imagers in all Lydar would be far better in the future than it was or had been.

As they neared the edge of the town, Quaeryt raised the heaviest shields he could, not because he expected any attack, but as another way of keeping in practice, then turned in the saddle. "Imagers! Full shields!" As he turned back to study the town, he could hear one set of words.

". . . not like the attacks on Nordeau . . ."

Quaeryt wanted to shake his head at Threkhyl's muttered comment. Instead, he ignored it and concentrated on learning what he could about Clianto and what the town might tell him about Antiago.

"Can't believe how much warmer it is here than even in Kephria," observed Skarpa. "Not even a sign of Antiagon troopers."

"There hasn't been time for Aliaro to learn that we're here." Quaeryt glanced to the slightly higher hills to the east, where he spied a white-walled villa, large, but not sprawling, and certainly not close to the size of a Bovarian or Telaryn high holding. Perhaps two milles farther south along the eastern hills was a second villa, somewhat smaller, whose walls were a pinkish off-white. A single rider galloped along the last few hundred yards of the road leading to the first villa, but no dust rose in his tracks, suggesting a far better surface than Quaeryt had seen on most roads in Bovaria.

The dwellings on the outskirts of the town were built of some sort of brick covered with stucco and then whitewashed, although the wash on many houses had faded or been turned faintly rose-colored by dust from the reddish dirt. Roofs were either flat or gently sloped, suggesting that excessive rain was not a problem.

While Quaeryt saw a few men and women farther toward the center of town hurrying into buildings, the streets, lanes, and alleys were empty as Southern Army rode down the main street. Not all shutters were closed, but most were. Those that were not likely could not be easily closed, Quaeryt suspected. Just as he was about to suggest that they stop in the central square to water mounts and see what they could learn, two riders in green livery rode out of a side street and turned their mounts south.

Quaeryt thought about trying to image, but the riders were already more than a hundred yards away, and anything he did at that distance that would be effective would likely also be fatal. "Zhelan! Send a squad after those two!"

"Yes, sir! Second squad! Forward!"

Second squad moved out after the liveried riders, but not at a gallop.

"Young idiots," snorted Skarpa. "Charging off will tire their mounts too fast. Older riders would have walked their mounts down a side street and sneaked out of town. We never would have seen them."

"Jhalet's got some of the best mounts and riders," said Zhelan from behind the two senior officers. "If anyone can catch them, he can."

Quaeryt said nothing, well aware that he still knew far too little about horses and how to pace them. Instead, as first company reined up in the square, he quietly surveyed the buildings, taking in what likely passed for a chandlery, then a small cloth factorage.

On the west side was one of the pair of two-story structures in view, the other being the inn, and the only stone building fronting the square. After several moments, a white-haired man wearing dark gray trousers and a white shirt emerged from the stone structure and walked slowly toward Skarpa and Quaeryt, finally halting a good five yards away and bowing before speaking. "Honored sirs."

It took a moment for Quaeryt to understand his words, as heavily accented as they were, so much so that the way the older man spoke was almost like another language. Quaeryt was glad it wasn't. Having three languages in Lydar was bad enough. "Are you the councilor for Clianto?"

"No, sir. I am Khelito. I am the administrator appointed by the Autarch." The man's voice was pleasant, but edged with concern. "What would you have of us, honored sirs?"

"Water, and some supplies," replied Skarpa.

"We have little. Clianto is not a wealthy town. Might I ask why armed men in strange uniforms are riding through Antiago?"

Skarpa looked to Quaeryt.

"The uniforms are those of Telaryn," explained Quaeryt. "Lord Bhayar of Telaryn has combined Bovaria with Telaryn. Autarch Aliaro's ships have attacked Telaryn ships without provocation, and a number of Bovarian High Holders have fled into Antiago rather than pledge allegiance to Lord Bhayar. That is why we are here."

"There are no High Holders here, honored sir."

"I am certain that is so, administrator"—Quaeryt almost said councilor—"but we are on our way to deal with the Autarch."

"Then, Lord Bhayar intends to take our lands and make Antiago part of Telaryn?"

"He intends to make all Lydar one land. He has no intention of taking your lands. He will only take the lands of those who raise arms against him or who aid those who do."

"We have no arms to raise. We have little enough to aid ourselves."

"You have fine olive orchards." The plea of poverty was getting on Quaeryt's nerves, given that the town looked moderately prosperous.

"We do not own the orchards. Shahib Folinero does."

"Is one of the villas to the east his?"

Khelito laughed gently. "No. The larger one belongs to Orchard Master Ghario. He manages the orchards for the Shahib. The lesser one belongs to Orchard Master Zheno. He manages the orchards to the south for Shahiba Shenia."

"And they both live in Liantiago?"

"Of course. How could it be otherwise?"

"You don't see Antiagon armsmen near here, I take it?"

"Not often. Last spring, many marched through here on their way north." The administrator shrugged. "They must have returned to Liantiago another way. They did not return by the north road."

"Do you collect the tariffs for Autarch Aliaro?"

"Who else would do so?" Khelito's voice was tinged with puzzlement, as if any other arrangement would have been unthinkable.

"Who collects them from you?"

"Those who come from Liantiago who serve the most noble Autarch."

"Who are these collectors?"

"They are the regional tariff collectors."

"Do armsmen accompany them? How many?"

"I have not counted them. There are not many."

"Who besides collectors and armsmen?" Quaeryt could tell that Skarpa was puzzled at the line of questioning.

"I would not know who they are, only that the tariff collectors defer to them."

"Do the armsmen defer more to those you do not know than to the tariff collectors?"

There was the slightest trace of hesitation before Khelito replied, "I could not say, honored sir."

While Skarpa issued orders for regiments to water their mounts and then re-form on the south side of the town, Quaeryt dismounted and continued to talk with the town administrator.

"What maps do you have of the land, and the way to Suemyran?"

"Maps? There might be one . . ."

More than a glass later, when the regiments were re-formed on the south side of town, and several wagons loaded with grain for the mounts, Quaeryt watched as Jhalet led second squad—and two men in green livery with gold piping on their jackets and trousers, their hands bound, and their mounts on leads—back up the road.

"One of them threw this into a false olive hedgerow," reported Jhalet, riding up beside Quaeryt and extending a brown leather dispatch folder.

Both captive riders looked to be young, if older than Quaeryt's youngest undercaptains, and neither looked directly at Quaeryt. "Who do you serve?"

The younger of the two shook his head.

The other rider said, "High Holder Chaelaet." He glanced at the other. "They'll find out soon enough."

Quaeryt glanced toward Skarpa, who had ridden over. He held up the case. "Do you want to read it first?"

"Go ahead."

Quaeryt turned to Jhalet. "If you would hold the prisoners over there until we finish?"

"Yes, sir."

After waiting until the captives were out of earshot, Quaeryt opened the case and extracted the single folded and sealed sheet, breaking the green wax and unfolding the parchment, then began to read.

*Your most puissant power—*

*Most puissant power? Talk about trying to curry favor.* Quaeryt couldn't help but smile as he continued reading.

> *As a longtime admirer and ally, which you know well, I regret that I must be the bearer of tidings less than favorable. As I reported in an earlier dispatch, the tyrant Bhayar insisted on a fawning and impoverishing allegiance on the part of High Holders in southern Bovaria. When we refused to meet with his submarshal, he leveled five holds so thoroughly that nothing remains. It is said that this was accomplished by imagers, but I cannot verify this. The invading army is apparently comprised of three to four battle-tested regiments, mixed foot and mounted, far too large for our forces, but certainly not beyond your capabilities, especially since, knowing you to be a just and reasonable ruler, we would be willing to place our resources at your disposal in repelling the invaders . . .*

After finishing the letter or dispatch—Quaeryt wasn't sure what to call it—he extended it to Skarpa and waited.

When Skarpa finished, he smiled sardonically. "What do you think?"

"It's a veiled plea and bargain. Chaelaet is saying he and the other High Holders will support Aliaro if Aliaro will destroy us. But there's so much evasion and distortion . . ."

"Like his not being able to verify that you used imagers?"

"That, and the fact they all fled over the border to avoid meeting with us."

"They're all pissing-in-their pants scared of you and the imagers, and they're not about to admit it to Aliaro."

"Because they don't want him coming to terms with Bhayar and because they want him to destroy the invading force so that they can secede and become part of Antiago?"

"That's the way it looks. They know that they've burned their bridges with Bhayar."

"That's true . . . but they didn't have to."

"People are like that," Skarpa said. "They get an idea in their heads, and when things don't go the way they think they should, they don't think. They react and do something stupid . . . and they'll blame someone else."

"I need to see what else I can find out." Quaeryt gestured toward the two captives.

"Let me know." Skarpa slipped the dispatch back into the case and extended it back to Quaeryt. "Question them on the ride. We need to get moving."

"I'll do that. Don't you want to keep the letter?"

The submarshal shook his head. "I can't do anything with it, but it might help us both if you keep it safe. You'll see Bhayar sooner than I will." Skarpa smiled, then turned his mount.

"Only if he's displeased with me." *And that's getting more and more likely.*

Quaeryt eased the mare over to where Jhalet waited with the captives, but didn't begin questioning them until the entire column was moving south and he was riding between them behind Skarpa and Zhelan.

"What's your name?" Quaeryt asked the older captive.

"Erlaet."

"Where did you leave High Holder Chaelaet?"

"North of here . . . and east. Town called Vholia."

Quaeryt had to concentrate to understand, because the southern Bovarian accent was almost as heavy as that of the Antiagons. "How far south from Chaelaet?"

"Two days' ride."

Two quints and scores of questions later, he'd discovered very little else that shed light on where Chaelaet and the other fleeing High Holders might be, at least not until he could talk with someone who knew the geography and towns along the Lohan Hills.

For the next three days, under slightly hazy but sunny skies, Southern Army marched and rode southward through towns invariably similar in architecture and agriculture to Clianto and the lands surrounding it. Early on Meredi morning, Quaeryt and Skarpa sat at opposite sides of a small table in the study of a villa in Nankico, a town perhaps half the size of Laaryn. The villa was normally used by the orchard manager of a Shahib Alzonio, who was resident, unsurprisingly, in Liantiago.

"We should reach Suemyran late the day after tomorrow," said Skarpa. "That's if we don't run into trouble."

"I'd think that Aliaro might at least have a garrison or outpost there," ventured Quaeryt.

"You think we should see about surprising a post when we don't even know if there is one and where it might be?"

"I was thinking about sending a battalion around Suemyran and setting up a hidden picket line on the road to Barna. The local commander, if there is one, or the town administrator might just send a courier or a messenger to Barna and then on to Liantiago. We don't have to know where the post is—just the route that a messenger might take."

"And you have your maps," said Skarpa.

The entire time Southern Army had been on the move, Quaeryt had made inquiries in all the towns and hamlets through which they had passed and, after Clianto, especially at the larger villas about maps of Antiago. The best maps had come from the villas, along with a growing confirmation that the Shahibs and Shahibas of Antiago were effectively the equivalent of High Holders—and that all of them seemed to live near Liantiago. Two maps in particular depicted the roads in and around Suemyran in detail.

"They all show the same roads to the west. Both of them—the old road and the new road."

"That might help. It can't hurt. You'd planned on sending one of Alazyn's battalions?"

"Whichever one he recommends," Quaeryt replied.

"It can't hurt."

"You think someone has already sent a message to Aliaro?"

"I'd be astounded if someone hasn't."

"It won't be any of the town administrators," replied Quaeryt. "They're not the type to volunteer anything unless they have to, and we haven't raided town treasuries." *As much because there wasn't anything in them.* "More likely one of the orchard managers who's sent a message to Liantiago to explain what happened to the grain and flour and mutton we've taken."

"Aliaro will find out soon enough. One way or another."

"But which Shahib will want to tell him?" asked Quaeryt, recalling just how few High Holders ever wanted to tell Bhayar anything negative—unless it enhanced their position, and Quaeryt couldn't see how any Antiagon Shahib could benefit from reporting a Telaryn army.

*Although someone is bound to find a way to turn it to their benefit. Some holders and their like always do.*

"Someone will." Skarpa paused. "I don't trust any of those town administrators."

"I'd agree. They're hiding what they feel, in a way that shows long practice. I have to wonder if the Autarch sends imagers out with the tariff collectors. You noticed how several of the administrators never answered my questions about who came with them?"

"More here than meets the eye." Skarpa nodded. "Do you think the *Montagne* has returned by now?"

"We're inland, but we haven't seen any sign of storms. We should have if the weather over the Gulf has been bad. Then again, I'm not sure I trust Nykaal to press much, even in fair seas. I wouldn't be surprised if Calkoran didn't return before Khaern and his last battalions."

"I'd put the wager on Calkoran," said Skarpa dryly. "Do you think Aliaro will send ships and troops to try to retake Kephria?"

"It's always possible, but it will take time. By then, hopefully, we'll have given him a more immediate worry." Quaeryt didn't mention his concerns about Vaelora. There was little enough he could do now, and he'd given Baarl orders to withdraw if the Antiagons appeared in overwhelming force.

"Anything else?"

"Besides what we've already talked over?" Quaeryt shook his head. "Supplies will always be a problem."

"Before long, we'll have other problems."

"Like Antiagon Fire, cannon, musketeers, and Antiagon imagers?"

"Don't you think so?"

"It's all possible, but we do have the advantage that we're attacking from behind their defenses. It's pretty clear that because of the Lohan Hills, the Sud Swamp, and the high deserts along the southern coast, the autarchs have always felt their warships were their best defense, and that attacks would come against Kephria and Liantiago . . . or Westisle."

Skarpa shook his head. "You may be right, but except for the wall, there weren't many defenses in Kephria. There have to be more somewhere?"

"We saw five warships on the way to Kherseilles, and a pair of different ones on the return, and that was just in the Gulf of Khellor."

"What about imagers?"

"The Autarch has them. How many I don't know," admitted Quaeryt. "I'm not certain anyone knows. There have to be troopers because Aliaro wouldn't have sent an entire regiment to Bovaria without others remaining here. We know about the Antiagon Fire."

"I don't know," said Skarpa. "There has to be more."

"I'm sure there is," replied Quaeryt. "It's just not here. That makes sense. There's not much of value here, either, except olive orchards and crops. I'd wager that most of the defenses are around Liantiago and Westisle."

"You're saying we'll have an easy time of it until we get near there?"

Quaeryt offered a rueful smile. "I'll never say that. I will say that it will get harder as we near Liantiago. But you know that."

Skarpa nodded, then rose. "Time to head out."

Although Skarpa and Quaeryt had discussed sending just one battalion to seal off the road from Suemyran to Barna and on to Liantiago, on Meredi evening the submarshal had drawn Quaeryt aside and said, "I'd feel better if you'd take all of Nineteenth Regiment and first company—just in case. They just might have a regiment and imagers."

So, in the dimness well before sixth glass on Jeudi morning, behind scouts and outriders, Quaeryt and Alazyn led Nineteenth Regiment and first company to the west and south of Suemyran, along a side road that was little more than a lane, if lightly graveled and well packed. The leaves of the olive orchards to the west of the lane looked gray in the early light, and the shoots in the fields to the east were already almost knee-high. Quaeryt had no idea what the plants might be, except that they were not maize, because maize took great amounts of water, and the ditches that flanked the fields were empty.

"The old road runs almost three milles to the south of the new road . . . if the maps are correct," he said to Alazyn. "That's where this lane joins it. If the Antiagons withdraw from Suemyran, they'll send most, if not all, of their troopers on the new road. Still . . . we need to cover the older road, just in case. How big a force do you think we should dispatch?"

"I'd recommend a battalion, sir, with couriers standing by. That way, we can shift battalions as needed."

"Which battalion?"

"Fourth. Major Daelor is good at independent operations."

*Meaning that he'd like to be the subcommander.* "Fourth it is. You can brief him and send the battalion off once we reach the new road."

By a quint past sixth glass, Nineteenth Regiment had reached the "new" road, the first paved thoroughfare Quaeryt had seen in Antiago—except for the short section of road Threkhyl had laid down through the taudis on the north side of Kephria. Before long, based on reports from the scouts, Quaeryt and Alazyn agreed that the best location to set up a possible ambush and entrapment was where the road curved around a low hill and past a small pond fed by a stream.

Two battalions could move from behind the hill to block the road on the west, and the third could move up behind any Antiagon force on the east. While there were fields on the south side of the road, they were open and offered little cover, should the Antiagons attempt to flee southward. There was a lane leading south, farther back to the east, along which Major Daelor had taken fourth battalion to reach the old road to Barna. Just in case there might be stragglers who would try to reach the lane, Quaeryt had Alazyn station one company a half mille farther south along the lane.

Then they settled in to wait.

"How big a force do you think they have in Suemyran?" Alazyn finally asked.

"They might not have any troopers at all. Or they might have a full regiment. I think it's unlikely they'll have more than a battalion this far from the coast . . . but we just don't know."

"Do you know why they didn't have more troopers in Kephria?"

"No. Not really. I'd guess that it's because there's really nothing to protect there, and because, until we came along, there wasn't any real threat, either. Although they squabbled, Kharst and Aliaro were essentially allies . . . at least in the sense that both opposed Bhayar."

"But didn't they fight over Kephria and Ephra?"

"Aliaro shelled Ephra. Kharst raided Kephria, and then Aliaro killed the raiders. That was it. They both decided, it appears, that Kephria and Ephra weren't worth any more fighting."

"I could have told them that after looking at them," replied Alazyn dryly.

"Sometimes, rulers don't see what others do."

By eighth glass, Quaeryt was about to believe that his idea of cutting off any Antiagon withdrawal had been a bad idea—or at least that there hadn't been any forces to cut off. A quint later, a scout reined up beside him on the backside of the hill.

"Sir . . . the Antiagons are coming."

"How many?"

"More than a company, less than two. All mounted and one wagon."

"Thank you." Quaeryt turned to Alazyn. "I think we have enough force that we might not even have to fight, but the men need to be prepared."

The subcommander nodded.

Quaeryt waited until the Antiagon troopers were on the road almost between the hill and the pond before the three battalions moved into position.

The Antiagon force consisted of perhaps a company of riders in maroon and white uniforms, riding quickly, followed by a single wagon heaped high with items covered by a canvas tarp and drawn by two dray horses. The driver kept looking back over his shoulder, perhaps because there was no rear guard, then reined up the team as he saw third battalion close off the road to the east.

Quaeryt had taken a position on the lower gentle slope of the hill, high enough that he could see the road and all his forces. He watched, ready to order an attack, as the Antiagon company reined up.

An officer near the front of the column, likely a captain, rode forward.

"You can surrender, Captain," said Quaeryt, image-projecting his voice, "or you can be attacked and likely perish to the last man. If you surrender, you and your men will be disarmed and taken prisoner."

"How do I know that?" shouted the captain in the thick Antiagon accent or dialect.

At that moment the wagon driver turned the team, skidding slightly on the shoulder of the road, then flicked the reins as he guided the wagon back east toward the side land heading south.

"Undercaptain Lhandor, image off the wagon wheels!"

"Yes, sir!"

"Major Zhelan, send a squad to capture the wagon and driver!"

Only then did Quaeryt see two men along the side of the lane, apparently working on repairing a ditch. Both looked stunned as the team and wagon rolled in their direction, especially as the front wheels of the wagon vanished, and the wagon bed slammed down on the lane, then dug in. In moments, the wagon bed, the traces, and the horses were a tangled mess, and one was screaming in agony. A second look told Quaeryt that the wagon bed had skidded into one of the workers and knocked him down on the shoulder of the road.

Quaeryt glanced back to the Antiagon captain, who had turned in the saddle and watched the wagon crash before looking back to Quaeryt. "Surrender or not?"

"We will take your word, sir. We have neither imagers nor our Fire."

"I'll send a squad down to collect your weapons." Quaeryt turned. "Lhandor, Horan, you accompany the squad to collect arms. Your job is to shield the troopers collecting the weapons."

"Yes, sir."

As the two imager undercaptains moved forward to join the designated squad, Quaeryt turned to Alazyn. "We'd best send a messenger to Major Daelor." Then he glanced back. "Major Zhelan, if you'd assign a squad to accompany Undercaptain Khalis to see about injuries in that wagon crash and to see about repairing the wagon."

"Yes, sir."

In less than a quint, the Antiagon prisoners had been disarmed and were surrounded. Quaeryt rode down the slope, accompanied by five troopers from first company and Voltyr, and gestured for the Antiagon officer to join him.

"I'm Quaeryt, Commander, Telaryn forces. You are?"

"Captain Sentio A'Rhedir, Commander."

"We need to take a look at your wagon, Captain, and your teamster."

The faintest expression of puzzlement crossed the tanned face of the dark-haired Antiagon officer. "As you wish, Commander."

As they neared the wrecked wagon, Quaeryt saw Khalis kneeling by the injured ditch worker.

The undercaptain looked up. "The wagon skidded into him and broke his leg. I've splinted it as well as I can. He'll need a real healer, though."

"Can you and Voltyr image the wagon back together?"

"If someone will unload it." Voltyr grinned. "We've learned more about wheelwrighting since the first time."

"What's in the wagon?" Quaeryt asked the captain.

"Weapons, rations, a paychest, spare riding gear, farrier supplies . . ." Sentio shrugged.

"Fine. We'll have some of your men unload it."

"But . . . they're troopers, not loaders."

"At the moment they're prisoners," Quaeryt said dryly.

"Ah . . . yes."

Quaeryt glanced sharply at the captain, who immediately looked down.

True to their word, Voltyr and Khalis did return the wagon back to working order, although it took almost a glass before it was in shape to be reloaded.

"You will bring him back to Suemyran?" asked Sentio as two troopers hoisted the injured worker onto the seat beside the trooper who had taken over as teamster.

"There's no reason not to, is there?"

"But he will be leaving his lands."

"We don't have time to seek out the local healer." *If there even is one.*

"He will be punished for leaving his lands."

Quaeryt tried not to show his astonishment, given that the worker had been injured because the Antiagon driver had tried to escape. Even so, he didn't have a good reply, knowing that he and Skarpa didn't have the forces necessary to garrison and govern even the major towns and cities along the way to Liantiago. Finally he said, "We can only do what we can."

Sentio did not reply.

"What were your duties in Suemyran?" Quaeryt asked the Antiagon captain once Nineteenth Regiment and the prisoners were riding back eastward toward Suemyran.

"We were posted here because of the bandits in the Khoro area. We sent patrols along the roads so that the cargoes of olive oil and other crops were not disturbed. No one ever raided where we patrolled."

"What were they raiding?" asked Quaeryt, curious because one of the maps had shown Khoro as a small town to the west of Suemyran, practically at the foot of the rugged and rocky hills that separated the orchard regions of Antiago from the inhospitable high desert badlands of the south and east. He had to wonder what there might be of value there.

"Who could tell?" replied the captain. "We never caught any of them, and the locals wouldn't tell us. They are not very bright, you know?"

Quaeryt suspected that the locals were far brighter than Sentio knew, if only because they knew enough to keep secrets. "Where are you from?"

"Liantiago."

"Are all officers from Liantiago?"

"I would not say that all are, but most I have known are from Liantiago or from villas nearby."

"What does your father do?"

"He is of the Ascendency, of course."

"The Ascendency?"

"The Ascendents are the families who are the foundation of prosperity."

"The large factors and landholders, the ones who own the olive orchards in the north and the palm oil plantations south of Liantiago?"

"And those who have built the great trading fleets."

"Your father is one of those? A Shahib?"

"His fleet is modest compared to some."

"How many older brothers do you have?"

"Five."

Quaeryt almost nodded, but continued his questions as they rode.

Quaeryt and Nineteenth Regiment had not even reached the western edge of Suemyran when a squad from Southern Army rode toward them.

"Submarshal Skarpa holds the city," announced the squad leader. "The Antiagons had a small post, but it was deserted."

"We captured the company that held the post. If you'd carry that message back to the submarshal."

"Yes, sir."

By the first glass of the afternoon, Quaeryt and Nineteenth Regiment were riding along the wide central boulevard of Suemyran toward the central square. On one low rise along the western end of the city Quaeryt noted close to a hundred large villas. Two quints later, he was meeting with Skarpa in the gaming room of the largest inn of Suemyran, located on the north side of the main square. The inn was built like a two-story villa around a central courtyard that held a fountained garden.

"What do you think we should do with the prisoners?" asked Skarpa.

"Take their uniforms, weapons, and mounts, and leave them here. I doubt that many, if any, will want to walk to Barna . . . or Liantiago. Otherwise, we'd have to leave a detachment to guard them, and that doesn't make much sense, one way or the other."

"I don't like it, but it makes sense." Skarpa paused. "What about those two riders of Chaelaet's?"

"Leave them here, too."

"What do we do with whatever forces we encounter in Barna? If there's a detachment posted here, there's bound to be one there."

Quaeryt shrugged. "I think we'll have to make that decision when we get there. We may not have a decision to make, either. They may be ordered to fight to the last man . . . or to withdraw to Liantiago."

"Or to harass us all the way there."

Quaeryt nodded, but he was still thinking about the reaction of Captain Sentio and what it might mean . . . and what lay ahead of them in Barna and in Liantiago.

Over the next eight days, while Quaeryt had the sense that they were being watched as they rode westward toward Barna, none of the scouts could find any tracks that might have supported that feeling, and the people in the towns through which they passed seemed to know nothing about any Antiagon troopers.

On Solayi, near midmorning under a clear and bright winter sky, not that it seemed much like winter, Quaeryt stiffened in the saddle, glancing toward the northwest and a slightly higher hill, covered only at the top with trees bearing gold-tinted green leaves. Quaeryt hadn't seen any trees like them until the past few days, and every time he'd seen them, he'd observed that each stand was on a hilltop unconnected to any other forested area.

"Gets to you after a while, doesn't it?" asked Skarpa. "You have the feeling people are watching, but you never see them, and no one knows anything about them."

"Or no one wants to tell you anything about them. It seems like everyone is too frightened to say anything about Aliaro or whatever Shahib owns the lands."

"Don't know what it is, but they're scared. They're not scared of the Antiagon troopers. They're cautious around them, but not frightened," added Skarpa.

*It has to be imagers, because there isn't any other thing it could be . . . or something else of power having to do with the Autarch or the Shahibs.* That bothered Quaeryt—a lot—because he wanted to build the imagers into a force to support Bhayar, but he didn't like the aura of quiet fear he'd seen in the cities and towns of Antiago so far. *Would it be different if only High Holders and wealthy factors had to worry?* He didn't have an answer for that question . . . as he didn't for so many.

"You're worried about an Antiagon attack," observed Quaeryt. "Where would you attack us?"

"Right now," replied Skarpa, not quite humorously. "We don't know exactly where we are, and we're really not in the best fighting formation, because you can't travel as fast if you're set for battle."

"There's no cover nearby," Quaeryt pointed out.

"If they put cannon on one of those hills and aimed down along the road, we'd take casualties even if we broke and regrouped immediately. With all their warships, they must have cannon somewhere here in Antiago."

"Cannon are heavy. That's why Kharst didn't have many except close to Variana."

Skarpa grinned. "The road is paved, and how many large cities are left before us?"

"You're saying we should expect cannon . . . soon."

"I've ordered the scouts to look for any traces of heavy wear on the road or especially leaving it, and they're scouting in squads."

"So that someone is likely to return if they run into trouble?"

The submarshal nodded. "I don't like it when things are too quiet and they shouldn't be."

"That's why you have the scouts farther out than usual." Quaeryt was just repeating what Skarpa had said earlier, trying to see if the older officer would add anything.

"The last thing we need to do is find ourselves riding into massed cannon, even with you and the imagers. Riding into heavy cannon fire in terrain we don't know with a force as small as we have . . ."

"In short, when you've got almost thirty regiments you can take some fire, but not with six."

"And not when we're more likely to be facing gunners who know what to do with their weapons."

That unfortunately made sense, and that was why Skarpa and Quaeryt had gone over orders with the regimental commanders on what to do if the Antiagons attempted to shell the column from a distance. Basically, those orders were a refinement on what Quaeryt had done in the last battles against the Bovarians—to move quickly, at an angle.

Skarpa cleared his throat. "You said you thought the Antiagons wouldn't wait until we got too close to Barna or Liantiago. That, if they attacked us at all, they'd do so away from towns or cities."

"You don't think so?"

"I'd be interested in why you thought so. We couldn't maneuver as well in a town or city."

"Have you noticed how well kept the towns are, even the older buildings in them?"

Skarpa nodded, even as his eyes scanned the road ahead and the gentle rolling hills, their heights generally tree-covered.

"I'm just guessing, but everything I've seen or heard suggests that they try to preserve what they have. Using troops and cannon inside a city would go against that. If they're using imagers to build things—or repair them—what they can do at any one time has to be limited."

"Limited? Your imagers rebuilt the entire Chateau Regis in less than three weeks."

"They refinished it and modified some things, and we had the largest gathering of imagers in the history of either Bovaria or Telaryn. The autarchs may have been using imagers longer, and they may have gathered a greater number of imagers from those that they have, but Antiago is a smaller and less populous land—"

"Frig!" Skarpa gestured ahead to where a puff of smoke appeared above the trees on the hillside a good three-fifths of a mille ahead on the north side of the road. On the road to the south of the hilltop, a scouting patrol appeared, galloping back over a low rise in the road, and one trooper was waving a red banner—danger—trying to get Skarpa's attention.

Almost instantly, the shoulder of the road ahead on the south side of the pavement erupted into a geyser of dirt, stones, and gravel.

"First company! On me!" Holding his imaging shields barely extended away from himself and the mare, Quaeryt urged her forward and to the north side of the road, across a field at an angle toward a stand of trees near the top of a ridge. The imager undercaptains and first company rode close behind him. As he glanced back, he could see Skarpa and Fhaen leading Third Regiment southeast at a quick trot.

Another explosion, even closer to him, so that stones and gravel rattled off his shields, momentarily blocked a better view of what the various regiments were doing. Quaeryt looked to the west, noting the location of the haze of smoke that marked from where the cannon were firing, then guided the mare more to the north so that first company would end up behind the trees.

The time it took first company to reach the trees, the same ones with the gold-tinged leaves, seemed like a full glass, but was far less than half a quint. Once Quaeryt had the company temporarily out of sight, he immediately raised sight shields and led them, at a fast walk, down the far side of the ridge and then along the fields to the west, trying to gauge how to reach the lower edge of the woods from which the Antiagon gunners were firing.

The field grass was barely ankle high as he led first company toward the larger hill from which the cannon were firing, but then, Quaeryt reflected, it was still supposedly late winter, and the meadows and fields in most of Bovaria and Telaryn were still likely cold and possibly frozen, and certainly still snow-covered in Tilbor. He could almost feel the passage of cannonballs across the sky to the south before they landed and exploded, but with the ridge between him and the road, he had no idea how effective the Antiagon gunners were being. He did know that he and first company had to put the cannon out of action as soon as possible.

The grassy field sloped down to a depression before slowly rising toward the trees that held the cannon still firing eastward at Southern Army. As he rode closer, all Quaeryt could see was a narrow expanse of dirt and mud, an indication that a stream had run there intermittently. Once he felt that first company was close enough that the cannon could not be depressed enough to fire at first company, he dropped the concealment shields and raised full shields across the front of the column.

"Imagers! Shields!"

Quaeryt had barely issued the order when a hail of arrows arched out from the trees, the clattered off his shields.

Under the cover of the archers, two squads of troopers in maroon and white uniforms advanced from the woods, half of them bearing long pikes.

"Advance and plant!" called a voice from the trees.

"Threkhyl," said Quaeryt in a low voice image-projected to the undercaptain, "bring the trees down on them."

A sound like rainfall followed a series of creaks and cracking sounds as the greenish gold leaves shivered while the limbs and the trunks bearing those limbs shuddered and then toppled northward onto the advancing pikemen.

Only a handful of the pikemen escaped the tangle of leaves, branches, and limbs, but behind the welter of fallen trees some hundred yards wide were several hundred troopers bearing small round shields larger than bucklers and blades longer than the sabres of first company. Behind them were archers, not quite a company's worth, Quaeryt judged, although it was hard to tell with so many of them partly concealed by the shadows of the tall trees with their green-golden leaves.

Almost absently, Quaeryt noted that the trees were planted in rows. *Another kind of orchard?*

Above them on the hillside, the sound of yet another round being fired echoed down the slope, reminding Quaeryt that the objective was not the archers and the troopers in the woods, but the cannon on the slopes above.

Unfortunately, bringing down the line of trees had made charging the archers all but impossible. *And you'll lose too much of first company if you don't deal with the archers.*

"Imagers! Iron darts on the archers!"

As the archers began to fall, the footmen glanced around, then began to break. With that so did the remaining archers.

"Khalis, Lhandor, Voltyr! Hot iron to the cannon!" Quaeryt followed his order by imaging scores of hot iron splinters to the area where the cannon appeared to be. When there was no apparent reaction, he tried again, and a faint flash of pain seared across his eyes, then faded. He took a deep breath.

For several moments nothing seemed to happen. Then the top of the hillside erupted into a geyser of flame, and the ground under the mare's hoofs shook for several moments before subsiding. The remaining handful or so of Antiagon troopers staying in the trees glanced uphill, then turned and sprinted for the woods to the west.

"First company! Hold!" ordered Quaeryt.

"Hold!" echoed Zhelan.

Quaeryt quickly scanned the tree debris between first company and where the Antiagon force had been, but he saw no movement, but it was more likely that any surviving Antiagons were lying low than that the toppling trees had killed or wounded them all.

The flames rising from the top of the hill faded into an orangish yellow light, but did not die away. Slowly, as first company re-formed and as fourth squad took charge of the few handfuls of Antiagon prisoners, that orangish light began to intensify. Before long, thick gray smoke began to billow upward, and a sweetish, almost perfume-like odor filled the air, rather than the acrid scents Quaeryt associated with fire.

"The whole top of the hill's on fire," declared Horan. "Must be oil nut trees."

Quaeryt had read about oil nut trees, but he'd never seen them, nor had he realized how fiercely they might burn. He turned to Zhelan. "The fire's spreading, and it's hot. There's no way we can track down or capture the Antiagons who fled. We need to finish re-forming and head back to Southern Army."

"We're ready to go, sir." Zhelan paused. "We don't know if the rest of Southern Army was attacked, do we?"

Quaeryt appreciated the gentle reminder that they had no idea what they might be heading back toward. "Once we leave here, I'll try to hold concealment shields until we have a better idea of what to expect."

"Yes, sir." The major turned in the saddle. "Head out! On the commander!"

Quaeryt eased the mare forward.

Even after he'd ridden several hundred yards east, he could feel the heat from the burning oil trees on his back, and he had no doubt that the troopers in fourth squad and the prisoners they were marching with felt it even more strongly.

Once first company began to circle back toward the road, Quaeryt asked Zhelan, "Do you have any idea of our casualties?"

"Five wounded, maybe a few more. No deaths so far. The archers were the problem, and the imagers' shields protected most of the men."

"I can't believe the oil nut trees."

"They use the oil for lamps. Must work well," said Zhelan blandly.

Quaeryt couldn't help smiling, but he kept looking at other hilltops and at the road. The section of road to the west of where Southern Army had been was clear, although there were small craters on both sides of the road and places in the road itself where the cannonballs had hit and left shattered stone and small depressions.

Southern Army was largely formed up by the time first company reached the section of the main road east of where Quaeryt had been when the initial cannon fire had begun. Quaeryt saw bodies in maroon and white everywhere. Most of the fallen looked either too young or too old to be proper troopers. Leaving first company in the vanguard position for the continued advance on Barna, Quaeryt rode back to meet Skarpa.

The submarshal gestured toward the raging fire on the hilltop to the west. "What did you do?"

"We blew up the cannon. The fire happened because they were hidden in an oil nut tree plantation. I'd wager that's why all those hilltops with the trees that have golden green leaves are surrounded by pastures and meadows. What happened here?"

"They sent a mounted regiment against us." Skarpa offered a wry smile. "I did tell you that they'd find out we were heading toward Liantiago no matter what we did."

"You were right."

"In a way." Skarpa shook his head. "They were barely trained. They lost over a thousand troopers before the rest broke and fled. There wasn't any point in trying to chase them down. They're scattered all over the countryside."

"And Southern Army?"

"We lost fifty or so, but we've got another hundred fifty, maybe two hundred wounded. The whole thing was designed to see how much they could bleed us without risking really trained troopers, or likely even their best gunners or cannon. Terrible waste of men." The submarshal frowned. "Unless they intend to keep doing the same thing all the way to Liantiago."

"That could be a problem," admitted Quaeryt, "but I can't believe they have that many troops to spare." After a moment he asked, "Did you run into any musketeers?"

"No. Did you?"

"Not a one. A company of archers, but no musketeers."

"Cannon, but no musketeers. That's strange," mused Skarpa. "Can't be because muskets are too heavy, not if they're lugging cannon up on hilltops."

"You think it could be because they don't use muskets on their ships?"

"I have no idea, but it bothers me. I don't want to be surprised the way we were in Bovaria."

Neither did Quaeryt, and he had to admit to himself that it bothered him as well, but there were more than a few aspects to Antiago that were troubling—and they'd likely become even more troubling if he and Skarpa were successful in removing Aliaro and controlling Liantiago.

Southern Army found the small city of Barna both like and unlike Suemyran. Unlike Suemyran, Barna was split into two sections, one on each side of the Arnio River, a very modest and comparatively shallow watercourse, and had a much greater proportion of two-storied and large dwellings than did Suemyran, not to mention far more villas on the surrounding hills. Quaeryt did notice that none of the villas were located near stands of oil nut trees. As in Suemyran, the inhabitants made no protests upon the entry of Southern Army. The dwellings were finished in stucco of various off-white shades . . . but all, even those in the poorest quarters, were reasonably well maintained. The main streets were all paved, and the paving stones were in good repair.

Once more Skarpa had commandeered the inns and the larger dwellings, and on Lundi evening, after all the troopers had been fed and the officers had eaten, while Telaryn squads patrolled the streets, he and Quaeryt sat in the gaming room in The Inn Bountiful, an expansive structure built as a rectangle around a central garden courtyard.

"All the warehouses are empty," Skarpa said. "They had to have moved everything days before we arrived."

"Nineteenth Regiment has gathered some from the storehouses of the villas out in the hills. They didn't expect us to show up," said Quaeryt.

"I'd wager that they were quietly offended," commented Skarpa.

"They were. Very quietly though, as if to say that matters weren't done that way." *As if regiments, even those of the Autarch, do not bother the stores of the Shahibs.* "Most of them were still more than half empty . . ."

"Most of the larger dwellings are empty, too. The owners departed well before we arrived, but the crafters and shopkeepers are still here."

"They're the ones who fear that they'll lose everything if they abandon their shops."

"Good thing we're not staying here. If we were, we'd have to start foraging off the people," Skarpa observed.

"I wonder where they sent all the provisions in the city storehouses. We didn't find many wagons accompanying that regiment."

"Back to Liantiago, I'd wager. They had to know that they might need them."

"They also had to know that the attack on us would fail."

"I don't know that I believe that," said Skarpa.

"Did we capture any officers?"

Skarpa frowned. "No . . . now that I think about it. Some squad leaders, and we found several undercaptains who were killed, but no senior officers."

"They didn't use any Fire, and there wasn't a catapult anywhere in sight. That, along with their performance, suggests barely trained men, as you pointed out. In turn, that means . . ."

"They expected the assault to fail, and the officers knew it, and rode off," finished Skarpa. "Then why make the attack at all?"

"So the Autarch could see what casualties they could inflict without using their best troopers? To make us overconfident? To be able to tell the Shahibs and Shahibas that he was making every effort to stop the invaders?" Quaeryt shrugged. "Any answer we come up with is just a guess." *And even if we win—when we win—we still may never know.*

After discussing the plans for leaving Barna on the next morning, Quaeryt left the gaming chamber and waited in the back hall until he caught sight of the innkeeper. Mhario was a tall, thin, but muscular figure of a man with a lightly tanned face.

"Innkeeper?"

"Yes, Shahib Commander?"

"Is not your inn, The Inn Bountiful, the most renowned in all of Barna?"

"It is well regarded, Shahib."

"Do not some of the most influential people in the city dine here upon occasion?"

"That has been known to happen."

"And have they not talked of many things?"

"Many people talk of many things. That is true."

"Did some not talk about the fact that we might be occupying the city?"

"I could not say, sir."

"How long did the Antiagon regiment stay in Barna before it marched out to fight?"

"I could not say, Shahib. A few days, perhaps."

"Did any of the officers dine here?"

"They may have. I cannot recall everyone who dines here, you understand." The innkeeper smiled apologetically.

"Have the prices of goods gone up recently, the things you buy for the inn and the public room?"

"I could not . . ." The innkeeper paused, as if realizing that what seemed to be a standard reply was hardly credible. "They have not so far. I fear that they will, from inquiries I have made."

"When did you find out about the Autarch's decision to strip the warehouses here and send all the provisions to Liantiago?"

"Honored Shahib . . . I know nothing of that."

"Surely, you must have heard something." Quaeryt projected friendliness and concern.

"All I know, honored sir, is that provisions will be hard to come by."

For all that Quaeryt tried over the next quint, even with image projection, to obtain more information, in the end, he knew little more than he had after the first few questions.

So he made his way out to the stables, where he looked over where the mare was stabled, checking her manger and her feed bag, just hoping that one of the stable boys or the ostler would show up. Before long, one did, a boy who couldn't have been much older than ten.

"Nice mare, she is, sir."

"She's a good mount, and she's been more than good to me." Quaeryt offered a copper. "I'd appreciate it if you'd see to her properly."

"Yes, sir." The copper vanished. The urchin-like boy pushed back raggedly cut hair and grinned.

"You must have stabled a few mounts belonging to the officers of that regiment that passed through here."

"Nhallio wouldn't let me. He wanted their coin." The stable boy shook his head. "They didn't give him any. Hard men they were."

"Sometimes, the officers who get power too young are the hardest."

"None of the ones who came here were young. All of 'em older than you, sir."

"I imagine innkeeper Mhario was most polite to them."

"Had to be. He sent the girls off when he heard they were coming. Bessya almost didn't make it. She had to hide in the loft. Should have seen her shake when she snuck out. Mhario told me to stay out of sight."

"You did, I hope."

"Right that I did."

"Did you see them loading provisions?"

"Nah . . . the nearest storehouse is down on the river, two blocks over. Jaeklo said they took everything, even the old mule."

"They say where it was all going?"

"Nope . . ." After a moment the boy added, "They all took the west road, though. No place else to go but Liantiago. The drivers were real teamsters, too. Not troopers."

"The officers say anything about fighting or the like?"

"Not so as I could hear." The youth frowned. "One of 'em said something was a bloody waste. Couldn't hear what. Another . . . he said there'd be a lot of dead heroes." There was a pause. "There were, weren't there?"

"The troopers they sent against us weren't very good. They shouldn't have been fighting." Quaeryt shook his head, then handed over another copper. "Keep them safe."

"That I will, sir."

Then the boy slipped away into the dimness.

Quaeryt smiled, sadly, then gave the mare a solid pat, before turning and making his way from the stable.

He would have liked to have written to Vaelora, or even better to have received a missive from her, but there was little point in using troopers as dispatch riders . . . at least not until Liantiago was securely in Telaryn hands. *Will it ever be?*

He pushed that thought away as he walked across the side courtyard back to the inn.

Meredi dawned hazy, and by midmorning thick gray clouds rolled in from the west, promising the first rain since before Southern Army had taken Kephria. By noon a warm but light drizzle was falling, but the rain's warmth seemed to vanish when the droplets struck men, mounts, or the road and the ground, creating a knee-high mist and a dampish chill that settled over the land, cloaking the sheep that had earlier seemed ubiquitous . . . if always at a goodly distance from the stone-paved road that stretched westward through the endless low rolling hills.

"Looks like this will last for days," observed Zhelan, who rode beside Quaeryt while Skarpa was headed back along the column to check with his regimental commanders. "Reminds me of the fall in Cheva. The mist and rain would come in right after harvest and stay until it snowed. Sometimes, the mist turned to an ice fog and stayed."

"You make it sound pretty dismal," said Quaeryt.

"It was. That was when I joined up. Late fall when I was seventeen. I told my father I couldn't take another cold damp year. He said I'd take it and like it. I walked off and joined the old Ninth Regiment—that was one place I knew he couldn't get me."

"Did he try?"

"No idea. We rode off to deal with Tilbor, and I never went back."

"You didn't write?"

"Wasn't much point in it. What would I have said? That I didn't miss the beatings? Or Ma crying when she didn't think anyone saw? Besides, he couldn't read. She couldn't either. I barely knew my letters. Learned more when I saw that those who could read and write got promoted."

"Those who could read and write *and* fight?" suggested Quaeryt.

"Anyone can fight. Fighting smarter is harder—"

*Crumptt!* The shoulder of the road ahead of Quaeryt exploded, and gobbets of mud and wet grass struck his shields and splattered everywhere.

The mist and drizzle were just heavy enough that at the moment Quaeryt had no idea from where the Antiagons were firing, only that it had to be from somewhere to the east of Southern Army, and most likely not too far from the road.

"First company! Left! On me!" Quaeryt had no reason to head left, but that decision was as much as because the last time he'd led first company to the right. He urged the mare off the pavement and across the shoulder, through a shallow stretch of water that had pooled in a depression below the shoulder, and then up onto the grassy expanse that stretched southward for a good half mille.

Another explosion—this one on the south side of the road and less than ten yards east of the middle of first company—sprayed more mud, dirt, gravel, and debris across the troopers—and Quaeryt's shields and those of the imager undercaptains—he hoped. The next cannonball exploded well behind first company, but when Quaeryt glanced back, it seemed as though the entire road and the road shoulders as well were a mass of explosions.

He looked to the east and could make out, just barely, what he thought was a flash of orange from a distant hilltop, possibly a good mille or more away. He could see that there was no way that he and first company could reach the gun emplacement through the rain and over wet ground with any speed, not before the heavy bombardment wreaked havoc on Southern Army. The warm drizzle had made the ground even softer and more treacherous than a colder rain might have.

Behind him, more explosions wracked the road, and he could hear men yelling, and the screams of at least one horse.

*Warm rain . . . heat. Do you dare? The whole invasion was your idea. How can you not try?*

Trying to draw strength and warmth from the rain and the clouds, Quaeryt concentrated on sending thousands of tiny red-hot iron needles to the area where he had seen the drizzle-cloaked cannon smoke.

Instantly he was cloaked in ice, cold and so imprisoning that he could not breathe. He tried to escape and found that neither his arms nor his legs could move. Nor could he move anything else, no matter how hard he tried. Then, just as suddenly, the ice shattered, and he rocked forward in the saddle gasping for breath.

Two thunderclaps rocked him—one a distant explosion and the other a white hammering slashing impact that rocked his skull, then slashed his vision into tattered shards before another hammer pummeled him into darkness.

When the darkness lifted, Quaeryt was lying on his back, shivering, even though someone had wrapped a blanket around him.

"Sir . . . can you see me?"

Quaeryt blinked, trying to make out who was speaking. Finally, he saw a face. "Khalis . . . that you?"

"Yes, sir. Can you sit up and drink? It'll be cold, but it will help."

"Yes . . . I think . . ." Quaeryt managed, with the undercaptain's help, to get to a sitting position, but his hands were shaking so much that Khalis had to help him hold the water bottle as he sat on a second blanket. After several swallows, his vision began to clear, but the shaking continued, despite his riding jacket and the blanket around him. From where he sat, he could see, intermittently, that a light dusting of snow covered the ground for almost half a mille. Beyond that, the ground was brown and wet. The clouds overhead looked lighter in color, but those farther east were still thick and gray.

"The cannon . . . did . . . get them . . . ?"

"Yes, sir. The whole hilltop exploded." There was a slight pause. "It was more than a mille away. You imaged hot iron that far?"

"I . . . tried."

"You succeeded, sir. The scouts reported that there's nothing left except shattered bronze . . . and ashes. They couldn't get too close."

"They put the cannon . . . in another oil nut tree orchard?"

"Yes, sir."

Quaeryt frowned. "How long has it been?"

"Sir?"

"Since the Antiagons started shelling us."

"Two glasses or so."

*Two glasses?* Quaeryt sat there for several moments without speaking.

"You might drink some more lager, sir."

Quaeryt did.

He finally stopped shaking and was able to stand when Skarpa rode up from whatever he had been doing, dismounted, and walked over to Quaeryt.

*He's been totaling the casualties, no doubt.* Quaeryt waited.

"It's good to see you on your feet, Commander. Even if you look as white as deep winter ice."

"I'm glad to be on my feet."

"You know I don't like it when the only thing that saves us from huge losses is something you do that almost kills you." Skarpa looked at Quaeryt. "Someday, you'll do too much."

"It didn't kill me."

"It would have if Zhelan hadn't smashed you out of that ice coffin you created for yourself . . . and then kept you from falling out of the saddle." The submarshal gave a nod to Zhelan, who had edged closer to the three.

Quaeryt didn't want to dwell on his idiocy in getting himself frozen in ice. "Were there any Antiagon troopers that attacked?"

"No. We didn't see any, and the scouts haven't found any tracks. This time they were relying on cannon. They had the entire road ranged, it looks like."

"How many did we lose?" Quaeryt found he was holding his breath.

"A hundred and fifty outright, another sixty, seventy with wounds."

Quaeryt let his breath out slowly. "That's all?"

"That was all they had time for. You took them out of action in a fraction of a quint. At the rate they were firing they might have had twenty cannon. They could have taken out an entire regiment before long." Skarpa paused. "Are you sure you'll be all right?"

"Nothing seems to be broken. I'm sore all over, and it's hard to see, but that's happened before."

Skarpa looked to Khalis. "Try to keep him from doing anything else for a while."

"Yes, sir."

After Skarpa had mounted and ridden off, Quaeryt looked to Zhelan. "Thank you. I know I wouldn't be here—"

"Lots of men wouldn't be here if you hadn't done what you did."

"How bad was it for first company?"

"Four men in third squad have shrapnel wounds."

"How serious?"

"Cuts and bruises except for one. A rock broke his arm. It's shattered. He'll likely lose it."

Quaeryt couldn't help but wince, but the wince brought on another wave of pain so agonizing that he couldn't see for a time.

"You need to be careful for a while, sir," interjected Khalis.

"That's . . . clear."

"The scouts have located some villas a few milles ahead. We'll be taking quarters there until the weather clears."

That was fine with Quaeryt.

Later, as he rode slowly eastward, he wondered why the ice hadn't happened before. He hadn't been encased in ice at Ferravyl or at the battle at Variana. *Except you made an effort to hold shields against it both times.* This time, he'd been so worried about the casualties to Southern Army that he hadn't even thought about strengthening his shields. *Anything you do without thinking it through . . .* He didn't need to finish the thought.

The drizzle turned into freezing rain on Jeudi and was gone by Vendrei morning, when Southern Army resumed its progress toward Liantiago under a cool sun and clear skies. By that afternoon, it was clear that everyone knew the Telaryn forces were coming. Every village and town along the road was largely deserted, with barred doors and shutters fastened tight.

By Samedi morning much of Quaeryt's soreness had subsided, and he only had a faint headache, but he was still wearing his riding jacket fastened shut because he still felt chill, even in full sunlight that was as warm as fall in Tilbor. As he rode through seemingly empty hamlet after hamlet, town after town, Quaeryt couldn't help but wonder why the people closer to Liantiago seemed more worried or concerned than those farther away had been. *Or is it because they're more worried about Aliaro and the Shahibs than about Southern Army?* Then again, his thoughts along that line might just be wishful thinking, but how could he tell?

Solayi morning, after Southern Army had been on the road for a glass or so, Skarpa eased his mount in beside Quaeryt and his mare. "How are you feeling this morning?"

"Fairly well . . . a little chill at times. Otherwise . . ." Quaeryt shrugged.

"A little chill isn't bad after almost being frozen to death. I still wish—"

"That I wouldn't do things like that?" Quaeryt laughed. "I wish I could think of better ways to deal with matters."

"You can when you deliver homilies," Skarpa pointed out.

"That's because I have time to think about them. When something unexpected happens in the field, I don't have that time." Quaeryt looked quizzically at Skarpa. "You think that it would be useful for the army to have services? Is that it?"

"It wouldn't hurt," replied Skarpa with a grin. "I had hoped. Some of the officers, especially the junior officers . . ."

"I'll do what I can."

"You always do. That's why I keep saying that you'll end up high in Bhayar's councils."

"I may be listened to, but I doubt I'll ever hold a rank or position higher than this."

"You keep saying that, but you're a commander."

"And you're a submarshal."

"Only because of you." Skarpa paused. "Don't think Kharllon and Meurn haven't alluded to that."

"And they're where they are because of Deucalon and Myskyl."

"Myskyl, I think. He seems to have a way of persuading people."

"I can't say I've found him very persuasive," said Quaeryt dryly.

"You're one of the few. Bhayar might find him persuasive as well, except for you. Don't think Myskyl doesn't know it."

"I wonder how he likes the frozen north."

"He's either avoided it or settled himself into a high holding with a compliant widow."

"If not both."

Once Skarpa rode off, Quaeryt began to split his attention between the road ahead and the hills flanking it, because he didn't want to be caught in another cannonade, and possible ideas for a homily. Since he had left *Rholan and the Nameless* with Vaelora, he wasn't going to be able to page through that volume for ideas. As the glasses passed, though, there were no more cannon attacks, and not even a trace of Antiagon forces.

*Why? Why not more attacks as we near Liantiago?*

The only idea that Quaeryt had was that Aliaro's forces were limited, and that he was saving them for the defense of Liantiago. In a way, that made perfect sense, because, given the way Antiago was governed, it was clear that without taking the capital city and capturing or removing Aliaro and his ministers and high officials, the entire Southern Army campaign would end up as an almost useless exercise. *Not to mention undercutting everything you and Vaelora tried to accomplish in Khel.*

After pushing that line of thought away—for the moment—Quaeryt tried to concentrate once more coming up with an idea for a decent homily.

By the fourth glass of the afternoon, Southern Army was settled into camp—a group of villas in the hills some ten milles from the outskirts of Liantiago—if both the maps and the millestones were to be believed. Unsurprisingly, the buildings had been largely stripped . . . except of common items such as heavy kitchen tables and common bedsteads and mattresses—and there were absolutely no supplies.

In the late twilight at sixth glass, those who wanted to attend services gathered on the slope below the main villa, where Quaeryt stood on the terrace. By image-projecting his voice, he made his way through the opening and invocation, a hymn, and the confession—and that had always disturbed him, but the men and officers seemed to need it. Before he knew it, he was beginning the homily.

". . . and, as are all evenings under the Nameless, it is a good evening. If you don't think so, you might recall that there are still several yards of snow covering Tilbor at the moment, and most likely a cold and drizzling rain is cloaking Solis right now, while the ground around Variana is either frozen solid or icy mud . . . and it's no longer drizzling here . . . and no one is firing cannon at us." Quaeryt paused for a moment. "All those examples could give you reasons for thinking it is a good evening. Whether for thinking it's a good evening or one not so good, all of us have reasons for why we think matters are the way they are. When we left Suemyran for Barna, I kept wondering why these stands of trees with gold-tinged leaves were only planted on hilltops and why nothing except low grass was planted around them. When some cannon powder exploded, those of us in first company found out the reason why those trees were planted where they were. When they catch fire, they burn hot and fast." Quaeryt did his best to image-project a sense of wry humor.

"But there's a problem with reasons and reasoning. We assume that there must be a reason for everything, and we tend to assume that other people reason in the same way and with the same motives as we do. When we discover that they do not, we often decide that such people are tools of the Namer or that they are not so bright as we are. Yet who is to say that those people are not in turn looking at us and thinking that we are tools of the Namer?

"Why do I say this? Because reasoning is a tool. It is a tool of the mind, but like any tool it can be used for good or ill. An advocate who is skilled with words might well be able to reason well enough to convince any listener that Rholan the Unnamer was the Namer and the Namer was really the Nameless. The tool is only so good as the man who wields it, and there are two parts involved in using any tool. The first is how well it is used, and the second is the purpose for which it is used . . .

"If the purpose for which reason is used is to distort what is and has been or if a man uses reason to persuade others to do that which is evil, then reason is no more than Naming through the use of clever words and logic . . ."

His concluding words were simple enough. ". . . When we reason, let us strive to seek what is and not what we would wish to be, for reason in pursuit of passion, rather than in seeking truth, is Naming merely raised to a higher level of deception."

Once the officers and men had dispersed, Quaeryt walked toward the end of an outbuilding to the west of the others. There he stopped, and under the stars, and the nearly full orb of Artiema, he looked down the long slope toward the ribbon of road he could barely see. That line of gray stretched east and west across the rolling hills. Aware of someone approaching, he glanced up to see Commander Kharllon stopping several yards away.

"It's a long and narrow road," said Kharllon, gesturing toward the road below.

"But well paved," replied Quaeryt noncommitally.

"I'd heard that you had been a chorister," offered Commander Kharllon. "It does show."

Quaeryt offered a polite smile. "Actually, I was a scholar."

"There's not that much difference, is there? Both study the unknown and the impractical."

"Much like officers in peacetime, when war isn't a problem, don't you think?" replied Quaeryt gently. "Too often, what's practical is defined as what we need now, as opposed to what we will need, or what we could do to avoid needing it in the future."

"Those who are effective in the present often assume that what they see is what others need."

"Isn't that true of all of us?" replied Quaeryt with a soft laugh. "We all think that what we understand is what others should as well. We often get angry when we find they don't see matters as we do."

"But the most dangerous men are those who are most persuasive, especially when their views are, shall we say, at variance with those who wield power."

"Absolutely," agreed Quaeryt. "That's most likely why Rholan vanished. He was too persuasive and lacked the power to protect his vision of what should be."

For several moments, Kharllon did not speak, merely looked at Quaeryt. Finally, he said, "It will be interesting to see what comes of this campaign."

"The unification of all Lydar under Lord Bhayar, I would hope," replied Quaeryt.

"So would I, but holding all Lydar together might prove even more daunting than conquering it."

"It all depends on which vision those in power embrace, I would judge," said Quaeryt.

"With that, I would agree." Kharllon inclined his head. "Good evening, Commander. By the way, it was an excellent homily."

Quaeryt watched as the older senior officer walked away, then looked back down at the road. In the east, Erion was rising.

On Lundi morning a thin mist drifted in from the west, suggesting to Quaeryt that an even heavier fog might be covering the ground to the west. Either way, with the mist or fog there was less chance for another cannon attack on Southern Army, and Skarpa seemed slightly less worried as he ordered his forces onto the road westward.

Once the order of march was established, with first company leading and Third Regiment riding immediately behind, Skarpa joined Quaeryt. "That was a decent homily last night."

"Decent is a good word for it. It wasn't one of my best. Kharllon thought it was good."

"He talked to you?"

"Not for long. He delivered a not-so-veiled message . . . something along the lines that I was a dangerous man because I was persuasive and my views were . . . at variance . . . with those who were in power. He wasn't that direct, but that was what he meant."

"What did you say?"

"I told him that was why Rholan vanished . . . and tried to suggest that my interests lay in seeing all Lydar united under Bhayar. He agrees with that, but not with what he feels I want to come after that."

"Did he say what he thought that might be?"

"No, and I didn't ask him to explain. In turn, he refrained from more than generalities. That seemed best." Quaeryt looked directly at Skarpa. "You have something on your mind, don't you? That feeling that something might happen?"

"Not exactly. We've seen cannon, and we've seen troopers, but we haven't seen musketeers or imagers or Antiagon Fire," said Skarpa. "That worries me."

"They might not have that many imagers . . . or some of their imagers might not have talents that suited to battle." Quaeryt was thinking about Baelthm, whose value in battle was limited largely to self-protection and the ability to stop one or two enemy troopers.

"I can come up with reasons why we might not see imagers . . . but not

Antiagon Fire. That's what they're known for. We even encountered it in Bovaria. Why not here?"

"There's one possibility," suggested Quaeryt. "We always ran into it when they had a fortified position with catapults behind walls. Or when they had regiments of troops."

"That's a thought. It doesn't reassure me." Skarpa shook his head.

"It doesn't reassure me, either, but I don't have any other ideas—except that we'll probably run into it sooner or later."

"That's what I worry about." After riding with Quaeryt for almost a glass, Skarpa left to brief the scouts, and then rode back along the column to see to each regimental commander.

As Quaeryt rode eastward, he studied the land as well as he could, but saw nothing but recently planted fields and shuttered cots—with occasional villas on more distant hills. Midday came and went, although Quaeryt couldn't have told by the sun because the hazy high clouds had thickened enough to block any hint of its position.

Sometime close to first glass, Skarpa returned and reined in beside Quaeryt. "The scouts have found some tracks ahead, but there's nothing heavy."

"Like cannon?"

"No. A squad of riders, maybe a few more. It looks like they were scouting the road and the shoulders."

"How far ahead?"

"A mille or so."

"How recent are they?"

"Probably yesterday. Might have been the day before."

"Do the tracks continue toward us?"

"No. They stop and retrace their way. That's what the scouts report."

Quaeryt tried to make out what lay ahead, but the combination of uncertain light diffusing through the high hazy clouds and the patches of mist made a clear view difficult. Still, he could see several low hills on each side of the road, rising above the recently planted fields between first company and the nearest hill. The closest hills were more like gentle rises on the north side of the road, with crests little more than twenty yards high, and the closest part of their bases were several hundred yards back from the edge of the road. All were wooded, but not with oil nut trees, and some of the woods extended almost into the fields.

"What are you thinking?" asked the submarshal.

"That sounds like ranging the road."

"My thought as well. I've asked the scouts to check any tracks leaving the road, especially on the side lanes. I'm calling a halt to give everyone a rest while they do."

That made sense to Quaeryt, because the column was on a section of road situated in the middle of rolling rises so low that the land around Southern Army seemed almost flat, and the scattered cots were shuttered tight, without a trace of smoke from the chimneys. The hills immediately ahead looked to be the beginning of the more rugged lands that surrounded Liantiago and the bay that held Westisle.

"The hills beyond those little ones could hide a lot," added Skarpa.

Quaeryt nodded, his eyes on the nearer hills.

"We'll have to see what the scouts find. I'll let you know." With that, Skarpa rode off.

Quaeryt gathered Zhelan, Ghaelyn, and the imager undercaptains at the side of the road.

"We have problems ahead, Commander?" asked Zhelan.

"We might," Quaeryt admitted. "There are Antiagon tracks up ahead."

"Be hard to see in places with all that fog," added Ghaelyn, first company's undercaptain.

"We could be facing anything," said Quaeryt. "Or nothing. But we're getting close to Liantiago, and it's been several days since we've been attacked. I think cannon are unlikely because they're heavy, and we haven't seen enough tracks, not yet, for there to be too many troopers. To my way of thinking, that means we just might be hit with Antiagon Fire next. If that's so, it will come from the hills. I'll be posting imager undercaptains with each of the five squads of first company, and I'll give the order for shields at the first sign of an attack." Quaeryt looked at the undercaptains, especially at Threkhyl, before continuing. "If any of you see anything coming before I do, raise your shields and call out the attack. If there is an attack, they may wait until the first part of the company has passed." He paused. "Is that clear?"

"Yes, sir."

Quaeryt turned to Zhelan and Ghaelyn. "If we get attacked by Antiagon Fire, the men need to stay close to their imager—unless the attack takes him out. That's because the imagers can shield against the Fire. So you need to have your squad leaders watch the undercaptains."

"Yes, sir."

Quaeryt continued with the details for another half quint, including assigning each undercaptain to a squad. Even so, he and first company had to wait another three quints before Skarpa again returned to inform Quaeryt.

"There are tracks up all the hills, but they don't lead anywhere. They just end a hundred yards or so upslope and into the woods . . . like they rode up and decided that the hill wasn't suitable for what they had in mind." Skarpa shook his head. "I still don't like it."

"You think that they started with the hills the farthest from Liantiago and then worked back toward the city."

"It looks that way."

"But you're not convinced?"

"No, but we can't ride up every hill from here to Liantiago, either. Not unless we intend to take a season to get there."

"Where exactly do the tracks coming toward us end?" asked Quaeryt.

"Up ahead . . . do you see where that sty over the low stone wall is?"

"That's what, a half mille from the first of the hills?"

"About that," Skarpa confirmed. "Do you think they've measured out to that point?"

"Not necessarily, but after that point, I'm going to be worrying and very careful."

"Good. I'll let you and first company remain as the vanguard."

"And you'll drop back with Third Regiment?"

"Of course."

"I do so appreciate your confidence . . . and don't tell me that this whole campaign was my idea. I could scarcely forget it."

Skarpa grinned, then said, "I won't."

"Thank you." Quaeryt shook his head ruefully, then watched as Skarpa turned his mount and rode back to Third Regiment. "Company! Mount up!" Once his men were mounted, he gave the order, "Forward!"

Beside him, Zhelan turned in the saddle and relayed the order.

Although he watched closely after they passed the sty on the stone wall, Quaeryt did not actually extend his personal shields to cover those around him and first squad until they were some four hundred yards from the first hill. At a hundred yards, he gave the order for shields, and he kept studying the first hill as they rode past it, gauging the distance—some hundred yards between its base and the edge of the road. Then he looked to the second and smaller one ahead, just slightly farther from the road.

As they rode closer and then passed the second hill . . . nothing happened.

Quaeryt looked ahead to the taller and somewhat more rugged hills that separated the rolling fields from lower lands around Liantiago.

"Fire grenade! Fire grenade!" came the call from somewhere behind Quaeryt.

He jerked his head around in time to see a splash of crimson-green-yellow flame rebounding from someone's shields—Lhandor's, he thought—and then there were splashes of flame everywhere, the heat intense despite the shields.

With the mist that rose from the fields, it took Quaeryt several moments to make out from where the fire grenades were being launched—from the second and lower hill slightly farther from the road. Then it took him more time to make out several of the dark objects being catapulted out of the trees—and he began to image them back to where he thought the catapults were, one after the other. Some exploded in flight, and others vanished . . .

In that time he obviously missed some grenades because lines of the crimson-greenish-yellow flames continued to explode against imager shields—at least Quaeryt hoped that happened to be the case.

He kept trying to intercept and redirect more of the grenades—and then they stopped. A wave of crimson-greenish-yellow flame rose from an entire section of the lower hill where Quaeryt thought the Antiagon catapults were. Only then did he call a halt to the company and re-form the troopers, ready to make a sweep of the hill, if necessary.

As they watched, in perhaps half a quint, an oval of woods vanished in flame—and not a single Antiagon fled the woods at the base of the hill, not from what he could see.

Quaeryt turned to Zhelan. "How badly were we hurt?"

"You and the imagers kept most of the men from severe burns. A few in fifth squad have splotches in various places. Nothing more."

That was a relief of sorts, but he knew that some of the fire grenades had likely impacted Third Regiment.

"Here comes the submarshal," said Zhelan quietly.

Quaeryt turned in the saddle and watched as Skarpa rode over and reined up beside him.

"Why didn't everything go up in flames, the way the cannon emplacement did?" asked the submarshal.

"These are hardwoods," said Quaeryt. "Maybe they're harder to burn, or the Antiagon Fire might have consumed everything so quickly that it didn't have a chance to spread. It's also been cooler and damper." He shrugged. "Other than that . . . I just don't know."

Skarpa laughed. "You don't like to admit you don't know, do you?"

"How did you ever guess that?" replied Quaeryt dryly.

"I have watched you upon occasion."

"Once the fire up there dies out totally, I'd like to take a look," said Quaeryt.

"You think you can find out something after everything's burned out?"

"I'd like to look. Besides, I don't think it would hurt to have the scouts really look over the next few milles before we proceed."

"I've already dispatched them."

"Thank you."

It was more than a glass later before Quaeryt and Skarpa rode through the still-smoldering woods on the south side of the hill, accompanied by a squad from Third Regiment. When they reined up at the edge of the cleared area, Quaeryt could see the charred and collapsed remnants of four catapults.

"Shouldn't they have burned to nothing?" asked Skarpa.

"I'd have thought so, but . . ." Quaeryt looked more closely across the clearing. He thought he could make out the forms of at least ten bodies. His eyes went to the charred framework of the first catapult, then to the second and finally to the third and fourth. All had been burned and partly collapsed in the same fashion.

"What is it?" asked Skarpa.

"You were asking about imagers, remember? These catapults were imaged, I'm fairly sure. I'm guessing that they brought one of them out here, along with some imagers, and used the one as a model for the others. They were imaged out of some kind of wood that's resistant to fire. They likely imaged the Antiagon Fire grenades into being as well."

"Could your imagers—"

"Not without knowing what's inside of them. You might recall that imaging even something as simple as a wheel takes observation and knowledge."

"I still . . . if they can do that . . ."

"I've been able to try different forms of imaging for a little more than a year. From what I can tell, the autarchs have been using imagers for a lot longer."

Skarpa sighed. "I suppose that's true, but . . ."

"I know. The more we find out, the more there is to find out."

"I still don't see how the scouts missed their tracks," said Skarpa. "And we didn't see any traces on the way up, either."

"If they had an imager with them, he could have imaged away all sign of tracks, and even imaged an extra tree or some underbrush in place." *Or he could have used concealment shields,* but Quaeryt wasn't about to admit that possibility publicly, especially not if word might get to Kharllon and Meurn.

When they finally headed back down toward the main road, Quaeryt asked, "What sort of casualties did we take—besides those in first company?"

"Less than fifty, mostly in Third Regiment, and most of those were in the first company."

Quaeryt feared that some of those might well have resulted from grenades deflected from fifth squad, but that was unavoidable, and the casualties would have been far higher without first company and the imagers leading the way.

Skarpa called a halt at fourth glass of Lundi afternoon, at a group of older villas just shy of the short stretch of rugged hills leading down to the lower lands that formed an arc around the bay on which Liantiago was located. Then he called a meeting of all the regimental commanders in the dining room of the largest villa, which held nothing but a long battered table and even more battered straight-backed chairs gathered from various places in the largely stripped villa. Once all seven regimental commanders and Quaeryt were present, from the head of the table Skarpa began, "We have several milles of hills ahead, five or six. At the west end, they drop steeply down to the lands around the bay. The mist is thickening, and it's already hard to see anything in the hills. The scouts haven't had time to cover more than a mille ahead. After what happened earlier today, I'd like to give the scouts plenty of time to scour those hills."

"Do you think that will give the Antiagons more time to form their defenses?" asked Commander Kharllon.

"If they don't have them already in place, I'd be astonished," replied Skarpa. "A little caution on our part won't give them that much more time, and it could save us quite a few troopers." He smiled politely. "I believe that Marshal Deucalon made that observation a number of times when he was commanding Northern Army on the advance up the Aluse."

"At times he did." Kharllon smiled in return.

Quaeryt could almost hear the words left unspoken—"but not in a case like this." He was about to say something when Alazyn cleared his throat.

"I'm one of the most junior here, but it seems to me that the submarshal will get the blame if anything goes wrong. Or have I missed something? It also seems to me that the submarshal's old regiment and Commander Quaeryt's first company have been taking the lead—and the brunt of the attacks. Now . . . I don't decide any of that. I just follow orders, but it does seem a little strange to me when those who've been shielded are the ones urging against caution and a prudent advance."

For a moment there was silence around the table. Then Kharllon looked at Alazyn, his eyes hard. Meurn looked aghast, but Quaeryt could see that

Fhaen was having trouble concealing a smile. Both Fhaasn and Dulaek looked to Paedn, the senior subcommander. No one looked directly at Quaeryt.

Quaeryt thought he knew why Skarpa did not immediately reply, and he kept a pleasant expression on his face and waited.

Paedn laughed, warmly. "A subcommander not afraid to offer the obvious. Don't look so astonished, Meurn. It does happen, now and again." The senior subcommander looked to Kharllon. "You asked a good question, and you got a good answer. At least, I thought it was a good one, especially coming from a commander known to move far more quickly than the marshal. Why do you have reservations?"

"It seems to me that the Antiagons are unprepared. I'd prefer to keep them that way," replied Kharllon, his voice open and pleasant.

"So would we all, I think, but the hills ahead are the last place from where they can mount a surprise attack. We escaped major casualties in the attack earlier today, but I wouldn't be surprised if fending off those fire grenades left our imagers somewhat . . . depleted." Paedn looked to Quaeryt.

"Several of them would not be able to offer the same level of imaging," replied Quaeryt.

"After any battle, some troopers would like to claim that," said Kharllon dryly.

"The submarshal has six imager undercaptains," replied Quaeryt. "There are six regiments. If one or two of your regiments were at half strength, you'd likely be more cautious." He paused just slightly, before adding, "I'd like to think you would be."

Fhaen smothered a grin.

"As always," replied Kharllon, "that would depend on the circumstances."

"As it does here," said Skarpa firmly. "Do any of you have any special needs or circumstances of which I should be aware?"

"We could use some boots or a bootmaker before long," said Meurn. "Or even tanned leather for boot soles."

"I'll see what I can do," said Skarpa.

"Would you like some fatted steers, too?" murmured someone, but Quaeryt didn't see who it was, although he suspected Alazyn.

Once Skarpa dealt with other questions involving supplies, set the duty and standby regiments for the evening, and dismissed the senior officers, Quaeryt walked outside and nodded for Alazyn to join him.

"I know, sir. I shouldn't have said anything, even in Northern Army he was like that. Always saying things without saying them. No one would say anything."

"That might have been because he's one of the marshal's favorites."

"That's why he's here, isn't it?"

"I wouldn't be surprised, but no one told me anything like that, and they didn't tell the submarshal, either."

"It doesn't matter. I never expected to make subcommander, and I'll be Namer-fired if I'll scrape and bow to a commander who hides behind other regiments."

"Don't scrape and bow. Smile warmly and politely to him from now on. That will upset him more than anything, now."

Alazyn grinned. "I can do that."

After a few more moments with Alazyn, Quaeryt watched as the dark-haired officer hurried back to his regiment. There wasn't any doubt in his mind that Alazyn had worked his way up through the ranks—and would probably have spent the rest of his time in service as a permanent undercaptain or captain if Kharst hadn't attacked Ferravyl. *But then, you'd probably have rotted away as a princeps somewhere . . . with a very unhappy wife.* He couldn't help but smile at the irony in that observation, since two years earlier he would have been astonished to have been named a princeps.

He shook his head and made his way to the small building that would serve first company, where he summoned the imager undercaptains. After relaying what Skarpa had in mind, he then looked at Horan. "Have you ever imaged leather?"

The middle-aged imager laughed. "More than once. Wasn't much of a cobbler or bootmaker, but leather I could do."

"One of the foot regiments needs boot leather. Is that possible?"

"Should be. Let's see what I can do. Be a welcome change from what we've been doing."

More than a glass later, just before the cooks were about to begin feeding the troopers, Quaeryt made his way back to the villa Skarpa was using, and then to the study.

The submarshal looked up from the maps on the table too small to be a proper desk. "I haven't heard yet."

"Oh . . . it's not about that. We have a wagon filled with tanned boot leather out here. I thought you might like to let Subcommander Meurn know about it."

"One of your imagers?" Skarpa brushed hair that was more gray than

Quaeryt remembered back off his forehead, then looked directly at the commander.

"He used to be a trapper and lived out from others. The leather looks to be good and sturdy."

"Leave the wagon here. I'll send word. Meurn won't like it."

Quaeryt nodded.

"How do you expect me to deal with Kharllon after what happened?" asked Skarpa, half humorously.

"Keep him in reserve until we reach Liantiago. Then have Fourteenth Regiment lead an attack." Quaeryt's tone was ironically dry.

"You're serious, aren't you?"

"It doesn't hurt to have a heroic senior officer now and again."

"I would ask, wouldn't I?"

"You're in charge."

"I wonder, at times, if any of us are truly in control. Or are we playthings in a vast game between the Namer and the Nameless?"

"Rholan wondered that as well. At least, he said that professing a great destiny was inviting the Namer and the Nameless to make one a plaque in a game."

"Is that why you disclaim everything?" asked Skarpa.

"No."

"Why then?"

"Most would not believe that what I seek is possible. Too many of the few who could see it is possible would do anything they could to stop it."

"And what do you seek that is so dangerous?"

"Among other things, a fairer and more just world for those without power and privilege."

"You're right," said Skarpa with a bark of laughter. "If the High Holders of Lydar believed you could bring that about, they'd line up with cannon and Antiagon Fire . . . for both you and Bhayar."

*And that's just part of what I seek.* "So I don't say much, except that I'm a loyal supporter of Lord Bhayar."

"What does Lord Bhayar think?"

"He knows I'm absolutely loyal."

Skarpa nodded slowly. "Another reason why you gather enemies."

"If it weren't that, it'd be something else. There's always something."

"There is. Speaking of that, you might also suggest to Alazyn that Kharllon does carry grudges."

"I already talked to him."

"Good. How many attacks do you think the Antiagons will make before we reach the city?"

"As many as they think they can without great losses. I'd expect something tomorrow, from the hills, and maybe even a fortified position somewhere short of the city. The fortified position might be long on walls and Antiagon Fire and short on troopers."

"To see what losses they can inflict without taking too many casualties."

"That's my thought. Has Kharllon offered any observations?"

"Of course not. He's just expressed the utmost confidence in my ability to direct an attack on a city that's supposedly never even been threatened, let alone taken."

"Oh?"

"By his quiet silence and his obedience . . . not by anything else." Skarpa snorted.

"I assume you want first company in the van tomorrow."

"Where else?"

"We'll be ready." With a nod, Quaeryt slipped away, leaving Skarpa and his maps.

A quint past seventh glass on Mardi morning saw first company riding down the lane from the old and tired villas toward the gray stone of the road leading westward to the rugged hills—and Liantiago beyond. The sky was clearer than it had been in days, and a brisk and chill wind blew out of the northeast.

Just before first company turned onto the main road, Skarpa rode up and eased his mount in beside Quaeryt's mare. "The scouts haven't found any tracks at all."

"None? Not on the road or on the shoulders or the side lanes?"

"No." Skarpa offered a crooked smile. "They say that there's not even a place where the Antiagons could make an attack. I'd say that means an attack. They've removed all tracks, and a road without any tracks suggests it held many. I'd like to know just how many."

"That's what they don't want us to know. Is there any place where it's more obvious that the road has been swept clean or the shoulders smoothed?"

"The scouts didn't see any signs of that."

"That means that they've kept everyone off the road, at least for the last day or so." That suggested something to Quaeryt . . . something . . . but he couldn't pin it down.

"Just keep your eyes open and your imagers ready," said Skarpa, before turning his mount back to rejoin Third Regiment.

"Yes, sir."

The morning was still as first company rode eastward past the first of the irregular hills of a reddish sandstone, where, in places, small evergreens clung precariously to crevices in the stone. Those hills stood several hundred yards from the roadbed, but over the next half mille, the road curved and began to descend toward a pass apparently between two taller and more rugged sandstone hills.

As first company neared that gap, Quaeryt could see that the road descended straight into a gorge that had been widened, the reddish stone walls cut back at a forty-five degree angle and smoothly finished. On each side of the roadway was a comparatively wide shoulder, a good twenty yards between the low stone rain gutters at the edge of the pavement and the base of the sandstone slope that angled upward and for a good two hundred yards, although the rugged top of the hill was less than 150 yards above the roadbed and likely that far back from the road. The part of the road that followed the cut through the hillside was not that long, certainly no more than four hundred yards before the road reached a wider and more open valley descending toward the lowlands.

"Do you see anyone or anything?" he asked Zhelan, riding beside him.

"No, sir. I can't even see where anyone could hide."

Neither could Quaeryt, but the narrow section between the two stone slopes worried him, even though he couldn't see any place for an attacker to hide, especially given the steepness and openness of the flattened and smoothed sandstone walls.

As he rode closer and closer to the beginning of the gorge, Quaeryt kept glancing toward the upper side of the road cut on the south side, just ahead. He couldn't see anyone . . . or even any shadows. *No shadows! There have to be shadows with the sun to the south.*

"Company halt!"

Quaeryt concentrated, trying to image out a section of the slope below the area that held no shadows. Abruptly the smooth slope vanished, to reveal men and catapults stationed on a ledge cut behind a chest-high wall of the same sandstone. Immediately above was another shorter ledge and wall, behind which stood archers.

Quaeryt extended his shields, as he did ordering, "Imager shields!"

Simultaneously, arrows sleeted from the upper ledge down toward first company.

Pain hammered at Quaeryt's skull from the effort of holding shields and trying to gouge out a large chunk of the mountainside. Even as he watched, the reddish stone immediately below the ledge vanished, but only a thin line perhaps a yard wide and deep. Then the stone above that shivered and cracks began to form, widening and growing, and the lower ledge began to crumble.

For a moment Quaeryt just held his shields, trying to shield the company from the arrows, and to recover from the effort of trying to handle two imaging efforts at once. Then he saw that one of the catapults was already in motion. He immediately imaged away a support on the far side of the device. While he'd hoped that would have flung the Antiagon Fire along the ledge, instead it just dropped onto the ledge and exploded into the telltale crimson-yellow-green flame. Then the lower ledge crumbled, and Antiagon troopers flailed as they lost their footing and slid down the sandstone toward the base of the gorge . . . and the roadway below.

The archers on the upper ledge had begun to aim their shafts farther to the east, at the first companies of Third Regiment, well beyond the shields of first company.

Then . . . fire grenades appeared from somewhere else, exploding into flame against the imager shields.

"To the west! Behind those scrubby pines!" called out an undercaptain—Voltyr, Quaeryt realized.

The scrubby pines to which Voltyr pointed hadn't been there a moment before—or, rather, they'd been concealed by an imaging shield of some sort, as had the Antiagons working the second set of catapults.

"Iron darts!" ordered Quaeryt, even as he concentrated on intercepting fire grenades and imaging them at the upper ledge and the archers there.

While some of the imagers managed darts, many of the Antiagons working on the fire grenade catapults ducked below the sandstone ledge wall before the Telaryn imagers could create the darts so that a handful of darts clunked against the soft stone, gouging shallow holes and spraying reddish sand.

A line of Antiagon Fire flared across the ledge holding the archers, and several jumped over the ends of the wall and tried to slide down the sandstone away from the rubble of the first ledge below them. One seemed to manage it, and immediately began to run down the road to the west. Another lost control and tumbled head over heels into an unmoving lump at the bottom of the gorge. Others skidded into the rugged rocks that filled the gouge beneath the first ledge that Quaeryt had destroyed.

Quaeryt returned his attention to the remaining catapults, where he did manage to return two or three of the fire grenades. Before long, Antiagon Fire was raging behind the ledge wall on the emplacement west of the pine trees.

Then Quaeryt saw a shower of rock cascading down from the north slope of the road cut . . . and above that a larger mass of stone breaking loose from somewhere.

Immediately he thought about drawing heat from somewhere to support his imaging—but there was nothing to draw from. The rock hadn't absorbed that much sunlight, and there was no water anywhere. Still . . . he concentrated on creating an angled wall into place, no more than a yard and a half high, running from the east to west as it descended along the northern sandstone slope. Waves of pain cascaded over him, and he doubled over in the saddle, with flashes of light burning into his skull.

All he could do was watch as the chunks of sandstone and other rock cascaded downslope toward his angled barrier.

The first and smaller rocks hit the wall and largely bounced westward, and downhill. So did most of what followed, but more than a few stray rocks and boulders bounced over the barrier and rolled or slid down into the gorge—building up next to the sandstone wall.

Dust followed, and when that began to clear, Quaeryt took a deep breath.

Most of the rocks and rubble had not reached the road. Even so, there was a mass almost a yard high and twenty yards long covering the roadbed, beginning some fifteen yards ahead of where first company had stopped. Beyond that rubble Quaeryt could see several scouts and outriders, but he had no idea if all of them had escaped. He could only hope.

Even as a last skitter of rocks slid to a stop atop the pile of rock partially blocking the road, Quaeryt kept looking around, ignoring the pain and flashes in his vision, seeing yet another Antiagon defensive emplacement. Where the first walled ledge had been there was only an angular and blacked gash in the sloped sandstone, its base partly filled with boulders and fragments of sandstone, some blackened. Above that, the upper ledge was blackened and empty. Above the top of the gash, where the original ledge had been, Quaeryt saw an oblong opening, with what looked to be stairs behind it. *That's how they got there.*

He kept looking, but could see no sign of any surviving Antiagons. There were no more fire grenades and no more archers. Nor was there any sign of more rockslides. Had the one been triggered by an imager? Quaeryt had no way of knowing and even sending someone to the top of the gorge wall likely wouldn't reveal anything. Still . . . they probably needed to have a squad investigate the tunnels to the ledges and see what lay behind them.

"That was something."

Quaeryt turned in the saddle to see Skarpa rein up.

The submarshal looked at the mass of rubble covering the road, then at the blackened ledges, and finally at Quaeryt. "How did you know?"

"I didn't, not exactly. I just knew it had to be an attack that relied on something other than a mass of troopers. When I couldn't see shadows where there should have been shadows . . ."

Skarpa raised his eyebrows.

Quaeryt went on to explain, then said, "Then there was the attack outside of Barna. They used barely trained troopers. The first Antiagon Fire attack—that took an imager and no more than twenty troopers. And . . . Antiago is a smaller land that makes most of its wealth from trading. Traders don't like to spend any more than they have to. Antiago has never had to maintain that many troopers, and I doubt Aliaro has that many to spare. So . . . he won't hazard them until he has to. Also, the more he can weaken us without using his best, the more likely they'll be able to turn us away."

"That would be a victory of sorts for him. He has to know that we're not equipped for a long siege or attack on Liantiago."

"He knows that and so do we."

Skarpa gestured toward the remaining ledges cut into the soft sandstone walls, ledges blacked and charred, with the remnants of Antiagons and catapults. "That's almost an unassailable position."

"They didn't think about having their own Fire used against them."

"Or your having imagers strong enough to cut away the stone under their feet." Skarpa's eyes went to the rubble beside and partially covering the road.

"The imagers can remove that, but you might want to send a company to investigate how the Antiagons got to those ledges."

"I already have," replied Skarpa. "I also told them to bring in anyone they capture."

"That would help in knowing how many imagers they have and how good they are."

"Do you think they used imagers to cut those ledges just for us?"

"I wondered that at first, but I don't think so. They were likely imaged, but not recently. There are trees growing in places that suggest the ledges were created some time ago. Also there are rivulets and channels in the sandstone that were made by rain. All that takes time. They might have used imagers recently to improve the old ledges and walls."

"How long will it take to clear this?"

"Less than two glasses, I'd judge, but we'll have to see."

"If you could make a narrow path first . . ."

"To get the scouts and a vanguard through? We can do that." Quaeryt nodded.

Once Skarpa headed back to Third Regiment, Quaeryt turned to the undercaptains. "We've got some road-clearing to do. We'll begin with a narrow path wide enough for a single mount." He gestured. "Threkhyl . . . Horan . . .

you two start. Remove the rocks and earth in smaller piles. There's more to image away than meets the eye."

"Yes, sir."

As the two imagers began to image away rock and sand, Quaeryt looked westward and downhill, but he could not make out either the bay or Liantiago.

By the time the imagers had cleared the road, and the scouting parties had returned with but a handful of surviving Antiagon troopers, it was past noon before Southern Army emerged from the bottom of the gorge and began to ride along a section of the road that sloped down, if ever so gradually, toward a lower line of hills. Those hills, unlike the irregular sandstone hills, were green with spring grass and intermittent olive orchards. The villas were also larger, and Quaeryt could make out several hamlets, although all were on lanes back off the main paved road by at least a mille, if not more, and most seemed to be located on or near slopes that showed rocky outcroppings, suggesting that where the common people built was controlled in some fashion, either by the Shahibs or the Autarch or even by a certain popular reluctance to be too close to the main road.

Before all that long, Skarpa rejoined Quaeryt, since first company remained as the vanguard.

"What did you discover from the captives?" asked Quaeryt.

"Not too much. Their commander sent two companies and two imagers. One company was of archers, and the other was of catapultists. Supposedly one imager was a master and the other his assistant. They were told to destroy the attackers and return." Skarpa snorted.

"Did they believe that was possible with so small a force?"

"Some did, it appears. That's not likely to happen again. At least a squad escaped with the master imager. You or your imagers got the assistant . . ."

*That suggests that the master imager might have some sort of shields,* thought Quaeryt.

"There's a hidden back trail down to the main road. One of the companies from second battalion found it, but the Antiagons were so far gone that even their dust had settled."

"So it's likely they know we have imagers, and the size of our force," said Quaeryt, "but not necessarily how many imagers. Did any of the captives know how many imagers there might be in Liantiago?"

"I did ask, but all they could tell me was that the imagers lived in special walled quarters inside the palace walls, and that only a few ever left

Liantiago. None of them had ever seen more than two imagers together—almost always a master and his apprentice."

Quaeryt frowned. *Was that a form of dissimulation? Or did it represent how Antiagon imagers were trained?*

"You have that look . . ."

"A master and apprentice system . . ." Quaeryt shook his head. "That sounds too traditional . . . but maybe it's merely a pretense to avoid people asking too many questions."

"Does it matter?"

"Not for now," replied Quaeryt. *But it's something to look into, especially why the Autarch uses that system . . . if he even does.*

Skarpa, Quaeryt, and first company continued to lead the way along the well-kept paved road. After they had ridden another glass, they came to the crest of a low rise, beyond which were low rolling hills, covered with already green pastures or meadows, that extended from just below him to the outskirts of Liantiago some five milles away.

Skarpa called a halt, after which he and Quaeryt surveyed the terrain before them. Liantiago was located on the southeastern end of a sheltered bay that extended more than a hundred milles from the Gulf of Khellor. In the center of the bay was the island of Westisle, itself some forty milles long and five to eight across. The size and sheltered nature of the bay provided the best port and anchorage in all of Lydar. All that Quaeryt recalled from his years at sea. What he didn't recall was the size of Liantiago, stretching as it did more than five milles along a curving shoreline. What he also did not recall was the imposing stone complex that dominated a low hill rising from the middle on the northern end of the city and overlooking the harbor. That had to be Aliaro's palace, what with its white stone walls and fortifications.

*White stone?* That suggested stone hardened and shaped by experienced and talented imagers. While it was clear that Aliaro had imagers, what Quaeryt and Skarpa had no way of knowing was how many the Autarch might have . . . or how accomplished they might be. The stone fortifications suggested both numbers and talent . . . but had the walls been built in the past . . . or more recently?

"Makes Variana and Solis look small," observed Skarpa.

"It does. It's also interesting that there aren't any other cities in Liantiago of any size."

"With one that size, why would the autarchs need any more?"

"The autarchs might not, but the traders and merchants and people might."

"Meaning what?" asked Skarpa.

"That the Autarch doesn't want too many people too far away from him, suggesting that he doesn't have that effective a government for controlling large groups of people at a distance. That might make matters easier for Bhayar to rule here."

"There's the small matter of defeating Aliaro's forces before we can consider that," said Skarpa dryly.

Quaeryt laughed lightly. "You're right about that."

Once below the gorge, the road that led to Liantiago through the remaining lower and gentler hills turned out to be wider. It was also paved in hard white stone and wide enough for three wagons abreast, with room to spare. Although the lines of the stone were sharp and clean, from the way the turf from which the hot-weather grasses sprouted had been cut back and from the occasional large mansions and small palaces set back from the road, each with elaborate gates—all closed—and paved lanes cut into the gentle hillside, it was clear that the road dated back some considerable time.

*If not so far back as the roads of the Naedarans,* thought Quaeryt. *Had some of the Naedarans fled to Antiago? Or had Aliaro's imagers come from elsewhere?*

While it was hard to determine, given their distance from the main road, most of the imposing structures appeared shuttered, and not a single wisp of smoke rose from any chimney, as if most inhabitants had either fled or were hiding within. Nor had Quaeryt seen any individual even on more distant lanes or fields. In fact, he had seen no livestock, not even a dog.

Just ahead of first company, the road curved gently to the north around the base of another hill, one planted at the top with oil nut trees. Some hundred yards to the south of the road was a depression not quite deep enough to be a gorge or a canyon but too narrow to be a valley and too deep to be a mere swale, at the bottom of which was a small stream. Quaeryt judged that the miniature canyon/valley was perhaps two hundred yards across and fifteen to twenty yards deep. *Just deep enough and steep enough to make it a barrier to any sort of maneuver.*

Even before the outriders reached the point where the road began to curve to the west-northwest, Skarpa rode up and ordered a halt, then eased his mount over beside Quaeryt. "About a mille ahead, at the top of a slight rise, between that hill and that valley to the south, there's a wall right across the road. The wall looks to be a half mille long. The stonework on each side of the road towers looks old. The wall between the towers looks new. The scouts report that there might be at least several regiments there."

"So they imaged a short section of wall between the towers?"

"Or they built it quickly," replied Skarpa sardonically.

"Is there any way to go around the wall?" asked Quaeryt.

"Either down through the valley or uphill through the oil nut trees. I imagine that they're ready to fire the trees themselves if we tried that."

"So why don't we fire the trees . . . and wait?"

"I'd thought about that, but . . . unless you or your imagers could do that, we'd likely lose a lot of men even trying to get close."

"I assume that there's no other easy or short way to get around the wall."

"I've had the scouts searching, but there's another gorge to the north . . ."

"So we'd have to retrace our way up the gorge that holds the main road and then find another road down to Liantiago?"

"If there is one," said Skarpa. "We didn't see any signs of main roads. There are likely farm roads or lanes, but they'll be narrow."

"And we might face another force if we attempted riding back up into the gorge. Or some other kind of trap."

"Even if we didn't, trying to reach Liantiago on back roads gives them more of an advantage."

"But not more than the advantage of fortifications," Quaeryt pointed out.

"I was hoping you and the imagers . . ."

"I'd have to look to see what might be possible."

"I thought you might. That's why I called a halt," said Skarpa. "You're not to do it by yourself with just a squad."

"I'll take Khalis and Horan."

"Not Voltyr?"

"You'll need him if anything happens while we're gone." Quaeryt turned to Zhelan. "Major . . . I'll need a squad to accompany me and two undercaptains on a scouting mission."

"Yes, sir. Third squad is ready."

"Thank you." Quaeryt looked back. "Undercaptains Khalis and Horan, forward!"

As Horan reined up beside Quaeryt, his face held a slightly puzzled expression, while Khalis offered a tentative smile.

Quaeryt ignored both expressions. "Once we near the curve in the road, Khalis, I want a concealment shield over the squad. If at any time you think you can't maintain it, let me know before that happens. Is that clear?"

"Yes, sir."

"Horan . . . I want you to study the hill to the north and the valley to the south. I need to know whether you can remove a section of the hill wide enough for a battalion to ride along such a cut around the end of the wall. I'd also like your thoughts on a bridge across the valley short of the wall and another one back across farther west and behind the wall."

The older undercaptain nodded, thoughtfully, as if his unspoken question had been answered.

Quaeryt turned his mount slightly, in order to address all the imager undercaptains. "The Antiagons have imagers. We don't know how many, and we don't know how strong they are. We also don't know how they will deploy those imagers after what we did in the gorge. They'll doubtless have Antiagon Fire and catapults. They will have cannon as well." He ignored the sarcastic expression on Threkhyl's face. "Until we do know what else they may use, when we first move into range of muskets, arrows, or imaging, you need to hold your shields. It's more than likely that the stone wall ahead is only the first barrier we'll encounter as we near the outskirts of the city."

By the time Quaeryt had finished speaking, third squad had ridden forward, ready to escort Quaeryt and the two undercaptains. Quaeryt turned the mare and eased her over to the squad leader. "I'd like two outriders, but only five yards in front of us." That was to make sure that they stayed within the limits of Khalis's concealment shield. "We'll take this at a fast walk. The two undercaptains will flank me, and you'll be immediately behind."

"Yes, sir."

In moments, the two rankers were leading the group out along the road.

After the first hundred or so yards, Quaeryt ordered, "Concealment shield now, Khalis. Third squad, quiet riding."

"Yes, sir."

Almost half a mille later, they came to the end of the curve in the road, and to a point almost even with the highest part of the low hill to the right. Some four hundred yards ahead was the stone wall that extended from the rear of the hill across the road and to the valley to the southwest. Even at that distance, Quaeryt could see that behind the stonework waited troopers in maroon uniforms. Some ten yards behind the stonework were catapults, spaced ten yards or so apart, with more than twenty of them in all.

Quaeryt didn't see any cannon, but he had no doubt that there must have been some, possibly in the trees on the upper slopes of the hill, trained down onto the open fields on each side of the road and ready to rake the approaches to the wall. *Another reason to fire the trees before we start any sort of attack.*

He held up his hand. "Squad, halt." Then he added, "Undercaptains, take a good look at all that."

The towers immediately flanking the road were square, some ten yards high, and clearly dated back many years, possibly more than a century, as did the two sections of the wall on each side of the towers, a wall that looked to be some five yards thick. The wall between the towers had no gates, and not even embrasures below the crenellations that topped the stonework, and the white stone was definitely much newer.

"Could you flatten that stonework for a width of thirty or forty yards?" Quaeryt asked Horan.

"Be easier to move some of the hill to make a ramp up and around the end of the wall, sir," Horan finally said.

"How wide do you think you could make it?"

"Wide enough for four horses, I'd think. If they stayed close together."

"What about bridges over the valley?"

"No, sir. I saw what all of you did at Ferravyl, and it'd take a lot more than that."

Quaeryt had thought the same, but had his reasons for asking. "And a ramp over the south end of the wall?"

"I could do the north end, and Threkhyl could do the south. He might be able to flatten the wall. He's still stronger than I am for that."

*But not for shields, I'd wager.* "Khalis . . . could you remove that center section of wall?"

"Yes, sir. That's less than twenty yards across. Well . . . less than thirty, anyway."

Quaeryt couldn't help but smile slightly, if ironically. A year and a half earlier, he couldn't have removed one of the wall stones. Now, that was nothing to all but one of the imagers he commanded. He nodded. "Time to head back, outriders, undercaptains, squad leader. Please keep holding that concealment, Khalis." He turned his mare.

"If I might ask," ventured Khalis, after they had covered about a hundred yards of the return to Southern Army, "what you have in mind, sir . . ."

"Anything where we don't have to attack a walled fortification directly. Do you have any suggestions, Undercaptain?" asked Quaeryt gently.

"If we just removed the front of the entire wall at the base, it wouldn't take as much effort . . ."

Quaeryt thought for a moment, then shook his head. "That would just leave a jumble of stone that would be a barrier to us, especially to a mounted regiment . . ." He let the words drift off for a moment, as something struck him. "Keep that thought in mind, though. It might be a very good tactic if we have to deal with manned high walls in Liantiago."

"What about toppling their catapults just before we get in range?" asked Horan. "We wouldn't need shields as much."

"It's a good idea, especially if it spreads Antiagon Fire across their ranks, but we'd still need shields against arrows and musket fire."

As they rode back around the curve, Quaeryt began to image burning hunks of wax into the leaves of the oil nut trees on the hill to the north of the road, concentrating on the southern side, overlooking the approach to the wall and towers. Wax was easier than iron fragments, and he also had no idea exactly where any Antiagons might be . . . if there were any at all, but he couldn't believe that there were none on such a strategic position. He might be destroying the grove and the crop of some Shahib, but he didn't wish to risk Southern Army having to deal with either a concealed Antiagon force or a cannon position that could rake any advance. He kept looking up at the tree-covered crest of the hill as he rode back toward where Skarpa and Southern Army waited—out of sight of the wall and its towers, but certainly obvious to any scouts or troopers on the hill.

Initially, even a half a quint after Quaeryt's fire-imaging, there were only puffs of smoke here and there, and in many places, the smoke just vanished. In more than a handful, though, perhaps in as many as a double handful, the thin trails of smoke thickened, followed by tongues of flame that expanded rapidly. By the time that the scouting squad was back in sight of Southern Army, patches of the trees were in full flame. Quaeryt didn't see anyone fleeing the fire. *But you wouldn't. They'd run back toward the wall on the side of the hill away from us.*

Before long, the entire hilltop was aflame. Then, abruptly, a geyser of dirt and vegetation erupted from the upper southern side of the hill, accompanied by one large explosion and followed by several others.

For a moment Quaeryt just watched, although he kept riding.

"Why didn't they fire on us earlier?" asked Khalis. "We were certainly in range even before we went to scout."

"They weren't positioned to fire on where Southern Army halted, and I'd guess that because cannon are heavy and hard to move, they worried that they wouldn't have time to reposition them to cover the approach to the wall. That's where they could do the most damage because that's where our forces would be the closest together."

Skarpa was waiting at the front of first company and gestured for Quaeryt to join him. Quaeryt rode over and reined up.

"I appreciate your taking out that cannon emplacement. It did warn them about some of our capabilities, but they probably know those already." Skarpa's smile was rueful. "I don't see much point in waiting until tomorrow. They might just decide to bring up cannon or something else unpleasant." Skarpa coughed and cleared his throat. "And most of Southern Army hasn't fought today. Can your imagers handle it?"

"Here's what I'd suggest," said Quaeryt. He began to explain.

When he finished, Skarpa nodded slowly, then said, "That's fine if they don't immediately turn cannon and catapults on the attack points."

"We can't do much against cannon, except use concealment shields until we begin the attack, but some of the imagers can cripple the catapult towers." Quaeryt paused. "I don't know that we can take them all out. They must have twenty of them along the wall."

"I'd think they'd have more. It is what they do best."

"They likely do in Liantiago, but here . . . there's no protected storage for the fire grenades, and you wouldn't want them too close together." *Not if you value your troopers.*

"That might be why they had the cannon on the hill. Some of the cannon, anyway," said Skarpa. "If I were their commander, I'd have more set back and ranged to fire over the walls into the approaches to the wall."

"Then they probably do, and we'll need to use concealment shields as long as we can and try to advance without raising enough dust that it lingers behind the regiments."

Skarpa gestured to a junior squad leader. "Commander Quaeryt and I would like to see all the regimental commanders immediately."

"Yes, sir."

Skarpa turned back to Quaeryt. "You can't do anything like you did at Ferravyl or Variana?"

Quaeryt shook his head. "It's not that warm. There's no rain and no water that near."

"I don't pretend to understand why that's important, but I'll take your word for it."

"Massive imaging takes heat."

"That's why all the ice and snow?"

Quaeryt nodded. "Without that . . ." He shook his head.

"The more I learn, the more I wouldn't want to be in your boots."

For those reasons, and for others Quaeryt wasn't about to mention, he was getting more and more uncomfortable in his own boots.

Once the seven commanders arrived, Skarpa laid out the plan of attack, looking around the senior officers when he had finished.

"You realize that coordinating the attack will be difficult using hand signals instead of horn signals," offered Kharllon.

"I do understand that, Commander," replied Skarpa, "but it is not necessary for the attacks to be perfectly coordinated. A surprise attack on three points that is not exactly timed is far better than a perfectly timed assault that is anticipated and expected. Would you not agree?"

"Do we have any idea what defenses they have besides the wall?" asked Kharllon, his question making clear the fact that he didn't intend to reply to Skarpa's gentle question.

"Some twenty catapults armed with Antiagon Fire grenades, most likely one or two cannon emplacements, and an undetermined number of troopers," replied Skarpa. "Probably at least three regiments. They have far less experience than your men."

"How do we know that?" asked Meurn, after looking to Kharllon.

"They haven't fought anyone in generations," replied Quaeryt. "Even if they're well trained, it's not the same."

Subcommander Dulaek cleared his throat. "Are we to give quarter?"

"To those who throw down their weapons and surrender immediately," replied Skarpa. "We're not interested in slaughtering if it's not necessary."

While Quaeryt nodded, he thought, *One way or another, that's not likely to be an issue, not with as much Antiagon Fire behind those walls as needed by that number of catapults.*

After several more questions, Skarpa released the commanders to their regiments. Quaeryt remounted the mare and rode back to the imager undercaptains, accompanied by Alazyn, who had said nothing during the senior officers' briefing.

"You didn't look all that pleased with Commander Kharllon's questions," observed Quaeryt, his eyes on the subcommander.

"He was asking questions so he could cover his back if things go wrong."

"Another reason why we need to make certain they don't." *It's also why Skarpa has him leading one of the attacks.*

Once he returned to first company, Quaeryt quickly briefed Zhelan, Ghaelyn, and the undercaptains. "The attack will begin with three separate assaults, each under concealment. Lhandor and Threkhyl, you'll be with the submarshal and Commander Fhaen. Voltyr and Horan with Fourteenth Regiment and Commander Kharllon, and Khalis, Baelthm, and I will support Subcommander Alazyn and Nineteenth Regiment . . ." He went on with the overall plan before discussing certain details.

"Voltyr . . . you need to stay close enough to Commander Kharllon to make certain that nothing slows the attack or goes wrong with it."

"And remove any unforeseen impediments?"

"If necessary . . . but only if necessary. You should be able to handle the concealment, and Horan should be able to create a causeway wide enough for Fourteenth Regiment to swing north of the defenders and attack their rear. If you see a cannon emplacement . . . do what you can. You're likely to be the one close enough and with the best view for that."

"Yes, sir." Voltyr nodded slowly.

"Good. You and Horan head out and join Fourteenth Regiment." Quaeryt then went over his instructions with Threkhyl and Lhandor before sending them to join Skarpa. Then he turned to Khalis. "You're going to have to remove as large a section of that wall as you can . . . but leave yourself enough strength to deal with the catapults."

"Yes, sir."

Almost two quints passed before Fourteenth, Nineteenth, and Third Regiments were in position to ride forward. Because maintaining concealment during the entire set of maneuvers would have been far too hard on all the imagers, once Fourteenth Regiment was in place, Paedn's Fourth Regiment moved up behind it, as did Meurn's Fifteenth behind Quaeryt and Nineteenth Regiment, and Dulaek's Sixth Regiment behind Skarpa and Fhaen's Third Regiment. Fhaasn's Twenty-sixth Foot was behind Fifteenth, but to the west of the road. The three lead regiments were a good half mille from the wall, with their backups separated from them by several hundred yards. Once the lead regiments had reached a point several hundred yards from the wall, the backup forces were to begin their advance, again in an angled fashion.

On Skarpa's signal, Khalis raised a concealment shield over the first company and Nineteenth Regiment, as did Voltyr over Fourteenth Regiment, and finally Lhandor over Third Regiment. Quaeryt thought it most likely that most, if not all, Antiagon observers would be puzzled by the concealment because they would still observe regiments in the same general position as before, if fewer in number, and might even think that the larger initial numbers were an imaging illusion. Even if the Antiagon commander did not happen to be deceived, the concealment would make it difficult to determine where the attackers were and what their movements were.

"Forward," ordered Quaeryt quietly, raising and then lowering his arm.

First company began to walk their mounts toward the central section of the wall, but at an angle, since Quaeryt and Skarpa had positioned all the regiments, not directly in front of their objective, but so that they would not move directly forward toward the wall. That way, if there were cannon or, as they neared the wall, other missiles, the defenders could not attempt merely to adjust the distance in trying to calculate where the Southern Army regiments might be. Further, since there were wide spaces between the regiments, any blanket barrage would waste a great deal of ammunition.

*Of course, if they drop something directly blindly into a regiment, the casualties will be higher, or the strain on the imager will be greater . . . if not both.* Again, Quaeryt was basing his tactics on the fact that no one in Lydar had ever used imagers the way he was—at least not since the time of the Naedarans, if then—and they hadn't had muskets, cannon, or Antiagon Fire.

First company and Nineteenth Regiment had advanced less than two hundred yards before what sounded almost like a sighing whistle passed overhead. Although Quaeryt couldn't see it, the *crumpt* well behind Nineteenth Regiment told Quaeryt all that he needed to know. "Forward! Fast trot!" As he gave the order, he extended shields across the front of first company, trusting that he could hold them at least until they reached a point close to the walls . . . or where Khalis would remove the stone.

More explosions echoed across the fields before the walls, but behind Nineteenth Regiment, demonstrating that the Antiagons not only had cannon emplacements, but that there were more than a few handfuls of cannon in those positions. From what Quaeryt could tell, most of the impact explosions occurred well to the south behind the advancing forces, but he hoped that the reserve battalions followed Skarpa's orders and had moved quickly—at an angle—once they came under fire. *Not that you can do anything about that now.*

As he rode toward the highway just in front of the gate, Quaeryt took a quick look at the two towers, but only saw a handful of troopers behind the crenellations of each tower. None of the nearer catapults appeared to be in motion, either. Could it be that the Antiagons were still concentrating on the secondary regiments? He pushed that thought away.

At that moment, from nowhere came a series of blows on Quaeryt's shields, strong enough to rock him in the saddle. Dropping away from his shields were iron darts—all aimed at the front ranks of first company—and that meant an imager on the walls who had deduced where first company happened to be.

"Image now!" Quaeryt ordered Khalis, before glancing back over his shoulder to make certain that Baelthm was close behind him.

Khalis said nothing, but in moments the section of wall between the towers flanking the stone-paved high had vanished—and reappeared as a flat paved square extending a good forty yards back. That newly created square was empty, except for wisps of mist curling up from the stone—a good indication that whatever forces had manned the wall or sheltered behind it were now entombed under it.

"Forward! Through the wall!" ordered Quaeryt.

First company and the first battalions of Nineteenth Regiment were through the gap in the white stonework, the hooves of their mounts clattering on the cold white paving that Khalis had laid down, before any of the defenders flanking the towers even began to react. At that point, Quaeryt dropped the concealment and strengthened his shields.

The appearance of riders amid the defenders engendered shouts, but whether those were of defiance or surprise Quaeryt certainly couldn't tell.

"First company! On me!" He turned the mare toward the defenders on the left, shifting his half-staff to his right hand. "Baelthm! Do what you can to the nearest catapult." After narrowing his personal shields to a wedge extending little more than the width of two horses, he urged the mare to move faster.

Even before the troopers turned toward the Southern Army troopers, from nowhere came another series of blows on Quaeryt's shields, again powerful enough to push him back in the saddle. Quaeryt had no idea from where they had come, but the sooner his troopers were close to the Antiagons, the harder it would be for Antiagon imagers to attack the Telaryn troopers.

Behind him, he heard Alazyn's command. "First battalion on the commander. Second to the right on me!"

Whatever imaging Baelthm did was sufficient, because the launching arm of the nearer catapult sagged, and a fire grenade exploded as the arm fell, with crimson-yellow-green flames oozing down the framework.

Quaeryt imaged a few handfuls of red-hot iron fragments into what looked to be the magazine for the catapult. In instants, flames roared up the catapult, and Antiagon troopers raced away from the flaming structure.

Another blast of *something* washed over his shields, and this time, Quaeryt attempted to image it back from wherever it had come.

Another wave of flame flared to Quaeryt's left, from narrow embrasures in the middle level of the western road tower . . . followed by a quick gust of cool air.

Quaeryt braced for another imaging attack . . . but there was none.

Ahead, the flames from the burning catapult or from the midsection of the tower didn't deter many of the defenders, who resolutely turned to face Quaeryt and first company. That resolution helped them little when his shields, loosely anchored to the mare and the other mounts of first company, thrust the defenders facing Quaeryt to one side or the other, unbalanced, and easy targets for Zhelan and his men.

A group of archers stood on the parapet of the wall ahead, beginning to fire shafts into the riders well behind Quaeryt.

Quaeryt imaged iron darts across the archers, and most of them went down. A flash of light momentarily blinded him so that all he could do was hold his seat as the mare charged forward through more defenders.

When his vision cleared, he found that the troopers of first company, and Khalis and Baelthm, had caught up with him, and that most of the nearby defenders were falling back, if not outright fleeing.

Farther ahead on the parapets stood another group of archers, whose shafts arched toward him and first company, but before most of them could release another shaft, iron darts were penetrating their necks.

Quaeryt glanced to Khalis, whose face was momentarily locked in concentration before relaxing slightly. "Good job!"

"We don't need casualties behind us, sir."

*No, we don't.* Quaeryt nodded, then scanned the area. Another catapult was turning toward the attackers. He imaged away the rear support and directed the fire grenade downward into the areas below. He must have missed the wood or the magazine, because nothing happened, except for the fact that the crew immediately fled. He looked farther to the west-southwest, concentrating on the next catapult, but not before the weapon had released another fire grenade. All Quaeryt could do was to image it onto the Antiagon troopers on the wall farther from him and first company . . . and ignore the flames and agony as he kept riding through the thinning ranks of the defenders and strewing them sideways and into the sabres of the lead ranks of first company.

Before that long, there were no defenders—and no working catapults—remaining close to first company, except the wounded and the dead, but he could see a mass of them farther to the southwest, still resisting Skarpa's attack through a gap in the wall—a gap that only looked to be some twenty yards wide.

"First company! First battalion! Forward!" Once more Quaeryt urged the mare forward, hoping that a rear attack on the Antiagons might break the will of the defenders ferociously blocking the Telaryn advance through the gap in the white stone wall.

As he rode forward, he imaged away the supports on the nearest catapult ahead, and then the one after that, but at the same time, he couldn't help but think that either Threkhyl or Lhandor should have done some imaging ahead of Third Regiment, anything to put a gap in the defenders. *But maybe they couldn't.*

Only the last few ranks of the defenders attempting to stop Third Regiment's advance saw or heard the approach of first company and Nineteenth Regiment's first battalion, even though a squad leader on the wall was shouting and gesturing—until Quaeryt cut him down with an imaged iron dart.

More flashes of light across Quaeryt's eyes persuaded him to reduce his shields and just concentrate on the area around him—especially in case there was another Antiagon imager around.

After perhaps half a quint, the remaining defenders caught between Third and Nineteenth Regiments began to break. Then . . . in what seemed moments, most were gone, and Quaeryt gestured and ordered, "Company! Halt!" That was to avoid riding into the advancing riders from Third Regiment.

"Sir! There!" shouted Khalis, pointing to the wall and an unroofed space that had chest-high walls on each side but was unwalled on the side away from the main wall.

Quaeryt jerked his head around. Two figures stood there, one apparently an officer and the other an older gray-haired man in a white jacket and maroon cuffs. To one side, lying on the parapet stones, was another white-jacketed figure.

The sharp-faced officer whirled toward the older man in the white jacket and the maroon cuffs, his blade clearly aimed at the man's neck. Quaeryt imaged the blade from the hilt. The officer looked stunned, but only for a moment as an iron dart from Khalis caught him on the back of the neck.

The older man glanced from the falling officer in the general direction of Quaeryt, his eyes widening, although he appeared not to be looking at the commander or Khalis. Then a gold disk appeared in his hand . . . and he swayed. He mouthed several words—words that, to Quaeryt, might have been "never to the ancients"—before he pitched forward onto the stone, and then toppled off the parapet to the stone pavement that extended several yards back from the base of the wall.

Before Quaeryt could say anything or ride forward, two massive explosions, one right after the other, filled the air, clearly coming from somewhere north of the eastern end of the wall. Quaeryt turned in the saddle, but all he could see were two pillars of thick smoke. *Powder bags or cannonballs . . . or both?* He stood in the stirrups, looking back to the northeast, trying to see what had happened there, but from what he could determine, the fighting around the wall had ended there as well and since no troopers in maroon were headed toward them, and the uniforms he could see were greenish, that meant that Kharllon had been successful . . . and that the fighting had ended possibly even sooner than it had for Nineteenth and Third Regiments. That suggested that either Volytr or Horan had torched the cannon emplacements, and that Kharllon would find a way to inflate his success, sooner or later. In any case, Fourteenth and Fourth Regiments looked to be in control, and he'd find out soon enough what had happened.

"What was that?" asked Khalis, easing his mount up beside Quaeryt.

"Let's hope it was Voltyr setting off Antiagon powder."

"No . . . the two fighting on the wall here, and the one who jumped off."

"He didn't jump. He was an imager. He imaged the gold to kill himself."

"You can do that?"

"You can." Quaeryt didn't remind Khalis that he'd pointed that out months before. "That's why imaging golds is dangerous."

"But why did he do it?"

Quaeryt shook his head. "The officer didn't want him taken captive, and he apparently didn't want it, either."

"That doesn't make sense."

Quaeryt was all too afraid that it did. He looked around for Zhelan, finally spotting the major some twenty yards away, giving orders to a squad leader. While he waited for Zhelan to finish, he decided to repeat a few things to Khalis. "Gold is one of the heaviest metals and one of the hardest to image . . ."

When Zhelan had finished, Quaeryt cut short his impromptu homily and rode over and reined up short of the major.

"Sir?"

"If there are any captives wearing white uniforms with maroon cuffs, I want to see them immediately. But have the men be careful with them. Some might be imagers."

The major's eyebrows lifted.

"That's a guess on my part, but one of the imagers was wearing that kind of uniform." Quaeryt gestured back toward the body on the stone pavement. "He killed himself, rather than let himself be captured."

Zhelan shook his head.

"I won't keep you. I imagine the submarshal will be here before long." Quaeryt nodded and eased the mare back to where Khalis and Baelthm waited, easing out his water bottle and hoping that the watered lager would help his throbbing head and various aches he hadn't realized that he had.

He still wondered why Threkhyl hadn't been able to image a larger gap in the Antiagon stonework.

As Quaeryt waited for reports from Alazyn and Zhelan, he surveyed the battlefield, trying to determine exactly what the Antiagon strategy had been, yet so far as he could determine, the Antiagon commander had apparently decided that a strong stone wall, imagers, and Antiagon Fire and cannon could turn away Southern Army. *And they could have, except for our imaging.* Was that what had happened to the Naedarans? That they lost, one way or another, enough imagers that they could no longer maintain their power? *Can you make that point, convincingly enough, to Bhayar?*

Alazyn rode toward Quaeryt and reined up, putting an end to Quaeryt's reflections and concerns.

"How bad was it?" asked Quaeryt.

"Not so bad as it could have been. A hundred twenty dead, two hundred seventy one wounded, and we'll likely lose half of them—third company in fourth battalion got hit with three fire grenades at once."

Quaeryt winced. Fourth battalion had turned to the northeast after going through the gap in the wall, and there hadn't been any imagers to bring down those catapults. *You only have so many imagers,* he reminded himself.

"Could have been worse, except one of the imagers with Fourteenth Regiment brought down the other catapults."

"Voltyr, most likely. Were there many casualties after that?"

"Not for us. Some of the foot regiments lost men until the Fourteenth Regiment got the cannon."

"Are there many prisoners?"

Alazyn shook his head. "There were two kinds of Antiagon troopers. Some fought well, and most of them died. The others fled well, and it didn't make sense to chase after them. We didn't pick up many mounts, either. Most of their troopers were foot. No musketeers, though."

"We haven't seen one musketeer here."

"Wonder what the Antiagons have against them?" asked Alazyn.

Quaeryt had no idea, even though he'd puzzled over the lack of musketeers earlier. "It can't be that they don't know how."

"We don't have many, either," Alazyn pointed out.

"Lord Bhayar decided against fielding musketeers for several reasons. First, they slow down most regiments. Second, they weren't much good in Tilbor. And third, each musket has to be forged separately because the barrels burst if they're cast, and forging enough muskets to make a difference would have reduced the number of regiments he could have raised." Quaeryt was actually guessing at the third reason, but Bhayar had talked about the first two, even before he'd sent Quaeryt to Tilbor.

"Won't always be like that," suggested Alazyn.

"No," said Quaeryt with a laugh. "That's why we have to get Lydar unified now."

"Do you really think we can do it?"

"I think we have to try." Quaeryt paused. "Don't you?"

After a moment the subcommander nodded. "If you don't need more from me, sir . . ."

"Go . . ." said Quaeryt.

No sooner had Alazyn ridden away than Zhelan rode up, accompanied by a squad. Riding beside him, rather thoroughly wrapped in chains, was an Antiagon trooper—or rather, Quaeryt suspected from the white jacket and the youthful face, an apprentice imager, with a large bruise across his forehead.

"I sent squads up and down the wall, sir," said Zhelan after he reined up. "They found seven bodies wearing those white uniforms. Four were older men, and three were much younger. There was one youngster in white. He'd been knocked out, and we wrapped him in chains before he woke."

"Where did you find chains?"

"Around the catapults. They must have chained slaves to them."

The more Quaeryt found out about Antiago, the less he liked what he was discovering.

The major gestured. "He won't talk to us."

Quaeryt turned in the saddle, and image-projected his voice. "Undercaptain Khalis!" Then he looked back to Zhelan. "We'll see what we can do."

Khalis immediately rode over from where he had been waiting with first squad. As he reined up, the black-haired youth in the white jacket with the maroon cuffs looked at Quaeryt. His eyes widened as he took in Quaeryt's silver white hair and eyebrows. Then he shuddered, but the shudder passed, and his eyes came to rest on Khalis. An expression, half puzzled, half quizzical, crossed his honey-shaded face.

"Talk to him," murmured Quaeryt.

Although Quaeryt had not directed Khalis to speak in Pharsi, the undercaptain did so.

The Antiagon imager's face expressed surprise, but he did reply, if in only a few words.

Khalis spoke again, and the Antiagon studied Quaeryt, then looked away.

"Ask him about why that officer tried to kill the older imager here," prompted Quaeryt.

Khalis spoke again in Pharsi, and the younger imager replied.

"He says that the life of any imager or apprentice who tries to leave Aliaro's service is forfeit. So is that of all members of their family."

"So why is he alive?"

Khalis spoke again and listened. "He's not a very good imager, and he's an orphan. He was assigned to the most difficult master."

"So he actually learned something?" Quaeryt let a little sardonicism permeate his voice.

Khalis offered a faint smile before speaking once more.

"He believes so, but you would have to judge."

"Not at the moment. Right now, we'll need to restrain him, but he doesn't need to be wrapped in chains." Quaeryt rode closer to the young imager and unwound some of the chains around his arm and right hand, then concentrated on imaging an iron wristband with an attached shackle, and then imaged one of the lengths of chain to the shackle. Lights flashed before his eyes, and he felt light-headed by the time he finished.

The Antiagon apprentice paled and began to shake. Finally, he spoke to Khalis.

"What did he say?" Quaeryt paused, then took another swallow of the watered lager.

"That you have proved to be his master, and the chain is unnecessary."

That didn't make sense to Quaeryt. At least one of the Antiagon imagers had been able to create iron darts and direct them at first company.

"Only the masters can image iron like that," added Khalis.

"Do you think you can handle him?" asked Quaeryt. "I'd like to see if we could eventually use him."

"I can see," replied Khalis. "Right now, he's just scared."

"Try to keep him respectful and worried without making him piss himself." Quaeryt glanced up to see Threkhyl and Lhandor riding toward him. "What's his name?"

When Khalis asked, the response was "Elsior."

"Just wait over there. I need to talk to Threkhyl and Lhandor."

"Yes, sir," replied Khalis.

"Will you need anything more, sir?" asked Zhelan quietly, as if not wishing to interrupt, but wanting to call attention to his other duties.

"I'm sorry to have kept you, Major. Not at the moment."

As Zhelan rode off, Quaeryt waited until the two arriving imagers reined up before speaking. "Threkhyl . . . you seemed to have trouble imaging a wide gap in the wall. What happened?"

"That was as wide as we could make it, sir." Threkhyl's tone was almost belligerent. "Took the two of us."

Lhandor looked to Quaeryt. "I had to drop the concealment early to help Threkhyl. It was like there was metal or something inside the stone. Then, all of a sudden it was gone."

*An imager, trying to use shields to protect the wall?* Quaeryt frowned, then asked, "Could it have been shielded somehow?"

Lhandor tilted his head slightly, as if considering. "It might have been. I've never tried to image through someone's shields. It might have been easier after we broke through, but . . . well . . . I couldn't image more."

Threkhyl shook his head. "Me neither."

"Against shields, you did well." Quaeryt saw Skarpa riding toward him. "We need to talk about this later, but I need to discuss some matters with the submarshal. Don't forget to drink a lot of watered ale or lager and eat some biscuits. That will help you recover your strength. If you'd join Khalis and his friend over there. He can fill you in."

"Yes, sir."

Quaeryt managed another swallow of watered lager and a few bites of a hard biscuit before Skarpa arrived, escorted by a half squad from Third Regiment, all of whom reined up well away from the two senior officers.

"It was a good thing you could attack the rear here," said Skarpa. "The gap in the wall wasn't wide enough to get enough troopers through quickly enough. When you attacked from the rear, a lot of them panicked, and we could break through."

"I'm just glad I saw it in time," replied Quaeryt.

"You're good about that." Skarpa paused. "They had more than five regiments here . . ."

"And several master imagers and apprentices, from what we've discovered."

"One junior imager for each senior one?"

"I'd guess so . . . at least in the field. We captured one . . ." Quaeryt went on to explain what had happened. ". . . and for the moment, he's over there with Khalis."

"Are you going to try to recruit him?"

"If we can. Since he hasn't seen much kindness, and since his life is forfeit in Antiago, there just might be a chance."

"You're an opportunist in everything, Quaeryt."

"When it makes sense."

Skarpa laughed. "You have a way of assuring that."

"Not always." Quaeryt couldn't help thinking about how matters hadn't worked out for him and Vaelora in Extela. *But they've worked out better for the people.* He had to remember that, not that anyone else besides Vaelora would. *And Bhayar . . . perhaps.*

"I still don't understand why the Antiagons waited so long to use their cannon," mused Skarpa.

"When was the last time they actually fought a war—on the ground?" asked Quaeryt, not quite rhetorically.

"You're the scholar. You tell me."

"A real war? I'm not sure they ever have. There were some skirmishes along the Lohan Hills in the time of Bhayar's great grandsire. I'd be willing to wager they've never had that many armsmen, and most of them have probably been used as naval marines. Who really ever wanted to attack the place against Antiagon Fire?"

"You do."

"It's only as part of a greater goal, and I'm wagering that it will cost far less than trying to use force to take Khel." *And that's an enormous wager . . .* So enormous that Quaeryt didn't even want to dwell on it, even in his mind.

"It would take someone like you and a ruler like Bhayar . . ."

Quaeryt said nothing.

Skarpa shook his head. "I need to see Kharllon."

"Do you want to ride on this afternoon?"

"I'll let you know."

"Yes, sir."

After Skarpa left, Quaeryt was about to ride east along the wall in search of Voltyr and Horan when he caught sight of the pair riding toward him. As they neared, and then reined up, he could see that both looked exhausted.

"Are you two all right? I was getting concerned that one or both of you might have been hurt when the cannon emplacement went up."

"We're fine." Voltyr offered a disgusted expression. "I had to suggest to Commander Kharllon that the submarshal would be less than pleased if we didn't return as directed to first company."

"The implication being that he was the senior commander and his commands were to be obeyed over mine."

"Almost wasn't an implication," growled Horan. "Begging your pardon, sir, but Commander Kharllon makes the most ornery jackass I ever had look reasonable. Except he does it with greasy words."

Quaeryt decided not to address that. "Did you run into problems with the wall?"

"Couldn't do a thing with the wall at first, not until I imaged a bunch of dirt on the end of it next to the hill. Felt like someone was shielding it. Just guessed where he was standing and dropped big rocks on him. Needed some help from Voltyr to finish the cut through the hill."

"Threkhyl and Lhandor had some difficulty at the other end, too." If Aliaro had even stronger imagers in Liantiago, Horan's suggestion about undermining the walls, perhaps below the shields of those imagers, might be the only way to deal with fortifications. *You'll just have to see.* "Did you ever see the imager? They wear white uniforms with maroon cuffs."

Voltyr nodded, as if that confirmed a suspicion. "Four . . . well . . . sort of. The two on the wall . . . their shields held for a bit . . . so they were only half buried."

"Or stoned," said Horan, with a hoarse laugh.

"That makes four, plus their apprentices," said Quaeryt. He turned and gestured. "Undercaptains! On me! Khalis, bring Elsior, too." He waited for a time, until all the undercaptains were facing him, mounted in a semicircle.

"All of you did well. Extraordinarily well. This is the first full battle we've had where there were other imagers. Four from what we can tell, all with apprentices." Quaeryt gestured toward the captive. "Elsior is the only one who survived. He wasn't that well treated, and he didn't kill himself like some of the others who seemed to think we're evil ancients from history." He looked to Khalis. "Has he said anything about that."

"No, sir. Not about that."

"We'll go over that later." From the way Khalis had phrased his answer, Quaeryt could sense that he had more to say, but not before the other undercaptains. "Now . . . we all had difficulty dealing with the imagers we faced. It's likely that those defending Liantiago will be at least as strong, if not stronger, and we may not be able to overcome their defenses so easily. I'll be talking with each of you individually to learn exactly how you dealt with the imagers here, and to go over possible other ways of dealing with them." He paused. "Is there anything any of you think we all should know?"

Voltyr cleared his throat. "Some of the men working the catapults were chained to them. That was where we were."

"We saw the same thing in the middle of the wall and at the west end," Quaeryt replied. "It may happen again, but we can't afford to leave the catapults alone."

"No, sir," agreed Voltyr. "I guess what I'm saying is that I don't like what I'm seeing here in Antiago."

Khalis, Horan, and Lhandor nodded. So did Baelthm, if almost surreptitiously, while Threkhyl snorted.

"Anything else?"

"Do you know what the submarshal has in mind?"

"He said he'd let us know shortly." Quaeryt offered a rueful smile. "Try and rest a bit, and drink some more watered ale or lager and get something to eat. I'll start going over things with Undercaptain Voltyr."

Almost a glass passed before Quaeryt finished talking to all the undercaptains except for Khalis, whom he'd saved for last. While all could supply details to what Quaeryt had seen and deduced, none supplied any real additional information about the Antiagon imagers or the tactics and strategy adopted by the defenders.

Quaeryt couldn't help but wonder what Khalis might have found out in talking to the captive apprentice imager. "What have you learned from Elsior?"

"He does speak Bovarian . . . or Antiagon, I guess you'd call it, as well as Pharsi, but his accent is so strong that it's hard to understand. For me, Pharsi is easier. He's also scared of you. He hasn't taken his eyes off you the whole time."

"Most of you could do what I did—that he saw, anyway."

"I told him that. I even imaged an iron loop to prove it. That upset him, but not as much as you did."

"What else?"

"You were right about one apprentice to each master. They're assigned to a master when they're fourteen."

"Do they learn from other masters?"

"Not often. Sometimes, if there's a skill one master has that the others don't, they'll let him teach a few other apprentices, but not all."

"Just so the knowledge of that skill doesn't disappear," said Quaeryt. "How long has Elsior been an apprentice?"

"Less than a year."

"Does he know how many imagers there are in Liantiago?"

"Not exactly. The Autarch never lets them meet as a group. He's only seen eleven masters that he knows about."

"If that's all Aliaro has, that means he's got about as many left as we have." *Maybe not even as many, but that's hardly likely.*

"Begging your pardon, sir, but shouldn't he have more?"

"I'd be surprised if he doesn't have more, but not too many more. There aren't many imagers born, and Telaryn is twice the size of Antiago and probably has four or five times the people, if not more. Also, there are more imagers born to those of Pharsi ancestry, and I don't think there are that many Pharsi in Antiago . . . at least not outside the capital. Did you find out anything more about the defenses or what the imagers might do in Liantiago?"

"He said he doesn't know, except that the walls around the palace are high and thick and that the stone has been hardened over the years. They kept him away from the imagers who are assigned to the palace . . ."

"The imagers they sent out here were the ones they trusted least?"

"I don't know," replied Khalis. "He didn't say anything like that."

"Are there other walls or defenses in Liantiago? Besides those around the palace?"

"No . . . he said that the city has no walls except around the palace. Some of the villas of the wealthy Shahibs have walls, though."

Another half glass passed before Quaeryt finished talking to Khalis—and having him ask more questions of Elsior—but he didn't learn much more. That didn't surprise him.

In the end, on Meredi afternoon, after the battle over the wall across the road into Liantiago, Skarpa had Southern Army advance into the western edge of the city proper, where his forces took over two adjoining walled villas that provided some barriers to the attacks he and Quaeryt anticipated, but which never occurred.

Quaeryt took a small room on the main level of the small villa, but while he slept soundly, he woke just before dawn with a jolt. He washed and dressed quickly, conferred briefly with Zhelan, told the imager undercaptains to get ready to move out, and then went looking for Skarpa. He found the submarshal in the study of the larger villa, studying a map laid out on a whitewood conference table that matched the elegantly carved desk, the chairs upholstered in a green velvet, and the settee before the built-in whitewood bookcases. Each corner of the map was weighted down with a leather-bound book, one of which looked older, to Quaeryt, than anything he'd seen in the scholarium in Solis, reminding him, again, that he really needed to replace the book he'd borrowed and lost in the shipwreck, although the replacement would have to be with a different volume, since he doubted that another copy of the one he had lost existed.

"What are you thinking?" asked Skarpa.

"About a lost book." Quaeryt shook his head. "It's a long story. Some other time. And you?"

"I'm worried," Skarpa said bluntly, brushing back hair that seemed grayer than Quaeryt recalled.

"Why?"

"Because the scouts haven't discovered a single barrier on the avenue leading north to the palace. There are no troopers anywhere in sight in the city, and every house and shop between us and the palace is shuttered and abandoned. We settled in here last evening, and by midnight, everyone was gone. There hasn't been a single Antiagon scout seen, and there's no sign of any troopers anywhere but inside the walls of the palace complex."

"What about the rest of the city?"

"We haven't checked more than a mille or two, except toward the harbor. Everything's closed and shuttered, but there are traces of people farther away, just not within a mille or so of the palace."

"You're suggesting that Aliaro has weapons that will destroy this entire quarter of Liantiago . . . and us with it. And that someone warned the people . . . or they know that."

Skarpa barked a laugh. "He must have said he does, and maybe he does. The thing is . . . the scouts also reported that no one has left the palace complex, and there are more walls and more catapults behind those walls this morning."

"So he had imagers building walls last night, and that means he has imagers to spare . . ." Quaeryt paused. "It all could be a bluff."

"He hasn't sent us a warning or anything like that. That's one thing that makes me think it's anything but a bluff."

Quaeryt nodded. "He didn't send any messages when he shelled Ephra after Rex Kharst attacked the harbor at Kephria."

Skarpa stood and gestured at the map before him on the table. "The scouts—and my own eyes—tell me that the map is accurate. Accurate enough for us, anyway." He pointed. "The palace is in the center of this square. It's called the Square of the Autarch."

"Somehow, that doesn't surprise me."

"I didn't think it would. By the way, each side is about fifteen hundred yards long. There is a low wall, two yards high, around the square. Where there were gates there's now solid stone. The north wall of the square is fifty yards from a sheer cliff, and the hill is sculpted to be hard to climb. Looks like one of the autarchs had imagers carve the hill that way. It's too far from the palace for archers and too close for cannon, even if we had them."

Quaeryt took several moments to study the map. "The gardens are all in the rear of the palace it looks like."

"There are at least three separate gardens, all separated by walls three to four yards high. With all the ponds and pools and walls, trying to get to the palace from the rear . . ."

"Wouldn't be a good idea."

"What would be a good idea?" Skarpa looked at Quaeryt.

"Not trying to attack the palace at all, but getting close enough to bring it down on Aliaro's crown."

"What if he's not there?"

"Where else would he be? Your scouts haven't seen any large bodies of men leaving. The harbor's been empty for the last two days, and they couldn't have pulled out everyone who's in the palace. The earlier battles showed that they can't match us on open ground or in the field. So they're going to concentrate their forces and make us come to them. I told you earlier. They know that until we take Liantiago, we haven't won."

"Aliaro could have fled," Skarpa pointed out.

"It won't make any difference. Once the palace is destroyed, so is his authority. But that's why he'll be there."

"I don't see that."

"Think about it. Everywhere we've been there's been little or no local control. Everyone defers to either the Autarch or their Shahib, out of fear of their power. Everything's referred to Liantiago. That's where the decisions are made. What happens if the palace is gone and Southern Army holds Liantiago?"

"Everything falls apart."

"Exactly. Aliaro has to know that. So do his ministers or advisors. He can't leave, because if he does, and they defeat us, they'll know that they don't need him. If he does, and we take the palace, his life is forfeit anywhere he goes, and everyone will be looking for him. So he can't leave, and he won't let them leave."

"You make it sound like, win or lose, we've got problems."

"The problems are much less if we win—when we win. As Bhayar's regional governor, you replace Aliaro, and life goes on—with more than a few changes, although you'll have to make them gradually, just like Rescalyn did in Tilbor."

"Regional governor? Aren't you assuming a lot?"

"You really think Bhayar will give up Antiago? He'll have to let you be governor for a while, and promote you to marshal. That way, you get a generous stipend. If he really wants to replace you, though, he'll probably give you a small high holding in an out-of-the-way place. If he did any less, he'd face trouble from the other senior officers."

"We can talk about your dreams for me after we deal with Aliaro," replied Skarpa dryly. "How do you propose that we bring down the palace?"

"By not letting Aliaro know that's our intention." Quaeryt went on to explain what he had in mind.

When he had finished, Skarpa nodded slowly, then asked, "Will it work?"

"I think it will . . . but until we try it, who knows? What I do know is that we have to get the Antiagon imagers involved from the beginning, and the imager undercaptains have to be able to handle them . . . at least for a little while. That's why we'll use three columns, and why I want the approaches by Fourteenth and Third Regiments to lag the initial attack by first company and Nineteenth Regiment."

Skarpa looked squarely at Quaeryt. "Answer me honestly. Do you really think we should attack? Why?"

"From a tactical point of view, I can't think of a single good reason to attack—except that I don't know anything else that will work. And after seeing what I've seen just so far, I'd find it hard to live with myself if we walked away. I also think that trying to get out of here without getting rid of Aliaro and his imagers would be almost as bad as fighting and losing."

Skarpa nodded slowly. "I have the same feelings. Just looking at the palace complex tells me that." He took the books off the corners of the map and rolled it up. "Now we just have to brief the senior officers . . . and ignore Kharllon's unbelieving expression when I tell him that we're going to attack the most fortified stronghold in all Lydar without cannon, siege engines, and with only a handful of imagers when the other side has as many troopers, scores of catapults, archers, and likely twice as many imagers. Except I'll leave all that out." Skarpa snorted. "Good thing I believe you."

*Let's just hope you can deliver.* In the back of Quaeryt's mind was the fear that someday he wouldn't be able to deliver. *Except that already happened. You couldn't deliver Khel, and that's why you're here.* After a moment, he had another thought. *A perfect example of tripling an already risky wager.*

He said nothing, just turned and followed Skarpa.

Almost to the instant when the first distant bells rang seventh glass—since all of the anomens near the palace were silent—Quaeryt led first company and Nineteenth Regiment out through the white stone gates of the villa to the southeast of the palace complex and onto the wide white stone boulevard leading to the Square of the Autarch.

Kharllon's expression had been close to incredulous, as Skarpa had predicted, and the senior commander had asked twice whether he would have to complete an assault on the palace walls, despite Skarpa's assurance that such would not be required.

Quaeryt's own briefing of the imager undercaptains, all now with him and first company, had been direct and simple. "We have to look like we're the spearhead of a full assault on the palace and get their imagers to try to stop us. Threkhyl . . . you and Horan need to take out as many catapults as you can. Horan, you've got the ones on the right, Threkhyl the ones on the left. Khalis, Lhandor, you'll be shielding; Khalis, the left; Lhandor, the right. Voltyr . . . you'll be standing by to handle whatever new they throw at us."

As first company led the way up the wide boulevard, the only sounds that

Quaeryt heard were those of hooves on stone and the low susurration of muted voices.

Every street, lane, and alley they passed was silent and empty under the clear sky and early morning sun. *No rainstorms to help, and we're more than a half mille from the harbor, but there haven't been that many storms since we've been in Antiago.* That wasn't surprising, given the land's reputation for being hot, dry, and sunny.

Quaeryt noticed several other things. All the ways, from boulevard to streets to lanes to alleys, were paved . . . and all the buildings looked to be about the same age and constructed in the same style. *Because that's what the autarchs wanted? Or because this entire part of Liantiago was destroyed and rebuilt? Both?* Either way it suggested very strong local control . . . and a great deal of imaging.

When they were less than two blocks from the Square of the Autarch, the one- and two-story stone dwellings and shops gave way to taller and more ornate private dwellings, clearly with central courtyards—most likely for Shahibs or wealthy factors, if not both, and possibly for high functionaries at the palace.

Quaeryt glanced toward the palace—an imposing white stone structure, with walls within walls, beginning with the low stone wall around the square. Behind that was the recently imaged mid-square wall, a good hundred yards back from the outer wall and another hundred forward of the palace walls, four yards high, with catapults behind the second wall. Then there was the palace wall proper, more than thirty yards high and running all the way around the palace, which in turn rose another forty yards above the walls with six towers, each at a point on the hexagonal main building within the hexagonal walls.

Quaeryt quickly returned his attention to the immediate tasks at hand. He could see men scrambling into position on the scores of catapults behind the higher walls in the middle of the square, walls whose whiteness confirmed that they had been recently imaged into place on the level stone surface of Autarch's Square, a stone plaza some three quarters of a mille on a side, without a single fountain, statue, or other ornamentation—a different kind of declaration of power, Quaeryt felt.

"Voltyr . . . take down the center part of the square wall . . . but so that it doesn't block our advance. And stand ready to open the gaps for the other two regiments."

"Yes, sir."

No sooner had the first ranks ridden through the gap in the outer square wall than a fire grenade, and then another, arched from behind the mid-square wall, toward first company. Quaeryt imaged them back toward the catapults, but the first grenade started to explode, and then turned to ice pellets that showered harmlessly on the white paving stones of the square. The second grenade just vanished.

*They know as much as you do . . . and likely more. We need to keep them busy, then.*

"Threkhyl and Horan! Start to work on taking down those catapults."

Immediately two catapults sagged, and then two more.

Quaeryt imaged a flurry of red-hot iron needles into the areas where he thought the catapult magazines of fire grenades would be.

Not only did he feel resistance, but nothing happened.

He couldn't say he was totally surprised.

One of the catapults suddenly was surrounded with an icy mist, but a third one exploded into fragments.

"Got the bastard anyway!" Threkhyl's voice held satisfaction and determination.

"Voltyr! Open the other gaps!" ordered Quaeryt, knowing that he needed to keep the Antiagon imagers concentrating on the attackers.

This time, as the vanguards of the flanking regiments moved into the square, arrows arched from somewhere, not toward first company, but toward Fourteenth Regiment and Third Regiment.

Quaeryt managed to block the first flights with short, broad shields, trying not to use too much energy, yet understanding all too clearly that, somehow, the Antiagon imagers knew where the Telaryn imagers were.

Two more catapults went down with explosions, and another collapsed in a shower of ice.

For a long instant . . . the entire square was silent.

Then . . . a shower of flame—not merely a few score fire grenades—but a huge curtain of flame, a vast expanse of Antiagon Fire that turned the very sky crimson-yellow-green, arched down toward the Telaryn forces.

"Shields!" ordered Quaeryt.

While Khalis and Lhandor created a wedge-shaped shield over the center of Southern Army, the near-curtain of Antiagon Fire cascaded down each side of the shield, growing and building with intensity enough that Quaeryt could sense that that immense concentration of heat could easily incinerate the troopers on each side of first company and Nineteenth Regiment, as well as those in Fourteenth Regiment and Third Regiment.

*Heat! Of course.* With that much heat so close, Quaeryt didn't even have to draw that much from the Antiagon forces, as he concentrated on imaging away rock and soil from under the entire palace, from well below where the shields of the Antiagon imagers were anchored and locked, yet he did extend a thread of imaging to the harbor . . . just in case. Even as he concentrated and hurried, he made, from well below where the shields of the Antiagon imagers were anchored and locked, a huge empty space, imaging the material that had been there into the air above the rear of the palace. Even as he concentrated and hurried, he made certain that he imaged away more rock from under the rear of the palace complex than from the front so that when it all collapsed the rubble would largely tumble away from the Telaryn forces.

"Hold shields!"

The ground trembled . . . then shook . . . and a huge groaning drowned out everything.

Behind the high hexagonal walls, the palace shivered, and the tall towers began to shake, and then collapse . . . except that the entire palace complex shuddered, sagged, and then dropped from sight—just as a small mountain of soil, gravel, and stones cascaded from the sky into the depression from which not even the top of the palace walls protruded.

The stone paving under the mare's hooves shook and trembled, and the trembling got worse. From the corners of his eyes, even as Quaeryt tried to hold shields to protect first company, he could see buildings in the distance trembling and shaking.

Gale force winds whipped toward him, so cold that ice pellets dropped everywhere, but he still tried to hold his shields . . .

. . . until a wall of whiteness, so cold he could do nothing . . . toppled from nowhere onto him . . . and froze him in burning ice.

The first thing Quaeryt saw when his eyes opened was white . . . white everywhere. He was covered in blankets and shivering, so much so that he couldn't focus his eyes on anything.

"Sir . . . ?"

"I'm . . . alive . . . I think." His entire body ached, and he couldn't stop shivering. "What happened?"

"Submarshal Skarpa says the city is ours. The part of it that's left after all the shaking."

"Left?" Quaeryt shivered so violently he couldn't say more.

"You need to drink some watered lager, sir . . . anything." Khalis rose from the chair beside the bed and guided a mug to Quaeryt's lips, holding it steady against his shivering.

Quaeryt could only take small sips, but after a time the worst of the shivering stopped, as did most of the twitching in his eyes. The throbbing in his head did not subside.

Despite the white walls of the bedchamber where he lay, the light coming through the windows was muted and gloomy. "What glass . . . ?"

"It's just past the third glass of the afternoon, sir. It's darker than you'd expect. Most of the city was covered in fog, yesterday and most of today. The sun's finally burning it off. That's because of all the ice that coated the ruins and the square."

"What day is it?"

"Jeudi afternoon, sir."

*Two days . . . better than the last time . . . you hope.*

"You need to drink more, sir."

Quacryt didn't object, and he wasn't shaking so much when he finished another series of swallows rather than sips.

"Don't try to get up, sir," said Khalis as he set the mug on the table beside the wide bed. "I'll be right back. Commander Skarpa wanted to know when you were awake."

"I'm not going anywhere," said Quaeryt dryly. He had the feeling that his head might fall off if he even tried to stand . . . if his legs didn't collapse first.

As Khalis left, Quaeryt turned his head and looked toward the window. *Ruins and shaking?* Beyond was a garden, although he could see that beyond an ornamental tree he did not recognize there was a wall . . . and there were cracks and gaps in the mortar between the stones. There were also cracks in the plaster finish of the outside wall of the bedchamber.

*But why would imaging a pit beneath the palace cause ruins elsewhere?* He frowned, before recalling that the paving stones of the Autarch's Square had been shaking so hard that the mare had struggled to keep her footing. *But why?*

He turned his head and closed his eyes, but the flashes of light that interrupted his vision were even more disconcerting against the closed lids, and he opened them again, just as Khalis returned to the bedchamber.

"The submarshal will be here shortly, sir."

"What about first company? All the undercaptains?"

"We're all fine . . . well, except for bruises and cuts, little things like that."

"From all the shaking?"

"And the falling buildings everywhere."

*Falling buildings? Why . . .* Quaeryt didn't question what Khalis had clearly experienced, but why would the impact of the palace on whatever lay below the hole he'd imaged have caused so much shaking that it toppled buildings farther away than around the square?

Behind Khalis, the door opened, and Skarpa stepped through.

Khalis inclined his head and departed, closing the chamber door behind himself.

Skarpa walked over to the bed and looked down at Quaeryt. "You look like hogshit, Quaeryt."

"I don't think I feel quite that bad." *Almost, but not quite.*

"Good. I'd tell you that you need to stop doing this, but I don't think there's any place left in Lydar that will need your way of dealing with things." Skarpa snorted. "There's not even much left of the north side of the city. It's a good thing that most of our forces were on or near the square. Whatever you did brought down most of the buildings. Good thing most of the locals had fled, too. The problem was that not enough of them left." He paused. "What exactly did you do besides create a big hole and drop the palace into it?"

"That's all . . ." Quaeryt coughed, and the paroxysm sent waves of pain through his entire body. For several moments he couldn't move or see.

The submarshal waited.

Finally, Quaeryt could speak and see again, if in flashes. "I . . . just imaged a hole under the palace and all the rocks and sand and gravel and stone up above it, and . . . let it all fall."

"The entire city was shaking for a time, might have been a good half glass, give or take a quint. No one was keeping track."

"Casualties . . . ?" Quaeryt ventured.

"We lost over a thousand to stray Antiagon Fire, flying rubble and falling houses . . . most of them were in Fhaasn's Twenty-sixth Foot. They weren't even on the boulevard around the Autarch's Square when everything came apart. They got hit hard when the big dwellings on the south end of the square came down." Skarpa looked at Quaeryt. "As for the Antiagons . . . maybe two hundred of the troopers near the mid-square wall survived. No one in the palace complex . . . no imagers, so far as we can tell."

"The rest of the city?"

"Who knows? At least three or four hundred people were killed, maybe more than a thousand. Could have been more. Several thousand were likely hurt."

"You declare yourself regional governor?"

"Acting regional governor. Even Kharllon agreed to that. He's been pretty quiet. I've already gotten a handful of letters from some Shahibs, pledging allegiance to Bhayar. Appears that you scared them a bit."

"More . . . than I intended," Quaeryt admitted. "I still don't understand why the whole city shook."

"I wouldn't pretend to know. But in some places closer to the square it was pretty bad. There was a school . . . children of factors and Shahibs . . . the whole thing came apart . . ." Skarpa shook his head. "One of your undercaptains broke down and sobbed . . . something about one of the little girls being like his own daughter . . ."

"Do you know who that was?"

"I didn't see it. Zhelan told me. He didn't say who. I was a little occupied."

*Baelthm, Horan, or maybe Threkhyl. The others can't have had children. Not yet, anyway.* "What else should I know?"

Skarpa offered a shrug. "We're still getting control of the city."

Quaeryt wanted to frown, but he felt tired . . . so tired. Skarpa was hiding something from him, he was certain. "The imagers . . . are they . . ."

"They're all fine . . . except for bruises and the like." Skarpa's tone was firm and assured. "You need more rest. We'll talk later."

Quaeryt wanted to say more, to ask what Skarpa was hiding, but the flashes across his eyes were coming more often, and they hurt more . . . and then the white darkness rose around him again.

Quaeryt dozed and woke, and dozed and woke all through Jeudi night, but when he finally opened his eyes sometime after dawn on Vendrei morning, his thoughts weren't so jumbled. The flashes across his eyes had almost vanished, and the throbbing in his head was down to a dull ache. Unfortunately, that diminution of acute pain made him aware of soreness in his right thigh and upper arm, both of which were heavily bruised. He was also strong enough to prop himself up and reach for the mug of watered lager and slowly drink it. He'd almost finished it when Khalis appeared.

"How are you feeling, sir?"

"Much better." Quaeryt wasn't even tempted to reply with something along the lines of he couldn't have felt much worse. He had felt worse, much worse. "How did I get so bruised, Khalis? Did I get knocked off my mount?"

"Ah . . . not exactly, sir."

"What happened, then?"

"All that shaking . . . it caused gaps in the paving stones, and your mare, her forelegs got crushed in between two stones. She tried not to go down . . . but she did. So did you."

Quaeryt winced. The mare had carried him all the way across Lydar . . . and then to have her brought down by his acts . . . and paving stones . . .

"I'm sorry, sir. That was just the way it was."

"Those things happen. I just wish . . ." He shook his head. "You told me the undercaptains were all right, if bruised." He paused. "What about the rest of first company?"

"There were some broken arms and legs, the major said—from horses and men going down. No one was killed that I heard."

"I need to talk to the submarshal." Quaeryt slowly swung his legs over the side of the bed and put his feet on the stone floor. "Do I have a uniform somewhere?"

"Yes, sir . . . but . . ."

"I need to find the submarshal."

"He's in the study . . ."

"I'll get dressed and find him." *Skarpa won't tell you anything if you're still lying in a bed and looking helpless.*

After dressing, if slowly, Quaeryt did have to sit on the edge of the bed and drink more of the watered lager, as well as slowly chew a too-hard biscuit. Then he rose. "Point me in the right direction, Undercaptain."

"I'll show you, sir. It's only down the hall."

Quaeryt didn't argue with that, but rose slowly and followed the young Pharsi undercaptain through the door and then through what looked to be a lady's study to a wide tiled hallway.

Two doors down stood a pair of troopers, but neither said a word as Khalis opened the door and announced, "Submarshal, Commander Quaeryt to see you."

Quaeryt didn't wait for an acknowledgment, but walked in and took one of the whitewood chairs opposite the table desk, trying not to sink into it. His legs were feeling weaker than he would have liked. The door closed behind him.

Skarpa looked up from the papers and maps surrounding him. "You're up early."

"What weren't you telling me yesterday?" Quaeryt demanded.

"What do you mean?"

"You know exactly what I mean. You were hiding something. What is it?"

The submarshal sighed, deeply, and his brow furrowed. "I'd hoped you wouldn't notice."

"I did. What didn't you tell me?"

"We found out early yesterday that when Aliaro heard about what we did at Kephria he sent three warships and some imagers north."

*Vaelora . . . with only half a regiment to support her, and not a single imager!* "Where did you find that out?"

"From the assistant harbormaster." Skarpa paused. "It might not be that bad."

"How could it not be that bad?" demanded Quaeryt.

"When he found out we were marching on Liantiago several days after that, Aliaro sent a fast schooner or ketch after them. The harbormaster didn't know why, but I'd wager it was to recall them to defend Liantiago."

"That wouldn't have stopped them from leveling and burning what was left of Kephria," Quaeryt pointed out.

"The schooner might have traveled faster."

"Not that much faster. The Antiagon warships are all built for speed.

Have you seen the *Montagne*? Or the *Solis*? Are there any other ships either here or in Westisle?"

"No one's seen either. There is a large schooner in Westisle. I had the captain sail it here."

"Put me on that ship . . . I can recover on the trip."

"I thought you'd say that," replied Skarpa wryly. "What about Liantiago? What if those imagers return and you're gone?"

"Voltyr and Threkhyl can provide any imaging you need. Have them watch the harbor and sink any Antiagon ship that tries to enter the port. They can do that. It's hard enough to image over water. I imagine it's even harder if you're in it or under it. As regional governor, you'll need some imagers anyway, and I planned on leaving them."

"Nice of you to tell me."

"You didn't want to hear my plans. Remember? And . . . Nineteenth Regiment can stay as well. The other undercaptains and first company can come with me." Even speaking that many words left Quaeryt feeling light-headed.

"You're not as well as you think."

"No . . . but Vaelora is Bhayar's sister."

Skarpa laughed harshly. "I worry more about you and your imagers than about Lord Bhayar. I already told the captain to be ready to sail before noon. Major Zhelan is readying first company, but the ship can't take any mounts. It'll be crowded enough with your imagers and the troopers. And I've sent a small paychest. You'll need it for supplies."

"Thank you. As for not having mounts, we'll make do."

"I did find a carriage, and you will ride in it, Commander. I won't be responsible for you falling off a mount when you shouldn't be up at all."

"Yes, sir."

"There are times when you can be impossible, you know?"

"If I weren't, you wouldn't be acting governor of Antiago, and Bhayar would likely be dead and Solis in the hands of Rex Kharst."

"Quaeryt . . . I know you're worried about Vaelora . . . but . . . don't take it out on me."

"I'm sorry. I am worried. She's not that far from having a child, only a month or so." *Maybe less.* "And she's not the kind to offer herself up." *Especially not after the way Aliaro treated her sister.*

"She and Baarl—and Khaern, if he's back—would certainly withdraw from an attack by imagers," Skarpa pointed out.

"I left that order—if they had any warning. But when Kharst attacked Kephria, Aliaro shelled Ephra and used his imagers to incinerate the attackers with no warning whatsoever." *And you weren't much different in your attacks on the cities of Liantiago. Is the Nameless returning the favor?* Quaeryt couldn't help but wonder that, even as he still doubted that there even was a Nameless.

"Just get yourself ready . . ." said Skarpa. "I'll make sure that everything else is on board and waiting for you."

"Thank you . . . and I'm sorry . . . It's just . . ."

"I do understand . . . Now get yourself out of here. Don't be too proud to ask Khalis or the others to help you."

"I won't." Quaeryt rose, deliberately, and inclined his head. "Thank you . . . again." Then he walked slowly to the study door.

In less than a glass, he was riding out from the villa in a white carriage, accompanied by Khalis and escorted by almost a company of troopers from Third Regiment.

*How could you not have seen this? How? And with Vaelora expecting?* She'd said that he'd need every imager. *But did you have to listen to her?* He'd assumed that Aliaro would have understood that Kephria was merely the first city to fall. *That was a terrible assumption.* He didn't even want to dwell on the fact that it might have cost him Vaelora—and their daughter.

Yet there was nothing he could do—now—beyond what he was about to do.

He forced himself to look at the buildings. From what he could tell, the villa in which he had been recovering was south and west of the Autarch's Square, possibly more than a half mille away. Yet, as he continued through the streets of Liantiago, every building near the villa showed some signs of damage, if as little as shutters hanging askew, or cracks in the outside walls. In more than a few instances, though, an entire dwelling had collapsed in on itself. Several times, the driver had to slow the carriage to ease it over or around raised paving stones, although, after another half mille, the damage was far less apparent. By the time the carriage had reached the harbor, there were almost no signs of damage, except for an occasional broken window, shutters askew, or fragments of roof tiles on the ground or sidewalks.

The three-masted schooner waiting at the long main pier was a comparatively large vessel, a good forty-five yards from stem to stern, with even a low sterncastle.

Voltyr and Threkhyl met the carriage even before Quaeryt could think about getting out. Standing behind them was Alazyn.

"Sir? The submarshal said that you'd ordered us to remain here to support him, but that you might have additional orders for us," said Voltyr.

"There may be imagers here that we don't know about. That's one reason why the submarshal may need you. The Autarch dispatched several to deal with Kephria. If they elude us, they may return here. For that reason, you are to attack and sink any Antiagon warship that attempts to port here."

Voltyr raised his eyebrows.

"Do you want to face another imager as strong as those who defended the palace? The *only* reason an Antiagon warship would be attempting to land immediately would be if they have an imager on board. Any other warship would likely stand off and send in someone under a parley flag. If that happens, make certain that the warship anchors offshore and keep them there until you get a dispatch from me. If you don't, then you'll have to discuss things with the submarshal and exercise your own judgment." Quaeryt laughed softly, and even that hurt. "You'll have to rely on your own judgment in many matters, I suspect. Just remember that your fate, and the fate of all imagers, rests on our ability to support Lord Bhayar and to consolidate his rule over all Lydar. Anything else—anything—is likely to be fatal for imagers. Do you understand?"

"Yes, sir." Voltyr nodded.

"I'm taking Elsior with Lhandor, Khalis, and Baelthm because his life is forfeit here . . . and maybe we can get him to join us. At the same time, I'd like you to keep your eye out for young imagers. You know how to train them."

"You're saying that we're likely to be here for a while, then?"

"You could be here for a month . . . or a year." *If not longer.* "Remember, when all of this started, I thought I'd be gone from Solis no more than two seasons. That was almost two years ago."

Threkhyl started to open his mouth, and Quaeryt looked hard at him. Threkhyl closed his mouth.

Quaeryt kept looking at Threkhyl. "You need to follow Voltyr's lead, his advice, and his orders. It might just keep you alive."

After a moment the ginger-bearded imager replied, "Yes, sir."

As the two undercaptains stepped back, Alazyn moved forward. "Sir? Any orders for me?"

Quaeryt frowned for a moment. "You're here to support the submarshal. You're also here to protect the imagers so that they can protect you as well. Don't let yourself or Nineteenth Regiment be separated from the imagers. Undercaptain Voltyr may gather and train other imagers. While technically you are his superior, listen to him and see if you can accommodate any needs he has."

Alazyn nodded. "I heard what you said to them."

"They weren't just words."

"No, sir. I've seen that."

Quaeryt smiled. "You're a perceptive officer, Alazyn. I appreciate that." He lowered his voice. "Be most careful around Commander Kharllon."

"Yes, sir." Alazyn offered a hand to help Quaeryt from the carriage.

As Quaeryt eased himself to his feet, several rankers hurried down to take his gear, such as it was. He walked slowly the distance to the foot of the gangway, his eyes flicking to the bow of the ship where carved letters, painted black, gave the name as *Zephyr*.

The dark-haired captain, younger than Quaeryt had expected, possibly only ten years older than Quaeryt, despite his weathered skin, stood just beyond the quarterdeck, his face impassive . . . for a moment, until he saw Quaeryt's silver-white hair, honey-colored skin, and dark eyes. Quaeryt couldn't read his reaction, but it was clear Quaeryt's appearance had given him pause.

"Permission to come aboard, Captain?"

The Antiagon smiled, if briefly. "Some do remember courtesy."

His accent was so heavy that it took Quaeryt a moment to catch his words and reply. "We try . . . when we can." Quaeryt crossed the gangway and then stopped short of the captain. "I'm Commander Quaeryt."

"Sario A'Basiol, sir."

"I would that we were not meeting this way, Captain, but matters are urgent. I don't know what you've been told, but speed is necessary. The late Autarch dispatched several ships to attack the Telaryn forces in Kephria under the command of Lord Bhayar's sister."

For a moment the captain did not react, but then Quaeryt caught the slightest swallow.

"The lady is also my wife," Quaeryt added, speaking slowly and as clearly as possible. "Whatever happened is not your fault, and I will not hold it against you. Failing to make the best speed possible, I will. I have some experience at sea. I was a junior quartermaster for several years."

The captain inclined his head. "I appreciate the explanation. I understand your concerns. We will do our best." After a moment, he added, "My quarters are yours, sir."

"Thank you." Quaeryt nodded in return. He just hoped he could make it to those quarters before his legs gave out.

# 69

Once the *Zephyr* cleared the harbor of Liantiago on Vendrei, Quaeryt allowed himself to sleep. He didn't do much besides sleep, occasionally eat, and even more occasionally check the ship's heading and progress until after noon on Samedi. His sleep was interrupted often by the same thought—*Why didn't you think that Aliaro would retaliate? How could he have known that Kephria was just the first city you planned to attack?*

When he finally felt stronger and more lucid, but no less guilty and worried, and fearful that he might have lost Vaelora through that stupidity, he sent for Zhelan, in order to begin planning for whatever eventualities they might encounter on the voyage or when they reached the waters off Kephria and Ephra.

"You're looking better, Commander," were Zhelan's first words when he entered the cabin, a space that was far more modest than the captain's quarters on the *Montagne*, but then, those quarters had been designed to serve Lord Chayar, if necessary, not that Bhayar's father had used them more than once, on a voyage from Tilbora back to Solis, as Quaeryt recalled.

"I think that means that you think I'll recover fully in time," replied Quaeryt, gesturing to one of the chairs around the small oblong table at which he had earlier seated himself. "What do you think of the captain and the crew?"

"I'm no seaman, but they seem to be doing their best. I did tell the captain you wanted to be told of any ships the lookouts sighted, no matter what the glass of day or night."

"Good. Thank you. How is first company holding up?"

"We're down to eighty-one men, and that includes five with broken arms, and one with a broken leg. That doesn't include the undercaptains or the captive imager."

"That's not too bad," said Quaeryt dryly, "considering what I've asked of them."

"What do you plan for when we reach Kephria?"

"I have the feeling that we won't find much there. I can't imagine that Aliaro's imagers and the guns on his warships have left much of either

Ephra or Kephria, and probably not much of Geusyn. I only hope that Vaelora and Baarl—and Khaern and Calkoran and their men—if they managed to reach Geusyn—could withdraw without horrendous casualties." Quaeryt shook his head. "I just didn't think. Aliaro just thought it was another attack on Kephria, and that Bhayar was repeating what Kharst did."

"Not everyone looks as far out as you, sir."

"Thank you. That's a polite way of saying that it's stupid to assume someone knows what you're going to do when they have no way of knowing. And you're right. It was stupid. Now . . . all I can do is hope, and try to make sure that the Antiagons don't cause any more damage because of my idiocy."

Zhelan nodded.

Quaeryt smiled wryly. "You're a good officer and a good man, Zhelan. You've saved my ass and that of the men on more than a few occasions."

"I've saved your pride, sir, and you've saved the men more times than I'd like to count."

"You've saved them as well. Now . . . my thoughts are that we really don't want to fight anyone. I'd just as soon sink the Antiagon ships and let it go at that. The problem is that the ships may not be there, and the imagers may be. If neither is there, all we can do is pick up the pieces." *And hope that we have some vestiges of a force left . . . and Vaelora. Please let her be there.* "I'd like your thoughts."

"I assume you or the other imagers can use concealments for the *Zephyr* . . ."

"We can, but a fast-moving schooner will leave a wake longer than we could extend a concealment, unless we're headed directly toward them. With three or four vessels . . ."

Quaeryt and Zhelan talked for close to a glass. Then Quaeryt had more watered lager and some biscuits and a bit of hard cheese.

After that, Khalis asked for a quint or so with Quaeryt, and he entered the cabin with Lhandor and Elsior. The three of them settled into two chairs on the other side of the oblong table, with Elsior on a stool between them.

"Before we start, sir . . . later . . . Horan wants to talk to you alone."

"Anytime," Quaeryt agreed. There wasn't much else he could do at the moment, although he felt much stronger than he had a day earlier, not that he was up to doing any imaging.

"Right now, Elsior has something to say," offered Khalis.

"Go ahead," Quaeryt said slowly . . . and gently.

"Are we sailing to Bovaria?"

"We are. It is now part of Telaryn."

"The others, the undercaptains, they say that they are free."

"They are as free as the other junior officers. No more. No less."

"They are paid?"

"The same as other undercaptains."

"You taught them to be better imagers."

"As well as I could."

Elsior's questions—and Quaeryt's answers—went on for almost a quint. Then, abruptly, he said, "I would like to be one of them."

"I am flattered," replied Quaeryt, "but might I ask why you have decided so quickly?"

"I have been afraid all my life. They are not afraid."

"We all fear the dangers of battle, and the dangers of imaging."

"That is a different fear."

Quaeryt couldn't argue with that. He nodded and waited.

"I had feared . . . if I offered allegiance to you . . . then Aliaro's imager assassins would track me across all Lydar." Elsior's eyes dropped. "They say you will have a place for imagers, a place where they will be free."

"As free as they are now. It will be a place that is part trooper and part school." Quaeryt decided not to try to explain more. Not at the moment. "It will be in Variana."

"I would like that."

*So would we all . . . if matters were but that simple.* "Is there anything else, Undercaptains?"

"Could you tell us what comes next, sir?" asked Lhandor.

"I wish I knew. We have to see what happened in Ephra and Kephria, and deal with the Antiagon imagers Aliaro sent out . . . if we can. If we can't, we have to reestablish a presence in what's left of Kephria or Geusyn." Quaeryt offered a shrug. "We just have to see. I'll let you know as I know."

"Thank you, sir."

After the three Pharsi left, Horan eased through the cabin door.

Quaeryt motioned for him to sit down, then took several long swallows of the watered lager, not as good as that which he imaged, but he wasn't about to try any imaging yet, although his headache was almost gone, and the flickering flashes of light no longer interrupted his sight.

"You wanted to see me?"

"Yes, sir."

Quaeryt waited.

"Sir . . . I don't know as I can do this . . . imaging . . . anymore." The burly imager took a deep breath. "When the whole palace came down . . . you know . . . there were bodies everywhere. There was this school . . . the walls just came apart . . . One of them . . . she was a girl . . . a little girl . . . and she looked like my daughter . . . There was a boy, too . . ." Horan shook his head. "There were others . . ." He looked helplessly at Quaeryt.

"Imaging is one thing when it's directed at troopers. It's another when it hurts children and the innocent. Is that it?"

"Yes, sir . . . except . . . no, sir . . . there were so many bodies there."

"There were far more bodies outside Variana," Quaeryt said quietly.

"But . . . they weren't children . . . she could have been my daughter . . ."

Quaeryt couldn't help but wonder about Vaelora—and the unborn daughter she carried. *What if she and Vaelora died because of your mistake?*

"Sir . . . ?"

"I'm sorry. I do understand. I don't know what to say." Quaeryt paused, thinking. Finally, he went on. "I won't ask you to do anything against others . . . but until this is settled, could I ask you to stay with us and to provide shields? That would not harm others, and it would keep troopers and officers from greater harm."

Horan took a deep breath. "I could do that, sir. Thank you, sir."

"I will request, if anyone asks, to tell them that you asked about your future duties and that we discussed them."

"Yes, sir. I can do that."

After Horan left, Quaeryt looked blankly at the closed cabin door.

By Solayi morning, the first day of Maris and, by the calendar, the first day of spring, Quaeryt felt far better, and could even hold light shields for a quint or so before having to drop them and rest. The weather remained the same, sunny and cool, with a wind out of the northwest that allowed fair speed and only moderate swells. Lundi was no different, and since his legs were steadier, Quaeryt had pulled on his riding jacket and stood on the low sterncastle beside Captain Sario, his eyes scanning the horizon, even though he knew that the lookout aloft would most likely see the sail of another vessel long before he did.

"How long have you been captain and master of the *Zephyr*?" asked Quaeryt conversationally.

"I have been captain for three years." Sario offered a tight smile. "I cannot say I am master, for the ship belongs to the family."

"Are you from Westisle?"

"Yes." After several moments the captain added, "Almost all merchanters port out of Westisle."

"Because it's farther from Liantiago?" Quaeryt let a sardonic tone creep into his words.

Sario did not reply.

"Lord Bhayar won't punish you for what you say. Neither will I. Besides, Bhayar has all of two warships at present." *If that. Who knows what might have happened to the* Montagne *and the* Solis *if they encountered the Antiagon imagers?* "He's always been friendly and fair to merchanters in Telaryn, and he is now to those in Bovaria." *So long as they don't try to cheat him.* "That won't change. In fact, you'll likely do better because all the ports in Lydar will be open to you."

"One of the officers said you know Lord Bhayar well."

"We have known each other since we were students. We had the same tutor."

"And it is true that you married his sister?"

Quaeryt laughed softly, trying not to think what might have happened to Vaelora. "He was the one who insisted on it. We were both fortunate." Quaeryt's voice turned somber. "I hope we still are."

"A man who has loved truly and been loved so is always fortunate, even when the Nameless turns from him."

"I'd rather be more fortunate than that, Captain."

"So would we all, sir."

Quaeryt paused. "I'm sorry. You sound like a man who has experienced love and loss. I would not pry . . ."

"She died in childbirth. So did our son. I was not there. I was here." Sario's words were clipped.

"I am truly sorry." After several moments Quaeryt asked, "Has your family always been from Westisle?"

"So far as we know."

"Did you help build the *Zephyr*?"

Sario looked at Quaeryt. "How did you know that?"

"I watched you. You know every sound, and you don't have to look. You know exactly what to tell your crew when the least little thing is not right."

"Any good captain should know that."

"The hull is cedar, isn't it? From Hassyl?"

"Loboro. In the hills west of Hassyl. We have lands there."

"The *Zephyr* is a fast ship, I suspect."

"One of the fastest," admitted Sario. "Except for the *Boreal*."

"She's a family ship, too, I take it?"

"Of course." Sario did smile, if but for a moment. "You have the look and the manner of what some would call a lost one."

"I've been called that. My parents died of the plague or the Red Death when I was so young I barely remember them. I didn't even realize I was Pharsi until much later. My hair used to be whitish-blond." *Until Variana.*

"I would not ask what . . ." Sario paused, as if uncertain as to how much to ask.

"Sail ho!" came the cry from the lookout aloft.

"What ships?" called Sario, immediately looking forward with greater intensity.

"Looks to be three ships, sir! Two Antiagon men-of-war and a ketch."

"What's their bearing?" called Quaeryt.

"A quint to starboard, sir!"

Sario looked to Quaeryt.

"Bring her onto a direct closing course, Captain."

"There are three vessels, sir, and two are warships."

"Closing course, as close to head to head as possible, if you would, Captain."

Sario turned to the helmsman. "Half quint starboard."

Quaeryt gestured to the duty ranker posted at the sterncastle ladder. "Have the undercaptains report to me."

"Yes, sir."

Zhelan appeared almost immediately. "Sir?"

"Antiagon warships. Likely the ones Aliaro dispatched to Kephria and then recalled. Whether they are or not, we'll have to deal with them."

"Sir . . ." ventured Zhelan, "I would not like to be the one to suggest this . . ."

"But they might have captives or prisoners? Is that it?"

"It is possible, is it not?"

"Possible, but hardly likely. The last time Kephria was attacked, Aliaro's imagers killed every last one of the Bovarians. Second, I doubt that they would know that Vaelora's there. Third, the very last thing she would allow would be to be captured. Fourth, neither would Baarl or Khaern." *Yet . . . even with all those reasons . . .* Quaeryt shook his head. "So unlikely we can't afford to consider it."

"What about cannon, sir? We have none."

"That's another reason for the concealment and for a course straight at them. They shouldn't be able to see us, and most guns are mounted midships. They'll have to get close enough to see our wake to guess at where we are, and then they'll have to turn to use them, and we should be close enough to use imaging by then." *You hope.*

Zhelan's nod only signified that he had heard Quaeryt's explanation, not that he agreed with it.

While he and the major waited for the undercaptains, Quaeryt strained to see the sails reported by the lookout, but even as the imagers gathered, he still could not see any sign of the ships. Finally, he turned to the undercaptains.

"We have three Antiagon ships headed toward us. The lookout reports that two are warships. The third may be the ship sent to fetch them back to Liantiago. They likely have imagers aboard, as well as Antiagon Fire. We can't let them get past us. Nor can we let them avoid us. The *Zephyr* is faster than they are, but they outnumber us. We'll need to approach under concealment, and then attack." Deciding not to mention cannon, he turned to Horan. "If you'd see to a concealment for now, and we'll need shields when we're closer."

"Yes, sir."

"Lhandor . . . I'll need you to remove a large chunk of the stem of the lead vessel, but not until we're closer. Khalis . . . you'll need to see to the second one. I'd like enough removed that she goes down fast."

"Yes, sir."

"Baelthm . . . just stand by to see what you can do."

The oldest imager nodded solemnly.

A quint passed before Quaeryt could easily make out the three sets of sails, and there was no doubt that the lookout had identified the vessels correctly. The first two flew the maroon battle ensign of Antiago, while the third, a ketch, bore no ensign, although the rigging was clearly Antiagon.

"There's no sign of another ship?" Quaeryt asked Sario.

"No, sir. The lookout would have called it out."

*Just where is the other warship? Still off Kephria?* Was it possible that the *Montagne* or the *Solis* might have encountered it and sunk it? Or had the Antiagons sunk or damaged both Telaryn warships?

Quaeryt watched and forced himself to wait as the Antiagon ships drew nearer. Finally, he turned to Horan. "We'll need shields now."

"Yes, sir."

The distance continued to close, and the Antiagons continued to hold their heading and course.

"In another few hundred yards, Lhandor . . ." Quaeryt began.

A large flare of Antiagon Fire exploded in midair, less than fifty yards from the bow of the *Zephyr*. At that moment Quaeryt could see the nearest ship begin to turn to bring her guns into play, and then a puff of smoke from the forward gun port.

*Those are pretty good indicators that these are some of the ships that went to Kephria. But how did they know where we are?* Quaeryt glanced to Horan. He could see the perspiration on the big undercaptain's forehead . . . although his shields had held. *But at least one of the imagers at the road wall had known where first company had been, even behind a concealment.* "Just keep holding those shields, Horan." Quaeryt turned, glad that whatever the Antiagon had fired had not struck the *Zephyr*. "Image the first vessel, Lhandor."

Abruptly the first five yards of the Antiagon warship vanished. Totally. What remained of the forecastle and the bow plowed into the swells, and the entire vessel shuddered, coming to a halt in what seemed to be a handful of yards.

Quaeryt imaged two yard-wide holes in the hull amidships, just in case. Flashes of light flared across his eyes, and he could feel the unsteadiness in his legs. "The second ship, Khalis."

Another fireball slammed into Horan's shields, and then a third, before the stem section of the second ship vanished, and it too plowed into the swells and began to nose down.

Quaeryt could see the ketch swinging hard to port trying to get the wind full in its sails, in hopes of outrunning what had struck the two larger vessels. "Khalis . . . can you stop the third ship?"

"I'll see, sir."

A portion of the ketch's stem disappeared, but not a large section, and Khalis went to his knees on the deck. "Harder to image over water."

Abruptly parts of the sails of the ketch caught fire, and then the mainmast swayed and then toppled, as if some of its stays had parted. From beside the others, Baelthm staggered and sat down hard on the sterncastle deck.

"I can do a little more," said Lhandor.

Another hole appeared at the waterline of the ketch, just aft of midships.

Almost inexplicably, both warships exploded into pillars of fire, burning fiercely.

"What?"

"How did that happen?"

It took Quaeryt a moment to realize what had happened. "Water . . . you must have opened the forward magazines to the sea, and cracked or severed a fire grenade or shell. That sometimes happens with Antiagon Fire."

"They must not have had much left," said Sario from behind the imagers. "Otherwise, the entire ship would have vanished. I saw that happen once when I was a boy."

*Must not have had much left?* Quaeryt managed to keep his face impassive as he watched the ketch, hoping he did not have to image anymore, and wondering if he even could, but the fire had spread, and the smaller vessel was markedly lower in the water than even moments before.

"Can you circle here, Captain, until we're certain?"

"Yes, sir." Sario's voice had returned to the impassive tones with which he had spoken earlier.

Quaeryt understood. He also knew that the captain didn't understand all that was at stake, and there was no way to explain it, not to a merchant captain who loved ships and cared for those who sailed them. "Imagers. Stand down, but stay on deck here."

Lhandor sat down, and Khalis actually stretched out on his back on the hard planks, his face pale and damp. "We'll need some watered ale or lager here," Quaeryt called to the duty ranker.

"Yes, sir."

In moments, several rankers appeared with water bottles.

After another quint Quaeryt directed Sario to have the *Zephyr* resume its course for Kephria. By then, the undercaptains looked less worn-out. Quaeryt finally dismissed them, but he kept looking back, long after they had left behind the scattered debris remaining, moved up and down by the regular swells of the Gulf.

Behind him stood Zhelan, equally silent.

After a time, Sario eased over to Quaeryt. "You gave them no chance."

"You saw those fireballs they sent at us."

"Why did they do that? The *Zephyr* is an Antiagon schooner, with an Antiagon rig."

"Because we raised imaging defenses, and that told the imagers on the warships that we were not friendly. I had not realized that they could detect those defenses," Quaeryt admitted.

"Did you have to destroy them all?"

"Not to have done so would have risked too much." *At Liantiago, Aliaro would have given us no chance. Nor did he give Kharst's imagers any chance. And then there was Chaerila.* Quaeryt smiled sadly. "There are times when to afford mercy is foolish. This was one of those times."

"These are terrible times, when whole ships go down in moments, and cities topple into dust."

"I hope we can end these times before long," replied Quaeryt. *But how many warriors and leaders have thought that? Did Hengyst? Or Chayar? Or Kharst when he took Khel?*

The captain eased away.

Quaeryt continued to watch where the third—and smaller—Antiagon vessel had gone down.

He kept thinking. *Three warships and a courier or sloop or that ketch . . . What happened to the other ship? Is it still off Kephria? Or have we missed it entirely? And what did they do in Kephria?*

Quaeryt was all too afraid that he knew. The only question was if anyone survived . . . and who.

On Mardi, the weather held, as did the wind, but Captain Sario remained distant, although by Meredi afternoon, his occasional comments and responses to Quaeryt were less clipped and almost pleasant at times. Quaeryt found himself pacing the deck on the sterncastle, searching for sails and listening, but all that the lookout had sighted were two fishing vessels and a beaten-up Ferran trader with what Sario called a "bastard rig." He was again able to hold full shields, if not for so long as he would have liked, and his headache had vanished, as had the intermittent flashes that had disrupted his eyesight.

"You always pace like that, Commander?" asked the captain.

"Not when I'm riding," returned Quaeryt with a smile, not that he felt like smiling, worrying as he did about Vaelora and Eleventh Regiment and what had likely happened to Ephra, Kephria, and possibly Geusyn.

Sario frowned, then opened his mouth, as if to speak, then closed it as the lookout called from above.

"Sail ho! Antiagon warship, flying a battle ensign."

Sario looked to Quaeryt. "You want a closing course again?"

"If you would."

Once the captain called out the orders to the helmsman, he turned to Quaeryt. "Are you going to sink this one, too?" asked Sario.

"If we can. It's likely to have another imager aboard and Antiagon Fire."

"Why? Haven't you won?"

"Not until Aliaro's imagers are all dead."

"That won't bring your wife back."

"No . . . it won't, and I can hope she's survived . . . but I also have to answer to her brother. What would you do?"

"You don't think he'd be reasonable?"

"After his older sister died in Liantiago and Aliaro barely acknowledged it?" asked Quaeryt dryly. "Or the dead daughter she tried to give birth to?"

"Oh . . ." Sario's voice dropped off for a moment. "You're close to him."

"At times." *When he wishes it.* "He tries to be fair, and from what I've seen of the other rulers in Lydar, he does a much better job of it."

"Even those in Khel?"

"The High Council seems fair enough, but after the Red Death and the Bovarian depredations, Khel is too weak to stand alone. Bhayar has offered terms to the High Council. They're considering them."

"What sort of terms?" asked Sario warily.

"He's trying to work out a way to let the Council handle local matters while having the same laws and tariffs as in all the rest of Lydar." Strictly speaking, that wasn't quite true. That was what Quaeryt and Vaelora were working toward.

"Why do they get more favorable terms?"

"Well . . . they didn't attack Telaryn the way Kharst did, and they didn't send troops to support Kharst against Telaryn, and they didn't attack Telaryn ships that weren't bothering them . . . among other things."

"Are those things true?"

"Every last one of them. We fought Antiagon troopers and their Antiagon Fire when we marched up the Aluse to take Variana. When the *Montagne* was carrying Bhayar's sister to Khel as an envoy, Antiagon warships attacked."

"That was not wise," temporized Sario, "but . . ."

"Should we have invaded and destroyed much of Liantiago on that basis?" Quaeryt offered a sad smile and a shrug. "We did it not because of those provocations but because those provocations indicated that there would always be fights and conflicts so long as Antiago and Telaryn were separate."

"The worst of acts are often justified by the best of reasons."

"They are," agreed Quaeryt. "Sometimes those reasons are right. Sometimes they are wrong. We often live to see where they were wrong. We seldom live to see where they were right." He turned and ordered, image-projecting his voice, "Undercaptains on deck!"

As usual, Zhelan was the first to appear. "Another Antiagon, sir?"

"That's what the lookout reports—flying a battle ensign."

"You think they'll attack?"

"If we raise a concealment. If we don't, they'll likely try to board, and I'd rather not deal with them at close quarters. Imaging isn't terribly effective against cannon." Quaeryt paused. Was that the reason why the Antiagon ships were so effective? Cannon at long range, and imaging and Antiagon Fire up close? It certainly fit in with the pattern of power he'd observed in Antiago—demand absolute obedience and destroy anyone who failed to obey. And that pattern made sense, in a way, for a land that was not all that wealthy.

"Sir?" pressed Zhelan.

"Sorry. I was thinking." Quaeryt glanced around as the undercaptains formed up.

When they were all there, including Elsior, he began to speak. "There's another Antiagon warship headed toward us . . . flying a battle ensign. We'll handle this in the same way as we did the last one. Just stand by for the moment."

"Yes, sir."

When the Antiagon was still barely visible from the deck, Quaeryt turned. "A concealment shield, if you would, Horan."

"Yes, sir."

Quaeryt had decided to see how the Antiagon responded to the concealment and the shields before making a final decision as to what to do with the warship. So he—and the captain and the imager undercaptains—watched and waited.

As in the case of the other Antiagon warships, the oncoming vessel continued directly toward the *Zephyr* until only a few hundred yards separated them. At that point, the ship began to turn to bring its guns to bear, and a huge fireball exploded against Horan's shields, with such force that the undercaptain staggered, even though his shields were linked to the *Zephyr* itself.

"Lhandor! Shields!"

"Yes, sir! Shields in place."

"Horan . . . release your shields. Khalis, image away the stem of the Antiagon. Now!"

Almost simultaneously, the first seven or eight yards of the attacker's bow vanished, and another massive fireball flared against Lhandor's shields.

As the stricken vessel nosed into the swells and shuddered to a halt, without a single gun firing, thankfully, Quaeryt imaged out a chunk of the hull midships. He didn't even feel light-headed.

Another firebolt, far smaller than the first or second, splashed against Lhandor's shields.

Then Quaeryt could see crew members jumping off the waterlogged vessel. Some were caught in midair as the ship exploded with such violence that debris rained down from Lhandor's shields, and the Pharsi undercaptain turned pale.

Quaeryt immediately extended his own shields. "Lhandor . . . you can release shields." He just hoped he didn't have to weather another explosion, but he continued to hold the shields, even as he began to feel light-headed, until he was certain that there were no hidden survivors who might be imagers.

Belatedly, he also realized why the Antiagons tended to attack without quarter—with all that they carried, they were also more than vulnerable, unless they could force another ship to surrender by pounding it with guns from a distance. *But why didn't anyone consider that?*

The answer was strangely obvious when he thought about it. Neither Bovaria nor Telaryn, nor Tilbor, when it had been ruled by the Khanar, had ever built a fleet because they were not trading powers, and the High Council of Khel probably hadn't had the resources to do so.

"Imagers. Stand down."

After another quint passed with no sign of other vessels, Quaeryt dismissed the undercaptains.

"Do you think we'll see more Antiagons?" asked Zhelan.

"I have no idea," Quaeryt admitted. "Over the past months, we've taken care of more than a few warships, but I have no idea how many the autarchs had. Once we get to Kephria, I hope we won't have to worry about that anymore."

"Someone will," predicted Zhelan.

"For a while. What exactly will they do? I doubt they usually carry imagers, and they'll eventually have to port somewhere. If every port in Lydar belongs to Bhayar . . ."

"They'll surrender or become pirates."

"Most of those left will likely surrender, especially if Bhayar grants them a pardon if they serve him." *And he should, since he really doesn't have a fleet.*

"You think he should?"

"We're not hunting down defeated Bovarian troopers or Antiagon troopers. I don't see the difference, and he'll get some serviceable warships."

"It might work," Zhelan grudged, before easing away from Quaeryt.

After several moments Sario eased closer to the commander. "The captains of those ships, they would like to remain captains. They will hear what you have done here. If Lord Bhayar grants a pardon, most will serve him."

"I would hope so." Quaeryt was hoping that Bhayar would follow his advice, or that he'd suggest something along those lines without Quaeryt even mentioning it . . . and that the Antiagon captains would do as Sario predicted.

"Did you notice, Captain, that we did nothing until we were attacked?" Quaeryt asked gently.

"I saw that." Sario shook his head. "Why did they do that?"

"Because they know that we are a threat to everything they believe in." Quaeryt gestured to the undercaptains. "In Liantiago, imagers live in buildings lined with metal. Each imager is apprenticed to an older imager, and they never left those buildings except to enforce the will of the Autarch. My undercaptains have a few more rules than the other undercaptains, but they have been able to do what the others do." *And you're fighting as much to keep those comparative freedoms as for Bhayar.*

"But will they have those freedoms once Lord Bhayar rules all?"

"That is part of what we seek, and the way I have tried to train them makes that far more likely."

For a long moment the captain did not speak. Finally, he said, "Then you are the one that Aliaro should have feared, not Lord Bhayar."

Quaeryt shook his head. "Without Lord Bhayar, this would not have happened."

"From what I have seen and from what my crew has overheard, without you Lord Bhayar would not be feared and Rex Kharst would rule much of Lydar."

Quaeryt laughed softly. "All things great or terrible come from more than one man, or even one group of men, no matter what the scholars say or write." *And the only question is whether Bhayar remembers this . . . except that it's your job—and Vaelora's—to make him remember.* He tried not to think about how things would be if something had happened to her.

Before long, he was again pacing the deck and looking to the northeast, as if his glances and pacing could speed the *Zephyr* even more swiftly toward a destination he feared for as much as he hoped to see before long.

By early Vendrei morning Quaeryt was alternating standing on and pacing across the low sterncastle of the *Zephyr*, running full before the wind, as she angled in toward the thin and wispy trails of smoke rising from Kephria. To the west, not even smoke rose from the flattened and burned-out heap of rubble that had been Ephra. Quaeryt glanced to the schooner's foremast, where flew the best replica of the Telaryn banner that Lhandor had been able to draw and Baelthm had been able to image. From the aft mast flew a replica, as well as Quaeryt could remember it, of Bhayar's personal banner.

Marshaled on the main deck was first company, weapons and gear ready, at Zhelan's urging, although Quaeryt had his doubts whether such would be necessary, one way or the other. Behind Quaeryt, on the port side, were the imager undercaptains, while Zhelan stood beside their commander.

Quaeryt studied the harbor, as devastated as he had expected, if not more so. The bright sun brought the destruction into a clear focus. The harbor itself was empty, with not even a trace of a vessel or the smallest rowboat or skiff. The only colors visible beside the blue-gray of the water and that of dull brown mud were shades of gray and black—and a thin line of whitish smoke coming from the old fort beside the long main pier, the southernmost one. On the pier, the few remaining bollards were mere charred husks of what they had once been. To the south of the pier was the fort, a square stone structure constructed on a raised knoll. The walls that formed three sides of a rectangle were pitted and shattered in places, blackened in others, and the small building that had comprised the rear east wall was only a heap of rubble.

Quaeryt turned his eyes more northward where, against the south side of the old river wall, was the northernmost stone pier, rising out of the mud and charred debris. From that pier the shoreline angled eastward downstream of the river wall, forming the northern side of the small harbor. What had been a muddy flat stretching southeast was now a stretch of baked mud and ashes that also covered parts of the old boulevard that had bordered the northern part of the harbor. Where there had been dwellings and shops, there remained nothing but charred brick and stone walls, half tumbled down. Not a single structure—except the stone fort—remained recognizable.

Quaeryt glanced back toward Sario, who stood to the side and slightly forward of the helmsman.

"Sir?"

"Bring her in toward the southern pier, the long one." Quaeryt turned. "At the seaward end on the north side."

"Yes, sir."

"They destroyed the entire town," said Zhelan. "It was *their* town, and they burned it to the ground."

"That's because the people failed—in the eyes of the Autarch," Quaeryt said.

"I don't feel quite so bad about Liantiago right now," murmured the major.

As the *Zephyr* neared the pier, Quaeryt could see an officer—Khaern, Quaeryt thought from the graying and faded red hair under the visor cap—and a squad of troopers waiting near the end of the long main stone pier. They did not move as Sario maneuvered the *Zephyr* alongside and a crewman leapt from the bow to the pier, line in hand. The seaman had to run the line around the base of the charred bollard, barely above the stone of the pier itself. Another crewman leapt off near the stern and ended up tying the line around and under one of the pier stones.

As Quaeryt stepped off the gangway and toward Khaern, he took in the pier itself. The gray stone was more worn, chipped, and weathered than he recalled, and blackened in spots. In other places, intense heat—likely from Antiagon Fire—had actually cracked the stone. Quaeryt looked at the subcommander, his face gaunt, with circles under his eyes. "I came as soon as I could."

"We thought you would—"

"Vaelora? How is she?"

"She's the reason we're mostly all alive, sir," replied the subcommander.

"How is she?" asked Quaeryt impatiently.

"She was hurt, but she says she'll be fine. She told me to tell you that. Two of the village healers are taking care of her."

"Where is she?"

"She's in the fort . . . over there." Khaern pointed. "The only things left are the stone structures. The Antiagons sailed up with three big warships and shelled the larger buildings. Some of the shells were Antiagon Fire. Then they landed almost a regiment of troopers and burned everything that would burn. From what we could see, they began by attacking here, but then they leveled and burned Ephra, and then the imagers—there were three of them—accompanied the troopers to Geusyn—"

"They burned it to the ground, didn't they?" asked Quaeryt.

"Yes, sir, but your wife had us send word, and most of the people escaped."

"How badly was she hurt?"

"She said to tell you that she will be fine, sir."

That was the same answer the subcommander had given before, and it didn't satisfy Quaeryt, but he could see Khaern had his own concerns. So he said quickly, "On the way here, we destroyed three Antiagon warships and a ketch. Since they had imagers, I'd like to think that they were the ones who fired Kephria. No one survived. Not that such is much consolation for the deaths and destruction here."

"Ah . . . what about Liantiago, sir?"

"Oh . . . Submarshal Skarpa holds Liantiago, and it appears that Antiago belongs to Lord Bhayar. There's nothing left of the palace or any of the troopers and imagers who defended it." Quaeryt paused. "If there's nothing urgent . . . I'd like to see Vaelora."

"No, sir, there's nothing urgent."

Quaeryt glanced toward the ship. "Zhelan! You're in command for now. Have the men disembark and unload."

"Yes, sir."

"If you'd lead the way, Subcommander?"

Khaern turned, and Quaeryt stepped up beside him, almost losing his balance as the heel of the boot on his bad leg caught the edge of an upraised pier stone.

"Are you all right, sir?"

"I'm fine." *The question is how Vaelora is.* "How many men did you lose?"

"Only about a hundred, sir."

"With all this?" Quaeryt gestured at the seemingly endless grayness of destruction. "How did you do it?"

"Ah . . . I didn't, sir. Without the Lady Vaelora . . ."

"Go on."

"It was a Jeudi, well before dawn. Lady Vaelora ran down the stairs at the River Inn and told me to get all the officers and men and mounts out of the town. She said that the Antiagons were coming and that nothing would be left of the town." Khaern shook his head. "I didn't believe her at first, but there were lights and shapes on the water . . . We'd gotten a battalion out when the first cannonballs struck the town. One way and another, we pulled back to north side of the wall, way back, almost to those rocky hills, while the cannonballs kept coming. Lady Vaelora—she directed the battalions where to go while I was getting the rest of them out of Kephria."

"Where is everyone?" asked Quaeryt. "There's nowhere to stay, and I don't see a camp."

"We've only got a company here, sir. That's because Lady Vaelora said we had to maintain a presence here. Most of Calkoran's men—"

"He's here?"

"They arrived a little more than two weeks after you left, and I and the rest of Eleventh Regiment came two days later, just before the Antiagons attacked. Well . . . four days before they did, just long enough for that bastard Nykaal to claim he never saw them."

"He said that?"

"No, sir. We've never seen him or the other captain since they dropped us off. Didn't really see much of him, either, on the trip here, just his officers, especially the junior officers, ensigns, whatever they're called. Anyway, we've got battalions garrisoned in the smaller towns along the hills to the east, at least for now."

At the end of the pier, Khaern turned south and then followed a path through the rubble at the east end of the fort and inside the solid stone structure. In the middle of the south side of the fort was a low bed. A gray-haired woman saw Quaeryt and Khaern and eased away from the bed. Khaern stopped.

Quaeryt moved quickly toward Vaelora.

She offered a wan smile, and tired as it was, he could feel the relief that she could do that much. Still . . . regardless of what Khaern had said, Vaelora looked worn and tired, and there was a bruise on her left cheek, and a scabbed scar across her forehead just below the hairline that angled into her hair, which had been cut short, barely longer than a boy's. In places, that wavy hair was almost frizzy. *How close had she been to Antiagon Fire?*

Quaeryt's eyes took in her form, slender under the blankets . . . and he knew. He swallowed, and his eyes burned. "How . . . did it happen?"

"I got hit . . . with a tree. It was a branch. One of the Antiagon cannonballs came over the wall, the big wall. I was there . . . trying to tell the majors and Calkoran where to send the men so that the cannonballs wouldn't hit them. It didn't even hurt all that much . . ."

Then Quaeryt was on his knees beside the low bed, his arms around her.

". . . but then it hurt so much . . . she was so pretty . . . even . . ." Great racking sobs convulsed Vaelora.

All Quaeryt could do was hold her.

In time, the sobs subsided, and she eased away from his shoulder. "I'm all right. We . . . we really can . . ."

There were more sobs, and Quaeryt's face was as damp as Vaelora's, even as he tried to reassure her. "It will be all right . . . do love you . . ."

In time, they gathered themselves together once more.

"How did you know the Antiagons were coming when they were?" Quaeryt asked.

"I didn't at first. I did, but I didn't. You remember that I told you I had a farsight vision that I thought was well in the future . . ."

"Yes . . ." ventured Quaeryt warily. "You wouldn't tell me."

"You know why. What you said about it might have colored what I recalled—and that would be dangerous. I didn't know what to make of it. It was just a vision of a harbor with burning buildings . . . and I didn't even recognize it . . . with the fire . . . and then I had another vision . . ." Tears began to stream down Vaelora's cheeks once more. "Someday . . . I'll tell you about it."

Quaeryt just held her once more.

After several moments she blotted her face and went on. "I woke up, and I looked out the inn window . . . and I saw a light out in the Gulf . . . and another one." She looked at Quaeryt. "I *knew* then. Khaern didn't want to believe me, but he saw the lights too, and we started to rouse the men and get them moving. He agreed that it was better to take precautions. He might have been humoring me. He insisted I go with the first company . . . The cannonballs came down first, near the water, and . . . we just did what we had to. I think hundreds of townspeople died. They didn't believe us, and by the time they did . . . some of them couldn't get away."

"But how did you escape the troopers?"

Vaelora shook her head. "They never came after us. They used cannon the first day. The second day, they used Antiagon Fire . . . Then they spent a day destroying Ephra before they came back and used the troopers to get the imagers far enough north along the river to burn down Geusyn. Once it was gone, they got back on the ships and left."

*Trying to get back to Liantiago in case we were attacking?* That was likely, but Quaeryt doubted that he'd ever know for certain. Nor did it matter . . . now.

"They're all dead," he said. "At least, we destroyed three warships and a ketch."

"What about Aliaro?" Vaelora's voice was cold.

"He's dead. Everyone in the palace and everyone in the Autarch's Square who was trying to defend the palace is dead. Skarpa holds Liantiago as acting regional governor."

"That was too good a death for him." Her voice caught. "I was going to name her Chaerila . . ."

For several moments Quaeryt could say nothing as he held her hands in his.

Then, abruptly, Vaelora cleared her throat and looked at Quaeryt. "Once I recover fully, dearest, I will need some new clothes. Most everything got burned up, and I was a little . . . occupied."

Quaeryt swallowed. *Clothes? How could she* . . . Then he almost shook his head, realizing that she was trying to divert him . . . and herself. He managed to offer a smile. "We should be able to manage that, after all you've been through."

"I didn't lose everything, though. Almost, but I did save this." Vaelora held up a small leatherbound volume.

Somehow, *Rholan and the Nameless* didn't seem so terribly important as, still on his knees, he leaned forward and put his arms around her once more.

# POPE JOAN

# POPE JOAN

*A Novel*

*Donna Woolfolk Cross*

Crown Publishers, Inc.
*New York*

Published by Crown Publishers, Inc., 201 East 50th Street, New York, New York 10022. Member of the Crown Publishing Group.

CROWN is a trademark of Crown Publishers, Inc.

Printed in the United States of America

Design by Linda Kocur

ISBN 0-517-59365-3

For my father, William Woolfolk,

*and there are no words*

*to add*

# ACKNOWLEDGMENTS

For research assistance I am indebted to Lucy Burgess at Cornell, Caroline Suma at the Pontifical Institute for Medieval Studies in Toronto, Eileen DeRycke at Syracuse University, Elizabeth Lukacs of Lemoyne College, Dr. Paul J. Dine, Dr. Arthur Hoffman, and Mr. John Lawrence, as well as the library staff of Vassar and Hamilton Colleges, the University of Pennsylvania, and the University of California in Los Angeles. Special thanks go to Linda McNamara, Gail Rizzo, and Gretchen Roberts of Onondaga Community College, who labored with tireless energy and resourcefulness to obtain numerous rare books for me from various libraries both in this country and abroad. Thanks also to Lil Kinney, Liz Liddy, and Susan Brown, skilled researchers who succeeded in unearthing a good deal of little-known information about the ninth century.

Many people read the manuscript at various stages and brought to it their own special expertise. I am grateful to Dr. Joseph Roesch, Roger Salzmann, Sharon Danley, Thomas McKague, David Ripper, Ellen Coin, Maureen McCarthy, Virginia Ruggiero, John Starkweather, and my mother, Dorothy Woolfolk. Their suggestions made the book immeasurably better.

I would also like to thank my agent, Jean Naggar, who was willing to take a chance on a partial manuscript; Irene Prokop, my first editor at Crown, whose warmth and enthusiasm for the book were so encouraging; and Betty A. Prashker, who took over as editor when Irene moved on.

I owe heartfelt gratitude to those who supported and heartened me through seven years of research and writing: my daughter, Emily, and my husband, Richard, front-line warriors; my sister-in-law, Donna Willis Cross, who believed in me and in this book even when my own faith faltered; Mary Putman, who shouldered extra burdens so I could be free to write; Patricia Waelder and Norma Chini, staunch allies who made sure I got the uninterrupted time I needed; Susan Francesconi, whose companionship during our long walks together did much to preserve my sanity; Joanna Woolfolk, Lisa Strick, James MacKillop, and Kathleen Eisele. As William Shakespeare said, "I am wealthy in my friends."

Above all, I would like to thank my father, William Woolfolk, to whom this book is justly dedicated; without his constant guidance and encouragement it would never have been written.

# POPE JOAN

# PROLOGUE

It was the twenty-eighth day of Wintarmanoth in the year of our Lord 814, the harshest winter in living memory.

Hrotrud, the village midwife of Ingelheim, struggled through the snow toward the canon's *grubenhaus.* A gust of wind swept through the trees and drove icy fingers into her body, searching the holes and patches of her thin woolen garments. The forest path was deeply drifted; with each step, she sank almost to her knees. Snow caked her eyebrows and eyelashes; she kept wiping her face to see. Her hands and feet ached with cold, despite the layers of linen rags she had wrapped around them.

A blur of black appeared on the path ahead. It was a dead crow. Even those hardy scavengers were dying this winter, starved because their beaks could not tear the flesh of the frozen carrion. Hrotrud shivered and quickened her pace.

Gudrun, the canon's woman, had gone into labor a month sooner than expected. *A fine time for the child to come,* Hrotrud thought bitterly. *Five children delivered in the last month alone, and not one of them lasted more than a week.*

A blast of wind-driven snow blinded Hrotrud, and for a moment she lost sight of the poorly marked path. She felt a swell of panic. More than one villager had died that way, wandering in circles only a short distance from their homes. She forced herself to stand still as the snow swirled around her, surrounding her in a featureless landscape of white. When the wind let up, she could just make out the outline of the path. Again she began to move forward. She no longer felt pain in her hands and feet; they had gone completely numb. She knew what that could mean, but she could not afford to dwell on it; it was important to remain calm.

*I must think of something besides the cold.*

She pictured the home in which she had been raised, a *casa* with a prosperous manse of some six hectares. It was warm and snug, with walls of solid timber, far nicer than their neighbors' homes, made of simple wooden lathes daubed with mud. A great fire had blazed in the central hearth, the smoke spiraling up to an opening in the roof. Hrotrud's father had worn an expensive vest of otter skins over his fine linen *bliaud,* and her mother had had silken ribbons for her long, black hair. Hrotrud herself had had two large-sleeved tunics, and a warm mantle of the finest wool. She remembered how soft and smooth the expensive material had felt against her skin.

It had all ended so quickly. Two summers of drought and a killing frost ruined the harvest. Everywhere people were starving; in Thuringia there were rumors of cannibalism. Through the judicious sale of the family possessions, Hrotrud's father had kept them from hunger for a while. Hrotrud had cried when they took away her woolen mantle. It had seemed to her then that nothing worse could happen. She was eight years old; she did not yet comprehend the horror and cruelty of the world.

She pushed her way through another large drift of snow, fighting off a growing light-headedness. It had been several days since she had had anything to eat. *Ah, well. If all goes well, I will feast tonight. Perhaps, if the canon is well pleased, there will even be some bacon to take home.* The idea gave her renewed energy.

Hrotrud emerged into the clearing. She could see the blurred outlines of the grubenhaus just ahead. The snow was deeper here, beyond the screen of trees, but she drove ahead, plowing through with her strong thighs and arms, confident now that safety was near.

Arriving at the door, she knocked once, then immediately let herself in; it was too cold to worry about social courtesies. Inside, she stood blinking in darkness. The single window of the grubenhaus had been boarded up for winter; the only light came from the hearth fire and a few smoky tallows scattered about the room. After a moment, her eyes began to adjust, and she saw two young boys seated close together near the hearth fire.

"Has the child come?" Hrotrud asked.

"Not yet," answered the older boy.

Hrotrud muttered a short prayer of thanks to St. Cosmas, patron saint of midwives. She had been cheated of her pay that way more than once, turned away without a *denar* for the trouble she had taken to come.

At the hearth fire, she peeled the frozen rags from her hands and feet, crying out in alarm when she saw their sickly blue-white color. *Holy Mother, do not let the frost take them.* The village would have little use for a crippled midwife. Elias the shoemaker had lost his livelihood that way. After he was caught in a storm on his way back from Mainz, the tips of his fingers had blackened and dropped off in a week. Now, gaunt and ragged, he squatted by the church doors, begging his living off the charity of others.

Shaking her head grimly, Hrotrud pinched and rubbed her numbed fingers and toes as the two boys watched in silence. The sight of them reassured her. *It will be an easy birth,* she told herself, trying to keep her mind off poor Elias. *After all, I delivered Gudrun of these two easily enough.* The older boy must be almost six winters now, a sturdy child with a look of alert intelligence. The younger, his round-cheeked, three-year-old brother, rocked back and forth, sucking his thumb morosely. Both were dark-avised, like their father; neither had inherited their Saxon mother's extraordinary white-gold hair.

Hrotrud remembered how the village men had stared at Gudrun's hair when the canon had brought her back from one of his missionary trips to Saxony. It had caused quite a stir at first, the canon's taking a woman. Some said it was against the law, that the Emperor had issued an edict forbidding men of the Church to take wives. But others said it could not be so, for it was plain that without a wife a man was subject to all kinds of temptation and wickedness. Look at the monks of Stablo, they said, who shame the Church with their fornications and drunken revelry. And certainly it was true that the canon was a sober and hardworking man.

The room was warm. The large hearth was piled high with thick logs of birch and oak; smoke rose in great billows to the hole in the thatched roof. It was a snug dwelling. The wooden timbers that formed the walls were heavy and thick, and the gaps between them were tightly packed with straw and clay to keep out the cold. The single window had been boarded over with sturdy planks of oak, an extra measure of protection against the *nordostroni,* the frigid northeast winds of winter. The house was large enough to be divided into three separate compartments, one containing the sleeping quarters of the canon and his wife, one for the animals that sheltered there in harsh weather—Hrotrud heard the soft scuffle and scrape of their hooves to her left—and this one, the central room, where the family worked and ate and the children slept. Other than the bishop, whose house was made of stone, no one in Ingelheim had a finer home.

Hrotrud's limbs began to prickle and throb with renewed sensation. She examined her fingers; they were rough and dry, but the bluish cast had receded, supplanted by a returning glow of healthy reddish pink. She sighed with relief, resolving to make an offering to St. Cosmas in thanksgiving. For a few more minutes, Hrotrud lingered by the fire, enjoying its warmth; then, with a nod and an encouraging pat for the boys, she hurried around the partition to where the laboring woman was waiting.

Gudrun lay on a bed of peat topped with fresh straw. The canon, a dark-haired man with thick, beetling eyebrows that gave him a perpetually stern expression, sat apart. He nodded at Hrotrud, then returned his attention to the large wood-bound book on his lap. Hrotrud had seen the book on previous visits to the cottage, but the sight of it still filled her with awe. It was a copy of the Holy Bible, and it was the only book she had ever seen. Like the other villagers, Hrotrud could neither read nor write. She knew, however, that the book was a treasure, worth more in gold *solidi* than the entire village earned in a year. The canon had brought it with him from his native England, where books were not so rare as in Frankland.

Hrotrud saw immediately that Gudrun was in a bad way. Her breathing was shallow, her pulse dangerously rapid, her whole body puffed and swollen. The midwife recognized the signs. There was no time to waste. She reached into her sack and took out a quantity of dove's dung that she had carefully collected in the fall. Returning to the hearth, she threw the dung on the fire, watching with satisfaction as the dark smoke began to rise, clearing the air of evil spirits.

She would have to ease the pain so Gudrun could relax and bring the child forth. For that, she would use henbane. She took a bundle of the small, yellow, purple-veined flowers, placed them in a clay mortar, and skillfully ground them into powder, wrinkling her nose at the acrid odor that was released. Then she infused the powder into a cup of strong red wine and brought it to Gudrun to drink.

"What is that you mean to give her?" the canon asked abruptly.

Hrotrud started; she had almost forgotten he was there. "She is weakened from the labor. This will relieve her pain and help the child issue forth."

The canon frowned. He took the henbane from Hrotrud's hands, strode around the partition, and threw it into the fire, where it hissed briefly and then vanished. "Woman, you blaspheme."

Hrotrud was aghast. It had taken her weeks of painstaking search to gather that small amount of the precious medicine. She turned toward the canon, ready to vent her anger, but stopped when she saw the flinty look in his eyes.

"It is written"—he thumped the book with his hand for emphasis—" 'In sorrow shalt thou bring forth children.' Such medicine is unholy!"

Hrotrud was indignant. There was nothing unchristian about *her* medicine. Didn't she recite nine paternosters each time she pulled one of the plants from the earth? The canon certainly never complained when she gave him henbane to ease the pain of *his* frequent toothaches. But she would not argue with him. He was an influential man. One word from him about "unholy" practices, and Hrotrud would be ruined.

Gudrun moaned in the throes of another pain. *Very well,* Hrotrud thought. If the canon would not allow the henbane, she would have to try another approach. She went to her sack and withdrew a long piece of cloth, cut to the True Length of Christ. Moving with brisk efficiency, she wound it tightly around Gudrun's abdomen. Gudrun groaned when Hrotrud shifted her. Movement was painful for her, but that could not be helped. Hrotrud took from her sack a small parcel, carefully wrapped in a scrap of silken fabric for protection. Inside was one of her treasures—the anklebone of a rabbit killed on Christmas Day. She had begged it off one of the Emperor's hunting party the previous winter. With utmost care, Hrotrud shaved off three thin slices and placed them in Gudrun's mouth.

"Chew these slowly," she instructed Gudrun, who nodded weakly. Hrotrud settled back to wait. From the corner of her eye, she studied the canon, who frowned in concentration on his book till his brows almost met over the bridge of his nose.

Gudrun moaned again and twisted in pain, but the canon did not look up. *He's a cold one,* Hrotrud reflected. *Still, he must have some fire in his loins, or he wouldn't have taken her to wife.*

How long had it been since the canon brought the Saxon woman home, ten—or was it eleven?—winters ago. Gudrun had not been young, by Frankish standards, perhaps twenty-six or twenty-seven years old, but she was very beautiful, with the long white-gold hair and blue eyes of the *aliengenae.* She had lost her entire family in the massacre at Verden. Thousands of Saxons had died that day rather than accept the truth of Our Lord

Jesus Christ. *Mad barbarians,* Hrotrud thought. *It wouldn't have happened to me.* She would have sworn to whatever they asked of her, would do it now for that matter, should the barbarians ever sweep through Frankland again, swear to whatever strange and terrible gods they wished. It changed nothing. Who was to know what went on in a person's heart? A wise woman kept her own counsel.

The fire sparked and flickered; it was burning low. Hrotrud crossed to the pile of wood stacked in the corner, chose two good-sized logs of birch, and put them on the hearth. She watched as they settled, hissing, into the fire, the flames licking upwards around them. Then she turned to check on Gudrun.

It was a full half hour since Gudrun had taken the shavings of rabbit bone, but there was no change in her condition. Even that strong medicine had failed to take effect. The pains remained erratic and ineffectual, and Gudrun was weakening.

Hrotrud sighed wearily. Clearly, she would have to resort to stronger measures.

The canon proved to be a problem when Hrotrud told him she would need help with the birthing.

"Send for the village women," he said peremptorily.

"Ah, sir, that is impossible. Who is there to send?" Hrotrud raised her palms expressively. "I cannot go, for your wife needs me here. Your elder boy cannot go, for though he seems a likely lad, he could get lost in weather such as this. I almost did myself."

The canon glared at her from under his dark brows. "Very well," he said, "I will go." As he rose from his chair, Hrotrud shook her head impatiently.

"It would do no good. By the time you returned, it would be too late. It is *your* help I need, and quickly, if you wish your wife and babe to live."

"*My* help? Are you mad, midwife? That"—he motioned distastefully toward the bed—"is women's business, and unclean. I will have nothing to do with it."

"Then your wife will die."

"That is in God's hands, not mine."

Hrotrud shrugged. "It is all one to me. But you will not find it easy, raising two children without a mother."

The canon stared at Hrotrud. "Why should I believe you? She's given birth before with no trouble. I have fortified her with my prayers. You cannot know that she will die."

This was too much. Canon or not, Hrotrud would not tolerate his questioning her skill as a midwife. "It is *you* who know nothing," she said sharply. "You have not even looked at her. Go see her now; then tell me that she is not dying."

The canon went to the bed and looked down at his wife. Her damp hair was pasted to her skin, which had turned yellowish white, her dark-rimmed eyes were hollow and sunken into her head; but for the long, unsteady exhalation of breath, she might have been already dead.

"Well?" prodded Hrotrud.

The canon wheeled to face her. "God's blood, woman! Why didn't you bring the women with you?"

"As you said yourself, sir, your wife's given birth before without a speck of trouble. There was no reason to expect any this time. Besides, who would have come in weather such as this?"

The canon stalked to the hearth and paced back and forth agitatedly. At last he halted. "What do you want me to do?"

Hrotrud smiled broadly. "Oh, little enough, sir, little enough." She led him back to the bed. "For a start, help get her up."

Standing on either side of Gudrun, they grabbed her under the arms and heaved. Her body was heavy, but together they managed to lift her to her feet, where she swayed against her husband. The canon was stronger than Hrotrud had thought. That was good, for she would need all his strength for what came next.

"We must force the babe down into position. When I give the command, lift her as high as you can. And shake hard."

The canon nodded, his mouth set grimly. Gudrun hung like a dead weight between them, her head fallen forward on her chest.

"Lift!" shouted Hrotrud. They hoisted Gudrun by the arms and began to shake her up and down. Gudrun screamed and fought to free herself. Pain and fear gave her surprising strength; the two of them were hard put to restrain her. *If only he had let me give her the henbane,* Hrotrud thought. *She would be half-sensible by now.*

Quickly they lowered her, but she continued to struggle and cry out. Hrotrud gave a second command, and again they hoisted, shook, then lowered Gudrun to the bed, where she lay half-fainting, murmuring in her barbarous native tongue. *Good,* Hrotrud thought. *If I move quickly, it will all be over before she regains her senses.*

Hrotrud reached into the birth passage, probing for the opening to the womb. It was rigid and swollen from the long hours of ineffectual labor. Using her right index fingernail, which she kept long for just this purpose, Hrotrud tore at the resistant tissue. Gudrun groaned, then went completely limp. Warm blood poured over Hrotrud's hand, down her arms, and onto the bed. At last she felt the opening give way. With an exultant cry, Hrotrud reached in and took hold of the baby's head, exerting a gentle downward pressure.

"Take her by the shoulders and pull against me," she instructed the canon, whose face had gone quite pale. Nevertheless he obeyed; Hrotrud felt the pressure increase as the canon added his strength to hers. After a few minutes, the baby started to move down into the birth passage. She kept pulling steadily, careful not to injure the soft bones of the child's head and neck. At last the crown of the babe's head appeared, covered with a mass of fine, wet hair. Hrotrud eased the head out gently, then turned the body to permit the right shoulder, then the left, to emerge. One last, firm tug and the small body slid wetly into Hrotrud's waiting arms.

"A girl," Hrotrud announced. "A strong one too, by the look of her," she added, noting with approval the infant's lusty cry and healthy pink color.

She turned to meet the canon's disapproving stare.

"A girl," he said. "So it was all for nothing."

"Do not say so, sir." Hrotrud was suddenly fearful that the canon's disappointment might mean less for her to eat. "The child is healthy and strong. God grant that she live to do credit to your name."

The canon shook his head. "She is a punishment from God. A punishment for my sins—and hers." He motioned toward Gudrun, who lay motionless. "Will she live?"

"Yes." Hrotrud hoped that she sounded convincing. She could not afford to let the canon think he might be doubly disappointed. She still hoped to taste meat that night. And there was, after all, a reasonable chance that Gudrun *would* survive. True, the birthing had been violent. After such an ordeal, many a woman came down with fever and the wasting disease. But Gudrun was strong; Hrotrud would treat her wound with a salve of mugwort mixed in fox's grease. "Yes, God willing, she will live," she repeated firmly. She did not feel it necessary to add that she would probably bear no more children.

"That's something, then," the canon said. He moved to the bed and stood looking down at Gudrun. Gently he touched the white-gold hair, darkened now with sweat. For a moment, Hrotrud thought he was going to kiss Gudrun. Then his expression changed; he looked stern, even angry.

*"Per mulierem culpa successit,"* he said. "Sin came through a woman." He dropped the lock of hair and stepped back.

Hrotrud shook her head. *Something from the Holy Book, no doubt.* The canon was a strange one, all right, but that was none of her affair, God be thanked. She hurried to finish cleaning the blood and birth fluids off Gudrun so she could start back home while there was still daylight.

Gudrun opened her eyes and saw the canon standing over her. The beginnings of a smile froze on her lips as she saw the expression in his eyes.

"Husband?" she said doubtfully.

"A girl," the canon said coldly, not troubling to hide his displeasure.

Gudrun nodded, understanding, then turned her face to the wall. The canon turned to go, stopping briefly to glance at the infant already safely ensconced in her pallet of straw.

"Joan. She will be called Joan," he announced, and abruptly left the room.

# 1

Thunder sounded, very near, and the child woke. She moved in the bed, seeking the warmth and comfort of her older brothers' sleeping forms. Then she remembered. Her brothers were gone.

It was raining, a hard spring downpour that filled the night air with the sweet-sour smell of newly plowed earth. Rain thudded on the roof of the canon's grubenhaus, but the thickly woven thatching kept the room dry, except for one or two small places in the corners where water first pooled and then trickled in slow, fat drops to the beaten earth floor.

The wind rose, and a nearby oak began to tap an uneven rhythm on the cottage walls. The shadow of its branches spilled into the room. The child watched, transfixed, as the monstrous dark fingers wriggled at the edges of the bed. They reached out for her, beckoning, and she shrank back.

*Mama,* she thought. She opened her mouth to call out, then stopped. If she made a sound, the menacing hand would pounce. She lay frozen, unable to will herself to move. Then she set her small chin resolutely. It had to be done, so she would do it. Moving with exquisite slowness, never taking her eyes off the enemy, she eased herself off the bed. Her feet felt the cool surface of the earthen floor; the familiar sensation was reassuring. Scarcely daring to breathe, she backed toward the partition behind which her mother lay sleeping. Lightning flashed; the fingers moved and lengthened, following her. She swallowed a scream, her throat tightening with the effort. She forced herself to move slowly, not to break into a run.

She was almost there. Suddenly, a salvo of thunder crashed overhead. At the same moment something touched her from behind. She yelped, then turned and fled around the partition, stumbling over the chair she had backed into.

This part of the house was dark and still, save for her mother's rhythmic breathing. From the sound, the child could tell she was deeply asleep; the noise had not wakened her. She went quickly to the bed, lifted the woolen blanket, and slid under it. Her mother lay on her side, lips slightly parted; her warm breath caressed the child's cheek. She snuggled close, feeling the softness of her mother's body through her thin linen shift.

Gudrun yawned and shifted position, roused by the movement. Her eyes opened, and she regarded the child sleepily. Then, waking fully, she reached out and put her arms around her daughter.

"Joan," she chastised gently, her lips against the child's soft hair. "Little one, you should be asleep."

Speaking quickly, her voice high and strained from fear, Joan told her mother about the monster hand.

Gudrun listened, petting and stroking her daughter and murmuring reassurances. Gently she ran her fingers over the child's face, half-seen in the darkness. She was not pretty, Gudrun reflected ruefully. She looked too much like *him,* with his thick English neck and wide jaw. Her small body was already stocky and heavyset, not long and graceful like Gudrun's people's. But the child's eyes were good, large and expressive and rich hued, green with dark gray smoke rings at the center. Gudrun lifted a strand of Joan's baby hair and caressed it, enjoying the way it shone, white-gold, even in the darkness. *My hair.* Not the coarse black hair of her husband or his cruel, dark people. *My child.* She wrapped the strand around her forefinger and smiled. *This one, at least, is mine.*

Soothed by her mother's attentions, Joan relaxed. In playful imitation, she began to tug at Gudrun's long braid, loosening it till her hair lay tumbled about her head. Joan marveled at it, spilling over the dark woolen coverlet like rich cream. She had never seen her mother's hair unbound. At the canon's insistence, Gudrun wore it always neatly braided, hidden under a rough linen cap. A woman's hair, her husband said, is the net wherein Satan catches a man's soul. And Gudrun's hair was extraordinarily beautiful, long and soft and pure white-gold, without a trace of gray, though she was now an old woman of thirty-six winters.

"Why did Matthew and John go away?" Joan asked suddenly. Her mother had explained this to her several times, but Joan wanted to hear it again.

"You know why. Your father took them with him on his missionary journey."

"Why couldn't I go too?"

Gudrun sighed patiently. The child was always so full of questions. "Matthew and John are boys; one day they will be priests like your father. You are a girl, and therefore such matters do not concern you." Seeing that Joan was not content with that, she added, "Besides, you are much too young."

Joan was indignant. "I was four in Wintarmanoth!"

Gudrun's eyes lit with amusement as she looked at the pudgy baby face. "Ah, yes, I forgot, you are a big girl now, aren't you? Four years old! That does sound very grown-up."

Joan lay quietly while her mother stroked her hair. Then she asked, "What are heathens?" Her father and brothers had spoken a good deal about heathens before they left. Joan did not understand what heathens were, exactly, though she gathered it was something very bad.

Gudrun stiffened. The word had conjuring powers. It had been on the lips of the invading soldiers as they pillaged her home and slaughtered her family and friends. The dark, cruel soldiers of the Frankish Emperor Karolus. "Magnus," people called him now that he was dead. "Karolus Magnus." Charles the Great. Would they name him so, Gudrun wondered, if they had seen his army tear Saxon babes from their mothers' arms, swinging them round before they dashed their heads against the reddened stones? Gudrun withdrew her hand from Joan's hair and rolled onto her back.

"That is a question you must ask your father," she said.

Joan did not understand what she had done wrong, but she heard the strange hardness in her mother's voice and knew that she would be sent back to her own bed if she didn't think of some way to repair the damage. Quickly she said, "Tell me again about the Old Ones."

"I cannot. Your father disapproves of the telling of such tales." The words were half statement, half question.

Joan knew what to do. Placing both hands solemnly over her heart, she recited the Oath exactly as her mother had taught it to her, promising eternal secrecy on the sacred name of Thor the Thunderer.

Gudrun laughed and drew Joan close again. "Very well, little quail. I will tell you the story, since you know so well how to ask."

Her voice was warm again, wistful and melodic as she began to tell of Woden and Thor and Freya and the other gods who had peopled her Saxon childhood before the armies of Karolus brought the Word of Christ with blood and fire. She spoke liltingly of Asgard, the radiant home of the gods, a place of golden and silver palaces, which could only be reached by crossing Bifrost, the mysterious bridge of the rainbow. Guarding the bridge was Heimdall the Watchman, who never slept, whose ears were so keen he could even hear the grass grow. In Valhalla, the most beautiful palace of all, lived Woden, the father-god, on whose shoulders sat the two ravens Hugin, Thought, and Munin, Memory. On his throne, while the other gods feasted, Woden contemplated what Thought and Memory told him.

Joan nodded happily. This was her favorite part of the story. "Tell about the Well of Wisdom," she begged.

"Although he was already very wise," explained her mother, "Woden always sought greater wisdom. One day he went to the Well of Wisdom, guarded by Mimir the Wise, and asked for a draft from it. 'What price will you pay?' asked Mimir. Woden replied that Mimir could ask what he wished. 'Wisdom must always be bought with pain,' replied Mimir. 'If you wish a drink of this water, you must pay for it with one of your eyes.' "

Eyes bright with excitement, Joan exclaimed, "And Woden did it, Mama, didn't he? He did it!"

Her mother nodded. "Though it was a hard choice, Woden consented to lose the eye. He drank the water. Afterward, he passed on to mankind the wisdom he had gained."

Joan looked up at her mother, her eyes wide and serious. "Would *you* have done it, Mama—to be wise, to know about all things?"

"Only gods make such choices," she replied. Then, seeing the child's persistent look of question, Gudrun confessed, "No. I would have been too afraid."

"So would I," Joan said thoughtfully. "But I would *want* to do it. I would want to know what the well could tell me."

Gudrun smiled down at the intent little face. "Perhaps you would not like what you would learn there. There is a saying among our people. 'A wise man's heart is seldom glad.' "

Joan nodded, though she did not really understand. "Now tell about the Tree," she said, snuggling close to her mother again.

Gudrun began to describe Irminsul, the wondrous universe tree. It had stood in the holiest of the Saxon groves at the source of the Lippe River. Her people had worshiped at it until it was cut down by the armies of Karolus.

"It was very beautiful," her mother said, "and so tall that no one could see the top. It—"

She stopped. Suddenly aware of another presence, Joan looked up. Her father was standing in the doorway.

Her mother sat up in bed. "Husband," she said. "I did not look for your return for another fortnight."

The canon did not respond. He took a wax taper from the table near the door and crossed to the hearth fire, where he plunged it into the glowing embers until it flared.

Gudrun said nervously, "The child was frightened by the thunder. I thought to comfort her with a harmless story."

"Harmless!" The canon's voice shook with the effort to control his rage. "You call such blasphemy harmless?" He covered the distance to the bed in two long strides, set down the taper, and pulled the blanket off, exposing them. Joan lay with her arms around her mother, half-hidden under a curtain of white-gold hair.

For a moment the canon stood stupefied with disbelief, looking at Gudrun's unbound hair. Then his fury overtook him. "How dare you! When I have expressly forbidden it!" Taking hold of Gudrun, he started to drag her from the bed. "Heathen witch!"

Joan clung to her mother. The canon's face darkened. "Child, begone!" he bellowed. Joan hesitated, torn between fear and the desire somehow to protect her mother.

Gudrun pushed her urgently. "Yes, go. *Go quickly.*"

Releasing her hold, Joan dropped to the floor and ran. At the door, she turned and saw her father grab her mother roughly by the hair, wrenching her head back, forcing her to her knees. Joan started back into the room. Terror stopped her short as she saw her father withdraw his long, bone-handled hunting knife from his corded belt.

*"Forsachistu diabolae?"* he asked Gudrun in Saxon, his voice scarcely more than a whisper. When she did not respond, he placed the point of the knife against her throat. "Say the words," he growled menacingly. *"Say them!"*

*"Ec forsacho allum diaboles,"* Gudrun responded tearfully, her eyes blazing defiance, *"wuercum and wuordum, thunaer ende woden ende saxnotes ende allum . . ."*

Rooted with fear, Joan watched her father pull up a heavy tress of her mother's hair and draw the knife across it. There was a ripping sound as the silken strands parted; a long band of white gold floated to the floor.

Clapping her hand over her mouth to stifle a sob, Joan turned and ran.

In the darkness, she bumped into a shape that reached out for her. She squealed in fear as it grabbed her. The monster hand! She had forgotten about it! She struggled, pummeling at it with her tiny fists, resisting with all her strength, but it was huge, and held her fast.

"Joan! Joan, it's all right. It's me!"

The words penetrated her fear. It was her ten-year-old brother Matthew, who had returned with her father.

"We've come back. Joan, stop struggling! It's all right. It's *me.*" Joan reached up, felt the smooth surface of the pectoral cross that Matthew always wore, then slumped against him in relief.

Together they sat in the dark, listening to the soft, splitting sounds of the knife ripping through their mother's hair. Once they heard Mama cry out in pain. Matthew cursed aloud. An answering sob came from the bed where Joan's seven-year-old brother, John, was hiding under the covers.

At last the ripping sounds stopped. After a brief pause the canon's voice began to rumble in prayer. Joan felt Matthew relax; it was over. She threw her arms around his neck and wept. He held her and rocked her gently.

After a time, she looked up at him. "Father called Mama a heathen."

"Yes."

"She isn't," Joan said hesitantly, "is she?"

"She *was.*" Seeing her look of horrified disbelief, he added, "A long time ago. Not anymore. But those were heathen stories she was telling you."

Joan stopped crying; this was interesting information.

"You know the first of the Commandments, don't you?"

Joan nodded and recited dutifully, "Thou shalt have no other gods before me."

"Yes. That means that the gods Mama was telling you about are false; it is sinful to speak of them."

"Is that why Father—"

"Yes," Matthew broke in. "Mama had to be punished for the good of her soul. She was disobedient to her husband, and that also is against the law of God."

"Why?"

"Because it says so in the Holy Book." He began to recite, " 'For the husband is the head of the wife; therefore, let the wives submit themselves unto their husbands in everything.' "

"Why?"

"Why?" Matthew was taken aback. No one had ever asked him that before. "Well, I guess because . . . because women are by nature inferior to men. Men are bigger, stronger, and smarter."

"But—" Joan started to respond, but Matthew cut her off.

"Enough questions, little sister. You should be in bed. Come now." He carried her to the bed and placed her beside John, who was already sleeping.

Matthew had been kind to her; to return the favor, Joan closed her eyes and burrowed under the covers as if to sleep.

But she was far too troubled for sleep. She lay in the dark, peering at John as he slept, his mouth hanging slackly open.

*He can't recite from the Psalter and he's seven years old.* Joan was only four, but she already knew the first ten psalms by heart.

John wasn't smart. But he was a boy. Yet how could Matthew be wrong? He knew everything; he was going to be a priest, like their father.

She lay awake in the dark, turning the problem over in her mind.

Toward dawn she slept, restlessly, troubled by dreams of mighty wars between jealous and angry gods. The angel Gabriel himself came from Heaven with a flaming sword to do battle with Thor and Freya. The battle was terrible and fierce, but in the end the false gods were driven back, and Gabriel stood triumphant before the gates of paradise. His sword had disappeared; in his hand gleamed a short, bone-handled knife.

# 2

The wooden stylus moved swiftly, forming letters and words in the soft yellow wax of the tablet. Joan stood attentively near Matthew's shoulder as he copied out the day's lessons. From time to time he stopped to wave a candle flame over the tablet to keep the wax from hardening too quickly.

She loved to watch Matthew work. His pointed bone stylus pushed the shapeless wax into lines that held for her a mysterious beauty. She longed to understand what each mark meant and followed every movement of the stylus intently, as if to discover the key to the meaning in the shape of the lines.

Matthew put the stylus down and leaned back in the chair, rubbing his eyes. Sensing an opportunity, Joan reached over to the tablet and pointed to a word.

"What does that say?"

"Jerome. That is the name of one of the great Fathers of the Church."

"Jerome," she repeated slowly. "The sound is like my name."

"Some of the letters are the same," Matthew agreed, smiling.

"Show me."

"I'd better not. Father wouldn't like it if he found out."

"He won't," Joan pleaded. "Please, Matthew. I want to know. Please show me?"

Matthew hesitated. "I suppose there is no harm in teaching you to write your own name. It may be useful one day when you are married and have a household of your own to manage."

Placing his hand over her small one, he helped her trace the letters of her name: J-O-H-A-N-N-A, with a long, looped *a* at the end.

"Good. Now try it yourself."

Joan gripped the stylus hard, forcing her fingers into the odd, constricted position, willing them to form the letters she pictured in her mind. Once, she cried aloud in frustration when she could not make the stylus go where she wished.

Matthew soothed her. "Slowly, little sister, slowly. You are only six. Writing does not come easy at that age. That is when I started also, and I remember. Take your time; it will come to you in the end."

The next day, she rose early and went outside. In the loose earth surrounding the livestock pen, she traced the letters over and over again until she was sure she had them right. Then she proudly called Matthew over to witness her handiwork.

"Why, that's very good, little sister. Really very good." He caught himself with a start and muttered guiltily, "But it will not do for Father to find out about this." He scuffed at the dirt with his feet, erasing the marks she had made.

"No, Matthew, no!" Joan tried to pull him away. Disturbed by the noise, the pigs started a chorus of grunting.

Matthew bent to embrace her. "It's all right, Joan. Don't be unhappy."

"B-but you said my letters were good!"

"They *are* good." Matthew was surprised by how good they were; better than John could do, and he was three years older. Indeed, if Joan weren't a girl, Matthew would have said that she would make a fine scribe one day. But it was better not to put wild ideas in the child's head. "I could not leave the letters for Father to see; that is why I erased them."

"Will you teach me more letters, Matthew? Will you?"

"I have already showed you more than I should have."

She said with grave seriousness, "Father won't find out. I won't ever tell him, I promise. And I will erase the letters very carefully when I am done." Her deep-set gray-green eyes held his intently, willing him to agree.

Matthew shook his head in rueful amusement. She was certainly persistent, this little sister of his. Affectionately he chucked her under the chin. "Very well," he agreed. "But, remember, we must keep it our secret."

After that, it became a kind of game between them. Whenever the chance presented itself, not nearly as often as Joan would have liked, Matthew would show her how to trace letters in the earth. She was an eager student; though wary of the consequences, Matthew found it impossible to resist her enthusiasm. He, too, loved learning; her eagerness spoke directly to his heart.

Nevertheless, even he was shocked when she came to him one day carrying the huge, wood-bound Bible that belonged to their father.

"What are you doing?" he cried. "Put that back; you should never have touched it!"

"Teach me to read."

"What?" Her audacity was astonishing. "Now, really, little sister, that's asking too much."

"Why?"

"Well . . . for one thing, reading is a lot more difficult than merely learning the abecedarium. I doubt you could even learn to do it."

"Why not? You did."

He smiled indulgently. "Yes. But I am a man." This was not quite true, as he had not yet attained thirteen winters. In a little over a year, when he turned fourteen, he would truly be a man. But it pleased him to claim the privilege now, and besides, his little sister didn't know the difference.

"I *can* do it. I know I can."

Matthew sighed. This was not going to be easy. "It's not only that, Joan. It is dangerous, and unnatural, for a girl to read and write."

"Saint Catherine did. The bishop said so in his sermon, remember? He said she was loved for her wisdom and learning."

"That's different. She was a saint. You are just a . . . girl."

She was silent then. Matthew was pleased at having won the debate so handily; he knew how determined his little sister could be. He reached for the Bible.

She started to give it to him, then pulled it back. "Why is Catherine a saint?" she asked.

Matthew paused, his hand still extended. "She was a holy martyr who died for the Faith. The bishop said so in his sermon, remember?" He could not resist parroting her.

"Why was she martyred?"

Matthew sighed. "She defied the Emperor Maxentius and fifty of his wisest men by proving, through logical debate, the falseness of paganism. For this she was punished. Now come, little sister, give me the book."

"How old was she when she did this?"

What odd questions the child asked! "I don't want to discuss it any further," Matthew said, exasperated. "Just give me the book!"

She backed away, keeping tight hold of it. "She was old when she went to Alexandria to debate the Emperor's wise men, wasn't she?"

Matthew wondered if he should wrest the book from her. No, better not. The fragile binding might come loose. Then they would both be in more trouble than he cared to think about. Better to keep talking, answering her questions, silly and childish as they were, until she tired of the game.

"Thirty-three, the bishop said, the same age as Christ Jesus at His crucifixion."

"And when St. Catherine defied the Emperor, she was already admired for her learning, like the bishop said?"

"Obviously." Matthew was condescending. "How else could she have bested the wisest men in all the land in such a debate?"

"Then"—Joan's small face was alight with triumph—"she must have learned to read *before* she was a saint. When she was just a girl. Like me!"

For a moment Matthew was speechless, torn between irritation and surprise. Then he laughed aloud. "You little imp!" he said. "So that's where you were headed! Well, you have a gift for disputation, that's for certain!"

She handed him the book then, smiling expectantly.

Matthew took it from her, shaking his head. What a strange creature she was, so inquisitive, so determined, so sure of herself. She was not at all like John or any other young child he had ever met. The eyes of a wise old woman shone forth from her little girl's face. No wonder the other girls in the village would have nothing to do with her.

"Very well, little sister," he said at last. "Today, you begin to learn to read." He saw the gleeful anticipation in her eyes and hastened to caution her. "You must not expect much. It is far more difficult than you think."

Joan threw her arms around her brother's neck. "I love you, Matthew."

Matthew extricated himself from her grasp, opened the book, and said gruffly, "We will begin here."

Joan bent over the book, picking up the pungent smell of parchment and wood as Matthew pointed out the passage, "The Gospel of John, chapter one, verse one. *In principio erat verbum et verbum erat apud Deum et verbum erat Deus*": "In the beginning was the Word and the Word was with God and the Word was God."

✦ ✦ ✦

The summer and fall that followed were mild and fruitful; the harvest was the best the village had had in years. But in Heilagmanoth, snow fell, and the wind drove in from the north in icy blasts. The window of the grubenhaus was boarded up against the cold, snow drifted high against its walls, and the family stayed indoors most of the day. It was more difficult for Joan and Matthew to find time for lessons. On good days the canon still went on his ministry, taking John with him—for Matthew he left to his all-important studies. When Gudrun went into the forest to gather wood, Joan would hurry to the desk where Matthew bent over his work and open the Bible to the place where they had left off the previous lesson. In this way Joan continued to make rapid progress, so that before Lent she had mastered almost all of the Book of John.

One day, Matthew withdrew something from his scrip and held it out to her with a smile. "For you, little sister." It was a wooden medallion attached to a loop of rope. Matthew ringed the loop around Joan's head; the medallion swung down onto her chest.

"What is it?" Joan asked curiously.

"Something for you to wear."

"Oh," she said, and then, realizing that something more was needed, "Thank you."

Matthew laughed, seeing her puzzlement. "Look at the front of the medallion."

Joan did as he told her. Carved into the wooden surface was the likeness of a woman. It was crudely done, for Matthew was no woodworker, but the woman's eyes were well made, even striking, looking straight ahead with an expression of intelligence.

"Now," Matthew directed her, "look at the back."

Joan turned it over. In bold letters ringing the edge of the medallion, she read the words "Saint Catherine of Alexandria."

With a cry, Joan clasped the medallion to her heart. She knew what this gift signified. It was Matthew's way of acknowledging her abilities and the faith he had in her. Tears welled in her eyes. "Thank you," she said again, and this time he knew she meant it.

He smiled at her. She noticed dark circles around his eyes; he looked tired and drawn.

"Are you feeling well?" she asked with concern.

"Of course!" he said, just a shade too heartily. "Let's begin the lesson, shall we?"

But he was restless and distracted. Uncharacteristically, he failed to catch her up when she made a careless error.

"Is there anything wrong?" Joan asked.

"No, no. I am a little tired, that is all."

"Shall we stop, then? I don't mind. We can go on tomorrow."

"No, I am sorry. My mind wandered, that's all. Let's see, where were we? Ah yes. Read the last passage again, and this time be careful of the verb: *videat,* not *videt.*"

The next day Matthew woke complaining of a headache and a sore throat. Gudrun brought him a hot posset of borage and honey.

"You must stay in bed for the rest of the day," she said. "Old Mistress Wigbod's boy has the spring flux; it may be that you are coming down with it."

Matthew laughed and said it was nothing of the kind. He worked several hours at his studies, then insisted on going outside to help John prune the vines.

The next morning he had a fever, and difficulty swallowing. Even the canon could see that he looked really ill.

"You are excused from your studies today," he told Matthew. This was an unheard-of dispensation.

They sent to the monastery of Lorsch for help, and in two days' time the infirmarian came and examined Matthew, shaking his head gravely and muttering under his breath. For the first time Joan realized that her brother's condition might be serious. The idea was terrifying. The monk bled Matthew profusely and exhausted his entire repertoire of prayer and holy talismans, but by the Feast of St. Severinus, Matthew's condition was critical. He lay in a feverish stupor, shaken by fits of coughing so violent that Joan covered her ears to try to shut them out.

Throughout the day and into the night the family kept vigil. Joan knelt beside her mother on the beaten earth floor. She was frightened by the alteration in Matthew's appearance. The skin on his face was stretched taut, distorting his familiar features into a horrible mask. Beneath his feverish flush was an ominous undertone of gray.

Above them, in the dark, the canon's voice droned into the night, reciting prayers for his son's deliverance. *"Domine Sancte, Pater omnipotens, aeterne Deus, qui fragilitatem conditionis nostrae infusa virtutis tuae dignatione confirmas . . ."* Joan nodded drowsily.

"No!"

Joan wakened suddenly to her mother's wailing cry.

"He is gone! Matthew, my son!"

Joan looked at the bed. Nothing appeared to have changed. Matthew lay motionless as before. Then she noticed his skin had lost its feverish flush; he was entirely gray, the color of stone.

She took his hand. It was flaccid, heavy, though not so hot as before. She held it tightly, pressing it to her cheek. *Please don't be dead, Matthew.* Dead meant that he would never again sleep beside her and John in the big bed; she would never again see him hunched over the pine table, brow furrowed in concentration as he labored at his studies, never again sit beside him while his finger moved across the pages of the Bible, pointing out words for her to read. *Please don't be dead.*

After a while, they sent her away so her mother and the village women could wash Matthew's body and prepare it for burial. When they were done, Joan was allowed to approach to pay her final respects. But for the unnatural grayness of his skin, he looked to be merely sleeping. If she touched him, she imagined he would wake, his eyes would open and gaze upon her again with teasing affection. She kissed his cheek, as her mother instructed her. It was cold and oddly unresistant, like the skin of the dead rabbit Joan had fetched from the cooling shed only last week. She drew back quickly.

Matthew was gone.

There would be no more lessons now.

She stood alongside the livestock pen, staring at the patches of black earth beginning to show under the melting snow, the earth in which she had traced her first letters.

"Matthew," she whispered. She sank to her knees. The wet snow penetrated her woolen cloak, soaking through to the skin. She felt very cold, but she could not go back in. There was something she had to do. With her forefinger, she traced the familiar letters from the Book of John in the wet snow.

*Ubi sum ego vos non potestis venire.* "Where I am you cannot come."

✦ ✦ ✦

"We will all do penance," the canon announced after the burial, "to atone for the sins that have visited God's wrath upon our family." He made Joan and John kneel in silent prayer on the hard wooden board that served as the family altar. They stayed there all that day with nothing to eat or drink until at last, with the coming of night, they were released and permitted to sleep in the bed, big and empty now without Matthew. John whimpered with hunger. In the middle of the night, Gudrun woke them, her finger pressed warningly to her lips. The canon was asleep. Quickly, she handed them several pieces of bread and a wooden cup filled with warm goat's milk—all the food she dared smuggle from the larder without arousing her husband's suspicions. John gobbled down his bread and was still hungry; Joan shared her portion with him. As soon as they were done, Gudrun took away the wooden cup and left, pulling the woolen covers up under their chins. The children nestled together for comfort and were quickly asleep.

With the first light, the canon woke them, and without breaking fast, sent them to the altar to resume their penance. The morning came and went, and the dinner hour, and still they remained on their knees.

The rays of the late afternoon sun slanted onto the altar, spilling through the slit in the grubenhaus window. Joan sighed and shifted position on the makeshift altar. Her knees were sore, and her stomach growled. She struggled to concentrate on the words of her prayer, *"Pater Noster qui es in caelis, sanctificetur nomen tuum, adveniat regnum tuum . . ."*

It was no use. The discomforts of her present situation kept intruding. She was tired and hungry, and she missed Matthew. She wondered why she did not cry. There was a sensation of pressure in her throat and chest, but the tears would not come.

She stared at the small wooden crucifix that hung on the wall before the altar. The canon had brought it with him from his native England when he had arrived to carry out his missionary work among the heathen Saxons. Fashioned by a Northumbrian artist, the Christ figure had more power and precision than most Frankish work. His body stretched on the cross, all elongated limbs and emaciated ribs, the lower half twisted to emphasize His mortal agony. His head was fallen back, so that the Adam's apple bulged—a strangely disconcerting reminder of His human maleness. The wood was deeply etched to reveal the tracks of blood from His many wounds.

The figure, for all its power, was grotesque. Joan knew she should be filled with love and awe at Christ's sacrifice, but instead she felt revulsion. Compared with the beautiful, strong gods of her mother, this figure seemed ugly, broken, and defeated.

Beside her, John started to whimper. Joan reached out and took his hand. John took punishment hard. She was stronger than he was, and she knew it. Though he was ten years old, and she only seven, she found it entirely natural that she should nurture and protect him, rather than the other way around.

Tears started to form in his eyes. "It's not fair," he said.

"Don't cry." Joan was worried that the noise might bring Mama—or worse yet, Father. "Soon the penance will be over."

"That's not it!" he responded with wounded dignity.

"What's the matter, then?"

"You wouldn't understand."

"Tell me."

"Father will want me to take over Matthew's studies. I know he will. And I can't do it; I can't."

"Perhaps you can," said Joan, though she understood why her brother was worried. Father accused him of laziness and beat him when he did not progress in his studies, but it was not John's fault. He tried to do well, but he was slow; he always had been.

"No," John insisted. "I'm not like Matthew. Did you know that Father planned to take him to Aachen, to petition for his acceptance in the Schola Palatina?"

"Truly?" Joan was astonished. The Palace School! She had no idea that her father's ambitions for Matthew had reached so high.

"And I can't even read Donatus yet. Father says that Matthew had mastered Donatus when he was only nine, and I am almost ten. What will I do, Joan? What will I do?"

"Well . . ." Joan tried to think of something comforting to quiet him, but the strain of the last two days had driven John into a state past all caring.

"He will beat me. I know he will beat me." Now John started to wail in earnest. *"I don't want to be beaten!"*

Gudrun appeared in the doorway. Nervously casting a glance into the room behind her, she hurried over to John. "Stop it. Do you want your father to hear you? Stop it, I tell you!"

John rocked clumsily off the altar, threw his head back, and bawled.

Oblivious to his mother's words, he continued to wail, tears streaming down red-blotched cheeks.

Gudrun gripped John's shoulders and shook him. His head flopped wildly, back to front; his eyes were closed, his mouth hanging open. Joan heard the sharp click of teeth as his mouth snapped shut. Startled, John opened his eyes and saw his mother.

Gudrun hugged him to her. "You will not cry anymore. For your sister's sake, and mine, you must not cry. All will be well, John. But now you will be quiet." She rocked him, soothing and remonstrating at the same time.

Joan watched thoughtfully. She recognized the truth in what her brother said. John was not smart. He could not follow in Matthew's footsteps. But— Her face flushed with excitement as a thought struck with the force of revelation.

"What is it, Joan?" Gudrun had seen the odd expression on her daughter's face. "Are you unwell?" She was concerned, for the demons that carried the flux were known to linger in a house.

"No, Mama. But I have an idea, a wonderful idea!"

Gudrun groaned inwardly. The child was full of ideas that only got her into trouble.

"Yes?"

"Father wanted Matthew to go to the Schola Palatina."

"I know."

"And now he will want John to go in Matthew's place. That is why John is crying, Mama. He knows he cannot do it, and he's afraid that Father will be angry."

"Well?" Gudrun was puzzled.

"*I* can do it, Mama. I can take over Matthew's studies."

For a moment Gudrun was too shocked to respond. *Her* daughter, her baby, the child she loved best—the only one with whom she had shared the language and the secrets of her people—*she* to study the sacred books of the Christian conquerors? That Joan would even consider such a thing was deeply wounding.

"What nonsense!" Gudrun said.

"I can work hard," Joan persisted. "I like to study and learn about things. I can do it, and then John won't have to. He isn't good at it." There was a muffled sob from John, whose head was still buried in his mother's chest.

"You are a girl; such things are not for you," Gudrun said dismissively. "Besides, your father would never approve."

"But, Mama, that was before. Things have changed. Don't you see? Now Father may feel differently."

"I forbid you to speak of this to your father. You must be light-headed from lack of food and rest, like your brother. Otherwise you would never speak so wildly."

"But, Mama, if I could only show him—"

"No more, I say!" Gudrun's tone left no room for further discussion.

Joan fell silent. Reaching inside her tunic, she clasped the medallion of St. Catherine that Matthew had carved for her. *I can read Latin, and John cannot,* she thought stubbornly. *Why should it matter that I am a girl?*

She went to the Bible on the little wooden desk. She lifted it, felt its weight, the familiar grooves of the gilt-edged tracings on the cover. The smell of wood and parchment, so strongly associated with Matthew, made her think of their work together, of all he had taught her, all she still wanted to learn. *Perhaps if I show Father what I have learned . . . perhaps then he will see I can do it.* Once again, she felt a rise of excitement. *But there could be trouble. Father might be very angry.* Her father's anger frightened her; she had been struck by him often enough to know and fear the force of his rage.

She stood uncertainly, fingering the smooth surface of the Bible's wooden binding. On an impulse, she opened it; the pages fell open to the Gospel of St. John, the text Matthew had used when he first taught her to read. *It is a sign,* she thought.

Her mother was sitting with her back to Joan, cradling John, whose sobs had subsided into forlorn hiccuping. *Now is my chance.* Joan held the book open and carried it into the next room.

Her father was hunched in a chair, head bowed, hands covering his face. He did not stir as Joan approached. She halted, suddenly afraid. The idea was impossible, ridiculous; Father would never approve. She was about to retreat when he took his hands from his face and looked up. She stood before him with the open book in her hands.

Her voice was nervously unsteady as she began to read, *"In principio erat verbum et verbum erat apud Deum et verbum erat Deus . . ."*

There was no interruption; she kept on, gaining confidence as she read. "All things were made by Him; and without Him was not any thing made that was made. In him was life; and the life was the light of men. And the light shone in the darkness, and the darkness comprehended it not." The beauty and power of the words filled her, leading her onward, giving her strength.

She came to the end, flushed with success, knowing she had read well. She looked up and saw her father staring at her.

"I can read. Matthew taught me. We kept it a secret so no one would know." The words spilled out in a breathless jumble. "I can make you proud, Father, I know I can. Let me take over Matthew's studies and I—"

*"You!"* Her father's voice rumbled with anger. "It was you!" He pointed at her accusingly. "You are the one! You brought God's wrath down upon us. Unnatural child! Changeling! *You murdered your brother!*"

Joan gasped. The canon came toward her with arm raised. Joan dropped the book and tried to run, but he caught her and spun her round, bringing his fist down on her cheek with a force that sent her reeling. She landed against the far wall, striking her head.

Her father stood over her. Joan braced herself for another blow. None came. Moments passed, and then he began to make hoarse, guttural noises in his throat. She realized he was crying. She had never seen her father cry.

"Joan!" Gudrun hurried into the room. "What have you done, child?" She knelt beside Joan, taking note of the swelling bruise under her right eye. Keeping her body between her husband and Joan, she whispered, "What did I tell you? Foolish girl, look what you've done!" In a louder voice, she said, "Go to your brother. He needs you." She helped Joan up and propelled her quickly toward the other room.

The canon watched Joan darkly as she went to the door.

"Forget the girl, Husband," Gudrun said to distract him. "She's of no importance. Do not despair; remember, you have yet another son."

# 3

It was Aranmanoth, the wheat-blade month, in the autumn of her ninth year, when Joan first met Aesculapius. He had stopped at the canon's grubenhaus on his way to Mainz, where he was to be teaching master at the cathedral *schola*.

"Be welcome, sir, be welcome!" Joan's father greeted Aesculapius delightedly. "We rejoice in your safe arrival. I trust the journey was not too arduous?" He bowed his guest solicitously through the door. "Come refresh yourself. Gudrun! Bring wine! You do my humble home great honor, sir, with your presence." From her father's behavior, Joan understood that Aesculapius was a scholar of some standing and importance.

He was Greek, dressed in the Byzantine manner. His fine white linen chlamys was clasped with a simple metal brooch and covered with a long blue cloak, bordered with silver thread. He wore his hair short, like a peasant, and kept it smoothly oiled back from his face. Unlike her father, who shaved in the manner of the Frankish clergy, Aesculapius had a long, full beard—white, like his hair.

When her father called her over to be presented, she suffered a fit of shyness and stood awkwardly before the stranger, her eyes fixed on the intricate braid work of his sandals. At last the canon intervened and sent her off to help her mother prepare the evening meal.

When they sat down at the table, the canon said, "It is our custom to read from the Holy Book before we partake of food. Would you do us the honor of reading this night?"

"Very well," said Aesculapius, smiling. Carefully he opened the wooden binding and turned the fragile parchment pages. "The text is Ecclesiastes. *Omnia tempus habent, et momentum suum cuique negotio sub caelo . . .*"

Joan had never heard Latin spoken so beautifully. His pronunciation was unusual: the words were not all run together, Gallic style; each was round and distinct, like drops of clear rainwater. "For everything there is a season, and a time to every purpose under Heaven. A time to be born, and a time to die; a time to plant, and a time to pluck up that which is planted . . ." Joan had heard her father read the same passage many times before, but in Aesculapius's reading, she heard a beauty she had not previously imagined.

When he was finished, Aesculapius closed the book. "An excellent volume," he said appreciatively to the canon. "Written in a fair hand. You must have brought it with you from England; I have heard that the art still flourishes there. It is rare these days to find a manuscript so free from grammatical barbarisms."

The canon flushed with pleasure. "There were many such in the library at Lindisfarne. This one was entrusted to me by the bishop when he ordained me for the mission in Saxony."

The meal was splendid, the most lavish the family had ever prepared for a guest. There was a haunch of roast salted pork, cooked till the skin crackled, boiled corn and beetroot, pungent cheese, and loaves of crusty bread freshly baked under the embers. The canon brought out some Frankish ale, spicy, dark, and thick as country soup. Afterward, they ate fried almonds and sweet roasted apples.

"Delicious," Aesculapius pronounced at the end of the meal. "It has been a long while since I have dined so well. Not since I left Byzantium have I tasted pork so sweet."

Gudrun was pleased. "It is because we keep our own pigs, and fatten them before the slaughter. The meat of the black forest pigs is tough and unappetizing."

"Tell us about Constantinople!" John said eagerly. "Is it true the streets are paved with precious stones, and the fountains spew liquid gold?"

Aesculapius laughed. "No. But it is a marvelous place to behold." Joan and John listened gape-mouthed as Aesculapius described Constantinople, perched on a towering promontory, with buildings of marble domed in gold and silver rising several stories high, overlooking the harbor of the Golden Horn, in which ships from all over the world lay at anchor. It was the city of Aesculapius's birth and youth. He had been forced to flee when his family had become embroiled in a religious dispute with the basileus, something to do with the breaking of icons. Joan did not understand this, though her father did, nodding with grave disapproval as Aesculapius described his family's persecution.

Here the discussion turned to theological matters, and Joan and her brother were trundled off to the part of the house where their parents slept; as an honored guest, Aesculapius was to have the big bed near the hearth all to himself.

"Please, can't I stay and listen?" Joan pleaded with her mother.

"No. It is well past time for you to be asleep. Besides, our guest is done with telling stories. This schoolroom talk will not interest you."

"But—"

"No more, child. Off to bed with you. I will need your help in the morning; your father wishes us to prepare another feast for his visitor tomorrow. Any more such guests," Gudrun grumbled, "and we will be ruined." She tucked the children into the straw pallet, kissed them, and left.

John was quickly asleep, but Joan lay awake, trying to hear what the voices were saying on the other side of the thick wooden partition. Finally, overcome with curiosity, she got out of bed and crept over to the partition, where she knelt, peering out from the darkness to where her father and Aesculapius sat talking by the hearth fire. It was chilly; the warmth of the fire did not reach this far, and Joan was wearing only a light linen shift. She shivered but did not consider returning to the bed; she *had* to hear what Aesculapius was saying.

The talk had turned to the cathedral schola. Aesculapius asked the canon, "Do you know anything of the library there?"

"Oh yes," said the canon, obviously pleased to have been asked. "I have spent many hours in it. It houses an excellent collection, upwards of five and seventy codices." Aesculapius nodded politely, though he did not appear impressed. Joan could not imagine so many books all in one place.

The canon said, "There are copies of Isidore's *De scriptoribus ecclesiasticus* and Salvianus's *De gubernatione Dei*. Also the complete *Commentarii* of Jerome, with wondrously skilled illustrations. And there is a particularly fine manuscript of the *Hexaëmeron* by your countryman St. Basil."

"Are there any manuscripts of Plato?"

"Plato?" The canon was shocked. "Certainly not; his writing is no fit study for a Christian."

"Ah? You do not approve of the study of logic, then?"

"It has its place in the trivium," the canon replied uneasily, "with the use of proper texts such as those of Augustine and Boethius. But faith is grounded in the authority of Scripture, not the evidence of logic; out of foolish curiosity men do sometimes shake their faith."

"I see your point." Aesculapius's words were spoken more out of courtesy than agreement. "Perhaps, however, you can answer me this: How does it happen that man can reason?"

"Reason is the spark of the divine essence in man. 'So God created man in His own image; In the image of God created He him.' "

"You have a good command of Scripture. So you would agree, then, that reason is God-given?"

"Most assuredly."

Joan crept closer, moving out from behind the shadow of the partition; she did not want to miss what Aesculapius said next.

"Then why fear to expose faith to reason? If God gave it to us, how then should it lead us from Him?"

The canon shifted in his seat. Joan had never seen him look so uncomfortable. He was a missionary, trained to lecture and to preach, unaccustomed to the give-and-take of logical debate. He opened his mouth to reply, then closed it.

"Indeed," Aesculapius went on, "is it not *lack* of faith that leads men to fear the scrutiny of reason? If the destination is doubtful, then the path must be fraught with fear. A robust faith need not fear, for if God exists, then reason cannot help but lead us to Him. *'Cogito, ergo Deus est,'* says St. Augustine, *'I think, therefore God is.'"*

Joan was following the argument so intently that she forgot herself and exclaimed aloud in appreciative understanding. Her father looked sharply toward the partition. She darted back into the shadows and waited, scarcely breathing. Then she heard the hum of voices again. *Benedicite,* she thought, *they did not see me.* She crept softly back to the pallet, where John lay snoring.

Long after the voices ceased, Joan lay awake in the dark. She felt incredibly lighthearted and free, as if an oppressive weight had been lifted from her. It was *not* her fault that Matthew had died. Her desire to learn had not killed him, despite what her father said. Tonight, listening to Aesculapius, she had discovered that her love of knowing was not unnatural or sinful but the direct consequence of a God-given ability to reason. *I think, therefore God is.* In her heart, she felt the truth of it.

Aesculapius's words had turned a light on in her soul. *Perhaps tomorrow I can speak to him,* she thought. *Perhaps I will have a chance to show him I can read.*

The prospect was so pleasing that she could not let go of it. She did not fall asleep until dawn.

Early the next morning, her mother sent Joan into the woods to gather beechnuts and acorns as fodder for the pigs. Anxious to return to the house and Aesculapius, Joan hurried to complete the chore. But the ground of the autumn forest was thick with fallen leaves, and the nuts were hard to find; she could not go back until the wicker basket was full.

By the time she returned, Aesculapius was readying to leave.

"Ah, but I had hoped you would do us the honor of dining with us again," said the canon. "I was interested in your ideas on the mystery of the Triune Oneness and would like to discuss the subject further."

"You are kind, but I must be in Mainz this evening. The bishop expects me, and I am eager to take up my new duties."

"Of course, of course." After a pause the canon added, "But you do remember our conversation about the boy. Will you stay to observe his lesson?"

"It is the least I can do for so generous a host," Aesculapius said with studied politeness.

Joan took up her sewing and stationed herself in a chair a short distance apart, trying to be as inconspicuous as possible, so her father would not send her away.

She need not have worried. The canon's attention was focused entirely on John. Hoping to impress Aesculapius with the extent of his son's learning, he began the lesson by questioning John on the rules of grammar following Donatus. This was a mistake, for grammar was John's weakest subject. Predictably, he performed dismally, confusing the ablative with the dative case, botching his verbs, and in the end showing himself utterly unable to parse a sentence correctly. Aesculapius listened solemnly, the line of a frown creasing his forehead.

Red-faced with embarrassment, the canon retreated to safer ground. He began with the great Alcuin's catechism of riddles, in which John had been thoroughly drilled. John made it through the first part of the catechism well enough:

"What is a year?"

"A cart with four wheels."

"What horses pull it?"

"The sun and the moon."

"How many palaces has it?"

"Twelve."

Pleased with this small success, the canon moved on to more difficult parts of the catechism. Joan feared what was coming, for she saw that John was now in a state of near panic.

"What is life?"

"The joy of the blessed, the sorrow of the sad, and . . . and . . ." John broke off.

Aesculapius shifted in his chair. Joan closed her eyes, concentrating on the words, willing John to utter them.

"Yes?" prodded the canon. "And what?"

John's face lit with inspiration. "And a search for death!"

The canon nodded curtly. "And what is death?"

Stricken, John stared at his father like a netted deer who sees at last the approach of the huntsman.

"What is death?" repeated the canon.

It was no use. The near miss on the last question and his father's mounting displeasure destroyed the last of John's composure. He could no longer remember anything. His face crumpled; Joan saw that he was going to cry. Her father glared at him. Aesculapius looked on with pitying eyes.

She could stand it no longer. Her brother's distress, her father's anger, the intolerable humiliation before the eyes of Aesculapius overwhelmed her. Before she knew what she was doing, she burst out: "An inevitable happening, an uncertain pilgrimage, the tears of the living, the thief of man."

Her words struck the others like a thunderbolt. All three looked up at once, their faces registering a range of emotions. On John's there was chagrin, on her father's outrage, on Aesculapius's astonishment. The canon found his voice first.

"What insolence is this?" he demanded. Then, remembering Aesculapius, he said, "Were it not for the presence of our guest, you would be given a proper thrashing right now. As it is, your punishment will have to wait. Be gone from my sight."

Joan rose from her chair, fighting for control until she reached the door of the grubenhaus and pulled it shut behind her. Then she ran, as fast and hard as she could, all the way to the bracken at the edge of the forest, where she threw herself down on the ground.

She thought she would burst with pain. To have been disgraced before the eyes of the one person she had most wanted to impress! *It isn't fair. John didn't know the answer, and I did. Why shouldn't I give it?*

For a long time she sat watching the lengthening shadows of the trees. A robin fluttered to the ground nearby and began to peck in the bracken, hunting for worms. It found one and, puffing out its chest, strutted in a little circle, displaying its prize. *Like me,* she thought with wry recognition. *All puffed with pride over what I've done.* She knew pridefulness was a sin—she had been chastised for it often enough—yet she could not help the way she felt. *I* am *smarter than John. Why should he be able to study and learn and not me?*

The robin flew off. Joan watched it become a distant flutter of color among the trees. She fingered the medal of St. Catherine that hung around her neck and thought of Matthew. He would have sat with her, talked with her, explained things so she could understand. She missed him so much.

*You murdered your brother,* Father had said. A sick feeling rose in her throat as she remembered. Still her spirit rebelled. She *was* prideful, wanting more than God intended for a woman. But why would God punish Matthew for her sin? It didn't make sense.

What was it in her that would not let go of her impossible dreams? Everyone told her that her desire to learn was unnatural. Yet she thirsted for knowledge, yearned to explore the larger world of ideas and opportunities that was open to people of learning. The other girls in the village had no such interest. They were content to sit through mass without understanding a single word. They accepted what they were told and did not look further. They dreamed of a good husband, by which they meant a man who would treat them kindly and not beat them, and a workable piece of soil; they had no desire ever to go beyond the safe, familiar world of the village. They were as inexplicable to Joan as she was to them.

*Why am I different?* she wondered. *What is wrong with me?*

Footsteps sounded beside her, and a hand touched her shoulder. It was John.

He said sulkily, "Father sent me. He wants to see you."

Joan took his hand. "I'm sorry."

"You shouldn't have done it. You're only a girl."

This was hard to take, but she owed him an apology for shaming him before their guest.

"I was wrong. Forgive me."

He tried to maintain his pose of wounded virtue but could not. "All right, I forgive you," he relented. "At least Father isn't angry at *me* anymore. Now—well, come and see for yourself."

He pulled her up from the damp ground and helped her dust off the clinging pieces of bracken. Holding hands, they walked back toward the cottage.

At the door, John ushered Joan in ahead of him. "Go on," he said. "It's you they want to see."

*They?* Joan wondered what he meant, but she could not ask, for she was already facing her father and Aesculapius, who waited before the hearth fire.

She approached and stood submissively before them. Her father had a peculiar look on his face, as if he had swallowed something sour. He grunted and motioned her toward Aesculapius, who beckoned to her. Taking her hands in his, Aesculapius fixed her with a penetrating gaze. "You know Latin?" he said.

"Yes, sir."

"How do you come by this knowledge?"

"I listened, sir, whenever my brother had his lessons." She could imagine her father's reaction to this information. She dropped her eyes. "I know that I should not have done so."

Aesculapius asked, "What other knowledge have you gained?"

"I can read, sir, and write a little. My brother Matthew taught me when I was small." From the corner of her eye Joan saw her father's start of anger.

"Show me." Aesculapius opened the Bible, searched for a passage, then held the book out to her, marking the place with his finger. It was the parable of the mustard seed from the Gospel of St. Luke. She began to read, stumbling at first over some of the Latin words—it had been a while since she had read from the book: *"Quomodo assimilabimus regnum Dei aut in qua parabola ponemus illud?"*—"Unto what is the kingdom of God like? And whereunto shall I resemble it?" She continued without hesitation until the end: "Then he said, It is like a grain of mustard seed which a man took, and cast into his garden, and it grew, and waxed a great tree, and the fowls of the air lodged in the branches of it."

She stopped reading. In the silence that followed she could hear the soft rustle of the autumn breeze passing through the thatching on the roof.

Aesculapius said quietly, "And do you understand the meaning of what you have read?"

"I think so."

"Explain it to me."

"It means that faith is like a mustard seed. You plant it in your heart, just like a seed is planted in a garden. If you cultivate the seed, it will grow into a beautiful tree. If you cultivate your faith, you will gain the Kingdom of Heaven."

Aesculapius tugged at his beard. He gave no indication of whether he approved of what she had said. Had she given the wrong interpretation?

"Or—" She had another idea.

Aesculapius's eyebrows went up. "Yes?"

"It could mean that *the Church* is like a seed. The Church started small, growing in darkness, cared for only by Christ and the Twelve Apostles, but it grew into a huge tree, a tree that shades the whole world."

"And the birds who nest in its branches?" Aesculapius asked.

She thought quickly. "They are the faithful, who find salvation in the Church, just as birds find protection in the branches of the tree."

Aesculapius's expression was unreadable. Again he tugged solemnly at his beard. Joan decided to give it one more try.

"Also . . ." She reasoned it out slowly as she spoke. "The mustard seed *could* represent Christ. Christ was like a seed when he was buried in the earth, and like a tree when he was resurrected and rose toward Heaven."

Aesculapius turned to the canon. "You heard?"

The canon's face twitched. "She is only a girl. I am sure she did not mean to presume . . ."

"The seed as faith, as the Church, as Christ," said Aesculapius. "*Allegoria, moralis, anagoge.* A classic threefold scriptural exegesis. Rather simply expressed, of course, but still, as complete an interpretation as that of the great Gregory himself. And that without any formal education! Astonishing! The child demonstrates an extraordinary intelligence. I will undertake to tutor her."

Joan was dazed. Was she dreaming? She was afraid to let herself believe this was actually happening.

"Not, of course, at the schola," Aesculapius continued, "for that would not be permitted. I will arrange to come here once a week. And I will provide books for her to study in between."

The canon was displeased. This was not the outcome he had envisioned. "That's all very well," he said testily. "But what about the boy?"

"Ah, the boy? I'm afraid he shows no promise as a scholar. With further training, he might qualify as a country priest. The law requires only that they read and write, and know the correct form of the sacraments. But I should look no further than that. The schola is not for him."

"I can scarcely credit my ears! You will undertake to teach the girl, but not the boy?"

Aesculapius shrugged. "One has talent; the other has not. There can be no other consideration."

"A woman as scholar!" The canon was indignant. "She to study the sacred texts while her brother is ignored? I will not permit it. Either you teach both or neither."

Joan held her breath. Surely she could not have come this close only to have it taken away. She started to recite a prayer under her breath, then stopped. Perhaps God would not approve. She reached under her tunic and gripped the medallion of St. Catherine. *She* would understand. *Please,* she prayed silently. *Help me to have this. I will make a fine offering to you. Only please let me have this.*

Aesculapius looked impatient. "I have told you the boy has no aptitude for study. To tutor him would be a waste of time."

"Then it is settled," said the canon angrily. Joan watched, disbelieving, as he rose from his chair.

"A moment," said Aesculapius. "I see you are fixed in your intention."

"I am."

"Very well. The girl shows every sign of a prodigious intellect. She could accomplish much with the proper education. I cannot let such an opportunity pass. Since you insist, I will tutor them both."

Joan let her breath out in a rush. "Thank you," she said, as much to

St. Catherine as to Aesculapius. It was all she could do to keep her voice steady. "I will work to be deserving."

Aesculapius looked at her, his eyes filled with a penetrating intelligence. *Like a fire from within,* Joan thought. A fire that would light the weeks and months ahead.

"Indeed you will," he said. Underneath the thick, white beard there was the trace of a smile. "Oh yes, indeed you will."

# 4

## *Rome*

The vaulted marble interior of the Lateran Palace was deliciously cool after the blistering heat of the Roman streets. As the huge wooden doors of the papal residence swung shut behind him, Anastasius stood blinking, momentarily blinded in the darkness of the Patriarchium. Instinctively, he reached for his father's hand, then drew back, remembering.

"Stand tall, and do not cling to your father," his mother had said that morning as she fussed over his attire. "You are twelve now; time enough to learn to play the part of a man." She tugged firmly on his jeweled belt, pulling it into place. "And look squarely at those who address you. The family name is second to none; you must not appear to be deferential."

Now, recalling her words, Anastasius drew his shoulders back and lifted his head high. He was small for his age, a continuing source of grief for him, but he tried always to hold himself so as to appear as tall as possible. His eyes began to adjust to the dim light, and he looked around curiously. It was his first visit to the Lateran, the majestic residence of the Pope, and the seat of all power in Rome, and Anastasius was impressed. The interior was enormous, a vast structure containing the archives of the Church and the Treasure Chamber, as well as dozens of oratories, triclinia, and chapels, among them the celebrated private chapel of the Popes, the Sanctum Sanctorum. Before Anastasius, on the wall of the Great Hall, hung a huge *tabula mundi,* an annotated wall map depicting the world as a flat disk surrounded by oceans. The three continents—Asia, Africa, and Europe—were separated by the great rivers Tanais and Nile as well as the Mediterranean. At the very center of the world was the holy city of Jerusalem, bounded on the east by the terrestrial paradise. Anastasius studied the map, his attention riveted to the large open spaces, mysterious and frightening, at the outmost edges, where the world fell off into darkness.

A man approached, wearing the white silk dalmatic of the members of the papal household. "I give you greeting and the blessing of our Most Holy Father, Pope Paschal," he said.

"May he live long, that we may continue to prosper from his benevolent guidance," replied Anastasius's father.

The required formalities over, both men relaxed.

"Well, Arsenius, how is it with you?" said the man. "You are here to see Theodorus, I suppose?"

Anastasius's father nodded. "Yes. To arrange the appointment of my nephew Cosmas as *arcarius.*" Lowering his voice, he added, "The payment was made weeks ago. I cannot think what has delayed the announcement so long."

"Theodorus has been quite busy of late. There was that nasty dispute, you know, over the possession of the monastery at Farfa. The Holy Father was much displeased with the imperial court's decision." Bending close, he added in a conspiratorial whisper, "And even more displeased with Theo for championing the Emperor's cause. Be prepared: there may be little that Theo can do for you just now."

"The thought had occurred to me." Anastasius's father shrugged. "Nevertheless, Theo is still *primicerius,* and the payment has been made."

"We shall see."

The conversation halted abruptly as a second man, also clad in the white dalmatic, came toward them. Anastasius, standing close by his father's side, sensed the slight stiffening of his back. "May the blessings of the Holy Father be conferred upon you, Sarpatus," said his father.

"And on you, my dear Arsenius, and on you," the man replied. His mouth had an odd twist. "Ah, Lucian," he said, turning to the first man. "You were so intent on your conversation with Arsenius just now. Have you some interesting news? I should love to hear it." He yawned elaborately. "Life is so tedious here since the Emperor left."

"No, Sarpatus, of course not. If I had any news, I should tell you," Lucian replied nervously. To Anastasius's father he said, "Well, Arsenius, I must go now. I have duties to attend to." He bowed, turned on his heel, and quickly walked away.

Sarpatus shook his head. "Lucian has been edgy of late. I wonder why." He looked pointedly at Anastasius's father. "Well, well, no matter. I see that you have company today."

"Yes. May I present my son Anastasius? He is to take the exam to become a *lector* soon." Anastasius's father added with emphasis, "His uncle Theo is especially fond of him; that is why I brought him along with me to our meeting."

Anastasius bowed. "May you prosper in His Name," he said formally, as he had been taught.

The man smiled, amusement twisting the corners of his lips even more.

"My! The boy's Latin is excellent; I congratulate you, Arsenius. He will prove to be an asset to you—unless, of course, he shares his uncle's deplorable lack of judgment." He continued, precluding any reply, "Yes, yes, a fine boy. How old is he?" The question was addressed to Anastasius's father.

Anastasius replied, "I turned twelve just after Advent."

"Indeed! You look younger." He patted Anastasius's head.

A dislike for the stranger rose inside Anastasius. Drawing himself up as tall as possible, he said, "And I think that my uncle's judgment cannot be so very bad, or else how did he come to be primicerius?"

His father squeezed Anastasius's arm in warning, but his eyes were mild and there was a hint of a smile on his lips. The stranger stared at Anastasius, something—surprise? anger?—registering in his eyes. Anastasius met his gaze levelly. After a long moment the man broke the gaze and returned his attention to Anastasius's father.

"Such family loyalty! How touching! Well, well, let us hope that the boy's thinking proves to be as correct as his Latin."

A loud noise drew their attention to the far side of the hall as the heavy doors were opened.

"Ah! Here comes the primicerius now. I shall intrude upon you no longer." Sarpatus bowed elaborately and withdrew.

A hush fell over the assembly as Theodorus entered, accompanied by his son-in-law Leo, recently elevated to the position of nomenclator. He stopped just inside the doors to converse briefly with a few of the clerics and nobles standing nearby. In his ruby silk dalmatic and golden cingulum, Theodorus was by far the most elegantly attired of the group; he loved fine materials and favored a certain ostentation in his dress, a characteristic that Anastasius admired.

Finishing with the formal greetings, Theodorus scanned the hall. Catching sight of Anastasius and his father, he smiled and started across the floor toward them. As he drew closer, he winked at Anastasius, and his right hand moved toward the fold in his dalmatic. Anastasius grinned, for he knew what that meant. Theodorus, who had a love for children, always carried some special treats to hand out. *What will it be today?* Anastasius wondered, his mouth watering in anticipation. *A plump fig, a sweet vermilion sugarplum, perhaps even a piece of marzipan, creamy and rich, filled with ground sugared almonds and walnuts?*

Anastasius's attention was focused so intently on the fold in Theodorus's dalmatic that at first he did not see the other men. They came up quickly—three of them—from behind; one clapped a hand over Theodorus's mouth, drawing him backward. Anastasius thought it was some kind of prank. Smiling, he looked at his father for explanation; his heart leapt when he saw the fear in his father's eyes. He turned back and saw Theodorus struggling to break loose. Theodorus was a big man, but the contest was hopelessly unequal. The men surrounded him, pinning his arms, dragging him down. The front of Theodorus's ruby dalmatic was torn, the fine silk hanging in jagged ribbons, exposing patches of white skin. One of the attackers entwined his fingers in Theodorus's thick black hair and wrenched his head back. Anastasius saw a glint of steel. There was a scream, and then Theodorus's face seemed to explode in a fountain of red. Anastasius flinched as a fine spray hit his face. He reached up, then stared numbly at his hand. It was blood. Across the room someone shouted; Anastasius saw Leo, Theodorus's son-in-law, disappear beneath a swarm of attackers.

The men released Theodorus, and he fell forward onto his knees. Then he raised his head, and Anastasius screamed in terror. The face was dreadful. Blood poured from the black and empty holes where Theodorus's eyes had been, streaming from his chin onto his shoulders and chest.

Anastasius buried his face in his father's side. He felt his father's large hands on his shoulders and heard his voice, strong and unwavering. "No," his father said. "You cannot hide, my son." The hands impelled him, pushing him away, turning him back toward the grisly scene before him.

"Watch," the voice commanded, "and learn. This is the price exacted for lack of subtlety and art. Theodorus pays now for wearing his loyalty to the Emperor so openly."

Anastasius stood like a post while the attackers carried Theodorus and Leo to the center of the hall. Several times they stumbled and almost fell on the tile floor, slippery with blood. Theodorus was shouting something, but the words were unintelligible. With his mouth open and moving, his face was even more frightful.

The men forced Theodorus and Leo to their knees and pulled their heads forward. One man raised a long sword over Leo's neck and with one quick stroke, decapitated him. But Theodorus's neck was thick, and he continued to struggle; it took three or four sword strokes to cleave his head from his body.

Anastasius saw, for the first time, that the attackers wore the scarlet cross of the papal militia. "Father!" he blurted. "It's the guards! The guards of the militia!"

"Yes." He drew Anastasius close.

Anastasius fought against the rise of hysteria. "But why? Why, Father? Why would they do it?"

"They were ordered to."

"Ordered to?" said Anastasius. He tried to make sense of it. "Who would give such an order?"

"Who? Ah, my son, *think*." His father's face was ashen, but his voice was steady as he replied, "You must learn to think so you will never suffer such a fate. Consider now: Who has the power? Who is capable of giving such an order?"

Anastasius stood speechless, overwhelmed by the enormity of the idea that had begun to break upon him.

"Yes." His father's hands were gentle now on Anastasius's shoulders. "Who else," he said, "but the Pope?"

# 5

"No, no, *no.*" Aesculapius's voice was edged with impatience. "You must make your letters much smaller. See how your sister pens her lesson?" He tapped Joan's paper. "You must learn a greater respect for your parchment, my boy—there's a whole sheep gone to make just one folio. If the monks of Andernach sprawled their words across the page in that manner, the herds of Austrasia would be wiped out in a month!"

John cast a resentful glance at Joan. "It's too hard; I can't do it."

Aesculapius sighed. "Very well; return to practicing on your tablet. When you have achieved a better control, we will try the parchment again." He asked Joan, "Have you finished the *De inventione*?"

"Yes, sir," Joan replied.

"Name the six evidentiary questions used to determine the circumstances of human acts."

Joan was ready. *"Quis, quid, quomodo, ubi, quando, cur?"*—"Who, what, how, where, when, why?"

"Good. Now identify the rhetorical *constitutiones.*"

"Cicero specifies four different *constitutiones:* dispute about fact, dispute about definition, dispute about the nature of the act, and—"

There was a thud as Gudrun kicked the door open and entered, stooping from the weight of the heavy wooden water buckets she carried, one in each clenched hand. Joan rose to help her, but Aesculapius put a hand on her shoulder, returning her to her seat.

"And?"

Joan hesitated, her eyes still on her mother.

"Child, continue." Aesculapius's tone indicated that he would tolerate no disobedience.

Joan hastened to reply. "Dispute about jurisdiction or procedure."

Aesculapius nodded, satisfied. "Provide an illustration of the third *status.* Write it out on your parchment, and make sure it will be worth the keeping."

Gudrun bustled about, blowing up the fire, bringing the pot to boil, laying the table in preparation for the afternoon meal. Once or twice she looked over her shoulder resentfully.

Joan felt a stab of guilt but forced her attention back to her work. This time was precious—Aesculapius came only once a week—and her studies mattered more than anything else.

But it was hard, working under the weight of her mother's displeasure. Aesculapius obviously noticed it too, though he attributed it to the fact that the lessons took Joan away from household chores. Joan knew the real cause. Her studies were a betrayal, a violation of the private world she shared with her mother, a world of Saxon gods and Saxon secrets. By learning Latin and studying Christian texts, Joan aligned herself with the things her mother most detested—with the Christian God who had destroyed Gudrun's homeland and, more to the point, with the canon, her husband.

The truth was that Joan worked mostly with pre-Christian, classical texts. Aesculapius revered the "pagan" texts of Cicero, Seneca, Lucan, and Ovid, regarded as anathema by most scholars of the day. He was teaching Joan to read Greek using the ancient texts of Menander and Homer, whose poetry the canon regarded as nothing less than pagan blasphemy. Taught by Aesculapius to appreciate clarity and style, Joan never considered the question of whether Homer's poetry was acceptable in terms of Christian doctrine; God was in it, because it was beautiful.

She would have liked to explain this to her mother but knew it would make no difference. Homer or Bede, Cicero or St. Augustine—to Gudrun it was all one: it was not Saxon; nothing else mattered.

Joan's concentration had wandered; she blundered and made an ugly blotch on her parchment. She looked up to see Aesculapius regarding her with penetrating dark eyes.

"Never mind, child." His voice was unexpectedly gentle; usually he was harsh with careless errors. "It is no matter. Begin again here."

The townspeople of Ingelheim were gathered round the village pond, chattering animatedly. A witch was to be tried today, an event sure to inspire horror, pity, and delight—welcome respite from the daily drudgery of their lives.

*"Benedictus."* The canon began the blessing of the water.

Hrotrud tried to run, but two men seized her and dragged her back to where the canon stood, his dark brows meeting in frowning disapproval. Hrotrud cursed and struggled as her captors wrested her clawed hands behind her and tied them together with strips of linen cloth, causing her to cry out in pain.

*"Maleficia,"* someone muttered, close to where Joan and Aesculapius were standing among the crowd of witnesses. "St. Barnabas, preserve us from the evil eye."

Aesculapius said nothing but shook his head sadly.

He had arrived at Ingelheim that morning for the weekly lesson, but the canon had refused to let the children receive instruction, insisting they first attend the trial of Hrotrud, formerly the village midwife.

"For you will learn more about the ways of God from observing this holy trial than you will from any heathen writing," the canon had said, looking pointedly at Aesculapius.

Joan did not like delaying her lesson, but she was curious about the trial. She wondered what it would be like; she had never seen anyone tried for witchcraft. She was sorry that it was Hrotrud, however. Joan liked Hrotrud, who was an honest woman and no hypocrite. She had always spoken fairly to Joan, treating her kindly and not ridiculing her as so many of the villagers did. Gudrun had told Joan how Hrotrud had assisted at her birthing—a grueling ordeal, according to her mother, who credited Hrotrud with saving her life and Joan's that day. As Joan stared at the crowd of villagers, the thought came to her that Hrotrud had doubtless helped to birth almost everyone gathered there—those, at least, who had reached six winters or more. One would never know it from the way they gawked at her now. She had become an annoyance to them, a goad to their Christian charity, for ever since the wasting pain had crooked her hands, destroying her usefulness as a midwife, she had lived off the alms of her neighbors—that, and what little she could earn from selling medicinal herbs and philters of her own devising.

Her skill in this last had proved to be her undoing, for her ability to work cures for sleeplessness and pains of the tooth, stomach, and head appeared to the simple villagers to be nothing less than sorcery.

Finishing with the blessing of the water, the canon turned to Hrotrud. "Woman! You know the crime of which you are accused. Will you now freely confess your sins in order to ensure the salvation of your immortal soul?"

Hrotrud regarded him consideringly from the corners of her eyes. "If I confess, you will let me go free?"

The canon shook his head. "It is expressly forbidden in the Holy Book: 'You shall not permit a sorceress to live.' " He added, for authority, "Exodus, chapter twenty-two, verse eighteen. But you will die a consecrated death, and a swift one, and through it gain the immeasurable rewards of Heaven."

"No!" Hrotrud retorted defiantly. "I am a Christian woman, and no witch, and anyone who says otherwise is a foul liar!"

"Sorceress! You will suffer the fires of Hell for all eternity! Can you deny the evidence of your own eyes?" From behind his back the canon pulled a soiled linen belt, mutilated by a series of crude knots. He thrust it accusingly at Hrotrud, who started and stepped back.

"See how she shrinks from it?" someone whispered close to Joan. "She is guilty, sure, and should be burned!"

*Anyone would be startled by so sudden a move,* Joan thought. *Surely that is no proof of guilt.*

The canon held the belt up for the crowd to observe. "This belongs to Arno, the miller. It went missing a fortnight ago. Immediately thereafter he took to his bed, afflicted with a terrible pain in the bowels."

The faces in the crowd looked solemn. They did not especially like Arno, who was widely suspected of cheating with his weights. "What is the boldest thing in the world?" began a riddle that they loved to repeat. "Arno's shirt, for it clasps a thief by the throat every day!" Nevertheless, the illness of their miller was of grave concern to the entire community. Without him, none of their grain could be turned into flour, for by law no villager could mill his own harvest.

"Two days ago"—the canon's voice was dark with accusation—"this belt was discovered in the woods near Hrotrud's cottage."

There was an awed murmur from the crowd, punctuated by scattered cries: "Witch!" "Sorceress!" "Burn her!"

The canon said to Hrotrud, "You stole the belt and made the knots in it to aid your evil incantations, which have brought Arno to the very brink of death."

"Never!" Hrotrud shouted indignantly, struggling against the bonds that held her. "I did no such thing! I've never seen that belt before! I never—"

Impatiently, the canon signaled to the men, who hoisted Hrotrud like a sack of oats, swung her back and forth several times, then released her at the height of the last swing. Hrotrud cried out in fear and anger as she sailed through the air and dropped with a splash directly into the center of the pond.

Joan and Aesculapius were jostled as people strained forward, trying to see. If Hrotrud rose to the surface of the pond and floated, that meant the priest-blessed waters had rejected her; she would be revealed as a sorceress and a witch and burned at the stake. If she sank, her innocence was proved and she was saved.

In tense silence, all eyes remained fixed on the surface of the pond. Ripples circled slowly outward from the spot where Hrotrud had entered the water; otherwise the surface was still.

The canon grunted and signaled the men, who immediately dashed into the water and dived down to search for Hrotrud.

"She is innocent of the charges against her," the canon pronounced. "God be praised."

Was it only Joan's imagination, or did he look disappointed?

The men kept diving and surfacing with no result. At last one of them broke the surface holding Hrotrud. She lay limp in his arms, her face swollen and discolored. He carried her to the edge of the pond and put her down. She did not stir. He bent over her, listening for a heartbeat.

After a moment he sat up. "She is dead," he announced.

A murmur went up from the crowd.

"Most unfortunate," the canon said. "But she died innocent of the crime of which she was accused. God knows His own; He will give recompense and rest to her soul."

The villagers dispersed, some making their way over to where Hrotrud's body lay, examining it curiously, some breaking into little groups that murmured and chattered in low tones.

Joan and Aesculapius walked back to the grubenhaus in silence. Joan was deeply disturbed by Hrotrud's death. She was ashamed of the excitement she had felt beforehand about witnessing the trial. But then she had not expected Hrotrud to die. Surely Hrotrud was not a witch; therefore Joan had believed God would prove her innocence.

And He had.

But then why did He let her die?

She didn't speak about it until later, after she had resumed her lesson back at the grubenhaus. She lowered her stylus in the middle of writing and asked suddenly, "Why would God do it?"

"Perhaps He didn't," Aesculapius responded, taking her meaning at once.

Joan stared at him. "Are you saying that such a thing could have happened in spite of His will?"

"Perhaps not. But the fault may lie in the nature of the trial rather than in the nature of God's will."

Joan considered that. "My father would say that this is how witches have been tried for hundreds of years."

"True enough."

"But that doesn't necessarily make it right." Joan looked at Aesculapius. "What would be a better way?"

"That," he said, "is for you to tell me."

Joan sighed. Aesculapius was so different from her father, or even Matthew. He refused to tell her things, insisting instead that she reason her own way to the answer. Joan tugged gently on the tip of her nose as she often did when thinking out a problem.

Of course. She had been blind not to see it at once. Cicero and the *De inventione*—until now, it had been merely an abstraction, a rhetorical ornament, an exercise for the mind.

"The evidentiary questions," Joan said. "Why couldn't they be brought to apply in this case?"

"Explain," Aesculapius said.

"*Quid:* there is the fact of the knotted belt—that is indisputable. But surely there is an argument about what it means. *Quis:* Who put the knots in the belt and placed it in the woods? *Quomodo:* How was it taken from Arno? *Quando, Ubi:* When and where was it taken? Did anyone actually see Hrotrud with it? *Cur:* Why should Hrotrud wish harm to Arno?" Joan spoke rapidly, excited by the possibilities of the idea. "Witnesses could be brought forward and questioned. And Hrotrud and Arno too—they could be questioned. Their answers might have determined Hrotrud's innocence. And"—Joan concluded ruefully—"she would not have had to die to prove it!"

They were on dangerous ground, and they knew it. They sat together in silence. Joan was overwhelmed by the enormity of the concept that had burst upon her: the application of logic to divine revelation, the possibility of an earthly justice in which the assumptions of faith were governed by rational inquiry, and belief was supported by the powers of reason.

Aesculapius said, "It would probably be wise not to mention this conversation to your father."

The Feast of St. Bertin was just past, the days were growing shorter, and so, of necessity, were the children's lessons. The sun was low in the sky when Aesculapius finally stood up.

"That, children, is enough for today."

"May I go now?" John asked. Aesculapius waved in dismissal, and he bounded from his seat and hurried outdoors.

Joan smiled ruefully at Aesculapius. John's obvious dislike for their studies embarrassed her. Aesculapius was frequently impatient, even sharp, with John. But her brother was a slow and unwilling student. "I can't do it!" he would wail the moment he met some new difficulty. There were times when Joan would have liked to shake him and shout, "Try! Try! How do you know you can't do it unless you try!"

Afterward, Joan reproached herself for such thoughts. John could not help being slow. Without John there would have been no lessons at all these past two years—and life without lessons had become unthinkable.

As soon as John had gone, Aesculapius said seriously, "I have something to tell you. I have been informed that my services are no longer needed at the schola. Another scholar, a Frankishman, has applied to be teaching master, and the bishop finds him more suitable for the position than I."

Joan was bewildered. "How can this be? Who is the man? He cannot possibly know as much as you!"

Aesculapius smiled. "That statement shows loyalty, if not wisdom. I have met the man; he is an excellent scholar, whose interests are better suited to the teachings of the schola than mine." Seeing that Joan did not take his meaning, he added, "There is a place for the kind of knowledge you and I have pursued together, Joan, and it is not within the walls of a cathedral. Remember what I tell you, and be careful: some ideas are dangerous."

"I understand," Joan said, though she didn't, completely. "But—what will you do now? How will you live?"

"I have a friend in Athens, a countryman who has achieved success as a merchant. He wants me to tutor his children."

"You are leaving?" Joan was unable to believe what he was telling her.

"He is prosperous; his offer is generous. I have little choice but to accept."

"You mean to go to Athens?" It was so far away. "When will you go?"

"In a month. I would have gone by now save for the pleasure I have taken in our work together."

"But—" Joan's mind raced, trying to think of something, anything to prevent this awful thing from happening. "You could live here, with us. You could be our tutor, John's and mine, and we could have lessons every day!"

"That is impossible, my dear. Your father has barely enough to sustain your family through the winter as it is. There is no room at your hearth or at your table for a stranger. Besides, I must go where I can continue my own work. The cathedral library will no longer be permitted me."

"Don't go." Grief rose within her like a palpable substance, forming a hard knot at the base of her throat. "Please don't go."

"My dear girl, I must. Though truly I wish it were not so." He stroked Joan's white-gold hair fondly. "I have learned much from teaching you; I do not look to have so apt a pupil again. You have a rare intelligence; it is God-given, and you must not deny it"—he glanced meaningfully at her—"whatever the cost."

Joan was afraid to speak lest her voice betray her emotions.

Aesculapius took her hand in his. "You must not worry. You will be able to continue your studies. I will make arrangements. I do not know exactly where, as yet, or how, but I will. Yours is too promising an intellect to lie fallow. We will find the seeds with which to sow it, I promise." He grasped her hand tightly. "Trust me in this."

After he had gone, Joan did not move from her little desk. She sat alone in the gathering darkness until her mother returned, carrying logs for the hearth.

"Ah, so you are finished?" said Gudrun. "Good! Now come help me build the fire."

✦ ✦ ✦

Aesculapius came to see her the day he left, dressed in his long blue traveling cloak. In his hands he carried a package wrapped in cloth.

"For you." He placed the package in her hands.

Joan unwrapped the strips of linen, then gasped as she saw what they had concealed. It was a book, bound in the Eastern fashion with leather-covered wooden boards.

"It is my own," said Aesculapius. "I made it myself, some years ago. It is an edition of Homer—the original Greek in the front half of the book, and a Latin translation in the back. It will help you keep your knowledge of the language fresh until the time you can begin your studies again."

Joan was speechless. A book of her own! Such a privilege was enjoyed only by monks and scholars of the highest rank. She opened it, looking at line after line of Aesculapius's neat uncial letters, filling the pages with words of inexpressible beauty. Aesculapius watched her, his eyes filled with tender sadness.

"Do not forget, Joan. Do not ever forget."

He opened his arms to her. She went to him, and for the first time they embraced. For a long while they clung to each other, Aesculapius's tall, broad form cradling Joan's small one. When at last they parted, his blue cloak was wet with Joan's tears.

She did not watch as he rode away. She stayed inside where he had left her, holding on to the book, grasping it so tightly that her hands ached.

Joan knew her father would not permit her to keep the book. He had never approved of her studies, and now, with Aesculapius gone, there was no one to stop him from enforcing his will. So she hid the book, rewrapping it carefully in its cloth and burying it under the thick straw on her side of the bed.

She was on fire to read it, to see the words, to hear again in her mind the joyous beauty of the poetry. But it was too dangerous; someone was usually in or near the cottage, and she feared discovery. Her only opportunity was at night. After everyone was asleep, she could read without risk of sudden interruption. But she needed some light—a candle, or at least some oil. The family got only two dozen candles a year—the canon was loath to take them from the sanctuary—and these were carefully conserved; she could not use one unnoticed. But the church storehouse had a huge stockpile of wax—the coloni of Ingelheim were required to supply the sanctuary with a hundred pounds a year. If she could get hold of some, she could fashion her own candle.

It wasn't easy, but in the end she managed to pilfer enough wax to make a small candle, using a piece of linen cord for a wick. It was a makeshift job—the flame was scarcely more than a flicker—but it was enough to provide light for study.

The first night she was cautious. She waited until long after her parents had retired to their bed behind the partition and she could hear the canon's snoring before daring to move. Finally she slid out of bed, silent and watchful as a fawn, careful not to disturb John, who lay beside her. He slept soundly, his head burrowed beneath the covers. Gently Joan removed the book from its hiding place in the straw and carried it to the small pine desk in the far corner of the room. She took her candle to the hearth and lit it in the glowing embers.

Returning to the desk, she held the candle close to the book. The light was faint and unsteady, but with an effort she could make out the lines of dark black ink. The neat letters danced in the flickering light, beckoning, inviting. Briefly Joan paused, savoring the moment. Then she turned the page and began.

The warm days and cool nights of Windumemanoth, the wine harvest month, passed swiftly. The harsh nordostroni winds arrived earlier than usual, blowing in from the northeast in strong, bone-chilling gusts. Once again the window of the grubenhaus was boarded up, but the frigid winds penetrated every crevice; to keep warm, they had to leave the hearth fire burning all day long, filling the place with sooty smoke.

Every night after her family slept, Joan rose and studied for hours in the darkness. She exhausted her candle and was forced to wait impatiently till she had pilfered some more wax from the church storehouse. When at last she was able to resume work, she drove herself relentlessly. She finished the book and then returned to the beginning, this time studying the complicated verb forms and copying them painstakingly onto her tablet until she knew them by heart. Her eyes were red and her head ached from the strain of working in the bad light, but it never occurred to her to stop. She was happy.

The Feast of St. Columban came and went, and there was still no word, no news of any arrangements for formal tutoring. Nevertheless, Joan kept faith with Aesculapius's promise. As long as she had his book, there was no cause for despair. She was continuing to learn, to make progress. Surely, surely something would happen soon. A tutor would arrive in the village, asking for her by name, or she would be summoned by the bishop and told of her acceptance into a schola.

Joan started work a little earlier each night. Sometimes she did not even wait till she heard her father's snoring. When she spilled some hot wax on the desk, she did not even notice.

One night she was working out a particularly difficult and interesting problem of syntax. Impatient to get started, she settled in at the desk not long after her parents had retired. She had been working only a few minutes when she heard a muffled sound from behind the partition.

She snuffed the candle flame and sat like a stone in the darkness, listening, feeling the leap of her pulse in her throat.

Several moments passed. There was no further sound. It must have been her imagination. Relief washed through her like a warm current. Still, she let a long time pass before she rose from the desk, went to the hearth to relight the wick, and returned with the glowing taper. The spark flared brightly, creating a little circle of light around the desk. At the edge of the circle, where the light met the shadows, was a pair of feet.

Her father's feet.

The canon stepped out of the darkness. Instinctively, Joan moved to hide the book from him, but it was too late.

His face, lit from below by the unsteady flame, was ghastly, terrifying. "What wickedness is this?"

Joan's voice was a whisper. "A book."

"A book!" He stared at it as if he could scarcely believe the evidence of his eyes. "How do you come by this? What are you doing with it?"

"Reading it. It—it's mine, it was given to me by Aesculapius. It's mine."

The force of her father's blow caught her by surprise, knocking her off the stool. She lay on the ground in a heap, the earthen floor cool against her cheek.

"Yours! Insolent child! *I* am master in this house!"

Joan raised herself on one elbow and watched helplessly as her father bent over the book, squinting to make out the words in the uncertain light. After a few moments he jerked upright, making the sign of the cross in the air above the desk. "Christ Jesus, protect us." Without taking his gaze from the book, he beckoned to Joan. "Come here."

Joan got up from the floor. She was dizzy, and there was a painful ringing in one ear. Slowly she walked over to her father.

"This is not the language of Holy Mother Church." He pointed to the open page before him. "What is the meaning of these marks? Answer me truly, child, as you value your immortal soul!"

"It is poetry, Father." Despite her fear, Joan felt a swell of pride in the knowledge. She did not dare add that the poetry was by Homer, whom her father regarded as a godless heathen. The canon knew no Greek. If he did not look at the Latin translation in the back, perhaps he would not realize what she had done.

Her father placed both hands on Joan's head, his broad peasant's fingers encircling her head just above the brow. *"Exorcizo te, immundissime spiritus, omnis incursio adversarii, omne phantasma . . ."* His hands tightened, squeezing so hard that Joan cried out in fear and pain.

Gudrun appeared in the doorway. "By all that's holy, Husband, what is the matter? Be careful with the child!"

"Silence!" the canon barked. "The child is possessed! Her demon must be exorcised." The pressure of his hands increased until Joan thought her eyes would burst.

Gudrun seized his arm. "Stop! She is just a child! Husband, stop! Would you kill her in your madness?"

The excruciating pressure ceased abruptly as the canon released his grip. He wheeled and with a single blow propelled Gudrun to the other side of the room. "Begone!" he roared. "This is no time for woman's weakness! I found the girl practicing magic in the night! With a witch's book! She is possessed!"

"No, Father, no!" Joan shrieked. "It is not witchcraft! It is poetry! Poetry written in Greek, that is all! I swear it!" He reached for her, but she ducked under his arm and circled behind him. He turned and advanced on her, eyes dark with menace.

He was going to kill her.

"Father! Turn to the back! The back of the book! It is written in Latin! You will see it! It is in Latin!"

The canon hesitated. Hurriedly Gudrun brought him the book. He did not look at it. He stared at Joan, considering.

"Please, Father. Only look at the back of the book. You can read it for yourself. It is not witchcraft!"

He took the book from Gudrun. She ran to get the candle and held it close to the page so he could see. He bent to examine the book, his thick, dark brows knitted in concentration.

Joan could not stop talking. "I was studying. I read by night so no one would know. I knew you would not approve." She would say anything, confess anything to make him believe. "It is Homer. The book of the *Iliad*. Homer's poem. It is not witchcraft, Father." She started to sob. "Not witchcraft."

The canon paid no attention. He read intently, his eyes close to the page, his mouth silently forming the words. After a moment he looked up.

"God be praised. It is not witchcraft. But it is the work of a godless heathen, and therefore an offense against the Lord." He turned to Gudrun. "Build up the fire. This abomination must be destroyed."

Joan gasped. Burn the book! Aesculapius's beautiful book, which he had given to her in trust!

"Father, the book is valuable! It is worth money; we could fetch a good price for it or"—her mind raced—"you could present it to the bishop as a gift for the cathedral library."

"Wicked child, you are so far sunk in sin it is a wonder you have not drowned in it. This is no fit gift for the bishop, nor for any God-fearing soul."

Gudrun went to the corner where the wood was stored and selected a few small logs. Joan watched numbly. She had to find some way to keep this from happening. If only the pain in her head would stop, she could think.

Gudrun stoked the embers, preparing the hearth for the fresh wood.

"Hold a moment." Abruptly, the canon addressed Gudrun. "Leave the fire be." He fingered the pages of the book appraisingly. "It is true that the parchment is valuable and might be put to good use." He placed the book on the desk and vanished into the next room.

What did it mean? Joan looked at her mother, who shrugged in bewilderment. Directly to her left, John sat upright in the bed. Awakened by the noise, he stared at Joan with large, round eyes.

The canon returned, carrying something long and shiny. It was his bone-handled hunting knife. As always, the sight of it filled Joan with a strong and bewildering sense of dread. The dim play of forgotten memory teased the edges of her awareness. Then it was gone, before she could remember what it was.

Her father sat at the desk. Turning the knife at an oblique angle so the sharp edge lay flat against the page, he scraped at the vellum. One of the letters on the page disappeared. He gave a little grunt of satisfaction.

"It works. I saw it done, once, at the monastery of Corbie. It leaves the pages clean so they can be used again. Now"—he motioned peremptorily to Joan—"you do it."

This, then, was to be her punishment. Her hand would be the one to destroy the book, to obliterate the forbidden knowledge and with it all her hopes.

Her father's eyes glittered with malevolent expectation.

Woodenly, she took the knife and sat at the desk. For a long moment she stared at the page. Then, holding the knife as she had seen her father do it, she moved the blade slowly over the surface of the page.

Nothing happened.

"It doesn't work." She looked up hopefully.

"Like this." The canon placed his hand over hers, applying pressure with a small lateral movement of the blade. Another letter disappeared. "Try again."

She thought of Aesculapius, of his long hours of labor making this book, of the faith he had shown in her when he entrusted it to her. The page blurred as tears rose to her eyes.

"Please. Don't make me. Please, Father."

"Daughter, you have offended God with your disobedience. In penance, you will work day and night until these pages are wholly cleansed of their ungodly contents. You will take nothing but bread and water until the task is complete. I will pray for God to have mercy upon you for your grievous sin." He pointed to the book. "Begin."

Joan placed the knife on the page and scraped as her father had shown her. One of the letters flaked, paled, and then disappeared. She moved the knife; another letter was obliterated. Then another. And another. Soon an entire word was gone, leaving only the rough, abraded surface of the parchment.

She moved the knife to begin on the next word. ἀλήθεια. Aletheia. *Truth.* Joan stopped, her hand poised over the word.

"Continue." Her father's voice was stern, commanding.

Truth. The round lines of the uncial letters stood out boldly against the pale parchment.

A fierce denial rose within her. All the fear and misery of the night gave way before one overwhelming conviction: *This must not be!*

She put down the knife. Slowly she looked up to meet her father's eyes. What she saw there made her draw her breath in sharply.

"Take up the knife." The menace in his voice was unmistakable.

Joan tried to speak, but her throat constricted and no words came. She shook her head no.

"Daughter of Eve, I will teach you to fear the tortures of Hell. Bring me the switch."

Joan went to the corner and retrieved the long, black stick which her father used on such occasions.

"Prepare yourself," the canon said.

She knelt on the floor in front of the hearth. Slowly, for her hands were shaking, she unclasped her gray woolen mantle and pulled off her linen tunic, exposing the bare flesh of her back.

"Begin the paternoster." Her father's voice was a low rumble behind her.

"Our Father, who art in Heaven—"

The first lash struck cleanly between the shoulders, parting the flesh, sending a piercing shaft of pain up her neck into her skull.

"Hallowed be thy Name—"

The second lash was harder. Joan bit her arm to keep from crying out. She had been beaten before, but never like this, never with such relentless, implacable force.

"Thy Kingdom come—"

The third lash bit deep into her torn flesh, drawing blood. The warm wetness trickled down her sides.

"Thy will be done—" The shock of the fourth lash jolted Joan's head upwards. She saw her brother watching intently from the bed. There was an odd expression on his face. Was it fear? Curiosity? Pity?

"On earth as it is—" The lash descended again. In the flash of a second before pain forced her eyes shut, Joan recognized the look on her brother's face. It was exultation.

"In Heaven. Give us this day—" The lash struck heavily. How many was it? Joan's senses reeled. She had never had to endure more than five.

Lash. Distantly, she heard someone screaming.

"Our daily bread. And forgive us . . . forgive—" Her mouth moved, but she could not form the words.

Lash.

With what power of thought was left her, Joan suddenly understood. This time it would not end. This time her father would not stop. This time he would continue until she was dead.

Lash.

The ringing in her ears built to a deafening crescendo. Then there was nothing but silence, and merciful darkness.

# 6

For days the village buzzed with the news of Joan's beating. The canon had lashed his daughter to within an inch of her life, it was said, and would have killed her had his wife's screams not attracted the attention of some villagers. It had taken three strong men to drag him away from the child.

But it wasn't the savagery of the beating that caused people to talk. Such things were common enough. Hadn't the blacksmith knocked his wife down and kicked her in the face until all her bones were broken, because he was tired of her nagging? The poor creature was disfigured for life, but there was nothing to do about it. A man was master in his own home, no one questioned that. The only law governing his absolute right to dispense punishment as he saw fit was one that limited the size of the club he could use. The canon had not used a club, in any case.

What was really interesting to the villagers was the fact that the canon had so far lost control of himself. Such violent emotion was unexpected, unseemly, in a man of God—so naturally everyone delighted in talking about it. Not since he had taken the Saxon woman to his bed had they had so much to gossip about. In little groups they whispered together, breaking off abruptly when the canon passed by.

Joan knew nothing of this. For an entire day after the beating, the canon forbade anyone to go near her. All that night and the following day Joan lay on the floor of the cottage unconscious. Dirt from the beaten earth floor clung to her lacerated flesh. By the time Gudrun was permitted to tend her, the wounds had corrupted and a dangerous fever set in.

Gudrun nursed her solicitously. She cleaned Joan's wounds with fresh water and bathed them with strong wine. Then, working with utmost gentleness to avoid further damage to the raw flesh, she applied a cooling paste of mulberry leaves.

*It's all the fault of the Greek,* Gudrun thought bitterly, as she made a hot posset and fed it to Joan, lifting her head and trickling the liquid into her mouth a few drops at a time. *Giving the child a book, filling her head with worthless ideas.* She was a girl, and therefore not meant for book study. The child was meant to be with her, to share the hidden secrets and the language of her people, to be the comfort and balm of her old age. *Evil the hour the Greek entered this house. May the wrath of all the gods descend upon him.*

Nevertheless, Gudrun's pride had been sparked by the child's display of bravery. Joan had defied her father with the fierce, heroic strength of her Saxon ancestors. Once Gudrun too had been strong and brave. But the long years of humiliation and exile in an alien land had gradually drained the will to fight out of her. *At least,* she thought proudly, *my blood runs true. The courage of my people runs strong within my daughter.*

She stopped to stroke Joan's throat, helping her swallow the healing broth. *Get well, little quail,* she thought. *Get well, and return to me.*

The fever broke early in the morning of the ninth day. Joan woke to find Gudrun bending over her.

"Mama?" Her voice sounded hoarse and unfamiliar in her ears.

Her mother smiled. "So you have returned to me at last, little quail. For a time I feared I had lost you."

Joan tried to raise herself but fell back heavily onto the straw. Pain pierced her, bringing back memory.

"The book?"

Gudrun's face tightened. "Your father has scraped the pages clean, and set your brother to copying some new nonsense onto it."

So it was gone.

Joan felt inexpressibly weary. She was sick; she wanted to sleep.

Gudrun held out a wooden bowl filled with steaming liquid. "Now you must eat to regain your strength. See, I have made you some broth."

"No." Joan shook her head weakly. "I don't want any." She did not want to get her strength back. She wanted to die. What was left to live for? She would never break free from the narrow confines of life in Ingelheim. Life had closed her in; there was no further hope of escape.

"Take a little now," Gudrun prodded, "and while you eat, I will sing you one of the old songs."

Joan turned her head away.

"Leave such things to the foolishness of priests. We have our own secrets, don't we, little quail? We will share them again, as we used to." Gudrun stroked Joan's forehead gently. "But first you must get well. Sip some broth. It is a Saxon recipe, with strong healing properties."

She held the wooden spoon to Joan's lips. Joan was too weak to resist; she allowed her mother to trickle a little broth into her mouth. It was good, warm and rich and comforting. Despite herself, she began to feel a little better.

"My little quail, my sweetheart, my darling." Gudrun's voice caressed Joan softly, seductively. She dipped the wooden ladle in the steaming broth and held it out to Joan, who sipped some more.

Her mother's voice rose and fell in the sweet, lilting strains of the familiar Saxon melody. Lulled by the sound and her mother's caresses, Joan drifted slowly into sleep.

With the fever past, Joan's strong young body mended quickly. In a fortnight, she was on her feet again. Her wounds closed cleanly, though it was plain she would bear the marks for the rest of her life. Gudrun lamented over the scars, long, dark stripes that turned Joan's back into an ugly patchwork, but Joan did not care. She did not care about anything very much. Hope was gone. She existed, that was all.

She spent all her time with her mother, rising at daybreak to help her feed the pigs and chickens, collect eggs, gather wood for the hearth fire, and haul heavy bucketfuls of water from the creek. Later they worked side by side preparing the day's meal.

One day they were making bread together, their fingers working to shape the heavy dough—for yeast and other leavenings were rarely used in this part of Frankland—when Joan asked suddenly, "Why did you marry him?"

The question took Gudrun aback. After a moment she said, "You cannot imagine what it was like for us when the armies of Karolus came."

"I know what they did to your people, Mama. What I can't understand is why, after that, you came away with the enemy—with *him*?"

Gudrun did not reply.

*I've offended her,* Joan thought. *She will not tell me now.*

"By winter," Gudrun began slowly, "we were starving, for the Christian soldiers had burned our crops along with our homes." She looked past

Joan, as if picturing something distant. "We ate anything we could find—grass, thistles, even the seeds contained in the dung of animals. We were not far from death when your father and the other missionaries arrived. They were different from the others; they carried no swords or weapons, and they dealt with us like people, not brute beasts. They gave us food in return for our promise to listen to them preach the word of the Christian God."

"They traded food for faith?" Joan asked. "A sorry way to win people's souls."

"I was young and impressionable, sick unto death of hunger and misery and fear. Their Christian God must be greater than ours, I thought, or else how had they succeeded in defeating us? Your father took a special interest in me. He had great hopes for me, he said, for though I was heathen born, he was sure I had the capacity to understand the True Faith. From the way he looked at me, I knew he desired me. When he asked me to come away with him, I consented. It was a chance at life, when all around was death." Her voice dropped to a whisper. "It was not long before I realized how great a mistake I'd made."

Her eyes were red rimmed, brimming with barely suppressed tears. Joan put an arm around her. "Don't cry, Mama."

"You must learn from my mistake," Gudrun said fiercely, "so you do not repeat it. To marry is to surrender everything—not only your body but your pride, your independence, even your life. Do you understand? *Do you?*" She gripped Joan's arm, fixing her with an urgent look. "Heed my words, daughter, if you ever mean to be happy: *Never give yourself to a man.*"

The scarred flesh on Joan's back quivered with the remembered pain of her father's lash. "No, Mama," she promised solemnly, "I never will."

In Ostarmanoth, when warm spring breezes caressed the earth and the animals were set out to pasture, the monotony was broken by the arrival of a stranger. It was a Thursday—Thor's Day, Gudrun still called it when the canon was not around to hear—and the rumble of that god's thunder was sounding in the distance as Joan and Gudrun worked together in the family garden. Joan was pulling up nettles and destroying molehills, while Gudrun followed after her, tracing the furrows and crushing the clods with a thick oaken plank. As she worked, Gudrun sang and told tales of the Old Ones. When Joan answered in Saxon, Gudrun laughed with pleasure. Joan had just finished a row when she looked up and saw John hurrying across the field toward them. She tapped her mother's arm in warning; Gudrun saw her son, and the Saxon words died on her lips.

"Quick!" John was breathless from running. "Father wants you at the house now. Hurry!" He pulled Gudrun by the arm.

"Gently, John," Gudrun reprimanded. "You're hurting me. What has happened? Is anything wrong?"

"I don't know." John kept tugging on his mother's arm. "He said something about a visitor. I don't know who. But hurry. He said he'd box my ears if I didn't bring you right away."

The canon was waiting for them at the grubenhaus door. "It took you long enough," he said.

Gudrun stared at him coolly. A tiny spark of anger ignited in the canon's eyes; he drew himself up importantly. "An emissary is coming. From the Bishop of Dorstadt." He paused for effect. "Go and prepare a suitable meal. I will meet him at the cathedral and lead him here." He dismissed her with a wave of the hand. "Be quick, woman! He will arrive soon." He left, slamming the door behind him.

Gudrun's face was rigidly expressionless. "Start with the pottage," she said to Joan. "I'll go collect some eggs."

Joan poured water from the oaken bucket into the large iron pot the family used for cooking and set the pot over the hearth fire. From a woolen sack, almost empty now after the long winter, she took handfuls of dried barley and threw them into the pot. She noticed, with surprise, that her hands shook with excitement. It had been so long since she had felt anything.

But an emissary from Dorstadt! Could it have anything to do with her? After all this time, had Aesculapius finally managed to find a way for her to resume her studies?

She cut off a slab of salt pork and added it to the pot. No, it was impossible. It was almost a year since Aesculapius had left. If he had been able to arrange anything, she would have heard long ago. It was dangerous to hope. Hope had nearly destroyed her once; she would not be so foolish again.

Nevertheless, she could not still her excitement when the door opened one hour later. Her father entered, followed by a dark-haired man. He was not at all what she had imagined. He had the blunt, unintelligent features of a *colonus,* and he carried himself more like a soldier than a scholar. His tunic, bearing the insignia of the bishop, was rumpled and dusty from travel.

"You will do us the honor of supping with us?" Joan's father indicated the pot boiling on the hearth.

"Thank you, but I cannot." He spoke in Theodisk, the common tongue, not Latin, another surprise. "I left the rest of the escort at a *cella* outside Mainz—the forest path is too slow and narrow for ten men and horse—and came ahead alone. I must rejoin them tonight; in the morning we begin the return journey to Dorstadt." He withdrew a parchment scroll from his scrip and handed it to the canon. "From his Eminence the Lord Bishop of Dorstadt."

Carefully the canon broke the seal; the stiff parchment crackled as it was unrolled. Joan watched her father closely as he squinted to make out the writing. He read all the way to the bottom, then began again, as if searching for something he had missed. Finally he looked up, his lips tight with anger.

"What is the meaning of this? I was told your message had to do with me!"

"So it does." The man smiled. "Insofar as you are the child's father."

"The bishop has nothing to say about my work?"

The man shrugged. "All I know, Father, is that I am to escort the child to the schola in Dorstadt, as the letter says."

Joan cried out in a sudden rush of emotion. Gudrun hurried over and placed an arm protectively around her.

The canon hesitated, eyeing the stranger. Abruptly, he came to a decision. "Very well. It's true that it is a fine opportunity for the child, though it will be hard enough for me without his help." He turned to John. "Gather your belongings, and be quick. Tomorrow you ride for Dorstadt, to begin studies at the cathedral in accordance with the bishop's express command."

Joan gasped. *John* was being called to study at the schola? How could this be?

The stranger shook his head. "With all respect, Holy Father, I believe it's a girl child I'm supposed to bring back with me. A girl by the name of Johanna."

Joan stepped out of her mother's encircling arm. "I am Johanna."

The bishop's man turned to her. The canon stepped quickly between them.

"Nonsense. It's my son Johannes the bishop wants. Johannes, Johanna. *Lapsus calami.* A slip of the pen. A simple mistake on the part of the bishop's amanuensis, that is all. It happens often enough, even among the best of scribes."

The stranger looked doubtful. "I don't know . . ."

"Use your head, man. What would the bishop want with a girl?"

"It did strike me as odd," the man agreed.

Joan started to protest, but Gudrun drew her back and placed a warning finger over her lips.

The canon continued. "My son, on the other hand, has been studying the Scriptures since he was a babe. Recite from the Book of Revelation for our honored guest, Johannes."

John paled and began to stammer. *"Acopa . . . Apocalypsis Jesu Christi quo . . . quam dedit illi Deus palam fa . . . facere servis—"*

The stranger impatiently signaled a stop to the unsteady flow of words. "There is no time. We must leave immediately if we are to reach the cella before dark." He looked uncertainly from John to Joan. Then he turned to Gudrun.

"Who is this woman?"

The canon cleared his throat. "A Saxon heathen whose soul I am laboring to bring to Christ."

The bishop's man took note of Gudrun's blue eyes and slim form and the white-gold hair peeking out from under her white linen cap. He smiled, a broad, knowing, gap-toothed grin, then addressed himself directly to her.

"You are the children's mother?"

Gudrun nodded wordlessly. The canon flushed.

"What do you say, then? Is it the boy the bishop wants, or the girl?"

"Disrespectful dog!" The canon was furious. "You dare to question the word of a sworn servant of God!"

"Calm yourself, Holy Father." The man emphasized the word *holy* ever so slightly. "Let me remind you of the duty you owe to the authority I represent."

The canon glared at the bishop's man, his face purpling.

Again the man asked Gudrun, "Is it the boy? Or the girl?"

Joan felt Gudrun's arms tighten around her, drawing her close. There was a long pause. Then she heard her mother's voice behind her, musical and sweet, filled with the broad Saxon vowels that still marked her, unmistakably, as a foreigner. "The boy is the one you want," Gudrun said. "Take him."

"Mama!" Shocked at this unexpected betrayal, Joan could only utter the single, startled cry.

The bishop's messenger nodded, satisfied. "Then it is settled." He turned toward the door. "I must see to my horse. Have the boy ready as quickly as possible."

"No!" Joan tried to stop him, but Gudrun held her tight, whispering in Saxon, "Trust me, little quail. It is for the best, I promise you."

"No!" Joan struggled to free herself. It was a lie. This was Aesculapius's doing. Joan was certain of it. He had not forgotten her; he had found a way at last for her to continue what they had begun together. John wasn't the one being called to study at the schola. It was all wrong.

"No!" She twisted sharply, broke loose, and made straight for the door. The canon reached for her, but she evaded him. Then she was outside, running swiftly toward the retreating messenger. Behind her, in the cottage, she heard her father shouting, then her mother's voice, tense, tearful, raised in reply.

She caught up with the man just as he reached his horse. She tugged at his tunic, and he looked at her. From the corner of her eye, Joan saw her father advancing toward them.

There wasn't much time. Her message had to be convincing, unmistakable.

*"Magna est veritas et praevalebit,"* she said. It was a passage from Esdras, obscure enough to be recognized only to those well versed in the writings of the Holy Fathers. "The truth is great, and it will prevail." He was the bishop's man, a man of the Church, he would know it. And the fact that she knew it, that she spoke Latin, would prove that *she* was the scholar the bishop sought.

*"Lapsus calami non est,"* she continued in Latin. "There is no error in the writing. I am Johanna; I am the one you want."

The man looked at her, his eyes kind. "Eh? What's this, bright eyes? What a mighty stream of words!" He chucked her under the chin. "Sorry, child. I speak none of your Saxon tongue. Though having seen your mother, I begin to wish I did." He reached into a pouch tied to his saddle and withdrew a sugared date. "Here, have a sweet."

Joan stared at the date. The man hadn't understood a word. A scion of the Church, the bishop's emissary, and he had no Latin. How was it possible?

Her father's footsteps sounded close behind her. His arm gripped her painfully around the waist; then she was lifted off the ground and carried back toward the house.

"No!" she screamed. Her father's large hand covered her nose and mouth, pressing so hard she could not breathe. She kicked and struggled. Inside the cottage he released her, and she fell to the floor, gulping air. He raised his fist over her.

"No!" Suddenly Gudrun was between them. "You will not touch her." There was a tone in her voice that Joan had never heard before. "Or I will tell the truth."

The canon stared in disbelief. John appeared in the doorway, carrying a linen sack stuffed with his belongings.

Gudrun nodded toward him. "Our son needs your blessing for the journey."

For a long time the canon held her gaze. Then, very slowly, he turned to face his son.

"Kneel, Johannes."

John knelt. The canon placed his hand on his bowed head. "O God, Who didst call Abraham to leave his home and didst protect him in all his wanderings, unto Thee we commit this boy."

A thin stream of late afternoon sun filtered through the window, illuminating John's dark hair with a rich light.

"Watch over him and provide all things needful for his soul and body . . ." The canon's voice assumed a singsong rhythm as he prayed.

Keeping his head bowed, John looked up and met his sister's gaze, his eyes wide and frightened, eloquent with appeal. *He doesn't want to go,* Joan realized suddenly. Of course! Why had she not seen it before? She had not given a thought to John's feelings. *He is afraid. He cannot keep up with the demands of a schola, and he knows it.*

*If only I could go with him.*

A plan began to formulate in her mind.

". . . and when life's pilgrimage is over," the canon finished, "may he arrive safely at the heavenly country, through Christ Jesus our Lord. Amen."

The blessing over, John rose to his feet. Stolid, unresisting, like a sheep before the sacrifice, he endured his mother's embraces and his father's last-minute admonitions. But when Joan approached and put her arms around him, he clutched her and began to sob.

"Don't be afraid," she murmured reassuringly.

"Enough," the canon said. He placed an arm around his son's shoulder, shepherding him toward the door. "Keep the girl inside," he commanded Gudrun, and then they were gone. The door swung shut with a hollow thud.

Joan ran to the window and peered out. She saw John mount behind the bishop's emissary, his plain woolen tunic contrasting with the rich red of the stranger's robes. The canon stood nearby, his dark, squat figure outlined against the budding green of the landscape. With a last shout of farewell, they rode off.

Joan turned from the window. Gudrun stood in the middle of the room, watching her.

"Little quail . . . ," Gudrun began hesitantly.

Joan walked past her as if she did not exist. She took up her pile of mending and sat by the hearth. She needed to think, to prepare. There wasn't much time, and everything had to be worked out very carefully.

It would be difficult, probably even dangerous. The thought frightened her, but it made no difference. With a certainty at once wonderful and terrifying, Joan knew what she must do.

*It's not fair,* John thought. He rode sullenly behind the bishop's man, scowling at the insignia on the red tunic. *I don't want to go.* He hated his father for making him. He reached inside his tunic, searching for the object he had secretly placed there before he left. His fingers touched the smooth handle of the knife—his father's bone-handled knife, one of his treasures.

A small, vengeful smile touched John's lips. His father would be furious when he discovered it missing. No matter. By then John would be miles away from Ingelheim, and there was nothing his father could do about it. It was a small triumph, but he clung to it in the misery of his situation.

*Why didn't he send Joan?* John asked himself angrily. Black resentment simmered inside him. *It's all her fault,* he thought. Because of Joan, he had already endured over two years of lessons from Aesculapius, that tedious and evil-tempered old man. Now he was being sent away to the schola at Dorstadt in *her* place. Oh, it was Joan the bishop wanted, John was sure of it. It had to be Joan. *She* was the smart one, *she* knew Latin and Greek, *she* could read Augustine when he still hadn't mastered all the psalms.

He might have forgiven her that, and more besides. She was, after all, his sister. But there was one thing that John could not forgive: Joan was Mama's pet. He had overheard them often enough, laughing and whispering together in Saxon, then breaking off abruptly when he joined them. They thought he didn't hear them, but he did. Mama never spoke the Old Tongue with him. *Why?* John asked himself bitterly for the thousandth time. *Does she think I'd tell Father? I wouldn't—not for anything, no matter what he did, not even if he beat me.*

*It isn't fair,* he thought again. *Why should she prefer Joan to me? I'm her son, which everybody knows is better than a useless daughter.* Joan was a sorry excuse for a girl. She couldn't sew or spin or weave half as well as other girls her age. Then there was her interest in book learning, which everyone knew to be unnatural. Even Mama saw there was something wrong there. The other children in the village constantly mocked Joan. It was embarrassing, having her as a sister; John would gladly disclaim her, if he could.

Immediately after he had the thought, he felt a twinge of conscience. Joan had always been good to him, had stood up for him when Father was angry, even done his work for him when he couldn't understand. He was grateful for her help—she had saved him from many a beating—but at the same time, he resented it. It was humiliating. After all, he was her older brother. *He* was the one who should look after her, not the other way around.

Now, because of her, he was riding behind this strange man toward a place he did not know and a life he did not want. He pictured his life at the schola, trapped inside some dreary room all day, surrounded by piles of boring, awful books.

Why couldn't Father understand that he didn't want to go? *I'm not Matthew; I'll never be good at book studies.* Nor did he mean to be a scholar or a cleric. He knew what he wanted: to be a warrior, a warrior in the Emperor's army, battling to subdue the heathen hordes. He had gotten the idea from Ulfert, the saddler, who had gone with Count Hugo on the old Emperor's campaign against the Saxons. What wonderful tales the old man told, sitting in his workshop, his tools temporarily forgotten by his side, his eyes lit with the memory of that great victory! "Like the thrushes that fly over the autumn vineyards, pecking at the grapes"—John remembered every word exactly as old Ulfert had spoken them—"we flew over the land, a holy canticle on our lips, ferreting out the heathens hiding in the woods and marshes and concealed in the ditches, men and women and children alike. There was not one of us whose bucklers and swords were not red with blood that day. By sunset, there was no soul left alive who had not renounced their godless ways and sworn eternal allegiance on their knees to the True Faith." Then old Ulfert had brought out his sword, which he had wrested, still warm, from the dead hand of one of the heathens. Its handle shone with glassy gems; its shaft was a gleaming yellow. Unlike Frankish swords, which were fashioned of iron, it was made from gold—an inferior material, Ulfert explained, lacking the solidity and bite of Frankish weapons, but beautiful nonetheless. John's heart had swelled at the sight of it. Old Ulfert had held it out to him, and John had grasped it, feeling its balance, its weight. His hand fit the gemmed handle as if it were made for it. He swung the sword over his head; it sliced the air with a thrumming sound that kept rhythm with the singing in his blood. He had known then he was born to be a warrior.

There were rumors, even now, of a new campaign in the spring. Perhaps Count Hugo would answer the Emperor's call again. If so, John planned to go with him, no matter what Father said. He would be fourteen soon, a man's age—many had gone to war at that age, even younger. He would run off, if necessary, but he would go.

Of course, that would be difficult now that he was to be imprisoned in the schola at Dorstadt. Would word of the new conscript even travel so far? he wondered. And if it did, would he be able to get away?

The thought was upsetting, and he put it out of his mind. Instead, he called up his favorite daydream. He was in the front ranks of the battle, the silver banners of the count gleaming before him, drawing him forward. They were driving the scattered and defeated heathens before them. They flew from him, desperate and frightened, the women's long, white-gold hair waving in the wind. He ran them down, wielding his long sword with great skill, slashing and killing, offering no mercy, until finally they submitted to him, repenting their blindness and showing themselves willing to accept the Light.

The corners of John's mouth lifted in a drowsy smile as the steady beat of the horse's hooves signaled their progress through the darkening forest.

✦ ✦ ✦

There was a whirring sound, followed by a heavy thud.

"Unnhh." The bishop's man jolted backward. His shoulder rammed into John, jarring him from sleep.

"Hey!" John protested, but already the man was falling, the weight of his pendulous body dragging John irresistibly from the saddle.

They dropped to the ground together. John landed on top of the bishop's man, who lay unmoving where he fell. As John put his hand out to raise himself, his fingers closed around something long and round and smooth.

It was the shaft of an arrow, yellow feathers at the end. The tip was buried deep in the middle of the man's chest.

John rose to his feet, all his senses alert. From the thick trees on the other side of the path, a man emerged, dressed in tattered clothes. In his hands he carried a bow, and on his back a quiverful of yellow-feathered arrows.

*Does he mean to kill me too?*

The man came toward him. John looked around, seeking a path of escape. The trees grew dense in this part of the woods; if he ran, he might be able to elude the attacker.

The man was almost upon him, close enough for John to read the menace in his eyes.

John tried to run, but it was too late. The man grabbed him by the arm. John struggled, but the man, taller than he by a head and powerfully built, held him fast, lifting him slightly so that his toes barely touched the ground.

John remembered the knife. With his free hand, he reached inside his tunic; frantically his fingers sought the bone handle, found it, gripped it. He pulled the knife out and plunged it home in one swift motion. With an exhilarating rush, John felt it sink deep into the man's flesh, striking bone before John withdrew it with a wicked twist. The man swore and grabbed his wounded shoulder, letting go of John.

John ran into the woods. Sharp branches tore at his clothes and scratched his skin, but he kept running. Despite the moonlight, it was dark under the canopy of trees. Looking behind him to see if he was being pursued, John bumped into a beech with low-hanging branches. He leapt for the bottommost branch, caught it, and started to scramble up quickly, his lithe young body snaking expertly through the branches, stopping only when the limbs became too small and pliant to support his weight. Then he waited.

There was no sound except the soft rustle of leaves. Twice a night owl called, its cry echoing eerily in the stillness. Then John heard footsteps crashing through the forest. He gripped the knife, holding his breath, grateful for his plain brown cloak, which merged so well with the blackness of the night.

The footsteps came closer and closer. John could hear the man's ragged, uneven breathing.

The footsteps stopped directly beneath him.

Joan stepped out of the silent darkness of the grubenhaus into the moonlit night. Shapes of familiar objects loomed eerily, transformed by shadows. She shivered, recalling stories of *Waldleuten,* evil sprites and trolls that haunted the night. Gathering her cloak of rough gray hemp around her, she moved into the shadows, searching the changed landscape for the entrance to the path through the forest. The light was good—it lacked only two days till full moon—and in a moment she was able to make out the old oak, split by lightning, that marked the spot. She ran quickly across the field toward it.

At the edge of the woods she paused. It was dark in there, the moon filtered by the trees into pale threads of light. She looked back at the grubenhaus. Washed by moonlight, surrounded by the fields and animal pens, it was solid, warm, familiar. She thought of her comfortable bed, the coverings probably still warm from the heat of her body. She thought of Mama, to whom she had not even said good-bye. She took a step toward home, then stopped. All that mattered, all she wanted, lay in the other direction.

She entered the woods. The trees closed over her head. The path was strewn with rocks and underbrush, but she moved ahead swiftly. It was fifteen miles to the cella, and she had to be there before dawn.

She concentrated on keeping a steady pace. It was hard going; in the darkness it was easy to stray toward the edge of the path, where branches tore at her clothes and hair. The path became more and more uneven. Several times she tripped on rocks or broken roots; once she fell, bruising her hands and knees.

After several hours, the sky began to show light above the roof of trees. It was nearing dawn. Joan was exhausted, but she quickened her pace, half-walking, half-running down the path. She had to make it before they left. She had to.

Her left foot caught on something. She tried to regain her balance, but she was moving too quickly and she fell, breaking her fall clumsily with her arms.

She lay still, the breath knocked out of her. Her right arm hurt where a sharp twig had scraped it, but otherwise she did not seem to be injured. She pushed herself into a sitting position.

On the ground beside her, a man lay with his back to her. Sleeping? No. He would have wakened when she stumbled over him. She touched his shoulder; he rolled onto his back. The dead eyes of the bishop's emissary glared up at her, lips frozen in a gap-toothed grimace. His rich tunic was ripped and bloody. The middle finger of his left hand was missing.

Joan leapt to her feet. "John!" she shouted. She scanned the woods and the ground nearby, afraid of what she might find.

"Here." A patch of pale skin showed faintly in the darkness.

"John!" She ran to him, and they embraced, holding on to each other tightly.

"Why are you here?" John asked. "Is Father with you?"

"No. I'll explain later. Are you hurt? What happened?"

"We were attacked. A brigand, I think, after the emissary's gold ring. I was riding behind when the arrow struck him."

Joan said nothing, but hugged him closer.

He pulled out of her arms. "But I defended myself. I did!" His eyes glittered with a strange excitement. "When he came for me, I struck him with this!" He held up the canon's bone-handled hunting knife. "Got him in the shoulder, I think. Anyway, it stopped him long enough for me to get away!"

Joan stared at the blade, discolored with blood. "Father's knife."

John's expression turned sullen. "Yes. I took it. Why not? He made me go—I didn't want to."

"All right," Joan said briskly. "Put it away. We must hurry if we are to make it to the cella before dawn."

"The cella? But I don't have to go to Dorstadt now. After what happened"—he thrust his head in the direction of the murdered emissary—"I can go home."

"No, John. *Think*. Now that Father knows the bishop's intentions, he will not permit you to stay at home. He'll find some way to get you to the schola, even if he has to take you himself. Besides"—Joan pointed to the knife—"by the time we get back, he will have discovered that you took this."

John looked startled. Obviously he had not thought of that.

"It will be all right. I'll be there with you, I'll help you." She took his hand. "Come."

Hand in hand, under the steadily brightening sky, the two children made their way to the cella, where the rest of the bishop's men were waiting.

# 7

They arrived at the cella while the sun was still low in the sky, but the bishop's men were already awake, impatiently awaiting their companion's return. When Joan and John told them what had transpired, the men became suspicious. They took John's bone-handled knife and examined it carefully. Joan breathed a prayer of thanks that she had thought to clean it thoroughly in the forest stream, washing off all trace of blood. The men rode back to find their companion's body, taking Joan and John with them; the discovery of the yellow-feathered arrow confirmed the children's story. But what should they do with the body? It was out of the question to carry it all the way to Dorstadt, a fortnight's journey, not with the spring sun making the days so warm. In the end they buried their companion in the forest, marking the spot with a rough wooden cross. Joan said a prayer over the grave, which impressed the men, for, like their companion, they knew no Latin. Expecting to escort a girl child, the men did not, at first, want to take John.

"There's no mount for him," their leader said, "nor food neither."

"We can ride tandem," Joan offered. "And share a ration."

The man shook his head. "The bishop sent for *you*. There's no point bringing your brother."

"My father made a compact with your companion," Joan lied. "I was permitted to go only on condition that John accompany me. If he doesn't, my father will call me home again—and you'll be put to the trouble of escorting me back."

The man frowned; having just endured the discomforts of a long journey, he did not relish the prospect of another.

Joan pressed her advantage. "If that happens, I'll tell the bishop that I tried my best to explain the situation, and you wouldn't listen. Will he be pleased to learn that the entire misunderstanding was your fault?"

The man was stunned. He had never heard a girl speak so boldly. Now he understood why the bishop wanted to see her; she was a curiosity, that was for certain.

"Very well," he agreed grudgingly. "The boy can come."

It was an exhausting journey to Dorstadt, for the men of the escort were eager to get home and rode long and hard every day. The rigors of the journey did not trouble Joan; she was fascinated by the ever-changing landscape and the new world which every day opened before her. At last she was free, free from Ingelheim and the confines of her existence there. She rode through squalid little villages and bustling towns with equal delight, full of curiosity and wonder. John, however, quickly grew irritable from lack of sufficient food and rest. Joan tried to soothe him, but his ill humor was only inflamed by his sister's good-natured solicitude.

They reached the bishop's palace at noontide of the tenth day. The palace steward took one disapproving look at the two children, in their stained and rumpled peasants' garments, and gave orders for baths and clean clothing before he would permit them to be admitted to the bishop's presence.

For Joan, accustomed to hurried washings in the stream that ran behind the grubenhaus, the bath was an extraordinary experience. The bishop's palace had indoor baths, with heated water, a luxury she had never even heard of. She remained in the warm water for almost an hour while serving women scrubbed her till her skin glowed pink and almost raw. Her back, however, they cleansed with utmost gentleness, clucking their tongues sympathetically over the jagged scars. They washed her hair and twisted the long, white-gold mass into shining plaits that framed her face. Then they brought her a new tunic of green linen. The texture was so soft, the weaving so fine, Joan found it hard to believe it had been made by human hands. When she was dressed, the women brought her a looking glass set in gold. Joan lifted it and saw the face of a stranger. She had never viewed her own features, except in occasional distorted fragments reflected by the muddy water of the village pond. Joan was astonished by the clarity of the image in the mirror. She held the mirror up, scrutinizing herself critically.

She was not pretty, but she knew that. She did not have the high, pale forehead, delicate chin, and frail, slope-shouldered form so favored by minstrels and lovers. She had a ruddy, healthy, boyish look. Her brow was too low, her chin too firm, her shoulders too straight for beauty. But her hair—Mama's hair—was lovely, and her eyes were good—deep-set gray-green orbs, fringed with thick lashes. She shrugged and put the glass down. The bishop had not sent for her to discover if she was pretty.

John was brought in, equally resplendent in tunic and mantle of blue linen. The two children were taken to the palace steward.

"Better," the steward said, examining them appraisingly. "Much better. Very well, then, follow me."

They walked down a long corridor whose walls were covered with enormous tapestries intricately worked with gold and silver thread. Joan's pulse leapt nervously in her throat. She was going to meet the bishop.

*Will I be able to answer his questions? Will he accept me in the schola?* All at once she felt inadequate and unsure. She tried to remember a single thing she had studied, but her mind went blank. When she thought of Aesculapius, of the faith he had shown in her by arranging this interview, her stomach clenched.

They stopped before a huge pair of double-sided oaken doors. From inside came a din of voices and a clattering of plates. The palace steward nodded at the house knave positioned at the entrance, and the man swung the heavy doors open.

Joan and John walked into the room, then stopped, gaping. Some two hundred people were gathered in the hall, seated at long tables piled high with food. Platters filled with every variety of roasted meat—capons, geese, moorhens, and several haunches of stag—crowded together on the tables within easy reach of the diners, who pulled off chunks of flesh with their fingers and stuffed it in their mouths, wiping their hands on their sleeves. In the center of the largest table, half devoured but still recognizable, rested the enormous head of a roasted boar, larded with sauce. There were pottages and pasties, peeled walnuts, figs, dates, white and vermilion sugarplums, and many other dishes which Joan could not identify. She had never seen so much food in one place in her life.

"A song! A song!" Pewter cups banged on the wooden tables, rhythmic, insistent. "Come, Widukind, a song!" A tall, fair-skinned young man was prodded to his feet and rose, laughing.

*"Ik gihorta dat seggen dat sih urhettun aenon muo tin, hiltibraht enti hadubrant . . ."*

Joan was surprised. The young man sang in Theodisk, the common tongue—the canon would have called it the pagan tongue.

"This I have heard told, that warriors met singly, Hildebrand and Hadubrand between two armies . . ."

The men stood and joined in, holding their cups high. ". . . they let glide spears of ashwood, sharp showers; they stepped together and cleft the battle boards until their shields of limewood shattered hacked by the weapons . . ."

An odd song for a bishop's table. Joan glanced sidelong at John, but he was listening raptly, eyes alight with excitement.

With an exultant shout, the men finished the song. There was a loud scraping of wood as they sat, pulling the long planked benches up to the tables.

Another man rose with a taunting smile. "I heard of something rising in a corner . . ." He paused expectantly.

"A riddle!" someone cried, and the crowd bellowed its approval. "One of Haido's riddles! Yes! Yes! Let's have it."

The man called Haido waited till the noise abated. "I heard of something rising in a corner," he repeated, "swelling and standing up, lifting its cover. The proud-hearted bride grabbed at that boneless wonder with her hands . . ."

A knowing chuckle began to build among the guests.

". . . the prince's daughter covered that swelling thing with a swirl of cloth." Haido's smiling eyes raked the room challengingly. "What is it?"

"Look between your legs," someone shouted, "and you'll find the answer right enough!" This was followed by more laughter and a barrage of obscene gestures. Joan watched in astonishment. *This* was a bishop's residence?

"Wrong!" Haido retorted merrily. "You are all wrong!"

"The answer, then! The answer!" People shouted and banged their cups on the tables.

Haido paused a moment for dramatic effect.

"Dough!" he announced triumphantly, and sat down as a wave of shouting laughter shook the room.

When the noise subsided, the steward said, "Come with me," and led the two children to the far end of the hall, where the high table rested on its dais. The bishop sat in the center, still chuckling, dressed in magnificent yellow silk stained with drops of grease and wine. A soft down pillow cushioned his place on the bench. He did not look at all as Joan had imagined him. He was a big man, thick necked; the muscularity of his chest and shoulders showed through his thin silken tunic. His large belly and florid face were those of a man who enjoyed his food and wine. As they approached, he leaned over and held a crimson sweetmeat to the lips of a buxom woman seated beside him. She bit it, then whispered something in his ear, and they both laughed.

The palace steward cleared his throat. "My lord, the men have returned from Ingelheim with the child."

The bishop stared at the steward opaquely. "Child? Eh? What child?"

"The one you sent for, my lord. A candidate for the schola, I believe. Recommended to you by the Gr—"

"Yes, yes." The bishop waved impatiently. "I remember now." His arm rested lightly around the woman's shoulders. He looked at Joan and John. "Well, Widukind, am I seeing double?"

"No, Lord. The canon sent his son as well. The two of them arrived at the cella together and would not be separated."

"Well." The bishop's face shone with amusement. "What do you think of that? I ask for one and get two. Would the Emperor were so generous with his favors as this country prelate!"

The table roared with laughter. There were several shouts of "Hear, hear!" and "Amen!"

The bishop reached over and ripped a leg off a roast hen. He said to Joan, "Are you the scholar you have been made out to be?"

Joan hesitated, unsure of what to say. "I have studied hard, Eminence."

"Pah! Studying!" The bishop snorted. He took a bite of chicken. "The schola is filled with dunderheads who study but know nothing. What do you *know,* child?"

"I can read and write, Eminence."

"In Theodisk or in Latin?"

"In Theodisk, in Latin, and in Greek."

"Greek! Now that is something. Even Odo has no Greek, have you, Odo?" He grinned at a thin-faced man a few seats away.

Odo spread his mouth in a humorless smile. "It is a pagan tongue, Sire, a tongue of idolaters and heretics."

"Quite correct, quite correct." The bishop's tone was taunting. "Odo is always correct, aren't you, Odo?"

The cleric sniffed. "You know well, Eminence, that I do not approve of this latest whim of yours. It is dangerous, and ungodly, to allow a woman into the schola."

From the back of the hall a voice called out, "She's no woman yet, from the looks of her." Another tide of laughter swept the hall, accompanied by lewd remarks.

A burning warmth crept from Joan's throat up to her cheeks. How could these people behave so in the presence of the bishop?

"It is also pointless," the man called Odo continued when the noise died down. "Women are, by nature, quite incapable of reasoning." His eyes flicked over Joan dismissively, then returned to the bishop. "Their natural humors, which are cold and moist, are unpropitious for cerebral activity. They cannot comprehend the higher spiritual and moral concepts."

Joan stared at the man.

"I have heard that opinion expressed," the bishop said. He smiled at Odo with the look of a man who was enjoying himself immensely. "But how then do you explain the girl's scholarly attainments—her knowledge of Greek, for example, which even *you,* Odo"—he lingered over the words—"have not mastered?"

"She has boasted of her abilities, but we have seen no proof of them." Odo sniffed. "You are credulous, Sire. The Greek may have been less than honest in reporting her accomplishments."

This was too much. First this hateful man insulted her, and now he dared to attack Aesculapius! Joan's lips started to form an angry reply when she caught the sympathetic gaze of a red-haired knight seated beside the bishop.

*No.* He signaled her silently. She hesitated, struck by the message in his compelling indigo eyes. He turned to the bishop and whispered something. The bishop nodded and addressed the thin-faced cleric. "Very well, Odo, examine her."

"My lord?"

"Examine her. See if she is fit for study at the schola."

"Here, my lord? It hardly seems appro—"

"Here, Odo. Why not? We will all profit from the example."

Odo frowned. He turned to Joan. His narrow face aimed at her like an ax.

"*Quicunque vult*. What does it mean?"

Joan was surprised. So easy a question? Perhaps it was a trick. Perhaps he was trying to put her off her guard. Cautiously she responded, "It is the doctrine asserting that the three Persons of the Trinity are cosubstantial. That Christ was fully divine just as He was fully human."

"The authority for this doctrine?"

"The first council of Nicaea."

"*Confessio Fidei*. What is it?"

"It is the false and pernicious doctrine"—Joan knew what to say, having been cautioned by Aesculapius on this point—"which asserts that Christ was first a human being and only secondarily divine. Divine, that is, only through his adoption by the Father." She studied Odo's face, but it was unreadable. *"Filius non proprius, sed adoptivus,"* she added for good measure.

"Explain the false nature of this heresy."

"If Christ is God's Son by grace and not by nature, then He must be subordinate to the Father. This is a false heresy and an abomination," Joan recited dutifully from memory, "because the Holy Spirit proceeds not only from the Father but also from the Son; there is only one Son, and He is not an adopted son. *'In utraque natura proprium eum et non adoptivum filium dei confitemur.'* "

The people at the tables snapped their fingers in applause. *"Litteratissima!"* someone shouted across the room.

"Amusing little oddity, isn't she?" a woman's voice muttered close behind Joan, just a shade too loudly.

"Well, Odo," the bishop said expansively. "What do you say? Was the Greek right about Joan, or not?"

Odo looked like a man who has tasted vinegar. "It appears the child has some knowledge of orthodox theology. Nevertheless, this in itself does not prove anything." He spoke condescendingly, as if to a difficult child. "There is, in some women, a highly developed imitative ability which allows them to memorize and repeat the words of men, and so give the appearance of thought. But this imitative skill is not to be confused with true reason, which is essentially male. For, as is well known"—Odo's voice assumed an authoritative ring, for now he was on familiar ground—"women are innately inferior to men."

"Why?" The word was out of Joan's mouth before she was even aware of having spoken.

Odo smiled, his thin lips drawing back unpleasantly. He had the look of the fox when it knows it has the rabbit cornered. "Your ignorance, child, is revealed in that question. For St. Paul himself has asserted this truth, that women are beneath men in conception, in place, and in will."

"In conception, in place, and in will?" Joan repeated.

"Yes." Odo spoke slowly and distinctly, as if addressing a half-wit. "In conception, because Adam was created first, and Eve afterward; in place, because Eve was created to serve Adam as companion and mate; in will, because Eve could not resist the Devil's temptation and ate of the apple."

Among the tables, heads nodded in agreement. The bishop's expression was grave. Beside him, the red-haired knight gave no outward sign of his thoughts.

Odo smirked. Joan felt an intense dislike for this man. For a moment she stood silently, tugging on her nose.

"Why," she said at last, "is woman inferior in conception? For though she was created second, she was made from Adam's side, while Adam was made from common clay."

There were several appreciative chuckles from the back of the hall. "In place"—the words tumbled out as Joan's thoughts raced ahead and she reasoned her way through—"woman should be preferred to man, because Eve was created inside Paradise, but Adam was created outside."

There was another hum from the audience. The smile on Odo's face wavered.

Joan continued, too interested in the line of her argument to consider what she was doing. "As for will, woman should be considered *superior* to man"—this was bold, but there was no going back now—"for Eve ate of the apple for love of knowledge and learning, but Adam ate of it merely because she asked him."

There was shocked silence in the room. Odo's pale lips pressed together angrily. The bishop was staring at Joan as if he could not quite believe what he had just heard.

She had gone too far.

*Some ideas are dangerous.*

Aesculapius had warned her, but she had become so involved in the debate she forgot his advice. That man, that Odo, had been so sure of himself, so bent on humiliating her before the bishop. She had ruined her chance for the schola and she knew it, but she would not give the hateful little man the satisfaction of seeing her dismay. She stood before the high table with chin lifted, eyes blazing.

The silence stretched on interminably. All eyes were on the bishop, whose assessing gaze remained fixed on Joan. Then, slowly, very slowly, a long, low rumble of mirth escaped his lips.

The bishop was laughing.

Beside him, the buxom woman giggled nervously. Then the room erupted with noise. People cheered and pounded on the tables and laughed, laughed so hard the tears coursed down their faces and they had to wipe them off with their sleeves. Joan looked at the red-haired knight. He was grinning broadly. She met his eyes, and he winked at her.

"Come now, Odo," said the bishop, when at last he could draw breath, "you must admit it. The girl has outwitted you!"

Odo gave the bishop a poisonous look. "What of the boy, Eminence? Do you wish to have him examined as well?"

"No, no. We'll take him too, since the girl is so attached to him. We'll take them both! To be sure, the girl's education has been a bit"—he sought the right word—"unorthodox. But she is entirely refreshing. Just what the schola needs! Odo, you have acquired some new students. Take good care with them!"

Joan stared at the bishop in shock. What did he mean? Could Odo be the master of the schola? The one who would teach her?

What had she done?

Odo looked down his narrow nose at the bishop. "You have, of course, made arrangements for the child's accommodation? She cannot board in the boys' quarters."

"Ah . . . accommodations." The bishop hesitated. "Let us see . . ."

"My lord." The red-haired knight interrupted. "The child could stay with me. My wife and I have two daughters, who would make her welcome. She would be a good companion for my Gisla."

Joan looked at him. He was a man in the prime of life, some twenty-five years of age, strong, well favored, with high cheekbones and a fine, full beard. His thick hair, really an extraordinary color of red, was parted in the middle and curled thickly to his shoulders. His startling blue eyes were intelligent and kind.

"Excellent, Gerold." The bishop thumped him warmly on the back. "It is all settled. The girl will stay with you."

A servant came by with a tray heaped with sweetmeats. John's eyes widened at sight of the sugared treats, oozing with butter.

The bishop smiled. "Children, you must be hungry after your long trip. Come sit by me." He moved closer to the woman beside him, clearing a space between him and the red-haired knight.

Joan and John went around the table and sat. The bishop himself served them sweetmeats. John ate greedily, taking huge bites of the gooey treats, the white powder mustaching his mouth.

The bishop returned his attention to the woman seated beside him. They drank from the same cup, laughing, and he stroked her hair, disarranging her coif. Joan fixed her eyes on the plate of sweetmeats. She nibbled at one of them but could not finish it; the sugary sweetness was sickening. She yearned to be away from this place, away from the noise, the unfamiliar people, and the puzzling behavior of the bishop.

The red-haired knight named Gerold spoke to her. "You have had a long day. Would you like to leave?"

Joan nodded. Seeing them rise, John stuffed in one last mouthful of candy and got up.

"No, son." Gerold placed a hand on John's shoulder. "You stay here."

John said plaintively, "I want to go with her."

"Your place is here, with the other boys. When the meal is finished, the steward will show you to your quarters."

John paled, but he mastered himself and said nothing.

"That is an interesting piece." Gerold pointed to the bone-handled knife strapped to John's waist. "May I see it?"

John pulled it from his belt and handed it to Gerold. He turned it over, admiring the working on the handle. The blade glinted, reflecting the flickering torches around the room. Joan remembered how it had glowed in the candlelight of the grubenhaus, before it bit into the parchment of Aesculapius's book, erasing, destroying.

"Very fine. Roger has a sword whose handle has similar working. Roger." Gerold called to a youth at a table nearby. "Come show this young man your sword."

Roger held out a long iron sword with an elaborate handle.

John regarded it reverently. "May I touch it?"

"You can hold it if you like."

"You'll be given a sword of your own," Gerold said. "And a bow. A lance too, if you've the strength for it. Tell him, Roger."

"Yes. We have lessons every day in fighting and weaponry."

John's eyes registered surprise and delight.

"See the little nick here on the side of the blade? That's where I struck a blow against the heavy sword of the master of weapons himself!"

"Really?" John was fascinated.

Gerold said to Joan, "Shall we go? I think your brother will not mind our leaving now."

At the doorway, Joan turned to look back at John. With the sword across his lap, he was talking animatedly to Roger. She felt an odd reluctance to part from him. They had often been more rivals than friends, but John was her link to home, to a world familiar and comprehensible. Without him, she was alone.

Gerold had gone ahead and was striding down the corridor. He was very tall, and his long legs carried him quickly; Joan had to take little running steps to catch up.

For several minutes they did not speak. Then Gerold said abruptly, "You did well, back there with Odo."

"I do not think he likes me."

"No. He wouldn't. Odo guards his dignity closely, as a man guards his coins when there are hardly any left."

Joan smiled up at Gerold, liking him.

On an impulse, she decided to trust him.

"Was that the bishop's . . . wife?" She stumbled over the word, embarrassed. All her life she had been aware of the shameful impropriety of her parents' marriage. It was a child's awareness, never spoken or even fully acknowledged, but deeply felt. Once, observing Joan's sensitivity on the subject, Aesculapius had told her that such marriages were not uncommon among the lower clergy. But for a bishop . . .

"Wife? Oh, you mean Theda." Gerold laughed. "No, my lord bishop is not the marrying kind. Theda is one of his paramours."

Paramours! The bishop kept paramours!

"You are shocked. You needn't be. Fulgentius—my lord bishop—is not a man of pious disposition. He inherited the title from his uncle, who was bishop before him. He never took priest's orders and makes no pretense of holiness, as you will have noted. But you will find him a good enough man for all that. He admires learning, though he is not lettered himself. It was he who established the schola here."

Gerold had spoken to her plainly, not as a child but as someone who could be expected to understand. Joan liked that. But his words were troubling. Could it be right for a bishop, a prince of the Church, to live like this? To keep . . . paramours? Everything was so different from what she had expected.

They arrived at the outside doors to the palace. Pages dressed in red silk swung the huge oaken panels open; the brightness of the torchlit hall spilled into the darkness.

"Come," said Gerold. "You will feel better after a night's sleep." He strode quickly in the direction of the stables.

Uncertain, Joan followed him into the cool night.

"There it is!" Gerold pointed off to the left, and Joan followed the direction of his arm. In the distance she could just make out dark shapes of buildings outlined against the moonlit sky. "There's Villaris, my home—and yours now as well, Joan."

Even in the darkness, Villaris was magnificent. Situated commandingly on the slopes of a hill, it appeared enormous to Joan's wondering eyes. It consisted of four tall, heavy-timbered buildings connected through a series of courtyards and splendid wooden porticoes. Gerold and Joan rode through the sturdy oak palisades guarding the main entrance and past several outbuildings: a kitchen, a bakery, a stable, a corncrib, and two barns. They dismounted in a small forecourt, and Gerold handed his mount over to the waiting hands of the stable master. Resin torches placed at regular intervals lit their way down a long, windowless corridor upon whose thick oak walls rows of gleaming weapons were displayed: long swords, lances, spears, crossbows, and scramasaxes, the short, heavy, single-edged blades favored by the fierce Frankish infantrymen. They emerged into a large second courtyard ringed by covered porticoes and passed through into the great hall itself, a vast, echoing space hung with richly decorated tapestries. In the center of the room stood the most beautiful woman Joan had ever seen, apart from her own mother. But whereas Gudrun was tall and fair, this woman was small and slight, with ebony hair and large, proud, dark eyes. Coolly those eyes raked Joan, inspecting her with an expression that clearly found her wanting.

"What is this?" she asked abruptly as they drew near.

Ignoring her rudeness, Gerold replied, "Joan, this is my wife, Richild, the lady of this manor. Richild, may I present Joan of Ingelheim, who has today arrived to begin study at the schola."

Joan made an awkward attempt at a curtsy, which Richild regarded with contempt before returning her attention to Gerold. "The schola? Is this some kind of jest?"

"Fulgentius has admitted her, and she is to reside here at Villaris for the duration of her studies."

"Here?"

"She can share a bed with Gisla, who could use a sensible companion for a change."

Richild's graceful black eyebrows arched haughtily. "She looks like a colona."

Joan flushed with the insult.

"Richild, you forget yourself," Gerold admonished sharply. "Joan is a guest in this house."

Richild sniffed. "Well"—she fingered Joan's new green linen tunic—"at least she appears to be clean." She signaled imperiously to one of the servants. "Show her to the *dortoir.*" Without another word she swept from the room.

Later, lying on the soft straw mattress in the upstairs dortoir beside a snoring Gisla (who had not awakened even when Joan crawled in beside her), Joan wondered about her brother. Beside whom was John sleeping now—if, that is, he was able to sleep? She certainly could not; her mind was aswirl with troubling thoughts and emotions. She longed for the familiar surroundings of home, longed especially for her mother. She wanted to be held and caressed and called "little quail" again. She should not have run off the way she did—in silence and in anger, without a word of farewell. Gudrun had betrayed her with the bishop's emissary, it was true, but Joan knew that she had done it from an excess of love, because she could not bear to see her daughter leave. Now Joan might never see her mother again. She had leapt at the chance for escape without considering the consequences. For she could never return home, that was certain. Her father would kill her for her disobedience. Her place was here now, in this strange and friendless country, and here, for good or ill, she must remain.

*Mama,* she thought as she stared into the forbidding darkness of the unfamiliar room, and a single tear slid silently down her cheek.

# 8

The classroom, a small, stone-walled chamber adjacent to the cathedral library, remained cool and moist even on this warm fall afternoon. Joan loved its coolness and the rich smell of parchment that permeated the air, an enticement to explore the vast holding of books that lay just next door.

An enormous painting covered the wall at the front of the room. It was a picture of a woman dressed in the long, flowing robes of the Greeks. In her left hand she held a pair of shears; in her right, a whip. The woman represented Knowledge; her shears were to prune away error and false dogma, her whip was to reprimand lazy students. The brows of Knowledge were sharply drawn together, and the corners of her mouth curved down, creating a stern expression. The dark eyes glared from the painted wall, seeming to focus on the observer, their look hard and commanding. Odo had commissioned the work shortly after assuming the position of teaching master at the schola.

*"Bos mugit, equus hinnit, asinus rudit, elephans barrit . . ."*

On the left side of the room, the less advanced students chanted monotonously, practicing simple verb forms.

"Cows moo, horses neigh, donkeys bray, elephants roar . . ."

Odo motioned rhythmically with his right hand, setting the pace of the chant. Meanwhile, his eyes swept the room with practiced skill, monitoring the work of his other students.

Ludovic and Ebbo huddled together over one of the psalms. They were supposed to be memorizing it, but the tilt of their heads toward each other indicated that they had ceased to concentrate on their work. Without letting his other hand miss a beat of the chanting rhythm, Odo smacked both boys sharply on the backs of their heads with a long wooden rod. They yelped and bent over their tablets again, models of industriousness.

Nearby, John was working on a chapter of Donatus. He was clearly having great difficulty. He read slowly, painstakingly forming each vowel and consonant with his lips, stopping frequently to scratch his head in puzzlement over some unfamiliar word pattern.

Sitting apart from the others—for they would have nothing to do with her—Joan was intent on the task to which Odo had set her, preparing a gloss of a life of St. Antony. She worked quickly, her stylus traveling across the parchment with confidence and precision. She did not look up, nor did her attention waver for an instant. Her concentration was absolute.

Odo said shortly, "That is enough for today. This group"—he gestured toward the novices—"is dismissed. The rest of you will remain at your seats until I have checked your work."

The novices rose excitedly from their desks, exiting the room as quickly as decorum permitted. The other students put down their styluses and watched Odo expectantly, eager to be released to the pleasures of the warm afternoon.

Joan remained studiously bent over her work.

Odo frowned. The girl's zeal had admittedly surprised him. His hand itched to use the rod on her, but so far she had given him no occasion. She actually seemed to want to learn.

Odo walked to her desk and stood over her pointedly. She stopped working then, her expression registering surprise and even—was it possible?—disappointment.

"Did you call on me, sir? Pardon me; I was concentrating on my work and did not hear you," Joan said politely.

*She acts her part well,* Odo thought. *But I am not deceived.* Oh, she pretended respect and submission whenever he addressed her, but he read the truth in her eyes. In her soul, she mocked and challenged him. That Odo would not tolerate.

He bent to examine her work, shuffling the pieces of parchment in silence.

"The hand," he said, "is not sufficiently fair. See here—and here"—he stabbed at the parchment with one long, white finger—"you do not round your letters sufficiently. Child, what explanation can you offer for such sloppy work?"

Sloppy work! Joan was indignant. She had just glossed ten pages of text—far more than any of the other students could have done in twice the time. Her explanations were accurate and complete—even Odo did not try to deny that. She had seen his eyes flicker as they scanned the passage with her elegant handling of the subjunctive.

"Well?" Odo prodded her. He wanted her to defy him, to answer him boldly. *Arrogant and unnatural creature.* He knew she sought to violate the God-given order of the universe by usurping men's rightful authority over her. *Go ahead,* he willed her. *Speak your mind.* If she did, he would have her where he wanted her.

Joan fought to keep her emotions under control. She knew what Odo was trying to do. But no matter how hard he provoked her, she would not oblige him. She would not provide him with a reason to dismiss her from the schola. Keeping her voice flat, she replied dryly, "I have no excuse, sir."

"Very well," Odo said. "As punishment for your indolence, you will copy out the passage from First Timothy, chapter two, verses eleven and twelve, twenty-five times in a *good* hand before you leave."

Dark resentment boiled inside Joan. Nasty, narrow-minded man! If only she could tell him what she thought of him!

"Yes, sir." She kept her eyes lowered, so he could not read her thoughts.

Odo was disappointed. Still, the girl could not keep this up forever. Sooner or later—the thought made him smile—she would give herself away. When she did, he would be waiting.

He left her and went to check on his other students.

Joan sighed and picked up her stylus. First Timothy, chapter two, verses eleven and twelve. She knew it well enough; it was not the first time Odo had levied this punishment. It was a quotation from St. Paul: "I do not permit a woman to be a teacher, nor must a woman domineer over a man; she should be quiet and listen with due submission."

She was halfway through the writing when she first sensed something wrong. She looked up. Odo was gone. The boys were standing in a knot by the door, talking. That was odd. Usually they rushed from the room as soon as lessons were over. She watched them warily. John stood on the outer fringe of the little group, listening. She caught his eye, and he smiled and waved.

She smiled in return, then went back to her writing. But a tiny prickle of alarm raised the hairs on her neck. Were the boys planning something? They frequently teased and tormented her—Odo did nothing to stop them—and though she had steeled herself to their abuse, she still dreaded it.

Hurriedly she finished the last few lines and rose to leave. The boys were standing by the door. She knew they were waiting for her. She lifted her chin determinedly. Whatever they had in store for her, she would walk past quickly and have done with it.

Her cloak hung on a wooden peg near the door. Making an elaborate gesture of ignoring the boys, she retrieved it, fastened it carefully round her neck, and pulled up the hood.

Something heavy and wet pooled on the top of her head. Immediately she tugged at the hood, but it would not come off. The sticky wetness oozed downward. She reached up and touched it; her fingers came away coated with a thick, mucousy substance. *Gum arabic.* A common material in schoolrooms and *scriptoria,* it was used, with vinegar and charcoal, to make ink. She wiped her hand on her cloak, but the gum arabic clung stickily. Frantically, she pulled at the hood again and yelped as her hair was yanked painfully by the roots.

Her cry elicited a shout of laughter from the boys. She walked quickly toward the door. The group parted as she drew near, forming a line on either side.

*"Lusus naturae!"* they taunted her. "Freak of nature!"

Halfway down the line she saw John. He was laughing and shouting insults along with the others. She met his eyes; he flushed and looked away.

She kept walking. Too late she saw the flash of blue cloth near the floor. She tripped and fell clumsily, landing heavily on her side.

*John,* she thought. *He tripped me.*

She got to her feet, wincing as a sharp pain shot down her side. The disgusting slime oozed from under the hood onto her face. She wiped at it, trying to keep it out of her eyes, but it was no use. It slid glutinously over her eyebrows onto her lids, gumming her eyelashes, making it impossible to see clearly.

Laughing, the boys crowded in, shoving her back and forth, trying to make her fall again. She heard John's voice among the others, calling out insults. Through the thick film that covered her eyes, the room spun dizzyingly in alternating patterns of light and color. She could no longer make out the door.

She felt a sudden sting of tears.

*Oh no,* she thought. That was what they wanted—to make her weep and plead for mercy, to show some weakness, so they could mock her as a coward of a girl.

*They shall not have that. I will not give them that.*

She held herself straight, willing herself not to cry. This display of self-control only inflamed them, and they began to hit harder. The biggest of the boys struck her forcefully on the neck. The blow staggered her, and she fought to keep her feet.

A man's voice shouted in the distance. Had Odo come at last to put an end to this?

*"What is happening here?"*

This time she recognized the voice. Gerold. There was a tone in his voice she had never heard before. The boys backed away from her so suddenly she almost fell again.

Gerold's arm was around her shoulder, steadying her. She leaned into him gratefully.

"Well, Bernhar." Gerold addressed the biggest boy, the one who had hit her on the neck. "Wasn't it just last week I watched you at weapons practice, trying so desperately to keep out of range of Eric's sword that you could not manage a single strike? Yet I see that you have no difficulty fighting when your opponent is a defenseless girl."

Bernhar stammered an explanation, but Gerold cut him off.

"You may tell that to His Lordship the bishop. He will send for you when he learns of this. Which he will, this very day."

The silence around them was absolute. Gerold lifted Joan in his arms. She felt with some surprise the rippling power of his arms and back. He was so tall and lean, she had not realized he was so strong. She tilted her head away so the disgusting slime that covered her would not mar his tunic.

Halfway to his mount, Gerold turned. "One thing more. From what I have witnessed, she is braver than any of you. Yes, and smarter too, for all that she is a girl."

Joan felt the start of tears in her eyes. No one had ever spoken for her like that save Aesculapius.

Gerold was—different.

The bud of a rose grows in darkness. It knows nothing of the sun, yet it pushes at the darkness that confines it until at last the walls give way and the rose bursts forth, spreading its petals into the light.

*I love him.*

The thought was as startling as it was sudden. What could it mean? She could not be in love with Gerold. He was a nobleman, a great lord, and she was a canon's daughter. He was a mature man of twenty-five winters, and Joan knew he thought of her as a child, though in fact she was almost thirteen and would soon be a woman grown.

Besides, he had a wife.

Joan's mind was a whirl of confusing emotions.

Gerold lifted her onto his horse and mounted behind. The boys stood huddled before the door, not daring to speak. Joan leaned back into Gerold's arms, feeling his strength, drawing upon it.

"Now," Gerold said, spurring the horse into a canter, "I will take you home."

# 9

Count Gerold, *grafio vir illuster* of this far northeastern march of the imperial realm, flicked his new chestnut into a gallop as he neared the motte on which his manor stood. The horse responded smartly, anticipating a warm stable and a pile of fresh hay. Beside him, the horse carrying Osdag, Gerold's venery servant, also lengthened its stride, though the weight of the slaughtered stag tied across its back caused it to lag.

It had been a good day's hunt. On a whim, for usually a hunting sortie consisted of six or more men, Gerold had gone out with only Osdag and two of the brachet hounds as companions. Luck had been with them; almost immediately they found deer's spoor, which Osdag scooped up in his hunting horn and scrutinized with a trained eye. "A hart," he announced, "and a big one." They tracked him for the better part of an hour until they sighted him in a small clearing. Gerold lifted his ivory oliphant to his lips and blew a series of soft, one-pitch notes, and the brachet hounds leapt eagerly to the chase. It had not been easy bringing the beast to bay with only two men and two dogs, but they had cornered it at last, and Gerold had dispatched it with one quick thrust of his lance. It was, as Osdag had predicted, a fine, large beast; with winter coming on, it would make a welcome addition to the Villaris larder.

Some distance away, Gerold spied Joan sitting cross-legged on the grass. He sent Osdag ahead to the stables and rode toward her. He had grown surprisingly attached to the girl over the past year. She was a strange one, there was no denying it—too much alone, too solemn for her years, but with a good heart and a keen intelligence that Gerold found very appealing.

Drawing near to where Joan sat still as one of the reliefs on the cathedral door, Gerold dismounted and led the chestnut forward. Joan was so deep in concentration that he got within ten yards of her before she saw him. Then she rose to her feet, blushing. Gerold was amused. She was incapable of disguise—a trait Gerold found quite charming, as it was so different from . . . what he was used to. There was no mistaking her childlike infatuation with him.

"You were deep in thought," he said.

"Yes." She rose and came over to admire the chestnut. "Did he handle well?"

"Perfectly. He's a fine mount."

"Oh yes." She stroked the chestnut's shining mane. She had an excellent appreciation of horses, perhaps because she had grown up without them. From what Gerold had been able to make out, her family had lived as poorly as any coloni, though her father was a canon of the Church.

The horse nuzzled her ear, and she laughed delightedly. An attractive girl, Gerold thought, though she would never be a beauty. Her large, intelligent eyes were set deep, her strong jaw and wide, straight shoulders gave her a boyish appearance, heightened now by the short white-gold hair that curled around her face, reaching barely to the tops of her ears. After that episode at the schola, they had been obliged to cut her hair down to the scalp; there had been no other way to remove the gum arabic smeared through every strand.

"What were you thinking about?"

"Oh. Just something that happened at the schola today."

"Tell me."

She looked at him. "Is it true that the cubs of the white wolf are born dead?"

"What?" Gerold was accustomed to her odd questions, but this one was stranger than usual.

"John and the other boys were talking. There's going to be a hunt for the white wolf, the one in the forest of Annapes."

Gerold nodded. "I know the one. A bitch, and a savage one—it hunts alone, apart from any pack, and knows no fear. Just last winter it attacked a band of travelers and carried off a small child before anyone could lift hand to bow to stop it. They say it now has a belly full of kits—I suppose they mean to kill it before it gives birth?"

"Yes. John and the others are excited, for Ebbo said his father promised to take him along on the hunt."

"So?"

"Odo was adamant against it. He would personally see the hunt called off, he said, for the white wolf is a holy beast, a living manifestation of Christ's resurrection."

Gerold's eyebrows lifted skeptically.

Joan continued. " 'Its cubs are born dead,' Odo said, 'and then in three days' time their sire licks them into life. It is a miracle so rare and so holy that none has ever witnessed it.' "

"What did you say to that?" Gerold asked. He knew her well enough by now to know that she would have had something to say.

"I asked how this was known to be true, if it had never been witnessed."

Gerold laughed out loud. "I'll wager our schoolmaster did not appreciate the question!"

"No. It was irreverent, he said. And also illogical, for the moment of the Resurrection was also never witnessed, yet no one doubts *its* truth."

Gerold laid a hand on Joan's shoulder. "Never mind, child."

There was a pause, as if she were debating whether to say anything further. Suddenly she looked up at him, her young face intent and deeply earnest. "How *can* we be sure of the truth of the Resurrection? If no one ever witnessed it?"

He was so startled that he jerked on the reins, and the chestnut started. Gerold placed a hand on the russet flank, gentling him.

Like most of his peers in this northern part of the Empire, landed magnates who had reached their manhood under the reign of old Emperor Karolus, who held to the old ways, Gerold was a Christian in the loosest sense. He attended mass, gave alms, and was careful to keep the feasts and outward observances. He followed those teachings of church doctrine that did not interfere with the execution of his manorial rights and duties, and ignored the rest.

But Gerold understood the way of the world, and he recognized danger when he saw it.

"You did not ask that of Odo!"

"Why not?"

"God's teeth!" This could mean trouble. Gerold had no liking for Odo, a little man of narrow ideas and even narrower spirit. But this was exactly the kind of weapon Odo needed to embarrass Fulgentius and force Joan from the schola. Or—it did not bear thinking of—even worse.

"What did he say?"

"He did not answer. He was very angry, and he . . . reprimanded me." She flushed.

Gerold let out his breath in a soft whistle. "Well, what did you expect? You are old enough now to know that there are some questions one does not ask."

"Why?" The large, gray-green eyes, so much deeper and wiser than other children's, fixed on him intently. *Pagan eyes,* Gerold thought, *eyes that would never look down before man or God.* It troubled him to think what must have gone into the making of those eyes.

"Why?" she asked again, insistent.

"One simply doesn't, that's all." He was irritated by her prodding. Sometimes the girl's intelligence, which so far outpaced her physical growth, was unsettling.

Something—hurt, or was it anger?—flared briefly in her eyes and then was masked. "I should return to the house. The tapestry for the hall is nearing completion, and your lady may need help with the finishing." Chin lifted, she turned to go.

Gerold was amused. So much wounded dignity in one so young! The thought of Richild, his wife, requiring Joan's help with the tapestry was absurd. She had frequently complained to him about Joan's clumsiness with the needle; Gerold himself had witnessed the girl's frustrated efforts to force her awkward fingers to obey, and seen the sorry results of her labors.

His irritation dissipated, he said, "Don't be offended. If you wish to get on in the world, you must have more patience with your betters."

She peered at him sideways, assessing his words, then threw her head back and laughed. The sound was delightful, full throated and musical, wholly infectious. Gerold was charmed. The girl could be stubborn and quick to anger, but she had a warm heart and a ready wit.

He cupped her chin. "I did not mean to be harsh," he said. "It's just that you surprise me sometimes. You are so wise about some things, and so stupid about others."

She started to speak, but he held a finger to her lips. "I don't know the answer to your question. But I know the question itself is dangerous. There are many who would say such a thought is heresy. Do you understand what that means, Joan?"

She nodded gravely. "It is an offense against God."

"Yes. It is that, and more than that. It could mean the forfeit of your hopes, Joan, of your future. Of—your very life."

There. He had said it. The gray-green eyes regarded him unwaveringly. There was no going back now. He would have to tell her all of it.

"Four winters ago a group of travelers was stoned to death, not far from here, in the fields bordering the cathedral. Two men, a woman, and a boy, not much older than you are now."

He was a seasoned soldier, a veteran of the Emperor's campaigns against the barbarian Obodrites, yet his flesh crawled, remembering. Death, even horrible death, held no surprises for him. But he had recoiled from this killing. The men were unarmed, and the other two . . . The dying had taken a long time, the woman and the boy suffering the longest, since the men had tried to shield them with their bodies.

"Stoned?" Joan's eyes were wide. "But why?"

"They were Armenians, members of the sect known as Paulicians. They were on their to Aachen, and they were unfortunate enough to pass through just after a hailstorm struck the vineyards. In less than an hour, the entire crop was lost. In such times, people seek a reason for their troubles. When they looked around, there they were—strangers, and of a suspect set of mind. *Tempestarii,* they were called, who had used enchantments to unchain the violent storm. Fulgentius tried to defend them, but they were questioned and their ideas found to be heretical. Ideas, Joan"—he fixed her with a level gaze—"not so very different from the question you asked Odo today."

She fell silent, staring off into the distance. Gerold said nothing, giving her time.

"Aesculapius once said something like that to me," she said at last. "Some ideas are dangerous."

"He was a wise man."

"Yes." Her eyes softened with remembrance. "I will be more careful."

"Good."

"Now," she said, "tell me. How *do* we know that the story of the Resurrection is true?"

Gerold laughed helplessly. "You"—he rumpled the cropped white-gold hair—"are incorrigible." Seeing that she still waited for an answer, he added, "Very well. I'll tell you what I think."

Her eyes lit with eager interest. He laughed again.

"But not now. Pistis needs tending. Come find me before vespers and we will talk."

Joan's admiration shone undisguised in her eyes. Gerold stroked her cheek. She was hardly more than a child, but there was no denying that she moved him. Well, his own marital bed was cold enough, God knew, for him to enjoy the warmth of such innocent affection without too great a burden of conscience.

The chestnut nuzzled Joan. She said, "I have an apple. May I give it to him?"

Gerold nodded. "Pistis deserves a reward. He did well today; he'll make a first-rate hunter one day, or I'm much mistaken."

She reached into her scrip, withdrew a small greenish red apple, and held it out to the chestnut, who lipped it gently, then took the whole fruit into his mouth. As she withdrew her hand, Gerold saw a flash of red. She realized he had seen and tried to hide the hand, but he caught it and held it up to the light. A deep furrow of torn flesh and drying blood scored the tender inside of the palm, cut clear across.

"Odo?" Gerold said quietly.

"Yes." She winced as he gently fingered the edges of the wound. Odo had obviously used the rod more than once, and with considerable force; the wound was deep and needed immediate tending to prevent corruption from setting in.

"We must see to this right away. Return to the house; I will meet you there." It was an effort to keep his voice steady. He was surprised at the intensity of his emotion. Odo had undeniably been within his rights to discipline her. Indeed, it was probably for the best that he had struck her, for, having vented his anger in this way, he was less likely to carry the matter further. Nevertheless, the sight of the wound roused in Gerold a strong, unreasoning fury. He would have liked to throttle Odo.

"It is not so bad as it looks." Joan was watching him closely with those wise, deep eyes.

Gerold checked the wound again. It was deep, centered right in the most sensitive part of the hand. Any other child would have wept and cried out with pain. She had not said a word, even when questioned.

Yet just a few weeks ago, when they had to cut her hair to get the gum arabic out, she had screamed and fought like a Saracen. Later, when Gerold asked why she had resisted so, she could offer no clearer explanation than that the sound of the scissors ripping through her hair had frightened her.

A strange girl, no doubt of it. Perhaps that was why he found her so intriguing.

"Father!" Dhuoda, Gerold's younger daughter, burst into view, running down the hill of the motte toward where Joan and he stood among the trees. They waited till she drew up to them, flushed and panting from her run. "Father!" Dhuoda raised her arms expectantly, and Gerold grabbed her and swung her up and around while she squealed exuberantly. When he thought she had had enough, he set her down.

Flushed and excited, Dhuoda tugged on his arm. "Oh, Father, come see! Lupa has given birth to five pups. May I have one for my own, Father? Can it sleep on my bed?"

Gerold laughed. "We'll have to see. But first"—he held her firmly, for she had already turned to race back to the house ahead of him—"first take Joan back to the house; her hand is injured and needs looking after."

"Her hand? Show me," she demanded of Joan, who held out her hand with a rueful smile. "Ooooooh." Dhuoda's eyes widened in horrified fascination as she examined it. "How did it happen?"

"She can tell you on the way back," Gerold interrupted impatiently. He did not like the look of that wound; the sooner it was seen to, the better. "Hurry now, and do as I told you."

"Yes, Father." Dhuoda said to Joan sympathetically, "Does it hurt *very* much?"

"Not enough to keep me from reaching the gate first!" Joan replied, and broke into a run.

Dhuoda squealed with delight and took off after her. The two girls ran up the hill of the motte together, laughing.

Gerold watched, smiling, but his eyes were troubled.

Winter came, marked indelibly in Joan's mind by her passage into womanhood. She was thirteen and should have expected it, but still it took her by surprise—the sudden appearance of a dark brown stain on her linen tunic and the tightening pain in her abdomen. She knew immediately what it was—she had heard her mother and the women in Gerold's household talk about it often enough, and seen them washing out their rags each month. Joan spoke to a maidservant, who ran to bring her a tall pile of clean rags, winking knowingly as she handed them over.

Joan hated it. Not just the pain and the bother, but the very idea of what was happening. She felt betrayed by her own body, which appeared to be rearranging itself almost daily into new and unfamiliar contours. When the boys at the schola began to take mocking notice of her budding breasts, she bound them tightly with strips of cloth. It was painful, but the effect was worth it. Her gender had been a source of misery and frustration for as long as she could remember, and she meant to fight this emerging evidence of her femininity as long as possible.

Wintarmanoth brought an iron frost that gripped the land like an oppressive fist. The cold was enough to make one's teeth ache. Wolves and other forest predators prowled nearer the town than ever before; few villagers ventured abroad without a pressing reason.

Gerold urged Joan not to go to the schola, but she would not be dissuaded. Every morning, excepting the Sabbath, she donned her thick wool cloak and belted it tightly around her waist to keep out the wind; then, hunching her body against the cold, she walked the two miles to the cathedral. When the high, frigid winds of Hornung came, driving the cold across the roads in bitter gusts, Gerold had a horse saddled every day and rode Joan to and from the schola himself.

Though Joan saw her brother every day at the schola, John never spoke to her now. He was still dismally slow at his studies, but his skill in the use of sword and lance had won the respect of the other boys, and he visibly flourished in their companionship. He had no wish to jeopardize his newfound sense of belonging by acknowledging a sister who was an embarrassment. He turned away whenever she approached.

The girls of the town kept their distance as well. They regarded Joan with suspicion, excluding her from their games and gossip. She was a freak of nature—male in intellect, female in body, she fit in nowhere; it was as if she belonged to a third, amorphous sex.

She was alone. Except, of course, for Gerold. But Gerold was enough. Joan was happy just to be near him, to talk and laugh and speak of things she could discuss with no one else in the world.

One cold day after she and Gerold had returned from the schola, he beckoned to her. "Come," he said, "I have something to show you."

He led her through the winding hall of the manor to the solar and the small cabinet in which he kept his papers. From it he withdrew a long, rectangular object and handed it to her.

A book! Somewhat old and frayed at the edges, but intact. In fine gold letters on the wooden cover was written the title: *De rerum natura. De rerum natura*. The great work of Lucretius! Aesculapius had frequently spoken of its importance. There was only one copy extant, it was said, and that one kept close and carefully in the great library of Lorsch. Yet here was Gerold offering it to her as casually as if it were a choice piece of meat.

"But how . . . ?" She lifted wondering eyes to his.

"What is written may be copied," he answered with a conspiratorial smile. "For a price. A considerable price, in this case. The abbot bargained hard, saying he was short of scribes. And, indeed, it has taken more than ten months to complete the work. But here it is. And not one denarius more than it's worth."

Joan's eyes glowed as she fingered the cover of the book. In all her months at the schola, she had never been allowed to work with texts such as this. Odo absolutely forbade her to read the great classical works in the cathedral library, restricting her to the study of sacred texts, which were, he said, the only ones suitable for her weak and impressionable female mind. Proudly she had not let him see how deeply this grieved her. *Go ahead, bar your library,* she thought defiantly. *You cannot put bars on my mind*. Nevertheless, it had been infuriating, knowing what treasures of knowledge were locked away from her. Gerold had seen that; he always seemed to know what she was thinking and feeling. How could she help but love him?

"Go on," Gerold said. "And when you have done, come to me and we will talk over what you have read. You will be most interested in what he has to say."

Joan's eyes opened wide in astonishment. "Then you—"

"Yes. I have read it. Does that surprise you?"

"Yes. I mean no—but—" Joan's cheeks pinkened as she stumbled for a reply. She had not known he could read Latin. It was rare for nobles and men of property to read and write at all. It was the job of the manor steward, a man of letters, to keep accounts and carry out any necessary correspondence. Naturally Joan had assumed . . .

Gerold laughed, plainly enjoying her embarrassment. "It's all right. You could not have known. I was some years studying at the Schola Palatina when old Emperor Karolus was alive."

"The Schola Palatina!" The name was legend. The school founded by the Emperor had turned out some of the finest minds of the day. The great Alcuin himself had been the master teacher.

"Yes. My father sent me, intending me for a scholar. The work was interesting, and I enjoyed it well enough, but I was young and hadn't the temperament to make a steady diet of it. When the Emperor called for men to campaign with him against the Obodrites, I went, though I was only thirteen. I was gone some years, perhaps would be there still, but then my eldest brother died, and I was called home to assume inheritance of this estate."

Joan regarded him wonderingly. He was a scholar, a man of letters! How could she not have known! She should have guessed from the way he had spoken with her about her studies.

"Off with you." Gerold shooed her away amiably. "I know you cannot wait. There's an hour yet before supper. But listen carefully for the bell."

Joan ran upstairs to the dortoir she shared with Dhuoda and Gisla. She went to her bed and opened the book. She read slowly, savoring the words, stopping occasionally to make note of a particularly elegant phrase or argument. When the light in the room faded with the dusk, she lit a candle and kept working.

She read on and on, completely forgetting the time and would have missed supper entirely had not Gerold, in the end, sent a servant to fetch her.

The weeks passed quickly, charged with the excitement of Joan and Gerold's work together. Waking each morning, Joan wondered impatiently how she would ever make it until after vespers, when, supper over and the necessary devotions past, she and Gerold could resume their study of Lucretius.

*De rerum natura* was a revelation—a wonder of a book, rich in knowledge and wisdom. In order to discover truth, Lucretius said, one had only to observe the natural world. It was an idea which made good sense in Lucretius's time but which was extraordinary, even revolutionary in anno domini 827. Nevertheless, it was a philosophy that appealed strongly to Joan's and Gerold's practical turn of mind.

It was, in fact, entirely because of Lucretius that Gerold trapped the white wolf.

Joan returned from the schola one day to find Villaris in an uproar.

The household dogs were barking themselves hoarse; the horses ran wildly round the perimeter of their corral; the entire bailey was echoing with a deafening series of terrifying growls.

In the middle of the forecourt, Joan found the object of all the excitement. A large white wolf fought and twisted and hurled itself furiously against the sides of an oblong cage. The bars of the cage, constructed of sturdy oakwood three inches thick, cracked and groaned under the fury of the beast's assault. Gerold and his men ringed the area warily, bows and spears at the ready, lest the creature should succeed in breaking loose. Gerold gestured to Joan to stay back. As she watched the she-wolf's strange pink eyes, glittering with hatred, Joan found herself willing the bars to hold firm.

After a time the wolf tired and stood panting, legs planted stolidly and head lowered, glowering. Gerold lowered his spear and came over to Joan.

"Now we put Odo's theory to the test!"

For a fortnight the two of them kept vigil, determined, if at all possible, to observe the very moment of birth. Nothing happened. The wolf sulked in her cage and showed no sign of an impending delivery. They had almost begun to doubt whether the beast was pregnant when she abruptly went into labor.

It happened during Joan's turn at the watch. The wolf alternately paced and shifted restlessly on the floor, as if unable to get comfortable. Finally she grunted and began to heave. Joan ran to get Gerold and found him in the solar with Richild. Bursting in upon them like a whirlwind, Joan dispensed with the normal courtesies. "Come quickly! It's started!"

Gerold rose immediately. Richild frowned and looked as if she would speak, but there was no time to waste. Joan spun around and ran back along the covered portico that led to the main courtyard. Gerold, who had stopped to fetch a lantern, followed close behind. Neither one of them witnessed the look on Richild's face as she watched them go.

By the time they reached the bailey, the wolf was straining hard. Joan and Gerold watched as the tip of one small paw began to emerge, followed by another, and then by a tiny, perfect head. Finally, with a last heave from the bitch, a small, dark body slid wetly onto the straw lining the bottom of the cage and lay still.

Joan and Gerold strained to see into the darkness of the cage. The newborn pup lay inert, completely covered by the birth sac, so they could hardly make out head from tail. His dam licked the sac off and ate it.

Gerold raised the lantern high against the bars of the cage to give more light. The newborn did not appear to be breathing.

The mother began to strain with the effort of a second delivery. Moments passed, and still the newborn cub did not move or give any sign of life.

Joan looked at Gerold with dismay. Was it so? Would it lie lifeless, waiting for its father to lick it into life? Had Odo been right, after all?

If so, then they had killed it, for they had taken it far from the father who would have given it life.

Once again the mother grunted; a second small body slid out, landing partly on top of the first. The impact jolted the firstborn, which twitched and let out a soft squeal of protest.

"Look!" The two of them prodded each other and pointed in exultant unison. They laughed, well pleased with the results of their experiment.

The two pups bumped their way over to their mother's side to nurse, even before she finished the throes of a third delivery.

Together, Gerold and Joan watched the beginning of this new family. Their hands reached out for each other in the dark, meeting and clasping in mutual understanding.

Joan had never felt so close to anyone in her life.

"We missed you at vespers." Richild glared at them reprovingly from the portico. "It is the Eve of St. Norbert, have you forgotten? It sets a poor example when the lord of the manor absents himself from the holy devotions."

"I had something else to attend to," Gerold replied coolly.

Richild started to respond, but Joan interrupted excitedly.

"We watched the white wolf give birth to her pups! They are not born dead, despite what people say," she announced jubilantly. "Lucretius was right!"

Richild stared at her as if she were mad.

"All things in nature are explainable," Joan continued. "Don't you see? The pups were born alive, with no reliance on the supernatural, just like Lucretius said!"

"What godless speech is this? Child, are you feverish?"

Gerold stepped quickly between them. "Go to bed, Joan," he said over his shoulder. "It is late." He took Richild by the arm and firmly steered her into the house.

Joan remained where she was, listening to Richild's voice echo shrilly through the calm evening air.

"This is what comes of educating the girl beyond her capacity to learn. Gerold, you must cease to encourage her in these unnatural pursuits!"

Joan slowly made her way back to her sleeping chamber.

They killed the white wolf after she weaned her pups. She was dangerous, having already attacked and carried off one small child, and such a man-killer could not be set free. Her last-born did not survive; it was a sickly thing that lived only a few days. But the other two grew into robust and active pups, whose playful antics delighted Joan and Gerold. One had a coat of brown and gray mottled fur, typical of the forest wolves in this part of Frankland; Gerold made a gift of him to Fulgentius, who derived a wicked pleasure in pointedly displaying him to Odo. The other pup, the firstborn, had his mother's snow white coat and singular, opalescent eyes; this one they kept. "Luke," Joan and Gerold called him, in Lucretius's honor, and their affection for the frisky, energetic pup strengthened the developing bond between them.

# 10

There was to be a fair in St.-Denis! The news was astonishing—there had not been a fair or a market in the entire kingdom for more years than most people could count. But some of the old ones—like Burchard, the miller—remembered a time when there had actually been two or three fairs a year in Frankland. So they said, though it was hard to credit the truth of it. Of course, those were in the days when Emperor Karolus of blessed memory was in his prime, and the roads and bridges still well maintained, no thieves or charlatans plying the ways, nor yet—God defend it!—the swift, savage terror of the Norsemen swooping down without warning upon the land. Now travel was too hazardous to make fairs profitable; merchants did not dare to transport precious goods over the unsafe roads, and people did not wish to chance their lives on the journey.

Nevertheless, there was to be a fair. And it would be a wonder, if even half of what the herald who brought the news said was true. There would be merchants from Byzantium bringing exotic spices, silks, and brocades; Venetian traders with cloaks of peacock feathers and embossed leather; Frisian slave dealers with their human cargo of Slavs and Saxons; Lombards with bags of salt piled high inside ships whose bright orange sails bore the signs of the zodiac; and all manner of amusements: rope dancers and acrobats, storytellers, jongleurs, performing dogs and bears.

St.-Denis was not close by—in fact, it was some one hundred fifty miles from Dorstadt, a fortnight's journey, over crumbling roads and fast-rushing rivers. But no one was daunted by that. Everyone who could get hold of a horse or mule or even a pony was going.

Gerold's entourage, as befitted that of a count, was large. Fifteen of Gerold's *fideles,* well armed, would ride with them, as well as several servants to attend the family. Joan was to go, and as a special courtesy—Joan was sure it was Gerold's idea—John was invited as well. Richild's preparations had been exacting; she had taken pains to ensure they would want for nothing in comfort and safety for the journey. For days now, wagons had been pulled into the castle bailey and loaded with goods.

The morning of the departure, Villaris was astir with activity. Grooms scurried about, feeding and loading the packhorses; the pantler and his scullions sweated over the great oven, whose tall chimney belched huge puffs of smoke; the blacksmith worked furiously at his forge, finishing the last of a supply of horseshoes, nails, and wagon fittings. Sounds blended and rose in noisy confusion: maidservants shouted shrilly to one another above the deeper calls and whistles of the grooms, cows mooed and stamped as they were hastily milked, one overladen donkey brayed loudly in protest against its load. The bustling activity stirred up a faint dust from the hard-packed earth; it rose into the air and hung in a shimmering mist, lit by the brilliant spring sunshine.

Joan lingered in the courtyard watching the last-minute preparations, enjoying the excitement. Luke pranced around her, ears pricked and opalescent eyes alight with expectation. He was going on the journey too, for, as Gerold had declared, the six-month-old pup had become so attached to Joan there was no separating them. Joan laughed and petted Luke, his white fur soft under her hand; he licked her cheek and sat back with his mouth stretched wide, as if he were laughing too.

"If you've nothing better to do than stand about gaping, give the pantler a hand." Richild gave Joan a push toward the kitchen, where the pantler waved flour-coated hands in a frenzy of activity. He had been up all night, baking rolls and pies for the journey.

By midmorning, the household was packed. The chaplain offered a brief prayer for the safe deliverance of the travelers, and the procession of wagons and horses moved out slowly onto the road. Joan rode in the first cart, behind Gerold and his men, along with Richild, Gisla, and Dhuoda, and the three villein girls who served as the ladies' personal attendants. The women jounced against the hard wooden seats as the cartwheels bumped over the pitted, uneven road. Luke trotted alongside, keeping a watchful eye on Joan. Joan looked ahead and saw John riding with the men, seated comfortably astride a fine roan mare.

*I sit a horse as well as he,* Joan thought. Gerold had spent many hours teaching her to ride, and she was now an accomplished horsewoman.

As if suddenly aware of her scrutiny, John turned around and gave her a knowing smile, at once intimate and malicious. Then he kicked his horse into a canter and rode up next to Gerold. They spoke; Gerold threw back his head and laughed.

Jealousy rose sharply within her. What could John have to say to Gerold that would amuse him so? They had nothing in common. Gerold was a learned man, a scholar. John knew nothing of such matters. Yet now he rode beside Gerold, talked with him, laughed with him, while she lurched along behind in this miserable dogcart.

Because she was a girl. Not for the first time she cursed the stroke of fate that had made her so.

"It is impolite to stare, Joan." Richild's dark eyes regarded Joan disdainfully.

Joan tore her eyes away from Gerold. "I'm sorry, my lady."

"Keep your hands folded on your lap," Richild remonstrated, "and your eyes turned down, as befits a modest woman."

Joan obediently followed her bidding.

"Proper deportment," Richild continued, "is a higher virtue in a lady than an ability to read—something you would know if you had been gently raised." She stared at Joan coolly for a few moments before returning her attention to her embroidery.

Joan watched her now out of the corner of her eye. She was certainly beautiful, in the pale, ascetic, slope-shouldered fashion of the day. Her creamy skin rose to an extremely high forehead, crowned by lustrous coils of thick black hair. Her eyes, fringed by long, dark lashes, were so deep a brown they appeared almost black. Joan felt a sharp pang of envy. Richild was everything that she was not.

"Come now, you must help us decide." Gisla, the elder daughter, beamed at Joan. "Which of my gowns should I wear for the wedding feast?" She giggled excitedly.

Gisla was fifteen, less than a year older than Joan, and already betrothed to Count Hugo, a Neustrian nobleman. Gerold and Richild were pleased, as the union was an advantageous match. The wedding was some six months away.

"Oh, Gisla, you have so many lovely things." And it was true. Joan had been astonished at the size of Gisla's wardrobe—enough to wear a different tunic every day for a fortnight if she chose. In Ingelheim, a girl had but one tunic, of strong woolen cloth if she was lucky, and she kept it carefully, for it would have to last many years. "I am sure Count Hugo will think you beautiful in any of them."

Gisla giggled again. A good-hearted but somewhat simple girl, she erupted into nervous laughter every time her affianced's name was mentioned.

"No, no," she said breathlessly. "You cannot wriggle out of it so easily. Listen. Mother thinks I should wear the blue, but I say the yellow. Come now, give me a proper answer."

Joan sighed. She liked Gisla, for all her giddiness and silly ways. They had shared a bed from the very first night, when Gerold had brought Joan home from the bishop's palace, weary and frightened. Gisla had welcomed Joan, been kind to her, and Joan would always be grateful. Still, there was no denying that conversation with Gisla could be trying, for her interests were entirely confined to clothes, food, and men. For the last few weeks, she had talked incessantly about the wedding, and it was beginning to try everyone's patience.

Joan smiled, making an effort to be obliging. "I think you should wear the blue. It matches your eyes."

"The blue? Really?" Gisla's brow furrowed. "But the yellow has the lovely lace trim on the front."

"Well, the yellow then."

"Still, the blue *does* match my eyes. Perhaps it would be better. What do you think?"

"*I* think that if I hear any more about that stupid wedding feast I shall scream," said Dhuoda. She was nine years old and resentful of all the attention her older sister had been getting over the past few weeks. "Who cares what color tunic you wear anyway!"

"Dhuoda, that remark is unbecoming a lady." Richild looked up from her embroidery to chastise her younger daughter.

"I'm sorry," Dhuoda said to Gisla contritely. But as soon as her mother looked away she stuck out her tongue at Gisla, who smiled back at her good-humoredly.

Richild said, "As for you, Joan, it is not for you to offer an opinion; Gisla will wear whatever *I* think best."

Joan flushed at the reprimand but said nothing.

"Count Hugo is such a handsome man." Bertha, one of the serving wenches, spoke up. A red-cheeked girl of no more than sixteen winters, she was new to household service, having been brought in a month ago to replace a girl dead of typhoid. "He looks so fine on his charger, with his ermine cloak and gloves."

Gisla giggled delightedly. Encouraged, Bertha continued. "And, mistress, from the way he looks at you, it cannot matter what tunic you wear. Come the wedding night, he'll have it off you quick enough!"

She laughed boisterously, pleased with her joke. Gisla tittered. The others in the wagon sat quietly, watching Richild.

Richild put down her embroidery, her eyes dark with anger. "What did you say?" she asked, in a tone ominously quiet.

"Uh—nothing, my lady," Bertha said.

"Oh, Mother, I am sure she did not mean—" Gisla tried ineffectually to intervene.

"Coarseness and filth! I will not suffer it in my presence!"

"I'm sorry, my lady," Bertha said, chastened. But she still smiled a little, not believing Richild could be truly angry.

Richild motioned Bertha to the open back of the cart. "Out."

"But, my lady!" Bertha wailed, at last comprehending the enormity of her error. "I did not mean—"

"Out!" Richild was adamant. "In penance for your impudence, you will walk the rest of the way."

It was a punishing journey to St.-Denis. Bertha looked ruefully at her feet, covered with rough, hemp-soled buskins. Joan felt sorry for her. Her remark had been heedless and ill advised, but the girl was young and new to service, and obviously had not meant to give offense.

"You will recite the paternoster aloud while you walk."

"Yes, my lady," Bertha said resignedly. She clambered out of the cart, took up a position alongside, and after a minute slowly began to recite, *"Pater Noster qui es in caelis . . ."* She spoke in an odd singsong style that emphasized all the wrong words. Joan was sure she had no idea what she was saying.

Richild returned to her embroidery. Her black hair shone in the sunlight as she bent her head over her stitching. Her lips were tight, her eyes hard with anger as she drove the needle through the thick cloth.

*She is an unhappy woman,* Joan thought. This was difficult to understand, for was she not married to Gerold? Yet theirs had been an arranged marriage, and although many such matches turned out to be happy ones, this one obviously had not. They slept in separate beds, and, if the servants' gossip was correct, had not known each other as man and wife for many years.

"Would you care to ride?" Gerold smiled down at her from astride his chestnut stallion. In his right hand he held the reins of Boda, a lively bay mare he knew Joan especially favored.

Joan blushed, embarrassed by what she had just been thinking. She had been so lost in thought that she had not seen Gerold ride back to retrieve Boda from the group of spare mounts and lead her toward the wagon.

"Ride with the men?" Richild frowned. "I won't permit it! It would not be proper!"

"Nonsense!" Gerold replied. "It does no harm, and the girl wants to ride, don't you, Joan?"

"I . . . I . . . ," she said awkwardly, caught in the middle and reluctant to further offend Richild.

Gerold raised an eyebrow. "Of course, if you'd rather remain in the wagon . . ."

"No!" Joan said quickly. "Please, I'd love to ride Boda." She stood in the cart and reached out her arms. Gerold laughed and caught her about the waist, swinging her high onto the saddle before him. Then, keeping the horses close, he hoisted her sideways onto Boda's back.

She settled into the saddle. In the wagon Gisla and Dhuoda looked on with surprise, Richild with glaring disapproval. Gerold appeared not to notice. Joan prodded Boda into a canter and rode quickly toward the front of the line. The smooth, rhythmic strides of the horse were a joy compared with the stiff jerking of the wagon. Luke ran alongside, tail held high, his laughing mouth registering a delight almost as great as Joan's.

She pulled up next to John, who could not conceal his dismay. Joan laughed, her spirits soaring. The road to St.-Denis would not be so long after all.

They crossed the tributary of the Rhine with no difficulty; the bridge there was sturdy and wide, one of those built in the days of Emperor Karolus and still maintained by the lord of that county. But the Meuse, at whose banks they arrived on the eighth day, presented a problem, for the bridge there had fallen into disrepair. The planks were rotten, and there were holes where one or two had dropped out completely, making passage impossible. Someone had improvised a rough bridge by tying a string of wooden boats together in a line; a person could cross by stepping through each of the boats in turn. But the boat bridge would not serve for so many people, horses, and wagons laden with goods. Gerold and two of his men ranged south along the riverbank, looking for a place to ford. An hour later they returned to report a likely spot two miles down where the river widened into shallows.

The party set off again, the wagons lurching wildly over the dense undergrowth along the riverbank. The women clutched the sides of their cart with both hands to keep from being thrown out. Bertha still walked alongside, her lips moving in unending recitation. The hemp on her buskins was worn through to the skin, and she had begun to limp; her toes were swollen, her soles cut and bleeding. Nevertheless, Joan noticed that she occasionally stole sidewards glances at Richild and her daughters and seemed to derive some small satisfaction from watching them pitch about in the wagon.

At last they reached the fording place. Gerold and several of the other mounted men rode down into the river first, to test the depth and levelness of the bottom. The water quickly swirled round them; it reached the bottom of their kirtles in midstream before it began to recede where the riverbed sloped upward to the opposite bank.

Gerold rode back, motioning the others forward. Without hesitation, Joan headed into the river, followed closely by Luke, who plunged in and swam with sure, confident movements. After a moment's hesitation, John and the others came after them.

The cold waters of the Meuse circled Joan. She gasped as the chill penetrated her clothes and reached her skin. Behind her the wagons slowly bumped down into the river, drawn forward by the mules. Bertha labored to keep up, pushing her way through the chilly water, which rose nearly to her shoulders.

Looking back, Joan saw that Bertha was in trouble. She rode toward her. The mare could carry both of them across with no trouble. She was no more than five feet away when the girl vanished, slipping beneath the surface of the water as quickly as if pulled by the feet. Joan halted, unsure what to do; then she urged her mount toward the widening rings of water marking the spot where Bertha had gone under.

"Stay back!" Gerold's hand grabbed the bridle, halting the mare. He broke a long branch off an overhanging birch, dismounted, and walked slowly back toward the bank, probing the riverbed. An arm's length away from the place where Bertha had disappeared, he stumbled and almost fell as the branch sank deep into the water.

"A hole!" He ripped off his mantle and dove in.

Suddenly everything was confusion. Men rode back and forth through the water, shouting instructions and beating the water with sticks.

Gerold was down there. They could be trampling him, hurting him, why couldn't they see that?

"Stop!" Joan screamed, but they paid no attention. She rode to Egbert, chief of Gerold's retainers, and grabbed him fiercely by the arm. "Stop!" she said.

Startled, Egbert was about to shrug her off, but she stared him down. "Tell them to stop; they are making it worse." He drew up, signaling the others. They reined in, ringing the water hole, and waited in tense concentration.

A minute passed. Behind them the first wagon gained the far bank and bumped safely onto land. Joan did not notice. Her eyes were fixed on the spot where Gerold had dived under.

Fear moistened her palms, made her hands slip on the reins. The bay mare, sensing trouble, whinnied and shifted. Luke threw back his head and howled.

*Deus Misereatur,* she prayed. *Dear God, take pity. Demand what sacrifice You will, only let him rise from this.*

Two minutes.

It was too long. He needed to come up for air.

She swung down out of the saddle into the cold water. She could not swim, but she did not stop to think of that. She began splashing wildly toward the hole. Luke leapt back and forth in front of her, trying to block her advance, but she shoved past him. Only one thought occupied all her mind—reach Gerold, pull him out, save him.

She was half a yard from the water hole when there was a splash and a plume of water. Gerold broke the surface in one leap and stood gasping, his red hair smeared across his face.

"Gerold!" Joan's exultant shout sounded clear above the cheers of the men. Gerold turned to her and nodded. Then he took a deep breath, ready to dive again.

"Look!" The mule driver in the first wagon pointed downriver.

A round blue object rose and fell gently against the far bank. Bertha's robe was blue.

They remounted and rode downriver. In the water, caught in branches and debris that had accumulated along the bank, Bertha was floating on her back, limbs thrown wide as if discarded, her lifeless features fixed into a terrible expression of helplessness and fear.

"Take her up." Gerold spoke brusquely to his men. "We will bear her to the church in Prüm for a decent burial."

Joan began to tremble violently, unable to pull her eyes away from Bertha. In death, she looked so much like Matthew had—the pale gray skin, the half-closed eyes, the slackened mouth.

Suddenly Gerold's arms were around her, turning her head away, pressing it to his shoulder. She closed her eyes and clung to him. The men dismounted and splashed into the water; she heard the soft, wet rustle of the river reeds as they released the weight of Bertha's body.

"You were coming after me back there, weren't you?" Gerold whispered, his mouth close to her ear. He spoke wonderingly, as if the realization had just struck him.

"Yes." She nodded, never taking her head from his shoulder.

"Can you swim?"

"No," she admitted, and felt Gerold's arms tighten around her as they stood together by the river's edge.

Behind them, the men slowly carried Bertha's body toward the wagons. The chaplain walked alongside, his head bowed as he recited the prayer for the dead. Richild was not praying with him. Her head was high, and she was staring at Joan and Gerold.

Joan stepped out of the circle of Gerold's arms.

"What is it?" His look was warm with affection and concern.

Richild was still watching them.

"N-nothing."

He followed the direction of her gaze. "Ah." Gently he lifted a stray lock of white-gold hair from her face. "Shall we rejoin the others then?"

Side by side they walked to the wagons. Then Gerold left to consult with the chaplain about the disposition of the body.

Richild said, "Joan, you will ride in the wagon for the rest of the journey. You will be far safer here with us."

It was useless to protest. Joan climbed into the wagon.

The men gently laid Bertha in one of the rear wagons, moving sacks aside to make room. A household servant, an older woman, cried out and threw herself onto Bertha's body.

The woman began the traditional keening wail for the dead. Everyone waited in a respectful, embarrassed silence. After a decent interval, the chaplain approached and spoke softly to the woman. She raised her head; her eyes, wild with grief and pain, fixed on Richild.

"You!" she screamed. "It was you, lady! You killed her! She was a good girl, my Bertha, she would have served you well! Her death is on your head, lady. On your head!"

Two of Richild's retainers grabbed the woman roughly and hurried her away, still screaming imprecations.

The chaplain approached Richild, wringing his hands in nervous apology. "She is Bertha's mother. Grief has driven the poor woman quite out of her senses. Of course the child's death was an accident. A tragic accident."

"No accident, Wala," Richild said sternly. "It was God's will."

Wala blanched. "Of course, of course." As Richild's chaplain, a private "house priest," Wala held a position little better than that of a common colonus; if he displeased her, she could have him whipped—or worse yet, cast out to starve. "God's will. God's will, lady, most assuredly."

"Go and speak to the woman, for the extremity of her grief has surely placed her soul in mortal danger."

"Ah, lady!" He fluttered long, white hands skyward. "Such heavenly forbearance! Such *caritas!*"

She dismissed him impatiently, and he hurried away, looking like a man who has been cut loose from the gallows just before the trap opens.

Gerold gave the command to start up, and the procession moved out, bumping along the riverbank back toward the road to St.-Denis. Behind them, in the rearmost wagon, the mother's screams gradually subsided into a steady, heart-wrenching sobbing. Dhuoda's eyes were moist with tears; even Gisla's unflagging high spirits were quenched. But Richild appeared entirely unshaken. Joan studied her appraisingly. Could anyone be that skillful at hiding her emotions, or was she really as cold as she appeared? Did the girl's death not weigh upon her conscience at all?

Richild looked at her. Joan turned her eyes away so she could not read her thoughts.

God's will?

No, my lady.

*Your* command.

✦ ✦ ✦

The first day of the fair was in full swing. People streamed through the huge iron gate that led to the open field fronting the Abbey of St.-Denis—peasants in ragged *bandelettes* and shirts of rude linen; noblemen and *fideles* in silk tunics crossed with golden baldrics, their wives elegantly bedecked in fur-trimmed mantles and jeweled headdresses; Lombards and Aquitanians in their exotic bouffant pantaloons and boots. Never had Joan seen so odd or so large a conglomeration of humanity.

On the field, the stalls of the merchants crowded closely together, their various goods displayed in a gaudy, incoherent riot of color and form. There were robes and mantles of purple silk, scarlet phoenix skins, peacock's feathers, stamped leather jerkins, rare delicacies such as almonds and raisins, and all manner of scents and spices, pearls, gems, silver and gold. Still more merchandise poured through the gates, heaped high on wagons or carried in unwieldy piles upon the backs of the poorer vendors, bent almost double under the weight. More than one of these would not sleep that night from the pain of muscles strained past endurance, but in this way they avoided the expensive tolls, the *rotaticum* and *saumaticum,* charged against goods carried in on wheeled vehicles and beasts of burden.

Inside the gate, Gerold said to Joan and John, "Hold out your hands." Into each of their outstretched palms, he placed a silver denarius. "Spend it wisely."

Joan stared at the shiny coin. She had seen denarii only once or twice before, and those at a distance, for in Ingelheim trade was accomplished by barter; even her father's income, the *decima* tithed from the peasants of his parish, had been offered in goods and foodstuffs.

A whole denarius! It seemed a fortune beyond measure.

They wandered down the narrow, crowded passageways between the stalls. All around vendors hawked their merchandise, customers bargained hotly over prices, and performers of every kind—dancers, jugglers, acrobats, bear and monkey trainers—plied their trades. The din of innumerable deals, jests, and arguments surrounded them on every side, conducted in a hundred dialects and tongues.

It was easy to get lost in the jostling crowds. Joan took John's hand—to her surprise, he did not protest—and kept close to Gerold's side. Luke stayed right behind them, inseparable, as always, from Joan. Their small group was soon parted from Richild and the others, who had walked more slowly. Halfway down the first row of stalls, they stopped and waited for the others to catch up. Off to their left, a woman stood screaming at a pair of merchants pulling at either end of a piece of linen cloth laid out beside a long wooden ruler measuring exactly one ell.

"Stop!" the woman shouted. "You dunderheads! You are stretching it!" And indeed, it appeared as if the men would rip the cloth in half to make the most of its measure.

There was a loud burst of shouting and laughter from a crowd circling a small open enclosure a short distance ahead.

"Come on." John pulled on Joan's arm. She hesitated, not wanting to leave Gerold, but he saw what John wanted and good-naturedly shooed them in that direction.

Another great shout rose from the crowd as they drew close. Joan saw a man fall to his knees in the center of the enclosure, clutching his shoulder as if it were hurt. Quickly he got back up to his feet, and now Joan could see that in his other hand he held a thick, sturdy birch bough. Another man stood in the ring, similarly armed. The two of them circled each other, swinging the heavy sticks with ferocious abandon. There was an odd, high-pitched squeal as a blood-spattered pig ran frantically between the two men, its stubby legs pumping like matched butter churns. The two men swung at the pig, but their aim was wild; the one who had just fallen shrieked as he took a solid hit on his nether parts. The crowd roared with laughter.

John laughed along with the others, his eyes lit with interest. He tugged on the sleeve of a short, pockmarked peasant who stood beside them. "What's going on?" he asked excitedly.

The man grinned down at him, the holes in his face widening as the skin creased. "Why, they're after the pig, lad, d'ye see? Him as kills it, takes it home for his table."

*Odd,* Joan thought, as she watched the two men compete for the prize. They swung their sticks forcefully, but their blows were random and undirected, falling on thin air or on each other more often than on the hapless pig. There was something strange about the appearance of the man facing her. She looked more closely and saw a milky whiteness where his pupils should have been. Now the other man turned to face her; his eyes looked normal enough, but they stared out fixedly into space, vacant and unfocused.

The men were blind.

Another blow found its mark, and the milky-eyed man staggered sideways, clutching his head. John jumped up, clapping his hands and shouting with laughter along with the rest of the crowd. His eyes glittered with a strange excitement.

Joan turned away.

"Psst! Young mistress!" a voice called out to her. Across the way, a vendor was gesturing at her. She left John cheering on the bizarre combat and went to the man's stall, fronted by a long table displaying an assortment of religious relics. There were wooden crosses and medallions of every kind and description, as well as holy relics of several locally popular saints: a strand of hair from St. Willibrord, a fingernail of St. Romaric, two teeth of St. Waldetrudis, and a scrap of cloth from the robe of the virgin martyr St. Genovefa.

The man pulled a vial from his leather scrip.

"Know what this holds?" His voice was so low she could barely hear him over the surrounding din. She shook her head.

"Several drops of the milk"—his voice dropped still further—"of the Holy Virgin Mother."

Joan was stunned. So great a treasure! Here? Surely it should be enshrined in some great monastery or cathedral.

"One denarius," the man said.

One denarius! She fingered the silver coin in her pocket. The man held the vial out to her, and she took it, its surface cool in her hand. She had a brief vision of the look on Odo's face when she returned with such a prize for the cathedral.

The man smiled, holding out his hand, fingers waggling to coax the coin from her.

Joan hesitated. Why would this man sell so great a treasure for such a sum? It was worth a fortune to some great abbey or cathedral in need of a holy relic for pilgrims to venerate.

She lifted the cap off the vial and peered inside. Halfway down the length of the tube, the pale surface of the milk shimmered smooth and blue-white in the sunlight. Joan reached down and touched it with the tip of her little finger. Then she looked up, her keen eyes scanning the area around the stall. She laughed, lifted the vial to her lips, and drank.

The man gasped. "Are you woodly?" His face was contorted with anger.

"Delicious," Joan said, recapping the vial and handing it back to him. "My compliments to your goat."

"Why, you . . . you . . . ," the man sputtered, unable to find the words to express his rage and frustration. For a moment it seemed as if he might come round the table after her. There was a low growl; Luke, who until then had been sitting quietly, moved in front of Joan, a deep line furrowing the length of his muzzle, lifted at the sides to reveal a row of menacing white teeth.

"What is that?" The vendor stared at Luke's glittering eyes.

"That," a voice said behind Joan, "is a wolf."

It was Gerold. He had come up quietly during her interchange with the vendor. He stood loosely, his arms at his sides, his body relaxed, but his eyes were hard with warning. The vendor turned away, mumbling something under his breath. Gerold put his arm around Joan's shoulders and led her away, calling to Luke, who growled at the vendor one more time, then ran to join them.

Gerold didn't speak. They walked together in silence, Joan quickening her pace to keep up with his long strides.

*He is angry,* she thought, her high spirits quenched as suddenly as a smothered hearth fire.

What was worse, she knew he was right. She had acted recklessly with the merchant. Hadn't she promised to be more careful? Why did she always have to question and challenge things? Why couldn't she learn it: *Some ideas are dangerous.*

*Maybe I* am *woodly.*

She heard a low rumble of sound; Gerold was laughing.

"The look on the man's face when you lifted the vial and drank! I shall never forget it!" He pulled her close in a warm hug. "Ah, Joan, you are my pearl! But tell me, how did you know that it wasn't the Virgin's milk?"

Joan grinned, relieved. "I was mistrustful from the first, for if the thing were truly holy, why would it fetch so small a price? And why did the vendor keep his goat tethered behind the stall, where it couldn't be seen? If it was received in barter, surely there was no need to hide it."

"True. But to actually *drink* the stuff"—there was another burst of laughter from Gerold—"surely you must have known something else."

"Yes. When I uncapped the vial, the milk was uncurdled and perfectly fresh, as if produced this morning, though the Virgin's milk would be over eight hundred years old."

"Ah"—Gerold smiled, his eyebrows arched, testing her—"but perhaps its great holiness kept it pure and uncorrupted."

"True," Joan admitted. "But when I touched the milk, it was still warm! So holy a thing might perhaps remain uncorrupted, but why should it be warm?"

"A pretty observation," Gerold said appreciatively. "Lucretius himself could have done no better!"

Joan beamed. How she loved to please him!

They had walked almost to the end of the long row of stalls, where the huge wooden cross of St.-Denis marked the boundary of the fair, protecting the holy tranquillity of the abbey brothers. This was where the parchment merchants had set up their stalls.

"Look!" Gerold spied them first, and they hurried over to inspect the merchandise, which was of very high quality. The vellum, in particular, was extraordinary: the flesh side of the skin was perfectly even, the color whiter than Joan had ever seen; the other side was, as usual, somewhat yellower, but the pittings where the calf's hair had been rooted were so tiny and shallow as to be almost invisible.

"What a pleasure it must be to write on such sheets!" Joan exclaimed, fingering them gently.

Gerold immediately called one of the merchants over. "Four sheets," he ordered, and Joan gasped, overwhelmed at his extravagance. Four sheets! It was enough for an entire codex!

While Gerold paid for his purchase, Joan's attention wandered to a few sheets of ragged-looking parchment scattered untidily toward the rear of the stall. The edges of the sheets were torn, and there was writing on them, very faint and obliterated in places by ugly brown stains. She bent close to read the writing better, then flushed with excitement.

Seeing her interest, the merchant hurried over.

"So young, and already a fine eye for a bargain," he said unctuously. "The sheets are old, as you see, but still good for their purpose. Look!"

Before she could speak, he took a long, flat tool and scraped it quickly across the page, effacing several letters.

"Stop!" Joan spoke sharply, remembering a different piece of parchment and a different knife. "Stop!"

The merchant looked at her curiously. "You needn't worry, lass, it's only pagan writing." He pointed proudly to the page. "See? Nice and clean and ready to write on!" He lifted the tool to demonstrate the trick again, but Joan grabbed his hand.

"I'll give you a denarius for them," she said tersely.

The man feigned being insulted. "They're worth three denarii, at least."

Joan took the coin from her scrip and held it out to him. "One," she repeated. "It's all I have."

The merchant hesitated, searching her face assessingly. "Very well," he said testily. "Take them."

Joan thrust the coin at him and gathered up the precious parchment before he could change his mind. She ran to Gerold.

"Look!" she said excitedly.

Gerold stared at the pages. "I don't recognize the letters."

"It's written in Greek," Joan explained. "And it's very old. An engineering text, I think. See the diagrams?" She pointed to one of the pages, and Gerold studied the drawing.

"Some kind of hydraulic device." His interest was kindled. "Fascinating. Can you provide a translation of the text?"

"I can."

"Then I might be able to rig it up."

They smiled at each other, conspirators in a fine new scheme.

"Father!" Gisla's voice pierced the noise of the crowd. Gerold turned, searching for her. He was taller by a head than anyone around him; in the sun his thick, red hair gleamed like colored gold. Joan's heart jumped unevenly in her chest as she watched him. *You are my pearl,* he had said. She grasped the papers tightly as she watched him, holding on to the moment.

"Father! Joan!" Gisla finally appeared, pushing her way through the crowd, followed by one of the household servants, his arms laden with goods. "I've been looking everywhere!" she remonstrated good-naturedly. "What have you got there?" Joan started to explain, but Gisla waved her aside. "Oh, just more of your silly old books. Look what *I* found," she enthused. She dangled a length of multicolored cloth. "For my wedding dress! Isn't it *perfect*?"

The cloth shimmered as Gisla displayed it. Examining it more closely, Joan saw that it was woven through with slender, perfect threads of gold and silver.

"It's astonishing," she said sincerely.

Gisla giggled. "I know!" Without waiting for a reply, she grabbed Joan's arm and started toward a stall some distance ahead. "Oh, look," she said, "a slave auction! Let's go see!"

"No." Joan hung back. She had seen the slave traders passing through Ingelheim, their human cargo bound together with heavy ropes. Many of them were Saxons, like her mother.

"No," she said again, and would not budge.

"Aren't you a goose!" Gisla tweaked Joan playfully. "They're only heathens. They don't have feelings, at least not like us."

"I wonder what's in here?" Joan said, anxious to distract her. She led Gisla toward a tiny stall at the end of the row. It was dark and sealed, every panel closed. Luke circled it, sniffing curiously at the walls.

"How strange," Gisla said.

In the bright afternoon sun, with business in full swing all around, the quiet, darkened stall *was* an oddity. Her curiosity piqued, Joan tapped gently on the closed shutter.

"Come in," a cracked voice spoke from within. Gisla jumped at the sound but did not back away. The two girls circled to the side of the stall and pushed cautiously on the planked timber door, which creaked and groaned as it opened inward, spilling slanting rays of light into the gloom.

They stepped inside. A strange smell pervaded the stall, cloying and sweet, like fermented honey. In the center of the enclosure, a tiny figure sat cross-legged—an old woman, dressed simply in a loose, dark robe. She appeared unbelievably ancient, perhaps seventy winters or more; her hair was gone, save for some fine white strands at her crown, and her head shook constantly as if she were afflicted with the ague. But her eyes shone alertly in the darkness, focusing on Joan and Gisla with shrewd assessment.

"Pretty little doves," she croaked. "So pretty and so young. What do you want of Old Balthild?"

"We just wanted to—to—" Joan faltered as she searched uneasily for an explanation. The old woman's gaze was unsettling.

"To find out what is for sale here," Gisla finished boldly.

"What's for sale? What's for sale?" The old woman cackled. "Something that you want but will never own."

"What?" Gisla asked.

"Something that is already yours though you have it not." The old woman grinned at them toothlessly. "Something beyond price and yet it can be bought."

"What *is* it?" Gisla said sharply, impatient with the old woman's riddles.

"The future." The old woman's eyes glittered in the dimness. "Your future, my little dove. All that will be and is not yet."

"Oh, you're a fortune-teller!" Gisla clapped her hands together, pleased to have deciphered the puzzle. "How much?"

"One *solidus.*"

One solidus! It was the price of a good milking cow, or a pair of fine rams!

"Too dear." Gisla was in her element now, confident and assured, a shrewd customer looking to strike a bargain.

"One *obole,*" she offered.

"Five denarii," the old woman countered.

"Two. One for each of us." Gisla withdrew the coins from her scrip and held them out on her palm for the woman to see.

The old woman hesitated, then took the coins, motioning the girls to the floor beside her. They sat; the woman clasped Joan's strong young hands in her shaking grasp and fixed her odd, disquieting gaze upon her. For a long time, she said nothing; then she began to speak.

"Changeling child, you are what you will not be; what you will become is other than you are."

This made little sense, unless it meant simply that she would soon be a woman grown. But then why had the old woman called her a "changeling"?

Balthild continued, "You aspire to that which is forbidden." Joan started with surprise, and the old woman tightened her clasp. "Yes, changeling, I see your secret heart. You will not be disappointed. Greatness will be yours, beyond your dreams, and grief, beyond your imaginings."

Balthild dropped Joan's hands and turned toward Gisla, who winked at Joan with an expression that said, *Wasn't that* fun?

The old woman took Gisla's hands, her bent, gnarled fingers curling around Gisla's smooth, pink ones.

"You will marry soon, and richly," she said.

"Yes!" Gisla giggled. "But, old woman, I did not pay you to tell me what I already know. Will the union be a happy one?"

"No more than most, but no less either," Balthild said. Gisla raised her eyes to the ceiling in mock despair.

"A wife you shall be, though never a mother," Balthild crooned, swaying with the rhythm of the words, her voice singsong, melodic.

Gisla's smile vanished. "Shall I be barren, then?"

"The future lies before you all dark and empty." Balthild's voice rose in a keening wail. "Pain shall be yours, and confusion, and fear."

Gisla sat transfixed, like a stoat held fast by the stare of a snake.

"Enough!" Joan pried Gisla's hands from the old woman's grasp. "Come with me," she said. Gisla obeyed, compliant as a babe.

Outside the stall, Gisla began to cry.

"Don't be silly," Joan soothed. "The old woman's mad, pay no attention to her. There is no truth in such fortune-telling."

Gisla would not be comforted. She cried and cried; finally, Joan led her to the sweetmeat stalls, where they bought sugared figs and gorged themselves until Gisla felt somewhat better.

That night, when they told Gerold what had happened, he was furious.

"What now, sorcery? Joan and Gisla, you will take me to this stall tomorrow. I have some words to say to this old woman who frightens young girls. In the meantime, Gisla, you must not give heed to such nonsense. Why did you even seek such false counsel?" To Joan he said reproachfully, "I would have thought that *you,* at least, would have known better."

Joan accepted the chastisement. Still, there was a part of her that wanted to believe in Balthild's powers. Hadn't the old woman said that she would realize her secret desire? If she was right, then Joan *would* achieve greatness, despite the fact that she was a girl, despite what everyone else believed possible.

But if Balthild was right about Joan's future, then she was also right about Gisla's.

When they returned to the stall with Gerold the next day, it was empty. No one could tell them where the old woman had gone.

In Winnemanoth, Gisla was married to Count Hugo. There had been some difficulty finding a date suitable for the immediate consummation of the marriage. The Church forbade all marital relations on Sundays,

Wednesdays, and Fridays, as well as for forty days before Easter, eight days after Pentecost, and five days before the taking of communion, or on the eve of any great feast or rogation day. In all, on some two hundred and twenty days of the year sexual intercourse was prohibited; when these, as well as Gisla's monthly bleeding time, were taken into account, there were not many dates left to choose from. But at last they settled on the twenty-fourth of the month, a date that pleased everyone save Gisla, who was impatient for the festivities to begin.

At last the great day arrived. The entire household rose before prime to fuss over Gisla. First she was helped into her long-sleeved, yellow linen undertunic. Over this was placed the resplendent new tunic fashioned from the shimmering silver and gold fabric purchased at the St.-Denis fair. It draped from her shoulders to the floor in graceful folds that were echoed in the wide sleeves opening out at her elbows. Around her hips was fastened a heavy kirtle set with good-luck stones—agate to guard against fever, chalk to defend against the evil eye, bloodstone for fertility, jasper for safe delivery in childbirth. Finally a delicate, finely worked silken veil was fastened on her head. It billowed to the ground, covering her shoulders and completely hiding her auburn hair. Standing there in her wedding dress, hardly able to move or even sit for fear of crumpling it, she looked, Joan thought, like an exotic game bird, stuffed and trussed and ready for carving.

*Not I,* Joan vowed. She did not mean to wed, although in seven months she would be fifteen, a more than marriageable age. In three more years, she would be an old maid. It was incredible to her that girls her age were so eager for marriage, for it immediately plunged a woman into a state of serflike bondage. A husband had absolute control of his wife's goods and property, her children, even her life. Having endured her father's tyranny, Joan meant never to give any man such power over her again.

Gisla, simple creature that she was, went to her bridegroom with eager enthusiasm, all blushes and nervous giggles. Count Hugo, magnificent in a tunic and mantle edged with ermine, waited for her at the sacred portal to the cathedral. She took his proffered hand and stood proudly while Wido, the steward of Villaris, publicly recited all the lands, servants, animals, and goods that Gisla brought as dowry. Then the wedding party entered the cathedral, where Fulgentius waited before the altar to perform the solemn wedding mass.

*"Quod Deus conjunxit homo non separet."* The Latin words issued halt-

ingly from Fulgentius's tongue. He had been a soldier before inheriting the bishopric late in life; having begun book study tardily, the proper forms of Latin were forever beyond him.

*"In nomine Patria et Filia . . ."* Joan winced as Fulgentius mangled the blessing, confusing his declensions so that instead of "In the name of the Father and the Son and the Holy Spirit" it came out "In the name of the Country and the Daughter."

Finishing with this part of the mass, Fulgentius turned, with obvious relief, to Theodisk.

"May this woman be amiable as Rachel, faithful as Sarah, fertile as Leah." He rested his hand kindly on Gisla's head. "May she bring forth many sons to bring honor to her husband's house."

Joan saw Gisla's shoulders shake and knew she was repressing a giggle.

"Let her copy the behavior of a dog who always has his heart and his eye upon his master; even if his master whip him and throw stones at him, the dog follows, wagging his tail." This seemed hard to Joan, but Fulgentius was regarding Gisla with a benign, even affectionate expression and obviously did not mean to offend. "Wherefore for a better and stronger reason," he continued, "a woman should have a perfect and indestructible love for her husband."

He turned to Count Hugo. "May this man be brave as David, wise as Solomon, strong as Samson. May his lands increase even as his fortune. May he be a just lord to this lady, never administering to her more than reasonable punishments. May he live to see his sons do honor to his name."

They began the exchange of vows. Count Hugo gave his promise first, then placed a ring of Byzantine turquoise on Gisla's fourth finger, which contained the vein leading to the heart.

It was Gisla's turn. Joan listened to Gisla recite her marriage vows. Her voice was high and merry, her mind untroubled by doubt, her future seemingly assured.

*What,* Joan wondered, *does* my *future hold?*

She could not continue at the schola forever—at most, she had another three years. She let herself daydream, picturing herself as teaching master at one of the great cathedral scholas, Rheims, perhaps, or even the Schola Palatina, her days spent exploring the wisdom of the ages with minds as eager and inquisitive as her own. The daydream was, as always, intensely pleasing.

*But*—the thought struck like a loosed shaft—*that would mean leaving Villaris. Leaving Gerold.*

She knew she would have to leave Villaris one day. But over the past few months, she had put that thought away, content to live in the present, in the joy of being with Gerold every day.

She let her gaze rest upon him. His profile was strong and well chiseled, his form tall and straight; his red hair curled thickly to his shoulders.

*The handsomest man I have ever seen,* she thought, not for the first time.

As if he had read her mind, he turned toward her. Their eyes met. Something in his expression—a momentary softening, a tenderness—thrilled her. In an instant the look had vanished, before she was even sure of it, but its warmth lingered.

*I am wrong to worry,* she thought. *Nothing needs to be decided yet.*

Three years was a long time.

A lot could happen in three years.

Returning from the schola the following week, Joan found Gerold waiting for her on the portico.

"Come with me." His tone indicated that he had a surprise in store. He motioned to her and started toward the foregate. Passing through the gated palisade, they followed the road for several miles, then abruptly turned aside into the woods, emerging a short time later into a small clearing, in the midst of which was a sunken hut. No longer inhabited, it had fallen into disrepair. But it must once have been a snug freeman's dwelling, for the wattle-and-daub walls still appeared tight, and the door was made of sturdy oak. It reminded Joan of her own home in Ingelheim, though this grubenhaus was far smaller and its thatched roof was holed with rot.

They stopped before it. "Wait here," Gerold commanded. Joan watched curiously as he circled the structure once, then returned and stood beside her, facing the door.

"Behold," Gerold said with feigned solemnity. Raising his hands above his head, he clapped loudly three times.

Nothing happened. Joan looked questioningly at Gerold, who stared at the hut expectantly. Evidently something was supposed to happen. But what?

With a loud groan, the heavy oak door began to swing open—slowly at first, then more quickly, exposing the vacant darkness within. Joan peered into the hut. No one was there. The door had moved on its own.

Astounded, Joan gaped at the door. A dozen questions thronged her brain, but only one found its way out. "How?"

Gerold raised his eyes to Heaven in mock piety. "A holy miracle."

Joan snorted.

He laughed. "Sorcery, then." He eyed her challengingly, enjoying the game.

Joan took up the challenge. She marched to the door and examined it. "Can you close it?" she asked.

Gerold raised his hands again. He clapped three times. After a pause, the door groaned and began to swing inward on its hinges. Joan followed as it moved, studying it. The heavy wooden panels were smooth and tightly jointed—no sign of anything unusual there. There was nothing unusual about the plain wooden handle, either. She examined the hinges. They were ordinary iron hinges. It was infuriating. She could not fathom what was making the door move.

The door was fast closed once more. It was a mystery.

"Well?" Gerold's indigo eyes were lit with amusement.

Joan hesitated, unwilling to forfeit the game.

Just as she was about to admit defeat, she heard something, a slender thread of sound coming from somewhere above her. At first she could not place it; the noise was familiar yet strangely out of place.

Then she recognized it. Water. The sound of trickling water.

She said excitedly, "The hydraulic device! The one in the manuscript from the St.-Denis fair! You built it!"

Gerold laughed. "Adapted it, rather. For it was designed to pump water, not to open and close doors!"

"How does it work?"

Gerold showed her the mechanism, located just under the decaying roof of the hut a full ten feet from the door, which was why she had not seen it. He demonstrated the complicated system of levers, pulleys, and counterweights, connected to two slender iron rods attached to the inside of the door so that they were barely visible. By stepping on a rope when he had circled the hut, Gerold had activated the device.

"Amazing!" she said when he finished explaining. "Do it again." Now that she understood how the device worked, she wanted to observe it in action.

"I can't. Not without fetching more water."

"Then let's fetch it," she said. "Where are the buckets?"

Gerold laughed. "You are incorrigible!" He pulled her close in an affectionate hug. His chest was hard and firm, his arms strong around her. Joan felt as if her insides were melting.

Abruptly, he let her go. "Come on, then," he said gruffly. "The buckets are over here."

They carried the empty buckets to the stream a quarter of a mile away, filled them, carried them back, poured them into the receptacle, then returned to fetch more. Three times they made the trip, and by the third they were feeling somewhat giddy. The sun was warm, the air full of spring promise, and their spirits high from the excitement of their project and the joy of each other's company.

"Gerold, look!" Joan called, standing knee-deep in the cool water of the stream. When he turned to her, she playfully slung the water from her bucket at him, wetting the front of his tunic.

"You imp!" he roared.

He filled his bucket and doused her in turn. So they continued, splashing each other in a flurry of sparkling spray, until Joan was hit by a stream of water from Gerold's bucket just as she was bending over to fill her own. Caught off balance, she slipped and fell heavily into the stream. The cool water closed over her head, and for a brief moment she panicked, unable to find her footing on the shifting pebbles of the riverbed.

Then Gerold's arms were around her, pulling her up, setting her on her feet.

"I've got you, Joan, I've got you." His voice, close to her ear, was warm and reassuring. Joan felt her whole body thrum to its cadence. She clung to him. Their wet clothes stuck to each other, molding their bodies together in unambiguous intimacy.

"I love you," she said simply. "I love you."

"Oh, my dearest, my perfect girl," Gerold murmured thickly, and then his mouth was on hers, and she was kissing him back, their passion fueled by the sudden release of emotions long held in check.

The very air seemed to hum in Joan's ears. *Gerold,* it sang. *Gerold.*

Neither of them guessed that from behind the little copse of trees on the crest of the hill, someone was watching.

✦ ✦ ✦

Odo had been on his way to Héristal to pay a visit to his uncle, one of the holy brothers of that abbey, when his mule had chanced to stray from the path in pursuit of a particularly succulent-looking patch of clover. He cursed the mule, pulling on its bridle and whipping it with a willow rod, but it was stubborn and would not be dissuaded. He had no choice but to leave the road and follow the stupid beast. Then he looked up, toward the stream, and saw.

*A learned woman is never chaste.* St. Paul's words, or were they Jerome's? No matter. Odo had always believed it to be true, and now he had the proof with his own eyes!

Odo patted the mule's flank. *You shall have an extra portion of feed tonight,* he thought. Then he reconsidered. Feed was expensive, and besides, the beast had only served as God's instrument.

Odo hurried back to the road. His errand would have to wait. First he must get to Villaris.

A short time later, the towers of Villaris loomed ahead. In his excitement, he had walked more quickly than usual. He passed through the gated palisade and was greeted by a guardsman.

Odo waved aside the greeting. "Take me to Lady Richild," he commanded. "I must speak with her at once."

Gerold removed Joan's arms from his neck and stepped back. "Come," he said, his voice heavy with emotion, "we must go back."

Woolly-headed with love, Joan moved to embrace him again.

"No," Gerold said firmly. "I must take you home now, while I have the will to do so."

Joan stared at him dazedly. "You don't . . . want me?" She lowered her head before he could answer.

Gerold cupped her chin gently, forcing her eyes to meet his. "I want you more than I have ever wanted any woman."

"Then why . . . ?"

"God's teeth, Joan! I am a man, with a man's desires. Do not tempt me beyond my limits!" Gerold sounded almost angry. Seeing the start of tears to her eyes, he gentled his tone. "What would you have me do, my love? Make you my mistress? Ah, Joan, I would take you right here on this sward if I thought it would make you happy. But it would spell your ruin, can't you see that?"

Gerold's indigo eyes held hers commandingly. He was so handsome that it took her breath away. All she wanted was for him to take her in his arms again.

He stroked her white-gold hair. She began to speak, but her voice broke. She breathed deeply, trying to steady her emotions, sick with shame and frustration.

"Come." Gerold took Joan's hand, folding it into his tenderly. She did not protest as he led her back to the road. Wordlessly, hand in hand, they walked the long, comfortless miles toward Villaris.

# 11

Lady Richild, Countess of Villaris," the herald announced as Richild swept regally into the bishop's reception hall.

"Eminence." She made a graceful reverence.

"Lady, you are welcome," Fulgentius said. "What news from your lord? God grant he has not met with misfortune on his journey?"

"No, no." She was pleased to find him so transparent. Of course he must wonder at the purpose of her visit! He must have thought—Gerold had been gone five days now, time enough to have met with some disaster on the dangerous roads.

"We have had no word of any difficulties, Eminence, nor do we expect any. Gerold took twenty men with him, well armed and well provisioned; he will not take any chances on the road, as he is on the Emperor's business."

"We heard as much. He is gone as *missus*—to Westphalia, is it?"

"Yes. To settle a dispute about *wergeld*. There are some minor matters of property to be settled as well. He will be away a fortnight or more." *Time enough,* she thought, *just time enough.*

They spoke briefly of local affairs—the shortage of grain at the mill, the repair of the cathedral roof, the success of the spring calving. Richild was careful to observe the necessary courtesies, but nothing more. *I am the scion of better stock than his.* Just as well to remind him of that before coming to the matter of her visit. Obviously he suspected nothing. So much the better; surprise would be her ally in this day's work.

Finally, she judged the time was right. "I have come to ask your help with a domestic matter."

He looked gratified. "Dear lady, I am only too happy to help. What is the nature of your difficulty?"

"It is the girl Joan. She is no longer a child; she"—Richild chose her words delicately—"has now reached womanhood. It is no longer seemly for her to remain under our roof."

"I see," Fulgentius said, though it was apparent he did not. "Well, I should think we could find some other lodg—"

"I have arranged an advantageous match," Richild interrupted. "With the son of Bodo, the farrier. He is a fine young man, well favored, and will be farrier himself when his father dies—there are no other sons."

"This comes as a surprise. Has the girl expressed any inclination for marriage?"

"Surely that is not for her to decide. It is a far better marriage than she has any right to expect. Her family is poor as coloni, and her odd ways have given her something of a . . . reputation."

"Perhaps," the bishop replied amiably. "But she seems devoted to her studies. And she could not, of course, continue at the schola if she married the farrier's boy."

"That is why I have come. As it was you who contracted to bring her to the schola, you would have to agree to her release."

"I see," he said again, though he still did not, quite. "And how does the count feel about the match?"

"He does not know of it. The opportunity only just offered itself."

"Well, then." Fulgentius looked relieved. "We will wait till his return. There's no need to rush the matter, surely."

Richild persisted. "The opportunity may not be open long. The boy is reluctant—seems he's taken a fancy to one of the town girls—but of course I have seen to it that this match will be far more beneficial for him. His father and I are agreed upon the dowry. The boy now says he will carry out his father's wishes—but he is young and of a changeable disposition. Best if the wedding take place immediately."

"Nevertheless . . ."

"I remind you, Eminence, that I am mistress of Villaris, and the girl has been placed in my care. I am fully capable of making this decision in my husband's absence. Indeed, I am better suited to make it. To speak frankly, Gerold's partiality for the girl clouds his judgment where she is concerned."

"I see," Fulgentius said, and this time he did, only too well.

Richild said quickly, "My concern is strictly monetary, you understand. Gerold has spent a small fortune obtaining books for the girl—a wasteful expense, since she has no possible future as a scholar. Someone must provide for her future; now I have done so. You must see that the match is a good one."

"Yes," Fulgentius admitted.

"Good. Then you agree to release her?"

"My apologies, dear lady, but my decision must attend upon the count's return. I assure you I will discuss the matter fully with him. And with the girl. For though the match is . . . advantageous, as you say, I am loath to commit her to it against her will. If the match proves agreeable to all, we will proceed with dispatch."

She started to speak, but he cut her off. "I know you believe the match will be compromised if it is not concluded immediately. But, forgive me, lady, I cannot agree. A fortnight, or even a month, will make little difference."

Again she tried to object, and again he silenced her. "I am quite decided. There is no point in further discussion."

Her cheeks burned with the insult. *High-handed fool! Who does he think he is to dictate to me? My family was living in royal palaces while his was still tilling fields!*

She eyed him levelly. "Very well, Eminence, if that is your decision, I must accept it." She began to pull on her riding gloves as if preparing to leave.

"By the way"—she kept her tone deliberately casual—"I have just had a letter from my cousin, Sigimund, Bishop of Troyes."

The bishop's face registered a gratifying respect. "A great man, a very great man."

"You know that he is to lead the synod which convenes in Aachen this summer?"

"So I had heard."

Now that she had ceased pressing him, his manner was once again relentlessly cheerful.

"Perhaps you have also heard what is to be the chief topic of discussion at this gathering?"

"I should be interested to learn," he responded politely. He obviously guessed nothing of where she was leading.

"Certain . . . irregularities"—she baited the trap carefully—"in the conduct of the episcopacy."

"Irregularities?"

He did not take her meaning. She would have to be plainer.

"My cousin plans to address the question of adherence to episcopal vows, especially"—she looked him directly in the eyes—"the vow of chastity."

The color drained from his face. "Indeed?"

"Apparently he means to make great issue of it at the synod. He's gathered a good deal of evidence about the Frankish bishoprics, which he finds most disturbing. But he is not so familiar with episcopacies in this part of the Empire and must therefore rely on local reports. In his letter he specifically requests me to share any information I may have about *your* episcopacy, Eminence." She used the title with open scorn and was gratified to see him flinch.

"I intended to reply before now," she went on smoothly. "But the details of the girl's betrothal kept me far too busy. Indeed, the plans for the wedding feast would make it impossible for me to respond at all. Of course, now that the wedding is to be delayed . . ." She let the end of the thought hang delicately.

He sat like a stone, silent, noncommittal. She was mildly surprised. He was going to be better at this than she had anticipated.

Only one thing gave him away. Deep inside his sleepy, heavy-lidded eyes, there was a tiny, unmistakable spark of fear.

Richild smiled.

Joan sat on a rock, troubled and sad. Luke lay down in front of her and put his head in her lap, staring up at her with his opalescent eyes.

"You miss him too, don't you, boy?" she said, gently ruffling the young wolf's white fur.

She was alone now, except for Luke. Gerold had been gone for over a week. Joan missed him with an ache that surprised her with its physicality. She could put her hand over the exact spot in her chest where the pain was most acute; it felt as if her heart had been removed from her body, beaten, and replaced.

She knew why he had gone. After what passed between them at the riverbank, he *had* to go. They needed time apart, time to let heads clear and passions cool. She understood, yet her heart rebelled.

*Why?* she asked for the thousandth time. *Why must it be this way?* Richild did not love Gerold, nor he her.

She reasoned with herself, rehearsing the arguments why this must be so, why it might even be for the best, but in the end she always came back to one unalterable fact: she loved Gerold.

She shook her head, angry with herself. If Gerold was strong enough to do this for her sake, could she be less so? What could not be changed must somehow be endured. She fixed her mind on a new resolve: when Gerold returned, things would be different. She would be content just to be near him, to talk and laugh as they always had . . . before. They would be like teacher and student, priest and nun, brother and sister. She would erase from her mind the memory of his arms around her, of his lips on hers . . .

Wido, the steward, came up suddenly beside her. "My lady wants to speak with you."

Joan followed him through the gated palisade into the forecourt, Luke trotting by her side. When they reached the main courtyard, Wido pointed to Luke. "Not the wolf."

Richild disliked dogs and forbade them to come inside the house walls, as they did on other manses.

Joan told Luke to lie down and wait in the courtyard.

The guard led her through the covered portico into the great hall, teeming with servants preparing the afternoon meal. They pushed their way through to the solar, where Richild was waiting.

"You sent for me, lady?"

"Sit down." Joan started for a nearby chair, but Richild motioned imperiously toward a wooden stool set before a small writing table. Joan sat down.

"You will take a letter."

Like all the noblewomen in this part of the Empire, Richild could neither read nor write. Wala, the Villaris chaplain, was usually her scribe. Wido could also write a little and sometimes served Richild in this capacity.

*Why, then, has she sent for me?* Joan wondered.

Richild tapped her foot impatiently. With a practiced eye, Joan surveyed the quills on the desk and selected the sharpest. She took a leaf of fresh parchment, dipped the quill in the inkwell, and nodded at Richild.

"From Richild, Countess, doyenne of the estate of Villaris," Richild dictated.

Joan wrote quickly. The scratching of the quill grated in the stony silence of the room.

"To the canon of the village of Ingelheim, Greetings."

Joan looked up. "My father?"

"Continue," Richild commanded in a tone that indicated she would tolerate no questions. "Your daughter, Joan, having attained almost fifteen years, and thus being of a marriageable age, will no longer be permitted to continue her studies at the schola."

Joan stopped writing altogether.

"As the girl's guardian, ever vigilant for her welfare," Richild continued, keeping up the pretense of dictation, "I have arranged an advantageous match with Iso, son of the farrier of this town, a prosperous man. The wedding will take place in two days. The terms of the arrangement are as follows—"

Joan jumped up, knocking over her stool. "Why are you doing this?"

"Because I choose to." A small, malicious smile lifted the corners of Richild's mouth. "And because I can."

*She knows,* Joan thought. *She knows about Gerold and me.* The blood rose into her neck and face so suddenly it felt as if her skin were on fire.

"Yes. Gerold told me everything about that pitiful little interlude by the riverbank." Richild laughed mirthlessly. She was enjoying this. "Did you really believe your clumsy kisses would please him? We laughed about them together that very night."

Joan was too shocked to respond.

"You are surprised. You shouldn't be. Did you think you were the only one? My dear, you are only the latest bead in Gerold's long necklace of conquests. You shouldn't have taken him so seriously."

*How does she know what passed between us? Did Gerold tell her?* Joan felt suddenly cold, as if caught in a chance wind.

"You do not know him," she said staunchly.

"I am his wife, you insolent child."

"You do not love him."

"No," she admitted. "But neither do I mean to be . . . discomforted by the worthless daughter of coloni!"

Joan tried to steady her thoughts. "You cannot do this without Bishop Fulgentius's approval. He brought me to the schola; you cannot remove me without his permission."

Richild held out a sheet of parchment, marked with Fulgentius's seal.

Joan read it quickly, then once again slowly, to be sure she had not made a mistake. There was no room for doubt; Fulgentius had terminated her studies at the schola. The document bore Odo's signature as well. Joan could imagine the pleasure it must have given him to pen it.

Richild's heart rejoiced as she watched Joan read. The arrogant little nobody was discovering just how insignificant she was. She said, "There is no point in further arguing. Sit down and finish taking the letter to your father."

Joan replied defiantly, "Gerold will not let you do this."

"Foolish child, it was his idea."

Joan thought quickly. "If this marriage were Gerold's idea, why did you wait until he left to arrange it?"

"Gerold is tenderhearted . . . to a fault. He lacks the heart to tell you. I have seen it happen before, with the others. He asked me to take care of the problem for him. And so I have."

"I don't believe you." Joan backed away, fighting back tears. "I don't believe you."

Richild sighed. "The matter is settled. Will you finish taking the letter, or shall I call Wala?"

Joan whirled and ran from the room. Before she reached the great hall, she heard the tinkle of Richild's bell, calling for her chaplain.

Luke was waiting where she had left him. Joan flung herself to her knees beside him. His body pressed against hers affectionately, his large head resting on her shoulder. His warm, comforting presence helped calm Joan's seething emotions.

*I mustn't panic. That's just what she wants me to do.*

She had to think, to plan what to do. But her thoughts spun round unproductively, all leading to the same place.

*Gerold.*

*Where is he?*

If he were here, Richild could not do this. *Unless of course she was telling the truth, and the marriage* was *Gerold's idea.*

Joan banished the traitorous thought. Gerold loved her; he would not let her be married off against her will to a man she didn't even know.

He might still return in time to stop it. He might—

*No.* She could not let her future hang on so slim a reed of chance. Joan's mind, numbed by shock and fear, was yet clear enough to understand that.

*Gerold is not due back for two more weeks. The wedding will take place in two days.*

She had to save herself. She could not go through with this marriage.

*Bishop Fulgentius. I must get to him, talk to him, persuade him that this wedding cannot take place.*

Joan was sure Fulgentius had not signed that document with a happy heart. Through dozens of small kindnesses, he had made it plain that he liked Joan and took pleasure in her achievements at the schola—particularly since they were so effective a thorn in Odo's side.

*Richild must have some hold over him to have gotten him to agree to this.*

If Joan could speak to him, she might convince him to call off the wedding—or at least delay it until Gerold's return.

*But perhaps he will not see me.* However he had been won round to the marriage, he would be reluctant—even embarrassed—to meet with her now. If she requested an audience, she would probably be denied.

She fought down fear, forcing herself to think logically. *Fulgentius will lead the high mass on Sunday. He will ride in procession to the cathedral beforehand. I'll approach him then, throw myself at his feet if I have to. I don't care. He* will *stop and hear me; I will make him.*

She looked at Luke. "Will it work, Luke? Will it be enough to save me?"

He tilted his head inquisitively, as if trying to understand. It was a mannerism that always amused Gerold. Joan hugged the white wolf, burying her face in the thick fur ringing his neck.

The notaries and other clerical officers came into view first, walking in stately procession toward the cathedral. Behind them, on horseback, rode the officials of the Church, the deacons and subdeacons, all splendidly attired. Odo rode among them, dressed in plain brown robes, his narrow face haughty and disapproving. As his gaze fell on Joan, standing with the group of beggars and petitioners awaiting the bishop, his thin lips parted in a malevolent smile.

At last the bishop appeared, robed in white silk, riding a magnificent steed caparisoned in crimson. Immediately behind rode the chief dignitaries of the episcopal palace: the treasurer, the controller of the wardrobe, and the almoner. The procession halted as ragged beggars pressed in eagerly all around, crying out for alms in the name of St. Stephen, patron saint of the indigent. Wearily the almoner distributed coins among them.

Joan moved quickly to where the bishop waited, his horse pawing the ground impatiently.

She fell to her knees. "Eminence, hear my plea—"

"I know this case," the bishop interrupted, not looking at her. "I have already rendered judgment. I will not hear this petitioner."

He spurred his horse, but Joan leapt up and grabbed the bridle, staying him. "This marriage will be my ruin." She spoke quickly and quietly, so no one else would hear. "If you can do nothing to stop it, will you at least delay it for a month?"

He made as if to ride on again, but Joan kept tight hold of the bridle. Two of the guards rushed over and would have pulled her away, but the bishop checked them with a wave of his hand.

"A fortnight?" Joan pleaded. "I entreat you, Eminence, give me a fortnight!" Mortifyingly, for she had resolved to be strong, she began to sob.

Fulgentius was a weak man, with many faults, but he was not hardhearted. His eyes softened with sympathy as he reached down to pat Joan's white-gold hair.

"Child, I cannot help you. You must resign yourself to your fate, which is, after all, natural enough for a woman." He bent down and whispered, "I have inquired after the young man who is to be your husband. He's a comely lad; you will not find your lot difficult to bear."

He signaled the guards, who pried Joan's hands from the bridle and shoved her back into the crowd. A path opened for her. As she passed through, trying to hide her tears, she heard the villagers' whispered laughter.

In the rear of the crowd, she saw John. She went to him, but he backed off.

"Stay away!" He scowled. "I hate you!"

"Why? What have I done?"

"You know what you've done!"

"John, what is it? What's wrong?"

"I have to leave Dorstadt!" he cried. "Because of you!"

"I don't understand."

"Odo told me, 'You don't belong here.' " John mimicked the schoolmaster's nasal intonation. " 'We only let you stay because of your sister.' "

Joan was shocked. She had been so involved in her own dilemma that she had not thought of the consequences for John. He was a poor student; they'd kept him on only because of his kinship to her.

"This marriage is not of my choosing, John."

"You've always spoiled things for me, and now you're doing it again!"

"Didn't you hear what I said to the bishop just now?"

"I don't care! It's all your fault. Everything's always been your fault!"

Joan was puzzled. "You hate book studies. Why do you care if they send you from the schola?"

"You don't understand." He looked behind her. "You never understand."

Joan turned and saw the boys of the schola huddled together. One of them pointed and whispered something to the others, followed by muffled laughter.

*So they already know,* Joan thought. *Of course. Odo would not spare John's feelings.* She regarded her brother with sympathy. It must have been difficult, almost unbearable, for him to be separated from his friends because of her. He had often joined with them against her, but Joan understood why. John never wanted anything more than to be accepted, to belong.

"You'll be all right, John," she said soothingly. "You're free to go home now."

"Free?" John laughed harshly. "Free as a monk!"

"What do you mean?"

"I'm to go to the monastery at Fulda! Father sent instructions to the bishop after we first arrived. If I failed at the schola, I was to be sent to join the Fulda brotherhood!"

So this was the source of John's anger. Once consigned to the brotherhood, he would not be able to leave. He would never be a soldier now, nor ride in the Emperor's army as he had dreamed.

"There may still be a way out," Joan said. "We can petition the bishop again. Perhaps if we both plead with him, he will—"

Her brother glared at her, his mouth working as he searched for words strong enough to express what he felt. "I . . . I wish you'd never been born!" He turned and ran.

Dispiritedly, she started back toward Villaris.

✦ ✦ ✦

Joan sat by the stream where she and Gerold had embraced only a few weeks ago. An eternity had passed since then. She looked at the sun; it lacked only an hour or two until sext. By this time tomorrow, she would be wed to the farrier's son.

*Unless . . .*

She studied the line of trees marking the edge of the woods. The forest surrounding Dorstadt was dense and broad; a person could hide in there for days, even weeks, without being discovered. It would be a fortnight or more before Gerold returned. Could she survive for that long?

The forest was dangerous; there were wild boars, and aurochs, and . . . wolves. She remembered the savage violence of Luke's dam as she fought against the bars of her cage, her sharp teeth glinting in the moonlight.

*I'll take Luke with me,* she thought. *He will protect me, and help me hunt for food as well.* The young wolf was already a skilled hunter of rabbits and other small game, which were plentiful this time of year.

*John,* she thought. *What about John?* She couldn't just run off without letting him know where she had gone.

*He can come with me!* Of course! It was the solution to both their problems. They would hide together in the woods and await Gerold's return. Gerold would set everything right—not only for her but for her brother.

She must get word to John. Tell him to meet her in the forest tonight, bringing his lance and bow and quiver.

It was a desperate plan. But she *was* desperate.

She found Dhuoda in the dortoir. Though she was only ten, she was a big girl, well developed for her age. Her resemblance to her sister Gisla was unmistakable. She greeted Joan excitedly. "I've just heard! Tomorrow is your wedding day!"

"Not if I can prevent it," Joan responded bluntly.

Dhuoda was surprised. Gisla had been so eager to wed. "Is he old, then?" Her face lit with childish horror. "Is he toothless? Does he have scrofula?"

"No." Joan had to smile. "He's young and comely, I am told."

"Then why—"

"There's no time to explain, Dhuoda," Joan said urgently. "I've come to ask a favor. Can you keep a secret?"

"Oh, yes!" Dhuoda leaned forward eagerly.

Joan pulled a piece of rolled parchment from her scrip. "This letter is for my brother, John. Take it to him at the schola. I would go myself, but I am expected in the solar to have a new tunic fit for the wedding. Will you do this for me?"

Dhuoda stared at the piece of parchment. Like her mother and sister, she could not read or write.

"What does it say?"

"I can't tell you, Dhuoda. But it's important, very important."

"A secret message!" Her face was aglow with excitement.

"It's only two miles to the schola. You can go and come in an hour if you hurry."

Dhuoda grabbed the parchment. "I'll be back before that!"

Dhuoda hurried through the main courtyard, dodging to avoid the servants and craftsmen who always filled the place this time of day. Her senses were alive with an intimation of adventure. She felt the cool smoothness of the parchment in her hand and wished she knew what was written on it. Joan's ability to read and write filled her with awe.

This mysterious errand was a welcome change from the boredom of her daily routine at Villaris. Besides, she was glad to help Joan. Joan was always nice to her; she took time to explain all kinds of interesting things—not like Mama, who was so often short-tempered and angry.

She was almost to the palisade when she heard a shout.

"Dhuoda!"

Mama's voice. Dhuoda kept going as if she hadn't heard, but as she passed through the gate, the porter grabbed her and forced her to wait. She turned to face her mother.

"Dhuoda! Where are you going?"

"Nowhere." Dhuoda thrust the parchment behind her. Richild caught the sudden movement, and her mouth set with suspicion.

"What is that?"

"N-nothing," Dhuoda stammered.

"Give it to me." Richild held out her hand imperiously.

Dhuoda hesitated. If she gave Mother the parchment, she would betray the secret Joan had entrusted her with. If she resisted . . .

Her mother glared at her, her dark eyes reflecting a building anger. Looking into those eyes, Dhuoda knew she had no choice.

✦ ✦ ✦

For this last night before Joan's wedding, Richild had insisted that she sleep in the small warming room adjoining her own chamber—a privilege customarily reserved only for sick children or favored servants. It was a special honor accorded to the bride-to-be, Richild said, but Joan was sure that she simply wanted to keep her under close observation. No matter. Once Richild was asleep, Joan could slip out of this room just as easily as the dortoir.

Ermentrude, one of the serving girls, came into the little room, carrying a wooden cup filled with spiced red wine. "From the Lady Richild," she said simply. "To honor you on this night."

"I don't want it." Joan waved it away. She would not accept favors from the enemy.

"But the Lady Richild said to stay while you drink it and then take the cup away." Ermentrude was anxious to do things right, being only twelve and new to household service.

"Have it yourself, then," Joan said irritably. "Or empty it on the ground. Richild will never know."

Ermentrude brightened. The idea had not occurred to her. "Yes, mistress. Thank you, mistress." She turned to go.

"A moment." Joan called her back, reconsidering. The wine brimmed the cup, rich and thick, shimmering in the dim light. If she was going to survive for a fortnight in the forest, she would need all the sustenance she could get. She could not afford foolish gestures of pride. She took the cup and gulped the warm wine greedily. It mustached her lips, leaving a strange sour taste. She wiped her mouth with her sleeve, then handed the cup to Ermentrude, who hurriedly left.

Joan blew out the candle and lay on the bed in the dark, waiting. The feather mattress surrounded her with alien softness; she was accustomed to the thin straw on her bed upstairs in the dortoir. She wished Richild had let her sleep in her own bed, beside Dhuoda. She had not seen Dhuoda since handing her the message, having been cloistered in Richild's chambers all afternoon while the serving women fussed over her wedding dress and assembled the clothing and personal items that would go with her as dowry.

Had Dhuoda given John the message? There was no way to be sure. She would wait for John in the forest clearing; if he did not come, she and Luke would go on alone.

In the adjoining room, she heard Richild's deep, slow breathing. Joan waited another quarter of an hour, to be sure Richild was asleep. Then she slipped silently from under the blankets.

She stepped through the door into Richild's chamber. Richild lay still, her breathing regular and deep. Joan slipped along the wall and out the door.

As soon as she had gone, Richild's eyes flew open.

Joan moved soundlessly through the halls until at last she reached the open air of the courtyard. She breathed deeply, feeling a bit giddy.

All was still. A single guard sat with his back to the wall near the gate, his head on his chest, snoring. Her lengthened shadow spilled across the moonlit earth, grotesquely huge. She moved her hand, and a giant gesture mocked her.

Joan whistled softly to Luke. The guard stirred and shifted in his sleep. Luke did not come. Keeping to the shadows, she started toward the corner where Luke usually slept; she would not risk waking the guard by making any further sound.

Suddenly, the ground seemed to shift beneath her. She felt a rise of nausea and dizzily held on to a post to steady herself. *Benedicite. I can't be sick now.*

Fighting the giddiness, she made her way across the courtyard. In the far corner she saw Luke. The young wolf lay on his side, his opalescent eyes staring blindly into the night, his tongue lolling limply out of his mouth. She bent to touch him and felt the coldness of his body beneath the soft white fur. She gasped and drew back. Her eyes fell on a half-eaten piece of meat on the ground. She stared at it dazedly. A fly settled on the bloody wetness surrounding the meat. It remained there, drinking, then flew upward, circling erratically before it dropped abruptly to the ground. It did not move again.

There was a loud humming in Joan's ears. The air seemed to undulate around her. She backed away, turning to run, but again the ground lurched and shifted, then rose suddenly to meet her.

She did not feel the arms that lifted her roughly from where she lay and carried her back inside.

The creaking of the wheels kept melancholy rhythm with the clopping of horses' hooves as the cart bumped along the road toward the cathedral, carrying Joan to her wedding mass.

She had been dragged awake this morning, too dazed to realize what had happened. She stood numbly while the servants fussed over her, putting on her wedding dress and fixing her hair.

But the effects of the drug were wearing off, and Joan began to remember. *It was the wine,* she thought. *Richild put something in the wine.* Joan thought of Luke, lying cold and alone in the night. A lump rose in her throat. He had died without comfort or companionship; Joan hoped he had not suffered long. It must have given Richild pleasure to poison his meat; she had always hated him, sensing the bond he represented between Gerold and Joan.

Richild was riding in the cart just ahead. She was magnificently dressed in a tunic of gleaming blue silk, her black hair coiled elegantly around her head and secured with a silver tiara set with emeralds. She was beautiful.

*Why,* Joan wondered dully, *didn't she just kill me too?*

Sitting in the cart drawing her ever closer to the cathedral, sick in body and heart, with Gerold far away and no way of escape, Joan wished that she had.

The wheels clattered noisily onto the uneven cobblestones of the cathedral forecourt, and the horses were reined to a stop. Immediately, two of Richild's retainers appeared alongside. With elaborate obsequiousness, they helped Joan from the cart.

An enormous crowd was gathered outside the cathedral. It was the Feast of the First Martyrs, a solemn religious holiday, as well as Joan's wedding mass, and the entire town had turned out for the occasion.

In front of the crowd Joan caught sight of a tall, ruddy, big-boned boy standing awkwardly beside his parents. The farrier's son. She noted his sullen expression and the dejected set of his head. *He doesn't want me for a wife any more than I want him for a husband. Why should he?*

His father prodded him; he came toward Joan and held out his hand. She took it, and they stood side by side as Wido, Richild's steward, read the list of items composing Joan's dowry.

Joan looked toward the forest. She could not possibly run and hide there now. The crowd encircled them, and Richild's men stood close beside her, eyeing her warily.

In the crowd Joan saw Odo. Gathered around him were the boys of the schola, whispering together as usual. John was not among them. She searched the crowd and found him standing off to one side, ignored by his companions. They were both alone now, except for each other. Her eyes sought his, seeking and offering comfort. Surprisingly, he did not look away but returned her gaze, his face openly registering his pain.

They had been strangers for a long time, but in that moment they were two again, brother and sister, leagued in understanding. Joan kept her eyes fixed on him, reluctant to break the fragile bond.

The steward stopped reading. The crowd waited expectantly. The farrier's son led Joan into the cathedral. Richild and her household swept in behind them, followed by the townspeople.

Fulgentius was waiting by the altar. As Joan and the boy came toward him, he motioned them to sit. First the holy feast would be celebrated, then the wedding mass.

*Omnipotens sempiterne Deus qui me peccatoris.* As usual, Fulgentius was mangling the Latin service, but Joan hardly noticed. He signaled an acolyte to prepare for the offertory and began the oblation prayer. *Suscipe sanctum Trinitas . . .* Beside her, the farrier's son bent his head reverently. Joan tried to pray, too, bowing her head and mouthing the words, but there was no substance to the form; inside her there was only emptiness.

The mixing of the water with the wine began. *Deus qui humanae substantiae . . .*

The doors of the cathedral burst open with a loud crack. Fulgentius abandoned his struggles with the Latin mass and stared incredulously at the entrance. Joan craned her neck, trying to make out the source of this unprecedented intrusion. But the people behind her blocked her view.

Then she saw it. An enormous creature, manlike but taller by a head than any man, stood outlined in the blinding light of the doorway, its shadow spilling into the dim interior. Its face was curiously expressionless and shone with a metallic gleam, the eyes so deep in their dark sockets that Joan could not make them out. Golden horns grew out of the top of its head.

Somewhere in the crowded assembly, a woman screamed.

*Woden,* Joan thought. She had long ago ceased to believe in her mother's gods, but here was Woden, exactly as her mother had described him, striding boldly up the aisle right toward her.

*Has he come to save me?* she thought wildly.

As he drew closer, she saw that the metallic face and horns were a mask, part of an elaborate battle helmet. The creature was a man and no god. From the back of his head, where the helmet ended, long golden hair curled down to his shoulders.

"Norsemen!" someone shouted.

The intruder continued past without breaking stride. Reaching the altar, he raised a heavy, two-sided broadsword and brought it down with savage force on the bald tonsure of one of the assisting clerics. The man dropped, blood spurting from the deep cleft where his head had been.

Everything erupted into chaos. All around Joan people were screaming and shoving to get away. Joan was dragged along with the crowd, packed so tightly between struggling bodies that her feet lost contact with the floor. The wave of terrified villagers swept toward the doors, then abruptly halted.

The exit was blocked by another intruder, dressed for battle like the first, except that he carried an ax instead of a sword.

The crowd swayed uncertainly. Joan heard shouting outside, and then more of the Norsemen—a dozen at least—piled through the doors. They came in at a run, shouting hoarsely and swinging enormous iron axes over their heads.

The villagers fought and climbed over one another to get out of the way of the murderous blades. Joan was pushed hard from behind and fell to the ground. She felt feet on her sides and back, and she threw up her arms to protect her head. Someone stepped heavily on her right hand, and she cried out in pain. "Mama! Help me! Mama!"

Struggling to extricate herself from the crush of bodies, she crawled sideways until she reached an open area. She looked toward the altar and saw Fulgentius surrounded by Norsemen. He was striking at them with the huge wooden cross that had hung behind the altar. He must have pried it from the wall, and now he swung it around with fierce strength as his attackers darted back and forth, attempting to strike him with their swords but unable to get inside the circle of his defense. As she watched, Fulgentius dealt one Norseman a blow that sent him flying halfway across the room.

She crawled through the noise and the smoke—was there a fire?—searching for John. All around her were shrieks, war cries, and howls of pain and terror. The floor was littered with overturned chairs and sprawled bodies, wet with spilled blood.

"John!" she called. The smoke was thicker here; her eyes burned, and she could not see clearly. "John!" She hardly heard her own voice over the din.

A rush of air on the back of her neck warned her, and she reacted instinctively, hurling herself to the side. The Norseman's blade, aimed for her head, tore a gash in her cheek instead. The blow threw her to the floor, where she rolled in agony, clutching her wounded face.

The Norseman stood above her, his blue eyes murderous through the appalling mask. She crawled backwards, trying to get away, but she could not move fast enough.

The Norseman raised his sword for the death blow. Joan shielded her head with her arms, turning her face aside.

The blow did not come. She opened her eyes to see the sword drop from her attacker's hands. Blood trickled from the corners of his mouth as he sank slowly to the floor. Behind him stood John, grasping the reddened blade of Father's bone-handled knife.

His eyes glittered with a strange exhilaration. "I took him right through the heart! Did you see? He would have killed you!"

The horror of it flooded her. "They will kill us all!" She clutched at John. "We must get away, we must hide!"

He shrugged her off. "I got another one. He came at me with an ax, but I got inside and took him through the throat."

Joan looked round frantically for somewhere to hide. A few feet ahead was the reredos. It was wrought of wood, fronted with gilded panels depicting the life of St. Germanus. And it was hollow. There might just be enough room . . .

"Quickly," she shouted to John. "Follow me!" She grasped the sleeve of his tunic, pulling him down beside her on the floor. Motioning him to follow, she crawled to the side of the reredos. Yes! There was an interstice, just big enough to squeeze through.

It was dark inside. Only a thin stream of light trickled in from the seam in front where the panels were inexpertly joined.

She squatted in the far corner, tucking her legs under to leave room for John. He did not appear. She crawled back to the opening and peered out.

A few feet away she saw him, bending over the body of the Norseman he had killed. He was pulling at the man's clothes, trying to pry something loose.

"John!" she shouted. "In here! Hurry!"

He stared at her, a mad, glittering gaze, his hands still working under the Norseman's body. She didn't dare shout again for fear she would reveal the precious hiding place. After a moment he gave an exultant yell and stood, holding the Norseman's sword. She gestured for him to join her. He lifted the sword in mocking salute and ran off.

*Shall I go after him?* She edged toward the opening.

Someone—a child?—screamed nearby, a hideous shriek that hung in the air, then abruptly ceased. Fear overwhelmed her, and she drew back. Tremulously she put an eye to the seam between the panels and peered out, searching for John.

There was fighting directly in front of her peephole. She heard the clang of metal on metal, caught a brief glimpse of yellow cloth, the gleam of an uplifted sword. A body thumped down heavily. The fighting moved off to the side, and she was looking straight down the nave toward the cathedral entrance. The heavy doors stood ajar, propped open by a grotesque jumble of bodies.

The Norsemen were herding their victims away from the entrance toward the right side of the cathedral.

The way stood clear.

*Now,* she told herself. *Run for the doors.* But she could not bring herself to move; her limbs seemed to be locked.

A man appeared at the edge of her narrow field of vision. He looked so wild and disheveled that for a moment she did not recognize him as Odo. He was lurching toward the entrance, dragging his left leg. In his arms he clutched the huge Bible from the high altar.

He was almost to the doors when two Norsemen intercepted him. He faced his attackers, holding the Bible aloft as if warding off evil spirits. A heavy sword sliced through the book and took him directly in the chest. For a moment he stood, astonished, clutching the two halves of the book in his hands. Then he fell backwards and did not move again.

Joan shrank back into the darkness. The screams of the dying were all around her. Hunched in a ball, she buried her head in her arms. Her rapid heartbeat sounded in her ears.

The screaming had stopped.

She heard the Norsemen calling out to one another in their guttural tongue. There was a loud noise of splintering wood. At first she did not understand what was happening; then she realized they were stripping the cathedral of its treasures. The men laughed and shouted. They were in high spirits.

It did not take them long to complete their plundering. Joan heard them grunting under the weight of their loot, their voices receding into the distance.

Rigid as a post, she sat in the dark and strained to hear. Everything was quiet. She inched toward the opening of the reredos until she reached the edge of the narrow crack of light.

The cathedral lay in ruins. Benches were overturned, hangings were torn off walls, statuary lay in pieces on the floor. There was no sign of the Norsemen.

Bodies lay everywhere, piled in careless heaps. A few feet away, at the bottom of the stairs leading to the altar, Fulgentius was sprawled beside the great wooden cross. It was splintered, the gilded crosspiece broken and wet with blood. Beside him lay the bodies of two Norsemen, their skulls crushed within their shattered helmets.

Cautiously, Joan crept forward until her head and shoulders were out of the reredos.

In the far corner of the room, something moved. Joan shrank back out of the light.

A pile of clothing twisted, then separated itself from the heap of bodies. Someone was alive!

A young woman rose, her back toward Joan. She stood, shakily, and then began to stagger toward the door.

Her golden dress was ripped and bloodied, and her hair, torn loose from its cap, tumbled over her shoulders in auburn coils.

Gisla!

Joan called her name, and she turned, swaying unsteadily, toward the reredos.

There was a sudden burst of laughter outside the cathedral.

Gisla heard and wheeled to run, but it was too late. A group of Norsemen came through the door. They fell on Gisla with a jubilant shout, lifting her above their heads.

They carried her to an open space beside the altar and spread-eagled her, pinning her down by the wrists and ankles. She twisted violently to free herself. The tallest of the men dragged her tunic up over her face and dropped full length on her. Gisla screamed. The man dug his hands into her breasts. The others laughed and shouted encouragement as he raped her.

Joan gagged, clamping hand over mouth to mask the sound.

The Norseman stood up, and another one took his place. Gisla lay slack and unmoving. One of the men took hold of her hair and twisted it to make her jump.

A third man took her, and a fourth; then they left her alone while they retrieved several sacks piled near the door. There was a ringing of metal as they hoisted them; the sacks must have been filled with more of the cathedral's plundered treasure.

It was for these that they had returned.

Before they left, one of the men strode over to Gisla, pulled her up, still limp and unresisting, and slung her over his shoulder like a sack of grain.

They left by the far door.

Deep inside the reredos Joan heard only the eerie, echoing stillness of the cathedral.

Light coming through the front seam of the reredos cast long shadows. There had been no sound for several hours. Joan stirred and crept cautiously through the narrow opening.

The high altar still stood, though stripped of its gold plating. Joan leaned against it, staring at the scene around her. Her wedding tunic was splattered with blood—her own? She could not tell. Her torn cheek throbbed with pain. Woodenly, she picked her way through the jumbled bodies, searching.

In a pile of corpses near the door, she came upon the farrier and his son, their arms sprawled as if each had tried to protect the other. In death the boy looked shrunken and old. Only a few hours ago, he had stood beside her in the cathedral, tall and ruddy and full of youthful strength and vigor. *There will be no marriage now,* Joan thought. Yesterday that thought would have filled her with profound relief and joy; now she felt nothing but numbing emptiness. She left him lying beside his father and continued her search.

She found John in the corner, his hand still gripping the Norseman's sword. The back of his head had been smashed in with a heavy blow, but the violence of his death had left no mark on his face. His blue eyes were clear and open; his mouth was drawn back slightly in what appeared to be a smile.

He had died a soldier's death.

She ran, stumbling, toward the door and pushed it open. It swung away from her crookedly, the hinges broken by the Norsemen's axes. She rushed outside and stood gasping, breathing the fresh, sweet air in great gulps, ridding herself of the stench of death.

The landscape was bare. Smoke curled upward in lazy spirals from heaps of rubble that only this morning had been a lively clutter of homes and buildings surrounding the cathedral.

Dorstadt was in ruins.

Nothing stirred. No one was left. All the townspeople had been gathered in the cathedral for the mass.

She looked east. Above the trees obscuring her view, black smoke mushroomed skyward, darkening the sky.

Villaris.

They had burned it.

She sat down on the ground and put her face in her hands, cradling her wounded cheek.

*Gerold.*

She needed him to hold her, comfort her, make the world recognizable again. Scanning the horizon with narrowed eyes, she half-expected him to appear, riding toward her on Pistis, red hair streaming behind him like a banner.

*I must wait for him. If he returns and does not find me, he will think I was carried off by the Norsemen, like poor Gisla.*

*But I can't stay here.* Fearfully she surveyed the ruined landscape. There was no sign of the Norsemen. Had they gone? Or would they be back, looking for more plunder?

*What if they find me?* She had seen what mercy an unprotected female could expect from them.

Where could she hide? She started toward the trees that marked the edge of the forest circling the town, slowly at first, then at a run. Her breath came sobbingly; at every step, she expected hands to grab her from behind, spinning her around to face the hideous, metallic masks of the Norsemen. Reaching the safety of the trees, she threw herself on the ground.

After a long while, she forced herself to sit up. Night was coming on. The forest around her was dark and foreboding. She heard a rustle of leaves and flinched in fear.

The Norsemen might be nearby, camping in these woods.

She had to escape from Dorstadt and somehow get word to Gerold about where she had gone.

*Mama.* She longed for her mother, but she could not go home. Her father had not forgiven her. If she returned now, bringing news of the death of his only remaining son, he would have his revenge upon her, that was certain.

*If only I were not a girl. If only . . .*

For the rest of her life she would remember this moment and wonder what power of good or evil had directed her thoughts. But now there was no time to consider. It was a chance. There might never be another.

The red sun glittered on the horizon. She had to act quickly.

She found John lying as she had left him, sprawled in the dim interior of the cathedral. His body was limp and unresistant as she rolled him onto his side. The death rigor had not yet set in.

"Forgive me," she whispered as she unclasped John's mantle.

When she was done, she covered him with her own discarded cloak. Gently she closed his eyes and arranged him as decently as she could. She stood, shifting her arms, adjusting to the weight and feel of her new clothes. They were not so different from her own, except for the sleeves, close-fitted at the wrists. She fingered the bone-handled knife she had taken from John's belt.

*Father's knife.* It was old, the white bone handle darkened and chipped, but the blade was sharp.

She went to the altar. Loosening her cap, she placed a mass of her hair upon the altar. It curled thickly over the smooth stone surface, almost white in the dimming light.

She lifted the knife.

Slowly, deliberately, she began to cut.

At twilight, the figure of a young man stepped from the door of the ruined cathedral, scanning the landscape with keen gray-green eyes. The moon was rising in a sky quickening with stars.

Beyond the rubble of buildings, the eastern road shimmered mackerel-silver in the gathering darkness.

The figure slipped furtively out of the shadow of the cathedral. No one was left alive to watch as Joan hurried down the road, toward the great monastery of Fulda.

# 12

The hall was crowded and clamorous, jammed with people who had traveled from miles around the small Westphalian village to witness the proceedings of the *mallus.* They stood shoulder to shoulder, jostling, scuffling the clean rushes that had been scattered across the beaten earth floor, uncovering the ancient accumulation of beer, grease, spittle, and animal excrement that lay beneath. The rank odor rose into the hot, close air. But no one gave it much mind, such odors being common in Frankish dwellings. Besides, the focus of the crowd's attention lay elsewhere: on the red-haired Frisian count who had come as missus to render judgment and deliver justice in the Emperor's name.

Gerold turned to Frambert, one of the seven *scabini* assigned to assist him in his work. "How many more today?" The mallus had convened at first light; it was now midafternoon, and they had been hard at it for over eight hours. Behind the high table at which Gerold sat, his retainers drooped wearily over their swords. He had brought twenty of his best men, just in case. Ever since the death of the Emperor Karolus, the Empire had been sinking into disarray; the position of imperial *missi* had become increasingly precarious. They were sometimes met with bold-faced defiance from wealthy and powerful local lords, men who were unused to having their authority questioned. The law was nothing if it could not be enforced; that was why Gerold had brought so many men, though this had meant leaving Villaris with only a handful of defenders. But the manor's strong wooden palisades were sufficient guarantee against the depredations of the solitary thieves and brigands who had been the only threat to the peace and security of the surrounding countryside for many years.

Frambert checked the list of complainants, written on a strip of parchment eight inches wide, its segments stitched together end to end to form a roll some fifteen feet long.

"Three more today, my lord," Frambert said.

Gerold sighed wearily. He was tired and hungry; his patience for dealing with the endless stream of petty accusations, countercharges, and complaints was wearing thin. He wished he were back at Villaris, with Joan.

*Joan.* How he missed her—her husky voice, her rich, deep laughter, her fascinating gray-green eyes, which regarded him with such knowledge and love. But he must not think of her. That was why he had agreed to serve as missus after all—to put distance between them, give him time to regain control of the ungovernable intensity of emotion that had been building inside him.

"Call the next case, Frambert," Gerold commanded, putting a check on his errant thoughts.

Frambert lifted the roll of parchment and read aloud, straining to be heard over the buzzing crowd.

"Abo complains of his neighbor Hunald, that he has unlawfully and without just compensation taken his livestock from him."

Gerold nodded knowingly. The situation was all too common. In these illiterate times, rare was the property owner who could keep written account of his holdings; the absence of such records left his fields open to all kinds of thievery and false dealing.

Hunald, a big, florid-faced man, dressed ostentatiously in scarlet linen, stepped forward to deny the charge.

"The beasts are mine. Bring me the reliquary." He pointed to the box of holy relics on the high table. "Before God"—he posed dramatically, raising his arms toward Heaven—"I will swear to my innocence on these sacred bones."

"They are my cows, my lord, not Hunald's, as well he knows," responded Abo, a small man whose quiet demeanor and simple dress made him a study in contrast with Hunald. "Hunald can swear as he likes; it will not change the truth."

"What, Abo, do you question God's judgment?" Hunald remonstrated. His voice registered the correct note of pious indignation, but Gerold caught the undertone of triumph. "Mark it, my lord Count, this is blasphemy!"

"Have you any proof the beasts are yours?" Gerold asked Abo.

The question was highly irregular; there were no laws of witness or evidence in Frankland. Hunald glowered at Gerold. What was this strange Frisian count trying to do?

"Proof?" This was a new idea; Abo had to think for a moment. "Well, Berta—that's my wife—can name every one, and so can my four children, for they have known them since they were babes. They can tell you which ones have a temper when milked, and which prefer clover to grass." Another thought struck him. "Bring me to them and let me call them; they will come to me readily, for they know the sound of my voice and the touch of my hand." A tiny flicker of hope ignited in Abo's eyes.

"Nonsense!" Hunald exploded. "Is this court supposed to accept the unthinking actions of dumb beasts before the sacred laws of Heaven? I demand just trial by compurgation. Bring the box of relics and let me swear!"

Gerold stroked his beard, considering. Hunald was the accused; he was within his rights to request the oath taking. God would not permit him to swear falsely with his hand on the holy relics, or so said the law.

The Emperor set great store by such trials, but Gerold had his doubts. There were certainly men who, caring more for the solid advantages of this world than for the vague and insubstantial terrors of the next, would not hesitate to lie. *If it came to that, I would do it myself,* Gerold thought, *if the stakes were high enough.* He would swear to a lie on a whole cartful of relics to protect the safety of anyone he loved.

*Joan.* Again her image rose irresistibly to his mind, and he forced it aside. There would be time enough for such thoughts when the day's work was done.

"My lord." Frambert spoke quietly into his ear. "I can vouch for Hunald. He is a fine man, a generous man, and this claim against him is falsely brought."

Below the level of the table, out of sight of the crowd, Frambert played with a magnificent ring, an amethyst set in silver, engraved with the figure of an eagle. He twirled it round his middle finger so Gerold could see how it gleamed in the light.

"Ah, yes, a most *generous* man." Frambert slipped the ring off his finger. "Hunald wished me to tell you that it is yours. A gesture of his appreciation for your support." A small, tentative smile played at the corners of his lips.

Gerold took the ring. It was a magnificent piece of work, the finest he had ever seen. He handled it, admiring its weight and the perfect workmanship of its artisan. "Thank you, Frambert," he said decisively. "This makes my judgment easier."

Frambert's smile widened into a broad, conspiratorial grin.

Gerold turned to Hunald. "You wish to submit yourself to the judgment of God."

"Yes, my lord." Hunald swelled with confidence, having witnessed the exchange between Gerold and Frambert. The servant with the box of relics stepped forward, but Gerold waved him back.

"We will seek God's judgment through the *judicium aquae ferventis.*"

Hunald and Abo looked blank; like everyone else in the room, they knew no Latin.

*"Kesselfang,"* Gerold translated.

"Kesselfang!" Hunald blanched; he had not thought of this. Ordeal by boiling water was a well-known form of trial, but it had not been employed in this part of the Empire for some years.

"Bring the caldron," Gerold commanded.

There was a moment of stunned silence. Then the room dissolved into a chaotic bustle of conversation and activity. Several of the scabini rushed outside to search the nearby houses for a pot with water already on the boil. Minutes later they returned, carrying a black iron caldron, deep as a man's arm from top to bottom, filled with steaming hot water. Placed on the hearth in the center of the room, the water soon foamed and bubbled.

Gerold nodded, satisfied. Given Hunald's talent for bribery, it might have been a smaller pot.

Hunald scowled. "My lord Count, I protest!" Fear had rendered him indifferent to appearances. "What about the ring?"

"My thought exactly, Hunald." Gerold held the ring up for all to see, then threw it into the caldron. "On the accused's suggestion, this ring shall be the servitor of God's judgment."

Hunald swallowed hard. The ring was small and slippery; it would be hellishly difficult to retrieve. But he could not refuse the trial without admitting his guilt and returning Abo's cows—and they were worth well over seventy solidi. He cursed the foreign count who was so inexplicably immune to the mutually beneficial exchange of favors that had characterized his dealings with other missi. Then he took a deep breath and plunged his arm into the pot.

His face creased with pain as the boiling water seared his skin. Frantically he groped round the bottom of the pot, searching for the ring. A howl of anguish broke from his lips as it slipped through his hand. His tortured fingers scuttled after it in pursuit and—praise God!—closed upon it. He withdrew his hand and held the ring aloft.

"Aaaaaaah." A fascinated moan passed through the crowd as they saw Hunald's arm. Blisters and boils were already starting to form over the angry red surface of his skin.

"Ten days," Gerold announced, "shall be the time of God's judgment."

There was a stir from the crowd, but it held no tone of protest. Everyone understood the law: if the wounds on Hunald's hand and arm healed within ten days, his innocence was proved, and the cattle were his. If not, he was guilty of theft, and the cattle would be returned to their rightful owner, Abo.

Privately Gerold doubted the wounds would heal in so short a time. This was what he had intended, for he had little doubt that Hunald was guilty of the crime. And if Hunald's wounds should happen to heal in the allotted time—well, the ordeal would make him think twice before stealing his neighbor's cattle again. It was rough justice, but it was all the law provided, and it was far better than none. *Lex dura, sed lex*. The imperial statutes were the sole pillars supporting the rule of law in these disordered times; strike them flat, and who knew what wild winds would blow across the land, casting down weak and powerful alike.

"Call the next case, Frambert."

"Aelfric accuses Fulrad of refusing to pay the lawful blood price."

The case seemed straightforward enough. Fulrad's son Tenbert, a boy of sixteen, had killed a young woman, one of Aelfric's coloni. The crime itself was not in dispute, only the amount of the blood price. The laws regarding wergeld were detailed and specific for every person in the Empire, depending on rank, property holdings, age, and sex.

"It was her own fault," said Tenbert, a tall, loose-jointed boy with mottled skin and a sullen expression. "She was only a colona; she should not have fought so hard against me."

"He raped her," Aelfric explained. "Came across her harvesting grapes in my vineyard and took a fancy to her. She was a pretty little thing of only twelve winters—still a child, really, and she didn't understand. She thought he meant to harm her. When she wouldn't submit willingly, he beat her senseless." There was a long murmur from the crowd; Aelfric paused, content to let it register. "She died the next day, bruised and swollen and calling out for her mother."

"You have no cause for complaint," Fulrad, Tenbert's father, broke in hotly. "Did I not pay the wergeld the next week—fifty gold solidi, a generous sum! And the girl only a common colona!"

"The girl is dead; she will not tend my vines again. And her mother, one of my best weavers, is gone woodly with grief and is of no use anymore. I demand the lawful wergeld—one hundred gold solidi."

"An outrage!" Fulrad spread his arms wide in appeal. "Your Eminence, with what I have given him, Aelfric can purchase twenty fine milk cows—which everyone knows are worth far more than a wretched girl, her mother, and the loom combined!"

Gerold frowned. This bartering over blood price was repellent. The girl had been about the same age as Gerold's daughter Dhuoda. The idea of this sullen, disagreeable youth forcing himself on her was grotesque. Such things happened all the time, of course—any colona who made it to the age of fourteen with her virtue intact was extraordinarily lucky, or ugly, or both. Gerold was not naive, he knew the way of the world, but he did not have to like it.

A huge leather-bound codex gold-stamped with the imperial seal rested on the table before him. In it were inscribed the ancient laws of the Empire, the *Lex Salica,* as well as the *Lex Karolina,* which included revisions and additions to the code of law issued by the Emperor Karolus. Gerold knew the law and had no need of the book. Nevertheless, he made solemn show of consulting it; its symbolic value would not be lost on the litigants, and the judgment he was about to render would require all of its authority.

"The Salic code is very clear on this point," he said at last. "One hundred solidi is the lawful wergeld for a colona."

Fulrad cursed aloud. Aelfric grinned.

"The girl was twelve years of age," Gerold continued, "and had therefore reached her childbearing years. By law her blood price must be tripled to three hundred gold solidi."

"What, is the court mad?" Fulrad shouted.

"The sum," Gerold continued equably, "is to be paid as follows: two hundred solidi to Aelfric, the girl's lawful lord, and one hundred to her family."

Now it was Aelfric's turn to be outraged. "One hundred solidi to her *family?*" he said incredulously. "To coloni? I am lord of the landholding; the girl's wergeld is mine by rights!"

"Are you trying to ruin me?" Fulrad interrupted, too absorbed in his own problem to take pleasure in his enemy's distress. "Three hundred solidi is almost the blood price of a warrior! Of a priest!" He moved aggressively toward the table where Gerold sat. "Even, perhaps"—the threat in his voice was unmistakable—"of a count?"

A short shriek of alarm came from the crowd as a dozen of Fulrad's retainers pushed their way to the front. They were armed with swords, and they looked like men who knew how to use them.

Gerold's men moved to counter them, their hands on their half-drawn swords. Gerold stayed them with a gesture of his hand.

"In the Emperor's name"—Gerold's voice rang out, steely as a knife blade—"judgment in this case has been rendered and received." His cool indigo eyes stared Fulrad down. "Call the next case, Frambert."

Frambert did not answer. He had slid out of his seat and was hiding under the table.

Several moments passed in tense silence, the restive, murmuring crowd utterly stilled.

Gerold sat back in his chair, giving every appearance of confidence and ease, but his right hand dangled carelessly above his sword, so close his fingertips brushed the cold steel.

Abruptly, with a muttered curse, Fulrad spun on his heel. Grabbing Tenbert roughly by the arm, he dragged him toward the door. Fulrad's men followed, the crowd giving way before them. As they passed through the door, Fulrad struck Tenbert a hard blow to the head. The boy's yelp of pain sounded through the hall, and the crowd exploded into raucous, tension-breaking laughter.

Gerold smiled grimly. If he knew anything about human nature, Tenbert was in for quite a beating. Perhaps it would teach him a lesson, perhaps not. Either way, it could no longer help the murdered girl. But her family would receive part of her wergeld. With it, they would be able to buy their freedom and build a better life for themselves, their remaining children, and their children's children.

Gerold signaled his men; they resheathed their swords and withdrew to their positions behind the judicial table.

Frambert crawled out from under the table and reoccupied his seat with an air of ruffled dignity. His face was pale, and his voice shook as he read off the last case. "Ermoin, the miller, and his wife complain of their daughter, that she has willfully and against their express command taken a slave to husband."

Again the crowd parted to let pass an elderly couple, gray haired, patrician, robed in fine cloth—testimony to Ermoin's success in his trade. Behind them came a youth, dressed in the worn and tattered tunic of a slave, and finally a young woman, who entered with head modestly bowed.

"My lord." Ermoin spoke without waiting to be addressed. "You see before you our daughter, Hildegarde, joy of our aging hearts, the sole surviving child of eight born to us. She has been tenderly reared, my lord—too tenderly, as we have learned to our grief. For she has repaid our loving kindness with willful disobedience and ingratitude."

"What redress do you seek from this court?" Gerold asked.

"Why, the choice, my lord," Ermoin said with surprise. "The spindle or the sword. She must choose, as the law requires."

Gerold looked grave. In his career as missus he had presided over one other such case; he did not relish witnessing another.

"The law, as you say, provides for such a circumstance. But it seems harsh, especially for one who has been raised so—tenderly. Is there no other way?"

Ermoin took his meaning. The man price could be paid, the boy bought out of slavery and made a freedman.

"No, my lord." He shook his head vehemently.

"Very well," Gerold said resignedly. There was no way to avoid it—the girl's parents knew the law and would insist on carrying out the ugly business to its conclusion.

"Bring a spindle," Gerold commanded. "And Hunric"—he gestured to one of his men—"lend me your sword." He would not use his own weapon; it had never yet bitten into undefended flesh, nor ever would while Gerold carried it.

Some moments of bustle and commotion ensued while a spindle was procured from a nearby house.

The girl looked up as it was carried in. Her father spoke sharply to her, and she quickly dropped her eyes. But in that brief moment, Gerold got a glimpse of her face. She was exquisite—huge carnelian eyes islanded in a sea of milky skin, a fine, delicate brow, sweetly curving lips. Gerold could understand her parents' fury: with such a face the girl might have captured the heart of a great lord, even a nobleman, and bettered her family's fortunes.

Gerold placed one hand on the spindle; with his other he raised the sword. "If Hildegarde chooses the sword," Gerold said loudly so all might hear, "then her husband, the slave Romuald, will immediately die by it. If she chooses the spindle, then she herself will become a slave."

It was a terrible choice. Once Gerold had witnessed a different girl, not so lovely but just as young, face the same alternatives. That one had chosen the sword and stood by while the man she loved was slain with it before her eyes. Yet what else could she have done? Who would willingly choose vile debasement, not only for herself but for her children, and all future generations of her line?

The girl stood silent and unmoving. She had not reacted with so much as a quiver when Gerold had explained the trial.

"Do you understand the significance of the choice you must make?" Gerold asked her gently.

"She does, my lord," said Ermoin, tightening his grip on his daughter's arm. "She knows exactly what to do."

Gerold could well imagine it. The girl's cooperation had doubtless been secured by means of dire threats and curses, perhaps even blows.

The guards flanking the young man took hold of his arms to prevent any struggle to escape. He eyed them scornfully. He had an interesting face—a low, common brow crowned with a thatch of coarse hair, but intelligent eyes, a well-formed jaw, and a fine, strong nose; he looked to have some of the old Roman blood.

He might be a slave, but he had courage. Gerold signaled the guards to stand off.

"Come, child," Gerold said to the girl. "It is time."

Her father whispered something in her ear. She nodded, and he loosed his grip on her arm and pushed her forward.

She raised her head and looked at the young man. The undisguised love that shone in her eyes took Gerold aback.

"No!" The girl's father tried to stop her, but it was too late. With her gaze fixed on her husband, she unhesitatingly approached the spindle, sat down, and started to spin.

✦ ✦ ✦

Riding home to Villaris the next day, Gerold thought about what had happened. The girl had sacrificed everything—her family, her fortune, even her freedom. The love he had seen in her face fired his imagination and moved him in ways he did not entirely understand. All he knew, with a conviction that swept everything else aside, was that he wanted it—that purity and intensity of emotion that made all else seem pale and meaningless. It was not too late for him; surely it was not too late. He was only twenty-nine—no longer young, perhaps, but still in the prime of his years.

He had never loved his wife, Richild, nor had she ever made any pretense of loving him. She would not, he knew, sacrifice so much as a single jeweled hair comb for him. Theirs had been a carefully negotiated marriage of fortunes and families. This was quite as things should be, and until recently Gerold had looked for no more. When, following Dhuoda's birth, Richild had announced that she wanted no more children, he had acceded to her wishes with no sense of loss. He had had no difficulty finding willing partners to share pleasures away from the marital bed.

But now, because of Joan, all that was changed. He pictured her in his mind, her fine, white-gold hair circling her face, her wise, gray-green eyes belying her years. His longing for her, stronger even than desire, tugged at his heart. He had never known anyone like her. Her probing intelligence, her willingness to challenge and question ideas the rest of the world accepted as unshakable truths, filled him with awe. He could talk to her as he could talk to no one else. He could trust her with anything, even his life.

It would be easy enough to make her his mistress—their last encounter at the riverbank had left no doubt about that. Uncharacteristically, he had held back, wanting something more, though he had not, at the time, known what.

Now he knew.

*I want her as my wife.*

It would be difficult, and no doubt costly, to free himself from Richild, but that did not matter.

*Joan will be my wife, if she will have me.*

With this resolve came a sense of peace. Gerold breathed deeply, reveling in the rich, exciting smells of the spring forest, feeling happier and more alive than he had for years.

✦ ✦ ✦

They were very near home. A low-lying cloud hung heavily in the air, obscuring Gerold's view of Villaris. Joan was there, waiting for him. Impatient, he urged Pistis into a canter.

An unpleasant scent filled the air, penetrating his senses.

Smoke.

The cloud over Villaris was smoke.

Then they were all riding recklessly through the forest at an open run, unmindful of the branches tearing at their hair and their clothes. They emerged into the clearing and reined in sharply, staring in bewilderment.

Villaris was gone.

Beneath the cloud of slowly spiraling smoke, a blackened pile of rubble and ash was all that remained of the home they had left only two weeks before.

"Joan!" Gerold shouted. "Dhuoda! Richild!" Had they escaped, or were they dead, buried beneath the smoldering heap of debris?

His men were on their knees in the middle of the heap, searching for anything recognizable—a scrap of clothing, a ring, a headpiece. Some of them wept openly as they tore at the rubble, fearful that any moment they would find what they were seeking.

Off to one side, under a pile of blackened beams, Gerold saw something that made his heart sink.

It was a foot. A human foot.

He ran over and began pulling off the beams, clawing at them with his hands till they bled, though he did not know it. Gradually, the body underneath was revealed. It was a man's body, so badly burned that the features were scarcely recognizable, but from the amulet around the neck Gerold knew that it was Andulf, one of the guards. In his right hand was a sword. Gerold bent to take it up, but the dead man's hand followed, refusing to loose its grip. The heat of the fire had melted the handle, fusing flesh and iron into one.

Andulf had died fighting. But whom? Or what? Gerold surveyed the landscape with a soldier's practiced eye. There was no sign of any encampment, no weapons or materials left behind to lend a clue to what had happened. The surrounding forest lay motionless in the bright spring afternoon.

"My lord!" His men had found the bodies of two more guards. Like

Andulf, they had died fighting, their weapons still in their hands. The discovery fueled a renewed search, but it was fruitless. There was no sign of anyone else.

*Where are they all?* They had left over two score people behind in Villaris—they couldn't all have vanished, without even a trace of bone or blood.

Gerold's heart pounded with a wild hope. Joan was alive, she must be alive. Perhaps she was nearby, hiding in the forest with the others who were missing—or perhaps they had fled to the town!

He mounted Pistis in a single leap, calling to his men. They rode into town at a gallop, slowing only when they reached the vacant, deserted streets.

Quietly, Gerold and his men scattered, reconnoitering, into the long row of silent houses. Gerold took Worad and Amalwin and rode on to the cathedral. The heavy oaken doors hung crookedly open on broken hinges. Warily they dismounted and approached, swords in hand. Climbing the steps, Gerold stumbled on something slippery. A pool of darkening blood lay atop the well-worn wood, fed by a slow, steady trickle from the other side of the door.

Gerold stepped inside.

For one merciful moment, the darkness of the interior obscured his sight. Then his vision cleared.

Behind him, Amalwin began to retch. Gerold felt his own gorge rise, but he swallowed hard, mastering himself. He covered his mouth and nose with his sleeve and moved forward into the nave of the church. It was difficult to avoid stepping on the densely sprawled bodies. He heard Worad and Amalwin cursing, heard the sound of his own rapid, shallow breath. He continued as in a dream, picking his way among the ghastly human debris, searching.

Near the high altar, he came across the members of his household. There was Wala, the chaplain, and Wido, the steward. Irminon, the chambermaid, lay nearby, her lifeless arms still cradling her dead babe. There was a howl from Worad, her husband, as he spied them. He fell to his knees and clasped them, pressed his hands to their wounds, smearing himself with their blood.

Gerold turned away. His eyes fell upon a familiar gleam of emerald and silver. Richild's tiara. She lay on her back beside it, her black hair spread across her body like a shroud. He picked up the tiara and went to replace it in her hair. At his touch Richild's head twisted grotesquely, then slowly rolled away from her body.

Startled, Gerold stepped backwards. His foot struck another body, and he almost fell. He looked down. At his feet lay Dhuoda, her body twisted as if she had tried to dodge her attacker's blow. With a groan, Gerold dropped to his knees beside his daughter's body. Gently he touched her, stroking her fine, soft child's hair, rearranging her limbs so she rested more comfortably. He kissed her cheek and passed his hand over the vacant eyes, closing them. It was all wrong. She should have been the one to perform these final respects for him.

With leaden expectation, he rose and resumed his grisly search through the sprawled bodies. Joan must be there somewhere, among the others; he had to find her.

He traversed the room, staring into every one of the cold, dead faces, recognizing in each of them the familiar features of a townsman, neighbor, or friend. But he did not find Joan.

Could she have somehow, miraculously, escaped? Was it possible? Gerold scarcely dared hope. He started to search the room again.

"My lord! My lord!" Voices rose urgently outside the cathedral. Gerold reached the door as the rest of his men came riding up.

"Norsemen, my lord! Down by the river! Loading their ships—"

But Gerold was already out the door, running toward Pistis.

They rode hell-bent for the river, their horses' hooves drumming on the hard earth of the road. They gave no thought to surprise; reckless with grief, they were fixed only on revenge.

Rounding a corner, they saw a long, shallow-drafted ship with a high wooden prow carved in the shape of a dragon's head with gaping mouth and long, curving teeth. Most of the Norsemen were already aboard, but a score remained onshore guarding the ship while the last of the booty was loaded.

With a great wordless battle shout, Gerold spurred forward, leveling his spear. His men followed close behind. The unmounted Norsemen dived and stumbled to get out of the way; several fell screaming beneath the trampling hooves. Gerold raised his barbed javelin, taking aim at the nearest Norseman, a gold-helmeted giant with a yellow beard. The giant turned, lifted his shield, and the javelin landed in it, shuddering.

Suddenly the air was filled with arrows; the Norsemen were shooting at them. Pistis reared wildly, then lurched to the ground, a feathered shaft in his eye. Gerold jumped clear, landing awkwardly on his left leg. He drew his sword and ran limping toward the giant, who was struggling to cut the javelin free from his shield. Gerold placed his foot on the butt of the javelin as it trailed on the ground, pulling the Norseman's shield down and away. The giant looked at Gerold with surprise and lifted his ax, but it was too late; with a single stroke Gerold took him through the heart. Without waiting to see him fall, Gerold whirled and struck at another Norseman, cleaving him through the head. Bloody shreds of tissue spattered Gerold's face, and he wiped his eyes to see. He was in the thick of the fighting now. He raised his sword, striking all around him with reckless exhilaration, the tightly coiled emotions of the past hour sprung forth in a welcome delirium of killing and blood.

"They're leaving! They're leaving!" The shouts of his men sounded in Gerold's ears; he looked toward the shore and saw the dragon-headed ship pulling away, its red sail fluttering in the wind. The Norsemen were fleeing.

A riderless black-maned bay danced nervously a few feet away. Gerold leapt on his back. The horse panicked and reared, but Gerold stayed with him, hands firm on the bridle. The bay turned smartly and headed for the shore. With a shout to his men to follow, Gerold rode straight into the water. An unused spear dangled from the saddle. Gerold withdrew the spear and hurled it with a force that almost propelled him over the neck of the bay. The spear sliced the air, its iron tip shimmering in the sun, and dropped into the water just short of the grinning dragon's mouth.

There was a burst of jeering laughter from the ship. The Norsemen called out derisively in their rough tongue. Two of them hoisted a golden bundle for display, only it wasn't a bundle, it was a woman hanging limply between them, a woman with auburn hair.

"Gisla!" Gerold shouted in an agony of recognition. What was she doing here? She should be safe at home with her husband.

Dazedly Gisla lifted her head. "Father!" she screamed. "Fatherrrrrr!" Her cry resonated in the fiber of his being.

Gerold spurred the bay, but he whinnied and backed off, refusing to advance any farther into the deepening dark water. He jabbed him in the hindquarters with his sword to force him to obey, but it only panicked him; he bucked wildly, his hooves flailing. A less skilled rider would have been thrown, but Gerold held on determinedly, fighting to bend the bay to his will.

"My lord! My lord!" Gerold's men were all around him, grabbing the bridle, pulling him back.

"It's hopeless, my lord." Grifo, Gerold's lieutenant, spoke clearly in his ear. "There's nothing more we can do."

The red sails of the Viking ship had ceased fluttering; they curved smoothly as the ship glided rapidly away from shore. There was no way to pursue it, no boats anywhere, even had Gerold and his men known how to sail them; the craft of shipbuilding had long been forgotten in Frankland.

Numbly, Gerold allowed Grifo to lead the bay to shore. Gisla's cry still echoed in his ears. *Fatherrrrrr!* She was lost, irretrievably lost. There had been reports of young girls taken during the Norsemen's increasingly frequent raids along the coast of the Empire, but Gerold had never thought, never imagined . . .

Joan! The thought struck him with the force of an arrow shaft, robbing him of breath. They had taken her too! Gerold's disordered thoughts spun round, seeking another possibility, but found none. The barbarians had abducted Joan and Gisla, stolen them away to unspeakable horrors, and there was nothing, nothing he could do to save them.

His eyes fell on one of the dead Norsemen. He leapt off the bay, grabbed the long-handled ax from the dead man's clenched hand, and began striking at the corpse. The limp body jumped with every blow. The golden helmet came off, revealing the beardless face of a young boy, but Gerold kept striking, raising the ax again and again. Blood spurted everywhere, drenching his clothes.

Two of his men moved to stop him, but Grifo held them back.

"No," he said quietly. "Let him be."

A few moments later Gerold released the ax and dropped to his knees, covering his face with his hands. Warm blood coated his fingers, sticking them together. Sobs rose explosively in his throat, and he no longer tried to resist. Brokenly and unashamedly he wept.

# 13

### *Colmar*
### *June 24, 833*
### *The Field of Lies*

Anastasius pulled aside the heavy curtains covering the opening of the Pope's tent and slipped inside.

Gregory, fourth of that name to occupy the Throne of St. Peter, was still at prayer, kneeling on the silken pillows placed before the exquisite carved ivory figure of Christ that occupied the place of honor in his tent. The figure had survived the perilous journey over ruined roads and bridges, through the high and treacherous passes of the Alps, without a scratch. It gleamed as brightly here, in a crude tent pitched on this alien Frankish land, as it had in the safety and comfort of Gregory's private chapel in the Lateran Palace.

*"Deus illuminatio mea, Deus optimus et maximus,"* Gregory prayed, his face alight with devotion.

Watching soundlessly from the entryway, Anastasius wondered, *Was I ever so simple in my faith?* Perhaps once, when he was very small. But his innocence had died the day his uncle Theodorus had been murdered in the Lateran Palace before his eyes. "Watch," his father had told him then, "and learn."

Anastasius had watched, and learned—learned how to conceal his true feelings behind the mask of manners, learned how to manipulate and deceive, even betray, if necessary. The rewards of that knowledge had been gratifying. At nineteen, Anastasius was already *vestiarius*—the youngest man ever to hold so high a position. Arsenius, his father, took great pride in him. Anastasius meant to make him prouder still.

"Christ Jesus, give me the wisdom I need this day," Gregory continued. "Show me the way to avert this unholy war and reconcile these rebellious sons to the Emperor their father."

*Is it possible that he does not know, even yet, what he stands to lose this day?* Anastasius could scarcely believe it. The Pope was such an innocent. Anastasius was only nineteen, less than half Gregory's age, and already he understood far more about the world.

*He is ill suited to be Pope,* Anastasius thought, not for the first time. Gregory was a pious soul, there was no denying that, but piety was an overrated virtue. The man had a nature better suited to the cloister than the papal court, whose subtle politics were forever beyond his reach. Whatever had Emperor Louis been thinking of when he had asked Gregory to make the long journey from Rome to the empire of the Franks to serve as mediator in this crisis?

Anastasius coughed discreetly, to attract Gregory's attention, but he was lost in prayer, gazing at the Christ figure with a look of exaltation.

"It is time, Holiness." Anastasius did not hesitate to interrupt the Pope's devotions. Gregory had been at prayer for over an hour, and the Emperor was waiting.

Startled, Gregory looked around, and seeing Anastasius, nodded, crossed himself, and stood, smoothing the bell-shaped purple *paenula* which he wore over the papal dalmatic.

"I see you have drawn strength from the Christ figure, Holiness," Anastasius said, helping Gregory put on the pallium. "I too have felt its power."

"Yes. It is magnificent, isn't it?"

"Indeed. Especially the beauty of the head, which is large in proportion to the body. It always reminds me of the first Epistle to the Corinthians: 'And the head of Christ is God.' A glorious expression of the idea that Christ combines in His person both natures, Godhood and manhood."

Gregory beamed appreciatively. "I don't think I have ever heard that thought so well expressed. You make a fine vestiarius, Anastasius; the eloquence of your faith is an inspiration."

Anastasius was pleased. Such papal praise might well translate into another promotion—to nomenclator, perhaps, or even primicerius? He was young, it was true, but such high honors were not beyond ambition. Indeed, they were but way stations on the path to the single overarching ambition of Anastasius's life: to be Pope himself one day.

"You overprize me, Sire," Anastasius said with what he hoped was becoming modesty. "It is the perfection of the sculpture, and not my inadequate words, which deserves your praise."

Gregory smiled. "Spoken with true *humilitas*." He put his hand fondly on Anastasius's shoulder and said gravely, "It is God's work we do this day, Anastasius."

Anastasius studied the Pope's face. *He suspects nothing. Good*. Obviously, Gregory still believed that he could mediate a peace between the Emperor and his sons, still knew nothing of the secret arrangements that Anastasius had so carefully and quietly carried out, following his father's explicit instructions.

"Tomorrow's dawn will see a new peace in this troubled land," Gregory said.

*That is true enough,* thought Anastasius, *though the peace will not be of the kind you envision*.

If all went as planned, tomorrow at dawn the Emperor would awake to find that his troops had deserted in the night, leaving him defenseless before the armies of his sons. It was all agreed upon and paid for; nothing that Gregory said or did this day would make the slightest whit of difference.

But it was important that the papal mediation occur as planned. Negotiating with Gregory would allay the Emperor's suspicions and distract his attention at this crucial juncture.

It would be judicious to offer Gregory some encouragement. "It is a great thing you do today, Holiness," Anastasius said. "God will smile upon it, and upon you."

Gregory nodded. "I know it, Anastasius. More surely at this moment than ever before."

"Gregory the peacemaker, they will call you, Gregory the Great!"

"No, Anastasius," Gregory reproved. "If I succeed in this day's work, it will be God's doing, not mine. The future of the Empire, upon which Rome's security depends, hangs in the balance today. If we win through, it will be with His help alone."

Gregory's selfless faith fascinated Anastasius, who regarded it as a freak of nature akin to having six fingers on one hand. Gregory was a genuinely humble man, Anastasius decided—but then, considering his talents, he had every reason to *be* humble.

"Accompany me to the Emperor's tent," Gregory said. "I would like you to be there when I speak with him."

*Everything is going smoothly,* Anastasius thought. When this was over, he had only to return to Rome and wait. Once Lothar was crowned Emperor in his father's place, he would know how to reward Anastasius for the work he had done here.

Gregory went to the door of the tent. "Come then. Let us do what must be done."

They walked out onto the open field crowded with the tents and banners of the Emperor's army. It was hard to believe that by tomorrow morning the colorful riot of activity would all be gone. Anastasius tried to imagine the look on Louis's face when he stepped outside his tent and found the quiet fields stretching bare before him.

Passing the royal guard, they arrived at the imperial tent. Just outside, Gregory paused to murmur one last prayer. *"Verba mea auribus percipe, Domine . . ."*

Anastasius watched impatiently while Gregory's full, almost feminine lips soundlessly formed the words of the fifth psalm: *". . . intende voci clamoris mei, rex meus et Deus meus . . ."*

*Pious fool.* At that moment Anastasius's contempt for the Pope was so strong that he had to make a conscious effort to keep his voice respectful.

"Shall we go in, Sire?"

Gregory raised his head. "Yes, Anastasius, I am ready."

# 14

## *Fulda*

In the shadowy predawn moonlight, the brothers of Fulda descended the night stairs and walked serenely in single file through the inner courtyard to the church, their gray robes merging seamlessly with the darkness. The quiet slap of their plain leathern sandals was the only sound to break the profound silence; even the larks would not awaken for several hours. The brothers entered the choir and, with the sureness of long habit, moved to their assigned positions for the celebration of vigils.

Brother John Anglicus knelt with the others, shifting knees with practiced, unconscious movements to find the most comfortable place on the packed earth floor.

*Domine labia mea aperies* . . . They began with a versicle, then moved on to the third psalm, following the form laid down by St. Benedict in his blessed rule.

John Anglicus liked this first office of the day. The unchanging pattern of the ceremony left the mind free to roam while the lips mouthed the familiar words. Several brothers were already starting to nod, but John Anglicus felt marvelously awake, all senses quickened and alert to this little world lit by flickering candle flames, bounded by the comforting solidity of the walls.

The feeling of belonging, of community, was especially strong this time of night. Daylight's sharp edges, so quick to expose individual personalities, likes and dislikes, loyalties and grudges, were submerged in the muted shadows and the resonant unison of the brothers' voices, hushed and melodic in the still night air.

*Te Deum laudamus* . . . John Anglicus chanted the Alleluia with the others, their bowed, cowled heads as indistinguishable as seeds in a furrow.

But John Anglicus was not like the others. John Anglicus did not belong here among this renowned and distinguished brotherhood. It was not through any defect of mind or character that this was so. It was an accident of fate, or of a cruel, indifferent God, that set John Anglicus irrevocably apart. John Anglicus did not belong among the brothers of Fulda, because John Anglicus, born Joan of Ingelheim, was a woman.

Four years had passed since she had presented herself at the abbey foregate disguised as her brother John. "Anglicus" they named her, because of her English father, and even among this select brotherhood of scholars, poets, and intellects, she soon distinguished herself.

The very same qualities of mind that as a woman had earned her derision and contempt were here universally praised. Her brilliance, knowledge of Scripture, and quick-wittedness in scholarly debate became matters of community pride. She was free—no, *encouraged*—to work to the very limit of her abilities. Among the novices, she was quickly promoted to *seniorus;* this gave her greater freedom of access to the renowned Fulda library—an enormous collection of some three hundred and fifty codices, including an extraordinarily fine series of classical authors—Suetonius, Tacitus, Virgil, Pliny, Marcellinus, among others. She ranged among the neatly rolled stacks in a transport of delight. All the knowledge of the world was here, it seemed, and all was hers for the asking.

Coming upon her reading a treatise of St. Chrysostom one day, Prior Joseph was surprised to discover that she knew Greek, a skill no other brother possessed. He told Abbot Raban, who immediately set her to work translating the abbey's excellent collection of Greek treatises on medicine; these included five of Hippocrates' seven books of aphorisms, the complete Tetrabiblios of Aëtius, as well as fragments of works by Oribasius and Alexander of Tralles. Brother Benjamin, the community physician, was so impressed with Joan's work that he made her his apprentice. He taught her how to grow and harvest the plants in the medicinal herb garden, and how to make use of their various healing properties: fennel for constipation, mustard for coughs, chervil for hemorrhages, wormwood and willow-bark for fevers—there were curatives in Benjamin's garden for every human ailment imaginable. Joan helped him compound the various poultices, purges, infusions, and simples that were the mainstay of monastic medicine, and she accompanied him to the infirmary to tend the sick. It was fascinating work, exactly suited to her inquisitive, analytical mind.

Between her studies and her work with Brother Benjamin, as well as the bells that rang regularly seven times a day, calling the brethren to canonical prayers, her days were busy and productive. There was a freedom and power in this man's existence that she had never experienced before, and Joan found that she liked it; she liked it very much.

"Perhaps I shouldn't be telling you this, for it will swell your head till it no longer fits the cowl," gossipy old Hatto, the porter, had said to her just the day before, smiling cheerfully to let her know he was only jesting. "But yesterday I heard Father Abbot tell Prior Joseph that you had the keenest mind of all the brethren and would one day bring great distinction to this house."

The words of the old fortune-teller from the St.-Denis fair echoed in Joan's ears: "Greatness will be yours, beyond your imaginings." Was this what she had meant? "Changeling," the old woman had called her and said, "You are what you will not be; what you will become is other than you are."

*That much is certainly true,* Joan thought ruefully, fingering the small hairless spot at the crown of her head, almost obscured by the thick ring of curly white-gold hair encircling it. Her hair—her mother's hair—had been Joan's only vanity. Nevertheless, she had welcomed being shaved. Her monk's tonsure, along with the thin scar on her cheek left by the Norseman's sword, enhanced her masculine disguise—a disguise upon which her life now depended.

When she had first come to Fulda, she faced each day full of apprehension, never knowing if some new and unanticipated aspect of the monastic routine would suddenly expose her identity. She worked hard to mimic a masculine carriage and demeanor but worried that she was giving herself away in dozens of unsuspected little ways, though no one seemed to take notice.

Fortunately, the Benedictine way of life was carefully designed to protect the modesty of every member of the community, from the abbot to the lowliest of the brothers. The physical body, sinful vessel, had to be concealed insofar as possible. The long, full robes of the Benedictine habit provided ample camouflage of her budding woman's shape; as an added precaution, however, she bound her breasts tightly with strong linen strips. The Rule of St. Benedict explicitly stated that the brothers must sleep in their robes and reveal no more than hands and feet even on the hottest nights of Heuvimanoth. Baths were prohibited, except for the sick. Even the *necessaria,* the community latrines, preserved brotherly modesty through the provision of sturdy concealing partitions between all of the cold stone seats.

Upon first adopting her disguise on the road from Dorstadt to Fulda, Joan had learned to contain her monthly bleeding with a thick wadding of absorbent leaves, which she could later bury. In the abbey, even this precaution proved unnecessary. She simply dropped the soiled leaves down the deep, dark holes of the necessaria, where they mixed indistinguishably with other excreta.

Everyone at Fulda accepted her unquestioningly as a boy. Once a person's gender was established, Joan came to realize, no one thought any more about it. This was fortunate, for discovery of her true identity would mean certain death.

It was that certainty that kept her, at first, from any attempt to contact Gerold. There was no one she could trust to bear a message, and no way for her to leave. As a novice she was closely watched at all hours of the day and night.

She had lain awake for hours on her narrow dormitory cot, tormented by doubt. Even if she could get word to Gerold, would he want her? When they had been together that last time at the riverbank, she had wanted him to make love to her—she blushed at the remembrance—but he had refused. Afterward, on the way home, he was distant and remote, almost as if angry. Then he had taken the first opportunity to go away.

"You shouldn't have taken him so seriously," Richild had said. "You are only the latest bead in Gerold's long necklace of conquests." Was Richild right? At the time it had seemed impossible to believe, but perhaps Richild had been telling the truth.

It would be absurd to risk everything, her very life, to contact a man who did not want her, who had perhaps never wanted her. And yet . . .

She had been at Fulda three months when she witnessed something that helped her decide what to do. She was passing through the grange court with a group of fellow novices on the way to their cloister when a lively commotion near the porter's gate drew their attention. She watched as an escort of mounted men rode through, followed by a lady, sumptuously arrayed in cloth of golden silk, as straight and elegant in the saddle as a marble pillar. She was beautiful, her delicate, rounded features and pale skin framed by a waterfall of lustrous, light brown hair, but her dark, intelligent eyes held a look of mysterious sadness.

"Who is she?" Joan asked, intrigued.

"Judith, wife of Viscount Waifar," replied Brother Rudolph, the master of novices. "A learned woman. They say she can read and write Latin like a man."

*"Deo, juva nos."* Brother Gailo crossed himself fearfully. "Is she a witch?"

"She has a great reputation for piety. She has even written a commentary on the life of Esther."

"Abomination," said Brother Thomas, one of the other novices. A homely young man with a melon face, cleft chin, and heavy-lidded eyes, Thomas was convinced of his own superior virtue and seized every opportunity to display it. "A gross violation of nature. What can a woman, a creature of base passions, know of such things? God will surely punish her for her arrogance."

"He already has," Brother Rudolph replied, "for though the viscount needs an heir, his lady is barren. Just last month, she was delivered of another stillborn babe."

The noble procession pulled up before the abbatial church. Joan watched Judith dismount and approach the church door with solemn dignity, carrying a single taper.

"You should not stare, Brother John," Thomas remonstrated piously. He frequently curried favor with Brother Rudolph at the expense of his fellow novices. "A good monk should keep his eyes chastely lowered before a woman," he quoted sanctimoniously from the rule.

"You are right, Brother," Joan replied. "But I've never seen a lady like that, with one eye blue and the other brown."

"Do not compound your sin with falsehood, Brother John. Both the lady's eyes are brown."

"And how do you know that, Brother," Joan inquired slyly, "if *you* did not look at her?"

The other novices burst into laughter. Even Brother Rudolph could not suppress a smile.

Thomas glared at Joan. She had made him look a fool, and he was not one to forget such an injury.

Their attention was distracted by Brother Hildwin, the sacristan, who hurried to interpose himself between Judith and the church.

"Peace be with you, lady," he said, using the Frankish vernacular.

*"Et cum spiritu tuo,"* she replied smoothly in perfect Latin.

Pointedly, Brother Hildwin addressed her again in the vernacular. "If you require food and lodging, we stand ready to accommodate you and your entourage. Come, I will escort you to the house for distinguished visitors and inform our lord Abbot of your arrival. He will doubtless wish to greet you in person."

"You are most kind, Father, but I do not require *hospitalitas,*" she replied again in Latin. "I only wish to light a candle in the church for my dead babe. Then I will be on my way."

"Ah! Then it is my duty, as sacristan of this church, to inform you, Daughter, that you may not pass through these doors while you are still"—he sought a suitable word—"unclean."

Judith flushed but did not lose her composure. "I know the law, Father," she said calmly. "I have waited the requisite thirty-three days since the birthing."

"The babe of which you were delivered was a girl child, was it not?" Brother Hildwin said with an air of condescension.

"Yes."

"Then the time of . . . uncleanliness . . . is longer. You may not enter the sacred confines of this church for sixty-six days after the birth of the child."

"Where is this written? I have not read this law."

"Nor is it fitting that you should, being a woman."

Joan started indignantly at the brazenness of the affront. With the force of remembered experience, she felt the shame of Judith's humiliation. All the lady's learning, her intelligence, her breeding stood for naught. The vilest beggar, ignorant and mud streaked, could enter the church to pray, but Judith could not, for she was "unclean."

"Return home, Daughter," Brother Hildwin continued, "and pray in your own chapel for the soul of your unbaptized babe. God has a horror of what is against nature. Lay down the pen and pick up a womanly needle; repent of pridefulness, and He may lift the burden He has placed upon you."

The flush in Judith's cheeks spread its color across her face. "This insult shall not go unanswered. My husband shall know of it directly, and he will not be pleased." This was a piece of face-saving bravado, for Viscount Waifar's temporal authority carried no weight here, and she knew it. Holding her head high, she turned toward her waiting mount.

Joan came forward from the little group of novices.

"Give me the candle, lady," she said, holding out her hand. "I will light it for you."

Surprise and distrust registered in Judith's beautiful dark eyes. Was this a further attempt to humiliate her?

For a long moment the two women stood looking at each other, Judith the epitome of feminine beauty in her golden tunic, her long hair framing her face in a becoming cloud, Joan, the taller of the two, boyish and unadorned in her plain monk's garb.

Something in the compelling gray-green eyes that met hers with such intensity persuaded Judith. Wordlessly she placed the slim taper into Joan's outstretched hand. Then she remounted and rode through the gate.

Joan lighted the candle before the altar as she had promised. The sacristan was furious. "Intolerable cheek!" he declared. And that night, to Brother Thomas's evident delight, Joan was required to fast in penance for her crime.

After this episode, Joan made a determined effort to put Gerold from her mind. She could never be happy living a woman's restricted existence. Besides, she reasoned, her relationship with Gerold was not what she had believed it to be. She had been a child, inexperienced and naive; her love had been a romantic delusion born of loneliness and need. Gerold had certainly not loved her, or he would never have left.

*Aegra amans,* she thought. Truly Virgil was right: love *was* a form of sickness. It altered people, made them behave in strange and irrational ways. She was glad she was done with it.

*Never give yourself to a man.* Her mother's words of warning came back to her. She had forgotten them in the fervor of her childish infatuation. Now she realized how lucky she had been to have escaped her mother's fate.

Over and over again Joan told herself these things, until at last she came to believe them.

# 15

The brothers gathered in the chapter house, seated in order of seniority on the *gradines,* tiers of stone seats lining the walls of the house. The chapter meeting was the most important assembly of the day outside of the religious offices, for it was here that the temporal business of the community was conducted and matters regarding management, monies, appointments, and disputes were discussed. This was also where brothers who had committed transgressions of the rule were expected to confess their faults and be assigned their penances, or risk accusation by others.

Joan always came to chapter with a certain trepidation. Had she inadvertently given herself away with some incautious word or gesture? If her true identity were ever to be revealed, this was where she would learn of it.

The meeting always began with the reading of a chapter from the Rule of St. Benedict, the book of monastic regulations which guided the everyday spiritual and administrative life of the community. The rule was read straight through from beginning to end, a chapter a day, so that over the course of a year the brethren heard it in its entirety.

After the reading and benediction, Abbot Raban asked, "Brethren, have you any faults to confess?"

Before he finished uttering the words, Brother Thedo leapt to his feet. "Father, I do confess a fault."

"What is it, Brother?" Abbot Raban said with weary patience. Brother Thedo was always the first to accuse himself of wrongdoing.

"I have faltered in the performance of the *opus manuum*. Copying a life of St. Amandus, I fell asleep in the scriptorium."

"Again?" Abbot Raban lifted an eyebrow.

Thedo bowed his head meekly. "Father, I am sinful and unworthy. Please exact the harshest of penances upon me."

Abbot Raban sighed. "Very well. For two days you will stand a penitent before the church."

The brothers smiled wryly. Brother Thedo was so frequently to be found doing penance outside the church that he seemed part of the decoration, a living, breathing pillar of remorse.

Thedo was disappointed. "You are too charitable, Father. For so grievous a fault, I ask to be allowed to do penance for a week."

"God does not welcome pridefulness, Thedo, even in suffering. Remember that, while you are asking His forgiveness for your other faults."

The reprimand struck home. Thedo flushed and sat down.

"Are there any other faults to confess?" Raban asked.

Brother Hunric stood. "Twice I came late to night office."

Abbot Raban nodded; Hunric's tardiness had been noted, but because he admitted his fault freely and did not try to hide it, his penance would be light.

"From now until St. Denis's day, you will keep night watch."

Brother Hunric bowed his head. The Feast of St. Denis was two days away; for the next two nights, he must stay awake and watch the progress of the moon and the stars across the sky so he could determine as closely as possible the arrival of the eighth hour of the night, or two A.M., and then awaken the sleeping brothers for the celebration of vigils. Such watches were essential to the strict observance of the night office, for the sundial was the only other way of measuring the passage of time, and of course it was of no use in darkness.

"During your watch," Raban continued, "you will kneel in unceasing prayer on a pile of nettles, that you may be sharply reminded of your indolence and prevented from compounding your fault with sinful sleepfulness."

"Yes, Father Abbot." Brother Hunric accepted the penance without rancor. For so grave an offense, the punishment could have been far worse.

Several brothers stood in their turn and confessed to such minor faults as breaking dishes in refectory, errors in scribing, mistakes in the oratory, receiving their corresponding penances with humble acceptance. When they were finished, Abbot Raban paused to make certain no one else wished to confess. Then he said, "Have any other infractions of the rule been committed? Let those who will speak, for the good of their brothers' souls."

This was the part of the meeting Joan dreaded. Scanning the rows of brethren, her gaze fell on Brother Thomas. His heavy-lidded eyes were regarding her with unmistakable hostility. She shifted uneasily in her seat. *Does he mean to accuse me of something?*

But Thomas made no move to rise. From the row of seats just behind him, Brother Odilo stood.

"On Friday fastday, I saw Brother Hugh take an apple from the orchard and eat it."

Brother Hugh leapt nervously to his feet. "Father, it is true I picked the apple, for it was hard work pulling up the weeds, and I felt a great weakness in my limbs. But, Holy Father, I did not eat the apple; I merely took a small bite, to strengthen me so I could go on with the opus manuum."

"Weakness of the flesh is no excuse for violation of the rule," Abbot Raban responded sternly. "It is a test, sent by God to try the spirit of the faithful. Like Eve, the mother of sin, you have failed that test, Brother—a serious fault, especially as you did not seek to confess it yourself. In penance, you will fast for a week and forgo all pittances until Epiphany."

A week of starvation, and no pittances—the extra little treats that supplemented the spartan monastic diet of greens, pulse, and occasionally fish—until well after Christ Mass! This last part would be especially hard to bear, for it was during this holy season that gifts of food poured into the abbey from all over the countryside, as Christians looked guiltily to the welfare of their immortal souls. Honey cakes, pasties, sweet roast chickens, and other rare and wonderful indulgences would briefly grace the abbey tables. Brother Hugh looked evilly at Brother Odilo.

"Furthermore," Abbot Raban continued, "in grateful return to Brother Odilo for his attention to your spiritual well-being, you will prostrate yourself before him tonight and wash his feet with humility and thankfulness."

Brother Hugh bowed his head. He would perforce do as Abbot Raban had charged, but Joan doubted he would feel grateful. Penitent acts were easier to enjoin than penitent hearts.

"Are there any other faults that need to be disclosed?" Abbot Raban asked. When no one responded, he said gravely, "It grieves me to report that there is one among us who is guilty of the wickedest of sins, a crime detestable in the sight of God and Heaven—"

Joan's heart gave a leap of alarm.

"—the breaking of his holy vow made to God."

Brother Gottschalk jumped to his feet. "It was my father's vow, not mine!" he said chokingly.

Gottschalk was a young man, some three or four years older than Joan, with curly black hair and eyes set so deep in their sockets they looked like two dark bruises. Like Joan, he was an oblate, offered to the monastery in infancy by his father, a Saxon noble. Now that he was grown a man, he wanted to leave.

"It is lawful for a Christian man to dedicate his son to God," Abbot Raban said sternly. "Such offering cannot be withdrawn without great sin."

"Is it not an equal sin for a man to be bound against his nature and his will?"

"If a man will not turn, He will whet His sword," Abbot Raban said portentously. "He hath bent His bow and made it ready. He hath prepared for him the instruments of death."

"That is tyranny, not truth!" Gottschalk cried passionately.

"Shame!" "Sinner!" "For shame, Brother!" Scattered cries of outrage punctuated a chorus of hissing from the brethren.

"Your disobedience, my son, has placed your immortal soul in grievous danger," Abbot Raban said solemnly. "There is but one cure for such a disease—in the just and terrible words of the Apostle: *Tradere hujusmodi hominem in interitum carnis, ut spiritus salvus sit in diem Domini*—such a man must be handed over for the destruction of his flesh, that his spirit may be saved on the day of the Lord."

At Raban's signal, two of the *decani juniores,* brothers in charge of monastic discipline, took hold of Gottschalk and pushed him to the center of the room. He offered no resistance as they shoved him to his knees and roughly pulled up his robes, exposing his naked buttocks and back. From one corner of the room where it was kept for just this purpose, Brother Germar, the senior deacon, retrieved a sturdy willow stick, at the end of which were affixed thick strands of knotted, wiry rope. Positioning himself carefully, he raised the scourge high and brought it down hard on Gottschalk's back. The slap of the lash reverberated throughout the hushed assembly.

The scarred skin on Joan's back quivered. The flesh has its own memory, keener than the mind's.

Brother Germar raised the scourge again and brought it down even harder. Gottschalk's whole body shuddered, but he clamped his lips together, refusing to give Abbot Raban the satisfaction of hearing him cry out. Again the scourge rose and fell, rose and fell, and still Gottschalk did not break.

After the usual seven lashes, Brother Germar lowered the scourge. Abbot Raban angrily signaled him to continue. With a look of surprise, Brother Germar obeyed.

Three more lashes, four, five, and then there was an awful crack as the scourge struck bone. Gottschalk threw back his head and screamed—a great, terrible, tearing cry from the center of his being. The appalling sound hung in the air, then subsided into a long, shuddering sob.

Abbot Raban nodded, satisfied, and signaled Brother Germar to stop. As Gottschalk was lifted and half-led, half-dragged from the hall, Joan caught a flash of white in the middle of his crimsoned back. It was one of Gottschalk's ribs, and it had completely pierced his flesh.

The infirmary was uncharactistically empty, for the day was warm and breezeless, and the old ones and the chronically ill had been taken outside for a touch of healing sun.

Brother Gottschalk lay prone on the infirmary bed, half conscious, his open wounds reddening the sheets. Brother Benjamin, the physician, bent over him, trying to staunch the bleeding with the aid of a few linen bandages, already completely saturated with blood. He looked up as Joan came in.

"Good. You are here. Hand me some bandages from the shelf."

Joan hurried to comply. Brother Benjamin peeled off the old bandages, threw them to the ground, and applied the new. Within moments, they were soaked through.

"Help me to shift him," Benjamin said. "The way he's lying, that bone is still making mischief. We must get that rib back into place, or we'll never stop the bleeding."

Joan moved to the opposite side of the bed, skillfully positioning her hands so that one quick forward motion would draw the bone back into place.

"Easy, now," Benjamin said. "Half sensible though he is, he'll feel it sharp. On my mark, Brother. One, two, *three*!"

Joan pulled while Brother Benjamin pushed. There was a fresh outpouring of blood; then the bone slid beneath the gaping flesh.

*"Deo, juva me!"* Gottschalk lifted his head in tortured petition, then fell back unconscious.

They sponged up the blood and cleansed Gottschalk's wounds.

"Well, Brother John, what needs doing next?" Brother Benjamin quizzed Joan when they had done.

She was quick with the answer. "Apply a salve . . . of mugwort, perhaps, mixed with some pennyroyal. Soak some bandages in vinegar, and apply them as a healing pad."

"Very good." Benjamin was pleased. "We shall put in some lovage as well, as a guard against infection."

They worked side by side, preparing the solution, the pungent smell of the new-crushed herbs rising headily around them. When the bandages were dipped and ready, Joan handed them to Brother Benjamin.

"You do it," he said, then stood back and watched approvingly as his young apprentice firmly pressed the ugly flaps of skin together and expertly positioned the bandages.

He came forward to inspect the patient. The bandaging was perfect—better, in fact, than he could have done himself. Nevertheless, he did not like the way Brother Gottschalk looked. His skin, cold and clammy to the touch, had gone white as new-sheared wool. His breathing came shallowly, and the pulse of his heart blood, faintly detected, was dangerously rapid.

*He's going to die,* Brother Benjamin realized with dismay, and the thought immediately followed: *Father Abbot will be furious.* Raban had exceeded himself in chapter and surely knew it; Gottschalk's death would serve as both reproach and embarrassment. And if news of it should reach King Ludwig . . . well, even abbots were not immune from censure and dismissal.

Brother Benjamin searched his mind for something more to do. His pharmacopoeia of medicines was useless, for he could not administer anything by mouth, not even water to replenish lost fluids, while his patient lay senseless.

John Anglicus's voice startled him from his reverie: "Should I start a fire in the brazier and set some stones to heating?"

Benjamin looked at his assistant with surprise. Packing a patient round with hot stones wrapped in flannel was standard medical procedure in winter, when the pervading chill was known to sap a sick man's strength, but now, in these last warm days of autumn . . . ?

"Hippocrates' treatise on wounds," Joan reminded him. She had given him her translation of the Greek physician's brilliant work only last month.

Brother Benjamin frowned. He enjoyed doctoring, and within the limited medical knowledge of the day, he was good at it. But he was no innovator; he felt more comfortable with safe, familiar remedies than with new ideas and theories.

"The shock of violent injury," Joan continued with a barely perceptible degree of impatience. "According to Hippocrates, it can kill a man with a penetrating chill that emanates from within."

"It is true that I have seen men die suddenly after injury, though their wounds did not appear to be mortal," Brother Benjamin said slowly. "*Deus vult,* I thought, God's will . . ."

The intelligent young face of John Anglicus was alight with expectancy, seeking permission to proceed.

"Very well," Brother Benjamin conceded, "fire up the brazier; it's unlikely to do Brother Gottschalk any harm, and it may do him good, as the pagan doctor says." He settled himself on a bench, grateful to rest his arthritic legs as his energetic young assistant bustled about the room, starting the fire and setting stones over it.

When the stones were hot, Joan wrapped them in thick layers of flannel cloth and carefully placed them all about Gottschalk. Two of the largest stones she positioned under his feet, so that they were slightly elevated, following Hippocrates' recommendation. She finished by laying a light woolen blanket over all, to hold in the warmth.

After a short while, Gottschalk's eyelids fluttered; he moaned and began to stir. Brother Benjamin went to the bed. A healthy pink tinge had returned to Gottschalk's skin, and he was breathing more normally. A quick check of his pulse revealed a strong, regular heartbeat.

"God be praised." Brother Benjamin breathed in relief. He smiled at John Anglicus across the bed. *He has the gift,* Brother Benjamin thought with an almost paternal pride, slightly tinged with envy. From the beginning the boy had shown brilliant promise—that was why Benjamin had asked for him as his assistant—but he had never expected him to come so far so fast. In just a few years, John Anglicus had mastered the skills it had taken Brother Benjamin a lifetime to acquire.

"You have the healing touch, Brother John," he said benevolently. "Today you have surpassed your old master; soon I will have nothing left to teach you."

"Do not say so," Joan responded with chagrin, for she was fond of Benjamin. "I still have much to learn, and I know it."

Gottschalk groaned again, his pinched lips drawing back to reveal his teeth.

"He begins to feel the pain," Brother Benjamin said. Working rapidly, he made a potion of red wine and sage, into which he infused a few drops of poppy juice. Such a preparation required the greatest care, for what could, in small doses, provide blessed relief from insupportable pain could also kill, the difference depending solely on the skill of the physician.

When he was done, Brother Benjamin handed the brimming cup to Joan, who carried it to the bed and offered it to Gottschalk. Proudly, he pushed it away, though the sudden movement caused him to cry out in pain.

"Drink it, Brother," Joan chided gently, and held the cup to Gottschalk's lips. "You must get well if you are ever to win your freedom," she added in a conspiratorial whisper.

Gottschalk flashed her a surprised look. He took a few sips, then drank rapidly, thirstily, like a man who comes upon a well after a hot day's march.

An authoritative voice sounded unexpectedly behind them. "Do not place your hopes in herbs and potions."

Turning, Joan saw Abbot Raban, followed by a score of the brethren. She put down the cup and rose.

"The Lord grants life to men and makes them sound. Prayer alone can restore this sinner to health." Abbot Raban signaled the brothers, who quietly surrounded the bed.

Abbot Raban led them in the prayer for the sick. Gottschalk did not join in. He lay unmoving, eyes closed as if asleep, though Joan could tell from his breathing he was not.

*His body will heal,* she thought, *but not his wounded soul.* Joan's heart went out to the young monk. She understood his stubborn refusal to submit to Raban's tyranny, remembering, too well, her own fierce struggle against her father.

"All praise and thanks to God." Abbot Raban's voice sounded clear above the rest of the brethren.

Joan joined in praising God, but in her mind she also gave thanks to the pagan Hippocrates, worshiper of idols, whose bones were dust many centuries before Christ was born, but whose wisdom had reached across the distant years to heal one of His sons.

"The wound's mending nicely," Joan reassured Gottschalk after she unwrapped the bandages and laid his back bare for inspection. Two weeks had passed since the day of his scourging, and already the broken rib had knit and the jagged edges of the wound sealed neatly together—though, like her, Gottschalk would bear the marks of his punishment for life.

"Thanks for the trouble you've taken, Brother," Gottschalk replied, "but it will all be to do over, for it's only a matter of time till he has me scourged again."

"You only provoke him with open defiance. A milder approach would serve you better."

"I will defy him with the last breath in my body. He is evil," he cried passionately.

"Have you thought of telling him you'll forgo your claim to the land in return for your freedom?" Joan asked. An oblate was always offered to a monastery along with a substantial gift of land; if the oblate subsequently left, the land presumably would revert as well.

"Don't you think I've offered that already?" Gottschalk replied. "It's not the land he's after; it's me, or rather my submission, body and soul. And that he'll never have, though he kill me for it."

So it was a contest of wills between them—one that Gottschalk could not possibly win. Best to get him away from here before something terrible happened.

"I've been giving some thought to your problem," Joan said. "Next month there's a synod in Mainz. All the bishops of the Church will attend. If you submitted a petition for your release, they would have to consider it—and their ruling would supersede Abbot Raban's."

Gottschalk said bleakly, "The synod will never contravene the will of the great Raban Maur. His power is too great."

"The ruling of abbots, even of archbishops, has been overturned before," Joan argued. "And you've a strong argument in the fact you were offered as an oblate in infancy, before you had reached the age of reason. I searched the library and found some passages from Jerome that would support such an argument." She pulled a roll of parchment from under her robe. "Here, see for yourself—I've written it all down."

Gottschalk's dark eyes brightened as he read. He looked up excitedly. "It's brilliant! A dozen Rabans could not refute so well made an argument!" Then the dark clouds rolled in again. "But—there's no way for me to present this before the synod. *He* will never grant me permission to leave, even for a day, and certainly not to go to Mainz."

"Burchard, the cloth merchant, can take it for you. His business brings him here regularly. I know him well, for he comes to the infirmary to fetch medicine for his wife, who suffers from headache. He's a good man and can be trusted to bear the petition safely to Mainz."

Gottschalk asked with suspicion, "Why are you doing this?"

Joan shrugged. "A man should be free to live the life he chooses." To herself she added, *And so, for that matter, should a woman.*

Everything went off as planned. When Burchard came to the infirmary to pick up the medicine for his wife, Joan gave him the petition, which he bore away tucked safely in his saddlebag.

A few weeks later, the abbey received an unexpected visit from Otgar, Bishop of Trier. After the formal greeting in the forecourt, the bishop requested and received immediate audience with the abbot in his quarters.

The news the bishop brought was astonishing: Gottschalk was released from his vows. He was free to leave Fulda when he chose.

He chose to leave at once, not wishing to remain one moment longer than necessary under Raban's baleful eye. Packing was no problem; though he had lived all his life at the monastery, Gottschalk had nothing to bring away with him, for a monk could not own any personal property. Brother Anselm, the kitchener, put together a sack of food to see Gottschalk through the first few days on the road, and that was all.

"Where will you go?" Joan asked him.

"To Speyer," he answered. "I've a married sister there; I can stay with her for a while. Then . . . I don't know."

He had fought for liberty so long and with so little hope he had not stopped to consider what he would do if he actually achieved it. He had never known anything but the monastic life; its safe and predictable rhythms were as much a part of him as breathing. Though he was too proud to admit to it, Joan read the uncertainty and fear in his eyes.

The brethren did not gather for a formal leave-taking, for Raban had forbidden it. Only Joan and a few other brothers whose opus manuum brought them across the forecourt at that hour were there to see Gottschalk walk through the gate, a free man at last. Joan watched him make his way down the road, his tall, spare figure growing smaller and smaller until it disappeared on the horizon.

Would he be happy? Joan hoped so. But somehow he seemed a man fated always to yearn after that which he could not have, to choose for himself the rockiest, most difficult path. She would pray for him, as for all the other sad and troubled souls who must travel roads alone.

# 16

On All Souls' Day, the brethren of Fulda gathered in the forecourt for the *separatio leprosorum,* the solemn liturgy segregating lepers from society. This year seven such unfortunates had been identified in the region surrounding Fulda, four men and three women. One was a youth of no more than fourteen, in whom the marks of the disease were as yet very indistinct; one an ancient woman of sixty or more, whose lidless eyes and absent lips and fingers attested to an advanced stage of the disease. All seven had been wrapped in black shrouds and herded into the forecourt, where they huddled in a wretched little band.

The brethren approached in solemn procession. First came Abbot Raban, drawn up tall in full abbatial dignity. To his right walked Prior Joseph, to his left, Bishop Otgar. Behind marched the remaining brethren in order of seniority. Two lay brothers brought up the rear of the procession, pushing a wheelbarrow heaped with earth taken from the graveyard.

"I hereby forbid you to enter any church, mill, bakery, market, or other place where people gather." Abbot Raban addressed the lepers with heavy solemnity. "I forbid you to use the common roads and paths. I forbid you to come near any living person without ringing your bell to give warning. I forbid you to touch children, or to give them anything."

One of the women began to wail. Two dark, wet patches stained the front of her worn woolen tunic. *A nursing mother,* Joan thought. *Where is her babe? Who will take care of it?*

"I forbid you to eat or drink in the company of anyone save lepers like yourselves," Abbot Raban continued. "I forbid you ever to wash your hands or face or any objects you may use at the riverbank, or at any spring or stream. I forbid you carnal knowledge of your spouse, or any other person. I forbid you to beget children, or to nurse them."

The woman's anguished wailing intensified, her tears coursing down her ulcerated face.

"What is your name?" With barely concealed irritation, Abbot Raban addressed the woman in the vernacular. Her unseemly display of emotion was marring the well-ordered symmetry of the ceremony, with which Raban had hoped to impress the bishop. For it was now apparent that Otgar had come to Fulda not merely to deliver the news of Gottschalk's release but also to observe and make report upon Raban's stewardship of the abbey.

"Madalgis," the woman snuffled in reply. "Please, lord, I must go home, for there are four fatherless little ones needing their dinner."

"Heaven will provide for the innocent. You have sinned, Madalgis, and God is afflicting you," Raban explained with elaborate patience, as if to a child. "You must not weep, but instead thank God, for you will suffer the less torment in the life to come."

Madalgis stood bewildered, as if she doubted she had heard aright. Then her face crumpled and her crying broke out anew, louder than before, her face crimsoning from the bottom of her neck to the roots of her hair.

*That's odd,* Joan thought.

Raban turned his back upon the woman. *"De profundis clamavi ad te, Domine . . ."* He began the prayer for the dead. The brethren joined in, their voices mingling in deep unison.

Joan mouthed the words mechanically, her eyes fixed on Madalgis with intent concentration.

Finishing with the prayer, Raban moved on to the final part of the ceremony, in which each of the lepers, in turn, would be formally separated from the world. He stood before the first, the relatively unmarked boy of fourteen. *"Sis mortuus mundo, vivens iterum Deo,"* Abbot Raban said. "Be dead unto the world, living in the eyes of God." He signaled to Brother Magenard, who plunged a spade into the wheelbarrow, lifted out a small pile of graveyard earth, and flung it at the boy, spattering his clothes and hair.

Five times the little ceremony was repeated, ending each time with the hurling of the earth. When it came Madalgis's turn, she tried to run, but the two lay brothers blocked her way. Raban frowned at her.

*"Sis mortuus mundo, vivens iter—"*

"Stop!" Joan shouted.

Abbot Raban broke off. Everyone turned to locate the source of this unprecedented interruption.

With all eyes upon her, Joan advanced toward Madalgis and examined her with rapid skill. Then she turned to Abbot Raban. "Father, this woman is no leper."

"What?" Raban struggled to keep his anger reined, so the bishop would not observe it.

"These lesions are not leprotic. See how her skin colors, fed by the blood beneath? This affliction of the skin is not infectious; it can be cured."

"If she is not a leper, then what has caused these ulcers?" Raban demanded.

"There could be several causes. It is difficult to say without further examination. But whatever the reason, one thing is certain: it is not leprosy."

"God has marked this woman with the visible manifestation of sin. We must not defy His will!"

"She is marked, but not by leprosy," Joan responded sturdily. "God has provided us with the knowledge to discern between those whom He has chosen to bear this burden, and those whom He has not. Will He be pleased if we consign to a living death one whom He Himself has not elected?"

It was a clever argument. With dismay, Raban saw the others were moved by it. "How do we know whether you have correctly interpreted the signs of God's will?" he countered. "Is your pride so great you would sacrifice your brethren to it—for in order to minister to this woman you must put all in jeopardy."

This elicited a buzz of concern. Nothing, save the unimaginable torments of Hell, inspired more horror, revulsion, and fear than the disease of leprosy.

With a howl, Madalgis threw herself at Joan's feet. She had been following the discussion without understanding, for Joan and Raban had been speaking in Latin, but she had managed to discern that Joan had interceded on her behalf, and that the argument was not going well.

Joan patted her shoulder, as much to quiet as to comfort her. "None of the brethren needs be put at risk, saving myself. With your leave, Father,

I will go with her to her home, bringing such medications as may be necessary."

"Alone? With a woman?" Raban's brows rose in pious horror. "John Anglicus, your purpose is perhaps innocent, but you are as yet a young man, subject to the baser passions of the flesh, from which it is my duty, as your spiritual father, to protect you."

Joan opened her mouth to respond, then closed it with frustration. No one could be safer from temptation by a woman than she, but there was no way she could explain that to Raban.

Brother Benjamin's rasping voice sounded behind her. "I will accompany Brother John. I am old, long past the time for such temptation. Father, you may trust in Brother John when he says the woman is no leper, for when he speaks with such certainty, he will not be wrong. His skill in such matters is very great."

Joan shot him a grateful glance. Madalgis clung to her, her wails tempered into muted whimpering by Joan's reassuring touch.

Abbot Raban hesitated. What he really wanted was to give John Anglicus a sound caning for his presumptuous disobedience. But Bishop Otgar was watching; Raban could not appear to be unbending or unmerciful. "Very well," he said grudgingly. "Brother John, after vespers you and Brother Benjamin may go from here with this sinner, and do what may be done in God's name to cure her of her affliction."

"Thank you, Father," Joan said.

Raban made the sign of the cross over them. "May God in His merciful goodness shield you from harm."

The mule carrying bags of medical supplies plodded along placidly, indifferent to the westering sun. Madalgis's cottage lay some five miles on; at this languid pace, they would be hard-pressed to arrive before dark. Joan prodded the mule impatiently. To humor her, the beast took five or six quick steps in succession, then settled back comfortably into its original gait.

As they walked, Madalgis chattered on with the nervous energy that often follows a great fright. Joan and Benjamin learned her whole sad story. Despite her destitute appearance, she was no colona but a freewoman whose husband had held independent title to a manse encompassing some twelve hectares. After his death, she had tried to support her family by working the land herself, but this heroic endeavor was abruptly curtailed by her neighbor, Lord Rathold, who coveted the prosperous manse. Lord Rathold had brought Madalgis's labors to the attention of Abbot Raban, who forbade her, upon threat of excommunication, ever to take up tiller or hoe again. "It is ungodly for a woman to do the work of men," he told her.

Faced with starvation, Madalgis had been forced to sell the manse and its house to Lord Rathold for a fraction of its worth, receiving in return only a few solidi and a tiny hut in a nearby settlement with a small piece of pasturage for her cows.

She had taken up cheese making; in this way she had managed to eke out a minimal subsistence, bartering the fruits of her labor for other food and necessities.

As soon as she caught sight of her home, Madalgis gave a glad cry and ran ahead, quickly disappearing inside. Joan and Brother Benjamin followed a few minutes later and discovered her buried beneath a breathless tumble of children, all laughing, crying, and talking at the same time. Seeing the two monks enter, the children cried out in alarm and surrounded Madalgis protectively, fearing she would be taken from them again. Madalgis spoke to them and their smiles returned, though they studied the two strangers curiously.

A woman came in, holding a babe in each arm. She made a respectful bow to the two monks, then hurried past to hand one of the infants to Madalgis, who seized it joyfully and put it to her breast, where it began to suck hungrily. The other woman seemed a dame of fifty years or more, but then Joan saw that though her face was drawn and lined with care, she was not so old as that—no more perhaps than twenty-nine or thirty.

*She has been nursing Madalgis's babe as well as her own,* Joan realized. With sympathy she noted the woman's leaking breasts and sagging abdomen and the unhealthy pallor of her skin. Joan had seen the symptoms before: women often bore their first child by the age of thirteen or fourteen and thereafter existed in a state of virtually perpetual pregnancy, bringing forth one babe after another with dreary regularity. It was not uncommon for a woman to have twenty or more pregnancies during her lifetime—though inevitably some of these were cut short by miscarriage. By the time a woman reached her time of change—if indeed she lived that long, for childbirth carried with it a considerable hazard—her body was wasted, her spirit broken by exhaustion. Joan made a mental note to make up a tonic of powdered oak bark and sage to fortify the woman against the coming winter.

Madalgis spoke to her oldest child, a gangly boy of twelve or thirteen. He went out the door and returned a minute later with a loaf of bread and a chunk of blue-veined cheese, which he offered to Joan and Brother Benjamin. Brother Benjamin took the bread but refused the cheese, for it was obviously rotten with mold. Joan also found the cheese repellent, but to please the boy, she broke off a tiny piece and put it in her mouth. To her surprise, it tasted wonderful—pungent, rich, astonishingly flavorful—far superior to any cheese at Fulda's tables.

"Why, it's delicious."

The boy grinned.

"What's your name?" she asked him.

"Arn," he answered shyly.

As she ate, Joan took note of her surroundings. Madalgis's home was a small, windowless hut rudely constructed of crossed lathes daubed with mud and stuffed with straw and leaves. There were large gaps in the walls, through which the cool night air now swept, stirring the smoke from the hearth fire into a choking cloud. In one corner there was a pen for animals; in another month, Madalgis would bring in her cows for the winter—a common practice among the poor. Doing so not only protected the precious livestock but also brought a much-needed extra source of warmth into their homes. Unfortunately, in addition to their body heat, the animals brought pests: ticks, biting flies, fleas, and a host of other vermin, which burrowed into the floor rushes and the straw sleeping pallets. Most poor folk were covered with painful bites and rashes, a fact documented in the local churches, whose walls featured graphic representations of Job, his body covered with ulcers, scraping at his sores with a knife.

Some people—and Joan suspected Madalgis was one of these—developed unusually strong reactions to the insect bites over time. Their skin swelled into great sores, which, further irritated by clothes of coarse and unclean wool, finally erupted into festering lesions.

The test of Joan's diagnosis would have to wait, however, as it was now full dark. *Tomorrow,* Joan told herself as she prepared for sleep, *tomorrow we'll begin*.

The next day they cleaned the little hut from top to bottom. The old rushes covering the ground were tossed out and the earth floor swept perfectly smooth and even. The sleeping pallets were burned, and new ones of fine fresh straw made up. Even the thatch roof, which had begun to sag and rot with age, was replaced.

The difficult part was persuading Madalgis to take a bath. Like everyone else, she washed her face, hands, and feet regularly, but the idea of total immersion was to her strange and even dangerous.

"I'll catch the flux and die!" she wailed.

"You'll die if you don't," Joan answered firmly. "A leper's existence is a living death."

The cool winds of Herbistmanoth had rendered the little creek that ran behind the settlement too cold for bathing. They had to haul the water up and heat it over the hearth fire, then pour it into a laundry tub. While the two monks stood with their backs to her, Madalgis lowered herself into the tub with a great deal of trepidation, then washed her body with soap and water.

After her bath, Madalgis donned a clean new tunic Joan had obtained from Brother Conrad, the cellarer, in anticipation of the need. Made of fine heavy linen, it was warm enough to see Madalgis through the winter yet was far smoother and less irritating than wool.

Bathed and cleaned, her house rid of vermin and gleaming from roof to floor, Madalgis immediately began to improve. Her lesions dried and began to show signs of healing.

Brother Benjamin was ecstatic. "You were right!" he said to Joan. "It isn't leprosy! We must return and show the others!"

"A few days more," Joan said cautiously. There must be no doubt whatsoever as to the cure when they returned.

"Show me another one," Arn pleaded.

Joan smiled at him. For the past few days she had been teaching the boy Bede's classical method of digital computation, and he had proved an apt and eager student.

"First you must show me that you remember what you've already learned. What do these represent?" She held up the last three fingers of her left hand.

"Units of one," the boy said unhesitatingly. "And these"—he indicated the left thumb and index finger—"are decimals."

"Good. And on the right hand?"

"These represent hundreds, and these, thousands." He lifted the appropriate fingers to illustrate.

"Very well, what numbers do you want to use?"

"Twelve, for that's my age. And"—he thought for a moment—"three hundred sixty-five, for that's the number of days in a year!" he said, proud to show off something else he had learned.

"Twelve times three hundred sixty-five. Let's see . . ." Joan's fingers moved swiftly, computing the total. "That's four thousand three hundred and eighty."

Arn clapped his hands with delight.

"You try it," Joan said, going through it again, more slowly, allowing time for him to mimic each motion. Then she had him do it on his own. "Excellent!" she said after he had executed it.

Arn grinned, delighted by the game and the praise. Then his round little face grew serious. "How high can you go?" he asked. "Can you do it with a hundred and a thousand? With . . . a thousand and another thousand?"

Joan nodded. "Just touch your chest like this . . . see? That gives you tens of thousands. And if you touch your thigh, like this, hundreds of thousands. So"—her fingers moved again—"one thousand one hundred times two thousand three hundred is . . . two million, five hundred and thirty thousand!"

Arn's eyes flew wide with wonderment. The numbers were so enormous he could scarcely conceive them.

"Show me another!" he begged. Joan laughed. She enjoyed teaching the boy, for he drank in knowledge thirstily. He reminded her of herself as a child. *What a shame,* she thought, *that this bright spark of intelligence was destined to be extinguished in the darkness of ignorance.*

"If I can arrange it," she said, "would you like to study at the abbey school? You could go on learning there—not just numbers, but reading and writing as well."

"Reading and writing?" Arn repeated in wonder. Those extraordinary skills were reserved for priests and very great lords, not for such as he. He asked anxiously, "Would I have to become a monk?"

Joan was amused. Arn was of the age when boys begin to develop a strong interest in the opposite sex; the idea of a life of chastity was understandably abhorrent to him.

"No," she said. "You would study at the Outer School, the one for lay students. But it would mean leaving home and living at the abbey. And you'd have to study hard, for the teaching master is very strict."

Arn didn't hesitate for a moment. "Oh yes! Yes, please!"

"Very well. We're returning to Fulda tomorrow. I'll speak to the teaching master then."

"At last!" Brother Benjamin breathed with relief. Straight ahead, where the pebbled road met the horizon, the gray walls of Fulda rose starkly, backgrounded by the twin towers of the abbatial church.

The little group of travelers had endured a wearisome journey from Madalgis's cottage, and the chill damp had aggravated Benjamin's rheumatism, making every step a torment.

"We'll be there soon," Joan said. "You'll have your feet up before the brazier in the warming room within the hour."

In the distance, the beating of the boards was announcing their arrival—for no one approached the gates of Fulda unheralded. At the sound, Madalgis clutched her babe nervously. It had been all Joan and Brother Benjamin could do to convince her that she had to return to the abbey; she had agreed at last only on condition that her children accompany her.

The brethren were gathered in the forecourt to greet them, lined up ceremoniously in order of rank, with Abbot Raban himself, silver haired and majestically erect, in the front.

Madalgis shrank back fearfully, hiding behind Joan.

"Come forth," Raban said.

"It's all right, Madalgis," Joan reassured her. "Do as Father Abbot says."

Madalgis advanced and stood trembling in the midst of the alien company. An audible sigh of astonishment passed through the ranks of brethren at the sight of her. The open, ulcerous nodes and lesions had all disappeared; except for a few dry and healing marks, the sun-browned skin of her face and arms showed forth clear and firm, blooming with renewed health. There could be no further doubt: even the most inexperienced could tell that the woman who stood before them was no leper.

"O wondrous sign of grace!" Bishop Otgar exclaimed in awe. "Like Lazarus, she has been restored from death to life!"

The brethren crowded around, sweeping the little group of travelers triumphantly toward the church.

✦ ✦ ✦

Joan's cure of Madalgis was regarded as nothing less than a miracle. All Fulda rang with John Anglicus's praise. When elderly Brother Aldwin, one of the community's two priests, died in his sleep one night, there was little doubt among the brethren as to who should succeed him.

Abbot Raban, however, was of a different mind. John Anglicus had entirely too bold and presumptuous a nature for his liking. Raban preferred Brother Thomas, who, though admittedly less brilliant, was far more predictable—a quality Raban valued.

But there was Bishop Otgar to consider. The bishop knew of Gottschalk's near-death from whipping, an event that reflected badly on Raban's abbacy. If Raban passed over John Anglicus in favor of a less qualified brother, it might raise further questions about his stewardship of the abbey. And if the king should receive bad report of him, he might remove him as abbot—an unthinkable outcome. Best to be prudent in his choice of priest, Raban decided—at least for the moment.

At chapter he announced, "As your spiritual father, the right to appoint a priest from among you belongs to me. After much prayer and reflection, I have decided upon a brother well suited for the office by virtue of his great learning: Brother John Anglicus."

There was a murmur of approval from the brethren. Joan flushed with excitement. *I, a priest!* To be admitted to the sacred mysteries, to administer the holy sacraments! It had been her father's cherished ambition for Matthew and, after Matthew died, for John. How rich an irony if that ambition were finally realized through his daughter!

Seated across the room, Brother Thomas glowered at Joan. *This priesthood is mine,* he thought bitterly. *I was Raban's choice; didn't he say as much only a few weeks ago?*

John Anglicus's cure of the leper woman had changed everything. It was infuriating. Madalgis was a nobody, a slave, or little better. What difference did it make if she went to the leprosarium—or lived or died for that matter?

That the prize should go to John Anglicus was bitter gall. From the very first, Thomas had hated him—hated the quickness of his wit, of which he had often felt the barb, hated the ease with which he had mastered his lessons. Such things did not come easily to Thomas. He had had to slave to learn the forms of Latin and memorize the chapters of the rule.

But what Thomas lacked in brilliance he made up for in persistence, and in the effort he put into the outward forms of faith. Whenever he finished with his meal, Thomas took care to lay his knife and fork down perpendicularly, in tribute to the Blessed Cross. He never drank his wine straight down like the others but partook of it reverently, three sips at a time, in pious illustration of the miracle of the Trinity. John Anglicus didn't trouble himself with such acts of devotion.

Thomas glared at his rival, so angelic looking with his fine halo of white-gold hair. *May Hell dry him up with its flames, him and the God-cursed womb that engendered him!*

The refectory, or monks' dining hall, was a masonry-walled structure forty feet wide and one hundred feet long, built large to accommodate all three hundred and fifty of the Fulda brethren at once. With seven tall windows on the south wall and six on the north, letting in direct sunlight year-round, it was one of the most cheerful of all the cloister buildings. The wide wooden beams and purlins supporting the rafters were colorfully painted with scenes from the life of Boniface, patron saint of Fulda; these added to the impression of brightness and light, so the room was as cheerful and pleasant now, in the cold, short days of Heilagmanoth, as it was in summertime.

It was noontime, and the brothers were assembled in the refectory for dinner, the first of the day's two meals. Abbot Raban sat at a long U-shaped table centered on the east wall, flanked by twelve brothers on his left and twelve on his right, representing Christ's apostles. The long planked tables bore simple plates of bread, pulse, and cheese. Mice scurried about on the earthen floor beneath, in furtive search of fallen crumbs.

In accordance with the Rule of St. Benedict, the brothers always took their meal without speaking. The strict silence was broken only by the clink of metal knives and cups and the voice of the lector for the week, who stood at the pulpit reading from the Psalms or the Lives of the Fathers. "As the mortal body partakes of earthly food," Abbot Raban liked to say, "so let the soul derive spiritual sustenance."

The *regula taciturnitis,* or rule of silence, was an ideal, commended by all but observed by few. The brothers had worked out an elaborate scheme of hand signs and facial gestures with which they communicated during meals. Entire conversations could be carried on in this manner, especially when, as now, the reader was poor. Brother Thomas read in a harsh, heavily accented voice that completely missed the lilting poetry of the Psalms; oblivious to his shortcomings, Thomas read loudly, his voice grating on the brethren's ears. Abbot Raban often asked Brother Thomas to read, preferring him to the monastery's more skilled readers, for, as he said, "too sweet a voice invites demons into the heart."

"Pssst." A muted hissing drew Joan's attention. She looked up from her plate to see Brother Adalgar signaling her across the table.

He held up four fingers. The number signified a chapter from the Rule of St. Benedict, a frequent vehicle for this kind of brotherly communication, which favored enigmatic references and circumlocutions.

Joan recalled the opening lines of chapter four: *"Omnes supervenientes hospites tamquam Christus suscipiantur,"* it read. "Let all who come be received like Christ."

Joan took Brother Adalgar's meaning at once. A visitor had come to Fulda—someone of note, or Brother Adalgar would not have troubled to mention it. Fulda received upward of a dozen visitors a day, rich and poor, fur-robed pilgrims and ragged paupers, weary travelers who came knowing that they would not be sent away, that here they would find a few days' rest, shelter, and food before continuing on their way.

Joan's curiosity was piqued. "Who?" she responded by a slight lift of her eyebrows.

At that moment Abbot Raban gave the sign, and the brothers rose from the table in unison, lining up in order of seniority. As they exited the refectory, Brother Adalgar turned to her.

*"Parens,"* he signed, and pointed at her emphatically. "Your parent."

With the calm, measured step and placid mien befitting a monk of Fulda, Joan followed the brethren out of the refectory. Nothing in her outward appearance betrayed her profound agitation.

Could Brother Adalgar be right? Had one of her parents come to Fulda? Her mother or her father? *Parens,* Adalgar had said, which could mean either. What if it was her father? He would not expect to see her but rather her brother, John. The idea filled Joan with alarm. If her father discovered her imposture, he would surely denounce her.

But perhaps it was her mother who had come. Gudrun would not betray her secret. She would understand that such a revelation would cost Joan her life.

*Mama.* It had been ten years since Joan had seen her, and they had parted badly. Suddenly, more than anything, Joan wanted to see Gudrun's familiar, beloved face, wanted to hold and be held by her, to hear her speak the lilting rhythms of the Old Tongue.

Brother Samuel, the hospitaler, intercepted her as she was leaving the refectory.

"You are excused from your duties this afternoon; someone has come to see you."

Torn between hope and fear, Joan said nothing.

"Don't look so serious, Brother; it isn't the Devil come for your immortal soul." Brother Samuel laughed heartily. He was a good-hearted, jovial man, fond of jests and laughter. For years Abbot Raban had chastised him for these unspiritual qualities, then finally given up and appointed him hospitaler, a job whose worldly duties of greeting and caring for visitors suited Brother Samuel perfectly.

"Your father is here," Samuel said cheerfully, glad to impart such good news, "waiting in the garden to greet you."

Fear splintered Joan's mask of self-control. She backed away, shaking her head. "I will not see him. I . . . I cannot."

The smile disappeared from Brother Samuel's lips. "Now, Brother, you don't mean that. Your father's traveled all the way from Ingelheim to speak with you."

She would have to offer some explanation. "There is bad blood between us. We . . . argued . . . when I left home."

Brother Samuel put his arm around her shoulders. "I understand," he said sympathetically. "But he *is* your father, and he has come a long way. It will be an act of charity to talk to him, if only for a little while."

Unable to disagree with this, Joan kept silent.

Brother Samuel took this for acquiescence. "Come. I will take you to him."

"No!" She shook off his encircling arm.

Brother Samuel was startled. This was no way to address the hospitaler, one of the seven obedientiary officers of the abbey.

"Your soul is troubled, Brother," he said sharply. "You need spiritual guidance. We will discuss this in chapter tomorrow."

*What can I do?* Joan thought in dismay. It would be difficult, if not impossible, to keep her true identity from her father. But a discussion in chapter could also be ruinous. There was no excuse for her behavior. If she was found to be disobedient, like Gottschalk . . .

"Forgive me, *Nonnus*"—she used the address of respect due a senior brother—"for my lack of temperance and humility. You took me by surprise, and in my confusion, I forgot my duty to you. I ask your pardon, most humbly."

It was a pretty apology. Brother Samuel's stern look dissolved into a smile; he was not a man to hold a grudge.

"You have it, Brother, most freely. Come. We will walk together to the garden."

As they made their way from the cloister past the livestock barns, the mill, and the drying kilns, Joan quickly calculated her chances. The last time her father had seen her, she had been a child of twelve. She had changed greatly in the ensuing ten years. Perhaps he would not recognize her. Perhaps . . .

They reached the garden with its neat rows of raised planting beds—thirteen in all, the number carefully selected to symbolize the holy congregation of Christ and the Twelve Apostles at the Last Supper. Each bed was exactly seven feet wide; this was also significant, for seven was the number of gifts of the Holy Ghost, signifying the wholeness of all created things.

In the rear of the garden, between beds of pepperwort and chervil, her father stood with his back to them. His short, squat body, thick neck, and resolute stance were immediately familiar. Joan pulled her head deep inside her voluminous cowl so the heavy material hung down in front, covering her hair and face.

Hearing their approach, the canon turned. His dark hair and beetling brows, which had once struck such terror in Joan, had gone completely gray.

*"Deus tecum."* Brother Samuel gave Joan an encouraging pat. "God be with you." Then he left them.

Her father crossed the garden haltingly. He was smaller than she remembered; she saw with surprise that he used a stick to walk. As he drew near, Joan turned away and, without speaking, gestured him to follow. She led him out of the sharp glare of the midday sun into the windowless chapel adjoining the garden, where darkness would provide better concealment. Inside, she waited for him to take a seat on one of the benches. Then she seated herself at the far end, keeping her head low so the cowl hid her profile.

*"Pater Noster qui es in caelis, sanctificetur nomen tuum . . ."* Her father began the Lord's Prayer. His folded hands shook with palsy; he spoke in the quavering, brittle tones of an old man. Joan joined her voice to his, their mingled words echoing through the tiny, stone-walled chamber.

The prayer completed, they sat for a while in silence.

"My son," the canon said at last, "you have done well. Brother Hospitaler tells me you are to be a priest. You have brought honor to our family, as I once hoped your brother would."

*Matthew.* Joan fingered the medallion of St. Catherine that hung around her neck, the one Matthew had given her so long ago.

Her father caught the gesture. "My eyesight has grown thick. Is that your sister Joan's medallion?"

Joan let go of it, cursing her stupidity; she had not thought to hide it.

"I took it as a remembrance . . . afterwards." She could not bring herself to speak of the horror of the Norsemen's attack.

"Did your sister die without . . . dishonor?"

Joan had a sudden image of Gisla, screaming in pain and fear while the Norsemen took turns with her.

"She died inviolate."

*"Deo gratias."* The canon crossed himself. "It was God's will, then. Headstrong and unnatural child, she could never have been at peace in this world; it is better so."

"She would not have said so."

If the canon caught the irony in her voice, he did not reveal it. "Her death was a very great grief to your mother."

"How fares my mother?"

For a long moment the canon did not respond. When at last he did, his voice was shakier than before.

"She is gone."

"Gone?"

"To Hell," the canon said, "to burn for all eternity."

"No." Understanding crowded the edges of Joan's consciousness. "No."

Not Mama with the beautiful face, the kind eyes, the gentle hands that brought kindness and comfort—Mama, who had loved her.

"She died one month ago," the canon said, "unshriven and unreconciled to Christ, calling upon her heathen gods. When the midwife told me she would not live, I did everything I could, but she would not accept the

Blessed Sacrament. I put the Sacred Host in her mouth, and she spat it out at me."

"The midwife? You don't mean . . ." Her mother was over fifty, well past childbearing years; she had begotten no more children after Joan was born.

"They would not let me bury her in the Christian cemetery, not with the unbaptized babe still in her womb." He began to cry, great, choking sobs that shook his entire body.

*Did he love her, then?* He'd had an odd way of displaying it, with his brutal rages, his cruelty, and his lust, his selfish lust that had killed her in the end.

The canon's sobs slowly quieted, and he began the prayer for the dead. This time Joan did not join in. Quietly, under her breath, she began to recite the Oath, invoking the sacred name of Thor the Thunderer, just as Mama had taught her so long ago.

Her father cleared his throat uncomfortably. "There is one thing, John. The mission in Saxony . . . do you think . . . that is, could the brothers use my help, in their work with the heathens?"

Joan was perplexed. "What about your work in Ingelheim?"

"The fact is, my position in Ingelheim has become difficult. The recent . . . misfortune . . . with your mother . . ."

At once Joan understood. The strictures against married clergy, only feebly enforced during the reign of Emperor Karolus, had tightened under the reign of his son, whose religious zeal had earned him the title Louis the Pious. The recent synod in Paris had strongly reinforced both the theory and practice of clerical celibacy. Gudrun's pregnancy, visible evidence of the canon's lack of chastity, could not have come at a worse time.

"You have lost your position?"

Reluctantly, her father nodded. "But *Deo volente,* I have the strength and skill to do God's work yet. If you could intercede for me with Abbot Raban . . . ?"

Joan did not reply. She was overfull with grief, anger, and pain; there was no room left in her heart for compassion toward her father.

"You do not answer me. You have grown proud, my son." He stood, his voice taking on something of its old commanding tone. "Remember, it was I who brought you to this place, and to your current position in life. *Contritionem praecedit superbia, et ante ruinam exaltatio spiritus,*" he remonstrated sternly. "Pride goeth before destruction and a haughty spirit before a fall. Proverbs, chapter sixteen."

*"Bonum est homini mulierem non tangere,"* Joan retorted. "It is well for a man not to touch a woman, First Corinthians, chapter seven."

Her father raised his cane to strike her, but the movement caused him to lose his balance, and he fell. She put out her hand to help him, and he pulled her down to him, holding her fast.

"My son," his voice pleaded tearfully in her ear, "my son. Do not desert me. You are all I have."

Repelled, she pulled back so violently that her cowl slipped off her head. Hastily she pulled it on again, but it was too late.

Her father's face held an expression of horrified recognition. "No," he said, aghast. "No, it cannot be."

"Father—"

"Daughter of Eve, what have you done? Where is your brother, John?"

"He is dead."

"Dead?"

"Killed by Norsemen, in the church at Dorstadt. I tried to save him, but—"

"Witch! Mooncalf! Demon from Hell!" He traced the sign of the cross in the air before him.

"Father, please, let me explain—" Joan pleaded desperately. She had to calm him before his raised voice drew the others.

He retrieved his stick and struggled awkwardly to his feet, his whole body trembling. Joan moved to assist him, but he warded her off and said accusingly, "You killed your elder brother. Could you not have spared the younger?"

"I loved John, Father. I would never have harmed him. It was the Norsemen, they came without warning, with swords and axes." She tightened her throat against mounting sobs; she had to keep talking, make him understand. "John tried to fight, but they killed everyone, everyone. They—"

He turned toward the door. "I must put a stop to this, to you, before you do any further harm."

She grabbed hold of his arm. "Father, don't, please, they will kill me if—"

He rounded on her fiercely. "Changeling devil! You should have died in your heathen mother's womb before ever you were born!" He struggled to free himself, his face purpling alarmingly. *"Let me go!"*

Desperately she held on. If he walked through that door, her life was forfeit.

"Brother John?" A voice sounded from the doorway. It was Brother Samuel, his kindly face creased with concern. "Is anything wrong?"

Startled, Joan loosed her grip on her father's arm. He pulled free and went to Brother Samuel.

"Take me to Abbot Raban. I must . . . I mush—" He broke off suddenly with a look of puzzled surprise.

He looked strange. His skin had gone an even deeper purple; his face twisted grotesquely, the right eye drooping lower than the left, the mouth crooked peculiarly to one side.

"Father?" She approached hesitantly, holding out her hand.

He lunged for her, his right arm flapping wildly as if no longer under his control.

Terrified, Joan backed away.

He shouted something unrecognizable, then fell forward like a hewn tree.

Brother Samuel called for help. Immediately five brethren materialized in the doorway.

Joan knelt beside her father and supported him in her arms. His head lay heavy and unresisting against her shoulder, his thin gray hair twined between her fingers. Looking into his eyes, Joan was shocked by the malignant hatred she saw there.

His lips worked with a ghastly determination. "M . . . m . . . m . . . !"

"Don't try to speak," Joan said. "You are not well."

He blazed at her with savage fury. With one last, explosive effort, he spat out a single word: *"M . . . m . . . m . . . Mulier!"*

*Woman!*

His head turned convulsively to the side and froze there, his eyes set in their baleful glare.

Joan bent over him, seeking any sign of breath from the stretched lips, any pulse from the wasted neck. After a moment, she closed the staring eyes. "He is dead."

Brother Samuel and the others crossed themselves.

"I thought I heard him speak before he died," Brother Samuel said. "What did he say?"

"He . . . he called upon Mary, mother of Christ."

Brother Samuel nodded sagely. "A holy man." To the others he said, "Carry him to the church. We will prepare his body with all due ceremony."

*"Terra es, terram ibis,"* Abbot Raban intoned. With the rest of the brethren, Joan stooped to scoop up a handful of earth, then tossed it into the grave, watching the dark, wet lumps smear unevenly across the smooth wood of her father's coffin.

He had always hated her. Even when she was little, before the lines of battle between them had been drawn, she had never elicited anything more from him than a sour, grudging tolerance. To him, she had always been only a stupid, worthless girl. Still, she was shocked to learn how willingly he would have exposed her, how unhesitatingly he would have consigned her to unspeakable death.

Nevertheless, as the last of the heavy earth was mounded on her father's grave, Joan felt an odd, unexpected melancholy. She could not remember a time when she had not resented her father, feared him, even hated him. Yet she felt a peculiar sense of loss. Matthew, John, Mama—all were gone. Her father had been her last link with home, with the girl she once had been. There was no Joan of Ingelheim anymore; there was only John Anglicus, priest and monk of the Benedictine house of Fulda.

# 17

## *Fontenoy, 841*

The meadow shimmered in the dim, gray light of early dawn, threaded through the middle with the sweetly curving lines of a silver creek. *An unlikely scene for a battle,* Gerold thought grimly.

Emperor Louis had been dead less than a year, but the smoldering rivalry among his three sons had already flared into full-fledged civil war. The eldest, Lothar, had inherited the title of Emperor, but the lands of the Empire were divided between Lothar and his two younger brothers, Charles and Ludwig—an unwise and dangerous arrangement that left all three sons dissatisfied. Even so, war might have been avoided had Lothar been more skilled in diplomacy. Peremptory and despotic by nature, Lothar treated his younger brothers with an arrogance that goaded them to league together in open rebellion against him. So the three royal brothers were finally come here to Fontenoy, determined to settle the differences between them with blood.

After considerable soul-searching, Gerold had cast his lot with Lothar. He knew Lothar's flaws of character well, but as the anointed Emperor, Lothar was the only hope for a united Frankland. The divisions that had racked the country over the past year had exacted a terrible toll: the Norsemen, taking advantage of the distraction the political upheaval afforded, had intensified their raids against the Frankish coast, wreaking great destruction. If Lothar could win a decisive victory here, his brothers would have no choice but to support him. A country ruled by a tyrant was better than no country at all.

The beating of the boards began, mustering the men. Lothar had arranged for an early mass to hearten his troops before the coming battle. Gerold left his solitary meditations and returned to the camp.

Robed in cloth of gold, the Bishop of Auxerre stood high upon a supply cart so all could see him. *"Libera me, Domine, de morte aeterna,"* he chanted in a ringing baritone as dozens of acolytes passed among the men, distributing the consecrated Host. Many of the soldiers were coloni and peasants with no previous experience at arms, men who would normally have been exempt from the imperial *bannum* requiring military service. But these were not normal times. Many had been torn from their homes without so much as an hour's leave to arrange their affairs or bid farewell to their loved ones. These last received the Host distractedly, being in no condition to prepare for death. Their minds were still firmly fixed upon the things of this world from which they had been so roughly severed: their fields, livelihoods, debts, their wives and children rawly left. Bewildered and frightened, they could not yet comprehend the enormity of their predicament, could not believe they were expected to fight and die on this unfamiliar ground for an Emperor whose name had, until a few days ago, been only a distant echo in their lives. *How many of these innocents,* Gerold wondered, *will live to see the sun set on this day?*

"O Lord of Hosts," the bishop prayed at the conclusion of the mass, "Champion against the enemy, Achiever of victories, grant us the shield of Thy aid, and the sword of Thy glory, for the destruction of our enemies. Amen."

"Amen." The air reverberated with the sound of thousands of voices. A moment later, the first narrow sliver of sun crested the horizon, spilling its light over the field, setting the tips of their spears and arrows gleaming like precious gems. A loud cheer went up from the men.

The bishop removed the pallium and handed it to an attending acolyte. Loosing his chasuble, he let it fall to the ground and stood revealed in a soldier's mail: *brunia,* the thick leather jacket soaked in heated wax and sewn with scales of iron, and *bauga,* metal leg guards.

*He means to fight then,* Gerold thought.

Strictly speaking, the bishop's holy office forbade him to spill another man's blood, but in practice this pious ideal was often ignored; bishops and priests fought alongside their kings like any other royal vassals.

One of the acolytes handed the bishop a sword engraved with the sign of the cross. The bishop swung the sword aloft so its golden cross glittered in the sun. "Praise Jesus Christ!" he shouted. "Forward, good Christians, to the kill!"

✦ ✦ ✦

Gerold was in command of the left flank, positioned on the rise of a hill bordering the southern end of the field. On an opposite hill, Lothar's nephew Pippin commanded the right flank, a large, well-armed contingent of Aquitanians. The vanguard, commanded by Lothar himself, was drawn up just beyond the trees fronting the eastern end of the field, directly facing the enemy.

Gerold's bay stallion tossed its head and whinnied impatiently. Leaning over, Gerold ran a hand over its russet neck, gentling it. Best to reserve all that coiled energy for the charge, when it should come. "Soon enough, boy," he murmured steadyingly, "soon enough."

He checked the sky. It was rising six, the first hour of the morning. The sun, still low on the horizon, shone directly into the eyes of the enemy. *Good,* Gerold thought. *It's an advantage we can use.* He watched Lothar for the signal to advance. A quarter of an hour passed, and no signal came. The rival armies stood at opposite ends of the field, eyeing each other warily across the green expanse. Another quarter of an hour passed. Then another. And another.

Gerold broke rank and rode down the hill to the front line of the vanguard, where Lothar sat mounted under a flurry of banners.

"Majesty, why do we delay? The men are impatient to advance."

Lothar looked down his long nose irritably. "I am the Emperor; it is not meet that I should go to my enemies." He had no liking for Gerold, who had entirely too independent a mind for his taste—the result, no doubt, of the years he had spent among the pagans and barbarians in the northern march of the Empire.

"But, Sire, see the sun! Now the advantage is ours, but within the hour it will be gone!"

"Trust in God, Count Gerold," Lothar replied loftily. "I am Heaven's anointed king; He will not fail to grant us victory."

From the finality of Lothar's tone, Gerold understood that there was no point in further argument. He bowed stiffly, wheeled his horse, and rode back to his position.

Perhaps Lothar was right, and God did mean to award them victory. But might He not also expect a little help from men?

It was rising ten; the sun was nearing midpoint. *Damn,* Gerold swore under his breath. *What on earth is Lothar thinking?* They had been waiting now almost four hours. The sun beat down on their iron mail, heating it until the men squirmed with discomfort. Those who had to relieve themselves were required to do so where they stood, for they could not break formation; the rank smell rose and hung about them in the breezeless air.

In these difficult circumstances, Gerold was glad to witness the arrival of a small corps of serving men, porting barrels of wine. The men were hot and thirsty; a strong cup of wine was just what was needed to revive their sagging spirits. A lusty cheer went up as the serving men began to circulate, ladling out cupfuls of thick red Frankish wine. Gerold took one himself and felt much the better for it. He did not, however, allow himself or his men more than this one drink. Where a little wine could bolster a man's courage, too much made him foolhardy and wild, a danger to himself and to his fellows.

Lothar showed no such concern. Benignly, he encouraged the drinking to continue. Shouting and chaffing, boasting of their skill at arms, the men of his vanguard jockeyed roughly for position, tripping over one another to win the honor of standing in the foremost rank, pushing and shoving like wayward boys—which indeed they were; except for a handful of experienced veterans, the greater part were no older than eighteen.

*"They are coming! They are coming!"*

The shout went up throughout the ranks. The opposing army was advancing, slowly as yet, so the unmounted men-at-arms and archers could keep in close proximity to the mounted cavalry which rode before them. The effect was solemn, majestic, more like a religious procession than the onset of a battle.

In Lothar's vanguard, there was a disorderly flurry as men scrambled to retrieve scattered helmets, lances, and shields. They had just managed to mount when the enemy cavalry spurred into a full forward charge, bearing down upon them with terrifying speed, causing the earth to reverberate with a deafening roar like that of a thousand thunderbolts.

The banners in the imperial vanguard dropped and rose, signaling the answering charge. The cavalry leapt forward, the horses' hooves tearing the smooth green turf as they drove ahead with straining necks.

Gerold's bay sprang in response; Gerold reined him in. "Not yet, boy." Gerold and his men must hold back; the left flank was to be last onto the field, after Lothar and Pippin.

Like two great waves, the opposing armies swept toward each other forty thousand strong, the pride of the Frankish nobility riding knee to knee in solid lines a half mile wide and equally deep.

With a wild shout, a group from the imperial vanguard burst out of formation, spurring their horses into a disorderly run, racing against one another for the glory of being the first to engage the enemy before the eyes of their Emperor.

Gerold watched with chagrin. If they kept going as they were, they would reach the brook too soon and be caught laboring through the water while the enemy fought them from the solid ground of the far bank.

Reckless with wine and youth, they rode straight into the creek and collided with the enemy with an ear-splitting crack like two gigantic bones breaking. They fought with fierce courage at great disadvantage, for they had to strike from below at the enemy on the bank, their aim thrown off as their horses stumbled for footing on the slippery rocks. Those who were cut down fell into the water, where, mired in mud and struggling to rise against the weight of their mail, they were trampled by their own panicked, plunging horses.

The men in the rows behind saw what lay ahead but were coming on at such speed they could not check themselves without being violently overridden by those following. They, too, were forced to plunge down the muddied slope into the water, now churning alternately white and red with blood, driving the survivors of the first charge forward willy-nilly onto the spears of the enemy.

Only the rear of the cavalry, which now included Lothar, was able to check in time; they wheeled their horses and rode back across the field at a wild, undisciplined gallop that brought them crashing straight into the ranks of unmounted men-at-arms marching up behind. These were thrown into frenzied disarray as they cast aside their weapons and hurled themselves sideways to avoid the headlong rush.

It was a rout. The only hope now lay with the flanks, led by Pippin and Gerold. Positioned as they were, they could sweep down onto the field beyond the brook and strike directly at King Ludwig in the center. Looking to the opposite slope, Gerold saw that Pippin and his Aquitanians were turned, fighting with their backs to the field. King Charles must have circled round and come at them from behind.

No help to be had there.

Gerold looked back toward the field. The greater part of Ludwig's men had crossed the brook in pursuit of the retreating Lothar, and thus unwittingly thinned their ranks, leaving the king momentarily exposed. It was a chance in a thousand, but a desperate chance was better than none.

Gerold stood in his stirrups, raising his lance. "Forward!" he shouted, "in the Emperor's name!"

"The Emperor!" The cry went up like a great baying of hounds and was left shuddering in the air behind them as they streamed headlong down the slope, a great flying wedge aimed directly toward the spot where Ludwig's standard floated scarlet and blue in the summer sunlight.

The small band of men who had remained with the king scrambled to close ranks before him. Gerold and his men bore down upon them, shearing a path through their ranks.

Gerold took his first man with the lance, running him cleanly through the chest, the shaft of the lance splintering from the force of the blow. The man somersaulted out of the saddle, taking the shattered lance with him. Armed only with his sword, Gerold hurled himself forward with savage determination, striking left and right in great, powerful sweeps, hewing his way doggedly through the press toward the fluttering standard. His men drove in to the sides and behind, widening his path.

Yard by yard, inch by inch, Ludwig's guard gave way before the onslaught. Then, abruptly, the way ahead stood clear. Directly before Gerold rose the royal standard, a red griffin emblazoned on a field of blue. Before it, mounted on a white charger, was King Ludwig himself.

"Yield," Gerold shouted at full pitch to carry over the din. "Yield and you shall live!"

For answer, Ludwig brought his sword crashing down against Gerold's. Grimly, they fought man to man, an equal match of strength and skill, until a nearby horse pitched violently sidelong, felled by an arrow, causing Gerold's bay to rear and flinch away violently. Ludwig pressed this momentary advantage with a well-timed blow at Gerold's neck. Gerold ducked and thrust to the inside beneath the king's raised sword arm, driving his own blade in between the ribs.

Ludwig coughed, a froth of blood rising at his mouth; slowly his body twisted and slipped sideways from the saddle, thumping to the trampled ground.

"The king is dead!" Gerold's men shouted exultantly. "Ludwig is slain!" The cry was flung back echoing through the ranks.

Ludwig's body hung from the saddle, one foot caught in the trappings. His horse reared, pawing the air and dragging the king's body across the torn earth. The conical helmet with its protective nose plate loosened and dislodged, revealing a flat, broad-nosed, completely unfamiliar face.

Gerold swore. It was a coward's trick, unworthy of a king. This was not Ludwig but his counterfeit, decked out like the king to deceive them.

There was no time to lament, for they were immediately surrounded by Ludwig's troops. Guarding one another's flanks, Gerold and his men strove to extricate themselves from the enemy's noose, fighting with fierce determination toward the outer perimeter of the circle.

A brief flash of green and a breath of fresh, sweet-scented air sent Gerold's heart soaring. Another few yards and they would be free, with open field and a clear run before them.

A man flung himself in Gerold's path, planting himself as solidly as a tree. Quickly Gerold took his measure—a big man, fleshy, large stomached, powerful in the arms, wielding a mace, a weapon of strength, not skill. Gerold feinted with his sword to the left; when the man turned to answer it, Gerold drew back quickly to deliver a biting cut on the other arm. The man swore and quickly switched the mace to his left hand.

From behind came a humming sound like a beating of birds' wings. Gerold felt a sudden, numbing pain in his back as an arrow drove through his right shoulder. Helplessly he watched his sword slip from his suddenly nerveless fingers.

The big man raised the heavy mace and swung. Even as Gerold moved to evade it, he knew that he was too late.

Something seemed to explode inside his head as the crushing blow landed, spinning him into obliterating darkness.

The stars shone down in imperturbable beauty upon the darkened field, strewn with the bodies of the fallen. Twenty thousand men who had wakened that morning lay dead or dying in that dark night—nobles, vassals, farmers, craftsmen, fathers, sons, brothers—the past greatness of an empire, and the blighted hope of its future.

Gerold stirred and opened his eyes. For a moment he lay looking up at the stars, unable to remember where he was or what had happened. A strong odor rose to his nostrils, unpleasant and sickeningly familiar.

Blood.

Gerold sat up. The sudden movement caused an explosion of pain inside his head, and pain brought back memory. He touched his right shoulder; the arrow that had struck him was still lodged there, cut clean through the flesh just under his arm from back to front. It must come out, or the wound would fester. Clamping his arm against his side, he snapped off the iron tip, then reached back his left hand and, with one swift motion, drew out the feathered shaft.

He gasped and swore against the white-hot pain, fighting to remain conscious. After a while the pain began to ease and he was able to take account of his surroundings. All around him the ground was strewn with flung swords, broken shields, severed limbs, tattered standards, stiffening corpses—the ghastly debris of battle.

From the hill where Charles and Ludwig were encamped, the sounds of a victory celebration spilled down, bibulous jests and raucous laughter that floated eerily over the deep silence below. The light of the victors' torches shone down flickeringly, illuminating the field with a ghostly pallor. From the Emperor's camp on the opposite hill, not a single sound came, nor fire burned; the hill was silent, dark and still.

Lothar was defeated. His troops, what remained of them, had scattered into the surrounding woods, seeking what cover they could find from the pursuing enemy.

Gerold rose, fighting down a wave of nausea. A few feet away he found his bay stallion, horribly wounded, his hind legs twitching. He had been speared from beneath; his innards spilled from the gaping wound in his belly. As Gerold moved toward him, a shape, small and furtive, started up defensively: a mangy, starveling dog, come to feast on the night's rich banquet. Gerold waved his arms threateningly, and the dog skulked away, sidelong, resentful. Gerold knelt beside the bay, stroking his neck, murmuring to him; in response to the familiar touch, the anguished twitching slowed, but the eyes stared out in an agony of pain. Gerold took his knife from his belt. Pressing hard to be sure to sever the vein, he drew it across the bay's neck. Then he held him, speaking soothingly into his ear, until at last the great legs ceased flailing and the smoothly muscled flank relaxed beneath his hands.

A murmur of voices sounded behind Gerold.

"Look! Here's a helmet should fetch a solidus at least!"

"Leave it," said another voice, lower and more authoritative. "It's worthless, cleaved clean through at the back, can't you see? This way, lads, there's better pickings over here!"

Cutpurses. The aftermath of war drew such lawless types from the roads and byways that were their customary haunts, for the dead were easier prey than the quick. They moved furtively in the dark, stripping their victims of clothes, armor, weapons, and rings—whatever might be of value.

A voice sounded close by: "This one's alive!"

There was the sound of a blow, and a cry that broke off abruptly.

"If there are others," another voice said, "deal them the same. We want no witnesses to put a noose around our necks."

In a moment they would be upon him. Gerold stood, swaying. Then, keeping well to the shadows, he slipped into the darkness of the woods beyond.

# 18

The brethren of Fulda remained largely unaffected by the feud among the royal Frankish brothers. Like a stone cast into a pond, the Battle of Fontenoy created great waves in the centers of power, but here, in the eastern march of the Empire, it caused scarcely a ripple. True, some of the larger landholders in the region had gone to serve in King Ludwig's army; according to law any freeman in possession of more than four manses had to answer the call to military service. But Ludwig's quick and decisive victory meant that all save two of these local men returned safe and sound to their homes.

The days passed as before, woven together indistinguishably in the unchanging fabric of monastic life. A string of successful harvests had resulted in a time of unprecedented plenty. The abbey granaries were full to bursting; even the lean, stringy Austrasian pigs grew fat from good feeding.

Then, abruptly, disaster struck. Weeks of unrelenting rain ruined the spring sowing. The earth was too wet to dig the small furrows necessary for planting, and the seeds moldered in the ground. Most disastrous of all, the pervasive damp penetrated the granaries, rotting the stored grain where it lay.

The famine of the following winter was the worst in living memory. To the horror of the Church, some even turned to cannibalism. The roads became more dangerous, as travelers were murdered not only for the goods they carried but for the sustenance their dead bodies could provide. After a public hanging in Lorsch, the starving crowd mobbed the platform and tore down the gallows, fighting over the still-warm flesh.

Weakened by starvation, people were easy prey for disease. Thousands died of the plague. The symptoms were always the same: headache, chills, and disorientation, followed by high fever and a violent cough. There was little anyone could do but strip the sufferers and pack them with cool cloths to keep their temperature down. If they survived the fever, they stood a chance of recovery. But very few survived the fever.

Nor did the sanctity of the monastic walls offer any protection against the plague. The first to be taken ill was Brother Samuel, the hospitaler, whose position brought him into frequent contact with the outside world. Within two days, he was dead. Abbot Raban ascribed this misfortune to Samuel's worldliness and immoderate fondness for jest; afflictions of the flesh, he affirmed, were only outward manifestations of moral and spiritual decay. Then Brother Aldoardus, acknowledged by all to be the embodiment of monkish piety and virtue, was struck down, followed in close order by Brother Hildwin, the sacristan, and several others.

To the surprise of the brethren, Abbot Raban announced that he was making a pilgrimage to the shrine of St. Martin to pray for the holy martyr's intervention against the plague.

"Prior Joseph will act for me in all things while I am gone," Raban said. "Give him due obedience, for his word is even as my own."

The abruptness of Raban's announcement, and his precipitate departure, occasioned a good deal of talk. Some of the brethren praised the abbot for undertaking so arduous a journey on behalf of all. Others muttered darkly that the abbot had absented himself in order to escape the local danger.

Joan had no time to debate such matters. She was kept busy from dawn till dusk saying Mass, hearing confession, and administering the increasingly frequent rites of *unctio extrema*.

One morning she noticed that Brother Benjamin was absent from his choir stall at vigils. Devout soul that he was, he never missed the daily offices. As soon as the service ended, Joan hurried to the infirmary. Entering the long, rectangular room, she breathed the pungent aroma of goose grease and mustard, known specifics for diseases of the lungs. The room was crowded to bursting; beds and pallets were placed side by side, and every one was occupied. Between the beds, the brothers whose opus manuum was in the infirmary circulated, straightening blankets, offering sips of water, praying quietly beside those too far gone to accept any other comfort.

Brother Benjamin was propped up in bed, explaining to Brother Deodatus, one of the junior brothers, the best way to apply a mustard plaster. Listening to him, Joan recalled the long-ago day when he had first taught her that same skill.

She smiled fondly at the memory. Surely, she thought, if Benjamin was still capable of directing things in the infirmary, he could not be critically ill.

A sudden fit of coughing interrupted Brother Benjamin's rapid flow of words. Joan hurried to his bed. Dipping a cloth in the bowl of rose-scented water that stood beside the bed, she held it gently to Benjamin's forehead. His skin felt incredibly hot. *Benedicite! How has he remained lucid with a fever so high?*

At last he stopped coughing and lay with eyes closed, breathing harshly. His graying hair ringed his head like a faded halo. His hands, those wide, squat plowman's hands possessed of such unexpected gentleness and skill, lay on the coverlet as open and helpless as a babe's. Joan's heart twisted at the sight.

Brother Benjamin opened his eyes, saw Joan, and smiled.

"You have come," he said raspingly. "Good. As you see, I am in need of your services."

"A bit of yarrow and some powdered willow-bark will have you right again soon enough," Joan said, more cheerfully than she felt.

Benjamin shook his head. "It's as priest, not as physician, that I need you now. You must help me into the next world, little brother, for I am done with this one."

Joan took his hand. "I'll not give you up without a fight."

"You've learned everything I had to teach you. Now you must learn acceptance."

"I won't accept losing you," she replied fiercely.

For the next two days, Joan battled determinedly for Benjamin's life. She used every skill he had ever taught her, tried every medicine she could think of. The fever continued to rage. Benjamin's large, well-fleshed body dwindled like the empty husk of a cocoon after the moth has flown. Beneath his feverish flush there appeared an ominous undertone of gray.

"Shrive me," he pleaded. "I wish to be in full possession of my senses when I receive the Sacrament."

She could deny him no longer.

*"Quid me advocasti?"* she began in the ceremonial cadences of the liturgy. "What do you ask of me?"

*"Ut mihi unctionem trados,"* he responded. "Give me unction."

Dipping her thumb in a mixture of ashes and water, Joan drew the sign of the cross on Brother Benjamin's chest, then laid a piece of sackcloth, symbol of penance, over the smudged design.

Benjamin was shaken with another violent fit of coughing. When it ended, Joan saw that he had brought up blood. Suddenly frightened, she hurried through the recitation of the seven penitential psalms and the ritual anointing of the eyes, ears, nose, mouth, hands, and feet. It seemed to take a very long time. Toward the end, Benjamin lay with his eyes closed, completely unmoving. Joan could not tell if he was still conscious.

At last the moment came to administer the viaticum. Joan held out the Sacred Host, but Benjamin did not respond. *It is too late,* Joan thought. *I have failed him.*

She touched the Host to Benjamin's lips; he opened his eyes and took it into his mouth. Joan made the sign of blessing over him. Her voice shook as she started the sacramental prayer: *"Corpus et Sanguis Domini nostri Jesu Christi in vitam aeternam te perducat . . ."*

He died at dawn, as the sweet canticles of lauds filtered through the morning air. Joan was plunged into a profound grief. Since the moment twelve years ago when Benjamin had taken her under his wing, he had been her friend and mentor. Even when her duties as priest took her from the infirmary, he had continued to help her, encourage her, support her. He had been a true father to her.

Unable to find consolation in prayer, Joan threw herself into work. Daily mass was more crowded than ever, as the specter of death brought the faithful flocking to the church in unprecedented numbers.

One day while Joan was tipping the communal chalice for one of the communicants, an elderly man, she observed his oozing eyes and the dusky, feverish flush of his cheeks. She moved on to the next in line, a slim young mother with a small, sweet-faced girl still in arms. The woman held the child up to take the Sacrament; the tiny rosebud lips opened to drink from the same spot where the old man's mouth had just been.

Joan pulled the chalice away. Taking a piece of the bread, she wet it in the wine and gave it to the child instead. Startled, the girl looked toward her mother, who nodded encouragement; it was a departure from custom, but the abbey priest surely knew what he was doing. Joan continued down the line, wetting the bread in the wine, until the entire congregation had received the Sacrament.

Immediately after mass, Prior Joseph summoned her. Joan was glad it was Joseph and not Raban she would have to answer to. Joseph was not a man to cling undeviatingly to tradition, not if there was good and sufficient argument for change.

"You made an alteration in the Mass today," Joseph said.

"Yes, Father."

"Why?" The question was not challenging, merely curious.

Joan explained.

"The sick old man and the healthy infant," Joseph repeated thoughtfully. "A repulsive incongruity, I agree."

"More than an incongruity," Joan responded. "I believe it may be one way the disease is transmitted."

Joseph was confounded. "How can that be? Surely the noxious spirits are everywhere."

"Perhaps it's not noxious spirits that are causing the sickness—not alone, anyway. It may be passed along by physical contact with its victims, or with objects that they touch."

It was a new idea, but not a radical one. That some diseases were contagious was well known; this was, after all, why lepers were strictly segregated from society. It was also beyond dispute that sickness often passed through entire households, carrying off members of a family within days, even hours. But the cause for this phenomenon was unclear.

"Transmitted by physical contact? In what manner?"

"I don't know," Joan admitted. "But today, when I saw the sick man, and the open sores about his mouth, I felt—" She broke off, frustrated. "I cannot explain, Father, at least not yet. But until I know more, I would like to leave off passing the communal cup and dip the bread in the wine instead."

"You would undertake this change on the basis of a mere . . . intuition?" Joseph asked.

"If I am wrong, no harm will derive from my error, for the faithful will still have partaken of both the Body and the Blood," Joan argued. "But if my . . . intuition proves correct, then we will have saved lives."

Joseph considered a moment. An alteration in the Mass was not to be undertaken lightly. On the other hand, John Anglicus was a learned brother, renowned for his skill at healing. Joseph had not forgotten his cure of the leper woman. Then, as now, there had been little to go on other than

John Anglicus's "intuition." Such intuitions, Joseph thought, were not to be scorned, for they were God-given.

"You may proceed for now," he said. "When Abbot Raban returns, he will of course render his own judgment upon the matter."

"Thank you, Father." Joan made her obeisance and left quickly, before Prior Joseph could change his mind.

*Intinctio,* they called the dipping of the Host, and apart from some of the elder brothers, who were set in their ways, the practice enjoyed widespread support among the brethren, for it was as satisfying to the aesthetics of the Mass as it was to the requirements of cleanliness and hygiene. A monk of Corbie, stopping by on his way home, was so impressed he carried the idea back to his own abbey, which adopted it as well.

Among the faithful, the frequency of new occurrences of the plague noticeably slowed, though it did not stop. Joan began to keep careful record of new cases of the disease, studying them in order to detect the cause of infection.

Her efforts were cut short by the return of Abbot Raban. Soon after his arrival, he summoned Joan to his quarters and confronted her with stern disapproval.

"The Canon of the Mass is sacred. How dare you tamper with it?"

"Father Abbot, the change is in form only, not in substance. And I believe it is saving lives."

Joan started to explain what she had observed, but Raban cut her off. "Such observations are useless, for they come not from faith but from the physical senses, which are not to be trusted. They are the Devil's tools, with which he lures men away from God and into the conceits of the intellect."

"If God did not wish us to observe the material world," Joan rejoined, "why then did He give us eyes to see, ears to hear, a nose to smell? Surely it is not sin to make use of the gifts He Himself has given us."

"Remember the words of St. Augustine: 'Faith is to believe what you do not see.' "

Joan responded without missing a beat, "Augustine also says that we could not believe at all if we did not have rational minds. He would not have us despise what sense and reason tell us must be so."

Raban scowled. His mind was of a rigidly conventional and unimaginative cast, so he disliked the give-and-take of reasoned argument, preferring the safer ground of authority.

"Receive thy father's counsel and obey it," he quoted sententiously from the rule. "Return unto God by the difficult path of obedience, for thou hast forsaken Him by following thine own will."

"But, Father—"

"No more, I say!" Raban exploded angrily. His face was livid. "John Anglicus, as of this moment, you are relieved of your duties as priest. You will study humility by returning to the infirmary, where you will assist Brother Odilo, serving him with due and proper obedience."

Joan started to protest, then thought better of it. Raban had been pushed to his limit; any further argument could place her in gravest jeopardy.

With an effort of will, she bowed her head. "As you command, Father Abbot."

Reflecting later upon what had happened, Joan saw that Raban was right; she had been prideful and disobedient. But of what use was obedience, if others must suffer by it? Intinction *was* saving lives; she was sure of that. But how could she convince the abbot? He would not tolerate further argument from her. But he might be persuaded by the weight of established authority. So now, in addition to the Opus Dei and her duties in the infirmary, Joan added hours of study in the library, searching the texts of Hippocrates, Oribasius, and Alexander of Tralles for anything that might support her theory. She worked constantly, sleeping only two or three hours a night, driving herself to exhaustion.

One day, poring over a section of Oribasius, she found what she needed. She was copying the crucial passage out in translation when she began having difficulty scribing; her head ached, and she could not hold the pen steady. She shrugged this off as the natural consequence of too little sleep and went on working. Then her quill inexplicably slipped from her grasp and rolled onto the page, scattering blobs of ink across the clean vellum, obscuring the words. *Curse the luck,* she thought. *I will have to scrape it clean and start over.* She tried to pick up the quill, but her fingers trembled so violently she could not get a grip on it.

She stood, holding on to the edge of the desk as dizziness swept over her. Stumbling to the door, she thrust herself outside just as the retching hit hard, doubling her up and thrusting her onto all fours, where she heaved up the contents of her stomach.

Somehow she managed to stagger to the infirmary. Brother Odilo made her lie down on an empty bed and put his hand to her forehead. It was cold as ice.

Joan blinked with surprise. "Have you come from the washing trough?"

Brother Odilo shook his head. "My hands are not cold, Brother John. You're burning with fever. I fear the plague has you in its grip."

*The plague!* Joan thought woozily. *No, that can't be right. I'm tired, that's all. If I can just rest for a while . . .*

Brother Odilo laid a cool strip of linen, steeped in rosewater, on her forehead. "Now lie quiet, while I soak some fresh linen. I won't be a minute."

His voice seemed to come from a long distance away. Joan closed her eyes. The cloth felt cool against her skin. It felt good to lie still with the sweet aroma around her, sinking peacefully into a welcome darkness.

Suddenly her eyes flew wide. They were going to cover her in a sheath of wet linen to bring the fever down. To do that they would have to strip her bare.

She had to stop them. Then she realized that no matter how strenuously she resisted—and in her present condition she would not be able to put up much of a fight—her protests would be dismissed as mere feverish ravings.

She sat up, swinging her feet off the bed. Immediately the pain in her head returned, pounding and insistent. She started for the door. The room whirled sickeningly, but she forced herself to keep going and made it outside. Then she headed quickly toward the foregate. As she drew near the gate, she took a deep breath, willing herself steady as she walked past Hatto, the porter. He looked at her curiously but made no move to stop her. Once outside, she headed straight for the river.

*Benedicite.* The abbey's little boat was there, moored with a single rope to an overhanging branch. She untied the rope and climbed in, leaning against the grassy bank to push off. As the boat swung away from the bank, she collapsed.

For a long moment the boat hung motionless in the water. Then the current took it, spinning it around before propelling it down the swiftly moving stream.

✦ ✦ ✦

The sky revolved slowly, twisting the high, white clouds into exotic patterns. A dark red sun touched the horizon, its rays burning hotter than fire, scorching Joan's face, searing her eyes. She watched fascinated as its outer edges shimmered and dissolved, forming human shape.

Her father's face floated before her, a ghastly, grinning death's-head stripped of flesh beneath the dark line of its brows. The lipless mouth parted. *"Mulier!"* it cried, but it was not her father's voice, it was her mother's. The mouth opened wider, and Joan saw that it was not a mouth at all but a hideous yawning gate opening into a great darkness. At the end of the darkness, fires burned, shooting up great blue-red pillars of flame. There were people in the flames, their bodies writhing in grotesque pantomimes of pain. One of them looked toward Joan. With a shock, Joan recognized the woman's clear blue eyes and white-gold Saxon hair. Her mother called to her, holding out her arms. Joan started toward her; suddenly the ground beneath dropped away and she was falling, falling toward the hideous mouth-gate. "Mamaaaaaaa!" she screamed as she fell into the flames . . .

She was in a snow-covered field. Villaris gleamed in the distance as the sun melted the snow on its roof, setting the water droplets sparkling like thousands of tiny gems. She heard the drumming of hooves and turned to see Gerold riding toward her on Pistis. She ran to him across the field; he drew up beside her, reached down, and hoisted her up before him. She leaned back, reveling in the tender strength of his encircling arms. She was safe. Nothing could harm her now, for Gerold would not permit it. Together they rode toward the gleaming towers of Villaris, the strides of the horse lengthening beneath them, rocking them gently, rocking, rocking . . .

The motion had ceased. Joan opened her eyes. Above the level edge of the boat, the treetops were silhouetted black and unmoving against the twilit sky. The boat had come to a stop.

A murmur of voices came from somewhere above her, but Joan could not make out the words. Hands reached down, took hold of her, lifted her from the boat. Dimly she remembered: she must not let them take her, not while she was still sick, she must not let them carry her back to Fulda. She struck out ferociously with her arms and legs, striking flesh. Distantly she heard cursing. There was a short, sharp pain against her jaw, and then nothing else.

◆ ◆ ◆

Joan rose slowly out of a pool of blackness. Her head was pounding, her throat so dry it felt as if it had been scraped raw. She ran a dry tongue over parched lips, drawing tiny drops of blood from the cracked flesh. There was a dull ache in her jaw. She winced as her fingers explored a sensitive bump on her chin. *Where did I get that?* she wondered.

Then, more urgently, *Where am I?*

She was lying on a feather mattress in a room she did not recognize. Judging by the number and quality of the furnishings, the owner of the dwelling was prosperous: in addition to the enormous bed in which she was lying, there were benches upholstered with soft cloth, a high-backed chair covered with cushions, a long trencher table, a writing desk, and several trunks and chests, very finely carved. A hearth fire glowed nearby, and a pair of fresh loaves had been newly placed on the embers, their warm aromas just beginning to rise.

A few feet away, a plump young woman stood with her back toward Joan, kneading a mass of dough. She finished, wiping the flour from her tunic, and her eyes fell on Joan. She moved briskly to the door and called out, "Husband! Come quickly. Our guest has awakened!"

A ruddy-faced young man, long and gangly as a crane, came hurrying in. "How is she?" he asked.

*She?* Joan started as she caught the word. She looked down and saw that her monk's habit was gone; in its place she was clothed in a woman's tunic of soft blue linen.

*They know.*

She struggled to lift herself from the bed, but her limbs were heavy and weak as water.

"You mustn't exert yourself." The young man touched her shoulder gently, easing her back into the bed. He had a pleasant, honest face, his eyes round and blue as cornflowers.

*Who is he?* Joan wondered. *Will he tell Abbot Raban and the others about me—or has he already? Am I truly his "guest," or am I a prisoner?*

"Th . . . thirsty," she croaked.

The young man dipped a cup into a wooden bucket beside the bed and withdrew it brimming with water. He held it against Joan's lips and tipped it carefully, starting a slow stream of droplets into her mouth.

Joan grabbed the cup, angling it so the water poured faster. The cool liquid was sweeter than anything she had ever tasted.

The young man cautioned, "Best not take too much too soon. It's been over a week since we've been able to get anything into you beyond a few spoonfuls."

Over a week! Had she been here so long? She could not remember anything after climbing into the little fishing rig. "Wh . . . where am I?" she stammered hoarsely.

"You're in the demesne of Lord Riculf, fifty miles downstream from Fulda. We found your boat in a tangle of branches along the river's edge. You were half out of your mind with fever. Sick as you were, you fought hard to keep us from taking you."

Joan fingered the tender bump on her jaw.

The young man grinned. "Sorry. There was no reasoning with you in the condition we found you in. But take comfort, for you gave almost as good as you took." He pulled up his sleeve, revealing a large, ugly-looking bruise on his right shoulder.

"You saved my life," Joan said. "Thank you."

"You're welcome. It was only fair return for all you've done for me and mine."

"Do I . . . know you?" she asked, surprised.

The young man smiled. "I suppose I *have* changed a good deal since last we saw each other. I was only twelve then, rising thirteen. Let's see . . ." He began to figure on his hands, using Bede's classical method of computation. "That was some six years ago. Six years times three hundred sixty-five days . . . why, that's . . . two thousand one hundred and ninety days!"

Joan's eyes widened with recognition. "Arn!" she cried, and was immediately swept up into his enthusiastic embrace.

They did not speak further that day, for Joan was still very weak, and Arn would not allow her to weary herself. After she had taken a few spoonfuls of broth, she immediately fell asleep.

She awoke the next day feeling stronger, and, most encouraging of all, ravenously hungry. Breaking fast with Arn over a plate of bread and cheese, she listened intently as he told her all that had transpired since they last saw each other.

"As you foresaw, Father Abbot was so satisfied with our cheese that he accepted us as *prebendarii,* promising us fair living in exchange for a hundred pounds of cheese a year. But this much you must know."

Joan nodded. The extraordinary blue-veined cheese of repellent appearance and exquisite taste had become a staple at the refectory table. Guests of the abbey, both lay and monastic, were so taken with its quality that there was increasing demand for it throughout the region.

"How fares your mother?" Joan asked.

"Very well. She married again, a good man, a farmer with a herd of his own, whose milk they put toward making more cheese. Their trade grows daily, and they are happy and prosperous."

"No less than you." With a sweep of her arm, Joan indicated the large, well-kept home.

"My good fortune I owe to you," Arn said. "For at the abbey school I learned to read and to figure with numbers—skills that came in handy as our trade grew and it became necessary to keep accurate accounts. Learning of my abilities, Lord Riculf took me for his steward. I manage his estate here and guard against poachers of game or fish—that's how I came upon your boat."

Joan shook her head wonderingly, picturing Arn and his mother as they had been six years ago, living in their squalid hut as wretched as coloni—doomed, so it seemed, to a life of grinding poverty and semistarvation. Yet Madalgis was now remarried, a prosperous tradeswoman, and her son steward to a powerful lord! *Vitam regit fortuna,* Joan thought. *Truly, chance governs human life—my own as much as any.*

"Here," Arn said proudly, "is my wife, Bona, and our girl, Arnalda." Bona, a pretty young woman with laughing eyes and a quick smile, was even younger than her husband—seventeen winters at most. She was already a mother, and her swelling stomach revealed that she was once again with child. Arnalda was a cherub, all round blue eyes and curly blond hair, pink cheeked and adorable. She smiled dazzlingly at Joan, revealing a set of winning dimples.

"A fine family," Joan said.

Arn beamed and motioned to the woman and child. "Come and greet . . ." He hesitated. "How shall I name you? 'Brother John' seems strange, knowing . . . what we know."

"Joan." The word was both alien and familiar to her ears. "Call me Joan, for that is my true name."

"Joan," Arn repeated, pleased to be trusted with this confidence. "Tell us, then, if you may, how it is that you came to live among the Benedictines of Fulda, for such a thing scarcely seems possible. How ever did you manage it? What brought you to do it? Did anyone share your secret? Did no one suspect?"

Joan laughed. "Time, I see, has not dulled your curiosity."

There was no point in deception. Joan told Arn everything, from her unorthodox education at the schola in Dorstadt to her years at Fulda and her accession to the priesthood.

"So the brothers still don't know about you," Arn said thoughtfully when she finished. "We thought perhaps you had been discovered and forced to flee. . . . Do you mean to return, then? You can, you know. I would die stretched upon the rack before anyone pried your secret out of me!"

Joan smiled. Despite Arn's manly appearance, there remained in him more than a bit of the little boy she had known.

She said, "Fortunately, there is no need for such a sacrifice. I got away in time; the brethren have no reason to suspect me. But . . . I am not sure that I *will* go back."

"What will you do, then?"

"A good question," Joan said. "A very good question indeed. As yet I don't know the answer."

Arn and Bona fussed over her like a pair of overanxious mother hens, refusing to let her rise from bed for several more days. "You are not yet strong enough," they insisted. Joan had little alternative but to resign herself to their solicitude. She passed the long hours by teaching little Arnalda her letters and numbers. Young as the child was, she had her father's aptitude for learning, and she responded eagerly, delighted by the attention of so diverting a companion.

When, at the end of the day, Arnalda was trundled off to sleep, Joan lay restlessly contemplating her future. Should she return to Fulda? She had been at the abbey almost twelve years, had grown up within its walls; it was difficult to imagine being anywhere else. But facts had to be faced: she was twenty-seven years old, already past the prime of life. The brethren of Fulda, worn down by the harsh climate, spartan diet, and unheated rooms of the monastery, seldom lived past forty; Brother Deodatus, the community elder, was fifty-four. How long could she hold out against the advances of age—how long before she would again be struck down by illness, forced anew to run the risk of disclosure and death?

Then, too, there was Abbot Raban to consider. His mind was firmly set against her, and he was not a man to turn from such a position. If she went back, what further hardships and punishments might she have to face?

Her spirit cried out for change. There was not a book in Fulda's library she had not read, not a crack in the ceiling of the dormitory she did not know by heart. It had been years since she had awakened in the morning with the happy expectation that something new and interesting might happen. She yearned to explore a wider world.

Where could she go? Back to Ingelheim? Now Mama was dead, there was nothing she cared about there. Dorstadt? What did she hope to find there—Gerold, still waiting, harboring his love for her after all these years? What folly. He was married again, more than likely, and would not be happy at Joan's sudden reappearance. Besides, she had long ago chosen a different life—a life in which the love of a man could play no part.

No, Gerold and Fulda both belonged to her past. She had to look determinedly toward the future—whatever that might be.

"Bona and I have decided," Arn said. "You must stay with us. It would be good to have another woman about the house to keep Bona company and help with the cooking and needlework—especially now, with the baby coming."

His condescension was irksome, but the offer was kindly meant, so Joan answered mildly, "That would prove a bad bargain, I fear. I was always a sorry seamstress, all thumbs with a needle and no use at all in the kitchen."

"Bona would be only too glad to teach y—"

"The truth is," she interrupted, "I have lived so long as a man I could not be a proper woman again—if, indeed, I ever was one! No, Arn"—she waved off his protest—"a man's life suits me. I like its benefits too well to be content without them."

Arn pondered this awhile. "Keep your disguise, then. It doesn't matter. You can help in the garden . . . or teach little Arnalda! You've charmed her already with your lessons and games, as once you did me."

It was a generous offer. She could not ask for greater ease or security than she would find in the bosom of this happy, prosperous family. But their world, snug and sheltered, was too small to contain her reawakened spirit of adventure. She would not trade one set of walls for another.

"Bless you, Arn, for a kind heart. But I've other plans."

"What are they?"

"I'm taking the pilgrim road."

"To Tours and the tomb of St. Martin?"

"No," Joan said, "to Rome."

"Rome!" Arn was stunned. "Are you mad?"

"Now the war is over, others will be making the same pilgrimage."

Arn shook his head. "My lord Riculf tells me that Lothar has not given up his crown, despite his defeat at Fontenoy. He has fled back to the imperial palace at Aachen and is looking for more men to fill the empty ranks of his army. My lord says he has even made overture to the Saxons, offering to let them return to worshiping their pagan gods if they will fight for him!"

*How Mama would have laughed,* Joan thought, *at such an unexpected turn of events: a Christian king offering to restore the Old Gods.* She could imagine what her mother would have said: the gentle martyr-God of the Christians might serve for ordinary purposes, but to win battles, one must call upon Thor and Odin, and the other fierce warrior-gods of her people.

"You cannot go, with things unsettled as they are," Arn said. "It's too dangerous."

He had a point. The conflict among the royal brothers had resulted in a complete collapse of civil order. The unguarded roads had become easy targets for roving bands of murderous brigands and outlaws.

"I'll be safe enough," Joan said. "Who'd want anything from a pilgrim priest, with nothing of value but the clothes upon his back?"

"Some of these devils would kill for the cloth, never mind the garment! I forbid you to go alone!" He spoke with an authority he would never have assumed had he still believed her to be a man.

She said sharply, "I am my own master, Arn. I go where I will."

Recognizing his mistake, Arn immediately retreated. "At least wait three months," he suggested. "The spice merchants come through then, peddling their goods. They travel well guarded, for they take no risks with their precious merchandise. They can provide you with safe escort all the way to Langres."

"Langres! Surely that is not the most direct route?"

"No," Arn agreed. "But it is the surest. In Langres there's a hostel for pilgrims headed south; you'll have no trouble finding a group of fellow travelers to keep you safe company."

Joan considered this. "You may be right."

"My lord Riculf made the same pilgrimage himself some years ago. He kept a map of the route he followed; I have it here." He opened a locked chest, took out a piece of parchment, and carefully unfolded it. It was darkened and frayed with age, but the ink had not faded; the bold lines stood out clearly, marking the route to Rome.

"Thank you, Arn," Joan said. "I'll do as you suggest. Three months' delay is not very long. It will give me more time with Arnalda; she's very smart, and coming along so well in her lessons!"

"Then it's settled." Arn began to roll up the parchment.

"I'd like to study the map a little longer, if I may."

"Take all the time you like. I'm off to the barns to oversee the shearing." Arn left smiling, pleased to have been able to persuade her so far.

Joan breathed deeply, filling her lungs with the sweet smells of early spring. Her spirit soared like a falcon loosed from its fetters, delivered suddenly to the miraculous freedom of wind and sky. At this hour, the brethren of Fulda would be gathered in the dark interior of the chapter house, crowded together on the hard stone gradines, listening to Brother Cellarer drone on about the abbey accounts. But she was here, free and unhindered, with the adventure of a lifetime before her.

With a surge of excitement, Joan studied the map. There was a good, wide road from here to Langres. There, the road turned south through Besançon and Orbe, descending along Lake St.-Maurice to Le Valais. At the foot of the Alps, there was a monastic hostelry where pilgrims could rest and provision themselves for the hard trek across the mountains through the Great St. Bernard—the best and most frequently traveled of the Alpine passes. Once over the Alps, the wide, straight line of the Via Francigena led down through Aosta, Pavia, and Bologna into Tuscany, and beyond it to Rome.

*Rome.* The world's greatest minds gathered in that ancient city; its churches held untold treasures, its libraries the accumulated wisdom of centuries. Surely there, amidst the sacred tombs of the apostles, Joan would find what she was seeking. In Rome she would discover her destiny.

She was settling her saddlebag on the mule—Arn had insisted she take one for the journey—when little Arnalda came running out of the cottage, her blond hair still tousled from her night's sleep.

"Where are you going?" the cherubic little face demanded anxiously.

Joan knelt so her face was level with the child's. "To Rome," she replied, "the City of Marvels, where the Pope dwells."

"Do you like the Pope better than me?"

Joan laughed. "I've never met him. And there is no one I like better than you, little quail." She stroked the child's soft hair.

"Then don't go." Arnalda threw her arms around Joan. "I don't want you to go."

Joan hugged her. The small child-body cuddled warmly against her, filling her arms and her heart. *I could have had a little girl like this, if I had chosen a different path. A little girl to hold and to cuddle—and to teach.* She remembered the desolation she had felt when Aesculapius had gone away. He had left her a book, so she could continue to learn. But she, who had fled from the monastery with only the clothes on her back, had nothing to give the child.

Except . . .

Joan reached inside her tunic and pulled out the medallion she had worn ever since the day Matthew had first placed it about her neck. "This is St. Catherine. She was very smart and very strong, just like you." She related the story of St. Catherine.

Arnalda's eyes grew round with wonder. "She was a *girl,* and she did that?"

"Yes. And so may you, if you keep working at your letters." Joan took the medallion from her neck and hung it around Arnalda's. "She is yours now. Look after her for me."

Arnalda clutched the medallion, her little face contorted in a determined effort not to cry.

Joan said good-bye to Arn and Bona, who had come outside to see her off. Bona handed her a parcel of food and an oiled goatskin filled with ale. "There's bread and cheese, and some dried meat—enough to see you through for a fortnight, by which time you will have reached the hostel."

"Thank you," Joan said. "I will never forget your kindness."

Arn said, "Remember, Joan. You are welcome here at any time. This is your home."

Joan embraced him. "Teach the girl," she said. "She is intelligent, and as hungry to learn as you were."

She mounted the mule. The little family stood around her, looking sad. It was her constant fate, it seemed, to leave behind those she loved. This was the price for the strange life she had chosen, but she had gone into it with eyes open, and there was no profit in regret.

Joan kicked the mule into a trot. With a last wave over her shoulder, she turned her face toward the southern road—and Rome.

# 19

### *Rome, 844*

Anastasius put down his quill, stretching his fingers to rid them of cramp. With pride, he studied the page he had just written—the latest entry in his masterpiece, the *Liber pontificalis,* or Book of the Popes, a detailed record of the papacies of his time.

Lovingly Anastasius ran his hand over the clean white vellum that lay ahead. On these blank pages the accomplishments, the triumphs, the glory of his own papacy would one day be recorded.

How proud his father, Arsenius, would be then! Though Anastasius's family had accumulated many titles and honors over the years, the ultimate prize of the papal throne had eluded them. Once it had seemed Arsenius might achieve it, but time and circumstance had conspired against him, and the opportunity had passed.

Now it was up to Anastasius. He must, he *would* vindicate his father's faith in him by becoming Lord Pope and Bishop of Rome.

Not immediately, of course. Anastasius's overarching ambition had not blinded him to the fact that his time had not yet come. He was only thirty-three, and his position as *primicerius,* though one of great power, was too secular a post from which to ascend to the Sacred Chair of St. Peter.

But his situation was soon to change. Pope Gregory lay on his deathbed. Once the formal period of mourning was over, there would be an election for a new Pope—an election whose outcome Arsenius had predetermined with a skillful blend of diplomacy, bribery, and threat. The next Pope would be Sergius, cardinal priest of the Church of St. Martin, weak and corruptible scion of a noble Roman family. Unlike Gregory, Sergius was a man who understood the way of the world; he would know how to express his gratitude to those who had helped him into office.

Soon after Sergius's election, Anastasius would be appointed Bishop of Castellum, a perfect position from which to ascend the papal throne after Sergius, in his turn, was gone.

It was a pretty picture, but for one detail—Gregory still lived. Like an aging vine, roots driven deep to suck sustenance from arid soil, the old man stubbornly clung to life. Prudent and contemplative in his personal life as in his papacy, Gregory was proceeding with infuriating slowness even in this final act of dying.

He had reigned for seventeen years, longer than any Pope since Leo III of blessed memory. A good man, modest, well intentioned, pious, Gregory was well loved by the Roman people. He had been a solicitous patron of the city's teeming population of impoverished pilgrims, providing numerous shelters and houses of refuge, seeing that alms were distributed with a generous hand on all feast days and processions.

Anastasius regarded Gregory with a complicated mix of emotion, equal parts wonder and contempt: wonder at the genuineness of the man's piety and faith, contempt for his simplicity and slow-wittedness, which left him constantly open to deceit and manipulation. Anastasius himself had often taken advantage of the Pope's ingenuousness, never more successfully than on the Field of Lies, when he had arranged for the betrayal of Gregory's peace negotiations with the Frankish Emperor Louis under his very nose. That little stratagem had paid handsomely; the benefactor, Louis's son Lothar, had known how to render gratitude into coin, and Anastasius was now a wealthy man. Even more important, Anastasius had succeeded in winning Lothar's trust and support. For a time, it was true, Anastasius had feared that his carefully cultivated alliance with the Frankish heir might come to naught—for Lothar's defeat at Fontenoy had been admittedly disastrous. But Lothar had managed to come to terms with his rebellious brothers in the Treaty of Verdun, a remarkable piece of political legerdemain that permitted him to retain both his crown and his territories. Lothar was once again undisputed Emperor—a fact that should prove very valuable to Anastasius in the future.

The sound of bells jolted Anastasius from his reverie. The bells tolled once, twice, a third time. Anastasius slapped his thighs jubilantly. At last!

He had already donned the robe of mourning when the expected knock came. A papal notary entered on silent feet. "The Apostolic One has been gathered to God," he announced. "Your presence, Primicerius, is requested in the papal bedchamber."

Side by side, without speaking, they threaded their way through the labyrinthine hallways of the Lateran Palace toward the papal quarters.

"He was a godly man." The notary broke the silence. "A peacemaker, a saint."

"A saint, indeed," Anastasius responded. To himself he thought, *What better place for him, then, than in Heaven?*

"When will come another?" The notary's voice cracked.

Anastasius saw the man was crying. He was intrigued by the display of genuine emotion. He himself was far too artful, too aware of the effect everything he said and did had on others, to engage in *lacrimae rerum*. Nevertheless, the notary's emotion reminded him that he should prepare his own show of grief. As they approached the papal bedchamber, he drew in his breath and held it, screwing up his face until he felt a sting behind his eyes. It was a trick he had, a way of bringing forth tears at will; he used it seldom, but always to good effect.

The bedchamber stood open to the gathering crowd of mourners. Inside Gregory lay on the great feather bed, eyes closed, arms, ritually crossed, clasped round a golden cross. The other *optimates,* or chief officers of the papal court, ringed the deathbed: Anastasius saw Arighis, the vicedominus; Compulus, the nomenclator; and Stephen, the vestiarius.

"The primicerius, Anastasius," the secretary announced as Anastasius entered. The others looked up to see him plunged into grief, his features etched with pain, his cheeks streaked with tears.

Joan raised her head, letting the rays of warm Roman sun spill onto her face. She was still unaccustomed to such pleasant, mild weather in Wintarmanoth—or January, as it was called in this southern part of the Empire, where Roman, not Frankish, customs prevailed.

Rome was not what she had imagined. She had envisioned a shining city, paved with gold and marble, its hundreds of basilicas rising toward Heaven in gleaming testimony to the existence of a true *Civitas Dei,* a City of God on earth. The reality proved far different. Sprawling, filthy, teeming, Rome's narrow, broken streets seemed engendered in Hell rather than Heaven. Its ancient monuments—those that had not been converted to Christian churches—stood in ruin. Temples, amphitheaters, palaces, and baths had been stripped of their gold and silver and left open to the elements. Vines snaked across their fallen column shafts; jasmine and acanthus sprouted from the crevices of their walls; pigs and goats and great-horned oxen grazed in their decaying porticoes. Statues of emperors lay strewn upon the ground; the empty sarcophagi of heroes were reemployed as washtubs, cisterns, or troughs for swine.

It was a city of ancient and seemingly irreconcilable contradictions: the wonder of the world, and a filthy, decaying backwash; a place of Christian pilgrimage, whose greatest art celebrated pagan gods; a center of books and learning, whose people wallowed in ignorance and superstition.

Despite these contradictions, perhaps because of them, Joan loved Rome. The seething tumult of its streets stirred her. In these teeming corridors the far corners of the world converged: Roman, Lombard, German, Byzantine, and Muslim jostling one another in an exciting mix of customs and tongues. Past and present, pagan and Christian were intertwined in a rich and diverting tapestry. The best and worst of all the world were gathered within these ancient walls. In Rome, Joan found the world of opportunity and adventure which she had sought all her life.

She spent most of her time in the Borgo, where the various *scholae,* or societies, of foreigners were clustered. Arriving over a year ago, she had naturally gone first to the Schola Francorum but found no admittance there, as the place was overbursting with Frankish pilgrims and immigrants. So she had gone on to the Schola Anglorum, where her father's English ancestry, as well as her surname, Anglicus, had gained her a warm welcome.

The depth and breadth of her education soon earned her a reputation as a brilliant scholar. Theologians came from all over Rome to engage her in learned discourse; they went away awed by the breadth of her knowledge and her quick-witted skill in disputation. How dismayed they would have been, Joan thought with an inward smile, had they known they had been bested by a woman!

Her regular duties included assisting at daily mass in the small church close beside the schola. After the midday meal, and a short nap (for it was the custom in the south to sleep away the sweltering afternoon hours), she went to the infirmary, where she passed the rest of the day tending the sick. Her knowledge of the medical arts stood her in good stead, for the practice of medicine here was nowhere near as advanced as in Frankland.

The Romans knew little of the healing properties of herbs and plants, and nothing of the study of urine to diagnose and treat disease. Joan's successes as a healer put her services much in demand.

It was an active, busy life, one that suited Joan perfectly. It offered all the opportunities of monastic life with none of the disadvantages. She could exercise the full measure of her intelligence without check or censure. She had access to the schola library, a small but fine collection of more than fifty volumes, and no one stood over her shoulder to question her if she chose to read Cicero or Suetonius rather than Augustine. She was free to come and go as she pleased, to think as she liked, to express her thoughts without fear of flogging and exposure. The time passed quickly, measured out contentedly in the fulfillment of each day's work.

So things might have continued indefinitely had the newly elected Pope Sergius not fallen ill.

Since Septuagesima Sunday, the Pope had been beset by an assortment of vague but troubling symptoms: bad digestion, insomnia, heaviness and swelling of the limbs; shortly before Easter, he was stricken with a pain so intense as to be almost unendurable. Night after night, the entire palace was kept awake by his screaming.

The society of physicians sent a dozen of its best men to attend the stricken Pope. They tried a multitude of devices to effect a cure: they brought a fragment of the skull of St. Polycarp for Sergius to touch; they massaged his afflicted limbs with oil taken from a lamp that had burned all night on the tomb of St. Peter, a measure known to cure even the most desperate of afflictions; they bled him repeatedly and purged him with emetics so strong his whole body was racked with violent spasms. When even these powerful curatives failed, they tried to dispel the pain through counter-irritation, laying strips of burning flax across the veins of the legs.

Nothing availed. As the Pope's condition worsened, the Roman people were gripped with alarm: if Sergius should die so soon after his predecessor, leaving the Throne of St. Peter vacant again, the Frankish Emperor, Lothar, might seize the opportunity to descend on the city and assert his imperial authority over them.

Sergius's brother Benedict was also beset by worry—not out of any fraternal sentiment but because his brother's demise represented a threat to his own interests. Having persuaded Sergius to appoint him papal missus,

Benedict had skillfully used that position to accrue the authority of the papal office for himself. The result was that, only five months into his papacy, Sergius ruled in name only; all real power in Rome was wielded by Benedict—to the considerable aggrandizement of his personal fortune.

Benedict would have preferred to have the title and honor of the papal office as well, but he had always known this to be beyond his reach. He had neither the education nor the polish for so great an office. He was a second son, and in Rome it was not the custom to divide property and title among heirs as in Frankland. As the firstborn, Sergius had been lavished with all the privileges the family could provide—the expensive clothes, the private tutors. It was terribly unfair, but there was nothing to be done about it, and after a while Benedict had left off sulking and sought consolation in worldlier pleasures, of which, he quickly discovered, Rome had no shortage. His mother had grumbled about his dissolute habits but made no serious attempt to curtail them; her interest and hopes had always been centered on Sergius.

Now, at last, the long years of being overlooked were at an end. It had not been difficult to get Sergius to appoint him papal missus; Sergius had always felt guilty about the preference he had been given over his younger brother. Benedict knew his brother was weak, but corrupting him had proved even easier than anticipated. After all the years of ceaseless study and monkish deprivation, Sergius was more than ready to enjoy life. Benedict did not try to lure his brother with women, for Sergius clung adamantly to the ideal of priestly chastity. Indeed, his feelings on this point approached obsession, so that Benedict was hard put to keep secret his own sexual adventuring.

But Sergius had another weakness—an insatiable appetite for the pleasures of the table. As he consolidated his own power, Benedict kept his brother distracted with an unending parade of gustatory delights. Sergius's capacity for food and wine was prodigious. He had been known to consume five trout, two roast hens, a dozen meat pasties, and a whole haunch of venison in a single sitting. After one such orgy, he had come to morning mass so gorged and bloated that he vomited up the Sacred Host onto the altar, to the horror of the congregation.

Following this shameful episode, Sergius resolved to reform, resuming the simple diet of bread and greens on which he had been raised. This spartan regimen restored him; he again began to take an interest in affairs of state. This had interfered with Benedict's profitable schemes. But Benedict bided his time. Then, when he judged Sergius had had enough of pious self-denial, he resumed tempting him with extravagant gifts: rich and exotic sweetmeats, pasties and pottages, roasted pigs, barrelfuls of thick Tuscan wine. Soon Sergius was off on another feeding binge.

This time, however, the bingeing had gone too far. Sergius became ill, dangerously ill. Benedict felt no compassion for his elder brother, but he did not want him to die. Sergius's death would spell the end of Benedict's own power.

Something had to be done. The physicians attending Sergius were an incompetent lot who attributed the Pope's sickness to powerful demons, against whose malignancy only prayer could avail. They surrounded Sergius with a multitude of priests and monks, who wept and prayed beside his bed day and night, raising their voices stringently toward Heaven, but it made no difference: Sergius continued to decline.

Benedict was not content to let his future hang upon the slender thread of prayer. *I must do something. But what?*

"My lord."

Benedict was roused from his reverie by the small, hesitant voice of Celestinus, one of the papal *cubicularii,* or chamberlains. Like most of his fellows, Celestinus was the scion of a rich and aristocratic Roman family that had paid handsomely for the honor of having their young son serve as chamberlain to the Pope. Benedict regarded the boy with dislike. What did this pampered child of privilege know of life, of the hard scrabble to raise oneself up from obscurity?

"What is it?"

"My lord Anastasius requests an audience with you."

"Anastasius?" Benedict could not place the name.

"Bishop of Castellum," Celestinus offered helpfully.

"You dare instruct me?" Furious, Benedict brought his hand down forcefully on Celestinus's cheek. "That will teach you respect for your betters. Now be off, and bring the bishop to me here."

Celestinus hurried away, cradling his cheek tearfully. Benedict's hand stung where it had contacted the boy; he flexed it, feeling better than he had in days.

Moments later Anastasius swept regally through the doors. Tall and courtly, the epitome of aristocratic elegance, he was well aware of the impression he made on Benedict.

*"Pax vobiscus,"* Benedict greeted him in mangled Latin.

Anastasius noted the barbarism but took care not to let his contempt show. *"Et cum spiritu tuo,"* he responded smoothly. "How fares His Holiness the Pope?"

"Poorly. Very poorly."

"I grieve to hear it." This was more than politeness; Anastasius truly was concerned. The time was not yet right for Sergius to die. Anastasius would not be thirty-five, the minimum age required in a Pontiff, for more than a year. If Sergius died now, a younger man than he might be elected, and it could be twenty years or more before the Chair of St. Peter stood vacant again. Anastasius did not intend to wait that long to realize his life's ambition.

"Your brother is skillfully attended, I trust?"

"He is surrounded night and day by holy men offering prayers for his recovery."

"Ah!" There was a silence. Both men were skeptical of the efficacy of such measures, but neither could own his doubt openly.

"There is someone at the Schola Anglorum," Anastasius ventured, "a priest with a great reputation for healing."

"Oh?"

"John Anglicus, I believe he is called—a foreigner. Apparently he is a man of great learning. They say that he can perform veritable miracles of healing."

"Perhaps I should send for him," said Benedict.

"Perhaps," Anastasius agreed, then let the matter drop. Benedict, he sensed, was not a man to be pushed. Tactfully, Anastasius shifted the discussion to another matter. When he judged a reasonable amount of time to have passed, he stood to leave. *"Dominus tecum, Benedictus."*

*"Deus vobiscus."* Benedict mangled the form once again.

*Ignorant oaf,* Anastasius thought. That such a man could rise so far in power was an embarrassment, a stain upon the reputation of the Church. With a bow and an elegant sweep of his robes, Anastasius turned and left.

Benedict watched him go. *Not a bad sort, for an aristocrat. I will send for this healer-priest, this John Anglicus.* It would probably cause trouble, bringing in someone who was not a member of the society of physicians, but no matter. Benedict would find a way. There was always a way, when one knew what one wanted.

✦ ✦ ✦

Three dozen candles blazed at the foot of the great bed in which Sergius lay. Behind them knelt a clot of black-robed monks, droning litanies in deep-voiced unison.

Ennodius, chief physician of Rome, raised his iron lancet and drew it deftly across Sergius's left forearm, slicing into the chief vein. Blood welled from the wound and dripped into a silver bowl held by Ennodius's apprentice. Ennodius shook his head as he examined the blood in the bowl. It was thick and dark; the peccant humor that was causing the Pope's illness was compacted in the body and would not be drawn out. Ennodius left the wound open, letting the blood flow longer than usual; he would not be able to bleed Sergius again for some days, for the moon was passing into Gemini, an unpropitious sign for bloodletting.

"How does it look?" Florus, a fellow physician, asked.

"Bad. Very bad."

"Come outside," Florus whispered. "I must speak with you."

Ennodius staunched the wound, pressing the flaps of skin together and applying pressure with his hand. The task of binding the wound with grease-coated leaves of rue wrapped in cloth he left to his apprentice. Wiping the blood from his hands, he followed Florus out to the hall.

"They've sent for someone else," Florus said urgently as soon as they were alone. "A healer from the Schola Anglorum."

"No!" Ennodius was chagrined. The practice of medicine within the city was supposed to be strictly confined to members of the physicians' society—though in actuality a small and unrecognized army of medical dabblers plied their questionable skills among the populace. These were tolerated, as long as they operated anonymously among the poor. But a forthright acknowledgment of one of these, coming from the papal palace itself, represented an undeniable threat.

"John Anglicus, the man is called," Florus said. "Rumor has it he is possessed of extraordinary powers. They say he can diagnose an illness merely by examining a patient's urine."

Ennodius sniffed. "A charlatan."

"Obviously. But some of these medical pretenders are quite artful. If this John Anglicus can mount even an appearance of skill, it could be damaging."

Florus was right. In a profession such as theirs, where results were often disappointing and always unpredictable, reputation was everything.

If this outsider should meet with success where they had been seen to fail . . .

Ennodius thought for a moment. "He makes a study of urine, you say? Well, then, we'll provide him with a sample."

"Surely the last thing we should do is help the foreigner!"

Ennodius smiled. "I said we'd provide him with a sample, Florus. I didn't say from whom."

Surrounded by an escort of papal guards, Joan walked quickly toward the Patriarchium, the enormous palace housing the papal residence as well as the multiplicity of administrative offices that constituted the seat of government in Rome. Bypassing the great Basilica of Constantine, with its magnificent line of round-arched windows, they entered the Patriarchium. Inside, they climbed a short flight of stairs which let upon the *triclinium major,* or great hall of the palace, whose construction had been commissioned by Pope Leo of blessed memory.

The hall was paved in marble and decorated with myriad mosaics, worked with a degree of artistry that left Joan awestruck. Never before had she seen colors so bright, nor figures so lifelike. No one in Frankland—bishop, abbot, count, not even the Emperor himself—could command such magnificence.

In the center of the triclinium, a group of men was gathered. One came forward to greet her. He was dark avised, with narrow, puffy eyes and a crafty expression.

"You are the priest John Anglicus?" he asked.

"I am."

"I am Benedict, papal missus and brother to Pope Sergius. I have had you brought here to cure His Holiness."

"I will do all I can," Joan said.

Benedict dropped his voice to a conspiratorial whisper. "There are those who have no wish to see you succeed."

Joan could well believe it. Many in the assemblage were members of the select and exclusive physicians' society. They would not welcome an outsider.

Another man joined them—tall, thin, with penetrating eyes and a beaked nose. Benedict introduced him as Ennodius, chief of the physicians' society.

Ennodius acknowledged Joan with the barest of nods. "You will discover for yourself, *if* you have the skill, that His Holiness is afflicted by demons, whose pernicious hold will not be dislodged by medicines or purgings."

Joan said nothing. She put little credence in such theories. Why look to the supernatural when there were so many physical and detectable causes of disease?

Ennodius held out a vial of yellow liquid. "This sample of urine was taken from His Holiness not an hour ago. We are curious to see what you can learn from it."

*So I am to be tested,* Joan thought. *Well, I suppose it's as good a way to start as any.*

She took the vial and held it up against the light. The group gathered round in a semicircle. Ennodius's beaked nose quivered as he watched her with vulpine expectancy.

She turned the vial this way and that until the contents showed clearly. Strange. She sniffed it, then sniffed again. She dipped a finger in, put it to her tongue, and tasted carefully. The tension in the room was now almost palpable.

Again she sniffed and tasted. No doubt about it.

A clever ruse, substituting a pregnant woman's urine for the Pope's. They had confronted her with a true dilemma. As a simple priest, and a foreigner, she could not accuse so august a company of deliberate deceit. On the other hand, if she did not detect the substitution, she would be denounced as a fraud.

The trap had been skillfully set. How to escape it?

She stood considering.

Then she turned and announced, straight-faced, "God is about to perform a miracle. Within thirty days, His Holiness is going to give birth."

Benedict shook with laughter as he led the way out of the triclinium. "The looks on those old men's faces! It was all I could do to keep from laughing out loud!" He was deriving an inordinate amount of pleasure from what had transpired. "You proved your skill and exposed their deceit without uttering a single word of accusation. Brilliant!"

As they approached the papal bedroom, they heard hoarse shouting from the other side of the door.

"Villains! Ghouls! I'm not dead yet!" There was a loud crash, as of something thrown.

Benedict opened the door. Sergius was sitting up in bed, crimson faced with fury. Halfway across the floor, a broken pottery bowl rocked wildly before a group of cringing priests. Sergius had snatched a golden cup from a bedside table and was about to hurl it at the hapless prelates when Benedict hurried over and pulled it from his grasp.

"Now, Brother. You know what the doctors said. You are ill; you must not exert yourself."

Sergius said accusingly, "I woke to find them anointing me with oil. They were trying to administer unctio extrema."

The prelates smoothed their robes with ruffled dignity. They appeared to be men of importance; one who wore the pallium of an archbishop said, "We thought it best, in view of His Holiness's worsening condition—"

"Leave at once!" Benedict interrupted.

Joan was astonished; Benedict must be powerful, indeed, to address an archbishop so uncivilly.

"Take thought, Benedict," the archbishop warned. "Would you endanger your brother's immortal soul?"

"Out!" Benedict swung his arms as if driving off a flock of blackbirds. "All of you!"

The prelates retreated hastily, exiting in shared indignation.

Sergius fell back weakly against his pillows. "The pain, Benedict," he whimpered. "I cannot bear the pain."

Benedict poured wine from a pitcher beside the bed into the golden cup and put it to Sergius's lips. "Drink," he said, "it will ease you."

Sergius drank thirstily. "More," he demanded as soon as he had drained it. Benedict poured him a second cup, and then a third. Wine spilled down the sides of Sergius's mouth. He was small boned but very fat. His countenance was a series of connecting circles: round face connecting to round chin, round eyes centered inside twin rings of flesh.

"Now," Benedict said, when Sergius's thirst was quenched, "see what I have done for you, Brother? I have brought someone who can help you. He is John Anglicus, a healer of great repute."

"Another physician?" Sergius said mistrustfully.

But he made no objection when Joan pulled back the covers to examine him. She was shocked at his condition. His legs were hugely swollen, the stretched flesh cracked and splitting from the strain. He was afflicted with a serious inflammation of the joints; Joan guessed the cause, but she had to make certain. She checked Sergius's ears. Sure enough, there they were: the telltale tophi, little chalky excrescences resembling crabs' eyes whose presence meant only one thing: Sergius was suffering an acute attack of gout. How was it possible that his doctors had not recognized it?

Joan ran her fingertips gently over the red, shiny flesh, feeling for the source of the inflammation.

"At least this one hasn't the hands of a plowman," Sergius conceded. It was astonishing he was still lucid, for he burned with fever. Joan felt his pulse, noting as she did the multiple wounds on his arm from repeated bleedings. His heartbeat was weak, and his coloring, now the fit of choler had passed, a sickly bluish white.

*Benedicite,* she thought. *No wonder he suffers from thirst. They have bled him within an inch of his life.*

She turned to a chamberlain. "Bring water. Quickly."

She had to reduce the swelling before it killed him. Thank heavens she had brought corm of colchicum. Joan reached into her scrip and withdrew a small square of waxed parchment, unfolding it carefully so as not to spill any of the precious powder. The chamberlain returned with a jug of water. Joan poured some into a goblet, then infused two drams of the powdered root, the recommended dosage. She added clarified honey to mask the bitter taste and a small dose of henbane to make Sergius sleep—for sleep was the best anodyne against pain, and rest the best hope for a cure.

She handed the goblet to Sergius, who gulped it thirstily. "Pah!" He spat it out. "This is water!"

"Drink it," Joan said firmly.

To her surprise, Sergius acquiesced. "Now what?" he asked after he had drained the cup. "Are you going to purge me?"

"I should have thought you'd had enough of such tortures."

"You mean to do no more than this?" Benedict challenged. "A simple draft and that is all?"

Joan sighed. She had encountered such reactions before. Common sense and moderation were not appreciated in the art of healing. People demanded more dramatic measures. The more serious the disease, the more violent the cure was expected to be.

"His Holiness is suffering from gout. I have given him colchicum, a known specific for the disease. In a few moments, he will sleep, and, *Deo volente,* the pain and swelling that have afflicted him will recede in a few days' time."

As if in demonstration of the truth of what she said, Sergius's ragged breathing began to ease; he relaxed against the pillows and closed his eyes peacefully.

The door swung open with a bang. In stalked a small, tensely coiled man with a face like that of a bantam cock spoiling for a fight. He brandished a roll of parchment beneath Benedict's nose. "Here are the papers. All that's needed is the signature." By his dress and manner of speech, he appeared to be a merchant.

"Not now, Aio," Benedict answered.

Aio shook his head fiercely. "No, Benedict, I will not be put off again. All Rome knows the Pope is dangerously ill. What if he dies in the night?"

Joan looked anxiously at Sergius, but he had not heard. He had slipped into a doze.

The man jingled a bag of coins before Benedict's eyes. "One thousand solidi, as agreed. Have the paper signed, now, and this"—he raised another, smaller bag—"is yours as well."

Benedict took the parchment to the bed and unrolled it on the sheet. "Sergius?"

"He is sleeping," Joan protested. "Do not rouse him."

Benedict ignored her. "Sergius!" He took his brother by the shoulder and shook him roughly.

Sergius's eyes blinked open. Benedict took a quill from the table beside the bed, dipped it in ink, and wrapped Sergius's hand around it. "Sign this," he commanded.

Dazedly, Sergius put the pen to the parchment. His hand shook, spilling the ink onto the parchment in an uneven scrawl. Benedict covered his brother's hand with his own and helped him trace the papal signature.

From where she stood, Joan saw the paper clearly. It was a *formata* appointing Aio Bishop of Alatri. The contract being made before Joan's very eyes was a bribe to buy a bishopric!

"Rest you now, brother," Benedict said, content now he had what he wanted. To Joan he said, "Stay with him."

Joan nodded. Benedict and Aio exited from the room.

Joan pulled the bedcovers over Sergius, smoothing them gently. Her chin was set in characteristic determination. Clearly, things in the papal palace were very much amiss. Nor were they likely to be righted as long as Sergius lay ill and his venal brother ruled in his stead. Her task was plain: restore the Pope to health, and that as quickly as possible.

For the next few days, Sergius's condition remained perilous. The constant chanting of the priests kept him from sound sleep, so at Joan's insistence their bedside vigil was terminated. Except for one brief excursion to the Schola Anglorum to retrieve more medicines, Joan did not leave Sergius's side. By day she carefully monitored his condition; by night she slept on a pile of cushions beside the bed.

On the third day, the swelling began to recede, and the skin covering it started to peel. In the evening, Joan woke from a restless sleep to find that Sergius had broken sweat. *Benedicite,* she thought. *The fever has passed.*

The next morning he awoke.

"How do you feel?" Joan asked.

"I . . . don't know," he said groggily. "Better, I think."

"You look a good deal better." The pinched look was gone, as was the unhealthy blue-gray cast of his skin.

"My legs . . . they're crawling!" He began to scratch at them violently.

"The itching is a good sign; it means the life is returning," Joan said. "But you must not irritate the skin, for there is still a danger of infection."

He withdrew his hand. But the itching sensation was too strong; a moment later he was clawing at his legs again. Joan administered a dose of henbane to calm him, and again he slept.

When he opened his eyes the next day, he was clearheaded, fully aware of his surroundings.

"The pain—it's gone!" He looked at his legs. "And the swelling!" The observation animated him; he pulled himself into a sitting position. Spying a chamberlain by the door, he said, "I'm hungry. Bring a raft of bacon and some wine."

"A plate of greens and a jug of water," Joan countermanded. The chamberlain hurried off before Sergius could protest.

Sergius's brows flew up with surprise. "Who are you?"

"My name is John Anglicus."

"You're not Roman."

"I was born in Frankland."

"The north country!" Sergius's eyes sharpened. "Is it as barbarous as they say?"

Joan smiled. "There are fewer churches, if that's what you mean."

"Why are you called 'Anglicus,' " Sergius asked, "if you were born in Frankland?" He was astonishingly alert in light of what he had been through.

"My father was English," Joan explained. "He came to preach the faith among the Saxons."

"The Saxons?" Sergius frowned. "A godless tribe."

*Mama.* Joan felt the old familiar surge of shame and love. She said, "Most are Christian now—as far as any can be who are brought to the Faith through fire and sword."

Sergius eyed her sharply. "You do not hold with the Church's mission to convert the heathen?"

"What value has any pledge exacted by force? Under torture, a person may confess to any number of lies, merely to put an end to pain."

"Yet our Lord bids us spread the word of God: 'Go, therefore, and teach all nations, baptizing them in the name of the Father and of the Son and of the Holy Spirit.' "

"True," Joan conceded. "But—" She broke off. She was doing it again—allowing herself to be drawn into imprudent and possibly dangerous debate—this time with the Pope himself!

"Go on," Sergius prodded.

"Forgive me, Holiness. You are not well."

"Nor yet too sick for reason," Sergius replied impatiently. "Go on."

"Well"—she chose her words carefully—"consider the order of Christ's commands: teach the nations first, then baptize them. We are not enjoined to bestow the sacrament of baptism before the mind embraces the Faith with rational understanding. First teach, Christ says, then dip."

Sergius contemplated her with interest. "You reason well. Where were you educated?"

"A Greek by the name of Aesculapius, a man of great learning, tutored me as a child. Later, I was sent to the cathedral school at Dorstadt, and later still to Fulda."

"Ah, Fulda! I have only recently received a volume from Raban Maur, beautifully illuminated, containing a poem of his own composition on the Holy Cross of Christ. When I write to thank him, I will tell him of your service to our person."

She thought she had put Abbot Raban behind her forever; would his tyrannous hatred follow her even here, blighting the new life she had made for herself? "You will not have good report of me from that quarter, I fear."

"Why is that?"

"The abbot holds obedience to be the greatest of the religious vows. Yet, to me, it has always come the hardest."

"And your other vows?" Sergius asked sternly. "What of them?"

"I was born into poverty and am accustomed to it. As for chastity"—she kept her voice free of any tinge of irony—"I have always resisted the temptations of women."

Sergius's expression softened. "I am glad to hear it. For in this matter, Abbot Raban and I do not agree; of all the religious vows, chastity is surely the greatest and most pleasing to God."

Joan was surprised that he should think so. The ideal of priestly chastity was far from universally practiced in Rome. It was not at all uncommon for a Roman priest to have a wife, as there was no prohibition against married men entering the priesthood, provided that they agreed to abjure all future conjugal relations—an agreement that predictably was observed more in the breach than in the practice. A wife rarely objected if her husband sought to become a priest, for she shared in the prestige of his position: "Priestess," the wife of a priest was respectfully titled, or "Deaconess," if the wife of a deacon. Pope Leo III had been married when he ascended the papal throne, and no one in Rome had thought worse of him for it.

The chamberlain returned with a silver dish of bread and greens that he placed before Sergius, who tore off a chunk of bread and bit into it hungrily. "Now," he said, "tell me all about you and Raban Maur."

# 20

It was, Joan came to understand, as if Sergius were two different people—one dissolute, vulgar, and mean, the other cultivated, intelligent, and considerate. She had read of such cases in Celsus: *animae divisae,* he called them, divided spirits.

So it was with Sergius. But in his case, it was drink that triggered the metamorphosis. Gentle and kind when sober, he became a terror under the influence of wine. The palace servants, always ready to gossip, told Joan that Sergius had once condemned one of them to death merely for failing to deliver his supper in time. He had sobered up in time to stop the execution, but not before the unfortunate man had already been caned and pilloried.

His doctors had not been so far wrong after all, Joan decided: Sergius *was* possessed, though the demons that drove him were not of the Devil's making but his own.

Having gotten a glimpse of his better qualities, Joan made it her mission to restore him. She put him on a strict diet of greens and barley water. Sergius grumbled but submitted, fearing a return of pain. When she judged he was ready, Joan instituted a regimen of daily walks in the Lateran garden. In the beginning, he had to be carried there in his chair, three attendants groaning under his weight. The first day he barely managed to hobble a few steps before collapsing into his chair. With Joan's persistent encouragement, each day he went a little farther; at the end of a month he was able to make a full circuit of the garden. The residual swelling around his joints subsided, and the skin regained a healthy pink color. His eyes lost their puffiness, and as the contours of his face emerged more clearly, Joan could see that he was a much younger man than she had first thought—no more, perhaps, than forty-five or fifty.

"I feel a new man," Sergius said to Joan one day during their daily stroll. It was spring, and the lilacs were already in bloom, their heady scent perfuming the air.

"No dizziness, no weakness, no pain?" Joan asked.

"None. Truly, God has wrought a miracle."

"You might say that, Holiness," Joan said with a sideways smile. "But think what your condition was when God alone was serving as your physician!"

Sergius tweaked Joan's ear in playful recrimination. "God sent you here to me to effect His miracle!"

They smiled together, liking each other.

*This is the moment,* Joan thought. "If you truly feel quite well . . ." She let the words hang, tantalizingly.

"Yes?"

"I was just thinking . . . the papal court is in session today. Your brother Benedict is presiding in your place as usual. But if you're feeling strong enough . . ."

Sergius said irresolutely, "Benedict is accustomed to presiding. Surely there is no need . . ."

"The people did not choose Benedict for their lord. They need you, Holiness."

Sergius frowned. There was a long silence.

Joan thought: *I spoke too soon, and too boldly.*

Sergius said, "You speak truly, John Anglicus. I have been too long neglectful of such matters." The sadness in his eyes gave his face a look of grave wisdom.

Joan replied gently, "The remedy, my lord, lies in the doing."

Sergius contemplated this. Then he wheeled abruptly, heading for the garden gate. "Come on, then!" he called back to her. "What are you waiting for?"

Joan hurried after him.

Two guards leaned against the wall outside the council room, chatting idly. Seeing Sergius, they jumped to attention and pulled the doors open. "His Holiness Pope Sergius, Bishop and Metropolitan of Rome!" one announced in a ringing voice.

Sergius and Joan swept into the room. There was a moment's astonished silence, followed by a loud scraping of benches as everyone stood respectfully. Everyone, that is, but Benedict, who remained seated in the papal chair with his jaw agape.

"Close your mouth, Brother, unless you mean to catch flies," Sergius said.

"Holiness! Is this wise?" Benedict exclaimed. "Surely you should not risk your health by observing these proceedings!"

"Thank you, Brother, but I feel quite well," Sergius said. "And I have come not to observe but to preside."

Benedict stood up. "I rejoice to hear it, as does all Rome." He sounded anything but rejoiceful.

Sergius settled comfortably into the cushioned chair. "What is the case in hand?"

Quickly the notary outlined the details. Mamertus, a wealthy merchant, was suing for permission to renovate the Orphanotrophium, a shelter and school for orphans housed in a decaying structure close by the Lateran. Mamertus proposed to rebuild it entirely and turn it into a hostel for pilgrims.

"The Orphanotrophium," Sergius mused. "I know the place well; I stayed there some while myself, after my mother died."

"Holiness, the building is fallen into ruin," Mamertus said. "It is an eyesore, a blot upon our great city. What I propose will turn it into a palace!"

"What will become of the orphans?" Sergius asked.

Mamertus shrugged. "They can seek charity elsewhere. There are almshouses that will receive them."

Sergius looked doubtful. "It is a hard thing to be turned out from one's home."

"Holiness, this hostelry will be the pride of Rome! Dukes will not scorn to sleep there, nor kings neither!"

"Orphans are no less dear to God than kings. Has Christ not said, 'Blessed are the poor, for theirs is the Kingdom of God'?"

"Holiness, I beg you to consider. Think what the existence of such an establishment can do for Rome!"

Sergius shook his head. "I will not sanction the destruction of these children's home. The petition is denied."

"I protest!" Mamertus said heatedly. "Your brother and I are already agreed upon the arrangement; the compact has been struck, and the payment delivered."

"Payment?" Sergius arched a brow.

Benedict shook his head at Mamertus in urgent signal.

"I . . . I"—Mamertus raised his eyes, searching for words—"I made an offering, a most generous offering, at the altar of St. Servatius to speed the success of this enterprise."

"Then you are blessed," said Sergius. "Such charity carries its own reward, for you will suffer the less in the life everlasting."

"But—"

"You have our gratitude, Mamertus, for calling the poor state of repair of the Orphanotrophium to our attention. Restoring it shall become our immediate concern."

Mamertus's mouth opened and closed several times like that of a beached fish. With a last glare at Benedict, he stalked from the room.

Sergius winked at Joan, who smiled back.

Benedict caught the exchange. *So that's the weave of the wool,* he thought. He chided himself for not having noticed it sooner. It had been a busy season for the pontifical court, the most profitable time of year for Benedict; his time had been so heavily given over to these matters that he had not paid sufficient attention to the degree of sway the little foreign priest had acquired over his brother.

*No matter,* he told himself. *What's done can be undone. Every man has his weakness.* It was just a matter of discovering what that was.

Joan hurried down the corridor on her way to the triclinium major. As Sergius's personal physician, she was expected to sup at his table—a privilege that allowed her to keep a close eye on everything the Pope ate and drank. His state of health was still far from robust; overindulgence could well bring on another attack of gout.

"John Anglicus!"

She turned to see Arighis, the vicedominus, or majordomo of the palace, coming toward her.

"A lady in the Trastevere is dangerously ill; you are called upon to attend her."

Joan sighed. Three times this week she had been called out on such an errand. The news of her cure of Pope Sergius had spread throughout the city. To the great dismay of the members of the physicians' society, Joan's services as a healer were suddenly very much in demand.

"Why not send a physician from the schola?" Joan suggested.

Arighis frowned. He was not accustomed to being challenged: as vicedominus, it was his right and his duty to exercise control over all matters relating to the papal household and its staff—a fact that this brash young foreigner did not seem to understand. "I have already committed your services."

Joan bristled at this assertion of authority; as Sergius's personal physician, she was not, strictly speaking, under Arighis's supervision. But the matter was scarcely worth battling over, and an urgent call for help must be answered, however inopportune the moment of its arrival.

"Very well," Joan agreed, "I'll get my bag of medicaments."

Arriving at the address, Joan found herself before a large residence, styled in the manner of an old Roman *domus.* A servant led her through a series of connecting courtyards and a garden to an interior chamber riotously decorated with brightly colored mosaics, stucco seashells, and fool-the-eye paintings designed to create the illusion of distant vistas and rooms. This fantastical room was suffused with a sweet smell, redolent of ripe apples. At the far side of the room stood a large feather bed, lit round with candles like an altar. In the middle of the bed, a woman was lying languorously.

She was the most beautiful woman Joan had ever seen, more beautiful than Richild, more beautiful even than her mother, Gudrun, whom Joan had believed until this moment to be the loveliest woman in creation.

"I am Marioza." The woman's voice was liquid honey.

"L-lady," Joan stammered, tongue-tied before such perfection. "I am John Anglicus, come in answer to your summons."

Marioza smiled, pleased with the effect she was having. "Come closer, John Anglicus," the honey-voice urged. "Or do you mean to examine me from there?"

The sweet-apple scent was stronger by the bed. Joan thought, *I know that scent.* But she could not, for the moment, place it.

Marioza held out a cup of wine. "Won't you drink my health?"

Politely, Joan drank, draining the cup according to custom. Up close, Marioza was even more beautiful, her skin a flawless ivory, her eyes huge, black-fringed orbs of deepest violet, darkened into ebony by the wide black pupils at the center.

*Too wide,* Joan suddenly realized. So great a dilation of the pupils was decidedly abnormal. The clinical observation broke the spell of Marioza's beauty. "Tell me, lady"—Joan set the cup down—"what ails you?"

"So handsome," she sighed, "and so businesslike?"

"I wish to help you, lady. What distress has called me to your side so urgently?"

"Since you insist"—Marioza pouted prettily—"it's my heart."

An unusual complaint for a woman of her age, Joan thought; Marioza could not be older than twenty-two. Well, such cases were known to occur, children born under an unlucky star with a worm in their hearts, every breath of their short existence a torment and a struggle. But those who suffered from such afflictions did not look like Marioza, whose whole being, apart from those mysteriously dilated pupils, radiated good health.

Joan took up Marioza's wrist and felt her pulse, finding it strong and regular. She examined Marioza's hands. The color was good, the tips of the fingers showing pink under the nails. The skin sprang back to the touch without mark or discoloration. Joan examined Marioza's legs and feet with equal care, again finding no sign of necrosis; everywhere Marioza's circulation appeared healthy and strong.

Marioza lay back against the pillows, watching through half-lidded eyes. "Looking for my heart?" she teased. "You'll not find it there, John Anglicus!" She pulled opened her silken bed robe, revealing a pair of flawless ivory breasts.

*Benedicite!* Joan thought. This must be the Marioza of legend, the most celebrated hetaera, or courtesan, in all of Rome! It was said that she numbered some of the most important men in the city among her clients. *She is trying to seduce me,* Joan realized. The absurdity of the idea caused her to smile.

Misinterpreting Joan's smile, Marioza was encouraged. This priest was not going to be so difficult to seduce as Benedict had indicated when he had purchased her services for that purpose. Priest or no, John Anglicus was nevertheless a man, and the man had not been born who could resist her.

With studied disinterest, Joan concentrated on her examination. She probed Marioza's sides, checking for bruised ribs; the pain from such an injury was often mistaken for a problem of the heart. Marioza did not wince or give any evidence of discomfort.

"What fine hands you have," she purred, arranging herself so the enticing curves of her body were displayed to advantage. "What fine, strong hands."

Joan bolted upright. "Satan's apple!"

*How like a priest,* Marioza thought, *to talk high-mindedly of sin at such a moment.* Well, she was no stranger to priests; she knew how to deal with these last-minute crises of conscience.

"Do not suppress your feelings, John, for they are natural and God-given. Is it not written in the Bible: 'The two shall become one flesh'?" Actually, Marioza was not sure the words came from the Bible, but she thought it likely; they had been told to her, under circumstances very similar to the present, by an archbishop. "Besides," she added, "no one will ever know what happens here between us, excepting ourselves."

Joan shook her head vehemently. "That's not what I meant. The scent in this room—it's mandragora—sometimes called Satan's apple." The yellow fruit was a narcotic; that explained Marioza's dilated pupils. "But where is the scent coming from?" Joan sniffed a candle near the bed. "What have you done, mixed the juice with candle wax?"

Marioza sighed. She had seen such reactions from virginal young prelates before. Embarrassed and unsure, they kept trying to turn the conversation to safer ground. "Come," she said, "leave off talk of potions. There are better ways for us to pass the time." She ran her hand across the front of John Anglicus's tunic, reaching for his privates.

Anticipating her, Joan jumped back. She snuffed the candle and took Marioza's hands firmly in her own. "Listen to me, Marioza. The mandragora—you use it for its aphrodisiac qualities, I know. But you must leave off, for its fumes are poison."

Marioza frowned. This was not going according to plan. Somehow she must get the man's mind off his doctoring.

There were footsteps in the hall below. No time left for persuasion. She grabbed the top of her robe with both hands and rent it with a strong downward pull. "Oh!" she gasped, "a pain comes now! Do but listen!" She clasped Joan's head and held it firmly to her breast.

Joan tried to pull away, but Marioza held her tight. "Oh, John," her voice was now pure liquid, "I cannot resist the force of your passion!"

The door burst open. A dozen papal guards stormed into the room and seized Joan, lifting her roughly off the bed.

"Well, Father, this is a strange kind of communion!" the leader of the guards said mockingly.

Joan protested. "This woman is ill; I was called here to physick her."

The man leered. "Indeed, many's the woman been cured of barrenness with such remedying."

There was a burst of raucous laughter. Joan said to Marioza, "Tell them the truth."

Marioza shrugged, her torn robe slipping from her shoulders. "They saw us. Why try to deny it?"

"Join the ranks, Priest!" jeered one of the guards. "The number of Marioza's lovers would fill the Colosseum to bursting!"

This was greeted with another explosion of laughter. Marioza joined in with the others.

"Come on, Father." The leader of the guards took Joan's arm, propelling her toward the door.

"Where are you taking me?" Joan demanded, though she knew the answer.

"To the Lateran. You'll answer to the Pope for this."

Joan wrenched herself from his grasp. To Marioza she said, "I don't know why you've done this, or for whom, but I warn you, Marioza: do not pin your fortunes on the favors of men, for they will prove as fleeting as your beauty."

Marioza's laughter died on her lips. "Barbarian!" she spat back contemptuously.

On a tide of laughter, Joan was carried from the room.

Flanked by the guards, Joan walked in silence through the darkening streets. She could not bring herself to hate Marioza. Joan might have ended as such a one herself had fate not led her down a different path. The streets of Rome were filled with women offering themselves for no more than the price of a meal. Many had first come to the Holy City as pious pilgrims, even nuns; finding themselves without shelter or the means to buy return passage, they turned to the ready alternative. The clergy thundered against these "handmaids of the Devil" from the safety of their pulpits. Better to die chastely, they said, than live in sin. *But they,* thought Joan, *have never known hunger.*

No, Marioza was not to be blamed; she was only a tool. *But in whose hands? Who stands to gain by discrediting me?* Ennodius and the other members of the physicians' society were certainly capable of such chicanery. But surely they would aim their efforts at discrediting her medical skill.

*If not them, then who?* The answer came at once: *Benedict.* Ever since the business of the Orphanotrophium, he had resented her, jealous of her influence with his brother. The realization heartened her; at least she knew who the enemy was. Nor did she mean to let Benedict get away with this. True, he was Sergius's brother, but she was his friend; she would make him see the truth.

Arriving at the Lateran, Joan was dismayed when the guards marched her straight past the triclinium, where Sergius was dining with the optimates and other high officials of the papal court, down the hall to Benedict's quarters.

"Well, well. What have we here?" Benedict said mockingly as Joan and the guards entered. "John Anglicus, surrounded by guards like a common thief?" To the leader of the guard he said, "Speak, Tarasius, and tell me the nature of this priest's crime."

"My lord, we apprehended him in the rooms of the whore Marioza."

"Marioza!" Benedict affected a look of grave disapproval.

"We found him in the strumpet's bed, wrapped in her embrace," Tarasius added.

"It was a trick," Joan said. "I was called there on the false pretext that Marioza needed physicking. She knew the guards were coming and clasped me to her bosom just before they entered."

"You expect me to believe you were overpowered by a woman? For shame, false priest."

"The shame is yours, Benedict, not mine," Joan replied hotly. "You contrived the whole affair in order to discredit me. You arranged for Marioza to call me on the pretense of being ill, then sent the guards, knowing they would find us together."

"I own it readily."

The admission took Joan aback. "You confess your deceit?"

Benedict took a goblet of wine from a table and sipped from it, savoring the taste. "Knowing you to be unchaste, and not liking to see my brother's trust in you abused, I sought proof of your perfidy, that is all."

"I am not unchaste, nor have you any reason to think me so."

"Not unchaste?" Benedict sneered. "Tell me again how you found him, Tarasius."

"My lord, he lay with the wanton in her bed, and she was naked in his arms."

"Tsk, tsk. Think how distressed my brother will be to hear such damning testimony—the more so because of the great trust he has placed in you!"

For the first time Joan realized the seriousness of her situation. "Do not do this," she said. "Your brother needs me, for he is not yet out of danger. Without proper medical attention, he will suffer another attack—and the next one could kill him."

"Ennodius will attend my brother from now on," Benedict replied curtly. "Your sinner's hands have done harm enough."

"*I* do him harm?" Outrage obliterated the last of Joan's control. "You dare say that—you, who have sacrificed your brother to your own jealousy and greed?"

Wetness slapped her in the face; Benedict had hurled the contents of his cup at her. The strong wine burned her eyes, bringing forth tears; it coursed down her throat, causing her to choke and sputter.

"Take him to the dungeon," Benedict commanded.

"No!" With a sharp cry, Joan broke from the guards. She had to get to Sergius before Benedict could poison his mind against her. She ran swiftly down the hall toward the triclinium.

"Stop him!" Benedict shouted.

The guards' footsteps sounded behind her. Joan turned a corner and raced desperately toward the blazing lights of the triclinium.

She was a few yards away when she was tackled and sent sprawling. She struggled to rise, but the guards pinioned her arms and legs. Helpless, she was lifted and borne away.

She was carried down unfamiliar corridors and stairs that descended so steeply and for so long Joan began to wonder if they would ever end. At last the guards drew up before a heavy oak-planked door, barred with iron; they raised the bar and creaked the door open, then set Joan on her feet and thrust her roughly inside. She stumbled into murky darkness and landed with her feet in water. With terrifying solidity, the door slammed shut behind her, and the darkness became absolute.

✦ ✦ ✦

The footsteps of the guards retreated down the hall. Joan edged forward with arms held out, feeling at the darkness. She reached for her scrip—they had not thought to take it from her, a small blessing. She felt inside, fingering the various packets and vials, recognizing each by its shape and size. At last she found what she was looking for—the box containing her flint and kindling and the small stump of candle she used to warm her potions. She took up the flint and tapped it sharply against the side of the iron box, striking sparks into the dry tinder of straw. In a moment it quickened into flame. She held the candle to the tiny fire until the wick caught and steadied, casting its yellow light around her in a gentle arc.

The light shone precariously in the darkness, revealing flickering shapes and outlines. The dungeon was large, some thirty feet long by twenty feet wide. The walls were fashioned of heavy stone, smeared and darkened with age. From the slipperiness of the floor, Joan guessed it was also made of stone, though it was impossible to be sure, for it was covered with several inches of slimy, stagnant water.

She raised the candle higher, spreading its circle of light. In a far corner a pale shape shimmered into view—a human form, wan and insubstantial as a ghost's.

*I am not alone.* Relief flooded her, followed immediately by trepidation. This was, after all, a place of punishment. Was the apparition a madman or a murderer—or perhaps both?

*"Dominus tecum,"* she said tentatively. The man did not respond. She repeated the greeting in the common tongue, adding, "I am John Anglicus, priest and healer. Is there aught I can do for you, Brother?" The man sat slumped against the wall, arms at his sides, legs spread wide. Joan moved closer. The light of the candle spilled onto the man's face—but it wasn't a face, it was a skull, a hideous death's-head covered with shreds of decaying flesh and hair.

With a cry, Joan turned and ran splashing toward the door. She pounded on the heavy oaken planks. "Let me out!" She knocked and pounded till her knuckles were rubbed raw.

No one replied. No one would come. They were going to leave her here to die alone in the dark.

She wrapped her arms around herself and held on tightly, trying to stop shaking. Gradually, the waves of terror and despair began to subside.

Another feeling rose inside her—a stubborn determination to survive, to fight the injustice that had put her here. Her mind, temporarily numbed by fear, once again began to reason. *I must not give up hope,* she thought resolutely. *Sergius will not consign me to this dungeon forever. He'll be furious at first, when he hears Benedict's version of what happened with Marioza, but in a few days he'll calm down and send for me. All I have to do is endure until then.*

She began a careful circuit of the dungeon. She came across the remains of three other prisoners, but this time she was prepared, and they were not so frightful as the first, for their bones had long ago been picked clean of flesh. Her exploration also yielded an important discovery: one side of the dungeon was higher than the other; on the elevated side, the foul, slimy water stopped several feet short of the wall, leaving a long strip of dry floor. Against the wall, a discarded woolen cloak lay crumpled, tattered and honeycombed with holes, but still a useful protection against the penetrating chill of the underground chamber. In another corner of the room she made a further find: a straw pallet floating atop the water. The mattress was thick and well made, and so tightly woven that the top had remained dry. Joan dragged it over to the high side of the room and sat down on it, placing the candle beside her. She opened her scrip and took out some hellebore, scattering the poisonous black powder around her in a wide circle, a line of deterrent against rats and other vermin. Then she took out a package of powdered oak bark and another of dried sage; these she crumbled and infused into a small vial of wine mixed with honey. Tipping the vial of precious liquid carefully, she took a deep draft to fortify her against the foul and noxious humors of the place. Then she lay down on the pallet, snuffed the candle, and pulled the tattered cloak up over her.

She lay still in the dark. She had done all she could for the moment. Now she must rest and guard her strength until the time Sergius would send for her.

# 21

It was the Feast of the Ascension, and the day's stational service was to be at the titular Church of St. Prassede. Though the sun had only just risen, spectators were already gathering, livening the street outside the Patriarchium with movement and color and chatter.

Soon the great bronze doors to the Patriarchium opened. The first to appear were the acolytes and others in minor clerical orders, walking humbly on foot. These were followed by a group of mounted guards, their sharp eyes raking the crowd for potential troublemakers. Behind them rode the seven regionary deacons and the seven regionary notaries, each preceded by a cleric bearing the banner with the *signa* of their ecclesiastical region. Then came the archpriest and the primicerius of the *defensores,* followed by their brethren. Finally Pope Sergius appeared, magnificently attired in a robe of gold and silver, astride a tall roan mare trapped in white silk. Immediately behind rode the optimates, the chief dignitaries of the papal administration, in order of importance: Arighis, the vicedominus, and then the vestiarius, the sacellarius, the arcarius, and the nomenclator.

The long procession crossed the open expanse of the Lateran courtyard and moved out with stately dignity, passing the great bronze statue of a she-wolf, *mater romanorum,* or mother of the Romans, believed by the ancients to have suckled Romulus and Remus. The statue had occasioned considerable controversy, for there were those who said it was blasphemy for a piece of pagan idolatry to stand before the walls of the papal palace, but others defended it with equal passion, praising its beauty and the excellence of its craftsmanship.

Just beyond the she-wolf, the procession turned north, passing beneath the great arch of the Claudian aqueduct, with its lofty, finely proportioned brickwork, onto the ancient Via Sacra, the sacred road that Popes had traversed for time beyond memory.

Sergius blinked back the piercing rays of the sun. His head ached, and the rhythmic swaying of his horse was making him dizzy; he gripped the reins to steady himself. *This,* he thought penitently, *is the price I pay for gluttony.* He had sinned again, gorging himself on rich food and wine. Despising his weakness, Sergius resolved, for the twentieth time that week, to reform.

With a pang of regret, he thought of John Anglicus. He had felt so much better when the foreign priest had been physicking him. But of course there could be no question of having him back, not after what he had done. John Anglicus was a detestable sinner, a priest who had broken the holiest of his vows.

"God bless the Lord Pope!" The cheering crowd brought Sergius's thoughts back to the present. He made the sign of the cross in blessing, fighting down nausea as the procession moved with stately dignity down the narrow line of the Via Sacra.

They had just passed the monastery of Honorius when the crowd scattered in sudden confusion as a mounted man rode in upon them. Horse and rider had been driven hard; the bay's mouth was lathered, its sides heaving. The rider's clothes were torn, his face blackened like a Saracen's with the mud of the road. He reined in and leapt to the ground in front of the procession.

"How dare you interrupt this sacred procession?" Eustathius, the archpriest, demanded indignantly. "Guards, strip this man and flog him. Fifty strokes will teach him a better respect!"

"He . . . is coming . . ." The man was so out of breath that the words were scarcely distinguishable.

"Hold." Sergius stayed the guards. "Who is coming?"

"Lothar," the man gasped.

"The Emperor?" Sergius said in astonishment.

The man nodded. "At the head of a large army of Franks. Holiness, he's sworn a blood revenge against you and this city for the grievance that's been done him."

A murmur of dismay came from the crowd.

"Grievance?" For a moment Sergius could not think what this could mean. Then it came to him. "The consecration!"

After Sergius's election, the city had gone ahead with the consecration ceremony without waiting for the Emperor's approval. This was a manifest breach of the charter of 824, which granted Lothar the right of imperial *jussio,* or ratification of an elected Pope prior to consecration. Nevertheless, the move had been widely applauded, for the people saw it as a proud reassertion of Roman independence from the distant Frankish crown. It was a clear and deliberate slight to Lothar, but as the jussio was more symbolic than substantive—for no Emperor had ever failed to confirm an elected Pope—no one believed Lothar would do much about it.

"Where is the Emperor?" Sergius's voice was a dry whisper.

"In Viterbo, Holiness."

Cries of alarm greeted this news. Viterbo was part of the Roman campagna, no more than ten days' march from Rome.

"My lord, he is a scourge upon the earth"—the man's tongue was loosed now he had caught his breath—"his soldiers plunder all before them, ransacking the farms, carrying off the livestock, pulling up the vines by their roots. They take what they want, and what they do not want, they burn. Those who get in their way they kill without mercy—women, old men, babes in arms—none are spared. The horror"—his voice cracked—"the horror of it cannot be imagined."

Terrified and uncertain, the people looked to their Pope. But there was no comfort to be found there. Before the Romans' horrified eyes, Sergius's face went slack, his eyes rolled up into his head, and he toppled forward senseless onto his horse.

"O, he is dead!" The cry of lamentation found an echo on a dozen other tongues. Quickly the papal guards surrounded Sergius, plucking him from his horse and bearing him away into the Patriarchium. The rest of the procession followed close behind.

The frightened crowd thronged the courtyard, threatening to break into a dangerous panic. The guards rode in among them with whips and drawn swords, sending them scattering along the narrow, dark streets to the solitary terror of their homes.

Alarm and agitation grew as refugees thronged through the city gates from the surrounding campagna, from Farfa and Narni, Laurentum and Civitavecchia. They came in droves, their meager possessions bundled on their backs, their dead piled in carts. All had similar tales of Frankish depredation and savagery. These terrifying accounts spurred the city's efforts to strengthen its defenses: day and night the Romans toiled energetically to remove the layers of debris that had accumulated against the city walls over the centuries, making them easier for an enemy to surmount.

The priests of the city were kept busy from prime to vespers, saying Mass and hearing confession. The churches were filled to bursting, the ranks of the faithful swelled with a multitude of unfamiliar faces—for fear had goaded many a fainthearted Christian into newfound faith. Piously they lighted candles and raised their voices in prayer for the safety of their homes and families—and for the recovery of the ailing Sergius, on whom all their hopes depended. *May the strength of God be with our Lord Pope,* they prayed, for surely he would have need of great fortitude to save Rome from the devil Lothar.

Sergius's voice rose and fell in the fluid melodies of the Roman chant, truer and sweeter than that of any of the other boys in the *schola cantorum*. The singing master smiled approval at him. Encouraged, Sergius sang out more loudly, his young soprano rising higher and higher in joyous ecstasy, till it seemed as if it would lift him into Heaven itself.

The dream receded, and Sergius awoke. Fear, vague and undefined, crowded the edges of his consciousness, setting his heart racing before he understood why.

With a nauseating lurch, he remembered.

Lothar.

He sat up. His head throbbed, and there was a foul taste in his mouth. "Celestinus!" His voice cracked like a rusted hinge.

"Holiness!" Celestinus rose sleepily from the floor. With his soft pink cheeks, round child's eyes, and tousled blond hair, he resembled a heavenly cherub. At ten, he was the youngest of the cubicularii; Celestinus's father was a man of great influence in the city, so he had come to the Lateran earlier than most. *Well,* Sergius thought, *he is no younger than I was when I was taken from my parents' home.*

"Bring Benedict," he commanded. "I would speak with him."

Celestinus nodded and hurried off, stifling a yawn.

One of the kitchen servants entered with a platter of bread and bacon. Sergius was not supposed to break fast until after his celebration of Mass—for the hands that touched the eucharistic gifts had to be free from any worldly stain. In private, though, such niceties of form were often disregarded—especially with a Pope of such prodigious appetite.

This morning, however, the smell of the bacon made Sergius's gorge rise. He waved the tray aside. "Take it away."

A notary entered and announced, "His Grace the Archpriest awaits you in the triclinium."

"Let him wait," Sergius responded curtly. "I will speak first with my brother."

Benedict's common sense in this crisis had proved invaluable. It had been his idea to take money from the papal treasury in order to buy off Lothar. Fifty thousand gold solidi should be enough to assuage even an Emperor's wounded pride.

Celestinus returned, not with Benedict but with Arighis, the vicedominus.

"Where is my brother?" Sergius asked.

"Gone, Holiness," Arighis replied.

"Gone?"

"Ivo the porter saw him ride out just before dawn with a dozen or so attendants. We thought you knew."

A rise of bile bathed Sergius's throat. "The money?"

"Benedict collected it last night. There were eleven coffers altogether. He had them with him when he left."

"No!" But even as Sergius's lips formed the denial, he knew the truth of it. Benedict had betrayed him.

He was helpless. Lothar would come, and there was nothing, nothing Sergius could do to stop him.

A wave of nausea overtook him. He leaned over the side of the bed, spilling the sour contents of his stomach onto the floor. He tried to rise but could not; pain stabbed at his legs, immobilizing him. Celestinus and Arighis ran to help him, lifting him back and down. Turning his head into the pillow, Sergius wept unrestrainedly, like a child.

Arighis turned to Celestinus. "Stay with him. I'm going to the dungeon."

Joan stared at the bowl of food before her. There was a small crust of stale bread, and some gray, indistinguishable chunks of meat, threaded through with wriggling maggots; the rotten odor rose to her nostrils. It had been several days since she had eaten, for the guards, whether from carelessness or design, did not bring food every day. She stared at the meat, hunger doing battle with judgment. At last she put the bowl aside. Taking up the crust of bread, she bit off a small piece, chewing it slowly, to make it last longer.

How long had she been here—two weeks? Three? She had begun to lose count. The perpetual darkness was disorienting. She had used her piece of candle sparingly, lighting it only to eat or to prepare medications from her scrip. Nevertheless, the candle was reduced to a tiny stub of wax, good for no more than another hour or two of precious light.

Even more terrible than the darkness was the solitude. The utter and unremitting silence was unnerving. To stay alert, Joan set herself a series of mental tasks—reciting from memory the entire Rule of St. Benedict, all one hundred and fifty psalms, and the Book of Acts. But these feats of memory soon became too routine to keep her attention engaged.

She remembered how the great theologian Boethius, similarly imprisoned, had found strength and consolation in prayer. For hours she knelt on the cold stone floor of the dungeon, trying to pray. But at the core of her being, she felt nothing but emptiness. The seed of doubt, planted in her childhood by her mother, had taken deep root within her soul. She tried to weed it out, to rise up into the solacing light of grace, but she could not. Was God listening? Was He even there? As day after day passed with no word from Sergius, hope gradually slipped away.

The loud clank of metal jolted her as the bar on the door was lifted. A moment later the door swung wide, pouring dazzling light into the blackness. Shielding her eyes against the glare, Joan squinted toward the opening. A man stood silhouetted against the light. "John Anglicus?" he called uncertainly into the darkness.

The voice was instantly familiar. "Arighis!" Joan swayed lightheadedly as she rose and made her way through the stagnant water toward the papal vicedominus. "Have you come from Sergius?"

Arighis shook his head. "His Holiness does not wish to see you."

"Then why—?"

"He is gravely ill. Once before you gave him medicine that helped him; have you any with you now?"

"I have." Joan took a packet of powder of colchicum from her scrip. Arighis reached for it, but Joan quickly drew it back.

"What?" said Arighis. "Do you hate him so much? Beware, John Anglicus, for to wish harm upon Christ's chosen Vicar is to place your immortal soul in the gravest peril."

"I do not hate him," Joan said, and meant it. Sergius was not a bad man, she knew, only weak and overtrusting of his venal brother. "But I will not give this medicine into untrained hands. Its powers are very great, and the wrong dose could be lethal." This was not entirely true, for the powdered root was not as potent as she pretended; it would take a very large dose to do any real harm. But this was her chance at freedom; she would not let the door close upon it again. "Besides," she added, "how do I know Sergius is suffering from the same ailment as before? To cure His Holiness, I first must see him."

Arighis hesitated. To free the prisoner would be an act of insubordination, a direct countermanding of the Lord Pope's order. But if Sergius died with the Frankish Emperor at the gates, the papacy, and Rome itself, might be forfeit.

"Come," he said, abruptly arriving at a decision. "I will take you to His Holiness."

Sergius lay against the soft silken pillows of the papal bed. The worst of the pain had passed, but it had left him drained and weak as a newborn kitten.

The door to the chamber opened, and Arighis entered, followed by John Anglicus.

Sergius started violently. "What is this sinner doing here?"

Arighis said, "He comes with a powerful medicine that will restore you to health."

Sergius shook his head. "All true physicking comes from God. His healing grace will not be transmitted through so impure a vessel."

"I am not impure," Joan protested. "Benedict lied to you, Holiness."

"You were in the harlot's bed," Sergius replied accusingly. "The guards saw you there."

"They saw what they expected to see, what they had been told to observe," Joan retorted. Quickly she explained how Benedict had contrived to trap her. "I did not want to go there," she said, "but Arighis insisted."

"That is true, Holiness," Arighis confirmed. "John Anglicus asked if I would not send one of the other physicians. But Benedict insisted that John Anglicus and no other should go."

For a long while, Sergius did not speak. Finally he said in a cracked voice, "If this is true, you have been grievously wronged." He burst out in despair, "Lothar's coming is God's just judgment against me for all my sins!"

"If God wanted to punish you, there are easier ways to do it," Joan pointed out. "Why sacrifice the lives of thousands of innocents when he could smite you with a single stroke?"

This took Sergius by surprise. With the customary self-absorption of the great, such a thought had not occurred to him.

"Lothar's coming is not a punishment," Joan persevered, "it is a test—a test of faith. You must lead the people with the strength of your example."

"I'm sick in body and in heart. Let me die."

"If you do, the will of the people dies with you. You *must* be strong, for their sake."

"What difference does it make?" Sergius said hopelessly. "We cannot prevail against Lothar's forces; it would take a miracle."

"Then," Joan said staunchly, "we will have to make one."

The day after Pentecost Sunday, the date of Lothar's anticipated arrival, the piazza before the basilica of St. Peter began to fill with members of the various scholae of the city, dressed in their best finery. Lothar had not made a formal declaration of hostilities, so the plan was to accord him the reception due a personage of his exalted position. The unexpected show of welcome might disarm him long enough for the second part of Joan's plan to take effect.

By midmorning all was in readiness. Sergius gave the signal, and the first group, the *judices,* rode out, the yellow banners bearing their signa fluttering above them. Behind them rode the defensores and the deacons; then, on foot, the various societies of foreigners—Frisians, Franks, Saxons, Lombards, and Greeks. They called to one another bravely as they traveled down the Via Triumphalis, past the decaying skeletons of pagan temples lining the ancient road.

*God grant they are not marching to their deaths,* Joan thought. Then she turned her attention to Sergius. He had made good progress over the past few days but was still far from well. Would he be strong enough to endure the day's ordeal? Joan spoke to a chamberlain, who fetched a chair, into which Sergius sank gratefully. Joan gave him some lemon water mixed with honey to fortify him.

Fifty of the most powerful men in Rome were now gathered on the broad porch before the doors of the basilica: all the major officials of the Lateran administration, a select group of cardinal priests, the dukes and princes of the city, and their retinues. The archpriest Eustathius led them all in a short prayer, and then they stood in silence. There was nothing left to do but wait.

With taut faces they kept their eyes trained to where the road bent out of sight beyond the green hedges and meadows of the Neronian plain.

Time passed with unbearable slowness. The sun inched higher in a cloudless sky. The morning breeze diminished, then died, leaving the banners draped limply against their staffs. Swarms of flies circled lazily overhead, their irksome droning loud in the still, expectant air.

More than two hours had passed since the procession rode out. Surely they should have returned by now!

A barely perceptible noise came from the distance. They listened with pricked ears. The noise rose again, sustained and unmistakable—the sound of distant voices raised in song.

*"Deo gratias,"* breathed Eustathius as the banners of the judices floated into view, topping the green horizon like yellow sails upon a sea. Moments later, the first riders appeared, followed by members of the various scholae, on foot. Behind them marched a dark multitude that stretched as far as the eye could see—Lothar's army. Joan drew in her breath; never before had she seen so great a host.

Sergius rose, leaning on his crosier for support. The vanguard of the procession drew up to the basilica and fanned out, creating a path through which the Emperor could pass.

Lothar rode through. Looking at him, Joan could well believe the tales of barbaric cruelty that had preceded him. He had a stocky body, crowned by a thick neck and massive head; his broad, flat face and shallow-set eyes registered a look of malevolent intelligence.

The two opposing groups faced each other, one dark and muddied from the rigors of the road, the other spotless and gleaming in their white clerical robes. Behind Sergius the roof of St. Peter's rose incandescently, its silver plates shimmering with the reflected light of the morning—the spiritual heart of the Church, the beacon of the world, the holiest shrine in all Christendom. Before such sacred grandeur, even Emperors had bowed.

Lothar dismounted, but he did not kneel to kiss the bottom step of the basilica in the customary show of reverence. Boldly he mounted the steps, followed by a group of armed men. The prelates gathered before the open doors of the basilica drew back in alarm; the papal guards surrounded Sergius protectively, their hands on their sword hilts.

All at once, the open doors of St. Peter's jolted and moved. Lothar jumped back. His men drew their swords, then stood bewildered, gazing wildly from one side to the other. But there was no one nearby. The doors swung slowly inward on their hinges as if supernaturally propelled. Then they closed with a final, definitive crack.

*Now.* Joan willed Sergius to act. As if he had heard her unspoken command, he drew himself up, extending his arms dramatically. Gone was the weak and sickly man of a few days ago; in his white *camelaucum* and golden robes, he looked imposing, magisterial.

He spoke in Frankish, to be sure Lothar's soldiers would understand. "Behold the hand of God," he intoned solemnly, "which has barred the holiest of His altars against you."

Lothar's men cried out fearfully. The Emperor stood his ground, wary and suspicious.

Now Sergius switched to Latin. *"Si pura mente et pro salute Reipublicae huc advenisti . . .* If you are come with a pure mind and goodwill toward the republic, enter, and welcome; if not, then no earthly power will open these doors to you."

Lothar hesitated, still mistrustful. Had Sergius conjured up a miracle? He doubted it, but he could not be certain: God's ways were mysterious. Besides, his own position was now considerably weakened, for his men were dropping in terror to their knees, their swords slipping from their hands.

With a forced smile, Lothar opened his arms to Sergius. The two men embraced, their lips meeting in the formal kiss of peace. *"Benedictus qui venit in nomine Domini,"* the choir chanted joyously. "Blessed is he who comes in the name of the Lord."

The doors jolted into motion again. As everyone watched, awestruck, the silver-plated panels swung outward until once again they stood full open. Arm in arm, with the joyous sounds of Hosanna ringing in their ears, Sergius and Lothar walked into the basilica to pray before the shrine of the Blessed Apostle.

The difficulties with Lothar were not yet over—explanations still needed to be offered, apologies tendered, advantages negotiated, concessions made. But the immediate danger was past.

Joan thought of Gerold and how amused he would have been to see the use she had made of his hydraulic trick with the door. She pictured him, his indigo eyes alight with humor, his head thrown back in the generous laugh she remembered so well.

Strange, the workings of the heart. One could go on for years, habituated to loss, reconciled to it, and then, in a moment's unwary thought, the pain resurfaced, sharp and raw as a fresh wound.

# 22

Gerold breathed with relief as he and his men descended the final slope of Mt. Cenis. With the Alps behind them, the worst of the journey was over. The Via Francigena stretched ahead, blessedly flat and well kept, for it still retained its ancient paving of stone, laid down by the Romans in a time before memory.

Gerold spurred his horse into a canter. Perhaps now they could make up for time lost. An unseasonably late snowfall had made the narrow Alpine pass extremely treacherous; two men had died when their mounts lost their footing on the slippery ground, plunging horses and riders to their deaths. Gerold had been forced to call a halt until conditions improved; the delay put them even farther behind the vanguard of the imperial army, which must now be drawing close to Rome.

No matter; Lothar would scarcely miss them. This rear division numbered only two hundred men—lordlings and small landholders who had arrived late to the spring muster at the Marchfeld. It was an insulting command for a man of Gerold's stature.

In the three years since the Battle of Fontenoy, Gerold's relationship with Emperor Lothar had gone from bad to worse. Lothar had gradually become more and more tyrannical, surrounding himself with toadying followers who flattered him at every turn. He had absolutely no tolerance for fideles like Gerold, who continued to voice his opinions honestly—as, for example, when he had advised against this current campaign against Rome.

"Our troops are needed on the Frisian coast," Gerold argued, "to defend against the Norsemen. Their raids are becoming more and more frequent—and destructive."

It was true. Last year the Norsemen had attacked St.-Wandrille and

Utrecht; the previous spring they had sailed brazenly down the Seine and burned Paris! This had sent a shock wave of fear over the countryside. If so great a city as Paris, in the very heart of the Empire, was not safe from the barbarians, then no place was.

Lothar's attention, however, was directed toward Rome, which had dared proceed with Pope Sergius's consecration without first asking for his sovereign approval—an omission which Lothar took as a personal affront.

"Send to Sergius and make your royal displeasure known," Gerold advised. "Punish the Romans by withholding payment of the *Rome-feoh*. But let us keep our fighting men here, where they are needed."

Lothar had been enraged at this challenge to his authority. In retaliation, he had assigned Gerold command of the rear division.

They made good progress on the paved road, covering almost forty miles before dusk, but they did not pass a single town or village. Gerold had all but resigned himself to another restless night bedded down by the side of the road when he caught sight of a spiral of smoke circling lazily above the treetops.

*Deo gratias!* There was a village ahead, or at least a settlement of some kind. Now Gerold and his men were assured of a comfortable night's sleep. They had not yet crossed the border into papal lands; the Kingdom of Lombardy, through which they now rode, was imperial territory, and hospitality required that travelers be courteously welcomed—if not to beds in the house, then at least to soft berths of hay in a warm, dry stable.

They rounded a curve and saw that the smoke was not coming from a welcoming hearth fire but from the still-smoldering remains of houses burned to the ground. It must have been a thriving settlement; Gerold made out the blackened outlines of some fifteen buildings. The blaze had probably been started by a chance spark from a carelessly tended lamp or hearth fire; such calamities were not uncommon where houses were built of wood and thatch.

Riding past the blackened timbers, Gerold was reminded of Villaris. It had looked much the same on that long-ago day when he returned to find it burned by the Norsemen. He remembered digging through the rubble searching for Joan, seeking, yet afraid to find. Amazing—it had been fifteen years since he had last seen her, yet her image was imprinted on his mind as if it were yesterday: the crop of white-gold hair that curled beguilingly about her forehead, the full, throaty voice, the deep-set gray-green eyes so much wiser than their years.

He forced her image from his mind. Some things were too painful to dwell upon.

A mile beyond the ruined settlement, at the high cross marking the spot where two roads converged, a woman and five ragged children were begging alms. As Gerold and his men rode up, the little family drew back fearfully.

"Be at peace, good mother," Gerold reassured her. "We mean you no harm."

"Have you any food to spare, lord?" she asked. "For the children's sake?"

Four of the children ran to Gerold, holding their hands out in mute appeal, their small faces tight and anxious with hunger. The fifth, a pretty, black-haired girl some thirteen years of age, hung back and clung to her mother.

Gerold withdrew from his saddlebag the square of oiled sheepskin that held his ration of food for the next few days. There remained a good-sized loaf of bread, a block of cheese, and some dried salt venison. He started to break the loaf in half, then saw the children watching. *Ah, well,* he thought, handing over the whole parcel. *It's only a few more days to Rome; I can get by on the biscuits in the supply wagon.*

With a glad cry, the children fell upon the food like a swarm of starveling birds.

"Are you from the village?" Gerold asked the woman, pointing to the blackened ruin behind them.

The woman nodded. "My husband is the miller."

Gerold hid his surprise. The ragged figure before him appeared to be anything but a prosperous miller's wife. "What happened?"

"Three days ago, after the spring planting, soldiers came. The Emperor's men. They said we had to swear allegiance to Lothar or die immediately by their swords. So of course we swore."

Gerold nodded. Lothar's doubts about this part of Lombardy were not entirely unjustified, for it was a relatively new addition to the Empire, acquired by Lothar's grandfather, the great Emperor Karolus.

"If you took the oath of loyalty," he asked, "how did your village come to be destroyed?"

"They didn't believe us. Liars, they called us, and threw torches onto our roofs. When we tried to put the fires out, they held us back with their swords. Our stores of grain they torched as well, though we begged them not to, for the children's sake. They laughed and called them traitors' spawn, who deserved to starve."

"Villains!" Gerold exclaimed angrily. He had tried many times to convince Lothar that he could not win his subjects' loyalty with the use of force but only through just dealing and the rule of law. As usual, his words had fallen on deaf ears.

"They took all our men," the woman continued, "except the very young and the very old. The Emperor was marching to Rome, they said, and needed men to swell the foot ranks." She started to weep. "They took my husband and two of my sons—the younger is only eleven!"

Gerold scowled. Things had come to a sorry pass when Lothar needed children to fight his battles.

"My lord, what does it mean?" the woman asked anxiously. "Is the Emperor going to make war against the Holy City?"

"I don't know." Until this moment, Gerold had thought Lothar meant only to intimidate Pope Sergius and the Romans with a show of force. But the destruction of this village was an ominous sign; in so vengeful a mood, Lothar was capable of anything.

"Come, good mother," Gerold said. "We will take you with us to the next town. This is no safe place for you and the children."

She shook her head fiercely. "I'll not budge from this spot. How will my husband and sons find us when they return?"

If *they return,* Gerold thought grimly. To the black-haired girl he said, "Tell your mother to come with us, for the sake of the little ones."

The girl stared mutely at Gerold.

"She means no discourtesy, lord," her mother apologized. "She would answer if she could, but she cannot speak."

"Cannot speak?" Gerold said, surprised. The girl looked sound and showed no sign of being simple.

"Her tongue's cut out."

"Great God!" The loss of a tongue was a common punishment for thieves and other miscreants not quick enough to dodge the law's harsh justice. But surely this innocent young girl was guiltless of any crime. "Who did this? Surely it was not—"

The woman nodded grimly. "Lothar's men used her unlawfully, then cut out her tongue so she could not accuse them of the shameful deed."

Gerold was stunned. Such atrocities were to be expected of heathen Norsemen or Saracens—not of the Emperor's soldiers, defenders of Christian law and justice.

Brusquely Gerold gave orders. His men went to the wagons and took out a sack of biscuits and a small barrel of wine, which they placed on the ground before the little family.

"God bless you," the miller's wife said feelingly.

"And you, good mother," Gerold said.

They rode on, passing other plundered and deserted settlements along the way. Lothar had left ruin behind him wherever he passed.

*Fidelis adjutor.* As sworn fidelis to the imperial crown, Gerold was bound in honor to serve the Emperor faithfully. But what honor was there in serving a brute like Lothar? The disregard with which the Emperor cast aside the law and all other standards of human decency surely wiped clean the slate of obligation.

Gerold would lead this rearguard of the imperial army into Rome as he had promised. But afterward, he resolved firmly, he would quit the service of the tyrant Lothar forever.

Beyond Nepi, the road deteriorated. The solid, hard-surfaced highway gave way to a narrow and decaying track, pitted with treacherous crevices and gulleys. The Roman paving was gone, the ancient stones removed and carted off for use in other construction—for such strong building materials were scarce in these dark times. Gerold read the marks of Lothar's passing in the dark earth, deeply rutted with the multiple tracks of wagons and horses. They had to take extra care with the horses, lest they lame themselves with an unlucky step.

During the night, a heavy rainfall turned the road into an impassable sea of mud. Rather than call another halt, Gerold decided to strike out through the open countryside and come round to the Via Palestrina, which would bring them into Rome through the eastern gate of St. John.

They rode swiftly through budding, sweet-scented meadows of gentian and woods sprouting with the gold-green leaves of spring. Emerging from a patch of dense scrub, they suddenly came upon a group of mounted men riding escort around a heavy wagon pulled by four strong cart horses.

"Greetings." Gerold addressed the man who appeared to be their leader, a dark-avised fellow with narrow, puffy eyes. "Can you tell us if we are headed toward the Via Palestrina?"

"You are," the man responded curtly. He turned to ride past.

"If you're bound for the Via Flaminia," Gerold said, "better think again. The road's washed out; your cart will be mired to its axles before you've gone ten yards."

The man said, "We're not headed there."

That was curious. Other than the road, there was nothing in the direction they were headed but deserted countryside. "Where are you going?" Gerold asked.

"I've told you all you need to know," the man snapped. "Ride on and leave an honest merchant to his business."

No ordinary merchant would address a lord so pridefully. Gerold's suspicions were aroused.

"What is your trade?" Gerold rode to the cart. "Perhaps you've something I'd be interested in buying."

"Leave that alone!" the man shouted.

Gerold wrenched the covers back, revealing the contents of the cart: a dozen bronze coffers secured with heavy iron locks, each marked unmistakably with the papal insignia.

*The Pope's men,* Gerold thought. *They must have been sent from the city to transport the papal treasure out of reach of Lothar's clutches.*

He toyed with the idea of commandeering the treasure and bringing it back to Lothar. Then he thought, *No. Let the Romans salvage what they may.* Pope Sergius would no doubt find a better purpose for the money than Lothar, who would only use it to finance more brutal and bloody military campaigns.

He was about to ride on when one of the Romans leapt from his horse and prostrated himself on the ground. "Mercy, lord!" he cried. "Spare us! We must not die unshriven with the weight of this great crime upon our souls!"

"Crime?" Gerold echoed.

"Hold your tongue, fool!" Their leader spurred his horse and would have trampled the other in the dirt, but Gerold intercepted him with drawn sword. Immediately Gerold's men drew their swords and surrounded the Romans, who, observing how greatly they were outnumbered, wisely kept their own blades scabbarded.

"Benedict's the one to blame!" the man on the ground sputtered in a burst of retaliatory anger. "It was his idea to steal the money, not ours!"

*Steal the money?*

The man called Benedict spoke placatingly. "I have no quarrel with you, lord, nor need our petty quarrels concern you. Let us pass in peace, and in token of our gratitude you may have one of these coffers." He smiled at Gerold conspiratorially. "There's gold enough inside to make you a wealthy man."

The offer and the manner of his making it resolved all doubt. "Bind him," Gerold commanded. "And the others. We'll take them and these coffers to Rome with us."

The triclinium was ablaze with the light of a hundred torches. A phalanx of servants stood behind the high table at which Pope Sergius sat, flanked by the high dignitaries of the city: the priests of each of the seven regions of Rome to his left; their temporal counterparts, the seven defensores, to his right. Perpendicular to this table, and just as grand, was another, at which Lothar and his retinue were placed at seats of honor. The rest of the company, some two hundred men altogether, sat on hard wooden benches drawn up before long tables in the middle of the room. Plates, ewers, goblets, and platters crowded together on the tables, whose cloths already carried the marks of innumerable spills and stains.

As it was neither a Wednesday nor a Friday, nor any other fast day, the meal was not confined to bread and fish but included flesh meat and other rich viands. Even for a Pope's table, it was an extraordinary repast: there were platters of capons smothered with white sauce and ornamented with pomegranate and crimson sweetmeats; bowls of soup, filled with tender morsels of rabbit and woodcock swimming in a thick cream, giving off an aromatic steam; jellies of crayfish and loach; whole pigs larded with grease; and huge plates of roasted roe deer, kid, pigeon, and goose. In the center of Lothar's table, a whole cooked swan was displayed as if alive, its gilded beak and silvered body resting upon a mass of greens artfully arranged to appear like waves of the sea.

Seated at one of the tables in the center of the room, Joan cast a worried eye over the extravagant display. Such rich delights might well tempt Sergius into dangerous overindulgence.

"A toast!" The Count of Mâcon rose from his place beside Lothar and raised his cup. "To peace and friendship between our two Christian peoples!"

"Peace and friendship!" everyone chorused, and drained their cups. Servants hurried along the tables, pouring more wine.

There followed a multitude of toasts. When at last they ran out of subjects for liquid tribute, the feasting began.

Joan watched with alarm as Sergius ate and drank with reckless abandon. His eyes began to swell, his speech to slur, his skin to darken ominously. She would have to give him a strong dose of colchicum tonight to prevent a return attack of gout.

The doors to the triclinium opened, and a group of guards marched in. Sidestepping to avoid the innumerable serving boys who scurried nimbly about the room fetching and clearing dishes, the guards made their way briskly to the front of the room. A sudden quiet fell as the guests broke off talking, craning their necks to make out the cause of this extraordinary intrusion. This hush was followed by a murmur of surprise as they caught a glimpse of the man who walked in the midst of the guards with bound hands and lowered eyes: Benedict.

The cheerful circles of Sergius's face collapsed like punctured bladders. "You!" he cried.

Tarasius, the leader of the guards, said, "A troop of Franks found him in the campagna. He had the treasure with him."

Benedict had had a good deal of time on the trip back to Rome to consider his predicament. He could not deny taking the treasure, having been caught in the act. Nor could he think of a plausible excuse for what he had done, though he had racked his brain trying. He finally decided that the best course was to throw himself upon his brother's mercy. Sergius was tenderhearted to the core—a weakness Benedict despised, though now he hoped to use it to his gain.

He dropped to his knees, lifting his bound arms toward his brother. "Forgive me, Sergius. I have sinned, and I repent most humbly and sincerely."

But Benedict had not counted on the effects of the wine on his brother's temper. Sergius's face crimsoned as he swung unexpectedly into rage. "Traitor!" he shouted. "Villain! Thief!" He punctuated each word with a violent thump of his fist on the table, setting the plates clattering.

Benedict paled. "Brother, I beseech you—"

"Take him away!" Sergius ordered.

"Where should we take him, Holiness?" Tarasius asked.

Sergius's head was spinning; it was difficult to think. All he knew was that he had been betrayed, and he wanted to strike back, to wound as he himself had been wounded. "He's a thief!" he said bitterly. "Let him be punished as a thief!"

"No!" Benedict shouted as the guards took hold of him. "Sergius! *Brother!*" The last word was left echoing as he was dragged from the hall.

The color drained from Sergius's face, and he dropped into his chair. His head fell back, his eyes rolled, his arms and legs began to shake uncontrollably.

"It's the evil eye!" someone shouted. "Benedict's put a spell on him!" The guests cried out in consternation, crossing themselves against the workings of the Devil.

Joan raced through the crowded tables to Sergius's side. His face was turning blue. She took hold of his head and pried his clenched jaws open. His tongue was folded back upon itself, blocking the airway. Grabbing a knife from the table, Joan inserted the blunt end into Sergius's mouth, slipping it into the folded loop of tongue. Then she pulled. There was a sucking sound as the tongue flipped forward. Sergius gasped and began to breathe again. Joan pressed down gently with the knife, keeping the airway open. After a moment, the paroxysm subsided. With a muted groan, Sergius went limp.

"Take him to his bed," she ordered. Several serving boys lifted Sergius from his chair and carried him toward the door as the crowd pressed round curiously. "Make way! Make way!" Joan shouted as they bore the unconscious Pope out of the hall.

By the time they reached his bedroom, Sergius was conscious. Joan gave him black mustard mixed with gentian to make him vomit. Afterward he was dramatically improved. She gave him a strong dose of colchicum, just to be safe, mixing in some poppy juice to help him rest soundly.

"He'll sleep till morning," she told Arighis.

Arighis nodded. "You look exhausted."

"I *am* rather tired," Joan admitted. It had been a long day, and she had not yet recovered fully from her weeks of confinement in the dungeon.

"Ennodius and others from the physicians' society are waiting outside. They mean to interrogate you about His Holiness's relapse."

Joan sighed. She did not feel up to fending off a barrage of hostile questions, but apparently there was no help for it. Wearily she started for the door.

"Just a moment." Arighis beckoned her to follow him. At the far side of the room, he moved aside one of the tapestries and pushed on the wall beneath. The wall slid sideways, leaving an opening some two and a half feet wide.

"What on earth?" Joan was astonished.

"A secret passage," Arighis explained. "Built in the days of the pagan Emperors—in case they needed to make a quick escape from their enemies. Now it connects the papal bedroom to the private chapel, so the Apostolic One can enter and pray undisturbed any time of day or night. Come." He took a candle and entered the passage. "This way you can avoid that pack of jackals, at least for tonight."

Joan was touched that Arighis would share his knowledge of the secret passageway; it was a sign of the growing trust and respect between them. They descended a steep circular flight of stairs that leveled out before a wall into which was set a wooden lever. Arighis pulled it, and the wall moved aside, opening a passage. Joan slipped through, and the vicedominus pulled the lever again. The opening disappeared, leaving no trace of its existence.

She was behind one of the marble pillars in the rear of the Pope's private chapel, the Sanctum Sanctorum. Voices sounded near the altar. This was unexpected; no one should be here at this hour of night.

"It's been a long time, Anastasius," one voice said in gruff, heavily accented tones she recognized as Lothar's. He had called the other one Anastasius; that must be the Bishop of Castellum. The two men had obviously withdrawn to the chapel to speak privately. They would not look kindly upon an intruder.

*What should I do?* Joan wondered. If she tried to slip quietly through the door of the chapel, they might see her. Nor could she retrace her steps to the papal chamber; the lever that controlled the secret passage was on the other side of the wall. She would have to stay hidden until the meeting concluded and both men left. Then she could slip out of the chapel unnoticed.

"Most distressing, His Holiness's attack this evening," Lothar said.

Anastasius replied, "The Apostolic One is very ill. He may not live out the year."

"A great tragedy for the Church."

"Very great," Anastasius agreed smoothly.

"His successor must be a man of strength and vision," Lothar said, "a man who can better appreciate the historic . . . understanding between our two peoples."

"You must use all your influence, my liege, to ensure that the next Pontiff is such a man."

"Don't you mean—a man like you?"

"Have you reason to doubt me, Sire? Surely the service I did you at Colmar proved my loyalty beyond all question."

"Perhaps." Lothar was noncommittal. "But times change, and so do men. Now, my lord Bishop, your loyalty is to be put to the test again. Will you support the oath taking, or no?"

"The people will be reluctant to swear loyalty to you, my liege, after the damage your army has visited upon the countryside."

"Your family has the power to change that," Lothar responded. "If you and your father, Arsenius, take the oath, others will follow."

"What you ask is very great. It would require something great in return."

"I know that."

"An oath is only words. The people need a Pope who can lead them back to the old ways—to the Frankish Empire, and to you, my liege."

"I can think of no one better able to do that than you, Anastasius. I shall do everything in my power to see that you are the next Pope."

There was a pause. Then Anastasius said, "The people *will* take the oath, Sire. I will make certain of it."

Joan felt a surge of anger. Lothar and Anastasius had just bartered for the papacy like a pair of merchants at a bazaar. In return for the privileges of power, Anastasius had agreed to hand the Romans over to the Frankish Emperor's control.

There was a knock on the door, and Lothar's servant entered.

"The count has arrived, my liege."

"Show him in. The bishop and I have concluded our business."

A man entered, dressed in a soldier's brunia. He was tall and striking, with long, red hair and indigo eyes.

Gerold.

# 23

A startled cry burst from Joan's lips.

"Who's there?" Lothar asked sharply.

Slowly Joan came out from behind the pillar. Lothar and Anastasius looked at her with astonishment.

"Who are you?" Lothar demanded.

"John Anglicus, my liege. Priest and physician to His Holiness Pope Sergius."

Lothar asked suspiciously, "How long have you been here?"

Joan thought quickly. "Some hours, Sire. I came to pray for His Holiness's recovery. I must have been more tired than I realized, for I fell asleep and only just awoke."

Lothar looked down his long nose disapprovingly. More likely the little priest had been trapped in the chapel when Anastasius and he had entered. There was no place to run and no place to hide. But it scarcely mattered. How much could he have overheard, and, more important, how much understood? Little enough. There could be no danger in the man; he was obviously no one of importance. The best course was to ignore him.

Anastasius had arrived at a different conclusion. Obviously John Anglicus had been eavesdropping, but why? Was he a spy? Not for Sergius, surely, for the Pope lacked the ingenuity to use spies. But if not, then for whom? And why? From now on, Anastasius decided, the little foreign priest would bear close watching.

Gerold was also studying Joan curiously. "You look familiar, Father," he said. "Have we met before?" He peered at her frowningly through the dim light. Suddenly his expression changed; he stared like a man who had just seen a ghost. "My God," he said chokingly. "It can't be . . ."

"You know each other?" Anastasius asked.

"We met in Dorstadt," Joan said quickly. "I studied some years at the cathedral school there; my *sister*"—she emphasized the word ever so slightly—"stayed with the count and his family during that time."

Her eyes flashed Gerold an urgent warning: *Say nothing.*

Gerold recovered his composure. "Of course," he said. "I remember your sister well."

Lothar broke in impatiently. "Enough of this. What have you come to tell me, Count?"

"My message is for your ears alone, my liege."

Lothar nodded. "Very well. The others may leave. We will speak again, Anastasius."

As Joan turned to go, Gerold touched her arm. "Wait for me. I would like to hear more . . . about your sister."

Outside the chapel, Anastasius went his way. Joan waited nervously under the baleful eye of Lothar's steward. The situation was extremely dangerous; one ill-considered word, and her true identity could be revealed. *I should leave now, before Gerold comes out,* she told herself. But she yearned to see him. She stood rooted there by a complex mix of fear and anticipation.

The chapel door opened, and Gerold emerged. "It *is* you, then?" he said wonderingly. "But how—?"

The servant was eyeing them curiously.

"Not here," Joan said. She led him to the little room where she kept her herbs and medicines. Inside, she lit the poppy oil lamps; they flared into life, enclosing the two in an intimate circle of light.

They stared at each other with the wonder of rediscovery. Gerold had changed in the fifteen years since Joan had last seen him; the thick, red hair was traced with gray, and there were new lines around the indigo eyes and wide, sensual mouth—but he was still the handsomest man she had ever seen. The sight of him set her heart hammering.

Gerold took a step toward her. All at once they were in each other's arms, holding on so tightly that Joan could feel the metal rings of Gerold's mail through her thick priest's robe.

"Joan," Gerold murmured. "My dearest, my pearl. I never thought to see you again."

"Gerold." The word blotted out all reasonable thought.

Gently his finger traced the faint scar on her left cheek. "The Norsemen?"

"Yes."

He bent and kissed it gently, his lips warm against her cheek. "They did take you, then—you and Gisla?"

*Gisla*. Gerold must never know, she must never tell him, the horror that had befallen his elder daughter.

"They took Gisla. I—I managed to escape."

He was astonished. "How? And to where? My men and I scoured the countryside looking for you but found no trace."

Briefly she told him what had happened—as much as she could tell in so hurried and constrained a circumstance: her escape to Fulda and acceptance as John Anglicus, the near-discovery of her identity and flight from the abbey, her pilgrimage to Rome and subsequent rise to the position of Pope's physician.

"And in all this time," Gerold said slowly when she had finished, "you never thought to send word to me?"

Joan heard the pain and bewilderment in his voice. "I—I did not think you wanted me. Richild said the idea of marrying me to the farrier's son was yours, that you had asked her to arrange it."

"And you believed her?" Abruptly he released her. "Great God, Joan, had we no better understanding between us?"

"I—I didn't know what to think. You had gone; I could not be certain why. And Richild knew—about us, about what happened at the riverbank. How could she have known, unless you told her?"

"I don't know. I only know that I loved you as I have never loved anyone before—or since." His voice tightened. "I drove Pistis almost beyond endurance on the road home, straining to catch sight of Villaris, for *you* were there, and I was wild with impatience to see you . . . to ask you to be my wife."

"Your wife?" Joan was dumbfounded. "But . . . Richild . . . ?"

"Something happened while I was gone—something that helped me see how empty my marriage was, how vital you were to my happiness. I was returning to tell you that I meant to divorce Richild, and marry you, if you would have me."

Joan shook her head. "So much misunderstanding," she said sorrowfully. "So much gone wrong."

"So much," he replied, "to make up for." He pulled her close and kissed her. The effect was like holding a candle to a wax tablet, dissolving what the years had written. Once again they were standing together in the river behind Villaris in the spring sunshine, young and giddy with new-discovered love.

After a long while he released her. "Listen, my heart," he said huskily. "I'm leaving Lothar's service. I told him so just now, in the chapel."

"And he agreed to let you go?" Lothar did not seem the kind of man to set aside willingly any man's obligation to him.

"At first he was difficult, but I got him to come round in the end. My freedom comes at a price; I've had to surrender Villaris with all its estates. I'm no longer a rich man, Joan. But I have the strength of my two arms, and friends who will stand by me. One of them is Siconulf, Prince of Benevento, whom I befriended when we served together on the Emperor's campaign against the Obodrites. He needs good men around him now, for he's being hard-pressed by his rival Radelchis. Will you come with me, Joan? Will you be my wife?"

Brisk footsteps outside the door jolted them apart. A moment later the door opened and a head peeked in. It was Florintinus, one of the palace notaries.

"Ah!" he said. "There you are, John Anglicus! I've been looking all over for you." He looked sharply from Joan to Gerold and back again. "Am I . . . interrupting anything?"

"Not at all," Joan said quickly. "What can I do for you, Florintinus?"

"I've a terrible headache," he said. "I wondered if you could prepare one of your palliatives for me."

"I'd be happy to," Joan said courteously.

Florintinus lingered by the door, exchanging idle conversation with Gerold while Joan quickly prepared a mixture of violet leaves and willow-bark, decocting it in a cup of rosemary tea. She gave it to Florintinus, and he left at once.

"We can't talk here," she said to Gerold as soon as he was gone. "It's too dangerous."

"When can I see you again?" Gerold asked urgently.

Joan thought. "There's a Temple of Vesta on the Via Appia, just outside of town. I'll meet you there tomorrow after terce."

He took her in his arms and kissed her again, softly at first, then with an intensity that filled her with aching desire. "Till tomorrow," he whispered. Then he went through the door, leaving Joan's head spinning with a dizzying mix of emotions.

Arighis peered sharply through the predawn light, checking the Lateran courtyard. All was in readiness. A lighted brazier had been placed alongside the great bronze statue of the she-wolf. A pair of sturdy fire irons were set inside the flaming brazier, their tips beginning to glow red from the heat of the flames. Nearby stood a swordsman, sharpened blade at the ready.

The first rays of the sun crested the horizon. It was an unusual hour for a public execution; such events normally took place after mass. Despite the earliness of the hour, a crowd of spectators was already gathered—the eager ones always arrived well in advance to secure the best position for viewing. Many had brought their children, who scampered about in excited anticipation of the gory spectacle.

Arighis had deliberately set the hour of Benedict's punishment for dawn, before Sergius awakened and changed his mind. Others might accuse him of proceeding with unseemly haste, but Arighis did not care. He knew exactly what he was doing, and why.

Arighis had held the high office of vicedominus for over twenty years; his entire life had been devoted to the service of the Patriarchium, to keeping the vast and complicated hive of pontifical offices that composed the seat of government in Rome running smoothly and efficiently. Over the years, Arighis had come to think of the papal household as a living entity, a being whose continuing welfare was his sole responsibility and concern.

That welfare was now threatened. In less than a year, Benedict had turned the Patriarchium into a center of corrupt power brokering and simony. Grasping and manipulative to the core, Benedict's very existence was a malignant canker upon the Papacy. The only way to save the patient was to amputate the diseased member. Benedict must die.

Sergius did not have the backbone for the deed, so it fell upon Arighis to shoulder the burden. He did so unhesitatingly, knowing that he acted for the good of Holy Mother Church.

Everything was in readiness. "Bring the prisoner," Arighis commanded the guards.

Benedict was marched in. Clothes rumpled, face drawn and ashen from a sleepless night in the dungeon, he anxiously searched the courtyard. "Where is Sergius?" he demanded. "Where is my brother?"

"His Holiness cannot be disturbed," Arighis said.

Benedict whirled on him. "What do you think you are doing, Arighis? You saw my brother last night. He was drunk; he didn't know what he was saying. Let me talk to him, and you will see: he will reverse the judgment against me."

"Proceed," Arighis commanded the guards.

The guards dragged Benedict to the center of the courtyard and forced him to his knees. They grabbed his arms and pulled them across the pedestal of the statue of the she-wolf so his hands rested levelly on the top.

Terror creased Benedict's face. "No! Stop!" he shouted. Raising his eyes toward the windows of the Patriarchium, he cried out, "Sergius! Sergius! Serg—!"

The sword sliced downward. Benedict screamed as his severed hands dropped to the ground, spurting blood.

The crowd cheered. The swordsman nailed Benedict's severed hands to the side of the she-wolf. According to ancient custom, they would remain there for one month as a warning to others tempted to the sin of thievery.

Ennodius the physician came forward. Pulling the hot irons from the brazier, he pressed them firmly against Benedict's bleeding stumps. The smell of burning flesh rose sickeningly in the air. Benedict screamed again and toppled into a faint. Ennodius bent to attend him.

Arighis leaned forward attentively. Most men died after such an injury—if not immediately from shock and pain then shortly afterward from infection or loss of blood. But some of the strongest managed to survive. One saw them on the streets of Rome, their grotesque mutilations revealing the nature of their crimes: severed lips, those who had lied under oath; severed feet, slaves who'd fled their masters; gouged-out eyes, those who had lusted after the wives or daughters of their betters.

The distressing possibility of survival was the reason Arighis had asked Ennodius and not John Anglicus to attend the condemned man, for the skill of the latter might be great enough to save Benedict.

Ennodius stood. "God's judgment has been rendered," he announced gravely. "Benedict is dead."

*Christ be praised,* Arighis thought. *The papacy is safe.*

Joan stood on line in the *lavatorium,* waiting her turn for the ritual hand washing before mass. Her eyes were swollen and heavy from lack of sleep; all night she had tossed restlessly, her mind filled with thoughts of Gerold. Last night, feelings she believed long buried had resurfaced with an intensity that astonished and frightened her.

Gerold's return had reawakened the disturbing desires of her youth. *What would it be like to live as a woman again?* she wondered. She was accustomed to being responsible for herself, to having complete control of her destiny. But by law a wife surrendered her life to her husband. Could she trust any man so far—even Gerold?

*Never give yourself to a man.* Her mother's words echoed like warning bells in her mind.

She needed time to sort out the turmoil of emotions in her heart. But time was one thing she didn't have.

Arighis appeared beside her. "Come," he said urgently. He pulled her out of line. "His Holiness needs you."

"Is he ill?" Worriedly, she followed Arighis down the corridor to the papal bedroom. Last night's rich food and wine had been purged from Sergius's body, and the strong dose of colchicum Joan had administered should have staved off a return attack of gout.

"He will be if he keeps carrying on as he is."

"Why, what's wrong?"

"Benedict is dead."

"Dead!"

"The sentence was carried out this morning. He died immediately."

*"Benedicite!"* Joan quickened her steps. She could imagine the effect this news would have on Sergius.

Even so, when she saw him she was shocked. Sergius was scarcely recognizable. His hair was disheveled, his eyes red and swollen from weeping, his cheeks covered with scratches where his nails had scored them. He was on his knees beside the bed, rocking back and forth, whimpering like a lost child.

"Holiness!" Joan spoke sharply into his ear. "Sergius!"

He kept on rocking, blind and deaf in an extremity of grief. Clearly there was no way to reach him in his present condition. Taking some tincture of henbane from her scrip, Joan measured out a dose and held it to his lips. He drank distractedly.

After a few minutes, his rocking slowed, then stopped. He looked at Joan as if seeing her for the first time.

"Weep for me, John. My soul is damned for all eternity!"

"Nonsense," Joan said firmly. "You acted in just accordance with the law."

Sergius shook his head. " 'Be not like Cain, who was of the Evil One and murdered his brother,' " he quoted from the First Letter of John.

Joan countered with an answering passage. " 'And why did he murder him? Because his own deeds were evil and his brother's righteous.' Benedict was not righteous, Holiness; he betrayed you and Rome."

"And now he is dead, by my own word! O God!" He struck his chest and howled in pain.

She had to divert him from his grief or he would work himself into another fit. She took him firmly by the shoulders and said, "You must make auricular confession."

This form of the sacrament of penance, in which one made private and regular confession *ad auriculam,* "to the ear" of a priest, was widespread in Frankland. But Rome still held determinedly to the old ways, in which confession and penance were made and given publicly, only once in a lifetime.

Sergius seized on the idea. "Yes, yes, I will confess."

"I'll send for one of the cardinal priests," she said. "Is there someone you prefer?"

"I will make my confession to you."

"Me?" A simple priest and a foreigner, Joan was an unlikely candidate to serve as confessor to the Pope. "Are you sure, Holiness?"

"I want no other."

"Very well." She turned to Arighis. "Leave us."

Arighis shot her a grateful look as he left the room.

*"Peccavi, impie egi, iniquitatem feci, miserere mei Domine . . ."* Sergius began in the ritual words of penitence.

Joan listened with quiet sympathy to his long outpouring of grief, regret, and remorse. With a soul so burdened and tormented, it was no wonder Sergius sought peace and forgetfulness in drink.

The confession worked as she had intended; gradually the wild passion of despair subsided, leaving Sergius drained and exhausted but no longer a danger to himself or others.

Now came the tricky part, the penance that had to precede forgiveness of sin. Sergius would expect his penance to be harsh—public mortification, perhaps, on the steps of St. Peter's. But such an act would only serve to weaken Sergius and the Papacy in Lothar's eyes—and that must be prevented at all costs. Yet the penance Joan imposed must not be too light or Sergius would reject it.

She had an idea. "In token of repentance," she said, "you will abstain from all wine and the meat of four-footed animals from this day forward until the hour of your death."

Fasts were a common form of penance, but they usually lasted only a few months, perhaps a year. A lifetime of abstinence was stern punishment—especially for Sergius. And the penance would have the added benefit of helping protect the Pope from his own worst instincts.

Sergius bowed his head in acceptance. "Pray with me, John."

She knelt beside him. In many ways, he was like a child—weak, impulsive, needful, demanding. Yet she knew he was capable of good. And at this moment, he was all that stood between Anastasius and the Throne of St. Peter.

At the end of the prayer, she rose. Sergius clutched at her. "Don't leave," he pleaded. "I can't be alone."

Joan covered his hand with her own. "I won't leave you," she promised solemnly.

Entering through the crumbling portals of the ruined Temple of Vesta, Gerold saw with disappointment that Joan had not yet arrived. *No matter,* he told himself; *it's early yet.* He sat down to wait with his back against one of the slim granite pillars.

Like most pagan monuments in Rome, the temple had been stripped of its precious metals: the gilt rosettes that had once adorned the coffers of the dome were gone, as were the golden bas-reliefs ornamenting the pediment of the *pronaos.* The niches lining the walls were empty, their marble statues having been carted off to the lime kilns to be turned into building material for the walls of Christian churches. Remarkably, however, the figure of the goddess herself survived, ensconced in her shrine under the dome. One of her hands had broken off, and the lines of her garment were roughened, eroded by time and the elements, but the statue still had remarkable power and grace of form—testimony to the skill of its heathen sculptor.

Vesta, ancient goddess of home and hearth. She represented all that Joan meant to him: life, love, a renewed sense of hope. He breathed deeply, drinking in the damp sweetness of the morning, feeling better than he had in years. He had been low of late, weary of life's stale, unchanging round.

He had resigned himself to it, telling himself it was the inevitable result of his years, for he was nearing forty-three, an old man's age.

Now he knew how wrong he had been. Far from being tired of life, he was hungry for it. He felt young, alive, vital, as if he had drunk from the fabled cup of Christ. The rest of his life stretched ahead bright with promise. He would marry Joan, and they would go to Benevento and live together in peace and love. They might even have children—it was not too late. The way he felt at this moment, anything was possible.

He started up as she came hurrying through the portal, her priest's robes billowing behind her. Her cheeks were rosy from the exertion of her walk; her cropped white-gold hair curled around her face, accentuating her deep-set gray-green eyes, eyes that drew him like pools of light in a darkened sanctuary. How ever had she succeeded in this man's disguise? he wondered. To his knowing eyes, she looked very womanly and wholly desirable.

"Joan." The word was part name, part supplication.

Joan kept a cautious distance between them. If once she let herself into Gerold's arms, she knew her resolve would melt.

"I've brought a mount for you," Gerold said. "If we leave now, we'll be at Benevento in three days' time."

She took a deep breath. "I'm not going with you."

"Not going?" Gerold echoed.

"I cannot leave Sergius."

For a moment he was too taken aback to say anything. Then he managed to ask, "Why not?"

"Sergius needs me. He is . . . weak."

"He's Pope of Rome, Joan, not a child in need of coddling."

"I don't coddle him; I doctor him. The physicians of the schola have no knowledge of the disease that afflicts him."

"He survived well enough before you came to Rome."

It was gentle mockery, but it stung. "If I leave now, Sergius will drink himself to death within a six-month."

"Then let him," Gerold answered harshly. "What has that to do with you and me?"

She was shocked. "How can you say such a thing?"

"Great God, haven't we sacrificed enough? The spring of our lives is already behind us. Let's not squander the time that is left!"

She turned away, so he would not see how much this affected her.

Gerold caught her by the wrist. "I love you, Joan. Come with me, now, while there's still time."

The touch of his hand warmed her flesh, sparking desire. She had a treacherous impulse to embrace him, to feel his lips on hers. Embarrassed by these weak and shameful feelings, she was suddenly, unreasonably angry with Gerold for having aroused them. "What did you expect?" she cried. "That I would run off with you the first moment you beckoned?" She let the wave of anger rise and crest within her, submerging her other, more dangerous emotions. "I've made a life here—a good life. I've independence and respect, and opportunities I never had as a woman. Why should I give it all up? What for? To spend the rest of my days confined to a narrow set of rooms, cooking and embroidering?"

Gerold said in a low voice, "If that's all I wanted in a wife, I'd have married long before now."

"Do so, then!" Joan retorted hotly. "I'll not stop you!"

A knot of bewilderment appeared between Gerold's brows. He asked gently, "Joan, what has happened? What's wrong?"

"Nothing is wrong. I've changed, that's all. I'm no longer the naive, lovesick girl you knew in Dorstadt. I'm my own master now. And I won't give that up—not for you, not for any man!"

"Have I asked you to?" Gerold responded reasonably.

But Joan did not want to hear reason. Gerold's nearness and her strong physical attraction to him were a torment, a snake coiled tightly around her will, strangling it. Savagely she tried to break its hold. "You cannot accept it, can you? The idea that I'm not willing to give up my life for you? That I'm one woman who's actually immune to your masculine charms?"

She had sought to wound, and she had succeeded.

Gerold stared at her as though he saw something new written upon her face. "I thought you loved me," he said stiffly. "I see I was mistaken. Forgive me; I'll not trouble you again." He went to the portal, hesitated, turned back. "This means we will never see each other again. Is that really what you want?"

*No!* Joan felt like crying. *It's not what I want! It's not what I want at all!* But another part of her cautioned her to hold back. "That's what I want," she said. Her voice sounded curiously distant in her own ears.

One more word of love and need from him, and she would have broken and run to his arms. Instead he wheeled abruptly and went through the portal. She heard him racing down the temple steps.

In another moment he would be gone forever.

Joan's heart rose like a cup filled to overbrimming. Then the cup tilted, spilling forth all her pent-up emotion.

She ran to the door. "Gerold!" she cried. "Wait!"

The loud clatter of hooves against stones drowned out her cry. Gerold rode swiftly down the road. A moment later he rounded a corner and was gone.

# 24

The Roman summer arrived with a vengeance. The sun beat down relentlessly; by midday, the cobblestones were hot enough to blister a man's feet. The stench of rotting garbage and manure, intensified by the heat, rose into the still air and hung over the city like a suffocating pall. Pestilential fevers raged among the poor who lived in the damp and decaying tenements lining the low-lying banks of the Tiber.

Fearful of contagion, Lothar and his army quit the city. The Romans rejoiced at their departure, for the burden of maintaining so large a host had strained the city's resources to the limit.

Sergius was hailed as a hero. The adulation of the people helped soften his grief over Benedict's death. Buoyed by newfound health and energy—gained in large measure from the spartan diet Joan had imposed in penance—Sergius was a man transformed. True to his promise, he began rebuilding the Orphanotrophium. The crumbling walls were reinforced, a new roof added. Tiles of fine travertine marble were stripped from the pagan Temple of Minerva and used to line the floor of the great hall. A new chapel was constructed and dedicated to St. Stephen.

Where previously Sergius had frequently been too tired or ill to say Mass, he now celebrated the holy service every morning. In addition, he was often to be found praying in his private chapel. He threw himself into his faith with the same fervor with which he had once pursued the pleasures of the table—for he was not a man to do things by halves.

Two years of mild winters and plentiful harvests resulted in a time of general prosperity. Even the legions of poor who crowded the streets of the city seemed a little less wretched, as the pockets of their more prosperous brethren loosened and almsgiving increased. The Romans offered prayers of thanksgiving at the altars of their churches, well content with their city and their Lord Pope.

They did not suspect—how could they?—the catastrophe that was about to descend upon them.

Joan was with Sergius during one of his regular meetings with the princes of the city when a messenger burst in upon them.

"What's this?" Sergius inquired sternly.

"Holiness." The messenger knelt in obeisance. "I bring a message of utmost importance from Siena. A large fleet of Saracen ships has set sail from Africa. They are on a direct course toward Rome."

"Toward Rome?" one of the princes echoed thinly. "Surely the report is mistaken."

"There is no mistake," the messenger said. "The Saracens will be here within a fortnight."

There was a moment of silence while everyone took in this astonishing news.

Another of the princes spoke. "Perhaps it would be wise to remove the holy relics to a place of greater safety?" He was referring to the bones of the apostle Peter, the most sacred relics in all of Christendom, which lay housed in their namesake basilica outside the protection of the city walls.

Romuald, the greatest of the assembled princes, threw back his head and laughed. "You don't think the infidels would attack St. Peter's!"

"What's to prevent them?" Joan asked.

"They may be barbarians, but they're not fools," Romuald replied. "They know the hand of God would smite them flat the moment they set foot inside the sacred tomb!"

"They have their own worship," Joan pointed out. "They do not fear the hand of our Christian God."

Romuald's smile died. "What heathen blasphemy is this?"

Joan stood her ground. "The basilica is an obvious target for plunder, if only for the treasure that lies within. For safety's sake, we should bring these sacred objects and the saint's sarcophagus within the city walls."

Sergius was doubtful. "We've had other such warnings before, and nothing came of them."

"Indeed," Romuald said mockingly, "if we took fright at every sighting of a Saracen ship, the sacred bones would have been moving back and forth like a pair of shuttles on a loom!"

A burst of appreciative laughter was instantly cut off by the Pontiff's disapproving frown.

Sergius said, "God will defend His own. The Blessed Apostle will remain where he is."

"At least," Joan urged, "let us send to the outlying settlements, asking for men to help defend the city."

"It's pruning time," Sergius said. "The settlements need every able-bodied man to work in the vineyards. I see no need to risk the harvest, upon which all depend, when there is no immediate danger."

"But, Holiness—"

Sergius cut her off. "Trust in God, John Anglicus. There is no stronger armor than that of Christian faith and prayer."

Joan bowed her head in submission. But inside she thought rebelliously: *When the Saracens are at the gates, all the prayer in the world will not help half so much as a single division of good fighting men.*

Gerold and his company were encamped just outside the town of Benevento. Within their tents the men were sleeping soundly after a long night of ribaldry—a boon Gerold had granted in reward for their resounding victory the day before.

For the past two years Gerold had commanded Prince Siconulf's armies, fighting to secure Siconulf's throne against the ambitious pretender Radelchis. A skilled commander who pushed his men hard while they were learning discipline and proficiency at arms, then trusted them to give good account of themselves on the field, Gerold had inflicted defeat after defeat on Radelchis's forces. Yesterday's victory was so resounding it had probably put an end to Radelchis's claim to the Beneventan throne forever.

Although armed sentries were posted all around the camp, Gerold and his men slept with swords and shields at their sides, where they were always ready at hand. Gerold took no chances, for an enemy could be dangerous even after defeat. The heat of revenge often drove men to rash and desperate action. Gerold knew of many encampments taken by surprise, their inhabitants slaughtered before they even had time to wake.

At the moment, however, such thoughts were far from Gerold's mind. He lay supine, arms behind his head, legs splayed carelessly. Beside him a woman covered in his cloak breathed soddenly, a rhythmic sound broken by occasional bursts of snoring.

In the light of dawn Gerold regretted the brief gust of passion that had brought her into his bed. There had been other such transient encounters over the years, each less satisfying and more forgettable than the one before. For Gerold still cherished in his heart the memory of a love that could never be forgotten.

He shook his head impatiently. It was idle to dwell upon the past. Joan had not shared his feelings, or she would not have sent him away.

The woman rolled onto her side. Gerold touched her shoulder and she woke, opening pretty brown eyes that stared back at him without depth or meaning.

"It's morning," Gerold said. He took a few coins from his scrip and handed them to her.

She jingled them and smiled happily. "Shall I come again tonight, my lord?"

"No, that won't be necessary."

She looked disappointed. "Didn't I please you?"

"Yes, yes, of course. But we're breaking camp tonight."

A short while later he watched her cross the field, her sandals slapping dully against the dry grass. Overhead the cloudy sky was lightening into a flat and pallid gray.

Soon it would again be day.

Siconulf and his chief fideles were already gathered in the great hall when Gerold entered. Dispensing with the usual courtesies, Siconulf announced abruptly, "I have just received word from Corsica. Seventy-three Saracen ships have set sail from the African coast. They are carrying some five thousand men and two hundred horse."

An astonished silence followed. So large a fleet was scarcely imaginable.

Eburis, one of Siconulf's fideles, gave a low whistle. "Whatever they intend, it's more than just another piratical raid upon our coast."

"They have set course for Rome," Siconulf said.

"Rome! Surely not!" said another of the fideles.

"Preposterous!" scoffed a third. "They'd never dare!"

Gerold scarcely heard them. His thoughts were racing ahead. "Pope Sergius will need our help," he said tautly.

But it was not Sergius he was thinking of. With a single stroke, the news of the approach of the Saracen fleet had erased all the bitter hurt and misunderstanding of the past two years. Only one thing mattered—to reach Joan and do everything within his power to protect her.

"What do you suggest, Gerold?" Siconulf asked.

"My prince, let me lead our troops to Rome's defense."

Siconulf frowned. "Surely the Holy City has defenders of her own."

"Only the *familia Sancti Petri*—a small and undisciplined group of papal militia. They will fall like summer wheat before the Saracens' blades."

"What about the Aurelian Wall? Surely the Saracens cannot breach it?"

"The wall seems strong enough," Gerold admitted. "But several of its gates are poorly reinforced. They won't withstand a sustained assault. And the tomb of St. Peter is entirely unprotected, for it lies outside the wall."

Siconulf considered this. He was reluctant to commit his troops to a cause other than his own. But he was a Christian prince, with a proper reverence for the Holy City and its sacred places. The idea of barbarian infidels defiling the Apostle's tomb was appalling. Besides, it occurred to him now that there might be some personal benefit in sending men to Rome's defense. Afterward, a grateful Pope Sergius might reward him with one of the rich papal patrimonies that bordered Siconulf's territory.

He said to Gerold, "You may have three divisions of troops. How long will you need to prepare to march?"

"The troops are battle hardened and ready. We can leave at once. If the weather holds, we'll be in Rome in ten days' time."

"Let us pray that will be sufficient. God go with you, Gerold."

In Rome, an eerie sense of calm prevailed. Since the initial warning from Siena two weeks before, there had been no further word of the Saracen fleet. The Romans gradually began to relax their vigilance, convincing themselves that the reports of an enemy fleet had been false, after all.

The morning of August 23 dawned bright with promise. The stational mass was held at the Cathedral of Sancta Maria ad Martyres, known in pagan days as the Pantheon, one of the loveliest of Rome's churches. It was an especially beautiful service, with the sun filtering through the circular opening in the basilica's great domed roof, casting a golden glow over the entire congregation. Returning to the Patriarchium, the choir joyously chanted, *"Gloria in excelsis Deo."*

The song died on their lips as they entered the sun-dazzled piazza of the Lateran and saw a crowd of citizens milling anxiously round a weary and mud-stained messenger.

"The infidels have landed," the messenger announced grimly. "The town of Porto is taken, its people slaughtered and its churches defiled."

"Christ aid!" someone cried.

"What will become of us?" wailed another.

"They will kill us all!" a third shouted hysterically.

The crowd threatened to break into a dangerous disorder.

"Silence!" Sergius's voice rang above the uproar. "Cease this unworthy display!" The voice of authority cut commandingly through the din, compelling obedience.

"What," he said, "are we sheep, to cower so? Are we babes, to think ourselves defenseless!" He paused dramatically. "No! We are Romans! And this is Rome, protectorate of St. Peter, key bearer of the Kingdom of Heaven! 'Thou art Peter,' Christ has said, 'and upon this rock shall I build my church.' Why should you fear? Will God suffer His sacred altar to be defiled?"

The crowd stirred. Scattered voices cried out in response: "Yes! Listen to the Lord Pope! Sergius is right!"

"Have we not our guards and our militia?" With a sweep of his arm, Sergius indicated the papal guards, who obliged by raising their lances and shaking them fiercely. "The blood of our ancestors runs in their veins; they are armed with the strength of Omnipotent God! Who shall prevail against them?"

The crowd let out a ragged cheer. Rome's heroic past was still a source of pride, the military triumphs of Caesar and Pompey and Augustus the common knowledge of every citizen.

Joan watched Sergius in wonderment. Could this heroic figure be the same ailing, ill-tempered, disheartened old man she had encountered two years ago?

"Let the infidels come!" Sergius cried. "Let them hurl their weapons against this sacred fortress! They will crack their hearts against our God-protected walls!"

Joan felt the excitement, the swelling crest that rose thrillingly and broke upon the crowd in a roiling tumult of emotion. Her own feet were too firmly planted in reality to be so easily swept away. *The world is not as we would have it,* she thought, *no matter how skillfully we may conjure it.*

The crowd were on their feet, heads lifted, faces aglow. All around Joan excited voices reverberated in unison: "Sergius! Sergius! Sergius! Sergius!"

At Sergius's command, the people spent the next two days fasting and praying. The altars of all the churches shone brightly, lit with a profusion of votive candles. Miracles were everywhere reported. The golden statue of the Madonna at the Oratory of St. Cosmas was said to have moved her eyes and sung a litany. The crucifix above the altar of St. Hadrian had shed tears of blood. These miracles were interpreted as signs of divine blessing and favor. Day and night the sound of *Hosanna* rang out from churches and monasteries, as the clergy of the city rose to the Lord Pope's challenge and prepared to meet the enemy with the invincible strength of their Christian faith.

Shortly after dawn on August 26, the cry came down from the walls. "They're coming! They're coming!"

The terrified shrieks of the people penetrated even the thick stone walls of the Patriarchium.

"I must go to the parapets," Sergius announced. "When the people see me, they will know they have nothing to fear."

Arighis and the other optimates protested, arguing that it was far too dangerous, but Sergius was adamant. In the end they reluctantly led him to the wall, careful to choose a place where the stones rose somewhat higher, affording better protection.

There was a great cheer as Sergius ascended the steps. Then all eyes turned toward the west. A great cloud of dust rose shimmering in the air. The Saracens emerged from it at a rapid gallop, their loose garments flapping behind them like the wings of giant birds of prey. A terrible war cry rang out, a long, high ululation that rose and hung shuddering in the air, sending a chill of terror down the spines of all who stood listening.

*"Deo, juva nos,"* one of the priests said tremblingly.

Sergius raised a small, gem-encrusted crucifix and cried, "Christ is our Savior and our Shield."

The city gates opened, and the papal militia marched out bravely to meet the enemy. "Death to the infidel!" they shouted, waving their swords and spears.

The opposing armies collided with a great noise of clashing steel, louder than the din of a thousand smiths. In minutes, it became evident the battle was hopelessly unequal; the Saracen cavalry rode straight over the front ranks of the Roman foot soldiers, cutting and slashing with their curved scimitars.

The militia in the rear could not see the slaughter up front. Still convinced of victory, they thronged forward, pushing against the backs of those before them. Line after line of men were driven relentlessly onto the Saracens' swords and fell, their bodies creating a treacherous stumbling ground for those who came after.

It was a massacre. Broken and terrified, the militia retreated in desperate disorder. "Run!" they screamed as they scattered across the field like seeds of grain before a wind. "Run for your lives!"

The Saracens did not trouble to pursue them, for their victory had gained them a much greater prize: the unprotected basilica of St. Peter. They surrounded it in a dark swarm. They did not dismount but rode their horses straight up the steps and through the doors in a great flying wedge.

Behind the walls, the Romans waited breathlessly. A minute passed. Then another. No thunderclap split the sky, no sea of flame poured from the heavens. Instead, the unmistakable noise of rending wood and metal issued from the basilica. The Saracens were pillaging the sacred altar.

"It cannot be," Sergius whispered. "Dear God, it cannot be."

A band of Saracens emerged from the basilica, waving the golden cross of Constantine. Men had died, it was said, simply for daring to touch it. Yet now the Saracens tossed it about mockingly, laughing as they pumped it up and down between their legs in obscene and beastly parody.

With a muted groan, Sergius dropped the crucifix and sank to his knees.

"Holiness!" Joan rushed to him.

He grimaced in pain, pressing one hand to his chest.

*A seizure of the heart,* Joan thought in alarm. "Take him up," she commanded. Arighis and several of the guards lifted the stricken Pope, cradling him in their arms, and carried him into a nearby house, where they laid him down on a thick straw mattress.

Sergius's breath was coming in labored gasps. Joan prepared an infusion of hawthorn berries and valerian root and gave it to him. It seemed to ease him, for his color improved and he began to breathe more easily.

"They're at the gates!" People were screaming outside. "Christ aid! They're at the gates!"

Sergius tried to raise himself from the bed, but Joan eased him back. "You must not move."

The effort had cost him; he pressed his lips together tightly. "Speak for me," he pleaded. "Turn their minds toward God. . . . Help them . . . Prepare them . . ." His mouth worked agitatedly, but no words came.

"Yes, Holiness, yes," Joan agreed. Clearly nothing else would pacify him. "I will do as you say. But now you must rest."

He nodded and lay back. His eyelids fluttered and closed as the medicine began to take effect. There was nothing to do now but let him sleep and hope the medicine would do its work.

Joan left him under the solicitous eye of Arighis and went out onto the street.

A rending noise, loud as a thunderclap, sounded close by. Joan started in fear.

"What's happening?" she called to a passing group of guards.

"The idolatrous swine are battering at the gate!" a guard called back as they marched past.

She returned to the piazza. Terror had driven the crowd into a frenzy. Men yanked the hairs violently from their beards; women shrieked and tore their cheeks with their nails till the blood ran. The monks of the Abbey of St. John knelt together in a solid clump, black cowls fallen from their heads, arms uplifted to Heaven. Several of their number tore off their robes and began to scourge themselves with split canes of wood in a frenzied attempt to propitiate the evident wrath of God. Frightened at this alarming display, children began to wail, their high-pitched voices threading reedily through the mad, discordant chorus.

*Help them,* Sergius had pleaded. *Prepare them.*

But how?

Joan climbed the steps to the wall. Picking up the crucifix Sergius had dropped, she thrust it aloft for all to see. The sun caught its gems, sparking a golden rainbow of light.

*"Hosanna in excelsis,"* she began loudly. The high, clear notes of the holy canticle rang out over the crowd, strong and sweet and sure. The people nearest the wall raised tear-streaked faces toward the familiar sound. Priests and monks joined their voices in the song, kneeling on the cobbled stones beside masons and seamstresses. *"Christus qui venit nomine Domini . . ."*

There was another great crash, followed by the sound of splintering wood. The gates gave an inward heave. Light filtered through where a narrow crack had been opened.

*Dear God,* Joan thought. *What if they break through?* Until this moment such a possibility had seemed unthinkable.

Memory flooded her. She saw the Norsemen bursting through the doors of the cathedral at Dorstadt, swinging their axes. She heard the awful screams of the dying . . . saw John lying with his head crushed in . . . and Gisla . . . Gisla . . .

Her voice trembled into stillness. The people looked up in alarm. *Go on,* she told herself, *go on,* but her mind seemed frozen; she could not remember the words.

*"Hosanna in excelsis."* A deep baritone sounded beside her. It was Leo, Cardinal Priest of the Church of the Sancti Quattro Coronati. He had climbed up beside her on the wall. The sound of his voice jolted her from her fear, and together they went on with the canticle.

"God and St. Peter!" A loud cry resounded from the east.

The guards on the walls were jumping up and down, cheering, shouting, "God be praised! We are saved!"

She looked over the wall. A great army was galloping toward the city, its fluttering banners emblazoned with the emblems of St. Peter and the cross.

The Saracens dropped their battering rams and ran for their mounts.

Joan squinted into the sun. As the troops drew nearer, she gave a sudden, sharp cry.

At the head of the vanguard, his lance already poised for the throw, tall and fierce and heroic as one of her mother's ancient gods, rode Gerold.

The ensuing battle was sharp and savage. The attack of the Beneventans had caught the Saracens offguard; they were driven back from the city walls and forced to retreat through the campagna all the way to the sea. At the coast, the infidels hauled their stolen treasure aboard their ships and set sail. In their haste to depart, they left great numbers of their brethren behind. For weeks Gerold and his men rode up and down the coast, hunting down scattered bands of the marauders.

Rome was saved. The Romans were torn between joy and despair—joy at their deliverance, despair at the destruction of St. Peter's. For the sacred basilica had been plundered beyond recognition. The ancient gold cross on the tomb of the Apostle was gone, as was the great silver table with the relief of Byzantium, given by Emperor Karolus the Great. The infidels had torn silver entablatures from the doors and gold plates from the floor. They had even—God darken their eyes!—carried away the high altar itself. Unable to remove the bronze coffin containing the body of the Prince of the Apostles, they had broken it open, scattering and defiling the sacred ashes.

All Christendom was plunged into grief. The footprints of the ages had been preserved within the previously undesecrated doors of this oldest and greatest of Christian temples. Untold generations of pilgrims, including the world's greatest princes, had prostrated themselves humbly upon its sacred pavement. Scores of Popes rested within its walls. The reverence of the West knew no more sacred spot. Yet this sanctuary of the True Faith, which neither Goths, nor Vandals, nor Greeks, nor Lombards had ever dared to defile, had fallen before a brigand horde from Africa.

Sergius blamed himself for the catastrophe. He withdrew to his rooms, refusing admittance to anyone save Joan and his closest advisers. And he took to drink again, downing cup after cup of Tuscan wine until at last he slipped into merciful oblivion.

The drinking had a predictable effect: his gout returned with a vengeance; to ease the pain, he drank even more. He slept badly. Night after night he woke screaming, tormented by nightmarish dreams in which he was visited by the vengeful specter of Benedict. Joan feared the strain this was putting on his already weakened heart.

"Remember the penance to which you agreed," she reminded him.

"It doesn't matter now," Sergius replied despondently. "I have no hope of Heaven. God has abandoned me."

"You must not blame yourself for what happened. Some things are beyond all mortal power to remedy or prevent."

Sergius shook his head. "The soul of my murdered brother cries out against me! I have sinned, and this is my punishment."

"If you will not think of yourself," Joan argued, "think of the people! Now, more than ever, they look to you for consolation and guidance."

She said it to hearten him, but the truth was otherwise. The people had turned against Sergius. There had been sufficient warning of the Saracens' approach, they said, plenty of time for the Lord Pope to have transported the holy sarcophagus inside the walls. Sergius's faith in God's deliverance, which at the time had been universally praised, was now universally condemned as the result of a sinful and disastrously mistaken pride.

*"Mea culpa,"* Sergius responded, weeping. *"Mea maxima culpa."*

Joan reasoned and scolded and cajoled, to no avail. Sergius's health deteriorated rapidly. Joan did everything she could for him, but it was no use. Sergius had set his mind on death.

Nevertheless, the dying took some time. Long after reason had departed and he had lapsed into unconsciousness, Sergius lingered, his body reluctant to relinquish the final spark of life. On a dark and sunless morning he finally died, his spirit slipping away so quietly that at first no one noticed the passing.

Joan genuinely mourned him. He had not been as good a man or a Pope as he might have been. But she had known, better than anyone else, what demons he had faced, had known how hard he had fought to free himself from them. That he had lost the fight in the end made the struggle no less honorable.

He was buried in the damaged basilica beside his predecessors, with a minimum of ceremony that bordered on the scandalous. The required days of mourning were barely observed, for the Romans had already turned their minds impatiently toward the future—and the election of a new Pope.

Anastasius stepped out of the blustering January winds into the welcoming warmth of his family's ancestral palace. It was the grandest residence in all of Rome, save of course the Patriarchium, and Anastasius was justly proud of it. The vaulted ceiling of the reception hall rose over two stories and was constructed of pure white marble from Ravenna. Its walls were painted with brightly colored frescoes of scenes from the lives of the family ancestors. One depicted a consul making a speech before the Senate; another a general seated on a black charger, rallying the troops; still another a cardinal receiving the pallium from Pope Hadrian. A panel of the front wall had been left blank in anticipation of the long-awaited day when the family would finally achieve its greatest honor: the coronation of one of its sons as Pope.

Usually the hall was the scene of bustling activity. Today, but for the presence of the family steward, it stood empty. Scorning to acknowledge the steward's effusive greeting—for Anastasius never wasted time on underlings—he went directly to his father's room. Arsenius would normally have been in the great hall at this hour, engaged with the city's notables in the devious and gratifying politics of power. But last month he had been stricken by a wasting fever that had drained his formidable energies, confining him to his room.

"My son." Arsenius rose from his couch at Anastasius's entrance. He looked gray and frail. Anastasius felt a curious, exhilarating surge of strength, his own youth and energy somehow enhanced by contrast with his father's diminishing powers.

"Father." Anastasius went to him with arms stretched wide, and they embraced warmly.

"What news?" Arsenius asked.

"The election is set for tomorrow."

"God be praised!" Arsenius exclaimed. It was just an expression. Though he held the exalted title of Bishop of Orte, Arsenius had not taken priest's orders and was not a religious man. His appointment to the bishopric had been a politic acknowledgment of the enormous power he wielded in the city. "The day cannot come too soon when a son of mine will sit upon the Throne of St. Peter."

"That outcome may no longer be as certain as we once thought, Father."

"What do you mean?" Arsenius asked sharply.

"Lothar's support of my candidacy may not be enough. His failure to defend Rome against the Saracens has turned many against him. The people question why they should pay homage to an Emperor who does not protect us. There's a growing sentiment that Rome should assert her independence from the Frankish throne."

Arsenius considered this carefully. Then he said, "You must denounce Lothar."

Anastasius was aghast. His father's mind, always so sharp and discerning, was obviously slipping.

"If I did that," he responded, "I'd lose the support of the imperial party, upon which our hopes depend."

"No. You will go to them and explain that you are acting strictly out of political necessity. Reassure them that no matter what you may be compelled to say, you are indeed the Emperor's man, and will prove it after your election with the award of valuable benefices and preferments."

"Lothar will be furious."

"By that time, it won't matter. We'll move directly to the ceremony of consecration after the election, without waiting for the imperial jussio. Under these circumstances no one will protest, for Rome obviously cannot remain leaderless one day longer than necessary under the continuing threat of the Saracens. By the time Lothar receives word of what has transpired, you'll be Lord Pope, Bishop of Rome—and there'll be nothing the Emperor can do to change it."

Anastasius shook his head admiringly. His father had taken measure of the situation at once. The old fox might be graying, but he had not lost any of his subtlety.

Arsenius held out a long iron key. "Go to the vaults and take what gold you need to win their minds to you. Damn!" he swore. "But for this God-cursed fever, I'd do it myself."

The key lay cool and hard in Anastasius's hand, imparting a gratifying sense of power. "Rest yourself, Father. I will take care of it."

Arsenius caught him by the sleeve. "Be careful, my son. It's a dangerous game you're playing. You have not forgotten what happened to your uncle Theodorus?"

Forgotten! The murder of his uncle in the Lateran Palace had been the defining moment of Anastasius's childhood. The look on Theodorus's face as the papal guards gouged out his eyes would haunt Anastasius till the day he died.

"I'll be careful, Father," Anastasius said. "Leave everything to me."

"Precisely," replied Arsenius, "what I intend."

*Ad te, Domine, levavi animam meam* . . . Joan prayed, kneeling on the cold stone of the Patriarchium chapel. But no matter how hard she prayed, she could not rise into the light of grace; the strong pull of a mortal attachment kept her rooted here below.

She loved Gerold. There was no longer any point in trying to evade or deny that simple truth. When she had seen him riding toward the city at the head of the Beneventan troops, her whole being had rushed toward him with a powerful conviction.

She was thirty-three years old. Yet she had no one to whom she was intimately connected. The practical realities of her disguise had not permitted anyone to get too close. She had been living a life of deceit, denying the truth of who she was.

Was this why God withheld His blessed grace? Did He want her to abandon her disguise and live the woman's life to which she had been born?

Sergius's death had freed her from any obligation to remain in Rome. The next Pope would be Anastasius, and there would be no place for Joan in his administration.

She had fought her feelings for Gerold for so long. What a blessed relief it would be just to let go, to follow the dictates of her heart and not her head.

What would happen when she and Gerold met again? She smiled inwardly, imagining the joy of that moment.

Anything was possible now. Anything might happen.

By noon on the appointed day of the election, a great crowd had gathered in the large open area to the southwest of the Lateran. According to ancient custom, formally affirmed in the constitution of 824, all Romans, lay and clergy, participated in the election of a new Pope.

Joan stood on tiptoe, straining to see over the tossing sea of heads and arms. Where was Gerold? Rumor had it that he had returned from his monthlong campaign against the Saracens. If so, he should be here. She was gripped with a sudden fear—had he gone back to Benevento without seeing her again?

The crowd parted respectfully as Eustathius, the archpriest, Desiderius, the archdeacon, and Paschal, the primicerius, came into the marketplace: the triumvirate of officials who by tradition ruled the city *sede vacante,* meaning in the interregnum between the death of one Pope and the election of another.

Eustathius led the people in a short prayer. "Heavenly Father, guide us in what we do here today, that we may act with prudence and honor, that hatred shall not destroy reason, and love shall not interfere with truth. In the Name of the holy and indivisible Trinity of the Father, Son, and Holy Spirit. Amen."

Paschal spoke next. "The Lord Pope Sergius having gone to God, it falls to us to elect his successor. Any Romans here assembled may speak and voice what sentiments God has inspired in them, that the general will may thereby be determined."

"My Lord Primicerius." Tassilo, the leader of the imperial faction and one of Lothar's agents, spoke up immediately. "One name commends itself above all others. I speak of Anastasius, Bishop of Castellum, son of the illustrious Arsenius. All the qualities of this man's nature commend him for the throne—his noble birth, his extraordinary scholarship, his indisputed piety. In Anastasius we will have a defender not only of our Christian faith but of our private interests as well."

"Of *your* interests, you mean!" a voice called mockingly from the crowd.

"Not at all," Tassilo retorted. "Anastasius's generosity and large-heartedness will make him a true father to you all."

"He's the Emperor's man!" the heckler cried again. "We want no tool of the Frankish throne for our Lord Pope!"

"That's right! That's right!" Several voices rose in vigorous agreement.

Anastasius ascended the platform. He raised his arms in a dramatic gesture, quieting the crowd. "My fellow Romans, you judge me wrongly. The pride of my noble Roman ancestors runs as strongly in my veins as in yours. I bend my knee before no Frankish overlord!"

"Hear, hear!" his supporters cheered enthusiastically.

"Where was Lothar when the infidel was at our gates?" Anastasius continued. "In failing to answer our need, he forfeited the right to call himself 'Protector of the Lands of St. Peter!' As Lothar's rank is exalted, I owe him honor; as he is a fellow Christian, I owe him courtesy, but my fealty is first and always to Mother Rome!"

He had spoken well. His supporters cheered again, and this time they were joined by others in the crowd. The tide of opinion was shifting toward Anastasius.

"It's a lie!" Joan cried. All around faces turned toward her in startled surprise.

"Who speaks?" Paschal peered into the crowd. "Let the accuser come forward."

Joan hesitated. She had spoken without thinking, sparked to anger by Anastasius's hypocrisy. But there was no backing out now. Boldly she mounted the platform.

"Why, it's John Anglicus!" someone said. A murmur of recognition swept the crowd; everyone knew or had heard of Joan's brave stand at the walls during the Saracen attack.

Anastasius blocked her way. "You have no right to address this assembly," he said. "You're not a Roman citizen."

"Let him speak!" a voice called out. Others took up the cry until at last Anastasius was forced to stand aside.

Paschal said, "Speak your accusation openly, John Anglicus."

Squaring her shoulders, Joan said, "Bishop Anastasius made compact with the Emperor. I overheard him promise to lead the Romans back to the Frankish throne."

"False priest!" "Liar!" The members of the imperial party began shouting in an attempt to drown her out.

Raising her voice over them, she described how she had overheard Lothar ask for Anastasius's help in getting the people to take the oath of loyalty, and how Anastasius had agreed in return for Lothar's support.

"This is a grave accusation," Paschal said. "What say you to it, Anastasius?"

"Before God the priest is lying," Anastasius said. "Surely my countrymen will not believe the word of a foreigner over that of a fellow Roman!"

"You *were* the first to support the oath taking!" someone called out.

"What of it?" countered another. "That proves nothing!"

A good deal of bickering followed. The debate grew heated, the mood of the crowd shifting first one way, then another as speaker after speaker rose to support or condemn Anastasius.

"My lord Primicerius!" Arighis, who until then had not spoken, came forward.

"Vicedominus." Paschal acknowledged Arighis respectfully, though with some surprise. Devoted and loyal servant to the papal throne that he was, Arighis had never meddled in politics. "Have you aught to add to this debate?"

"I do." Arighis turned to address the crowd. "Citizens of Rome, we are not free from danger. When spring comes, the Saracens may attempt another assault upon the city. Against this threat we must stand united. There can be no division among us. Whomever we choose for our Lord Pope, it must be one upon whom all can agree."

A murmur of assent swept through the crowd.

"Is there such a man?" Paschal asked.

"There is," Arighis replied. "A man of vision and strength, as well as learning and piety: Leo, Cardinal Priest of the Church of the Sancti Quattro Coronati!"

The suggestion was met with profound silence. So intent had they all been on debating the merits of Anastasius's candidacy, they had not stopped to consider anyone else.

"Leo's bloodlines are as noble as Anastasius's," Arighis went on. "His father is a respected member of the Senate. He has performed his duties as cardinal priest with distinction." Arighis saved his most telling point for last: "Can any of us forget how he stood bravely at the walls during the Saracen attack, rallying our spirits? He is a lion of God, another St. Lawrence, a man who can, who *will* protect us from the infidel!"

The exigency of the moment had spurred Arighis into uncharacteristic eloquence. Responding to the depth of his feeling, many in the crowd broke into a spontaneous cheer.

Sensing opportunity, the members of the papal faction took up the cry. "Leo! Leo!" they shouted. "We will have Leo for our lord!"

Anastasius's supporters mounted a countereffort on behalf of his candidacy. But the sentiment of the crowd had clearly changed. When it became apparent to the imperial faction that they could not carry the day, they swung their support to Leo. With one voice, Leo was proclaimed Lord and Pope.

Borne forward triumphantly on the shoulders of his countrymen, Leo ascended the platform. He was a short but well-formed man still in the prime of his years, his strong Roman features set off by a thick growth of curly brown hair and an expression that suggested intelligence and humor. With a sense of solemn occasion, Paschal prostrated himself before him and kissed his feet. Eustathius and Desiderius immediately followed suit.

All eyes turned expectantly toward Anastasius. For a fraction of a second he hesitated. Then he forced his knees to bend. Stretching himself full length upon the ground, he kissed the Pope-elect's feet.

"Rise, noble Anastasius." Leo offered him his hand, helping him to his feet. "From this day forth, you are Cardinal Priest of St. Marcellus." It was a generous gesture; St. Marcellus was among the greatest of Rome's churches. Leo had just presented Anastasius with one of the most prestigious sinecures in Rome.

The crowd cheered its approval.

Anastasius forced his lips into a smile as the bitter taste of defeat settled like dry ashes in his mouth.

✦ ✦ ✦

*"Magnus Dominus et laudibilis nimis."* The notes of the introit filtered through the window of the small room where Joan kept her medicaments. Because St. Peter's lay in ruins, the ceremony of consecration was being held in the Lateran Basilica.

Joan should have been in church with the rest of the clergy, witnessing the joyous coronation of a new Pope. But there was much to do here, hanging the new-picked herbs to dry, refilling jars and bottles with their appropriate medicines, setting things in order. When she was done, she scanned the shelves with their neatly stacked rows of potions, herbs, and simples—tangible testimony to all she had learned of the healing art. With a twinge of regret, she realized she would miss this little workshop.

"I thought I might find you here." Gerold's voice sounded behind her. Joan's heart gave a sudden leap of joy. She turned toward him, and their eyes met.

*"Tu,"* Gerold said softly.

*"Tu."*

They beamed at each other with the warmth of reestablished intimacy.

"Strange," he said, "I almost forgot."

"Forgot?"

"Each time I see you I . . . discover you all over again."

She went to him, and they held each other tenderly, gently.

"The things I said the last time we were together . . . ," she murmured, "I didn't mean—"

Gerold put a finger to her lips. "Let me speak first. What happened was my fault. I was wrong to ask you to leave; I see that now. I didn't understand what you have accomplished here . . . what you have become. You were right, Joan—nothing I can offer you could possibly compare."

*Except love,* Joan thought. But she didn't say it. She said simply, "I don't want to lose you again."

"You won't," Gerold said. "I'm not returning to Benevento. Leo has asked me to remain in Rome—as superista."

Superista! It was an extraordinary honor, the highest military position in Rome: commander in chief of the papal militia.

"There's work to do here—important work. The treasure the Saracens plundered from St. Peter's will only encourage them to try again."

"You think they will come back?"

"Yes." To any other woman Gerold would have lied reassuringly. But Joan was not like any other woman. "Leo is going to need our help, Joan—yours and mine."

"Mine? I don't see what I can do."

Gerold said slowly, "You mean no one has told you?"

"Told me what?"

"That you are to be nomenclator."

*"What?"* She could not have heard aright. The nomenclator was one of the seven optimates, or highest officials, of Rome—the minister of charity, protector of wards, widows, and orphans.

"But . . . I'm a foreigner!"

"That doesn't matter to Leo. He's not a man to be bound by senseless tradition."

She was being offered the opportunity of a lifetime. But accepting it would also mean the end of any hope of a life with Gerold. Torn by opposing desires, Joan did not trust herself to speak.

Misinterpreting her silence, Gerold said, "Don't worry, Joan. I'll not trouble you again with proposals of marriage. I know now we can never be together in that way. But it will be good to work together again, as we once used to. We were always a good team, weren't we?"

Joan's mind was whirling; everything was coming out so differently from the way she had imagined. Her voice, when she answered, was a whisper. "Yes. We were."

*"Sanctus, Sanctus, Sanctus."* The words of the sacred hymn reached their ears through the open window. The ceremony of consecration had concluded; the Canon of the Mass was about to begin.

"Come." Gerold held out his hand. "Let us go together to greet our new Lord Pope."

# 25

The new Pontiff took up his duties with a youthful vigor that caught everyone by surprise. Overnight, it seemed, the Patriarchium was transformed from a dusty monastic palace into a bustling hive. Notaries and secretaries hurried down the halls, arms filled with rolls of parchment plans, statutes, cartularies, and benefices.

The first order of business was to fortify the city's defenses. At Leo's behest, Gerold undertook a thorough circuit of the walls, making careful note of every point of weakness. Following his suggestions, plans were drawn up and the work of repairing the walls and gates of the city began. Three of the gates and fifteen of the wall towers were completely rebuilt. Two new towers were constructed on opposite banks of the Tiber where the river entered the city at the gate of Portus. Chains of reinforced iron were strategically connected to each opposing tower; when the chains were stretched across the river, they formed an impassable barrier to ships. The Saracens would not be able to gain entry to the city by *that* means at least.

There still remained the difficult question of how to protect St. Peter's. To consider the problem, Leo convened a meeting of the high clergy and the optimates, including Gerold and Joan.

Several suggestions were put forth: posting a permanent garrison of militia around the basilica, enclosing its open portico, fortifying the doors and windows with bars of iron.

Leo listened without enthusiasm. "Such measures will only serve to delay a forced entry, not prevent it."

"With respect, Holiness," Anastasius said, "delay *is* our best defense. If we can hold the barbarians back until the Emperor's troops arrive—"

"*If* they arrive . . . ," Gerold interrupted dryly.

"You must trust in God, Superista," Anastasius rebuked him.

"Trust in Lothar, you mean," Gerold said. "And I do not."

"Pardon me, Superista," Anastasius said with exaggerated politeness, "for pointing out the obvious, but there is really nothing else we *can* do at the moment, since the basilica lies outside the city walls."

Joan said, "We can bring it inside."

Anastasius's dark brows arched sardonically. "What do you propose, John—moving the entire building stone by stone?"

"No," Joan replied. "I propose extending the city walls around St. Peter's."

"A new wall!" Leo's interest was sparked.

"Wholly impractical!" scoffed Anastasius. "So great a project has not been undertaken since the days of the ancients."

"Time, then," Leo said, "for another."

"We haven't the funds!" Gratius, the arcarius, or papal treasurer, protested. "We could bankrupt the entire treasury, and the work still wouldn't be half done!"

Leo considered this. "We will raise new taxes. After all, it is only fitting that the new wall, which will serve for the protection of all, should be completed with the help of all."

Gerold's mind was already racing ahead. "We could begin construction here"—he pointed to a map of the city—"by the Castel Sant'Angelo. Run the wall sideward up the Vatican Hill"—he traced an imaginary line with his finger—"circle it round St. Peter's, and bring it down in a straight line to the Tiber."

The horseshoe-shaped line Gerold had drawn enclosed not only St. Peter's and the monasteries and *diaconae* surrounding it but also the entire Borgo, in which were located the teeming settlements of the Saxons, Frisians, Franks, and Lombards.

"It's like a city of its own!" Leo exclaimed.

"Civitas Leonina," Joan said, "the Leonine City."

Anastasius and the others looked on with chagrin as Leo, Gerold, and Joan beamed in happy conspiracy.

After weeks of consultation with the master builders of the city, the design for the wall was completed. It was an ambitious project. Formed of layers of tufa and tiles, the wall would stand a full forty feet high and twelve feet wide and be defended by no fewer than forty-four towers—a barrier that could withstand even the most determined siege.

In response to Leo's call, workers poured into the city from every town and colony of the papal campagna. They crowded into the hot and overcrowded tenements of the Borgo, straining the city's resources to the breaking point. Loyal and eager though they were, they were untrained, undisciplined workers, and their efforts proved difficult to organize. They showed up each day uncertain what to do, for there were not enough skilled builders to supervise their efforts. On the ides of May, an entire section of wall unexpectedly collapsed, killing several of the workers.

The clergy, led by the cardinal priests of the city, pleaded with Leo to abandon the project. The collapse of the wall was a clear indication of God's disfavor, they argued. The whole idea was folly; so tall a structure would never stand, and even if it did, it would never be completed in time to defend against the Saracens. Far better to direct the people's energies toward solemn prayer and fasting to turn aside the wrath of God.

"We will pray as if all depended on God, and work as if all depended on ourselves," Leo replied sturdily. Every day he rode out to check on the progress of the building and to urge the workers on. Nothing could deter him from his determination to see the wall completed.

Joan admired Leo's stubborn defiance of the skeptics. Utterly different from Sergius in character and temperament, Leo was a true spiritual leader, a man of drive and energy and enormous strength of will. But Joan's admiration for him was not shared by everyone. Sentiment in the city was divided between those who approved of the wall and those who opposed it. It soon became apparent that Leo's continued ability to govern was going to depend very much on the successful completion of the wall.

Anastasius was well aware of the situation and the opportunity it presented. Leo's obsession with the wall left him dangerously vulnerable. If the project proved a failure, the resulting popular disapproval might provide Anastasius with just the opportunity he needed. His supporters in the imperial party could march to the Lateran, remove the discredited Pope from office, and install their candidate in his place.

Once he was Pope, Anastasius would protect the holy basilica of St. Peter by renewing and strengthening Rome's ties to the Frankish throne. Lothar's armies would prove a far better defense against the infidel than Leo's impractical wall.

But, Anastasius reminded himself, he must tread cautiously. Best not to take an open stand against Leo, not while people were still waiting to see the end result of the Pontiff's daring enterprise.

The wisest course was to support Leo publicly while doing all he could to bedevil the building project. To this end, Anastasius had already managed to arrange for the collapse of a section of wall. It had not been difficult; a few of his most trusted men had stolen out in the night and undermined the foundation with a bit of surreptitious digging. But the collapse had proved to be only a minor setback. Clearly something more was needed—a disaster of sufficient proportion to put an end to the whole ridiculous project once and for all.

Anastasius's mind twisted this way and that, seeking a way to strike. Again and again he came up without an idea. He fought a rising frustration. If only he could reach down with a giant hand, pluck the entire structure off the ground, and cast it into the flames of Hell with one great, irrefutable stroke.

The flames of Hell . . .

Anastasius sat bolt upright, energized by the sudden appearance of an idea.

Joan woke to the new day slowly. For a moment she lay confused, staring at the unfamiliar configuration of wooden beams on the ceiling. Then she remembered: this was not the dormitory, but her own private quarters—one of the privileges of her exalted position as nomenclator. Gerold had also been awarded private quarters in the Patriarchium but had not slept there for several weeks, choosing instead to stay at the Schola Francorum in the Borgo, to be nearer the ongoing work on the wall.

Joan had seen him from a distance, riding around the construction site encouraging the workers or bending over a table discussing plans with one of the master builders. They had no opportunity to exchange anything more than a passing glimpse. Yet her heart rose excitedly each time she saw him. *Truly*, she thought, *this woman's body of mine is a traitor.*

With a deliberate effort, she fixed her attention on the day's work and the duties that awaited her.

The light of dawn was already coming through the window. With a start of surprise, she realized she must have overslept. If she didn't hurry, she would be late to her meeting with the head of St. Michael's hospice.

As she swung out of bed, she became aware that the light coming into her room was not the dawn. It could not be the dawn, for the window faced west.

She ran to the window. Behind the dark silhouette of the Palatine Hill, on the far side of the city, ribbons of red and orange light streamed into the moonless sky.

Flames. And they were coming from the Borgo.

Without pausing to slip into her shoes, Joan ran barefoot through the halls. "Fire!" she shouted. "Fire! Fire!"

Doors were thrown open as people spilled excitedly into the hall. Arighis came toward her, rubbing the sleep from his eyes.

"What's all this?" he demanded sternly.

"The Borgo is on fire!"

*"Deo, juva nos!"* Arighis made the sign of the cross. "I must wake His Holiness." He hurried off toward the papal bedroom.

Joan ran down the stairs and out the door. It was harder to see from here, for the numerous oratories, monasteries, and clergy houses surrounding the Patriarchium obscured the view, but she could tell the fire had spread, for the entire night sky was now illuminated with lurid brilliance.

Others were following Joan out to the portico. They fell to their knees, weeping and calling upon God and St. Peter. Then Leo appeared, bareheaded and in a simple tunic.

"Fetch the guard," he ordered a chamberlain. "Rouse the stableboys. Have them make ready every available horse and cart." The boy ran off to carry out his orders.

The horses were led up, restive and irritable at having been dragged from the comfort of their stables in the middle of the night. Leo mounted the foremost, a bay.

Arighis was aghast. "You do not mean to go yourself?"

"I do," Leo replied, taking up the reins.

"Holiness, I must object! It's far too dangerous! Surely it would be more fitting for you to remain here and lead a mass for deliverance!"

"I can pray just as well outside the walls of a church as within," Leo replied. "Stand aside, Arighis."

Reluctantly, Arighis complied. Leo spurred the bay and took off down the street. Joan and several dozen guards mounted and followed close behind.

Arighis frowned after them. He wasn't much of a rider, but his place was at the Pope's side. If Leo was bent upon this foolish course, then it was Arighis's duty to accompany him. He mounted awkwardly and set off after them.

They rode at a gallop, their torches reflecting wildly off the walls of the houses, their shadows chasing one another down the dark streets like demented ghosts. As they drew near the Borgo, the acrid smell of smoke rose to their nostrils, and they heard a great roar like the bellowing of a thousand wild beasts. Rounding a corner, they saw the fire straight ahead.

It was a scene out of Hell. The entire block was aflame, shrouded in a solid sheet of fire. Through a shimmering red haze, the wooden buildings writhed in the grip of the flames that consumed them. Silhouetted sharply against the fire, the figures of men capered about like the tortured souls of the damned.

The horses whinnied and backed away, tossing their heads. A priest came running toward them through the lowering smoke, his face smeared with sweat and soot.

"Holiness! Praise God you are come!" By his accent and manner of dress, Joan knew him for a Frank.

"Is it as bad as it looks?" Leo asked tersely.

"As bad, and worse," the priest replied. "The Hadrianium is destroyed, and the hospice of St. Peregrinus. The foreign settlements are gone as well—the Schola Saxonum is burned to the ground, along with its church. The houses of the Schola Francorum are in flames. I barely got out with my life."

"Did you see Gerold?" Joan asked urgently.

"The superista?" The priest shook his head. "He slept on one of the upper floors with the masons. I doubt if any of them got out; the smoke and fire spread too quickly."

"What about the survivors?" Leo asked. "Where are they?"

"Most have taken refuge in St. Peter's. But the fire is everywhere. If it isn't stopped, the basilica itself may be in jeopardy!"

Leo held out his hand. "Come with us; that's where we're headed now." The priest leapt up behind him on the bay, and they all rode off in the direction of St. Peter's.

Joan did not follow. She had a different thought in mind: to get to Gerold.

The line of fire rose solid and unbroken before her. No way to get through there. She circled around until she came to a line of blackened, ruined streets through which the fire had already passed, and turned down one that led in the direction of the Schola Francorum.

Scattered individual fires still burned on either side, and the smoke grew thicker. Fear tightened her throat, but she forced herself to go on. Her roan shied and fought, unwilling to advance; she shouted and kicked him, and he leapt forward skittishly. She passed through a landscape of horror—shriveled stumps of trees, hollowed skeletons of houses, charred and blackened bodies of those trapped in the act of fleeing. Joan's heart twisted within her; surely nothing living could have survived this holocaust.

Suddenly, improbably, the walls of a building rose before her. The Schola Francorum! The church and the buildings nearest it had been reduced to ashes, but wondrously, miraculously, the main residence still stood.

Her heart beat with renewed hope: perhaps Gerold *had* escaped! Or perhaps he was still inside, injured, needing help.

The roan stopped stiff, refusing to go farther. She kicked him again; this time he reared defiantly, tossing her to the ground. Then he took off at a wild gallop.

She lay stunned, the wind knocked out of her. Beside her lay a human corpse, shiny and black as melted obsidian, its back arched in the death agony. Gagging, she rose and ran toward the schola. She had to find Gerold; nothing else mattered.

Great burning pieces of ash were everywhere, on the ground, on her clothes, in her hair, suspended around her in a heavy, choking cloud. Hot embers scorched her bare feet; too late, she regretted not having put on her shoes.

The door to the schola came into view. Another few yards and she would be there. "Gerold!" she shouted. "Where are you?"

Wild and ungovernable as the wind that whipped it, the fire shifted direction, depositing a scatter of burning embers on the shingled roof, already dry as tinder from the fire's first passage. The embers glowed darkly and then caught; moments later, the whole building burst into flame.

Joan felt the hair on her scalp lift and fall in a violent rush of scorching air. The fire reached toward her with scalding tongues.

"Gerold!" she screamed again, driven back by the advancing flames.

Gerold had stayed up late into the night, poring over plans for the wall. When at last he snuffed out his candle, he was so exhausted he fell immediately into a deep and dreamless sleep.

He woke to the smell of smoke. *A lamp must be foundering,* he thought, and stood to put it out. The first breath he drew seared his lungs with a pain that drove him to his knees gasping for air. *Fire. But where is it coming from?* The thick smoke made it impossible to see more than a few feet in either direction.

The terrified cries of children sounded nearby. Gerold crawled in their direction. Frightened faces swam toward him in the darkness—two children, a boy and a girl, no more than four or five years old. They ran to him and clung, wailing piteously.

"It's all right." He pretended a confidence he did not feel. "We'll soon be out of here. Have you ever played horse-and-rider?"

The children nodded, wide-eyed.

"Good." He swung the girl onto his back, then the boy. "Hold on now. We're going to ride out."

He moved awkwardly with the added weight of the children on his back. The smoke had become even thicker; the children gasped and choked. Gerold fought a rising fear. Many victims of a fire died with no mark upon them, the breath stopped in their throats by smothering smoke.

Suddenly he was aware that he had lost his bearings. His eyes searched the darkness but could not make out the door in the ever-thickening smoke.

"Gerold!" A voice called through the choking gloom.

Bending low to get the best of the air, he lurched blindly toward the sound.

Before the walls of St. Peter's, a pitched battle was being waged against the advancing fire. A crowd had gathered to defend the threatened basilica—black-robed monks from the neighboring monastery of St. John and their cowled counterparts from the Greek monastery of St. Cyril; deacons, priests, and altarboys; prostitutes and beggars; men, women, and children from all the foreign scholae of the Borgo—Saxons, Lombards, Englishmen, Frisians, and Franks. Lacking any central coordination, the efforts of these disparate groups were largely ineffectual. They were making a chaotic attempt to locate vessels and jars and fetch back water from nearby wells and cisterns. A single well was surrounded with a great crowd of people while another stood entirely deserted. Shouting in a confusing variety of tongues, people pushed and shoved to get their vessels filled; jars collided and broke, spilling precious water on the ground. In the course of the struggle, the dipping beam of a well was broken; the only way to retrieve its water was to climb down the well shaft and pass the bucket up—a process so time consuming it was quickly abandoned.

"To the river! To the river!" people shouted, heading downhill to the Tiber. In the fear and confusion, some took off empty-handed, realizing only when they reached the riverbank that they had nothing to carry water in. Others brought enormous jars that, when filled with water, proved too heavy for their strength; halfway up the hill, they dropped them, weeping with grief and frustration.

In the midst of this chaos, Leo stood before the doors of St. Peter, as solid and immovable as the stones of the great basilica itself. People took heart from his presence. As long as their Lord Pope was here, all was not lost; there was still hope. So they kept battling the flames that moved forward inexorably as a tide, driving the line of sweating, straining firefighters relentlessly backwards.

To the right of the basilica, the library of the monastery of St. Martin was aflame; scraps of flaming parchment blew out the open windows and, borne by the wind, landed on the roof of St. Peter's.

Arighis tugged at Leo's sleeve. "You must leave now, Holiness, while there's still time."

Ignoring him, Leo continued praying.

*I'll call the guards,* Arighis thought desperately. *I'll have them carry him off by force.* As vicedominus he had the authority to do so. He hovered in tortured indecision. Could he bring himself to defy the Apostolic One, even to save him?

He spied the danger coming before anyone else. A great piece of silken altar cloth blew out through the burning walls of the monastery in a curling rope of fire. The wind caught it, straightening it into a blazing arrow headed straight for Leo.

Arighis hurled himself at Leo and pushed him out of the way. A moment later, the altar cloth slapped Arighis full in the face, searing his eyes, wrapping itself around his head and body in a white-hot caress. In an instant, his clothes and hair were on fire.

Blind and deafened by the flames, he ran leaping down the basilica steps until his legs gave way and he fell. In the last terrible moments while his body burned but his brain remained sharply aware, Arighis suddenly understood: this was his destiny, this the sacrificial moment toward which his entire life had been directed.

"Christ Jesus!" he screamed as the unspeakable pain pierced through to his heart.

The cloud of smoke lifted a little, and Gerold saw the open door ahead. Beyond it, Joan's image shimmered in the heated air, her white-gold hair a shining halo in the firelight. With a final effort, Gerold heaved himself and the children upright and lurched through the door.

Joan saw him emerge from the smoky haze and ran toward him. She helped the sobbing children down and held them close to her own body, while her eyes remained fixed on Gerold, who stood swaying, unable to speak or move.

"Thank God," she said simply.

But the message in her eyes spoke so much more.

They left the children in the care of a group of nuns and hurried to the basilica, where Gerold saw at once that the firefighters were stationed in the wrong place; they were battling the blaze at close range.

Gerold took command. He ordered the men to fall back a safe distance and create a firebreak by uprooting bushes, twigs, and everything that would burn, then spading over the grass and watering the earth down.

Seeing the sparks showering down upon the basilica, Joan seized a bucket of water from a passing monk and climbed up onto the roof. Others followed her: two, then four, then ten. They formed a human chain, passing full buckets up from below and returning empty buckets to be filled. Pass, pour, pass, fill, pass, pour, pass, fill—they toiled side by side, arms aching with the effort, clothes and faces smeared with grime, open mouths gasping for breath in the smothering air.

On the ground below them, the fire crept closer, flames slicking across grass that blackened in an instant. Gerold and the men labored desperately to increase the area of the firebreak.

On the steps of the basilica, Leo made the sign of the cross, his face turned imploringly to the heavens. "O Lord God," he prayed. "Hear us now as we cry out unto Thee!"

The advancing fire reached the break line. The flames swelled, girding to leap forward over the denuded ground. Gerold and his men attacked with more buckets of water. The flames hesitated, drew back hissing angrily, then began to consume themselves.

The basilica was saved.

Joan felt the wet welcome of tears on her face.

The first several days after the fire were spent burying the dead—those whose bodies could be found. The intense heat of the fire had reduced many of its victims to charred bones and ashes.

Arighis, as befitted his high position, was laid to rest with solemn ceremony. After a funeral mass in the Lateran, his body was interred in a crypt in a small chapel near the tombs of Popes Gregory and Sergius.

Joan mourned his loss. She and Arighis had not always gotten along, especially in the beginning, but they had come to respect each other. She would miss his quiet efficiency, his uncanny knowledge of every detail of the complicated inner workings of the Patriarchium, even the aloof pride with which he had carried out the duties of his office. It was fitting that he would now rest for all eternity near the Apostolic Ones, whom he had served with such devotion.

After the required days of mourning were observed, the grim accounting of the damage done by the fire began. The Leonine Wall, where the blaze had apparently started, had sustained only minor damage, but some three-quarters of the Borgo had been completely destroyed. The foreign settlements and their churches had been reduced to little more than blackened rubble.

That the Basilica of St. Peter had survived the holocaust was nothing short of a miracle—as it quickly came to be regarded. Pope Leo had stayed the fire, it was said, by making the sign of the cross against the advancing flames. This version of events was eagerly taken up by the Roman people, who were badly in need of reassurance that God had not turned against them.

They found an affirmation of their faith in Leo's miracle, fervently attested to by everyone who had been there. Indeed, the number of witnesses grew with every passing day, until it seemed that all of Rome must have been at St. Peter's that fateful morning.

All criticism of Leo was forgotten. He was a hero, a prophet, a saint, the living embodiment of the spirit of St. Peter. The people rejoiced in him, for surely a Pope who had worked such a miracle would be able to protect them from the Saracen infidels.

The rejoicing was not, however, universal. When word of Leo's miracle reached the Church of St. Marcellus, the doors were immediately closed and barred. All baptisms were postponed, all appointments abruptly canceled; those who inquired were told that no one could be admitted to the presence of Cardinal Priest Anastasius, for he was suddenly indisposed.

Joan was working day and night, distributing clothing, medicine, and other supplies to the hospices and charitable homes in the city. The hospices were crowded with casualties of the fire, and there were too few physicians to tend them all, so she lent a hand wherever she could. Some burned and blackened bodies were past healing; there was little she could do for them but administer doses of poppy, mandragora, and henbane to ease their death agonies. Others had disfiguring burns that threatened to become infected; to these she applied poultices of honey and aloe, known specifics for burns. Still others, whose bodies were untouched by fire, suffered from having breathed in too much smoke. These lingered in torment, fighting for life with every shallow breath.

Shattered by the cumulative effect of so much horror and death, Joan was again afflicted by a crisis of faith. How could a good and benevolent God let such a thing happen? How could He so terribly afflict even children and babies, who were surely not guilty of any sin?

Her heart was troubled as the shadow of her ancient doubt fell upon her once again.

One morning she was meeting with Leo to arrange for the papal storehouses to be thrown open to the victims of the fire when Waldipert, the new vicedominus, entered unexpectedly. He was a tall, bony man whose pale skin and blond hair revealed his Lombard ancestry. Joan found it odd to see this stranger in Arighis's robes of office.

"Holiness," Waldipert said with an obeisance, "there are two citizens without who seek immediate audience."

"Have them wait," Leo replied. "I will hear their petition later."

"Pardon, Holiness," Waldipert persisted. "I believe you should hear what they have to say."

Leo raised an eyebrow. Had it been Arighis, Leo would have accepted his word without question, for Arighis's judgment had been known and trusted, but Waldipert was new and untried; unfamiliar as yet with the limitations of his position, he might be clumsily overreaching himself.

Leo hesitated, then decided to give Waldipert the benefit of the doubt. "Very well. Admit them."

Waldipert bowed and left, returning moments later with a priest and a boy. The priest was dark complexioned and squarely built. Joan recognized him as a stalwart of the faith, one of the many who toiled in honorable and impoverished obscurity in the lesser churches of Rome. The boy appeared by his dress to be in one of the minor orders—a lector, or perhaps an acolyte. He was a well-made youth, fifteen or sixteen years old, compact and comely with large, open eyes that must have normally radiated a cheerful good-naturedness, though at the moment they were clouded with grief.

The newcomers prostrated themselves before Leo.

"Rise," Leo said. "Tell us on what business you have come."

The priest spoke first. "I am Paul, Holiness, by God's grace and yours priest of the house of St. Lawrence in Damasco. This boy, Dominic, came to the chapel today requesting auricular confession, which service I was glad to render. What he told me was so shocking that I brought him here to tell it to you."

Leo frowned. "The privacy of such confessions may not be violated."

"Holiness, the boy comes here willingly, for he is in great distress of mind and spirit."

Leo turned to Dominic. "Is this true? Speak honestly, for there is no shame in refusing to repeat the secrets of the confessional."

"I want to tell you, Lord Father," the boy replied tremblingly. "I *must* tell you, for my soul's sake."

"Go on, then, my son."

Dominic's eyes blurred with tears. "I didn't know, Holy Father!" he burst out. "I swear on the relics of all the saints I didn't know what would happen, or I would never have done it!"

"Done what, my son?" Leo asked gently.

"Set the fire." The boy broke into a torrent of violent sobs.

There was a stunned silence, broken only by the sound of Dominic's crying.

"*You* set the fire?" Leo asked quietly.

"I did, and may God forgive me!"

"Why would you do such a thing?"

The boy swallowed his tears, struggling to master himself. "He told me the building of the wall was a great evil, for the money and time being squandered on it would be put to better use repairing churches and relieving the misery of the poor."

"He?" Leo said. "Did someone order you to set the fire?"

The boy nodded.

*"Who?"*

"My Lord Cardinal Anastasius. Lord Father, he must have had the Devil's tongue in him, for he spoke so convincingly that what he said seemed right and good."

There was another long silence. Then Leo said seriously, "Be careful of what you say, my son. You are certain it was Anastasius who commanded you?"

"Yes, Lord Father. It was to be only a small blaze," Dominic said in a strangled voice, "just enough to burn the scaffolding on the wall. God knows it was easy enough—I soaked a few rags in lamp oil and wedged them under a corner of the scaffolding, then set them alight. At first the fire stayed confined to the scaffolding, just as my lord cardinal had said it would. But then the wind came up and took it and—and—" He dropped weakly to his knees. "Oh, God!" he cried in sick despair. "The innocent blood! I'd not do it again, not if a thousand cardinals commanded me!"

The boy cast himself at Leo's feet. "Help me, Lord Father. Help me!" He raised his tormented face. "I cannot live with what I've done. Pronounce me my penance; I will bear any death, no matter how terrible, for my soul would be clean again!"

Joan stood stock-still, transfixed between horror and pity. To the list of Anastasius's crimes must surely be added the evil perversion of this boy's nature. His simple, honest-hearted soul had never been meant to commit such a crime, nor to bear its heavy weight on his conscience.

Leo laid a hand on the boy's head. "There has been death enough already, my son. What benefit to the world would there be in adding yours to the tally? No, Dominic, the penance I impose upon you is not death, but life—a life spent in atonement and penitence. From this day forward, you are banished from Rome. You will take the pilgrim road to Jerusalem, where you may pray before the Holy Sepulchre for divine forgiveness."

The boy raised bewildered eyes. "Is that all?"

"The road to atonement is never easy, my son. You will find the journey hard enough."

That, Joan thought, remembering her own pilgrimage from Frankland to Rome, was truer than young Dominic could possibly understand. He would have to live out his days far from his native land, separated from family and friends, from all that he had ever known. Along the way to Jerusalem he would have to brave a host of dangers—precipitous mountains and treacherous gorges, roads infested with thieves and brigands, starvation and thirst and a thousand other perils.

"Spend your life in unselfish service to your fellow men," Leo went on. "In all things conduct yourself in such a way that the scale of your good deeds may yet outweigh this one great evil."

Dominic flung himself to the ground and kissed the hem of Leo's robe. Then he rose, pale and resolute, his face transformed as if washed by a heavenly rain. "I am bound by you, Lord Father. I will do all exactly as you have commanded. I swear it by the sacred Body and Blood of Christ our Savior."

Leo made a sign of blessing over him. "Go in peace, my son."

Dominic and the priest left the room.

Leo said gravely, "Cardinal Anastasius comes from a powerful family; we must do everything in strict accordance with the law. I will draw up a writ specifying the charges against him. John, come with me; I may need your help. And, Waldipert—"

"Yes, Holiness?"

Leo nodded approval at him. "Well done."

"You've done well to bring me this news, Vicedominus," said Arsenius. He was in a private room of his palace with Waldipert, who had just finished reporting the details of the meeting between Pope Leo and the boy Dominic. "Allow me to express my gratitude for your help."

Arsenius unlocked a small bronze chest that stood upon his desk, took out twenty gold solidi, and handed them to Waldipert, who quickly pocketed the coins.

"I am glad to have been of service, my lord Bishop." With the briefest of bows, Waldipert turned and left.

Arsenius took no offense at Waldipert's hasty departure; it was imperative for the vicedominus to get back to the Patriarchium before his absence was noticed.

Arsenius congratulated himself on his foresight in having identified Waldipert as a young man with a future many years ago, when he was only a chamberlain in the papal household. It had been costly, buying the man's loyalty all these years. But now that Waldipert was vicedominus, the investment would pay off handsomely.

Arsenius rang for his servant. "Go to the Church of St. Marcellus and bid my son come at once."

✦ ✦ ✦

Hearing the news, Anastasius sat down heavily in a chair opposite his father. Silently he cursed himself, humiliated that his father had learned how badly he had bungled things.

"Who would have guessed the boy would talk?" he said defensively. "To betray me, he had to condemn himself."

"It was a mistake to let him live," Arsenius said matter-of-factly. "You should have had his throat slit the moment the deed was done. Well, it's over now. We must look to the future."

"Future?" Anastasius echoed bleakly. "What future?"

"Despair is for the weak, my son, not for such as you and me."

"But what am I to do? Surely the situation is past all righting!"

"You must leave Rome. Now. Tonight."

"Oh, God!" Anastasius buried his face in his hands. His whole world was crumbling around him.

Arsenius said sternly, "Enough! Remember who and what you are."

Anastasius sat up, struggling to master himself.

"You will go to Aachen," Arsenius said, "to the Emperor's court."

Anastasius was bewildered. The sick fear gripping his heart was keeping him from thinking clearly. "But . . . Lothar knows I denounced him at the papal election."

"Yes, and knows as well why you were compelled to do so. He's a man who understands political necessity—how else do you think he managed to wrest the throne from his father and brothers? He's also a man in need of money." Arsenius took a leather pouch from his desk and handed it to Anastasius. "If the imperial feathers are still ruffled, this purse will help smooth them."

Anastasius stared dully at the heavy bag of coins. *Must I really leave Rome?* The idea of living out the remainder of his days among a tribe of barbarian Franks filled him with loathing. *Better, perhaps, to die now and have done with it.*

"Think of it as an opportunity," his father was saying. "A chance to win powerful friends at the imperial court. You'll need them, once you are Pope."

*Once I am Pope.* The words penetrated the heavy fog of Anastasius's despair. Then he was not being sent away forever.

"I'll look after your interests here, never fear," Arsenius said. "The tide of opinion cannot run in Leo's favor forever. Eventually it will crest, and then subside. When I judge the time to be ripe, I'll send for you."

The cold nausea that had gripped Anastasius began to recede. His father had not given up hope; therefore, neither must he.

"I've arranged for an escort," Arsenius said briskly. "Twelve of my best men. Come, I'll walk with you to the stables."

The twelve guards were mounted and ready, armed with sword and pike and mace. Anastasius would not want for protection on the dangerous roads. His mount stood nearby, tossing its head impatiently—a strong and spirited beast; Anastasius recognized it as his father's favorite stallion.

"There's two or three hours of daylight yet—enough to give you a good start," Arsenius said. "They'll not come for you today, for they've no way of knowing you suspect anything, and Leo will surely take the precaution of drawing up an official writ for your arrest. It'll be morning before they start looking, and then they'll try St. Marcellus first. By the time they think of coming here, you'll be well away."

Struck with a sudden concern, Anastasius said, "What about you, Father?"

"They've no reason to suspect me. If they try to question me as to your whereabouts, they'll find they have a wolf by the tail."

Father and son embraced.

*Can this actually be happening?* Anastasius wondered. Things were moving so quickly it was bewildering.

"God go with you, my son," Arsenius said.

"And with you, Father." Anastasius mounted and turned his horse quickly so his father would not see the start of tears to his eyes. Just beyond the gate, he turned back for a last look. The sun was westering, spilling lengthening shadows over the sweet slopes of the Roman hills, painting with red-gold hues the majestic skeletons of the Forum and the Colosseum.

Rome. Everything he had worked for, all he cared about, lay inside its sacred walls.

His last sight was of his father's face—pained but resolute, and steady and reassuring as the rock of St. Peter.

*"Membrum putridum et insanibile, ferro excommunicationis a corpore Ecclesiae abscidamus . . ."*

In the cool dark of the Lateran Basilica, Joan listened to Leo pronounce the solemn and terrifying words that would sever Anastasius from Holy Mother Church forever. She noted that Leo had chosen the *excommunicatio minor,* the lesser form of excommunication, in which the condemned was enjoined from administering or receiving the sacraments (save for the last rites, from which no living soul could be excluded) but not from all intercourse with his fellow Christians. *Truly,* Joan thought, *Leo has a charitable heart.*

All the clergy of Rome and its patrimonies were gathered to witness the solemn ceremony; even Arsenius was here, for he would not jeopardize his own position as Bishop of Horta with a futile public opposition. Leo suspected, of course, that Arsenius had been complicit in his son's flight from justice. But there was no proof to substantiate such a charge and no other ground for complaint against him, since it was certainly no crime merely to be a man's father.

As the candle representing Anastasius's immortal soul was upended and extinguished in the dirt, Joan felt an unexpected twinge of sadness. *A tragic waste,* she thought. So brilliant a mind as Anastasius's could have been used to do much good, if his heart had not been twisted by obsessive ambition.

# 26

Construction on the Leonine Wall, as the structure was now universally called, proceeded apace. The fire intended to destroy it had done little actual harm; the wooden scaffolding used by the workers had burned to the ground, and one of the western ramparts had been badly blackened, but that was all. The problems that had plagued the project from the beginning now blessedly ceased. Work continued steadily throughout the winter and the following spring, for the weather remained blessedly mild, marked by long, cool, sunny days with no drop of rain. A constant supply of good-quality stone came in from the quarries, and the workers from the various domains of the papal campagna settled in to the work, laboring side by side in productive unison.

By Pentecost, the topmost row of stone reached a man's height. No one called the project folly now; no one complained of the time and money lavished on it. The Romans felt a growing pride in the work, whose immensity harked back to the ancient days of Empire, when such prodigies of construction were a commonplace, not a rarity. When finished, the wall would be magnificent, monumental, a towering barrier even the Saracens could never scale or breach.

But time ran out. On the calends of July, messengers arrived in the city with terrifying news: a Saracen fleet was gathering at Totarium, a small island off the east coast of Sardinia, in preparation for another attack on Rome.

Unlike Sergius, who had looked to the power of prayer to protect the city, Leo chose a more aggressive course of action. He sent immediately to the great maritime city of Naples, requesting a fleet of armed ships to engage the enemy at sea.

The idea was bold—and chancy. Naples still nominally owed allegiance to Constantinople, though in reality it had been independent for years. Would the Duke of Naples help Rome in her hour of need? Or would he use the opportunity to join forces with the Saracens and strike a blow against the Roman See on behalf of the Eastern Patriarchate? The plan was fraught with danger. But what alternative was there?

For ten days the city waited in tense expectation. When at last the Neapolitan fleet arrived at Porto, on the mouth of the Tiber, Leo set forth warily to meet them accompanied by a large retinue of heavily armed militia under Gerold's command.

The Romans' anxieties were allayed when Caesarius, the commander of the fleet, prostrated himself before Leo and humbly kissed his feet. With a degree of relief he did not reveal, Leo blessed Caesarius, solemnly committing the sacred bodies of the apostles Peter and Paul to his protection.

They had survived the first roll of fortune's dice; on the next one all their futures would depend.

The next morning the Saracen fleet appeared. The broad-stretched lateen sails spread across the horizon like opened talons. Bleakly Joan counted them—fifty, fifty-three, fifty-seven—still they kept coming—eighty, eighty-five, ninety—were there this many ships in the world?—one hundred, one hundred and ten, one hundred and twenty! *Deo, juva nos!* The Neapolitan vessels numbered only sixty-one; with the six Roman biremes still in serviceable condition, that made a total of sixty-seven. They were outnumbered almost two to one.

Leo stood on the steps of the nearby Church of St. Aurea and led the frightened citizens of Porto in prayer. "Lord, Thou who saved Peter from sinking when walking on the waves, Thou who rescued Paul from the depths of the sea, hear us. Grant power to the arms of Thy believing servants, who fight against the enemies of Thy church, that through their victory Thy holy name may be glorified among all nations."

In the open air, the voices of the people reverberated with a resounding "Amen."

Caesarius shouted orders from the deck of the foremost ship. The Neapolitans hurled themselves against the oars, muscles straining. For a moment the heavy biremes stood motionless in the water. Then, with an enormous groan of creaking timber, the ships began to move. The double banks of oars rose and dipped and rose and dipped, flashing like gems; the wind caught the sails, and the great biremes drove ahead, their ironclad prows cleaving the turquoise water into twin shafts of foam.

The Saracen ships turned to meet them. But before the two opposing fleets could engage, an earsplitting thunderclap signaled the advent of a storm. The sky darkened as black clouds rolled in rapidly from the sea. The heavy-drafted Neapolitan ships were able to make it back to safe harbor. But the Saracen vessels, crafted with low freeboards for speed and maneuverability in battle, were too flimsy to ride out the storm. They pitched and heaved on the rising waves, tossed about like pieces of bark, their iron rams striking their sister ships, breaking them apart.

Several of the ships headed into port, but as soon as they reached land, they were set upon. Fanned by the violent anger that follows terror, the Romans slaughtered the crews without mercy, dragging them from their ships and suspending them from gibbets hastily constructed along the shore. Witnessing their comrades' fate, the other Saracen ships struck out desperately for the open sea, where they were broken apart by giant, roiling waves.

In the moment of unexpected victory, Joan was watching Leo. He stood on the steps of the church, arms upraised, eyes lifted to Heaven in thanksgiving. He looked saintly, beatific, as if touched by a divine presence.

*Perhaps he can work miracles,* she thought. Her knees bent willingly as she bowed down before him.

"Victory! Victory at Ostia!" The news was cried jubilantly through the streets. The Romans spilled forth from their houses, the papal storehouses were thrown open, and wine flowed freely; for three days the city indulged in wild and drunken celebration.

Five hundred Saracens were marched into the city before jeering, hostile crowds. Many were stoned or hacked to death along the route. The survivors, some three hundred in number, were taken in chains to a camp in the Neronian Plain, where they were confined and required to labor on the Leonine Wall.

With the addition of these extra hands, the wall rose more quickly. In three years, it stood complete—a masterpiece of medieval engineering, the most extraordinary construction the city had seen in over four hundred years. The whole of the Vatican territory was enclosed within a structure twelve feet thick and forty feet tall, defended by forty-four massive towers. There were two separate galleries, one above the other; the lower gallery was supported by a series of graceful arcades opening within. Three gates gave entrance: the Posterula Sant'Angeli; the Posterula Saxonum, so named because it opened into the Saxon quarter; and the Posterula San Peregrinus, the principal gate through which future generations of kings and princes would pass to worship at the holy shrine of St. Peter.

Remarkable as the wall was, this was only the beginning of Leo's ambitious plans for the city. Dedicated to "restoring all the places of the saints," Leo embarked upon a great plan of rebuilding. The ring of anvils sounded day and night throughout the city as work went on in one after another of the city's churches. The burned basilica of the Saxons was restored, as well as the Frisian church of San Michele and the Church of the Sancti Quattro Coronati, of which Leo had once been cardinal.

Most important of all, Leo began the restoration of St. Peter's. The burned and blackened portico was completely rebuilt; the doors, stripped of their precious metal by the Saracens, were covered with new, light-diffusing silver plates on which myriad sacred histories were carved with astonishing skill. The great treasure that had been carried off by the Saracens was replaced: the high altar was covered with new plates of silver and gold and decorated with a massive gold crucifix set with pearls, emeralds, and diamonds; above it a silver ciborium weighing over a thousand pounds was mounted upon four great pillars of purest travertine marble, ornamented with gilt lilies. The altar was lit by lamps hung on silver chains, garnished with golden balls, their flickering light illuminating a veritable treasure trove of jeweled chalices, wrought silver lecterns, rich tapestries, and silken hangings. The great basilica gleamed with a splendor that outshone even its former magnificence.

Observing the vast amounts of money pouring forth from the papal treasury, Joan felt troubled. Undeniably Leo had created a shrine of awe-inspiring beauty. But the majority of those who lived within sight of this glittering magnificence spent their days in brutish, degrading poverty. A single one of St. Peter's massive silver plates, melted into coin, would feed and clothe the population of the Campus Martius for a year. Did God's worship really require such sacrifice?

There was only one person in the world with whom Joan dared raise such a question. When she put it to him, Gerold considered soberly before replying. "I have heard it argued," he said finally, "that the beauty of a holy shrine provides the faithful with a different form of nourishment—food for the soul, not the body."

"It's difficult to hear the voice of God over the grumbling of an empty stomach."

Gerold shook his head affectionately. "You haven't changed. Remember the time you asked Odo how he could be certain the Resurrection had taken place, since there were no eyewitnesses?"

"I do." Joan flexed her hand ruefully. "I also remember how he answered me."

"When I saw the wound Odo gave you," Gerold said, "I wanted to strike him—and would have, if I hadn't known it would only make things more difficult for you."

Joan smiled. "You always were my protector."

"And you," he bantered, "always had the soul of a heretic."

They had always been able to talk like this, free from the world's restraints. It was part of the special intimacy that had bound them from the very first.

He looked at her now with a familiar warmth. Joan was keenly aware of him; she felt his nearness like a touch on her naked skin. But by now she was skilled at disguising her feelings.

She pointed to the pile of petitions on the table between them. "I must go hear these petitioners."

"Shouldn't Leo do that?" Gerold asked.

"He's asked me to see to it."

Lately Leo had been delegating more and more of his daily responsibilities to her so he could devote himself to the continuing plans for rebuilding. Joan had become Leo's ambassador to the people; she was so familiar a sight going about her charitable duties in the different regions of the city that she was hailed everywhere as "the little Pope" and greeted with some of the affection reserved for Leo himself.

As she reached for the pile of papers, Gerold's hand brushed hers. She drew her hand back violently, as if from a fire. "I . . . I'd better go," she said awkwardly.

She was immensely relieved, and a little disappointed, when he did not follow her.

Buoyed by the success of the Leonine Wall and the renovation of St. Peter's, Leo's popularity was soaring. *Restaurator Urbis,* he was called, Restorer of the City. He was another Hadrian, the people said, another Aurelius. Everywhere he went, crowds cheered him. Rome rang with his praises.

Everywhere, that is, but in the palace on the Palatine Hill, where Arsenius waited with gathering impatience for the day when he could call Anastasius home.

Things had not gone as expected. There was no way to depose Leo from the throne, as Arsenius had originally hoped, and even less hope that it would be left vacant through the happy accident of death: healthy and vigorous, Leo gave every evidence of living forever.

Now the family fortunes had suffered another blow. The week before, Arsenius's second son, Eleutheris, had died. He had been riding down the Via Recta when a pig darted between his horse's legs; the horse stumbled and Eleutheris fell, receiving a cut on the thigh. At first no one was concerned, for the wound was slight. But misfortune has a way of following upon misfortune. The wound became infected. Arsenius called in Ennodius, who bled Eleutheris profusely, but it availed nothing. Within two days his son lay dead. Arsenius immediately ordered a search for the owner of the pig; when he was discovered, Arsenius had his throat slit from ear to ear. But such revenge was cold comfort, for it could not bring back Eleutheris.

Not that there had been much love lost between father and son. Eleutheris was the exact opposite of his brother—soft, lazy, and undisciplined even as a child, he had scorned Arsenius's offer of a church education and chosen instead the more immediate gratifications of a lay existence—women, wine, gambling, and other forms of debauchery.

No, Arsenius mourned Eleutheris not for the man he had been or might have become, given time, but for what he had represented: another branch of the family tree, a branch that might yet have borne promising fruit.

For centuries, theirs had been the first family of Rome. Arsenius could trace his ancestry back in a direct line to Augustus Caesar himself. Yet this illustrious heritage was tarnished by failure, for none of its noble sons had ever achieved Rome's ultimate prize: the Throne of St. Peter. How many lesser men had sat upon that throne, Arsenius thought bitterly, and with what tragic result? Rome, once the wonder of the world, was sunk into ruinous and embarrassing decay. The Byzantines mocked it openly, pointing to the gleaming splendor of their own Constantinople.

Who but one of Arsenius's family, Caesar's heirs, could lead the city back to her former greatness?

Now Eleutheris was gone, Anastasius was the last of the line, the only remaining chance the family would ever have to redeem its honor, and Rome's.

And Anastasius was banished to Frankland.

Arsenius felt dark despair close in on him. He shook it off brusquely, like an unwanted cloak. Greatness did not attend upon opportunity; it seized it. Those who would rule had to be willing to pay the price of power, however great.

During mass on the day of the Feast of St. John the Baptist, Joan first noticed something wrong with Leo. His hands trembled while receiving the offerings, and he faltered uncharacteristically over the *Nobis quoque peccatoribus.*

When Joan questioned him afterward, he dismissed his symptoms as nothing more than a touch of heat and indigestion.

The next day he was no better, nor the next, nor the next. His head ached constantly, and he complained of burning pains in his hands and feet. Each day he became a little weaker; each day it took more effort for him to rise from bed. Joan grew alarmed. She tried every remedy she knew for wasting diseases. Nothing helped. Leo continued to sink toward death.

The voices of the choir rose loudly in the *Te Deum,* the final canticle of the Mass. Anastasius kept his face expressionless, trying not to grimace at the noise. He had never grown accustomed to the Frankish chant, whose unfamiliar tones grated upon his ears like the croaking of blackbirds. Remembering the pure, sweet harmonies of the Roman chant, Anastasius felt a sharp stab of homesickness.

Not that his time here in Aachen had been wasted. Following his father's instructions, Anastasius had set out to win the Emperor's support. He began by courting Lothar's friends and intimates, and making himself agreeable to Lothar's wife, Ermengard. He assiduously charmed and flattered the Frankish nobility, impressing them all with his knowledge of Scripture and especially of Greek—a rare accomplishment. Ermengard and her friends interceded with the Emperor, and Anastasius was readmitted to the royal presence. Whatever doubt or resentment Lothar might once have harbored against him was forgotten; once again Anastasius enjoyed the Emperor's trust and support.

*I have done everything Father asked, and more. But when will come my reward?* There were times, such as now, when Anastasius feared he might be left to languish forever in this cold, barbarian backwater.

Returning to his rooms after mass, he discovered a letter had arrived in his absence. Recognizing the hand as his father's, he took up a knife and eagerly cut the seal. He read the first few lines and cried out exultantly.

*The time is now,* his father had written. *Come claim your destiny.*

Leo lay on his side in bed, knees drawn up, suffering from sharp pains in his stomach. Joan prepared an emollient potion of egg whites beaten into sweetened milk, to which she added a little fennel as a carminative. She watched him drink it.

"That was good," he said.

She waited to see if he would keep it down. He did, then slept more restfully than he had in weeks. When he awoke hours later, he felt better.

Joan decided to put him on a diet of the potion, restricting all other food and drink.

Waldipert protested: "He's so weak; surely he needs something more substantial to keep his strength up."

Joan replied firmly, "The treatment is helping him. He must take no food other than the potion."

Seeing the determined look in her eyes, Waldipert backed down. "As you say, Nomenclator."

For a week, Leo continued to improve. His pain went away, his color returned, he even seemed to regain some of his old energy. When Joan brought him his evening dose of the healing potion, Leo eyed the milky mixture ruefully.

"How about a meat pasty instead?"

"You're getting your appetite back—a good sign. Best not to rush things, however. I'll look in on you in the morning; if you're still hungry, I'll let you try a bit of simple pottage."

"Tyrant," Leo responded.

She smiled. It was good to have him gibe with her again.

✦ ✦ ✦

Early the next morning, she arrived to find that Leo had suffered a relapse. He lay in bed moaning, too much in pain to reply when she spoke to him.

Quickly Joan prepared another dose of the emollient potion. As she did, her eyes fell upon an empty plate of crumbs on the table beside the bed.

"What's this?" she asked Renatus, Leo's personal chamberlain.

"Why, it's the meat pasty you sent him," the boy replied.

"I sent nothing," Joan said.

Renatus looked confused. "But . . . my lord Vicedominus said you ordered it specially."

Joan looked at Leo doubled over with pain. A horrible suspicion dawned.

*"Run!"* she told Renatus. "Call the superista and the guards. Don't let Waldipert leave the palace."

The boy hesitated only a moment, then ran from the chamber.

With shaking hands, Joan prepared a strong emetic of mustard and elder-root, spooning the mixture through Leo's tightened mouth. In a few moments, the cleansing spasm took him; his whole body heaved convulsively, but he brought up only a thin green bile.

*Too late. The poison has left his stomach.* Joan saw with distress that it had already begun its deadly work, tightening the muscles of Leo's jaw and throat, strangling him.

Desperately she tried to think of something else to do.

Gerold ordered a search of every room of the palace. Waldipert was nowhere to be found. Immediately he was declared criminal and fugitive, and an intensive hunt was instituted throughout the city and into the surrounding countryside. But they searched in vain; Waldipert had completely disappeared.

Just as they were about to give up the pursuit, they found him. He was floating in the Tiber, his throat slit from ear to ear, his face fixed in a grimace of surprise.

The clergy and high officials of Rome were gathered in the papal bedchamber. They stood in a tight knot at the foot of the bed, as if to draw comfort from one another's nearness.

The poppy oil lamps burned low in their silver cressets. With the first of the dawn light, the senior chamberlain came to extinguish them. Joan watched as the old man loosened the cables and lowered the rings with exceeding care so none of the precious substance would be wasted. The simple domestic gesture seemed oddly out of place in the room's charged atmosphere.

Joan had not expected Leo to last the night. Long ago he had stopped responding to voice or touch. For hours his breathing had followed the same inexorable pattern, growing steadily noisier and more stertorous until it reached an alarming crescendo, then abruptly ceased. There was a pause during which no one in the room drew breath; then the terrifying cycle began again.

A flutter of cloth drew Joan's attention. Across the room Eustathius, the archpriest, was weeping, pressing his sleeve across his mouth to muffle the sound.

Leo let out a long, loud, rattling exhalation, then fell quiet. The silence dragged on and on. Joan crossed to the bed. The life was gone from Leo's face. She closed his eyes, then fell to her knees beside the bed.

Eustathius cried out in grief. The bishops and optimates knelt in prayer. Paschal, the primicerius, crossed himself, then left to carry the news to those waiting outside.

Leo, *Pontifex Maximus, Servus Servorum Dei,* Primate of the Bishops of the Church, and Lord Pope of the Apostolic See of Rome, was dead.

Outside the Patriarchium, the wailing began.

Leo was laid to rest in St. Peter's, before the altar of a new oratory dedicated to him. Burials were performed quickly this time of year, for no matter how saintly the soul that had inhabited it, a body did not withstand corruption long in the heat of a Roman July.

Shortly after the funeral, the ruling triumvirate proclaimed that in three days' time there would be a pontifical election. With Lothar to the north, the Saracens to the south, and Lombards and Byzantines between, Rome's situation was too precarious to allow the Throne of St. Peter to remain vacant any longer.

*Too soon,* Arsenius thought with chagrin as soon as he heard the news. *The election is too soon. Anastasius cannot arrive before then.* Waldipert, that bungling fool, had ruined things completely. He had been given explicit instructions on how to administer the poison gradually, in small doses; in that way, Leo would have lingered for a month or more—and his death would have aroused no suspicion.

But Waldipert had panicked and administered too large a dose, killing Leo at once. Then he'd had the gall to come cringing to Arsenius, asking for his protection. *Well, he's beyond reach of the law now, though not in the way he intended,* Arsenius thought.

He had ordered men killed before; it was part of the price of power, and only the weak balked at paying it. But he had never had to strike down anyone he knew as well as Waldipert. Distasteful as that had been, it was unavoidable. If Waldipert had been captured and questioned, he would have confessed under torture all he knew. Arsenius had merely done what he had to in order to protect himself and his family. He would destroy anyone who threatened the security of the family, break him as one breaks the flea that has bitten one with one's fingernails.

Nevertheless, Waldipert's death had left him feeling depressed and uneasy. Such violent acts, however necessary, took an inevitable toll.

With an effort of will, Arsenius turned his mind to more pressing matters. His son's absence complicated affairs; his election to the papacy would now be more difficult, but not impossible. The first thing to do was to get Eustathius, the archpriest, to overturn the sentence of excommunication against him. That would take some politic maneuvering.

Lifting a jeweled silver bell from his desk, Arsenius rang for his secretary. There was much to do, and very little time in which to do it.

In her workshop in the Patriarchium, Joan stood at her bench, crushing dried hyssop flowers to a fine powder in her mortar. Twist and grind and twist and grind; the familiar motions of hand and wrist were soothing balm to the grief battering her heart.

Leo was dead. It seemed impossible. He had been so vital, so forceful; he had loomed so much larger than life. Had he lived, he might have done much to lift Rome out of the quagmire of ignorance and poverty in which it had languished for centuries; he had the heart for it, and the will. But not the time.

The door opened, and Gerold entered. She met his eyes, feeling his presence as keenly as if he had touched her.

"I've just received word," he said brusquely. "Anastasius has left Aachen."

"You don't think he's coming here?"

"I do. Why else should he leave the Emperor's court so suddenly? He's coming to claim the throne that was denied him six years ago."

"But surely he can't be elected; he's excommunicate."

"Arsenius is trying to prevail upon the archpriest to reverse the sentence of excommunication."

*"Benedicite!"* This was very bad news. After his years of exile in the imperial court, Anastasius was surely more the Emperor's man than ever. If he was elected, Lothar's power would extend itself over Rome and all its territories.

Gerold said, "He will not have forgotten how you spoke against him at Leo's election. It will be dangerous for you to remain in Rome with him as Pope. He's not a man to forgive an injury."

Coming on top of her still-raw emotions over Leo's death, this realization was too much. Joan's eyes brimmed with tears.

"Don't cry, my heart." Gerold's arms were around her, strong and sure and comforting. His lips brushed her temples, her cheek, sparking currents of response. "Surely you've done enough, sacrificed enough. Come away with me, and we'll live as we were always meant to—together, as husband and wife."

She had a dizzying glimpse of his face close to hers, and then he was kissing her.

"Say yes," he said fiercely. "Say yes."

She felt as though she were being pulled below the surface of her conscious mind and carried off by a powerful current of desire. "Yes," she whispered, almost before she knew what she was saying. "Yes."

She had spoken without volition, responding impulsively to the force of his passion. But as soon as the words were out of her mouth, a great calm descended upon her. The decision had been made, and it seemed both right and inevitable.

He bent to kiss her again. Just then the bell rang, summoning everyone to the afternoon meal. A moment later, voices and hurrying footsteps sounded outside the door.

With murmured endearments, they parted quickly, promising to meet again after the papal election.

On the day of the election, Joan went to pray in the small English church that had been her own when she first came to Rome.

Burned to the ground during the great fire, the church had been reconstructed with materials stripped from Rome's ancient temples and monuments. As Joan knelt before the high altar, she saw that the marble pedestal supporting it bore the unmistakable symbol of the Magna Mater, ancient goddess of earth, worshiped by heathen tribes in a time beyond memory. Beneath the crude design was inscribed in Latin, "On this marble, incense was offered to the Goddess." Obviously when the great slab of marble had been brought here, no one understood the symbol or its inscription. This was not especially surprising, for many of the Roman clergy were barely literate, unable to decipher the ancient lettering, much less understand its meaning.

The incongruity of the sacred altar and its pagan base seemed to Joan a perfect symbol of herself: a Christian priest, she still dreamed of her mother's heathen gods; a man in the eyes of the world, she was tormented by her secret woman's heart; a seeker of faith, she was torn between her desire to know God and her fear that He might not exist. Mind and heart, faith and doubt, will and desire. Would the painful contradictions of her nature ever be reconciled?

She loved Gerold; about that there was no question. But could she be a wife to him? Never having lived as a woman, could she begin now, so late in life?

"Help me, Lord," Joan prayed, raising her eyes to the silver crucifix atop the altar. "Show me the way. Let me know what I must do. Dear God! Lift me into Thy bright light!"

Her words flew up, but her spirit remained below, weighted down by incertitude.

A door cracked open behind her. She turned from her place before the altar to see a head insert itself in the opening and as quickly withdraw.

"He's in here!" a voice shouted. "I've found him!"

Her heart pounded with sudden fear. Could Anastasius have moved against her so quickly? She rose to her feet.

The doors swung open, and the seven *proceres* entered, proceeded by acolytes carrying the banners of their office. They were followed by the cardinal clergy and then the seven optimates of the city. Not until Joan saw Gerold among them was she sure she was not going to be arrested.

In slow procession the delegation came down the aisle and halted before Joan.

"John Anglicus." Paschal, the primicerius, addressed her in formal tones. "By the will of God and of the Roman people, you have been elected Lord Pope of Rome, Bishop of the Roman See."

Then he prostrated himself before her and kissed her feet.

Joan stared at him disbelievingly. Was this some kind of ill-considered jest? Or a trap to lure her into expressing disloyalty to the new Pope?

She looked at Gerold. His face was taut and grimly serious as he dropped to his knees before her.

The outcome of the election had taken everyone by surprise. The imperial faction, led by Arsenius, had stood staunchly for Anastasius. The papal faction countered by nominating Hadrian, priest of the Church of St. Mark. He was not the kind of leader who inspired confidence. Plump and short, with a face disfigured by smallpox, he stood with slumped shoulders, as if already burdened by the responsibility that had been placed upon him. He was a pious man, a good priest, but few would choose him to be the spiritual leader of the world.

Evidently Hadrian agreed with the general opinion, for he unexpectedly withdrew his name from nomination, informing those assembled that after much prayer and deep reflection he had decided to decline the great honor they would bestow on him.

This announcement caused a mild uproar among the members of the papal party, who had not been informed of Hadrian's decision in advance. There was a great deal of cheering from the imperialist side. Anastasius's victory now seemed certain.

Then a clamor arose from the rear of the assembly, where the lower ranks of the laity were gathered. "John Anglicus!" they shouted. "John Anglicus!" Paschal, the primicerius, sent guards to quiet them, but they would not be silenced. They knew their rights; the constitution of 824 gave all Romans, lay and clergy, high and low, the right to vote in a papal election.

Arsenius sought to head off this unexpected problem by making an open bid to buy the people's loyalty; his agents circulated swiftly through the crowd, offering bribes of wine, women, and money. But even these strong enticements did not prevail; the people were set against Anastasius, whom their beloved Pope Leo had seen fit to declare excommunicate. Vociferously they clamored for "the little Pope," Leo's friend and helpmate John Anglicus, and they would not be swayed.

Even so they might not have carried the day, for the ruling aristocracy would not have allowed its will to be overturned by a bunch of commoners, constitution or no. But the papal party, seeing in this popular insurgence an unlooked-for opportunity to block Anastasius from the throne, joined their voices to the people's. The deed was done, and Joan was elected.

Anastasius and his party were camped outside Perugia, some ninety miles from Rome, when the courier arrived with the news. Anastasius barely finished reading the message before he let out a cry of pain. Without a word to his bewildered companions, he turned and reentered his tent, tying the flaps to prevent anyone from entering after him.

From inside the tent the men of his escort heard wild and unrestrained sobbing. After a time the sobbing became a kind of animal howling that went on through most of the night.

Robed in scarlet silk woven with gold and seated on a white palfrey also clothed and bridled in gold, Joan rode in ceremony toward her coronation. From every door and window along the Via Sacra, streamers and banners fluttered in riotous color; the ground was strewn with sweet-smelling myrtle. Throngs of cheering people lined the street, pressing forward to catch a glimpse of the new Lord Pope.

Lost in her own reverie, Joan scarcely heard the noise of the crowd. She was thinking of Matthew, of her old master Aesculapius, of Brother Benjamin. They had all believed in her, encouraged her, but none could have dreamed of such a day as this. She could scarcely believe it herself.

When she had first disguised herself as a man, when she had been accepted into the Fulda brotherhood, God had not raised His hand against her. But would He truly allow a woman to ascend the sacred Throne of St. Peter? The question spun round in her mind.

The papal guards, led by Gerold, rode escort around Joan. Gerold kept his wary gaze fixed on the crowds lining the road. Now and again someone broke through the ranks of guards, and each time Gerold's hand strayed to the sword at his side, ready to defend Joan against attack. There was no occasion to draw his sword, however, for each time the interloper wanted only to kiss the hem of Joan's robe and receive her blessing.

In this slow and interrupted fashion, the long procession wound its way through the streets toward the Lateran. The sun was at midpoint in the sky when they drew up before the papal cathedral. As Joan dismounted, the cardinals, bishops, and deacons fell into place behind her. Slowly she climbed the steps and entered the shimmering interior of the great basilica.

Replete with ancient and elaborate ritual, the *ordo coronationis,* or coronation ceremony, took several hours. Two bishops led Joan to the sacristy, where she was solemnly vested in alb, dalmatic, and paenula before she approached the high altar for the singing of the Litany and the lengthy ritual of consecration, or anointing. During the recitation of the *vere dignum,* Desiderius the archdeacon and two of the regionary deacons held over her head an open book of the Gospels. Then came the mass itself; this lasted a good deal longer than usual because of the addition of numerous prayers and formularies befitting the importance of the occasion.

Throughout it all Joan stood solemn and erect, weighted down by the liturgical robes, as stiff with gold as those of any Byzantine prince. Despite the magnificence of her attire, she felt very small and inadequate to the enormous responsibility being laid upon her. She told herself that those who had stood here before her must also have trembled and doubted. And somehow they had carried on.

But they had all been men.

Eustathius, the archpriest, began the final benediction: "Almighty Lord, stretch forth the right hand of Thy blessing upon Thy servant John Anglicus, and pour over him the gift of Thy mercy . . ."

Will *God bless me now?* Joan wondered. *Or will His just wrath strike me down the moment the papal crown is placed upon my head?*

The Bishop of Ostia came forward bearing the crown on a cushion of white silk. Joan's breath caught in her throat as he raised the crown above her. Then the weight of the gold circlet settled upon her head.

Nothing happened.

"Life to our illustrious Lord John Anglicus, by God decreed our chief Bishop and Universal Pope!" Eustathius cried.

The choir chanted *Laudes* as Joan faced the assembly.

Emerging onto the steps of the basilica, she was greeted by a thunderous roar of welcome. Thousands of people had been standing for hours in the blistering sun to greet their newly consecrated Pope. It was their will that she should wear the crown. Now they spoke that will in one great chorus of joyous acclamation: "Pope John! Pope John! Pope John!"

Joan raised her arms to them, feeling her spirit begin to soar. The epiphany, which only yesterday she had striven in vain to achieve, now came unlooked for and unbidden. God had allowed this to happen, so it could not be against His will. All doubt and anxiety were dispelled, replaced by a glorious, glowing certainty: *This is my destiny, and these my people.*

She was hallowed by the love she bore them. She would serve them in the Lord's name all the days of her life.

And perhaps in the end God would forgive her.

Standing nearby, Gerold stared at Joan in wonderment. She was aglow, transformed by some unspeakable joy, her face a lovely shining lamp. He alone, who knew her so well, could guess at her inner, private hallowing of spirit, more important by far than the formal ceremony which had preceded it. As he watched her receive the acclamation of the crowd, his heart was torn by an unbearable truth: the woman he loved was lost to him forever, yet he had never loved her more.

# 27

Joan's first act as Pope was to undertake a walking tour of the city. Accompanied by an entourage of optimates and guards, she visited each of the seven ecclesiastical regions in turn, greeting the people and listening to their grievances and needs.

As she neared the end of her tour, Desiderius, the archdeacon, directed her up the Via Lata away from the river.

"What about the Campus Martius?" she said.

The others in the papal entourage looked at one another in consternation. The Campus Martius, the marshy, breezeless, low-lying region abutting the Tiber, was the poorest part of Rome. In the great days of the Roman Republic, it had been dedicated to the worship of the pagan god Mars. Now starving dogs, ragged beggars, and thieves wandered its once-proud streets.

"We daren't venture in there, Holiness," Desiderius protested. "The place is rife with typhus and cholera."

But Joan was already striding toward the river, flanked by Gerold and the guards. Desiderius and the others had no choice but to follow.

Rows of *insulae,* the narrow tenements of the poor, crowded together along the filthy streets edging the riverbank, their rotting timbers bending inward like the broken backs of ancient workhorses. Some of the insulae had collapsed; the heaps of rotten timber lay where they had fallen, blocking the narrow streets. Overhead stretched the ruined arches of the Marcian aqueduct, once one of the engineering wonders of the world. Now its broken walls dripped filthy water that collected underneath in black, stagnant pools, breeding grounds for disease.

Groups of beggars huddled over pots of foul-smelling food simmering on little fires made from twigs and dried dung. The streets were covered with a layer of slime left behind by repeated floodings of the Tiber. Refuse and excrement plugged the gutters; the stench rose unbearably in the summer heat, attracting swarms of flies, rats, and other vermin.

"God's teeth," Gerold muttered darkly beside her. "The place is a pesthole."

Joan knew the face of poverty, but she had never seen anything to equal this appalling, brutish squalor.

Two small children crouched before a cooking fire. Their tunics were so threadbare Joan could see the whiteness of their skin beneath; their bare feet were wrapped with strips of filthy rags. One, a little boy, was obviously sick with fever; despite the summer heat, he was shivering uncontrollably. Joan removed her linen paenula and tucked it gently around him. The boy rubbed his cheek against the fine cloth, softer than anything he had felt in his life.

She felt a tug on the hem of her robe. The smaller child, a round-eyed cherub of a girl, was looking up at her questioningly. "Are you an angel?" the small voice chirruped.

Joan cupped the child's dirty chin. "You're the angel, little one."

Inside the pot, a small piece of stringy, unidentifiable meat was beginning to brown. A young woman with lank yellow hair came lumbering wearily up from the river hauling a bucket of water. The children's mother? Joan wondered. She was scarcely more than a child herself—surely no more than sixteen.

The young woman's eyes lit hopefully as she saw Joan and the other prelates. "Alms, good fathers?" She held out a grimy hand. "A bit of coin for the sake of my little ones?" Joan nodded at Victor, the sacellarius, who placed a silver denarius in the girl's outstretched palm. With a happy grin, the girl set down the water bucket to pocket the coin.

Raw sewage was floating in the water.

*Benedicite!* Joan thought. The filth in that water was doubtless what had made the boy sick. But with the aqueduct in ruins, what choice did his mother have? She must use the polluted water of the Tiber or die of thirst.

By now, others had begun to notice Joan and her entourage. People crowded around, eager to greet their new Lord Pope. Joan reached out to them, trying to touch and bless as many as she could. But as the crowd grew, the people packed round so closely she could scarcely move. Gerold gave commands; the guards shouldered the crowd back, opening a path, and the papal entourage retreated back up the Via Lata to the open sunshine and breezy, healthful air of the Capitoline Hill.

"We must rebuild the Marcian aqueduct," Joan said during a meeting with the optimates the next morning.

The brows of Paschal, the primicerius, lifted with surprise. "The restoration of a Christian edifice would be a more appropriate way to begin your papacy, Holiness."

"What need do the poor have of more churches?" she replied. "Rome abounds with them. But a working aqueduct could save untold lives."

"The project is chancy," Victor, the sacellarius, said. "It may well be that it can't be done."

She couldn't deny this. Rebuilding the aqueduct would be a monumental, perhaps an impossible, undertaking, given the sorry state of engineering of the day. The books which had preserved the accumulated wisdom of the ancients regarding these complicated pieces of construction had been lost or destroyed centuries ago. The parchment pages on which the precious plans were recorded had been scraped clean and written over with Christian homilies and stories of lives of saints and martyrs.

"We have to try," Joan said firmly. "We cannot allow people to go on living in such appalling conditions."

The others kept silent, not because they agreed but because it would be impolitic to offer further opposition when the Apostolic One's mind was so obviously set upon this course.

After a moment Paschal asked, "Who do you have in mind to oversee the building?"

"Gerold," Joan replied.

"The superista?" Paschal was surprised.

"Who else? He directed the construction of the Leonine Wall. Many believed that could not be done, either."

In the weeks since her coronation, she had sensed Gerold's growing unhappiness. It was difficult for them both, being near each other all the time. She, at least, had her work, a clear sense of mission and purpose. But Gerold was bored and restless. Joan knew this without his having to tell her; they had never needed speech between them to know what the other was feeling.

When Gerold came to her, she laid out her idea for the rebuilding of the Marcian aqueduct.

His brow furrowed thoughtfully. "Near Tivoli, the aqueduct runs underground, tunneling through a series of hills. If that section has fallen into decay, it will not be easy to repair."

Joan smiled as she saw his mind already beginning to engage with the idea, anticipating the problems involved.

"If anyone can do it, you can."

"Are you sure this is what you want?" Gerold's eyes met hers in an look of unmistakable longing.

She felt herself respond to him. But she dared not let her feelings show. To acknowledge their intimacy, even here in private, would be to court disaster. Matter-of-factly she replied, "I can think of nothing that would be of greater benefit to the people."

He looked away. "Very well, then. Mind you, I'm not promising anything. I'll look into it, see what's possible. I'll do all I can to see the aqueduct restored to working order."

"That's all I ask," she said.

She was coming to understand in an altogether new way what it meant to be Pope. Though nominally a position of great power, it was actually one of great obligation. Her time was completely taken up with the burdensome round of liturgical duties. On Palm Sunday, she blessed and distributed palm branches in front of St. Peter's. On Holy Thursday, she washed the feet of the poor and served a meal to them with her own hands. On the Feast of St. Anthony she stood before the Cathedral of Sancta Maria Maggiore and sprinkled holy water on the oxen, horses, and mules that had been brought by their owners to be blessed. On the third Sunday after Advent, she laid her hands upon each of the candidates brought forward to be ordained as priests, deacons, or bishops.

There was also the daily mass to lead. On certain days, this became a stational mass, preceded by a procession through the city to the titular church in which the service would be held, stopping along the route to hear petitioners; the procession and service took most of the day. There were over ninety stational masses, including the Marian feasts, the ember days, Christ Mass, Septuagesima and Sexagesima Sundays, and most of the Sundays and ferias in Lent.

There were feast days honoring Saints Peter, Paul, Lawrence, Agnes, John, Thomas, Luke, Andrew, and Anthony, as well as the Nativity, the Annunciation, and the Assumption of the Virgin Mary. These were fixed or immovable feasts, meaning that they fell on the same day each year, like Christ Mass and Epiphany. Oblation, the Feast of St. Peter's Chair, the Circumcision of Christ, the Nativity of John the Baptist, Michaelmas, All Saints', and the Exaltation of the Cross were also fixed feasts. Easter, the holiest day of the Christian year, was a movable feast; its place in the calendar followed the time of the ecclesiastical full moon, as did its "satellite" holidays, Shrove Tuesday, Ash Wednesday, Ascension Day, and Pentecost.

Each of these Christian holidays was observed with at least four days of celebration: the vigil, or eve of the feast; the feast itself; the morrow, or day following; and the octave, or eighth day subsequent. All told, there were over one hundred and seventy-five Christian festival days, given over to elaborate and time-consuming ceremonial.

All of this gave Joan very little time to actually govern, or do the things she deeply cared about: bettering the lot of the poor and improving the education of the clergy.

In August, the arduous liturgical routine was interrupted by a synod. Sixty-seven prelates attended, including all the *suburbicarii,* or provincial bishops, as well as four Frankish bishops sent by the Emperor Lothar.

Two of the issues addressed at this synod held particular interest for Joan. The first was intinction, the practice of bestowing Communion by dipping the eucharistic bread into the wine, rather than partaking of them separately. In the twenty years since Joan had introduced the idea at Fulda as a way of preventing the spread of disease, it had become so popular that in Frankland it was now almost universal custom. The Roman clergy, who were of course unaware of Joan's connection with intinction, regarded the novel practice with suspicion.

"It is a transgression of divine law," the Bishop of Castrum argued indignantly. "For the Holy Book clearly states that Christ gave His body and blood *separately* to His disciples."

There were nods of agreement all around.

"My lord Bishop speaks truly," Pothos, the Bishop of Trevi, said. "The practice has no precedent among the writings of the Fathers, and therefore must be condemned."

"Should we condemn an idea simply because it is new?" Joan asked.

"In all things we should be guided by the wisdom of the ancients," Pothos answered gravely. "The only truth of which we can be sure is that which has been vouchsafed in the past."

"Everything that is old was once new," Joan pointed out. "The new always precedes the old. Is it not foolish to scorn that which precedes and cherish that which follows?"

Pothos's brow furrowed as his mind wrestled with this complex dialectic. Like most of his colleagues, he had no training in classical argument and debate; he was comfortable only when quoting authority.

A lengthy discussion followed. Joan could, of course, have imposed her will by decree, but she preferred persuasion to tyranny. In the end the bishops were won over by her reasoning. The practice of intinction would continue in Frankland, at least for the present.

The next issue to be addressed was of deep personal interest to Joan because it involved her old friend Gottschalk, the oblate monk whose freedom she had once helped to win. According to the report of the Frankish bishops, he was again in serious trouble. Joan was saddened by this news but not especially surprised; Gottschalk was a man who courted unhappiness as ardently as a lover pursues his mistress.

Now he stood accused of the serious crime of heresy. Raban Maur, formerly Abbot of Fulda, since promoted to Archbishop of Mainz, had gotten wind of some radical theories Gottschalk had been preaching regarding predestination. Seizing the opportunity to wreak revenge upon his old nemesis, the archbishop had ordered Gottschalk imprisoned and savagely beaten.

Joan frowned. The cruelty with which supposedly pious men like Raban treated their fellow Christians never ceased to astound her. Pagan Norsemen aroused less fury in them than a Christian believer who stepped the slightest bit aside from the strict doctrines of the Church. *Why,* she wondered, *do we always reserve our worst hatred for our own?*

"What is the specific nature of this heresy?" she asked Wulfram, the leader of the Frankish bishops.

"First," Wulfram said, "the monk Gottschalk asserts that God has foreordained all men to either salvation or perdition. Second, that Christ did not die on the cross for all men, but only for the elect. And lastly, that fallen man can do no good apart from grace, nor exercise free will for anything but evil."

*That sounds like Gottschalk,* Joan thought. A confirmed pessimist, he would naturally gravitate to a theory that predestined man for doom. But there was nothing heretical, or even especially new, about his ideas. St. Augustine himself had said exactly as much in his two great works *De civitate Dei* and the *Enchiridion*.

No one in the room appeared to recognize this, however. Though all reverenced the name of Augustine, evidently none had taken the trouble to actually read his works.

Nirgotius, Bishop of Anagni, rose to speak. "This is wicked and sinful apostasy," he said. "For it is well known that God's will predestines the elect but not the condemned."

This reasoning was seriously flawed, as predestining the one group inevitably implied predestining the other. But Joan did not point this out, for she also was troubled by Gottschalk's preaching. There was a danger in leading people to believe they could not earn their own salvation by avoiding sin and trying to act justly. After all, why should anyone trouble to do good works if Heaven's roll was already made up?

She said, "I concur with Nirgotius. God's grace is not a predestining choice, but the overflowing power of His love, which suffuses all things that exist."

The bishops received this warmly, for it accorded well with their own thinking. Unanimously they voted to refute Gottschalk's theories. At Joan's instigation, however, they also included a condemnation of Archbishop Raban for his "harsh and unchristian" treatment of the erring monk.

Forty-two canons were passed by this synod, dealing mostly with the reform of ecclesiastical discipline and education. At the end of the week, the assembly was adjourned. All agreed that it had gone very well, and that Pope John had presided with unusual distinction. The Romans were especially proud to be represented by a spiritual leader of such superior intellect and learning.

The goodwill Joan accrued from the synod did not, however, last very long. The following month, the entire ecclesiastical community was jarred to its foundations when she announced her intention to institute a school for women. Even those of the papal party who had supported Joan's candidacy were shocked: what manner of Pope had they elected?

Jordanes, the secundicerius, confronted Joan publicly on the matter during the weekly meeting of the optimates.

"Holiness," he said, "you do great injury in seeking to educate women."

"How so?" she asked.

"Surely you know, Holiness, that the size of a woman's brain and her uterus are inversely proportionate; therefore, the more a girl learns, the less likely she will ever bear children."

*Better barren of body than of mind,* Joan thought dryly, though she kept the thought to herself.

"Where have you read this?"

"It is common knowledge."

"So common, apparently, that no one has taken the trouble to write it down so all may learn from it."

"There is nothing to be learned from what is obvious to all. No one has written that wool comes from sheep, yet we all know it to be so."

There were smiles on all sides. Jordanes preened, pleased with the cleverness of his argument.

Joan thought for a moment. "If what you say is true, how do you account for the extraordinary fertility of learned women such as Laeta, who corresponded with St. Jerome, and who, according to his report, was safely delivered of fifteen healthy children?"

"An aberration! A rare exception to the rule."

"If I remember correctly, Jordanes, your own sister Juliana knows how to read and write."

Jordanes was taken aback. "Only a little, Holiness. Just enough to allow her to keep the household accounts."

"Yet according to your theory, even a little learning should have an adverse effect upon a woman's fertility. How many children has Juliana borne?"

Jordanes flushed. "Twelve."

"*Another* aberration?"

There was a long, embarrassed silence.

"Obviously, Holiness," Jordanes said stiffly, "your mind is quite made up on this matter. Therefore, I'll say no more."

And he didn't, at least not in that assembly.

"It was not wise to insult Jordanes publicly," Gerold said afterward. "You may have driven him into the arms of Arsenius and the imperialists."

"But he's wrong, Gerold," Joan said. "Women are as capable of learning as men. Am I not proof of that?"

"Of course. But you must give people time. The world can't be remade in a day."

"The world won't ever be remade, if no one tries to remake it. Change must begin somewhere."

"True," Gerold allowed. "But not now, not here—not with you."

"Why not?"

*Because I love you,* he wanted to say, *and I'm afraid for you.*

Instead he said, "You can't afford to make enemies. Have you forgotten who and what you are? I can protect you from many things, Joan—but not from yourself."

"Oh, come—surely it's not as serious as all that. Will the world come to an end because a few women learn to read and write?"

"Your old tutor—Aesculapius, wasn't it?—what was it you told me he once said to you?"

"Some ideas are dangerous."

"Exactly."

There was a long silence.

"Very well," she conceded. "I'll speak to Jordanes and do what I can to smooth his ruffled feathers. And I promise to be more politic in the future. But the school for women is too important; I won't give up on it."

"I didn't think you would," Gerold replied, smiling.

In September, the school for women was formally dedicated. St. Catherine's School, Joan named it in loving memory of her brother Matthew, who had first acquainted her with the learned saint. Each time she passed the little building on the Via Merulana and heard the sound of female voices reciting, she thought her heart would split with joy.

She was as good as her word to Gerold. She was politic and courteous to Jordanes and the other optimates. She even managed to keep her tongue in check when she heard Cardinal Priest Citronatus preach that upon resurrection women's "imperfections" would be remedied, for all human beings would be reborn as men! Calling Citronatus to her, she offered in the guise of a helpful suggestion that eliminating that line from his sermons might help him achieve a better effect with his female parishioners. Couched in such diplomatic terms, the suggestion went over well; Citronatus was flattered by the papal attention and did not preach the idea again.

Patiently and uncomplainingly Joan endured the daily round of masses, audiences, baptisms, and ordinations. So the long, cool days of autumn passed with no further incident.

On the ides of November, the sky darkened and it began to rain. For ten days the rain came down in great driving sheets, drumming against the shingled roofs of the houses so the inhabitants had to plug their ears to shut out the maddening noise. The ancient sewers of the city were soon overwhelmed; on the streets water collected in growing pools that met and joined in quick-moving streams, turning the basalt stones into a treacherous slipping ground.

And still the rain came down. The waters of the Tiber rose dangerously, overrunning the embankments from the city to the sea, flooding the fields of the campagna, destroying the croplands, carrying off the cattle.

Within the city walls, the first region to be inundated was the low-lying Campus Martius, with its teeming population of poor. Some fled to higher ground as soon as the water began to rise, but many remained behind, unaware of the consequences of delay and reluctant to leave their homes and meager possessions.

Then it was too late. The waters rose above the height of a man, preventing any attempt at escape. Hundreds of people were trapped inside the rickety insulae; if the waters continued to rise, they would drown.

In such circumstances, the Pope usually retired to the Lateran cathedral and held a solemn litany, prostrating himself before the altar and praying for the city's deliverance. To the surprise and consternation of the clergy, Joan did no such thing. Instead, she summoned Gerold to discuss plans for a rescue.

"What can we do?" she asked. "There must be some way to save those people."

He replied, "The streets surrounding the Campius Martius are completely flooded. There's no way to get there except by boat."

"What about the boats moored at Ripa Grande?"

"They're only light fishing skiffs—flimsy vessels for such rough waters."

"It's worth an attempt," she argued urgently. "We can't just stand by idly while people drown!"

Gerold felt a rush of tenderness toward her. Not Sergius, not even Leo, would have showed such concern for the wretched population of the

Campus Martius. Joan was different; seeing no distinction between rich and poor, she made none. In her eyes, all people were equally deserving of her care and attention.

"I'll call up the militia at once," he said.

They marched to the dock at Ripa Grande, where Joan used her authority to commandeer every dinghy in seaworthy condition. Gerold and his men got into the boats, and Joan spoke a few quick words of blessing over them, raising her voice to make herself heard over the pelting rain. Then she astonished everyone by clambering down into the boat with Gerold.

"What are you doing?" he asked in alarm.

"What does it look like?"

"You don't mean to come with us!"

"Why not?"

He gazed at her as if she were mad. "It's far too dangerous!"

"Where I am needed, I will go," she replied determinedly.

Eustathius, the archpriest, frowned down from the dock. "Holiness, think of the dignity of your position! You are Lord Pope, Bishop of Rome. Would you risk your life for a group of ragged beggars?"

"They are God's children, Eustathius, no less than you and I."

"But who will lead the litany?" he asked plaintively.

"You will, Eustathius. Do it well, for we have good need of your prayers." She turned impatiently to Gerold. "Now, Superista, will you row, or must I?"

Recognizing the look of stubborn determination in those gray-green eyes, Gerold took up the oars. There was no further time for debate, for the waters were rising quickly. He pulled on the oars, rowing strongly, and the boat drew away from the dock.

Eustathius shouted something after them, but his words were lost in the wind and driving rain.

The makeshift flotilla headed northwest toward the Campus Martius. The floodwaters had risen. The Tiber was coursing through this lower part of the city as if in its own channel. From the Porta Septimánia to the foot of the Capitoline Hill, every church and house was flooded. The column of Marcus Aurelius was half submerged; waves lapped at the upper door-sills of the Pantheon.

Nearing the Campus Martius, they saw evidence of the terrible damage the flood had wreaked. Wooden debris, remains of the collapsed insulae, drifted swiftly by; bodies floated on the surface of the water, turning with every shift of the current. The terrified inhabitants of the remaining tenements had retreated to the upper stories. They leaned from the windows with outstretched arms, crying piteously for help.

The boats spread out, one or two to a building. The waves made it difficult to hold them steady. Some people panicked and jumped too soon, missing the bobbing, circling vessels. Others landed too far to the front or side of one of the boats, overturning it. There was a melee in the water as those who could not swim tried desperately to cling to those who could while the oarsmen cursed roundly and tried to right their flimsy craft.

Eventually all the boats were righted and they set off, following a route to the Capitoline Hill, where they let off their passengers. From this point, it was an easy climb to the safety of dry ground. Then the flotilla turned back to rescue more people.

They made trip after trip, drenched to the skin, clothes plastered to their bodies, aching from effort and fatigue. At last it seemed they had everyone. They were headed back toward the Capitoline Hill when Joan heard a child's voice crying for help. Turning, she saw a small boy silhouetted in one of the windows. Perhaps he had been asleep and only just awakened, or perhaps he had been too frightened to come to the window before.

Joan and Gerold looked at each other. Without a word, he turned the boat around and rowed back, pulling up beneath the window from which the boy now leaned and fanning the oars to hold the boat steady.

Joan stood, holding out her arms. "Jump!" she said. "Jump and I'll catch you!"

The boy stayed where he was, round eyes staring down in terror at the heaving boat below.

She fixed him with a compelling stare, willing him to move. "Jump now!" she commanded.

Timidly the boy slung one leg over the windowsill.

She reached for him.

At that moment there was a deafening roar. The ancient Posterula St. Agatha, northernmost gate of the Aurelian Wall, had given way under the pressure of the rising water. The Tiber came bursting into the city in a tidal wave of terrifying force.

Joan saw the boy's face framed in the window, his mouth forming a tiny *O* of terror as the entire building began to break apart. At the same moment, she felt the boat beneath her lift and shudder as it was sent spinning wildly on the onrushing flood.

She screamed, clinging desperately to the sides as the flimsy boat careered down the rapids, threatening at every moment to overturn. Water gushed over the sides; she raised her head, gulping for air, and caught an instant's glimpse of Gerold crouching near the bow.

There was a stunning jolt as the boat suddenly came to a halt, sending her crashing into the side.

For a while she lay dazed and uncomprehending. When at last she looked about her, she saw walls, a table, chairs.

She was indoors. The stupendous force of the flood had driven the little boat straight through an upper window of one of the insulae into the room within.

She saw Gerold lying in the front of the boat, facedown in several inches of water. She crawled over to him.

When she turned him over, he was limp and unresponsive, not breathing. She dragged him from the boat onto the floor of the room. Rolling him onto his stomach, she began pressing down on his back to force water out of his lungs. Press and release, press and release. *He can't die,* she thought. *He mustn't die.* Surely God could not be so cruel. Then she recalled the doomed young boy in the house and thought: *God is capable of anything.*

Press and release. Press and release.

Gerold's throat heaved, bringing up a great rush of water.

*Benedicite!* He was breathing again. Joan examined him carefully. No broken bones, no open wounds. But there was a large blue-black swelling just below his hairline, where he had received a nasty blow. This must have been what had knocked him senseless.

*He should be coming round now,* she thought. But Gerold remained sunk in his unnatural sleep, his skin pale and moist, his breathing shallow, his pulse faint and dangerously rapid. *What's wrong?* she wondered anxiously. *What else can I do?*

"The shock of violent injury can kill a man with a penetrating chill." The words of Hippocrates, words that had once saved Gottschalk's life, came back to her now.

She must get Gerold warm, and quickly.

Blasts of wind and rain were coming through the gaping hole left by the passage of the boat. She rose and began to explore the small tenement dwelling. Behind the front room there was a second, smaller one, windowless and therefore warmer and dryer. And—*Deo gratias!*—in the middle of the room there was a small iron brazier stacked with a few pieces of wood. On a nearby shelf she found a flint and some kindling. In a chest in the corner, there was a blanket of heavy wool, tattered but mercifully still dry.

Returning to the front room, she grasped Gerold under the shoulders and half-carried, half-dragged him into the back room, setting him down beside the brazier. Taking up the box of kindling, she struck the flint against the iron. Her hands were shaking so hard she had to try several times before she drew a spark. At last she got the little pile of straw to catch. She placed the flaming kindling in the brazier, and it flared upwards, licking at the logs above. The damp wood hissed and spat, reluctant to take. At last a tiny core of red glowed in one of the logs. She fanned the fragile fire, nursing it along with practiced skill. Just as it began to take hold, a breeze swept in from the other room and extinguished it.

She looked despairingly at the cold logs. There was no more kindling, no way for her to start the fire again. Gerold still lay unconscious, his skin an ominous bluish white, his eyes sunk in their sockets.

There was only one thing left to do now. Quickly she removed his wet clothes, baring his taut, slenderly muscular body, marked here and there with the fading scars of battle. Then she covered him with the blanket.

She stood and, shivering in the frigid air, began to take off her own soaked clothes: first the paenula and dalmatic, then the undergarments, the alb, amice, and cingulum. When she was stripped to the skin, she crawled under the blanket and lay full length against Gerold.

She held him close, warming his body with her own, willing her strength, her life into him.

*Fight, Gerold, my dearest. Fight.*

She closed her eyes and concentrated on making the link between them. All else was apart. The little room, the quenched fire, the boat, the storm outside—none of it was real. There was only the two of them. They would live joined, or perish.

Gerold's eyelids fluttered. His hand flung out reflexively as if to tear away some invisible veil. At the same instant Joan saw through blackness a beckoning light and hurried with him toward it. Out of a far place they emerged together.

He woke. His indigo eyes regarded her without surprise; he knew she had been with him.

"My pearl," he murmured.

For a long while they lay silent, joined in wordless communication. Then he raised his arm to draw her closer, and his fingers brushed against the raised scars on her back.

"The marks of a lash?" he asked quietly.

She flushed. "Yes."

"Who did this to you?"

Slowly, haltingly, she told him of the beating she had received from her father when she refused to destroy Aesculapius's book.

Gerold said nothing, but the muscles in his jaw tightened. He bent over her and began to kiss each jagged scar.

Over the years, Joan had trained herself to rein her emotions in, to hold tight against pain, not to cry. Now the tears slid down her cheeks unchecked.

He held her tenderly, murmuring endearments, until her tears stopped. Then his lips were on hers, moving softly with a skill and tenderness that filled her with surging warmth. She slid her arms around him and closed her eyes, letting the sweet, dark wine of her senses rush over her, mind's will yielding at long last to body's desire.

*Dear God!* she thought. *I didn't know, I didn't know!* Was this what her mother had warned her against, what she had run from all these years? This wasn't surrender; it was a wondrous, glorious expansion of self—a prayer not of words but of eyes and hands and lips and skin.

"I love you!" she cried at the moment of ecstasy, and the words were not profanation but sacrament.

In the Great Hall of the Patriarchium, Arsenius waited with the optimates and members of the high clergy of Rome for news. When he had first received word of what Pope John had done, Arsenius could scarcely believe it. But then what else could one expect from a foreigner—and a commoner at that?

Radoin, second in command of the papal militia, entered the hall.

"What news?" Paschal, the primicerius, asked impatiently.

"We managed to rescue several score of the inhabitants," Radoin reported. "But I fear His Holiness has been lost."

"Lost?" Paschal repeated thinly. "What do you mean?"

"He was in a skiff with the superista. We thought they were following us, but they must have turned back to rescue another survivor. That was just before the gate of St. Agatha collapsed and sent a wall of water crashing into that area."

This news was followed by scattered cries of alarm and dismay. Several of the prelates crossed themselves.

"Is there any chance they survived?" Arsenius asked.

"None," Radoin replied. "The force of the flood swept away everything in its path."

"God have mercy upon them," Arsenius said gravely, using all his control to conceal his elation.

"Shall I give the order to sound the bells of mourning?" Eustathius, the archpriest, asked.

"No," Paschal replied. "We must not be precipitate. Pope John is God's chosen Vicar; it is yet possible that God has worked a miracle to save him."

"Why not return and search for them?" Arsenius suggested. He had no interest in a rescue, but he did need to assure himself that the Throne of St. Peter was again vacant.

Radoin replied, "The collapse of the northern gate has rendered the entire area impassable. We can do nothing more until the floodwaters subside."

"Then let us pray," said Paschal. *"Deus misereatur nostri et benedicat nobis . . ."*

The others joined in, bowing their heads.

Arsenius recited the words by rote, while his mind ranged to other matters. If, as it now appeared certain, Pope John had died in the flood, then Anastasius had a second chance at the throne. *This time,* Arsenius thought determinedly, *nothing must go wrong with the election*. This time he would use all his power to make certain his son's candidacy did not fail.

*". . . et metuant eum omnes fines terrae. Amen."*

"Amen," Arsenius echoed. He could hardly wait for the news the next day would bring.

✦ ✦ ✦

Waking toward morning, Joan smiled to see Gerold sleeping beside her. She let her eyes linger on his long, spare, proud face—as startling now in its manly beauty as when she had first glimpsed it across a banquet table twenty-eight years ago.

*Did I know even then,* she wondered, *in the very first moment? Did I know that I loved him? I think I did.*

At last she had come to accept what she had fought so long to deny—Gerold was part of her, *was* her in some unfathomable way she could neither explain nor deny. They were twin souls, linked inextricably and forever, two halves of one perfect whole that would never again be complete without both.

She did not let herself dwell upon the full implications of this wondrous discovery. It was enough to live in the present moment, in the supreme happiness of being here, now, with him. The future did not exist.

He lay on his side, his head close to hers, lips slightly parted, long, red hair tousled about his face. In his sleep, he looked vulnerable and young, almost boyish. Moved by an inexpressible tenderness, Joan reached out and gently smoothed a stray tendril off his cheek.

Gerold's eyes opened, gazing at her with so intense an expression of love and need that it left her breathless. Wordlessly he reached for her, and she went to him.

They were dozing again, entwined in each other's arms, when Joan started alert, aware of a strange sound. She lay still, listening with pricked ears. All was quiet. Then she realized that it wasn't noise that had awakened her but silence—the absence of the loud, steady drumming on the roof overhead.

The rain had stopped.

She rose and went to the window. The sky was overcast and gray, but for the first time in over ten days patches of blue showed on the horizon, with shafts of sunlight spilling through the clouds.

*Praise God,* she thought. *Now the flooding will end.*

Gerold came up behind her and put his arms around her. She leaned back against him, loving the feel of him.

"Will they come for us soon, do you think?" she asked.

"Very soon, now the rain's stopped."

"Oh, Gerold!" She buried her head in his shoulder. "I've never been so happy, nor so unhappy."

"I know, my heart."

"We can never be together again, not like this."

He stroked her bright hair. "We needn't go back, you know."

She looked at him with surprise. "What do you mean?"

"No one knows we're here. If we don't signal the rescue boats when they come, they'll go away. In a day or so, when the floodwaters recede, we'll slip away from the city by night. No one will come after us, for they'll think we both died in the flood. We'll be free and clear—and we'll be together."

She made no answer but turned to look out the window again.

He awaited her decision, his life, his happiness hanging in the balance.

After a while she turned back to him. Looking into the depths of those gray-green eyes, haunted with grief, Gerold knew that he had lost.

She said slowly, "I cannot walk away from the great responsibility with which I've been entrusted. The people believe in me; I can't abandon them. If I did, it would turn me into someone else, someone different from the person you love."

He knew he would never have more power over her than he had at this moment. If he used that power, if he took her in his arms and kissed her, she might yet agree to come away with him. But that would be unfair. Even if she yielded, it would be a surrender that might not last. He would not try to persuade her to do anything she might afterward regret. She must come to him of her own free will or not at all.

"I understand," he said. "And I'll not press you further. But there's something I want you to know. I'll say it only once, and never again. You are my true wife on this earth, and I your true husband. No matter what happens, no matter what time and fate may do to us, nothing can ever change that."

They dressed, to be ready when rescue should come. Then they sat together, holding each other close, Joan's head resting lightly on Gerold's shoulder. They were sitting like that, rapt in each other, when the rescue boats arrived.

✦ ✦ ✦

As they were rowed back toward the Patriarchium, Joan kept her head bowed as if in prayer. Aware of the watchful eyes of the guards, she did not dare look at Gerold, for she was not sufficiently in control of her feelings.

Arriving at the dock, they were immediately surrounded by a jubilant, cheering crowd. There was time for only one last backward glance before they were triumphantly borne off to their separate quarters.

# 28

*Papa populi*, they called her, the people's Pope. Over and over the story was told of how the Lord Pope had gone forth from his palace on the day of the flood, risking his life to save those of his people. Wherever Joan went in the city, she was given a riotous welcome. Her path was strewn with sweet-smelling petals of acanthus, and from every window people called down blessings upon her. She drew strength and solace from their love, dedicating herself to them with renewed fervor.

The optimates and high clergy, on the other hand, were scandalized by Joan's behavior on the day of the flood. For the Vicar of St. Peter to rush off to the rescue in a dinghy—why, it was absurd, an embarrassment to the Church and the dignity of the papal office! They regarded her with growing disaffection, amplified by the very real differences they had with her: she was a foreigner, and they were native-born Romans; she believed in the power of reason and observation, and they believed in the power of sacred relics and miracles; she was forward looking and progressive, and they were conservative, bound by habit and tradition.

Most had entered the ranks of the clerical bureaucracy in childhood. By the time they reached maturity, they were thoroughly steeped in Lateran tradition and quite inimical to change. In their minds there was a right way and a wrong way to do things—and the right way was what had always been done.

Understandably, they were disconcerted by Joan's style of governance. Wherever she saw a problem—a need for a hospice, the injustice of a corrupt official, a shortage in the food supply—she sought to move quickly to correct it. Frequently she found herself thwarted by the papal bureaucracy, the vast and cumbersome system of government that over the course of centuries had evolved into a labyrinthine complexity. There were literally hundreds of departments, each with its own hierarchy and its own jealously guarded responsibilities.

Impatient to get things done, Joan looked for ways to circumvent the ponderous inefficiency of the system. When Gerold ran short of funds for the ongoing work on the aqueduct, she simply withdrew the money from the treasury, bypassing the usual course of putting a request through the office of the sacellarius, or papal paymaster.

Arsenius, alert as ever to opportunity, did what he could to exploit the situation. Seeking out Victor, the sacellarius, he broached the subject with politic art.

"I fear His Holiness lacks a sufficient appreciation of our Roman ways."

"So he would, not being born to them," Victor responded noncommittally. A cautious man, he would not reveal his hand until Arsenius played his.

"I was shocked to hear that he withdrew funds from the treasury without going through your office."

"It was rather . . . inappropriate," Victor conceded.

"Inappropriate!" Arsenius exclaimed. "My dear Victor, in your place I would not be so charitable."

"No?"

"If I were you," Arsenius said, "I'd look to my back."

Victor dropped his air of studied indifference. "Have you heard anything?" he asked anxiously. "Does His Holiness mean to replace me?"

"Who can tell?" Arsenius replied. "Perhaps he means to dispense with the position of sacellarius altogether. Then he can take whatever funds he likes from the treasury without having to explain to anyone."

"He'd never dare!"

"Wouldn't he?"

Victor didn't answer. Like a skilled fencer, Arsenius gauged his timing and thrust home.

"I begin to fear," he said, "that John's election was a mistake. A serious mistake."

"The thought has occurred to me," Victor admitted. "Some of His Holiness's ideas—the school for women, for example . . ." Victor shook his head. "God's ways are certainly mysterious."

"God didn't put John on the throne, Victor; we did. And we can remove him."

This was too much. "John is Christ's Vicar," Victor said, deeply shocked. "I admit he's . . . odd. But to move forcibly against him? No . . . no . . . surely it has not come to that."

"Well, well, you may be right." Artfully Arsenius let the matter drop. There was no need to pursue it further; he had planted the seed and knew it could be trusted to grow.

Since their parting on the day of the flood, Gerold had not seen Joan. The remaining work on the aqueduct was not within the city but at Tivoli, some twenty miles distant. Gerold was closely involved with every aspect of the construction, from overseeing the design of the repair to supervising the work crews. Frequently he bent his own back to the work, helping lift the heavy stones and cover them with new mortar. The men were surprised to see the lord superista stoop to such menial work, but Gerold welcomed it, for only in hard physical labor did he find momentary respite from the aching sadness inside.

*Better,* he thought, *far better if we had never lain together like man and wife.* Perhaps then he could have gone on as before. But now . . .

It was as if he had lived all the years before in blindness. All the roads he had traveled, all the risks he had taken, all he had ever done or been had led to one person: *Joan.*

When the aqueduct was finished, she would expect him to resume his position as leader of the papal guard. To be near her again every day, to see her and know that she was hopelessly out of reach . . . it would be unendurable.

*I'll leave Rome,* he thought, *as soon as the work on the aqueduct is complete. I'll return to Benevento and resume command of Siconulf's army.* There was an appealing simplicity to a soldier's life, with its definable enemies and clear objectives.

He drove himself and his men relentlessly. Within three months' time, the work was completed.

The restored aqueduct was formally dedicated on the Feast of the Annunciation. Led by Joan, the entire clergy—acolytes, porters, lectors, exorcists, priests, deacons, and bishops—circled the massive peperino arches in solemn procession, sprinkling the stones with holy water while chanting litanies, psalms, and hymns. The procession halted, and Joan spoke a few words of solemn blessing. She looked up to where Gerold stood waiting atop the foremost of the arches, lean, long legged, taller by a head than the others around him.

She nodded to him, and he pulled a lever, opening the sluice gates. The cheers of the people rang out as the cold, pure, healthful waters of the springs of Subiaco, which lay some forty-five miles outside the city walls, flowed within the Campus Martius for the first time in over three hundred years.

Crafted in the imperial style, the papal throne was a massive, high-backed piece of richly carved oak studded with rubies, pearls, sapphires, and other precious gems, as comfortless as it was impressive. Joan had been ensconced in it for over five hours, granting audience to a stream of petitioners. Now she shifted restlessly, trying to ease the growing discomfort in her back.

Juvianus, the head steward, announced the next petitioner. "Magister Militum Daniel."

Joan frowned. Daniel was a difficult man, thorny and irascible—and he was a close associate of Bishop Arsenius. His presence here could only mean trouble.

Daniel entered briskly, nodding greeting at several of the notaries and other papal officials.

"Holiness." He saluted Joan with the most minimal of bows, then began with rude abruptness. "Is it true that at the March ordinations, you intend to install Nicephorus as Bishop of Trevi?"

"It is."

"The man's a Greek!" Daniel protested.

"Why should that matter?"

"So important a position must go to a Roman."

Joan sighed inwardly. It was true that her predecessors had used the episcopacy as a political tool, distributing bishoprics among the noble Roman families like so many choice plums. Joan disagreed with this practice, for it had resulted in a great number of *episcopi agraphici*—illiterate bishops, who had spawned all kinds of ignorance and superstition. How, after all, could a bishop correctly interpret the word of God to his flock if he could not even read it?

"So important a position," she replied equably, "should go to the person best qualified. Nicephorus is a man of learning and piety. He will make a fine bishop."

"You would think so, being yourself a foreigner." Daniel deliberately used the insulting term *barbarus* rather than the more neutral *peregrinus.*

There was an audible intake of breath from the others in the room.

Joan looked Daniel straight in the eye. "This has nothing to do with Nicephorus," she said. "You are guided by selfish motives, Daniel, for you want your own son Peter to be bishop."

"Well, why not?" Daniel said defensively. "Peter is well suited for the position by virtue of family and birth."

"But not by ability," Joan said bluntly.

Daniel's mouth gaped in astonishment. "You dare . . . you dare . . . my son—"

"Your son," Joan interrupted, "reads equally well from a lectionary placed right side up or upside down, for he knows no Latin. He has committed to memory the few scriptural passages he knows. The people deserve better. And in Nicephorus they shall have it!"

Daniel drew himself up, stiffly offended. "Mark my words, Holiness: you have not heard the end of this!"

And with that he turned and left.

Joan thought, *He will go straight to Arsenius, who will no doubt find some way to make further trouble.* About one thing Daniel was certainly right; she had not heard the end of this.

Suddenly she was inexpressibly weary. The air in the windowless room seemed to close in upon her; she felt queasy and faint. She tugged on her pallium, pulling it away from her neck.

"The lord superista," Juvianus announced.

Gerold! Joan's spirits rose. They had not spoken since the day of their rescue. She had hoped he would come today, though at the same time she feared their meeting. Aware of the watchful eyes of the others, Joan kept her face impassive.

Then Gerold entered, and her treacherous heart leapt at the sight of him. The flickering lamplight played across his features, illuminating the handsomely chiseled angles of his brow and cheekbone. He returned her gaze; their eyes locked in silent communication, and for a brief moment they were quite alone in the midst of that great company.

He came forward and knelt before the throne.

"Rise, Superista," she said. Did she imagine it, or was her voice somewhat unsteady? "This day your head is crowned with honor. All Rome is indebted to you."

"I thank you, Holiness."

"Tonight we will celebrate your great accomplishment with a feast. You shall sit at my table in the place of honor."

"Alas, I regret that I will not be able to attend. I leave Rome today."

"Leave Rome?" She was taken aback. "What do you mean?"

"Now that the great work with which you charged me is complete, I am resigning as superista. Prince Siconulf has asked me to return to Benevento to resume command of his armies—and I have accepted the post."

Joan kept her rigid posture on the throne, but her hands gripped the arms. "You can't do that," she answered brusquely. "I won't permit it."

The assembled prelates raised their eyebrows. True, it was unusual to resign so prestigious a post, but Gerold was a free Frank, at liberty to commit his services wherever he chose.

"In helping Siconulf," Gerold answered reasonably, "I will be continuing to serve Rome's interests as well, for Siconulf's territories provide a strong Christian bulwark against the Longobards and Saracens."

Joan set her mouth firmly. Turning to the others, she commanded, "Leave us."

Juvianus and the rest exchanged surprised glances, then exited the room with a flurry of respectful obeisances.

"Was that wise?" Gerold asked after they had gone. "Now their suspicions may be aroused."

"I had to talk to you alone," she replied urgently. "Leave Rome? What on earth can you be thinking of? No matter, I won't allow it. Let Siconulf find someone else to lead his armies. I need you here, with me."

"Oh, my pearl." His voice was a caress. "Look at us—we cannot so much as look at each other without betraying how we feel. A single unwary glance, a careless word, and your life could be forfeit! I *must* go, can't you see?"

Joan knew what he was saying, even knew he was right in a way. But it didn't matter. The prospect of his leaving filled her with dismay. Gerold was the one person who truly knew her, the only one upon whom she could absolutely depend.

She said, "Without you, I'd be utterly alone. I don't think I could bear it."

"You are stronger than you know."

"No," she said. She rose from the throne to go to him and swayed as a strong wave of dizziness swept her.

Instantly Gerold was at her side. He took her arm, supporting her. "You're ill!"

"No, no. Just . . . overtired."

"You've been working too hard. You need rest. Come, I'll help you to your quarters."

She gripped him fiercely. "Promise me you won't go until we've had a chance to talk again."

"Of course I won't leave." His eyes were filled with concern. "Not until you're feeling quite well again."

Joan lay on her bed in the quiet of her room. *Am I truly ill?* she wondered. *If so, I must discover the cause and treat it quickly before Ennodius and the other physicians of the schola get wind of it.*

She applied her mind to the problem, putting questions to herself as if she were her own patient.

*When did the first symptoms begin?*

Now she thought about it, she had not felt well for several weeks.

*What are the symptoms?*

Fatigue. Lack of appetite. A feeling of bloatedness. Queasiness, especially upon first arising . . .

Sudden terror struck her.

Desperately she thought back, trying to recall the time of her last monthly bleeding. Two months ago, perhaps three. She had been so busy, she had paid no attention.

All the symptoms fit, but there was one way to be certain. She leaned over and picked up the bedpan that rested on the floor beside her bed.

A short while later, she set it down again with shaking hands.

The evidence was unmistakable. She was with child.

Anastasius pulled off his velvet buskins and leaned back comfortably on the divan. *A good day,* he thought, pleased with himself. *Yes, it's been a very good day.* This morning he had shone at the imperial court, impressing Lothar and his entire retinue with his wisdom and learning.

The Emperor had asked his opinion of *De corpore et sanguine Domini,* the treatise that was causing such a stir among the country's theologians.

Written by Paschasius Radbertus, Abbot of Corbie, the treatise advanced the daring theory that the Eucharist contained the true Body and true Blood of Christ the Savior—not His symbolic but his actual, historic flesh: "that which was born of Mary, suffered on the cross, and rose from the tomb."

"What do you think, Cardinal Anastasius?" Lothar inquired of him. "Is the sacred Host Christ's Body in mystery, or in truth?"

Anastasius was ready with an answer. "In mystery, my liege. For it can be shown that Christ has two distinct bodies: the first born of Mary, the second represented symbolically in the Eucharist. *'Hoc est corpus meum,'* Jesus said of the bread and wine at the Last Supper. 'This is my body.' *But he was still present bodily with his disciples when he said it.* So clearly He must have meant the words in a figurative sense."

So clever was this argument that when he'd finished speaking, all had applauded him. The Emperor had lauded him as "another Alcuin." Plucking several hairs from his beard, he had presented them to Anastasius—a gesture of highest honor among these strange, barbarian people.

Anastasius smiled, reliving the pleasure of the moment. He poured wine from the pitcher on the table beside him into a silver cup, then picked up the parchment scroll containing the latest letter from his father. He broke the wax seal and unrolled the fine white vellum. His eyes scanned the scroll, reading with eager interest. He stopped at the report of the theft of the corpses of Ss. Marcellinus and Peter from their cemetery.

Not that the taking of saints' bodies from their tombs was unusual; Christian sanctuaries all over the world constantly clamored for these holy relics in order to attract throngs of the faithful with the promise of miracles. For centuries the practical-minded Romans had made capital out of this foreign obsession with relics by conducting a regular trade in them. The countless pilgrims who swarmed to the Holy City were willing to dole out substantial sums for a finger of St. Damian, a collarbone of St. Anthony, or an eyelash of St. Sabina.

But the bodies of Ss. Marcellinus and Peter had not been sold; they had been stolen, dragged ignominiously from their graves at night and smuggled out of the city. *Furta sacra*—the theft of sacred things—such crimes were called. They had to be stopped, for they robbed the city of its greatest treasures.

"After this disgraceful theft," his father wrote, "we asked Pope John to double the number of guards posted in the churchyards and cemeteries.

But he refuses. He says men are better employed in the service of the living than the dead."

Anastasius knew that John had put great numbers of the papal militia to work building schools, hospices, and houses of refuge. He had devoted his time and attention—and the greater part of the papal finances—to such secular projects, while the city's churches were left to languish. His own father's church had not received so much as a single golden lamp or silver candelabrum since John had taken office. Yet Rome's innumerable cathedrals, oratories, baptisteries, and chapels were her claim to glory. If they were not constantly embellished and improved, Rome could not hope to compete with the splendor of her eastern rival, Constantinople, which now brazenly called itself New Rome.

If—no, Anastasius corrected himself—*when* he was Pope, things would be different. He would lead Rome back to the days of her greatness. Under his solicitous patronage, her churches would once again gleam with fabulous riches, more resplendent than even the finest palaces of Byzantium. This, he knew, was the great work that God had put him on this earth to do.

He returned to reading his father's letter, but with diminishing interest, for the last part was taken up with items of minor importance: the list of names of those to be ordained at the coming Easter ceremonies had finally been published; his cousin Cosmas had married again, this time to a widowed deaconess; a certain Daniel, magister militum, was greatly aggrieved because his son had been passed over for a bishopric in favor of a Greek.

Anastasius sat up. A Greek to be bishop! His father seemed to regard the move as just another example of Pope John's regrettable lack of *romanità*. Was it possible that he had completely overlooked the possibilities of the situation?

*This,* Anastasius thought with mounting excitement, *is the chance for which I've been waiting.* At long last, fortune had delivered opportunity into his hands.

He rose quickly and went to his desk. Taking up a quill, he began to write. "Dear Father. Waste no time upon receiving this letter, but send the magister militum Daniel here to me at once."

Joan paced the floor of the papal bedroom. *How,* she asked herself, *could I have been so blind?* It had simply not occurred to her that she could be pregnant. After all, she was over forty-one, well past the normal time for childbearing.

*But Mama was older still when she quickened with child for the last time.*

And died in the birthing.

*Never give yourself to a man.*

Fear, cold and unreasoning, gripped Joan's heart. She struggled to calm herself. After all, what had happened to Mama might not happen to her. She was strong and healthy; she had a good chance of surviving childbirth. But even if she did, what then? In the watchful beehive that was the Patriarchium, there was no way to keep her labor and delivery secret, no way to hide the child when it came. Her womanhood would surely be discovered.

What kind of death would be considered sufficient punishment for such a crime? It was certain to be terrible. They might put her eyes out with red-hot irons and flay her to the bone. Or she might be slowly dismembered, then burned while still alive. Some such hideous end was inevitable when this child came.

If it came . . .

She put both hands on her abdomen; there was no hint of movement from the babe growing within. The thread of life was as yet wound very thin; it would not take much to break it.

She went to the locked chest where she kept her medicaments. She had transferred them from her herbarium soon after her consecration; they were easier to hand here and safer against theft. Her hands ranged among the various vials and bottles until she found what she was looking for. With swift skill, she infused a measure of ergot into a cup of strong wine. In small doses, it was a beneficial medicine; in larger doses, it could induce abortion—though it didn't always work and was not without serious risk to the woman taking it.

What other choice did she have? If she did not end this pregnancy, she would face a death far more horrible.

She lifted the cup to her lips.

The words of Hippocrates came unbidden to her mind: *The medical art is a sacred trust. A physician should use his skill to help the sick according to his ability and judgment, but absolutely never to do harm.*

Resolutely Joan pushed the thought aside. All her life this woman's body of hers had been a source of grief and pain, an impediment to everything she wanted to do and to be. She would not now let it rob her of her life.

She tipped the cup and drank.

*Never to do harm. Never to do harm. Never to do harm.*

The words burned into her, searing her heart. With a sob, she threw the empty cup to the ground. It rolled away, the last drops streaking an erratic scarlet pattern across the floor.

She lay in her bed and waited for the ergot to take effect. Time passed, but she felt nothing. *It's not working,* she thought. She was frightened and at the same time greatly relieved. As she sat up, she was taken by a great fit of trembling. Her whole body shook with uncontrollable spasms. Her heart pounded; when she felt at her wrist, her pulse was wildly erratic.

Pain gripped her. She was stunned by its intensity, like a hot knife plunged into her innards. She rolled her head from side to side, biting her lip to keep from crying out. She dared not risk drawing the attention of the papal household.

The next few hours passed in a kind of haze as Joan moved in and out of consciousness. At one point she must have hallucinated; it seemed to her that her mother sat with her, called her "little quail," and sang to her in the Old Tongue as she used to, placing cool hands on her fevered brow.

Before dawn she awoke, weak and shaky. For a long while, she lay quite still. Then she slowly began to examine herself. Her pulse was regular, her heartbeat strong, her skin color good. There was no effusion of blood, no sign of any lasting harm.

She had survived the ordeal.

But so had the child within her.

There was only one person she could turn to now. When she told Gerold of her condition, he reacted at first with shocked disbelief.

"Great God! . . . is it possible?"

"Evidently," Joan said dryly.

He stood for a moment, his gaze fixed and reflective. "Is that why you've been ill?"

"Yes." She did not mention the abortifacient; even Gerold could not be expected to understand that.

He took her in his arms and held her close, cradling her head against his shoulder. For a long moment they remained quite still, silently sharing what was in their hearts.

He said quietly, "Do you remember what I said to you on the day of the flood?"

"We said many things to each other that day," she replied, but she felt her pulse quicken, for she knew what he meant.

"I said you were my true wife on this earth, and I your true husband." He put his hand under her chin, raising her eyes to his. "I understand you better than you think, Joan. I know how your heart's been torn. But now fate has decided things for us. We'll go away from here and be together as we were meant to."

She knew he was right. There was nothing else to do. All the roads that had lain before her were narrowed now to a single path. She felt sad and anxious, and at the same time strangely excited.

"We can leave tomorrow," Gerold said. "Dismiss your chamberlains for the night. Once everyone's asleep, it shouldn't be difficult for you to slip out the side door. I'll be waiting there with women's garments for you to change into once we're outside the city walls."

"Tomorrow!" She had accepted the idea of leaving but had not realized it would be so soon. "But . . . they'll come looking for us."

"By the time they do, we'll be well away. And they'll be looking for two men, not a simple pilgrim husband and his wife."

It was a daring plan, but it could work. Nevertheless, she resisted it. "I can't leave now. There's still so much I want to accomplish here, so much that needs doing."

"I know, my heart," he said tenderly. "But there's no other choice; surely you must see that."

"Wait until after Easter," she offered. "Then I'll go with you."

"Easter! Why, that's almost a month away! What if someone guesses your condition before then?"

"I'm only four months along. Under these great robes of mine, I can keep the pregnancy hidden for another month."

Gerold shook his head emphatically. "I can't let you risk it. You must get away from here now, while there's still time."

"No," she answered with equal conviction. "I won't leave my people without their Pope on the holiest day of the year."

*She's frightened and upset,* Gerold thought, *and therefore not thinking clearly.* He would go along with her for the present, having small choice, but quietly he would make things ready for a quick departure. If at any time danger threatened, he would whisk her away to safety—by force if necessary.

On *nox magna,* the Great Night of the Easter celebration, thousands of people crowded in and around the Lateran cathedral to join in the celebration of the paschal vigil, baptism, and mass. The long service began on Saturday evening and would continue into the early hours of Easter morning.

Outside the holy cathedral, Joan lit the paschal candle, then handed it to Desiderius, the archdeacon, who carried it ceremoniously into the darkened church. Joan and the rest of the clergy followed after, chanting the *lumen Christi,* hymn to the light of Christ. Three times the procession paused on its way down the aisle while Desiderius lit the candles of the faithful from the paschal candle. By the time Joan reached the altar, the great nave was ablaze with a thousand tiny flames, their flickering light reflecting dazzlingly off the polished marble of the walls and columns in dramatic representation of the Light brought into the world by Christ.

*"Exultet jam angelica turba caelorum. Exultent divina mysteria!"*

Joyously, Desiderius began the *Exultet*. The time-honored chant, with its beautiful and striking ancient melody, rang in Joan's ears with special poignancy.

*I will never stand before this altar and hear these sweet sounds again,* she reflected. The thought brought a strong sense of loss. Here, amid this inspiring celebration of redemption and hope, she came closest to experiencing a true faith in God. *"O vere beata nox, quae expoliavit Aegyptios, ditavit Hebraeos! Nox, in qua terrenis caelestia junguntur . . ."*

Exiting the cathedral at the conclusion of the mass, Joan saw a man with torn and mud-stained clothes waiting on the steps. Taking him for a beggar, she signaled Victor, the sacellarius, to give him alms.

The man waved off the proffered coins. "I am no alms seeker, Holiness, but a messenger, come with urgent news."

"Let's have it then."

"Emperor Lothar and his army are marching through Paterno. At the rate they are traveling, they will be in Rome in two days' time."

A murmur of alarm rose from the prelates standing nearby.

"Cardinal Priest Anastasius rides with him," the messenger added.

Anastasius! His presence among the imperial entourage was a very bad sign.

"Why do you call him Cardinal Priest?" Joan asked reproachfully. "Anastasius no longer has claim to that title, being excommunicate."

"Beg pardon, Holiness, but so I heard the Emperor address him."

This was the worst news of all. The Emperor's disregard of Leo's sentence of excommunication was a direct, unmistakable defiance of papal authority. In such a frame of mind, Lothar was capable of anything.

That night, discussing this turn of events, Gerold pressed her again to keep her promise. "I have waited until after Easter, as you wished. You must leave now, before Lothar arrives."

Joan shook her head. "If the papal throne is vacant when Lothar arrives, he will use his power to have Anastasius elected Pope."

Gerold had no better liking for the idea of Anastasius as Pope than she did, but her safety was his first concern. He said, "There will always be some reason or other to keep us from leaving, Joan. We cannot delay forever."

"I will not abuse the people's trust by leaving them in *his* hands," she replied stubbornly.

Gerold had an almost irresistible impulse to simply pick her up and carry her off, away from the web of danger that was tightening around her. As if sensing his thoughts, Joan quickly spoke again.

"It's only a matter of a few days," she said in a conciliatory tone. "Whatever Lothar's purpose is in coming, he's unlikely to stay any longer than he needs to accomplish it. As soon as he's gone, I'll leave with you."

He weighed this for a moment. "And you'll offer no further argument against leaving?"

"No further argument," Joan promised.

The next day, Joan waited on the steps of St. Peter's while Gerold rode out to greet Lothar. Sentries were posted all along the Leonine Wall to keep watch.

A short time later the cry went up from the wall, "The Emperor has arrived!" Joan ordered the gate of San Peregrinus opened.

Lothar rode in first. Anastasius was at his side, brazenly wearing the cardinal's pallium. His high-browed patrician face registered a look of haughty pride.

Joan acted as though she were oblivious to his presence. She waited on the steps for the Emperor to dismount and come to her.

"Be welcome, Majesty, to this Holy City of Rome." She extended her right hand, the one that bore the papal ring.

Lothar did not kneel but bent stiffly from the waist to kiss the symbol of her spiritual authority.

*So far, so good,* she thought.

The first rank of Lothar's men parted, and she saw Gerold. His face was taut with anger, and around his wrists was a tight cord of rope.

"What is the meaning of this?" Joan demanded. "Why is the superista bound?"

Lothar replied, "He has been arrested on a charge of treason."

"Treason? The superista is my loyal helpmate. There is no one I trust more."

Anastasius spoke for the first time. "The treason is not against your throne, Holiness, but the imperial one. Gerold is accused of conspiring to return Rome to Greek control."

"Nonsense! Who makes such an unfounded charge!"

Daniel rode out from behind Anastasius and fixed Joan with a look of malignant triumph. "I do," he said.

Later, in the privacy of her room, Joan bent her mind to the problem, trying to think of a way to respond. It was, she realized, a diabolically clever plot. As Pontiff, she herself could not be put on trial. But Gerold could—and if he was found guilty, she would be implicated as well. The plan had the mark of Anastasius all over it.

*Well, he won't get away with it.* She set her chin defiantly. Let Anastasius do what he could. He would not prevail. She was still Pope, with power and resources of her own.

# 29

The Great Triclinium was a relatively new addition to the Patriarchium, but it was already rich in historical significance. The paint on these walls had only just dried when Lothar's grandfather Karolus Magnus and Pope Leo III met here with their followers to forge the epic agreement that would raise Karolus from King of France to Emperor of the Holy Roman Empire and change the face of the world forever.

The fifty-five years that had passed since then had done nothing to dim the splendor of the hall. Its three large apses were paved with slates of flawless white marble and adorned with finely hewn columns of porphyry carved with decorations of marvelous complexity. Above the marble revetment, the walls were covered with colorful murals depicting the life of the apostle Peter, each drawn with wondrous artistry. But even these marvels were outshone by the great mosaic that rested over the arch of the central apse. In it St. Peter was depicted magnificently enthroned, surrounded by a round saint's nimbus. To his right knelt Pope Leo and to his left Emperor Karolus, each one's head surrounded by a square nimbus, the sign of the living—for they had been alive at the time the triclinium was built.

In the front of the hall, Joan and Lothar were ensconced upon two great, jewel-encrusted thrones. They appeared *sedentes pariter,* meaning that they were seated with equal ceremony; the two thrones were carefully placed side by side, level with each other so as not to give an appearance of greater importance to either one. The archbishops, cardinal priests, and abbots of Rome were seated facing them on high-backed chairs of Byzantine design, softly cushioned in green velvet. The other *sacerdotes,* the optimates, and the rest of the leading men of the Franks and Romans stood behind, filling the great hall to capacity.

When everyone was in place, Gerold was led in by Lothar's men, hands still bound before him. Joan's lips tightened as she saw dark bruises on his face and neck; obviously he had been beaten.

Lothar addressed Daniel. "Come forward, Magister Militum, and speak your accusation so all may hear."

Daniel said, "I overheard the superista tell Pope John that Rome should form an alliance with the Greeks in order to rid the city of Frankish domination."

"Liar!" Gerold growled, and was immediately rewarded with a hard cuff from one of his guards.

"Stand off!" Joan spoke sharply to the guard. To Gerold she said, "You deny these charges, Superista?"

"I do. They are false and wicked lies."

Joan took a deep breath. She must take the plunge now, or not at all. Speaking loudly so all could hear, she said, "I confirm the superista's testimony."

There was a shocked murmur from the assembled prelates. By responding in this way, Pope John had turned himself from judge to accused, in effect putting himself on trial along with Gerold.

Paschal, the primicerius, interjected soberly, "Holiness, the accusation is not for you to support or deny. Remember the words of the great Karolus: *Judicare non audemos.* You are not on trial here, nor can you be judged by any earthly court."

"I know that, Paschal. But I am prepared to answer these charges of my own free will, in order to free men's minds from any unjust suspicion." She nodded to Florentinus, the vestiarius. Following their prearranged signal, he immediately came forward bearing a large volume, magnificently bound—the gospel-book, containing the holy word of the apostles John, Luke, Mark, and Matthew. Joan clasped the book reverently. In a ringing voice she declared, "Upon these sacred gospels, wherein the Word of God is revealed, I swear before God and St. Peter that such a conversation never took place. If I am not speaking truth, may God strike me where I stand."

The dramatic gesture appeared to have worked. During the awed silence that followed, no one moved or spoke.

Then Anastasius stepped forward, taking up a position beside Daniel. "I offer myself as *sacramentale* for this man," he declared boldly.

Joan's heart sank. Anastasius had responded with a perfect counterthrust. He had invoked the law of *conjuratio,* according to which guilt or innocence was proved by whichever side in a dispute was able to amass the greatest number of *sacramentales,* or oath helpers, to support his sworn word.

Quick to take measure of the situation, Arsenius rose from his seat and joined his son. One by one, others slowly came forward to stand with them. Jordanes, the secundicerius, who had opposed Joan in the matter of the school for women, was among them. So was Victor, the sacellarius.

Ruefully Joan recalled Gerold's repeated words of caution to her to take things slowly and be more politic with her opponents. In her eagerness to get things done, she had not paid sufficient heed to his advice.

Now the reckoning was come.

"I will serve as sacramentale for the superista." A voice sounded clearly from the rear of the assembly.

Joan and the others turned to see Radoin, second in command of the papal guard, shouldering his way through the crowd. Staunchly he stood beside Gerold. His action emboldened others; in short order Juvianus, the head steward, came forward, followed by the cardinal priests Joseph and Theodore and six of the *suburbican* bishops, as well as several dozen of the lesser clergy who, being closer to the people, could better appreciate what Joan had done for them. The rest of the assembly held back, unwilling to commit themselves.

When all who wished to had come forward, the count was made: fifty-three men on Gerold's side and seventy-four on Daniel's.

Lothar cleared his throat. "God's judgment is here made manifest. Stand forth, Superista, to receive your sentence."

The guards started toward Gerold, but he shook them off. "The charge is false, no matter how many choose to perjure themselves by supporting it. I claim the right of ordeal."

Joan drew her breath in sharply. Here, in the southern part of the Empire, the ordeal was by fire, not water. An accused man had to walk barefoot over a twenty-foot row of white-hot plowshares. If he made it over, he was judged innocent. But very few people survived the ordeal.

Across the room, Gerold's eyes blazed an urgent message at Joan: *Do not try to stop me.*

He intended to sacrifice himself for her. If he made it over the coals, his innocence—and hers—would be proven. But he would probably die in the proving.

*Just like Hrotrud,* Joan thought. The memory of the village midwife's grisly death brought a sudden flash of inspiration.

She said, "Before proceeding further, there are some questions I would like to put to the magister militum."

"Questions?" Lothar frowned.

Anastasius protested. "This is highly irregular. If the superista wishes to undergo the ordeal, that is his right. Or does His Holiness doubt the workings of divine justice?"

Joan responded evenly, "Not at all. Neither do I scorn the workings of God-given reason. What harm can there be in asking a few questions?"

Unable to think of a reasonable reply, Anastasius shrugged and fell silent. But his face registered his vexation.

Joan's brow furrowed as she concentrated on recalling Cicero's six evidentiary questions.

*Quis.*

"Who," she asked Daniel, "apart from you, was witness to this alleged conversation?"

"No one," he replied. "But the testimony of these sacramentales is surety for my word."

Joan went on to the next question.

*Quomodo.*

"How did you come to overhear so private a conversation?"

Daniel hesitated only a moment before replying. "I was passing by the triclinium on my way to the dormitory. Seeing the door standing open, I went to close it. That's when I heard the superista talking."

*Ubi.*

"Where was the superista standing at the time?"

"Before the throne."

"About where he is now?"

"Yes."

*Quando.*

"When did this happen?"

Daniel pulled nervously on the neck of his tunic. The questions were coming so fast he had no time to think. "Aah . . . on the Feast of St. Agatha."

*Quid.*

"What exactly did you overhear?"

"I have already told the court that."

"Were those the superista's actual words, or an approximate rendering of the conversation?"

Daniel smirked. Did Pope John think he was stupid enough to fall into so obvious a trap? He said firmly, "I reported the superista's words exactly as he spoke them."

Joan sat forward on the papal throne. "Let me see if I have understood you correctly, Daniel. According to your testimony, on the Feast of St. Agatha you stood outside the door of the triclinium and heard every word of a conversation in which the superista told me that Rome should form an alliance with the Greeks."

"Correct," Daniel said.

Joan turned to Gerold. "Where were you on the Feast of St. Agatha, Superista?" she asked.

Gerold answered, "I was in Tivoli, finishing the work on the Marcian aqueduct."

"Are there any who can bear witness to that?"

"Dozens of men labored beside me all day long. They can all testify to my whereabouts that day."

"How do you explain this, Magister Militum?" Joan asked Daniel. "Surely a man cannot be in two places at once?"

Daniel was now looking decidedly pale. "Ah . . . ah . . . ," he stammered, desperately seeking a reply.

"Might you be mistaken about the date, Magister Militum?" Anastasius prompted. "After all these months, so small a detail might well be difficult to recall."

Daniel seized the proffered chance. "Yes, yes. Now I think back, it happened earlier than that—on the Feast of St. Ambrose, not St. Agatha. A thoughtless mistake."

"Where there is one mistake, there may be others," Joan responded. "Let us return to your testimony. You say you heard every word that was spoken while you were standing outside the door?"

"Yes," Daniel answered slowly, mistrustful now.

"You have sharp ears, Magister Militum. Please demonstrate this extraordinary acuity for us by repeating this feat."

"What?" Daniel was completely at a loss.

"Go stand outside the door, as you were before. The superista will speak a few words. When you come back, tell us what he said."

"What kind of trumpery is this?" Anastasius objected hotly.

Lothar looked at Joan disapprovingly. "Surely, Holiness, the use of jongleur's tricks undermines the gravity of these proceedings."

"Majesty," Joan replied, "what I have in mind is no trick, but a test. If Daniel is telling the truth, he should be able to hear the superista as well now as he did then."

"My liege, I protest!" Anastasius said. "Such a thing is contrary to all the customary proofs of law."

Lothar considered the matter. Anastasius was right; the use of evidence to prove or disprove an accusation was a strange and novel idea. On the other hand, Lothar had no reason to believe Daniel was lying. No doubt he would pass Pope John's unusual "test"—and that would lend greater credence to his testimony. Too much rested on the outcome of this trial for there to be any question afterward as to its fairness.

Lothar waved his hand imperiously. "Let the test proceed."

Reluctantly Daniel crossed the length of the great hall and stood on the other side of the door.

Joan put a finger to her lips, signaling Gerold to keep silent. *"Ratio in lege summa justitia est,"* she said in a high, clear voice. "Reason is the highest justice in law." She nodded to the guard at the door. "Bring Daniel back.

"Well," she asked when he stood before her again. "What did you hear?"

Daniel groped for a likely answer. "The superista repeated his protestation of innocence."

Those who had come forward to stand witness for him cried out in shocked dismay. Anastasius turned away in disappointment. Lothar's perpetual dark frown deepened even more.

Joan said, "Those are not the words that were spoken. And it was not the superista but I who spoke them."

Cornered, Daniel burst out angrily, "What difference does it make if I actually overheard the conversation or not? Your actions have demonstrated your true sympathies! Did you not ordain the Greek Nicephorus as bishop?"

"Ah!" Joan said. "That brings us to the last of the questions: *Cur.* Why? Why did you make false report of such a conversation to the Emperor? You were not motivated by truth, Daniel, but by envy—because your own son was passed over for the position Nicephorus received!"

"Shame!" a voice shouted from the crowd, and was quickly echoed by others. "Traitor!" "Liar!" "Rogue!" Even Daniel's own sacramentales joined in the torrent of abuse, eager to dissociate themselves from him now.

Joan raised a hand, silencing the assembly. Expectantly they waited for her to pronounce sentence against Daniel. For so serious a crime, the punishment would surely be very great: first the tongue that had uttered the treasonous lie would be cut out, then Daniel would probably be drawn and quartered.

Joan had no inclination to exact so terrible a price. She had accomplished what she wanted, which was to vindicate Gerold. There was no need to take Daniel's life; he was an unpleasant little man, spiteful and covetous, but no worse or more wicked than others she had known. And, Joan was certain, in this instance he had been little more than a tool in Anastasius's hands.

"Magister Militum Daniel," she said gravely. "From this moment forward, you are stripped of your title with all its lands and privileges. You will leave Rome today and remain forever banished from the Holy City and its sacred shrines."

The crowd was hushed by this astonishing display of *caritas.* Eustathius, the archpriest, seized the moment. "Praise be to God and St. Peter, Prince of the Apostles, through whom the truth has been made manifest! And long life to our Lord and Supreme Pontiff, Pope John!"

"Long life!" the others shouted. The sound echoed off the walls of the room, shaking the lamps in their silver cressets.

"What did you expect?" Arsenius paced the floor of his room agitatedly in front of his son, who was seated at ease on one of the divans. "Pope John may be guileless, but he's no fool. You underestimated him."

"True," Anastasius conceded. "But it doesn't matter. I'm back in Rome—with the full support of the Emperor and his troops."

Arsenius stopped pacing. "What do you mean by that?" he asked sharply.

"I mean, Father, that I am now in a position to take what we could not win by election."

Arsenius stared. "Take the throne by force of arms? *Now?*"

"Why not?"

"You've been away too long, my son. You don't know how things stand here. It's true Pope John has made enemies, but there are many who support him."

"What do you suggest, then?"

"Be patient. Return to Frankland, trim your sails, and wait."

"For what?"

"For the winds of fortune to change."

"When will that happen? I have waited long enough to claim what is mine by right!"

"There is danger in moving too precipitously. Remember what happened to John the Deacon."

John the Deacon had been the opposing candidate in the election that had raised Sergius to the papal throne. After the election, the disappointed John had marched to the Patriarchium with a large group of armed retainers and forcibly occupied the throne. But the princes of the city rallied against him; within hours the Patriarchium was retaken and John deposed. The next day, Sergius was ceremoniously ordained as Pope—and John's severed head rested atop a pike in the Lateran courtyard.

"That won't happen to me, Father," Anastasius said confidently. "I've thought about this very carefully. God knows I've had time for thinking, stranded all these years in that alien backwater."

Arsenius felt the sting of his son's unspoken rebuke. "What exactly do you propose?"

"Wednesday is the Feast of Rogation. The stational mass is at St. Peter's. Pope John will lead the procession to the basilica. We'll wait until he is well away, then take the Patriarchium by storm. It will all be over before John even suspects what is happening."

"Lothar will not order his troops to attack the Patriarchium. He knows such an act would unite all Rome against him, even those of his own party."

"We don't need Lothar's soldiers to take the Patriarchium; our own guards can handle that. Once I'm clearly in possession of the throne, Lothar will come to my support—of that I'm certain."

"Perhaps," Arsenius said. "But taking the papal palace will not be easy. The superista is a formidable fighter, and he commands the loyalty of the papal guard."

"The superista's chief concern is for the Pope's personal safety. With Lothar and his army in the city, Gerold will be riding guard on the procession, along with the better part of his men."

"And afterward? Surely you realize Gerold will come against you with all the power at his disposal?"

Anastasius smiled. "Don't worry about Gerold, Father. I have a plan that will take care of him."

Arsenius shook his head. "It's too risky. If you should fail, it will mean the ruin of our family, the end of all we have worked toward these many years."

*He's afraid,* Anastasius thought. The realization brought a quiet satisfaction. All his life, he had relied upon his father's help and counsel and at the same time had resented the fact that it was so. For once, he was proving the stronger. *Perhaps,* Anastasius thought, regarding the old man with a mix of love and pity, *perhaps it was this very fear, this failure of the will at the crucial moment of testing, that kept him from greatness.*

His father was looking at him strangely. In the depths of those familiar and well-loved eyes, faded now with the years, Anastasius read concern and worry, but something more, something Anastasius had never seen there before—respect.

He put a hand on his father's shoulder. "Trust me, Father. I will make you proud, I promise."

The Holy Day of Rogation was a fixed feast, invariably celebrated on April 25. Like so many other of the fixed feasts—the Feast of Oblation, the Feast of St. Peter's Chair, the ember weeks, Christ Mass—the roots of its celebration could be traced all the way back to pagan times. In ancient Rome, April 25 was the date of the Robigalia, the heathen festival honoring Robigo, God of Frost, who just at this season could visit great damage on the budding fruits of the earth if not placated with gifts and offerings. Robigalia was a joyous festival, involving a lively procession through the city into the cornfields, where animals were reverently sacrificed, followed by races and games and other forms of merriment in the open fields of the campagna. Rather than try to suppress this time-honored tradition, which would only alienate those they sought to win to the True Faith, the early Popes wisely chose to keep the festival but give it a more Christian character. The procession on the Holy Day of Rogation still went to the cornfields, but it stopped first at St. Peter's Basilica, where a solemn mass was celebrated to honor God and implore, through the intercession of the saints, His blessing on the harvest.

The weather had cooperated with the occasion. The sky above was blue as new-dyed cloth and clear of any trace of cloud; the sun sparkled a golden light on the trees and houses, its heat relieved by a welcome touch of coolness from a northerly breeze.

Joan rode in the middle of the procession behind the acolytes and defensores, who went on foot, and the seven regionary deacons, who were mounted. Behind her rode the optimates and other dignitaries of the Apostolic Palace. As the long line with its colorful signs and banners moved through the Lateran courtyard, past the bronze statue of the mater romanorum, she shifted uncomfortably on her white palfrey; the saddle must have been badly fitted, for already her back hurt with a dull but painful ache that came and went at intervals.

Gerold was ranging back and forth along the side of the procession with the other guards. Now he drew up beside her, tall and breathtakingly handsome in his guard's uniform.

"Are you well?" he asked anxiously. "You look pale."

She smiled at him, drawing strength from his nearness. "I'm fine."

The long procession turned onto the Via Sacra, and Joan was immediately greeted with a roar of acclamation. Aware of the threat that the presence of Lothar and his army represented, the people had turned out in record numbers to demonstrate their love and support of their Lord Pope. They thronged the road to a depth of twenty feet and more on either side, cheering and calling out blessings, so the guards were forced to keep pushing them back in order for the procession to move through. If Lothar required any proof of Joan's popularity with the people, he had it there.

Chanting and waving incense, the acolytes made their way down the ancient street, traveled by the Popes since time beyond memory. The pace was even slower than usual, for there were a great many petitioners stationed along the route, and, as was the custom, the procession stopped frequently so Joan could hear them. At one of the stops, an old woman with gray hair and a scarred face flung herself on the ground before Joan.

"Forgive me, Holy Father," the woman pleaded, "forgive the wrong I've done you!"

"Rise, good mother, and be comforted," Joan replied. "You've done me no injury I know of."

"Am I so changed you do not even know me?"

Something in the ravaged face raised imploringly to hers struck a sudden chord of recognition.

*"Marioza?"* Joan exclaimed. The famous courtesan had aged thirty years since Joan last saw her. "Great God, what has happened to you?"

Ruefully Marioza raised a hand to her scarred face. "The marks of a knife. A parting gift from a jealous lover."

*"Deus misereatur!"*

Marioza said bitterly, "Do not pin your fortunes on the favors of men, you once told me. Well, you were right. The love of men has proved my ruin. It's my punishment—God's punishment for the evil trick I played upon you. Forgive me, Lord Father, or else I am damned forever!"

Joan made the sign of blessing over her. "I forgive you willingly, with my whole heart."

Marioza clutched Joan's hand and kissed it. The people nearby cheered their approval.

The procession moved on. As they were passing the Church of St. Clement, Joan heard a sudden commotion off to the left. A group of ruffians at the rear of the crowd were jeering and throwing stones at the procession. One struck her horse on the neck, and it reared wildly, slamming Joan against the saddle. A jolt of pain shot through her. Stunned and breathless, she clung to the golden trappings as the deacons hurried to her side.

Gerold spied the group of troublemakers before anyone else. He turned his horse and was riding in after them before the first volley of rocks even left their hands.

Seeing him come, the ruffians ran off. Gerold spurred after them. Before the steps of the Church of St. Clement, the men abruptly wheeled, pulled weapons from the hidden folds of their garments, and came at Gerold.

Gerold drew his sword, signaling urgently to the guards following him. But there was no answering call, no sound of hooves drumming up behind. He was alone when the men surrounded him in a jabbing, thrusting swarm. Gerold wielded his sword with economical skill, making each blow count; he injured four of his assailants, taking only a single knife wound in his thigh before they dragged him from his horse. He let himself go limp, feigning insensibility, but kept a tight hand on his sword hilt.

No sooner had he hit the ground than he sprang back to his feet, sword in hand. With a cry of surprise, the nearest attacker came at him with drawn sword; Gerold moved sideways, wrong-stepping him, and when the man faltered, Gerold brought his sword down on his arm. The man dropped, his half-severed arm spurting blood. Several others came at him, but now Gerold heard the shouts of his guard approaching from behind. Another moment and help would be at hand. Keeping his sword before him, Gerold backed away, keeping a wary eye on his ambushers.

The dagger took him from behind, slipping between his ribs with noiseless stealth, like a thief into a sanctuary. Before he was aware of what had happened, his knees buckled and he folded softly to the ground, marveling even as he did that he felt no pain, only the warm blood streaming down his back.

Above him he heard fresh sounds of shouting and clashing steel. The guards had arrived and were fighting off the attackers. *I must join them,* Gerold thought and went to reach for his sword on the ground beside him, but he could not stir a hand.

Catching her breath, Joan looked up and saw Gerold turn aside in pursuit of the rock throwers. She saw the other guards start to follow him, only to be checked by a group of men standing among the crowd on that side of the road; the group closed together, blocking the way as if acting on some unseen signal.

*It's a trap!* Joan realized. Frantically she cried warning, but her words were drowned in the noise and confusion of the crowd. She spurred her horse to go to Gerold, but the deacons kept tight hold of the bridle.

"Let go! Let go!" she shouted, but they held on, not trusting the horse. Helplessly Joan watched the ruffians surround Gerold, saw their hands reach up to grab him, clutching at his belt, his tunic, his arms, dragging him from his horse. She saw a last bright glint of red hair as he disappeared beneath the swirling crowd.

She slid off the horse and ran, shoving her way through the group of milling, frightened acolytes. By the time she reached the side of the road, the crowd was already parting, making way for the guards, who came toward her bearing Gerold's limp body.

They set him on the ground, and she knelt beside him. Blood was trickling in a thin froth from one corner of his mouth. Quickly she removed the long rectangle of the pallium from around her neck, wadded it, and pressed hard against the wound in his back, trying to staunch the flow of blood. No use; within minutes the thick fabric was soaked through.

Their eyes met in a look that was deeply intimate, a look of love and painful understanding. Fear gripped Joan, fear like she had never known before. "No!" she cried, and clasped him in her arms, as if by sheer physical closeness she could stave off the inevitable. "Don't die, Gerold. Don't leave me here all alone."

His hand groped the air. She took it in hers, and his lips moved in a smile. "My pearl," he said. His voice was very faint, as if speaking from a long distance away.

"Hold on, Gerold, hold on," she said tautly. "We'll take you back to the Patriarchium; we'll—"

She sensed his going even before she heard the death rattle and felt his body grow heavy in her arms. She crouched over him, stroking his hair, his face. He lay still and peaceful, lips parted, eyes fixed blindly on the sky.

It was impossible that he was gone. Even now his spirit might be retreating from her in a succession of mirror images. She might see him again if she tried. She raised her head and looked around her. If he were somewhere near, there would be a sign. If he were anywhere, he would let her know.

She saw nothing, experienced nothing. In her arms lay a corpse with his face.

"He is gone to God," Desiderius, the archdeacon, said.

She did not move. As long as she kept hold of him, he was not entirely gone, a part of him was still with her.

Desiderius took her arm. "Let us carry him to the church."

Numbly she heard and understood. He must not lie here in the street, open to the gaze of curious strangers. She must see him honored with all the proper rites and dignities; it was all that was left her to do for him now.

She laid him down gently, to keep from hurting him, then closed his staring eyes and crossed his arms on his chest so the guards could bear him away with dignity.

As she went to stand, she was taken with a pain so violent it doubled her over, and she fell to the ground gasping. Her body heaved with great spasms over which she had no control. She felt an enormous pressure, as if a weight had been dropped on her; the pressure moved lower until she felt it would surely split her apart.

*The child. It's coming.*

"Gerold!" The word shuddered into a terrible groan of pain.

Gerold could not help her now. She was alone.

*"Deus Misereatur!"* Desiderius exclaimed. "The Lord Pope is possessed of the Devil!"

People screamed and wept, cast into an extremity of terror.

Aurianos, the chief exorcist, hurried forward. Sprinkling Joan with holy water, he intoned solemnly, *"Exorcizo te, immundissime spiritus, omnis incursio adversarii, omne phantasma . . ."*

All eyes were fixed on Joan, watching for the evil spirit to issue forth from her mouth or ear.

She screamed as with one last, agonizing pain the pressure inside suddenly gave way, spilling forth from her in a great red effusion.

The voice of Aurianos cut off abruptly, followed by a long, appalled silence.

Beneath the hem of Joan's voluminous white robes, dyed now with her blood, there appeared the tiny blue body of a premature infant.

Desiderius was the first to react. "A miracle!" he shouted, dropping to his knees.

"Witchcraft," cried another. Everyone crossed themselves.

The people pressed forward to see what had happened, pushing and shoving and climbing over one another's backs to get a better view.

"Stay back!" the deacons shouted, wielding their crucifixes like clubs to keep the unruly crowd at bay. Fighting broke out up and down the long line of the procession. The guards rushed in, shouting rough commands.

Joan heard it all as if from a distance. Lying on the street in a pool of her own blood, she was suddenly suffused with a transcendent sense of peace. The street, the people, the colorful banners of the procession glowed in her mind with a strange brightness, like threads in an enormous tapestry whose pattern she only now discerned.

Her spirit swelled within her, filling the emptiness inside. She was bathed in a great and illuminating light. Faith and doubt, will and desire, heart and head—at long last she saw and understood that all were one, and that One was God.

The light grew stronger. Smilingly she went toward it as the sounds and colors of the world dimmed into invisibility, like the moon with the coming of dawn.

# EPILOGUE

***Forty-two Years Later***

Anastasius sat at his desk in the Lateran scriptorium, writing a letter. His hands, stiff and arthritic with age, ached with every stroke of the quill. Despite the pain, he went on writing. The letter was extremely urgent and had to be dispatched at once.

"To His Imperial Majesty the most worshipful Emperor Arnulf," he scrawled.

Lothar was long dead, having died only a few months after leaving Rome. His throne had gone first to his son Louis II, and then, after his death, to Lothar's nephew Charles the Fat, both weak and undistinguished rulers. With the death of Charles the Fat in 888, the Carolingian line begun by the great Karolus—or Charlemagne, as he was now widely known—had come to an end. Arnulf, Duke of Carinthia, had managed to wrest the imperial throne from a host of challengers. On the whole, Anastasius thought the change in succession a good one. Arnulf was smarter than Lothar, and stronger. Anastasius was counting on that. For something had to be done about Pope Stephen.

Just last month, to the horror and scandal of all Rome, Stephen had ordered the body of his predecessor Pope Formosus dragged from its grave and brought to the Patriarchium. Propping the corpse up in a chair, Stephen had presided over a mock "trial," heaped calumnies upon it and finished by cutting off three fingers of its right hand, the ones used to bestow the papal blessing, in punishment for Formosus's "confessed" crimes.

"I appeal to Your Majesty," Anastasius wrote, "to come to Rome and put an end to the Pope's excesses, which are the scandal of all Christendom."

A sudden cramp in Anastasius's hand shook the quill, scattering droplets of ink over the clean parchment. Cursing, Anastasius blotted up the spilled ink, then put down the quill and stretched his fingers, rubbing them to ease the pain.

*Odd,* he reflected with grim irony, *that a man such as Stephen should succeed to the papacy when I, so perfectly suited to the office by every qualification of birth and learning, was denied it.*

He had come close, so close to gaining the coveted prize. After the shocking revelation and death of the female Pope, Anastasius had occupied the Patriarchium, claiming the throne for himself with Emperor Lothar's blessing.

What might he not have accomplished had he remained on the throne! But it was not to be. A small but influential group of clerics had adamantly opposed him. For several months, the issue of the papal succession had been hotly debated, with first one side, then the other appearing to prevail. In the end, persuaded that a substantial group of Romans would never be reconciled to Anastasius as Pope, Lothar chose the expedient course and withdrew his support. Anastasius was deposed and sent in ignominy to the monastery of Trastevere.

*They all thought I was finished then,* Anastasius thought. *But they underestimated me.*

With patience, skill, and diplomacy, he had fought his way back, eventually winning the confidence of Pope Nicholas. Nicholas had raised him to the office of papal librarian, a position of power and privilege he had held for over thirty years.

Having reached the extraordinary age of eighty-seven, Anastasius was now revered and respected, universally praised for his great learning. Scholars and churchmen from all over the world came to Rome to meet him and to admire his masterwork, the *Liber pontificalis,* the official chronicle of the Popes. Just last month a Frankish archbishop by the name of Arnaldo had asked permission to make a copy of the manuscript for his cathedral, and Anastasius had graciously agreed.

The *Liber pontificalis* was Anastasius's bid for immortality, his legacy to the world. It was also his final revenge upon his detested rival, the person whose election on that black day in 853 had denied him the glory for which he had been destined. Anastasius obliterated Pope Joan from the official record of the Popes; the *Liber pontificalis* did not even mention her name.

It was not what he had most deeply desired, but it was something.

The fame of Anastasius the Librarian and his great work would ring down through the ages, but Pope Joan would be lost and forgotten, consigned forever to oblivion.

The cramp in his hand was gone. Picking up the quill, Anastasius once again began to write.

In the scriptorium of the Episcopal Palace at Paris, Archbishop Arnaldo labored over the last page of his copy of the *Liber pontificalis.* Sunlight streamed through the narrow window, illuminating a shaft of floating dust. Arnaldo put the finishing flourish on the page, looked it over once, then wearily set down the quill.

It had been a long and difficult labor, copying out the entire manuscript of *The Book of the Popes.* The palace scribes had been quite surprised when the archbishop had taken on the task himself rather than assign it to one of them, but Arnaldo had his reasons for doing so. He had not merely duplicated the famous manuscript; he had corrected it. Between the chronicles of the lives of Pope Leo and Pope Benedict, there was now an entry on Pope Joan, restoring her pontificate to its rightful place in history.

He had done this as much out of a feeling of personal loyalty as from a desire to see the truth told. Like Joan, the archbishop was not what he seemed. For Arnaldo, née Arnalda, was actually the daughter of the Frankish steward Arn and his wife, Bona, with whom Joan had resided after her flight from Fulda. Arnalda had been only a small girl then, but she had never forgotten Joan—the kind and intelligent eyes that had regarded her so attentively; the excitement of their daily lessons together; the shared joy of accomplishment as Arnalda had begun to read and write.

She owed Joan a great debt, for it was Joan who had rescued Arnalda's family from poverty and despair, pointed the way from the dark abyss of ignorance to the light of knowledge, and made possible the high station which Arnalda now enjoyed. Inspired by Joan's example, Arnalda had also chosen, on approaching adulthood, to disguise herself as a man in order to pursue her ambitions.

*How many others like us are there?* Arnalda wondered, not for the first time. How many other women had made the daring leap, abandoning their feminine identities, giving up lives that might have been filled with children and family, in order to achieve that from which they would otherwise have been barred? Who could know? It might be that Arnalda had unknowingly passed by another such changeling in cathedral or cloister, toiling along in secret and undisclosed sisterhood.

She smiled at the thought. Reaching inside her archbishop's robes, she clasped the wooden medallion of St. Catherine that hung around her neck. She had worn it constantly ever since the day Joan had given it to her over fifty years ago.

Tomorrow she would have the manuscript bound in fine leather embossed with gold and placed in the archives of the cathedral library. Somewhere, at least, there would remain a record of Joan the Pope, who, though a woman, was nevertheless a good and faithful Vicar of Christ. Someday her story would be found and told again.

*The debt is repaid,* Arnalda thought. *Requiesce in pace, Johanna Papissa.*

# AUTHOR'S NOTE

## *Was There a Pope Joan?*

> *"Partout où vous voyez une légende, vous pouvez être sûr, en allant au fond des choses, que vous trouverez une histoire."*
>
> "Whenever you see a legend, you can be sure, if you go to the very bottom of things, that you will find history."
>
> Vallet de Viriville

Pope Joan is one of the most fascinating, extraordinary characters in Western history—and one of the least well known. Most people have never heard of Joan the Pope, and those who have regard her story as legend.

Yet for hundreds of years—up to the middle of the seventeenth century—Joan's papacy was universally known and accepted as truth. In the seventeenth century, the Catholic Church, under increasing attack from rising Protestantism, began a concerted effort to destroy the embarrassing historical records on Joan. Hundreds of manuscripts and books were seized by the Vatican. Joan's virtual disappearance from modern consciousness attests to the effectiveness of these measures.

Today the Catholic Church offers two principal arguments against Joan's papacy: the absence of any reference to her in contemporary documents, and the lack of a sufficient period of time for her papacy to have taken place between the end of the reign of her predecessor, Leo IV, and the beginning of the reign of her successor, Benedict III.

These arguments are not, however, conclusive. It is scarcely surprising that Joan does not appear in contemporary records, given the time and energy the Church has, by its own admission, devoted to expunging her from them. The fact that she lived in the ninth century, the darkest of the dark ages, would have made the job of obliterating her papacy easy. The ninth century was a time of widespread illiteracy, marked by an extraordinary dearth of record keeping. Today, scholarly research into the period relies on scattered, incomplete, contradictory, and unreliable documents. There are no court records, land surveys, farming accounts, or diaries of daily life. Except for one questionable history, the *Liber pontificalis* (which scholars have called a "propagandist document"), there is no continuous record of the ninth-century Popes—who they were, when they reigned, what they did. Apart from the *Liber pontificalis,* scarcely a mention can be found of Joan's successor, Pope Benedict III—and *he* was not the target of an extermination campaign.

One ancient copy of the *Liber pontificalis* with a record of Joan's papacy still exists. The entry on Joan is obviously a later interpolation, clumsily pieced into the main body of the text. However, this does not necessarily render the account untrue; a subsequent annalist, convinced by the testimony of less politically suspect chroniclers, may have felt morally obliged to correct the official record. Blondel, the Protestant historian who examined the text in 1647, concluded that the entry on Joan was written in the fourteenth century. He based his opinion on variations in style and handwriting—subjective judgments at best. Important questions about this document remain. When was the passage in question written? And by whom? A reexamination of this text using modern methods of dating—which has never been attempted—might yield some interesting answers.

Joan's absence from contemporary church records is only to be expected. The Roman clergymen of the day, appalled by the great deception visited upon them, would have gone to great lengths to bury all written report of the embarrassing episode. Indeed, they would have felt it their duty to do so. Hincmar, Joan's contemporary, frequently suppressed information damaging to the Church in his letters and chronicles. Even the great theologian Alcuin was not above tampering with the truth; in one of his letters he admits destroying a report on Pope Leo III's adultery and simony.

As witnesses for the denial, then, Joan's contemporaries are deeply suspect. This is especially true of the Roman prelates, who had strong personal motives for suppressing the truth. On the rare occasions when a papacy was declared invalid—as Joan's would have been when her feminine identity was discovered—all of the deposed Pope's appointments immediately became null and void. All the cardinals, bishops, deacons, and priests ordained by that Pope were stripped of their titles and positions. No great surprise, then, that records kept or copied by these very men make no mention of Joan.

One need only look to the recent examples of Nicaragua and El Salvador to see how a determined and well-coordinated state effort can make embarrassing evidence "disappear." It is only after the distancing effect of time that the truth, kept alive by unquenchable popular report, gradually begins to emerge. And, indeed, there is no shortage of documentation for Joan's papacy in later centuries. Frederick Spanheim, the learned German historian who conducted an extensive study of the matter, cites no fewer than *five hundred* ancient manuscripts containing accounts of Joan's papacy, including those of such acclaimed authors as Petrarch and Boccaccio.

Today, the church position on Joan is that she was an invention of Protestant reformers eager to expose papist corruption. Yet Joan's story first appeared hundreds of years before Martin Luther was born. Most of her chroniclers were Catholics, often highly placed in the church hierarchy. Joan's story was accepted even in official histories dedicated to Popes. Her statue stood undisputed alongside those of the other Popes in the Cathedral of Siena until 1601, when, by command of Pope Clement VIII, it suddenly "metamorphosed" into a bust of Pope Zacharias. In 1276, after ordering a thorough search of the papal records, Pope John XX changed his title to John XXI in official recognition of Joan's reign as Pope John VIII. Joan's story was included in the official church guidebook to Rome used by pilgrims for over three hundred years.

Another striking piece of historical evidence is found in the well-documented 1413 trial of Jan Hus for heresy. Hus was condemned for preaching the heretical doctrine that the Pope is fallible. In his defense Hus cited, during the trial, many examples of Popes who had sinned and committed crimes against the Church. To each of these charges his judges, all churchmen, replied in minute detail, denying Hus's accusations and labeling them blasphemy. Only one of Hus's statements went unchallenged: "Many times have the Popes fallen into sin and error, for instance when Joan was elected Pope, who was a woman." Not one of the twenty-eight cardinals, four patriarchs, thirty metropolitans, two hundred and six bishops, and four hundred and forty theologians present charged Hus with lying or blaspheming in this statement.

As for the Church's second argument against Joan, that there was not sufficient time between the papacies of Leo IV and Benedict III for her to have reigned—this too is questionable. The *Liber pontificalis* is notoriously inaccurate with regard to the times of papal accessions and deaths; many of the dates cited are known to be wholly invented. Given the strong motivation of a contemporary chronicler to conceal Joan's papacy, it would be no great surprise if the date of Leo's death was moved forward from 853 to 855—through the time of Joan's reported two-year reign—in order to make it appear that Pope Leo was immediately succeeded by Pope Benedict III.*

History provides many other examples of such deliberate falsification of records. The Bourbonists dated the reign of Louis XVIII from the day of his brother's death and simply omitted the reign of Napoleon. They could not, however, eradicate Napoleon from the historical records because his reign was so well recorded in innumerable chronicles, diaries, letters, and other documents. In the ninth century, by contrast, the job of obliterating Joan from the historical record would have been far easier.

There is also circumstantial evidence difficult to explain if there was never a female Pope. One example is the so-called chair exam, part of the medieval papal consecration ceremony for almost six hundred years. Each newly elected Pope after Joan sat on the *sella stercoraria* (literally, "dung seat"), pierced in the middle like a toilet, where his genitals were examined to give proof of his manhood. Afterward the examiner (usually a deacon) solemnly informed the gathered people, *"Mas nobis nominus est"*—"Our nominee is a man." Only then was the Pope handed the keys of St. Peter. This ceremony continued until the sixteenth century. Even Alexander Borgia was compelled to submit to the ordeal, though at the time of his election his wife had borne him four sons, whom he acknowledged with pride!

The Catholic Church does not deny the existence of the pierced seat, for it survives in Rome to this day. Nor does anyone deny the fact that it was used for centuries in the ceremony of papal consecration. But many

* Two of the strongest material proofs against Joan's papacy are predicated on the assumption that Leo IV died in 855. (1) A coin bearing the name of Pope Benedict on one side and Emperor Lothar on the other. Since Lothar died on September 28, 855, and the coin shows Benedict and Lothar alive together, Benedict could obviously not have assumed the throne later than 855. (2) A decretal written on October 7, 855, by Pope Benedict confirming the privileges of the monastery of Corbie, again indicating that he was at that time in possession of the throne. But these "proofs" are rendered meaningless if Leo died in 853 (or even 854), for then there was time for Joan's reign before Benedict assumed the throne in 855.

Figure 1. The *sella stercoraria*.

argue that the chair was used merely because of its handsome and impressive appearance; the fact that it had a hole in it is, they say, quite irrelevant. The name *sella stercoraria* is supposedly derived from the words addressed to the Pope while he is seated in the chair: *"Suscitans de pulvere egenem, et de stercore erigens pauperem ut sedeat cum principibus . . ."*—"[God] raises the needy from dust and the poor from dung to sit with princes . . ."

This argument seems doubtful. The chair had obviously once served as a toilet, or possibly an obstetric chair. (See figure 1.) Is it likely that an object with such crude associations would be used as a papal throne without some very good reason? And if the chair exam is a fiction, how does one explain the innumerable jests and songs referring to it that were rife among the Roman populace for centuries? Granted, these were ignorant and superstitious times, but medieval Rome was a close-knit community: the people lived within yards of the papal palace; many of their fathers, brothers, sons, and cousins were prelates who attended papal consecrations and who would have known the truth about the *sella stercoraria*. There even exists an eyewitness account of the chair exam. In 1404, the Welshman Adam of Usk journeyed to Rome and remained there for two years, keeping close record of his observations in his chronicle. His detailed description of Pope Innocent VII's coronation includes the chair exam.

Another interesting piece of circumstantial evidence is the "shunned street." The Patriarchium, the Pope's residence and episcopal cathedral (now St. John Lateran) is located on the opposite side of Rome from St. Peter's Basilica; papal processions therefore frequently traveled between them. A quick perusal of any map of Rome will show that the Via Sacra (now the Via S. Giovanni) is by far the shortest and most direct route between these two locations—and so in fact it was used for centuries (hence the name Via Sacra, or "sacred road.") This is the street on which Joan reportedly gave birth to her stillborn child. Soon afterward, papal processions deliberately began to turn aside from the Via Sacra, "in abhorrence of that event."

The Church argues that the detour was made simply because the street was too narrow for processions to pass along until the sixteenth century, when it was widened by Pope Sixtus V. But this explanation is patently not true. In 1486, John Burcardt, Bishop of Horta and papal master of ceremonies under five Popes—a position which gave him intimate knowledge of the papal court—described in his journal what transpired when a papal procession broke from custom and traversed the Via Sacra:

*On going as in returning, [the Pope] came by way of the Coliseum and that straight road where . . . John Anglicus gave birth to a child. . . . For that reason . . . the Popes, in their cavalcades, never pass through that street; the Pope was therefore blamed by the Archbishop of Florence, the Bishop of Massano, and Hugo de Bencii the Apostolic Subdeacon . . .*

A hundred years *before* the street was widened, this papal procession passed down the Via Sacra with no difficulty. Burcardt's account also makes it plain that Joan's papacy was accepted at the time by the highest officials of the papal court.

Given the obscurity and confusion of the times, it is impossible to determine with certainty whether Joan existed or not. The truth of what happened in A.D. 855 may never be fully known. This is why I have chosen to write a novel and not a historical study. Though based on the facts of Joan's life as they have been reported, the book is nevertheless a work of fiction. Little is known about Joan's early life, except that she was born in Ingelheim of an English father and that she was once a monk at the monastery of Fulda. I have necessarily had to fill in some missing pieces of her story.

However, the major events of Joan's adult life as described in *Pope Joan* are all accurate. The Battle of Fontenoy took place as described on June 25, 841. The Saracens did sack St. Peter's in the year 847 and were later defeated at sea in 849; there was a fire in the Borgo in 848 and a flood of the Tiber in 854. Intinction gained popularity as a regular method of communion in Frankland during the ninth century. Anastasius was in fact excommunicated by Pope Leo IV; later, after his restitution as papal librarian for Pope Nicholas, he is widely credited as the author of the contemporary lives in the *Liber pontificalis.* The murders of Theodorus and Leo in the papal palace actually happened, as did the trial pitting the magister militum Daniel against the papal superista. Pope Sergius's gluttony and gout are matters of historical record as is his rebuilding of the Orphanotrophium. Anastasius, Arsenius, Gottschalk, Raban Maur, Lothar, Benedict, and Popes Gregory, Sergius, and Leo are all real historic figures. The details of the ninth-century setting have been meticulously researched: the information on clothing, food, and medical treatment is accurate.

I did make some adjustments in the interest of telling a good story. I needed a Viking raid on Dorstadt in the year 828, although it didn't actually take place until 834. Similarly, I had Emperor Lothar descend twice upon Rome to chastise the Pope, though in fact he actually dispatched his son Louis, King of Italy, to do the job for him the first time. The bodies of Ss. Marcellinus and Peter were stolen from their graves in 827, not 855; John the Antipope, Sergius's predecessor, was not killed after his deposition but merely imprisoned and then banished. Anastasius died in 878, not 897. These deliberate errata are, I trust, exceptions; on the whole I tried to be historically accurate.

Some things described in *Pope Joan* may seem shocking from our perspective, but they did not seem so to the people of the day. The collapse of the Roman Empire and the resulting breakdown of law and order led to an era of almost unprecedented barbarism and violence. As one contemporary chronicler lamented, it was "a sword age, a wind age, a wolf age." The population of Europe had been almost halved by a disastrous series of famines, plagues, civil wars, and "barbarian" invasions. The average life expectancy was very short: less than a quarter of the population ever reached their fifties. There were no longer any real cities; the largest towns had no more than two to three thousand inhabitants. The Roman roads had fallen into decay, the bridges on which they depended disappeared.

The social and economic order which we now call feudalism had not yet begun. Europe was as yet one country: Germany did not exist as a separate nation, nor did France, or Spain, or Italy. The Romance languages had not yet evolved from their parent Latin; there were no French or Spanish or Italian languages, only a variety of forms of degenerating Latin and a host of local patois. The ninth century marked, in short, a society in transition from one form of civilization, long dead, to another not yet born—with all the ferment and unrest that this implies.

Life in these troubled times was especially difficult for women. It was a misogynistic age, informed by the antifemale diatribes of church fathers such as St. Paul and Tertullian:

> *And do you not know that you are Eve?. . . You are the gate of the devil, the traitor of the tree, the first deserter of Divine Law; you are she who enticed the one whom the devil dare not approach . . . on account of the death you deserved even the Son of God had to die.*

Menstrual blood was believed to turn wine sour, make crops barren, take the edge off steel, make iron rust, and infect dog bites with an incurable poison. With few exceptions, women were treated as perpetual minors, with no legal or property rights. By law, they could be beaten by their husbands. Rape was treated as a form of minor theft. The education of women was discouraged, for a learned women was considered not only unnatural but dangerous.

Small wonder, then, if a woman chose to disguise herself as a man in order to escape such an existence. Apart from Joan, there are other women who successfully managed the imposture. In the third century, Eugenia, daughter of the Prefect of Alexandria, entered a monastery disguised as a man and eventually rose to the office of abbot. Her disguise went undetected until she was forced to reveal her sex as a last resort to refute the accusation of having deflowered a virgin. In the twelfth century, St. Hildegund, using the name Joseph, became a brother of Schönau Abbey and lived undiscovered among the brethren until her death many years later.*

The light of hope kindled by such women shone only flickeringly in a great darkness, but it was never entirely to go out. Opportunities were available for women strong enough to dream. *Pope Joan* is the story of one of those dreamers.

* There are other, more modern examples of women who have successfully passed themselves off as men, including Mary Reade, who lived as a pirate in the early eighteenth century; Hannah Snell, a soldier and sailor in the British navy; a nineteenth-century woman whose real name is unknown to us but who, under the name of James Barry, rose to the rank of full inspector-general of British hospitals; Loreta Janeta Velaquez, who fought for the Confederate side at the Battle of Bull Run under the name Harry Buford. Most recently, Teresinha Gomez of Lisbon spent eighteen years pretending to be a man; a highly decorated soldier, she rose to the rank of general in the Portuguese army and was discovered only in 1994, when she was arrested on charges of financial fraud and forced by the police to undergo a physical exam.